PENGUIN BOOKS

THE HIGHLAND OMNIBUS

Compton Mackenzie was born in West Hartlepool in 1883. He was educated at St Paul's School and Magdalen College, Oxford. During the First World War he became a Captain in the Royal Marines, becoming Director of the Aegean Intelligence Service. He wrote more than ninety books – novels, history and biography, essays and criticism, children's stories and verse, and was also an outstanding broadcaster. He founded and edited until 1961 the magazine the *Gramophone*, and was President of the Siamese Cat Club. He lived for many years on the Island of Barra in the Outer Hebrides, but later settled in Edinburgh. He was knighted in 1952. His last book was *My Life and Times: Octave Ten* (1971). Compton Mackenzie died in 1972.

COMPTON MACKENZIE

THE HIGHLAND OMNIBUS

THE MONARCH OF THE GLEN

WHISKY GALORE

THE RIVAL MONSTER

PENGUIN BOOKS

PENGUIN BOOKS

Published by the Penguin Group
Penguin Books Ltd, 27 Wrights Lane, London W8 5TZ, England
Penguin Books USA Inc., 375 Hudson Street, New York, New York 10014, USA
Penguin Books Australia Ltd, Ringwood, Victoria, Australia
Penguin Books Canada Ltd, 10 Alcorn Avenue, Toronto, Ontario, Canada M4V 3B2
Penguin Books (NZ) Ltd, 182–190 Wairau Road, Auckland 10, New Zealand

Penguin Books Ltd, Registered Offices: Harmondsworth, Middlesex, England

The Monarch of the Glen first published by Chatto & Windus 1941
Published in Penguin Books 1959
Copyright 1941 by Compton Mackenzie

Whisky Galore first published by Chatto & Windus 1947
Published in Penguin Books 1957
Copyright 1947 by Compton Mackenzie

The Rival Monster first published by Chatto & Windus 1952
Published in Penguin Books 1959
Copyright 1952 by Compton Mackenzie

Published in one volume by Penguin Books under the title *The Highland Omnibus* 1983
3 5 7 9 10 8 6 4

Copyright © the Estate of Compton Mackenzie, 1983
All rights reserved

Printed in England by Clays Ltd, St Ives plc
Set in Garamond (VIP)

CONTENTS

THE MONARCH OF THE GLEN

My dear Bob,

I do not propose to involve myself with any institution or any individual by saying why I particularly choose this moment to dedicate to you a farce; but I want to commemorate a friendship of twenty years, and this dedication gives me a chance to say how precious that friendship has been, is, and always will be to

Yours ever,
COMPTON MACKENZIE

Suidheachan,
Island of Barra,
14 July 1941

CONTENTS

Chapter 1

GLENBOGLE

Inadequate indeed would be the guidebook or traveller's tale that did not accord to Glenbogle a place of honour in the very forefront of Highland scenery and romance, and it is a tribute to Scottish thoroughness that no such guidebook exists. Here are a page or two from *Summer Days Among the Heather*:

Nobody who can spare the time should omit to explore Glenbogle. Apart from the wild magnificence of the natural scene Glenbogle literally teems with historic memories and romantic legends. It was in a cave in the rocky fastness of Ben Booey, the yellow mountain, that Bonny Prince Charlie spent several nights hidden from the 'redcoats'. Ben Booey (3,100 ft) with Ben Glass (2,890 ft), the grey mountain, and Ben Gorm (3,055 ft), the blue mountain, are the famous Three Sisters of Glenbogle celebrated in many a poem and many a picture. Loch na Craosnaich (the loch of the spear) will be noticed on the left-hand side of the road five miles up the glen from the main road between Fort William and Fort Augustus. It was here that the famous Hector MacDonald of Ben Nevis, known as Hector of the Great Jaw, speared eleven Macintoshes and drowned them in the waters of the loch. A further two hours' walk from Loch na Craosnaich will bring the visitor to the gates of Glenbogle Castle, the seat of MacDonald of Ben Nevis. The present Chieftain, Donald MacDonald of Ben Nevis, is the twenty-third of the famous line of Mac 'ic Eachainn (pron. *Mack 'ick Yacken*), and it is one of the boasts of the 'true and tender North' that a MacDonald of Ben Nevis in the direct male line still occupies the stronghold of the 'sons of Hector'.

The Castle itself is not shown to visitors, but permission to wander about the well-wooded policies is readily granted on application at the lodge by the main entrance-gate, on the pillars of which will be noticed the two stone water-horses mordant of the MacDonalds of Ben Nevis. Legend says that the first Mac 'ic Eachainn was pursued by two water-horses from sunrise till sunset all over Glenbogle and its guardian bens, and that at sunset, having found a claymore embedded in a granite boulder, he drew the weapon and immediately slew the two monsters. Thereupon a fairy woman appeared and promised that all the land within the line along which he had been pursued by the two water-horses should be his and his heirs, until the day of the seven whirlwinds or, as the more prosaic Sassenach would say, the end of the world. Tradition goes on to relate that the granite boulder in which the claymore was embedded is the actual cornerstone of Glenbogle Castle. Everybody who is privileged to gaze upon this stately pile, portions of which date back to the first half of the fourteenth century, will give a fervid assent to the motto of this branch of the great Clan Donald, *Beinn Nibheis Gu Brath* (*Anglicé* Ben Nevis For Ever).

Those who have promised themselves the pleasure of passing a summer's day exploring dark Glenbogle or wild Glenbogle as it is variously called, will do well to provide beforehand for the refreshment of the inner man. The grandeur and desolation which greet the eye on every side from the moment the wayfarer enters Glenbogle will amply compensate for the absence of any dwelling-place until the immediate surroundings of the Castle are reached. No, gentle reader, Glenbogle has no hotel, and the sophisticated traveller who expects teashops and restaurants should not wend his steps towards this historic spot. For him, however, who is content with a mossy bank for his resting-place, with water from the burn, and with the simple fare he carries in his knapsack, Glenbogle is 'Paradise enow'. Many a long summer's day has the present scribe dreamed away in that delectable spot 'far from the madding crowd', pondering upon the lore of the misty past and recapturing with the mind's eye the stirring scenes of auld lang syne. The scent of the bell-heather and the bog-myrtle, the buzzing of honey-bees, the babbling of the peaty burn, the solemn shapes of the old brooding hens, are not these better than the superficial luxury of our so-called civilization? If we go to Glenbogle when 'the world is too much with us' there is no doubt what our answer will be.

With a romantic sigh young Mrs Chester Royde laid down *Summer Days Among the Heather* and gazed out of the window in the North Tower of Glenbogle Castle at the Three Sisters of Glenbogle dreaming majestically in the flickering haze of a fine morning on the Twelfth of August. She had some reason to sigh romantically, for this was her first visit to the home of her forefathers, one of whom, much against his will, had been deported to Canada by the twentieth MacDonald of Ben Nevis, the great-grandfather of the present laird. As a girl Caroline Macdonald had suffered from the Lone Shieling complex. She had seen the fairies in a peach-orchard on the shores of Lake Ontario. She had repined at not having been christened Flora, but had derived a measure of consolation from the thought that Caroline was the feminine of Charles. Then Chester Royde Jr, who was in Canada on business for his father's great financial house in New York, had met Caroline Macdonald at a Toronto ball and she was persuaded to become Mrs Chester Royde Jr. Chester was no Prince Charlie. Indeed, Carrie's friends all said they were surprised, after the way Carrie Macdonald had talked so much about Celtic romance and second sight and Mrs Kennedy-Fraser's Hebridean songs, she should go and marry a fat pug-nosed New Yorker with a double chin already at twenty-five and a complexion like a marshmallow. Yet Carrie's friends weren't so much surprised as they pretended: Chester Royde Jr was the heir to the Royde millions, and well they knew it.

That was last year, and the honeymoon had been cut short on account of a crisis in the money market. So they had had a supplementary honeymoon this year in Europe and in London they had met Mrs MacDonald of Ben Nevis, who was down there with her two hefty daughters, Catriona and Mary. They were known to the ribald as the Three Sisters of Glenbogle, but this was an injustice to Mrs MacDonald, who was as large as her two girls put together and English at that. The yearly matrimonial campaign of Mrs MacDonald was short and sharp. They were always back in Glenbogle by the beginning of June.

The knowledge that a clanswoman of his was married to the heir of the Royde millions had filled Donald MacDonald, twenty-third of Ben Nevis, with the liveliest patriarchal emotions. Blood of an unusually disproportionate thickness compared with water coursed through his arteries, and the little veins upon his eagle's beak glowed like neon round a shop-window.

'You must come and visit Glenbogle,' he declared. 'Home of your forefathers, what? And we must work out our exact relationship.'

'But my great-great-grandfather was just a simple crofter. He left Glenbogle during the first clearance. In fact I'm afraid he was put out by the Ben Nevis of the time.'

'That was my great-grandfather Hector, twentieth of Ben Nevis. Yes, a bad business. Well, well, that's what comes of loyalty.'

'Loyalty?' Carrie Royde repeated, perplexed.

'Loyalty to the old Stuarts. We managed to keep the land, but it was only by raising regiments for the Government. And then of course once Highlanders had started settling in Canada the only sound economic policy was to settle as many more of them as possible. That was why my grandfather had to make a second clearance. He hated doing it of course, but it was for their own good, and where would the Empire be today if people like my great-grandfather hadn't taken the bull by the horns and faced up to hard facts? Yes, I'm sure we must be related. Distantly of course. But if you and your husband come up to Glenbogle we'll work it out.'

'Chester's young sister is coming over to us at the end of July.'

'Is she married?'

'Oh, no, Myrtle's only twenty. And one of the sweetest girls in the world.'

'Look here, Mrs Royde,' said the Chieftain earnestly, 'you and your husband and your sister-in-law simply must come up for the Twelfth and put in at least six weeks with us at Glenbogle. My eldest boy Hector's unfortunately out in India with his regiment, but my second boy Murdoch expects to be with us for part of August. He's in the Navy. And Iain, my youngest boy, who's at Cambridge, will be with us the whole of his vacation. In fact we shall be a very jolly party of young people.'

Thus it was that Mrs Chester Royde Jr found herself gazing from the window in the North Tower of Glenbogle Castle at the shapes of the Three Sisters of Glenbogle, dreaming majestically in the flickering haze of a fine Twelfth of August morning.

When the rest of the party had been mustered by their host to shoot the grouse or watch them being shot on his most prolific moors which swept between the braes of Strathdun and the braes of Strathdiddle, Carrie Royde, surrendering to the Lone Shieling complex of her youth, had expressed a desire to enjoy by herself the solitude of Glenbogle.

'I just want to make the most of this lovely weather, Ben Nevis,' she told the Chieftain. 'And I'm feeling kind of remote and mysterious. I feel as if anything might happen to me if I go and search for it alone.'

'Well, don't go and sprain your ankle or anything,' said Ben Nevis, who believed that a heavy bag of grouse was the way to make the most of the weather but had too much respect for the Royde millions to discourage anybody in close touch with them from the utmost extravagance of emotional self-indulgence.

'Carrie and I will find plenty to do to amuse ourselves,' Mrs MacDonald boomed confidently.

Carrie Royde threw a slanting glance from greenish eyes at her monumental hostess and said quickly that the very last thing she should think of being was the least responsibility.

'I know you have lots and lots to do without bothering yourself about me, dear Mrs MacDonald. So please, if I may just have a little packet of sandwiches and a few crackers I'll go wandering off by myself and spend the day with my dreams.'

'But won't that be rather dull for you?' the hostess suggested anxiously.

'You let her do as she likes, Trixie,' Ben Nevis adjured. 'She's going to look for the fairies. I can see it in her eye.'

Carrie put a finger to her lips and flashed a glance at the Chieftain, who went charging from the room to see that the party from the moors had gathered in the courtyard of the Castle, convinced that between him and that pretty little red-haired American–Canadian with her roots in the peat of his own moors there existed a secret understanding. Well, so much the better. If Murdoch could manage to make the running with that attractive little sister-in-law of hers, the closer the understanding between him and Mrs Chester Royde Jr there was the better. As he climbed up into the big pre-war Daimler (there was only one war to date fashion at the time of this tale) which was to drive him and most of his house-party to the Ballochy Pass where the ponies would be waiting for them, he wished regretfully that the Clanranalds were not in India, because, after all, Hector as the Younger of Ben Nevis was the son of his most entitled to benefit from the share of the Royde millions that would be Miss Myrtle Royde's portion. He looked round to where the engagingly plump little heiress was seated beside his second son Murdoch in the sports car whose noisiness and vulgarity he had hitherto deplored and reflected that after all there might be something in these foul products of the post-war age — sometimes.

He turned to his principal guest, Chester Royde Jr, who in his costume for the moors looked like a full-page colour advertisement in the pages of *Esquire* or *Vanity Fair* designed to haunt, to startle, and waylay the most casual reader.

'And this is really your first experience of our Twelfth, Royde?' he asked.

The cork-pop with which his guest answered him Ben Nevis had learnt by now to recognize as an affirmative.

'We're expecting plenty of birds this year.'

'That's fine,' the young financier twanged enthusiastically.

Up in the North Tower of the Castle Carrie Royde watched the cars down the glen turn off to the right and start winding slowly up the narrow road that led towards the Pass of Ballochy. Her Macdonald heart beat faster at the memories the name brought back. She opened *Summer Days Among the Heather* again:

It was in the Pass of Ballochy that in the year 1546 a party of marauding Macintoshes were surprised by the MacDonalds of Ben Nevis led by Mac 'ic Eachainn in person and every single one of them killed. Some years later Clan Chattan took its revenge for this defeat by descending into Strathdiddle, when the young men were raiding the Cameron country to the south, and baking thirty-two old and infirm Macdonalds in an oven. For this Hector the ninth of Ben Nevis exacted a terrible penalty from Clan Chattan when after marching from Glenbogle with the Macdonalds through a stormy December night in the year 1549 he caught the Macintoshes unawares on a Sunday morning and burned forty-five of them in church. While the unfortunate victims of Hector's vengeance were burning, Hector's piper Angus MacQuat improvised a tune and played it to drown their shrieks. This tune, called Mac 'ic Eachainn's Return to Glenbogle, is still played by a MacQuat whenever MacDonald of Ben Nevis returns after spending even a single night away from his Castle.

A poem by an unknown Gaelic bard of the sixteenth century celebrating the battle in the Pass of Ballochy was rendered into spirited English verse by the late lamented Reverend Colin MacKellaig, D.D., whose translations from the vernacular rendered a service to the 'land of bens and glens and heroes' second only to his faithful service for over sixty years as a Minister of the Gospel at first in his own Inverness-shire and then at the United Free Church in Dudden Gardens, Glasgow.

THE BATTLE OF THE PASS OF BALLOCHY

Sound the loud pibroch, ye sons of great Hector,
Lift your claymores and strike hard at the foe,
Hurry as fast as ye can from Glenbogle,
Clansmen of Hector, cry shame on the slow!

Whistle, ye winds, 'Mac 'ic Eachainn for ever!'
Roar, ye wild waters, 'Ben Nevis gu brath!'
Swift as the Bogle in spate, ye MacDonalds,
Fall on the Macintosh, drive him awa'.

Sharp are the claws of the cat of Clan Chattan,
Gleam their claymores in the Ballochy Pass:
But sharper the talons of Hector's own eagles
That swoop from Ben Booey, Ben Gorm, and Ben Glass.

Swoop on the Macintosh, rend him in pieces,
None of Clan Chattan this day shall survive,
Sons of Clan Donald, salute your great Chieftain;
Dead is the Macintosh, Hector's alive!

Faithful and fair is my own Mac 'ic Eachainn,
Mighty and mettlesome, stalwart and true.
Lord of Ben Nevis, Glenbogle, Glenbristle,
Strathdiddle, Strathdun, Loch Hoch, and Loch Hoo.

Mrs Chester Royde tossed her red locks. The echoes of ancestral voices prophesying war were ringing in her ears when she took from the butler the packet of sandwiches and set out to commune with her forefathers, the nettle-grown tumbled stones of whose cottages were strewn about the emptiness of wild Glenbogle. In one pocket of her green coat were the sandwiches, in the other a copy of *Gaelic Without Tears*.

Seldom can the long winding drive of Glenbogle Castle have been graced by a more becoming figure than that presented by Mrs Chester Royde Jr when she set out that morning to commune with her ancestors. She was wearing a skirt of the tartan of the Ben Nevis MacDonalds, the predominance of red in which did not detract from her own red hair, thanks to the judicious interposition of the green coat, and her green bonnet was brooched with the eagle's head of the Ben Nevis MacDonalds. Her host had presented her with a cromag as dainty as the crook of a Dresden shepherdess. The dark pines that bordered the drive seemed to light up when she passed as if touched by a fleeting sunbeam.

She paused a moment at the gate and looked up at the two water-horses mordant gnashing their teeth at one another from the lichen-covered pillars on either side. She turned to the vocabulary of her *Gaelic Without Tears* to see if she could find the Gaelic for water-horse, but it was evidently too difficult a word for such an elementary instructor and was not to be found. Just beyond the gate a Glenbogle estate painter was admiring the result of some recent work on a large noticeboard:

GLENBOGLE CASTLE   NO CAMPING

Thus the inscription ran in large black letters on a white ground. The spread of hiking had soured the milk of human kindness. No longer was permission readily granted on application at the lodge by the main entrance-gate to wander in the well-wooded policies of the Castle, as recorded by the author of *Summer Days Among the Heather*.

Carrie debated with herself for a moment whether she should venture to give the painter 'good day' in Gaelic, decided that one had to begin some time, looked up the phrase in her little brown volume, muttered her phonetics over to herself once or twice, and gulped:

'La math.'

There are few joys accessible to human beings more grateful than the joy of trying out a phrase from a conversation manual according to the pronunciation indicated in brackets alongside and finding that the subject of the experiment understands and responds. This joy was denied to Mrs Chester Royde. It was clear from the expression on the painter's face as he touched his cap that he was respectfully hoping the Castle guest would amplify her question if it was a question or if she had not really addressed him at all relieve his embarrassment by doing so.

Carrie Royde did not like being beaten. She turned back to *Gaelic Without Tears*. Yes, there it was. Good day. La math (*lah mah*). She tried again.

'La math.'

'I couldn't tell you, mistress, I'm afraid. I only came here from Glasgow two weeks ago.'

'Aren't you a Gaelic speaker?'

'No, mistress; I have nae a word of Gaelic.'

The Macdonald in Carrie was shocked by this revelation of Glenbogle's decline, but her disappointment was lightened by the reflection that the virginity of 'la math' was still intact and that the phonetics of *Gaelic Without Tears* had not betrayed her.

'What is the meaning of that notice?' she asked. For all this painter knew that might have been what 'la math' had meant.

'It's Mr MacDonald's orders,' she was told.

'Ben Nevis's orders?' she inquired, with a note of rebuke in her voice.

'Ay, mistress, that's right. Ben Nevis himself, as they call him up here. They've been plagued a lot by these hikers, as they call them, and I have orders to paint a couple of dozen of these notice-boards all about the estate.'

'Well, you have lovely weather for your painting.'

'Ay, it hasna rained for nearly a week. Most extraordinar', the fellows on the estate tell me. Begging your pardon, mistress, are you from London?'

'No; I'm an American Macdonald.'

'Well, well, is that so? I'm a Macdonald mysel'.'

'You must be very happy working in this part of the country, aren't you?'

'Och ay, I like it well enough. But it's no' Glasgow, ye ken. Were you never in Glasgow, mistress?'

'No, I never was.'

The painter shook his head sympathetically.

'Dinna fash yoursel', mistress. Och ay, you'll visit Glasgow one of these days. It's a bonny bonny city. Full of life, and the trams are sae convenient. I'll be back there mysel' in October. It's unco dreich in Glenbogle.'

Carrie Royde walked on along the road down the glen, and lightly though she swung her cromag her heart was heavy awhile to think of a Macdonald in this ancestral stronghold sighing for a city to which neither beauty nor romance ever accorded a testimonial. However, the bad taste of one degenerate Highlander was not enough to spoil the magic of the natural scene for long. Beside the road the Bogle babbling gently after nearly a week without rain kept her company. On the other side of the glen Ben Booey, Ben Gorm, and Ben Glass towered, their lower slopes empurpled as richly by heather as the nose of Mac 'ic Eachainn himself by wrath. Two buzzards which she had the pleasure of supposing were eagles hovered in the crystalline air. A bobbing stonechat clicked at her from a boulder. A lanky blue mountain-hare scampered up the brae on the left of the road. A shaggy Highland bull eyed her from a field on the other side of the little river, and with that and a barbed-wire fence between him and her she waved her cromag at him as carelessly as if he were in the foreground of a picture by Peter Graham.

For some three or four miles she followed the road down the glen until she came to a narrow grass-grown turning where a mouldering signpost pointed to GLENBRISTLE and beside it a freshly painted notice-board nailed to a larch-pole proclaimed NO CAMPING. Carrie Royde decided to follow this even wilder looking road. Mrs MacDonald had suggested driving along Glenbogle to pick her up and bring her back to lunch in case she grew tired of her own company. She was delighted by her own company and in no mood to be dragged out of ancestral reveries by her hostess. She was anxious to eradicate the belief prevalent in Glenbogle Castle that American visitors expected to be assiduously entertained all the time. Besides, she wasn't feeling at all American at this moment. She was feeling more like Deirdre than anybody since Deirdre said farewell to Scotland.

> Dearest Albyn,
> Land o'er yonder,
> Thou dear land of wood and wave.

These were as much of the words as she could remember, but she hummed to herself the tune in an ecstasy of romantic emotion, such an ecstasy that she kept quickening the tempo, and before she came to the end of the first verse *Deirdre's Farewell* had turned into *Oh, my darling, oh, my darling, oh, my darling Clementine*.

Soon, however, the profound silence of Glenbristle, unbroken even by the babble of the smallest burn, made even the humming of a tune correctly seem a sacrilegious interruption of the stillness.

Carrie became obsessed by an urgent intuition that the home of her great-great-grandfather before it was pulled down and he was sent away in an emigrant ship to Canada had been in Glenbristle and that his spirit was leading her to its site. Besides her own Celtic origins she had dabbled a bit in Yoga. So she took several very deep breaths and surrendered her will to the influence she felt all round her. Her corporal response was immediate. She seemed to be floating over rather than walking on the rough grass-grown road, and then on a green knoll about fifty yards up the brae on her right she saw the strewn stones and luxuriant nettles which still mark, sometimes centuries later, where once a human habitation stood. She had no doubt whatever that this knoll was the site of her ancestral home, and in high elation of spirit she made her way up to the top of it; and after meditating piously for a moment or two on the foundations of the cottage that were still clearly visible, this daughter of Glenbristle returning to it across a wide gulf of time and sea looked at her delicately diamonded wrist-watch, saw that it was high noon, and decided to eat her lunch.

'But there ought to be a burn close by,' she said aloud.

There was a burn close by, and convinced this was a clear case of ancestral memory Carrie Royde sat down on the grass cropped close by rabbits and untied the parcel of sandwiches the butler had made up for her.

'Yes,' she murmured, 'I certainly have been here before.'

When she had finished her lunch and drunk of the water of the burn from cupped hands she stuck a cigarette in a long tortoiseshell holder ringed with diamonds and studied *Gaelic Without Tears*. The boat is here. The boat is there. Is the boat here? Is the boat there? The boat is not here. The boat is not there. Is not the boat here? Is not the boat there? The boy says that the boat is here. The boy says that the boat is there. The boy says that the boat is not here. The boy says . . .

The boy's information about the boat's whereabouts became vaguer and vaguer as the outline of the hills opposite flickered in the heat of the sun, and beyond the tobacco-smoke the landscape lost all definite form, blending in a rich blur of purple and green and grey and blue and receding from her as she floated back into the past. Wrapped in a plaid and barelegged, she was gazing anxiously up the glen for signs of the redcoats searching for her Prince, when she fell fast asleep.

Chapter 2

THE SCUFFLE IN THE HEATHER

While Mrs Chester Royde Jr was asleep on that green knoll in Glenbristle the members of the house-party together with two or three of the neighbouring shots the Chieftain of Ben Nevis considered worthy of his best moor were enjoying their lunch after the most satisfactory bag registered on any morning of the Twelfth for six years.

'If we do as well this afternoon on Drumcockie, Hugh, we might lower the '22 record.'

This remark was addressed by the Chieftain to Hugh Cameron of Kilwhillie, a small button-headed man with long thin drooping moustaches, a faded kilt, and a faded eye. Although some ten years junior to Ben Nevis, he was his prime favourite among the Inverness-shire lairds. Their land nowhere marched together. Kilwhillie was a better fisherman; but Ben Nevis preferred the gun, and Kilwhillie was no match for him with a gun. Both were fond of whisky and both flattered themselves they could carry as much of it without a slip of the tongue or a trip of the toe as any two lairds on either side of the Great Glen. You could not call them boon companions, for there was a touch of Celtic melancholy about Kilwhillie, attributed by some to liver, which forbade the epithet; but their intimacy was as close as men in their class can achieve. It was beautifully expressed once by Mrs MacDonald when she said that Donald never slept so soundly and so peacefully as when Hughie Cameron had dined at Glenbogle. The Laird of Kilwhillie was unmarried, not from misogyny but because he had failed to persuade either of the two young women to whom he had proposed to accept him.

'And I don't intend to try again,' he used to assure Ben Nevis. 'I don't think this Bruce and the spider business has any bearing on marriage.'

And Ben Nevis, who always called it a pity when a good fellow got married, used to agree warmly with his friend, though sometimes he would remind him about the succession.

'There's not so much to succeed to now,' Kilwhillie would say, swallowing a dram recklessly. 'Let the Department of Agriculture take over what's left.'

But this was the kind of talk which suited a dying fire and an empty decanter. Up here in the heather on a fine Twelfth of August the mood was different.

'Splendid view, isn't it?' Ben Nevis exclaimed to his guests, with a justifiable touch of Highland pride, for indeed it was a splendid view over the wide level of Strathdun away to where flashed the silver of Loch Hoch, whose farthest bank marked the boundaries of Mac 'ic Eachainn's land.

Chester Royde eyed the Chieftain thoughtfully as he chewed slowly on a mouthful of chicken and ham. Then he turned to Kilwhillie, who was reclining next to him on the heather:

'What exactly lets anybody in on wearing kilts?' he asked. 'I mean to say, suppose I took a fancy to wearing kilts, would that strike a low note in Scotland?'

Kilwhillie, who was also chewing on a mouthful of chicken and ham, gulped it down and murmured, 'Kilt not kilts,' with a hint of reproachful pedantry.

'Are you only allowed one then?' the young financier asked. He did not like this kind of restriction.

'Only one at a time.'

'I got you. But what would happen if I were to wear one of these kilts? Would I be run out of the country on a rail or lynched or anything like that?'

'There's no objection to anybody's wearing the kilt,' said Kilwhillie. 'But there's always the question of the tartan. Some people who haven't themselves the right to a tartan wear their mother's tartan. But I'm against that. I believe it to be contrary to the best tradition. There's a tendency nowadays to introduce alien notions of female descent into the clan system, so that you actually get women claiming a Chiefship, which is preposterous.'

'I suppose now we have women lawyers and preachers and doctors they don't see why they shouldn't be Highland Chiefs. So you'd be against me wearing my wife's tartan, which by the way is the same as our host's. I tell you I was tickled to death when I found that out.'

'Personally I am strongly against wearing the tartan of one's wife. Some people without a tartan of their own who want to wear a tartan wear the Stewart tartan as subjects of King George.'

'But I'm not a subject of King George. And I guess George Washington never had a tartan.'

'The solution for you is to wear a kilt of hodden grey.'

'Grey? Is that the best you can do for me?' Royde exclaimed indignantly. 'I guess I'm better off as I am.' He contemplated his own polychromatic tweediness with frank admiration.

'Boswell in his account of his trip with Johnson through the Hebrides describes Malcolm Macleod as wearing a purple kilt.'

'Purple? Say, that's an idea.'

'But I've never seen a purple kilt in these days,' Kilwhillie added hastily.

'You will,' the young financier promised with fervour. 'But see here, this purple kilt is a secret between you and me. I want to give Carrie a surprise.'

'I shan't say a word about it,' Kilwhillie vowed.

And he meant it. A fine subject for Inverness-shire gossip if it leaked out that he was responsible for an American financier in a purple kilt! Why, it would be conspicuous even at the Oban Gathering.

'That's bully,' said Chester Royde in a tone of the deepest satisfaction. 'I'm crazy about the Highlands, Kilwhillie. I used to laugh at Carrie, but I tell you I've been bitten by this Highland bug myself. Now, see here, let me get this right, old man. Provided I stick to plain colours I'm O.K.? I mean to say purple, blue, green, anything I like so long as I keep off lines and checks and any kind of pattern?'

'It's unusual, of course, but . . .'

'I don't give a darn about it being unusual provided I'm not muscling in on somebody else's property.'

'You certainly wouldn't be doing that.'

'That's all I wanted to know. I mean to say, when I was in Canada I was adopted into the Carroway tribe of Indians with the name of Butting Moose. That's Chester Royde Jr among the Carroways, and that's the way I want to feel in the Highlands. The romance of the whole business has gotten a hold of me, Kilwhillie. I aim to buy a place up here.'

Kilwhillie's faded eyes were lighted up with that strange light which never was on sea or land, but is only to be seen in the eyes of a landed proprietor in the Highlands who hopes he has found a buyer for an overtaxed forest of twelve heads and a shooting-lodge that looks like a bunch of tarnished pepperpots.

'I could probably help you with my advice over that,' he murmured.

'I think I know the kind of place you want. When you've definitely made up your mind let me know. And if I may venture to offer a word of advice, don't talk about it till you have. Otherwise you'll be pestered with all sorts of shooting-properties you don't want to waste time looking at. I think Miss Royde's enjoying it up here with us.'

'Oh, Myrtle's enjoying herself fine.'

Myrtle Royde was seated between the two beefy sons of Ben Nevis – Murdoch the sailor and Iain the undergraduate. They, like their sisters Mary and Catriona, had inherited size and weight from their mother; they could indeed be called massive, particularly Iain, who was the heaviest Five that ever rowed in the Trinity Hall boat. It had been the impressive showing they made in the kilt which had prompted Chester Royde's emulation more than the superb appearance of Ben Nevis himself upon his native heath, with which he would probably never have dreamed of competing.

Myrtle undoubtedly was enjoying herself, but an observer would have been right in dissociating her enjoyment from the company of the two young men, whose conversation indeed was hardly more enlivening than a couple of megaliths. Ben Nevis had noticed optimistically the opportunities a two-seater sports car offered to develop an understanding between two young people. He forgot his second son's lack of conversation and was also unaware of the American point of view which makes dumbness and stupidity synonymous. Iain had more to say than Murdoch, but Myrtle Royde was twenty, and a month or two past the final stage when College boys are interesting to the majority of the female sex.

'Well, I envy you your lovely country,' she had exclaimed when Kilwhillie had commented to her brother on the enjoyment he had fancied in the brightness of her dark-brown eyes and the rosy flush upon her cheeks.

'It's not bad,' the sailor agreed.

'Not bad, indeed? Why, Lieutenant MacDonald, it's divine.'

Murdoch knitted his brows. He wished she would not call him Lieutenant MacDonald, and that if she must she would not pronounce it 'Lootenant'!

'I used to think my sister-in-law Carrie crazy when she was always on at Chester to take her to Scotland, but I understand it now. I wish I had Scotch ancestors myself. Look at that lovely lake shining away down there. We used sometimes to spend the summer in Vermont when we were children, and that's lovely too. But I think it's the romance here that gets me. Look at your father now. What a wonderful figure of a man he is! You can fancy him leading his clan into battle, can't you? Oh, I tell you I'm just in a sort of dream state. And so's Carrie. And I think Chester's pretty taken with it. I noticed a look in his eye I've never seen before when the pipers came in at dinner last night.'

'I think they're rather boring as a matter of fact,' said Iain.

'Mr MacDonald, how can you say that? Why, I was getting thrills all down my back every time they passed behind my chair.'

But Myrtle was spared further disillusionment by the voice of Ben Nevis asking if the guns were ready to move off.

'Drumcockie this afternoon, eh, Ben Nevis?' asked a thin elderly man in plus fours, with a white toothbrush moustache, his countenance dyed an indelible brownish-yellow by the Indian sun.

'Yes, and if we do as well as we did this morning, we ought to make a record.'

'Hope we do,' said the thin man.

Chester Royde asked Kilwhillie who the thin man was. He had not caught his name when they were introduced.

'Colonel Lindsay-Wolseley of Tummie.'

'Say, I don't have to call him Tummie, do I?' the young financier inquired anxiously.

'You can if you like, but he only bought Tummie after the war. I should call him "Colonel" if I were you.'

Chester Royde sighed his relief as he threw a leg across the hill pony that was to bear him to the grouse-teeming moor of Drumcockie.

Alas, for the high hopes of Ben Nevis! His dearest moor failed him. There were some birds. There could not fail to be some birds on Drumcockie. But compared with the number of birds there ought to have been the few that whirred towards the butts and death were nothing.

'What the devil are the beaters playing at, Duncan?' he demanded wrathfully, his eagle's beak darkening to the tint of an Anglican prelate's evening apron.

Big Duncan MacDonald, who looked like a major prophet in tweeds, shook his head.

'I'm thinking it's some of these hikers, Ben Nevis.'

'You think it's what?' the Chieftain gasped.

'Hikers.'

'Hikers? Hikers on Drumcockie?'

'They're after frightening every bird in the neighbourhood,' he declared, with a muttered imprecation in Gaelic.

'You're not seriously telling me, Duncan, that some of these abominable hikers have dared to defile Drumcockie on the Twelfth of August?'

'There were a party of sixteen of them camping in Strathdiddle last night.'

'In defiance of these notice-boards I've just had freshly painted?'

'My grandson Willie says they were camping right round the notice-board on the north bank of the loch.'

Mac 'ic Eachainn glared across Drumcockie Moor away to where the fair expanse of Loch Hoo crowned the head of Strathdiddle with gleaming silver.

'Why wasn't I told of this outrage before, Duncan?'

'Because I was not so anxious to spoil your eye, Ben Nevis. You should not have hit a bird this morning if you were after hearing about those hikers in Strathdiddle. I was hoping no harm would have been done, but there you are. While we were shooting Clacknaclock these hikers were at their devilment on Drumcockie.'

'Duncan,' his chief asked, 'how long have you been in my service?'

'Thirty-two years last June, Ben Nevis.'

'In the whole of that time have you ever known me go back on my word?'

'No, I don't believe you ever went back on your word, Ben Nevis.'

'Then when I tell you that whatever it costs me I am determined to rid my land of hikers you know I mean what I say.'

'You said the very same thing about rabbits, Ben Nevis, three years back,' his old henchman reminded him.

'Hikers don't breed like rabbits.'

'But you cannot trap hikers, Ben Nevis.'

'No, I can't trap them, thanks to the grandmotherly laws under which we suffer, but I can clear them off my land, and I will too. They're a fouler pest than rabbits. They're worse than bracken. Are hikers going to be able to do what the Macintoshes were never able to do? Am I or am I not the twenty-third MacDonald of Ben Nevis?'

'Gently now, gently, Ben Nevis. You're getting very red in the face. You mustn't excite yourself too much. It's very annoying, right enough. Och, it's terrible. But you mustn't let it boil your blood too much. If I call in the beaters we might move along to the Derrybeg. It's not too late at all.'

'I'm not going to shoot another bird today. The morning bag was the best for six years. I'm not going to spoil it. I want to find these hikers. Go and get hold of my two boys and Kilwhillie. I can't ask my other guests . . . no, stay where you are and I'll speak to them myself.'

The Chieftain strode across the moor, his kilt swinging, his sporran jiggling, his amaranthine nose cleaving the air. He came to the butt at which Colonel Lindsay-Wolseley was standing.

'Look here, Wolseley, you had a lot of experience on the North-West Frontier. I want your help. There's a band of filthy hikers loose in Strathdiddle.'

Colonel Wolseley looked a little apprehensive. He did not immediately perceive the link between Inverness-shire and Waziristan.

'What action exactly were you proposing to take, Ben Nevis?'

'I'm going to round the brutes up. They've ruined any hope of good sport on Drumcockie for today. And I *don't* see why they should get away with it.'

'You mean you're going to turn them off your land?'

'I'm going to lock them up in Glenbogle for a couple of nights and see if that'll give them the lesson they deserve.'

'You're proposing to use force?' the Colonel asked, amazement only kept in check by the traditions of his caste and calling.

'When these savages see themselves covered by half a dozen guns I don't assume they'll offer any resistance,' the Chieftain barked.

'But you can't threaten to shoot trespassers, Ben Nevis. You really can't.'

'I can and I will,' he declared.

'Well, I'm sorry, but I'm afraid I cannot take any part in such a proceeding. You must remember that I am Convener of the Police Committee of the County Council. It would put me in an impossible position. And if you'll take the advice of a friend, Ben Nevis, you'll avoid putting yourself in an impossible position by taking any such action as you contemplate. The proper course is to ask for their names and addresses and institute legal proceedings. If you take the law into your own hands you'll expose yourself to an action for assault and false imprisonment. You may get heavy damages against you.'

'Look here, Lindsay-Wolseley, I don't want you to take what I'm going to say personally. I've no desire to be offensive. But I'm not in the mood to be lectured about my actions. This band of miscreants camped last night on the banks of Loch Hoo, actually right round one of my freshly painted NO CAMPING notice-boards. Not content with that they've evidently been careering about all over Drumcockie this morning, and our Twelfth has been wrecked.'

'My dear Ben Nevis, do not misunderstand me. I sympathize profoundly over this beastly business. But when you ask me to take part with you in what amounts to a punitive expedition I should be no true friend of yours if I didn't try to dissuade you from such an action. I suppose you'll call me a cold-blooded Lowlander, but I do beg you to think twice before you embark upon a course of action the consequences of which may be . . . I mean to say, Ben Nevis, we landed proprietors cannot afford to stir up popular feeling in these democratic days.'

'Clap-trap!'

'What?'

'I said clap-trap, Lindsay-Wolseley. You're talking Bolshie clap-trap.'

'You are allowing your feelings to get the better of you, Ben Nevis,' the Colonel observed, a dull flush asserting itself beneath the brownish-yellow dye of the Indian sun.

'I have no desire to quarrel with you, Lindsay-Wolseley.'

'I accept that, Ben Nevis. So let us say no more about it,' the Colonel replied, with a gesture of old-world courtliness. 'I'm very sorry that the splendid sport you're been giving us has been interfered with by uninvited guests.'

'I suppose Bottley won't be any more anxious than you to round up these filthy hikers,' Ben Nevis growled, with a glance in the direction of Sir Hubert Bottley, the owner of the famous forest of Cloy which had been bought by his father, the first baronet, out of Bottley's Bottled Beans.

'I won't answer for him,' said the Colonel hurriedly. 'Bottley must decide for himself.'

'I shan't try to involve him or Rawstorne or Jack Fraser,' Ben Nevis said proudly. 'I think I can manage with my own people. We've managed for a good many years now. I only asked you, Wolseley, because I thought you might enjoy the kind of sport you must often have enjoyed at Peshawar. Well, I'm sorry to break up our day like this, but I must get my forces together.'

The Colonel saw it was useless to argue further with his friend. At any rate, he was glad to hear himself addressed again as 'Wolseley'. It indicated that his refusal to take part in the punitive expedition against the hikers was no longer resented. Lindsay-Wolseley was what Ben Nevis always called him when they found themselves in disagreement at a meeting of the County Council.

'That was the kind of thing which wrecked the 'Forty-five, Hugh,' the Chieftain observed to the laird of Kilwhillie when the ponies with the four recreant guns were lost to sight in a dip of the moor on the way back to the Pass of Ballochy and the waiting cars. 'However, thank God, the old loyalties haven't entirely disappeared!'

'You can't expect newcomers to feel as we do, Donald.' Then Hugh Cameron remembered his plan to sell Knocknacolly and its dilapidated lodge to Chester Royde Jr. 'Not *all* newcomers, that is.'

'Well', I'll say I'm enjoying myself,' the young financier declared. 'But what do we do if these hoodlums won't put their hands up, Ben Nevis?'

'I'm sending the beaters round to cut off their retreat. I don't think they'll resist. They're a weedy type. And there are some women with them. Extraordinary class of people altogether. I'm relying on you, Mary, and you, Catriona, to deal with these women. And what about you, Miss Royde?'

'Oh, please don't call me that, Ben Nevis. I don't feel a little bit like a daughter of the clan when you call me Miss Royde.'

'Very nice of you. Appreciate it very much. Well, what are you going to do, Myrtle? I think Murdoch had better look after you.'

'No, I know just what I'm going to do,' said Myrtle firmly. 'I'm going to stay right by you, Ben Nevis. I'm going to be your *vivandière*.'

The imaginative observer capable of rejecting the materialistic explanation that it was a sporting party walking up any game that was about would have derived from the spectacle of Mac 'ic Eachainn's line of battle the deepest romantic gratification. On the right as befitted MacDonalds was the Chieftain himself, a hefty son on either side of him, a daughter not less hefty on either side of their brothers, the tartan of the kilts and skirts in which red predominated recalling a dozen poems of battles fought by the MacDonalds of Ben Nevis. A few yards behind this line of red and immediately behind Mac 'ic Eachainn himself marched Myrtle Royde carrying a flask of whisky.

A pity Hector was out with his regiment in India, his father reflected. This was the very girl for him. Murdoch was too much of a slowcoach. He ought to have done better with the chances he had already had. And after all this jolly little girl with so much money in prospect would want an eldest son. She'd be sure to cotton on to Hector. He had a good mind to send an urgent cable telling Hector to apply for leave at once and fly home. It would cost a bit, but nothing venture nothing win. Ben Nevis looked round and smiled benignly at his *vivandière*, and the answering smile dimpling those cheeks decided him. He would cable Hector to obtain leave for urgent family reasons and come by plane.

The centre of Mac 'ic Eachainn's line of battle consisted of Chester Royde, whose fat face had taken on the severe lines of an Arizona sheriff riding after a gang of rustlers in the timeless air of Wild West romance, and his head-keeper, Duncan Macdonald, who looked like Elijah hot upon the trail of the priests of Baal. The left was commanded by Hugh Cameron of Kilwhillie, who had a couple of gillies with him.

For a quarter of an hour the line advanced steadily across Drumcockie's heather. Then as the moorland began to slope towards the braes of Strathdiddle Mac 'ic Eachainn uttered a shout.

'There they are!'

Yes, there they were in green corduroy shorts and brown corduroy shorts, in pink shirts and pale green shirts and coffee-coloured shirts, hatless, towzled, with long sticks and crêpe-soled shoes and knapsacks, there they were sitting round a fire they had just lighted to make tea and listening to a portable wireless, female hikers and male hikers to the number of sixteen.

Ben Nevis charged ahead of the others, and five of the hikers dived for their cameras to get snapshots of this magnificent specimen of the native fauna striding through the heather in the sun's eye. One young woman with smoked glasses and very short green corduroy shorts whose fat flaming thighs looked as if they were melting at the knees held up her hand when the Chieftain was almost on top of the party and asked him to stand still for a moment while she altered the focus of her Kodak.

'Who is in command of this party?' Ben Nevis bellowed.

The hikers looked at one another. The spirit of comradeship which had animated them ever since they had got out of the train from London at Perth and hiked their way to the bonny banks of Loch Hoo had made a leader superfluous.

'Who is in command of this party?' Ben Nevis bellowed again.

The loudness of his voice had by now convinced the hikers that the first specimen of the native fauna they had seen between Perth and Inverness was angry about something. They turned to the only member of the party over twenty-four. This was a dark desiccated little man of anything between forty and fifty with legs as thin and hairy as a spider's and the eyes of a kindly old maid, the sort of eyes one so often sees in confirmed scoutmasters.

'I am the Secretary of the N.U.H., sir,' he told Ben Nevis in a prim voice. 'Were you wanting information about anything?'

'I don't know what the N.U.H. is, but you must be aware that you are . . .'

'Excuse me, sir, the initials N.U.H. stand for National Union of Hikers. We are now a very large organization with branches in every one of our great cities. My name is Prew, Sydney Prew. I'm afraid I haven't a card with me. One disembarrasses oneself of such urban paraphernalia, does one not, when one takes to the open road?'

The combination of some peculiarly irritating quality in the timbre of Mr Prew's spinsterish voice, of the sight of his own armed forces closing in upon the hikers, and a dozen beaters advancing upon them from the rear, and of the recollection of his ruined Twelfth of August was too much for Donald MacDonald, the twenty-third of Ben Nevis. He was suddenly seized with an access of rage that must have been similar to the convulsion which had seized his ancestor Hector of the Great Jaw when in the year 1482 he speared eleven Macintoshes beside Loch na Craosnaich and drowned them in it one after another. Grasping the secretary of the N.U.H. by the collar of his khaki shirt, he shook him as a conscientious housemaid shakes a mat.

'This is assault and battery,' protested Mr Prew. 'I call on all you boys and girls to observe what this gentleman is doing. He is assaulting me. And please note I am making no resistance whatever. May I ask what is the meaning of this outrage?'

The sight of Mr Prew's inquiring face turned round with some difficulty owing to the grip upon his shirt-collar seemed to rouse Ben Nevis to fresh fury, and he shook him more violently than ever.

'I'll teach you to run amok among my birds. I'll teach you to camp out round one of my notice-boards forbidding camping. I'll teach you to light fires in the heather.'

By this time the shaker and the shaken were both so much out of breath that neither could speak, and the only sound that broke the heathery silence of the braes of Strathdiddle was the voice of a crooner coming from the portable wireless. Even those who disapprove of Mac 'ic Eachainn's assault upon Mr Prew will not blame him for dropping Mr Prew and giving the crooner the contents of his gun's two barrels.

'Look here, that's my portable,' a tall pink-faced young man expostulated. Whereupon Ben Nevis seized him by the front of his mauve shirt and shook him as violently as he had shaken Mr Prew. The young woman with the melting knees screamed in a rage and banged away at Ben Nevis with her hiker's staff. Catriona MacDonald caught hold of her by the back of her shorts and put a hefty arm round her neck. There was a general mêlée, but the male hikers, severely handicapped by the attempts of the female hikers to help them, were no match for Clan Donald.

'What will we do with them, Ben Nevis?' Duncan asked when the invaders were disarmed and surrounded.

'Bring them along to Ballochy, and I'll send the lorry for them when we get back to the Castle. You want to camp on my land, do you?' he snarled at Mr Prew. 'Very well, then you shall camp in the dungeons of Glenbogle Castle and see how you like that.'

'This is going to be a serious matter for you, Mr MacDonald,' said the Secretary of the N.U.H., his prim voice trembling with indignation, 'for I presume you are the Mr MacDonald who owns this land.'

Mac 'ic Eachainn turned away with a look of utter disgust. A gardener would as soon think of arguing with a slug as he would with Sydney Prew.

Chapter 3

ANCESTRAL VOICES

___

While such stirring events were happening on Drumcockie moor and the braes of Strathdiddle, Mrs Chester Royde Jr was asleep on that green knoll in the perfumed silence of Glenbristle.

When she awoke with a start about three o'clock to find two kilted forms gazing at her it is no matter for wonderment that she should have failed to disentangle them immediately from the romantic dream in which she had been wrapped and that for two or three all too brief moments she should have fancied that her attempt, with the help of Yoga, *Gaelic Without Tears* and dormant ancestral memories, to spirit herself back into the past had been successful, and that the young men, one in the vivid red and yellow of the Macmillan tartan, the other in the kaleidoscopic tartan of the Buchanans, were ancestral visions, their garb shining with celestial radiance. She recalled reading somewhere that Gaelic was the language of Eden, and thought it another good opportunity to murmur, 'La math.'

This time the phrase worked. The young man in the Macmillan tartan at once replied:

'La math. Tha è blath.'

'Blah?' Mrs Chester Royde echoed to herself. Was this fair shock-headed young man trying to be rude? The celestial radiance faded from the red and yellow of his kilt, for she had now perceived that the nimbus was caused by the newness of the material.

'Tha è blath,' the fair shock-headed young man repeated, feeling in the pocket of his doublet and drawing forth a copy of *Gaelic Without Tears* at the same instant as Mrs Royde discovered her copy and began turning over the pages.

'You'd better both speak English,' the second young man mumbled severely in the accent of Glasgow. 'Blah's just about what you're talking, Alan.'

'I've found "blath",' Carrie Royde exclaimed. 'It means warm. Yes, it is very warm indeed, isn't it? I see you're learning Gaelic from the same book as I'm using. But you're two exercises ahead of me.'

'I've been right through it once,' said the red and yellow kilt, with a touch of loftiness.

His companion grinned.

'What are you laughing at, James?' the red and yellow kilt demanded.

'I was not laughing, Alan. I was thinking to myself.'

Carrie did not want the peace of Glenbristle disturbed by a brawl, and she said quickly that Gaelic was a very difficult language.

'I thought at first it was because I was American,' she went on. 'But it seems to me just as difficult for English people.'

'I'm not English,' said the red and yellow kilt hotly, his shock of light-brown hair billowing with indignation at the disgraceful slur.

'Well, I'm not really American,' Carrie said soothingly. 'I'm a Canadian Scot married to an American. Royde is my name. But I was a Macdonald,' she added proudly.

'My name's Alan Macmillan, and this is my friend James Buchanan.'

'I'm so very pleased to meet you both. Are you staying near here?'

'We're camping further up the glen,' said Macmillan.

'Oh, you're camping, are you? I suppose you didn't see the notice-board?' Carrie asked.

'We saw the notice-board right enough,' Buchanan said. 'That's *why* we are camping in Glenbristle.'

'We don't recognize the right of lairds like Ben Nevis who have stolen the land from their clansmen to treat it as their own private property,' Macmillan explained.

'Why is Glenbristle a wilderness?' Buchanan asked in his best Glasgow University Union manner. 'I'll tell you why. It's because the grandfather and great-grandfather of the present owner cleared out the crofters and drove them to Canada.'

'It's strange you should say that,' Carrie Royde remarked pensively. 'You see those stones and nettles over there?'

'They show that there was a cottage here once,' Buchanan said.

'There certainly was,' Carrie declared impressively. 'The cottage of my great-great-grandfather who was evicted from Glenbristle in the first clearance.'

'That's interesting,' Alan Macmillan commented.

'It is very interesting,' Mrs Chester Royde Jr agreed emphatically.

'How do you know this was where your great-great-grandfather lived?' James Buchanan asked.

Carrie would have liked to say that the site had been revealed to her in a dream by the spirit of an ancestor, and if Alan Macmillan had been alone she might have succumbed to the temptation; but she felt that James Buchanan's bullet-head was too hard for such a tale, and instead attributed her knowledge of the evicted crofter's site to family tradition.

'I used to dream about Glenbristle when I was a little girl living on the shores of Lake Ontario. Once upon a time in a peach-orchard I saw . . .' she hesitated. It was a pity that a man privileged to wear that Joseph's coat of a tartan should be so evidently drab in his point of view about existence. Alan Macmillan might easily have seen the fairies himself, but of course he would never admit it in front of his prosaic friend.

'Are you camping round here?' Buchanan asked her.

'No; I'm staying at Glenbogle Castle.'

The two young men stiffened.

'Oh, please don't look so ferocious, both of you. If you knew Ben Nevis you'd think him most terribly kind.'

'We're not likely to have the honour of making his acquaintance,' said Alan Macmillan proudly.

'I wouldn't make it if we had,' Buchanan avowed. 'It's men like MacDonald of Ben Nevis who've brought Scotland to the position it's in today.'

'But surely Scotland is in a perfectly wonderful position,' the returned exile ejaculated.

'Practically dead,' Buchanan declared firmly.

'But that's not at all what we Canadians think. We think Scotland is the moving spirit of the British Empire.'

The two young men shook their heads compassionately.

'That's a sublimation of the libido,' Alan Macmillan asserted. 'Canadian Scots being mostly descendants of evicted Gaels long to score off their oppressors, and they sublimate this longing by being more imperialist than the imperialists who first exploited them a hundred years ago. I'm afraid James is right. Scotland is practically dead.'

'That's very discouraging news to hear on coming back to the land of one's forefathers. It certainly is. But why do you blame a nice man like Ben Nevis?'

'You needn't look beyond these empty glens for the answer to that one,' said Buchanan.

'Can't anything be done about it?' Carrie asked.

'We are doing our best,' he told her.

'Who are you?' she asked, piqued by the slight suggestion of portentousness in the emphasis on the first person plural.

The two young men looked at one another, each with a question in his eyes. Both almost imperceptibly shook their heads.

'It's a society we belong to,' said Alan Macmillan, after an awkward pause. He was upset by the thought that this pleasant red-haired Canadian should be fancying he and James distrusted her.

'A secret society,' James Buchanan added quickly.

'Isn't that thrilling?' Carrie exclaimed. 'I do wish you'd tell me more about it.'

'I'm afraid we can't very well,' Alan Macmillan said apologetically. 'You see, it's a political secret society. Look here, would you like to come up the glen to our camp? It's about a mile from here. We can give you some tea.'

'Why, I'd love a cup of tea. Aren't you an angel child?'

Buchanan's dark eyebrows beetled in his bullet-head. He did not trust Alan Macmillan's imperviousness to feminine wiles. However, if she thought she was going to be able to secure a tête-à-tête with Alan by pleading the view from up there as an excuse she was mistaken.

'Well, I must say I never expected to find two Highland beaux in Glenbristle,' Carrie said, when she and the two young men were walking up the glen towards their camp. And to herself she added the reflection that only in dreams had she ventured to hope she should behold anything so attractive as Alan Macmillan with his fair wavy hair and his melting blue eyes and clear-cut rose-browned features.

'What a gay tartan the Macmillan is,' she exclaimed. 'It makes my Ben Nevis MacDonald look quite dingy. My husband would go crazy about that. He just worships colour.'

'Is your husband staying at Glenbogle Castle?' Alan asked.

'Yes, he's away up on the moors today shooting grouse with our host.'

Had Carrie but known it, this was the very moment when on the braes of Strathdiddle Ben Nevis had just silenced the crooner with the contents of both barrels.

'The Twelfth of August, eh?' James Buchanan growled. 'That's all these lairds think about. Shooting stags and grouse and salmon . . .'

'You don't shoot salmon, James,' said his friend, a little irritably. He was inclined to deplore James's manners in criticizing lairds like this when the guest of the one on whose land they were camping was their guest.

'Salmon fishing I was going to say if you hadn't chipped in so smartly,' James Buchanan snapped.

'And your tartan is even more gay than Mr Macmillan's,' Carrie interposed. 'It has every colour imaginable in it.'

'Too many, I think,' said Alan.

'Not one too many,' James declared passionately. 'Just because the Macmillans can't think beyond two colours that doesn't say the Buchanans are to be bound by *them*. We let you have your red and yellow and kept a few of our own besides.'

'A few!' Alan exclaimed. 'You have the whole spectrum.'

'Look here, Alan Macmillan, I'd be glad to hear the reasons on which you base your right to sneer at the Buchanan tartan.'

'I was not sneering at it. I simply said I thought it was too polychromatic.'

'Alan, you're awful fond of trying to skate out of rash statements on long words. But that won't work with me. You sneered at the Buchanan tartan. I want to know why.'

'I was not sneering. I merely expressed my personal preference for fewer colours.'

'So our clan tartans are all to be re-designed to fit in with your private taste in colours. Well, that's a good one, right enough. Gosh! You really are the limit, Alan.'

Carrie felt it was time to intervene again.

'I'm sure Mr Macmillan would never think of changing that very lovely tartan of yours, Mr Buchanan.'

'He'd better try,' James muttered.

'Personally, I think they're both beautiful tartans. And, as I said just now, they make my own Ben Nevis MacDonald look quite drab. But I wish you'd tell me some more about this terrible condition of Scotland, because I assure you I do feel so distressed about it.'

For the rest of the way to the camp James Buchanan rattled off statistics, a confusing business always but rendered more confusing in his case by the indistinctness of his enunciation.

'So I think you'll admit, Mistress Royde, that I was not exaggerating when I said a while back that Scotland was practically dead,' he concluded.

Carrie came back to consciousness with a start.

'Indeed you certainly did not, Mr Buchanan. But I feel they ought to know all that in Canada . . . why, there are your tents I do declare.

Aren't they cute? . . . Yes, I think you and Mr Macmillan ought to come over to Canada and explain about the state of affairs in Scotland. I'm sure you'd have a most sympathetic audience. And I could give you letters of introduction to so many people who would be helpful.'

James Buchanan began to consider Mrs Chester Royde from a new angle. A visit to Canada with letters of introduction to the right people might lead to a good opening in business.

'I'm much obliged to you, Mistress Royde. I'll certainly think seriously about your offer.'

By now they had reached a grassy level at the foot of a steep rocky escarpment in the shelter of which were pitched the low green tents of her hosts.

'I feel I'm being entertained by two Jacobite fugitives,' Carrie declared, with a sigh of gratified romance.

'They wouldn't have been able to offer you tea,' Alan Macmillan reminded her.

'No, that's true. And I just can't tell you how much I'm looking forward to a cup of tea.'

Nor was Carrie disappointed by that cup of tea brewed with water from a near-by stream. It seemed the most delicious cup of tea she had ever drunk and afterwards when she sat smoking in the mellow afternoon sunshine, her back supported by a ledge of warm granite, she was confirmed in her belief that this glen welcomed her as a child of its own.

'I wish you two boys would tell me more about yourselves,' she said. 'And more about what you're going to do for Scotland. I can't help feeling I was brought to Glenbristle today for some purpose. I am aware of a most mysterious sort of psychic atmosphere all around me. I couldn't hope to put it into words, because of course if the atmosphere really is psychic you just can't put it into words. Yes, it's a very strange sensation. If I were a poet I would want to write a wonderful poem right now.'

'You'd better get Alan to write one for you,' said James Buchanan. 'He's a poet.'

'He is? Why, Alan, isn't that . . . oh dear, I hope you don't mind my calling you Alan?'

'Not at all,' Alan replied, scowling through a rich blush because he noticed what he fancied was a slightly derisive expression in James Buchanan's eyes.

'And what are you, Mr James? Are you a poet too?'

'No, I'm a lawyer,' said James Buchanan in the voice of a future Lord Justice Clerk.

'Ah, that's why you're so good at figures,' Carrie observed brightly. And she turned round to gaze reverently at the bard. 'I suppose your poetry is full of Celtic mysticism?'

'I hope not,' said the bard distastefully, who from what he and the young poets of the Scottish Renaissance believed was the sunny summit of Parnassus had been hurling savage epigrams at the Celtic twilight since his first term at Glasgow University.

'You hope not?' Carrie exclaimed in surprise. 'But surely that's the great gift we Celts can offer the world today?'

'If that's all we have to offer we won't get very far. What we have to teach the world is how to make the best of itself.'

'But isn't that a mystical message of spiritual hope?'

'Not at all,' the bard replied, with a hint of petulance. 'We have to teach the world how to make the best *practical* use of itself.'

'Aye, that's what the world has to learn,' James Buchanan agreed. 'And that's what a free Scotland could teach it.'

'Well, I must say you both puzzle me. I thought your idea for a free Scotland was to restore the spirit of the past and so set an example to the world of today. Surely spiritual values are what we all so badly need?'

'We don't object to spiritual values *quâ se*,' said the bard. 'But we have realized the danger of putting thought before action. Therefore although I write a good deal of poetry I know that what I call poetic action is the only poetry really worth while. For instance I consider that when James and myself camp here in Glenbristle in defiance of a notice-board forbidding camping that is more truly poetry than for me to write verse about deserted glens and lone shielings in the misty islands. That's just stale emotionalism. James and I are strictly practical people.'

'In every way,' James agreed.

'We told you about our secret society,' Alan went on.

'You didn't tell me very much about it,' Carrie put in reproachfully.

'That's another example of poetic action,' the bard insisted. 'It's an extremely practical society.'

'Well, of course I can't pass an opinion about that,' Carrie said, 'because I don't know what your aims are except what Mr James told me about statistics. I know you want to change all those statistics.'

The bard looked at the lawyer.

'I think we might tell Mistress Royde a few of our ideas, for instance that one about kidnapping MacDonald of Ben Nevis. Obviously we can't do that now because it would involve her.'

'You weren't going to kidnap Ben Nevis?' Carrie gasped.

'Only as part of a general campaign for kidnapping lairds,' the bard explained. 'But don't worry, Mistress Royde. There are plenty of others. We'll leave Ben Nevis out of the general campaign, at any rate for this year.'

'I'm afraid you'll think me terribly dense,' said Carrie. 'But I wish you'd explain just exactly what would be the practical value of kidnapping lairds.'

'The creation of a state of uneasiness among the landed class,' James informed her. 'The same with the rich business men. We aim to kidnap quite a few of them. Trades-union leaders too. Ministers. Sheriffs. Schoolmasters. The Editor of the *Glasgow Herald*. The Editor of the *Scotsman*. The general idea is to shake up complacency.'

'Take a man like MacDonald of Ben Nevis,' Alan urged. 'He's a friend of yours. But you must see how fatal that kind of stodgy comfortable existence is to any display of national energy. A man like that could do so much to give a lead to the country. But what does he do? Shoots, stalks, fishes, forbids camping on his land, and thinks he has fulfilled his political duty if he votes against a measure of reform which will put a halfpenny on the Inverness-shire rates. We're not going to kidnap him. I give you my word about that. But think how much being kidnapped would widen the point of view of a landed proprietor like that. Men of his type require mental shocks imaginatively applied. They move in a rut.'

'The whole country's moving in a rut,' said James solemnly. 'And the whole country's got to be jolted out of it.'

'By poetic action,' the bard insisted, rising to his feet and apparently ready to begin such action immediately.

'I'm so glad I chose today to visit Glenbristle,' Carrie said. 'I'm still a little hazy about just what you *are* going to do, but it's so wonderful to feel that something really is going to be done. I feel more positive than ever that I was guided to Glenbristle today by some higher power for a purpose. Do you have women in your secret society?'

'We have women members, yes,' James Buchanan answered doubt-fully.

'Well, won't you accept me as a member? I'd be so happy to help you kidnap anybody except Ben Nevis. I think I'd have to make him an exception because he has been so intensely hospitable, and I should feel a little mean about helping to kidnap him.'

'Well, of course personally, Mistress Royde, I would welcome you as a member,' said James, who had not forgotten that promise of hers to give him introductions to the right people in Canada. 'But I think it'll have to be referred to the Inner Council.'

'Of course James and I are both members,' the bard added encouragingly.

'I suppose you have an annual subscription?' Carrie asked.

'We have voluntary donations,' James replied. 'The trouble with annual subscriptions was that if a member got in arrears with his we couldn't expel him. It's not like a club or an ordinary society. Once you've admitted somebody to a secret society he knows too much. So we had to substitute voluntary donations for a regular subscription.'

'I hope you found that satisfactory,' Carrie asked.

'Oh, it's not too bad. We've had to spend a good deal on paint, but there's still a small balance in hand.'

'On paint?'

'Imphm! Painting slogans in Gaelic and English on public buildings.'

'I'm against that, James, don't forget,' said the bard sternly. 'It's pandering to words, and we can't afford to waste any energy on words.'

'Well, whether I'm admitted to your secret society or not,' said Carrie, 'I'd like to make a voluntary donation right away. There's no rule against that, I hope.'

'No, there's no rule against that,' James Buchanan admitted.

Carrie took out her vanity bag, pressed a spring, and from behind the mirror produced a hundred-dollar bill, which she offered to James. He looked at it, and his eyes were suddenly glazed as though by a well-timed upper cut.

'Losh, Alan,' he murmured, 'we'll be able to . . .' He put a hand up to his brow as if to shut out the too dazzling prospect conjured by this hundred-dollar bill. Then he turned to Carrie. 'But, look here, Mistress Royde, this is too much, at any rate before you're a member. We won't be able to convene the Inner Council before the end of next month at the earliest.'

'Oh, dear! Why, I'll probably be back in America by then,' Carrie sighed.

'I think we ought to take the responsibility of admitting Mistress Royde ourselves, James,' said the bard.

'But we're not a quorum, Alan.'

'This is a clear case for poetic action, in my opinion.'

'If we even had a third,' James Buchanan lamented.

'Well, we haven't,' said Alan Macmillan. 'And I'm positive this is a case for poetic action. If the rest of the Inner Council make a row about it I'll clear out of the S.B.A. and start another society.'

'Look here, Alan, if Mistress Royde doesn't mind I'd like to talk the matter over with you alone,' James suggested.

'Sure,' said Carrie. 'I'll walk back to where you found me by the ruins of my great-great-grandfather's cottage and you can come along and tell me what you've decided.' She smiled at the young men. 'Somehow I feel you'll discover a way.'

Carrie's presentiment was right. She had hardly been seated ten minutes on the knoll where she had fallen asleep after lunch than the red and yellow of the Macmillan and the rainbow of the Buchanan tartan came flashing down Glenbristle's grass-grown rocky road.

'Well?' she asked when the young men rejoined her.

'We're taking it upon ourselves to admit you to the Scottish Brotherhood of Action,' Alan Macmillan announced gravely. 'Will you please repeat the oath after me?'

'I think that's a very wonderful oath,' Carrie declared when she had echoed the bard's words and been initiated into the secret sign and countersign by which members of the Brotherhood recognized one another. 'Did you compose that oath, Alan?'

'Yes, I composed it, Mistress Royde,' said the bard modestly.

'I was positive you did. And listen, please don't call me Mrs Royde when we're just ourselves among the Brotherhood. Please call me "Carrie" then. How long do you expect to be camping in Glenbristle?'

'We were planning to move on nearer to Fort William tomorrow,' said James. 'I have to be back in Glasgow by the end of the week.'

'Isn't that too bad! And you, Alan?'

'I'll find a place to camp by myself for a week. I want to do some work.'

'I believe you're going to write a poem,' Carrie exclaimed.

The bard looked embarrassed. He felt such an admission might sound feeble after his stern words about action.

'I'm going to revise some poems I've already written.'

'Well, why don't you come back to Glenbristle when James goes to Glasgow?'

'Ach, you'd better stay where you are, Alan,' said James, who had been prepared for this development from long experience of the bard's effect on women and their effect on him. He had always found much to deplore in these effects, but that voluntary donation had made for an unusual tolerance. 'I'll stay another night and catch the bus to Fort William on Saturday.'

'I think I ought to be going back to the Castle now,' said Carrie. 'Will you both walk with me as far as Glenbogle?'

The Brotherhood was temporarily dissolved where the mouldering signpost hinted at Glenbristle and the garish new notice-board proclaimed NO CAMPING.

The two young men turned back along the rocky grass-grown road whence they had come. Mrs Chester Royde turned up Glenbogle in the direction of the Castle.

She had just entered the pine-darkened drive when she was passed by a lorry and saw to her astonishment that it was packed with young men and young women all shouting what sounded like abusive expressions at the tops of their voices.

'Ah, there you are, Mrs Royde,' her host shouted when she came into the Great Hall covered with targes and Lochaber axes, old muskets and stags' heads, and the portraits of the kilted chieftains of Hector's race. 'Have you heard about our bag?'

'No, did you have good sport?'

'Sixteen camping hikers. We've got the women locked up in the dungeon under the North Tower, and the men, if you can call them men, safely stowed away in the dungeon under the Raven's Tower — the one we call Mac 'ic Eachainn's Cradle.'

Carrie turned to her husband, who was standing in front of a welcome evening fire in the great hooded hearth, a whisky and soda in his hand.

'Chester, is this a joke?'

'Joke?' he echoed enthusiastically. 'No joke at all. Finest day's sport I ever had. Carrie, this little old country of yours is some country. I'm crazy about the way they do things here.'

And Ben Nevis, reflected Carrie, was the man whom the Scottish Brotherhood of Action wanted to shake out of a humdrum complacency and forcibly extricate from a rut.

Chapter 4

DINNER POSTPONED

It was the Lady of Ben Nevis among his immediate entourage who first ventured to question the wisdom of the Chieftain's high-handed action, catching him at the moment when he reached his dressing-room from the bath, herself already dressed for dinner. He found her there in black satin, a great catafalque occupying valuable space required for his own toilet.

'What do you want, Trixie?' he asked, a touch of slightly querulous apprehension in his tone which the consciousness that he had nothing on beneath his flower-silk dressing-gown did not allow him to neutralize by a masterful gesture of patriarchal authority.

'I want to have a little talk with you, Donald, before dinner,' the Lady of Ben Nevis boomed placidly. Dame Clara Butt answering a diapason of the Albert Hall organ was never more sure of herself. Mrs MacDonald's sway over her husband was a miniature (though perhaps miniature is an infelicitous word to use in her connection) of the sway which England exerts over Scotland. Mrs MacDonald, to put it shortly, had the money. Her father, a magnate of English business, had invested a considerable amount in the marriage of his only daughter to the Highland Chieftain, and he had taken care to see that his money was not lost by leaving a large sum in trust for her and her children after he had presented his son-in-law with enough to put the estate in order.

'Look at the time, Trixie,' said her husband reproachfully. 'And I have to shave as well as dress.'

'You can get on with your shaving and dressing while we have our little talk, Donald. You shouldn't have dallied so long talking to Hugh Cameron.'

Ben Nevis puffed out a sigh for feminine obstinacy and began to strop his razor.

'You know what I want to talk about, Donald?'

'Haven't the ghost of a notion,' he replied, with what they both knew was but a feeble simulation of defiance.

'It's this business on the moors this afternoon.'

'Oh, these hikers, you mean. Well, why are you worrying yourself about them?'

'I am worrying about them for many reasons, Donald, but chiefly on your account.'

'There's nothing to worry about on my account, as I told Lindsay-Wolseley this afternoon,' said Ben Nevis.

'Oh, Colonel Wolseley was worried, was he? I can't say I'm surprised, Donald. He's such a nice sensible man, and Mrs Wolseley is a very nice sensible woman. And such a good gardener. Her primulas are always a joy. What did Colonel Wolseley say?'

'Talked a lot of nonsense. These fellows who've spent half their lives in India always do. I suppose the sun affects them.'

'But what did he say, Donald?'

'I don't know exactly what he said, but he seemed to have some idea that my action wasn't legal. Well, if it isn't, all I've got to say is there's something very radically wrong with the law. Things have come to a pretty pass if bands of hikers can camp round notice-boards forbidding camping, and light fires on grouse-moors, and scare the birds, and sit listening to all this beastly jazz on the wireless in the middle of a landowner's preserves. I told Lindsay-Wolseley I was determined to give them a lesson and when I've made up my mind, Trixie, you know nothing will change it.'

'Yes; that's why I thought it wiser for us to have this little talk. I'm sure you already realize you've been too hasty.'

'I don't realize anything of the kind,' the Chieftain contradicted loudly. 'And I do wish you'd let me get on with my shaving. I'll be late for dinner, and you know what a point I make about punctuality. I've always tried to set an example. You have to in the West Highlands. We'd be starting dinner at midnight before we knew where we were if I didn't set an example.'

'There's no need for you to be late, Donald. If you'll give me the keys of the dungeons I'll try to arrange matters.'

The indignant swing round of the Chieftain's head at this request was too quick for the shaving-brush, which missed his cheek and profusely lathered the inside of his right ear.

'Arrange matters?' he fumed. 'How are you proposing to arrange matters?'

'Why, I shall tell Mrs Parsall to give them supper, and then they can be driven back to where they were camping beside Loch Hoo. Duncan

45

told me you'd given him orders to throw all their camping outfit into the loch. But I said you'd changed your mind and did not wish the tents disturbed.'

Ben Nevis stared at his Lady. Had the lather in his ear affected his hearing?

'You countermanded orders I'd given to Duncan?'

'Yes, dear, and now let me have the keys. I shall have plenty of time to put matters right before dinner,' she assured him tranquilly.

'Look here, Trixie, when I rounded up these hikers I didn't bring them to Glenbogle to be entertained. I brought them here to show them that they can't play fast and loose with a man like myself. They are going to remain in the dungeons at any rate for tonight. I may release them tomorrow with a warning. I shall decide about that tomorrow. Royde thinks I ought to keep them shut up for at least a week.'

'What *does* Mr Royde know about such matters?' Mrs MacDonald asked, the bitter-sweetness of the oboe audible for a moment in her tone. 'I'm sure Hugh doesn't think you ought to keep them here a week.'

'Hugh agrees with me that the time has come for landowners to take a firm stand. Ever since the Lloyd George Budget before the war we've allowed ourselves to be harried and bullied and persecuted and robbed right and left. Hugh agrees with me that a lead is required.'

'If Hugh Cameron thinks any good will come of your imprisoning hikers and campers on your own he certainly should be on a lead.' The oboe was reinforced by the bassoon.

'I don't mean that kind of a lead, Trixie. I mean the lead given by a leader.'

'Nobody is fonder of Hugh than I am, but if he's going to fill your head with all these extravagant ideas I shall not be fond of him any longer.' The deep rich diapason was again flooding the Chieftain's dressing-room.

'Hugh is loyal, Trixie. He holds fast to the old loyalties. Our ancestors stood back to back against the Macintoshes, and we don't intend to be bullyragged by hikers. Lindsay-Wolseley can't understand that kind of loyalty. He's a Lowlander.'

'And I am English, Donald, and I think there are occasions when common sense is more valuable in a friendship than loyalty.'

'Now, look here, Trixie,' he protested. 'I must ask you not to sneer at the old clan loyalties. And do let me get on with my dressing.'

'Very well, give me the keys and I'll leave you to yourself.'

'I will not give you the keys. If you go and let those hikers out and offer them supper they'll think I'm afraid of them. Before I know where I am they'll be threatening me with an action for assault and false imprisonment and I don't know what not.'

'Well,' said the Lady of Ben Nevis with dignified firmness, 'even if you keep the men of the party shut up I insist, Donald, I insist on your releasing the girls.'

This was no Queen Philippa humbling herself in tears to beg the lives of the burghers of Calais from an angry monarch. This was a woman who had frequently had her own way before and was determined to have it again.

'Girls!' Ben Nevis scoffed. 'I don't call a lot of unsexed young females in corduroy shorts girls. To be shut up in a dungeon for a bit without any jazz is just what they require.'

'The dungeon under the North Tower is no place for girls to spend the night in, Donald, however scantily they may be clothed. There's no kind of accommodation.'

'The decencies of a civilized existence are wasted on women like that,' Ben Nevis declared. 'They fought like wild cats. One of them went for me with her stick. And Catriona and Mary set about them.'

'I have already spoken to Catriona and Mary and expressed my surprise at their allowing themselves to be mixed up in such a disgraceful brawl,' Mrs MacDonald boomed.

'Disgraceful brawl?'

'Disgraceful brawl, Donald,' his wife boomed on a steady note.

'A short scuffle in the heather with sixteen male and female hikers is not a disgraceful brawl.'

'That is what people will call it, especially when they hear you encouraged your own daughters to take part in it. Now please give me the keys and I shall endeavour to undo a little of the harm you have done.'

'I should be much obliged if you would have the goodness to allow me to finish my dressing first,' said the Chieftain, grasping at haughtiness but landing in pomposity.

'I am not going to move from here, Donald, until you give me the key of the dungeon in which these girls have been shut up. I presume you will not attempt to use force with me.'

Mac 'ic Eachainn looked at his wife. Her eyes were steady as an owl's.

He hesitated. Then he produced from the pocket of his dressing-gown a bunch of very large keys.

'If you're going to let the women out you may as well let the men out too,' he said sulkily. His wife rose with a sigh of relief. 'But you are not to offer them supper,' he added. 'I refuse to have them fed. You hear that, Trixie?'

'I shall certainly offer them supper, Donald. And I shall be extremely relieved in my mind if they accept the invitation, for in that case we might hope they would be willing to consider the incident closed.'

'*They* would be willing?' Ben Nevis exploded. 'Let them think themselves lucky that I don't keep them locked up for a week on bread and water as I'd intended.'

'Donald!' his wife boomed.

'What is it now?'

'Don't be childish. It detracts from your dignity.'

With this the Lady of Ben Nevis swept from her lord's dressing-room, and retired to her own stronghold, which was still known as the Yellow Drawing-room, though it had not been either yellow or a drawing-room since twenty-five years ago, Hector, the twenty-second of Ben Nevis, died and was succeeded by the present Chieftain, who was the second son, his elder brother Hector having died in boyhood. Mrs MacDonald had devoted herself loyally to the customs of her adopted country from the moment her dowry had enabled Ben Nevis to put his castle and his land in order, but she had felt the need of having at least one room in the castle that apart from the view from the windows of the Three Sisters of Glenbogle might have been a room in the Grosvenor Square house of her father. She had seen that her proposal to substitute for the carpet and curtains of the bridal chamber a softer design and more becoming colour than the Ben Nevis MacDonald tartan had wounded Donald, and she had abandoned the notion at once. She would have liked to strip from the walls their frieze of substantial Victorian wallpaper depicting stags in every attitude a stag can put itself into, and when the attitudes were exhausted no less than eight sets of stags repeating the same set of attitudes all round the room. There were moments when the steel-engravings of MacDonalds overwhelming Macintoshes in battle palled upon her and when views in water-colour of the Three Sisters of Glenbogle, with that perpetual view of them from the windows, seemed superfluous. However, she always recognized that they were dear to the heart of the Chieftain she had married and she had never complained.

Only to the Yellow Drawing-room had she left nothing except its name, and of its chintzy privacy made for herself a refuge that was for ever England.

Mrs MacDonald laid the keys of the dungeon door upon a small table which shivered under the impact and when a kilted gillie that was the equivalent of a footman answered her bell she bade him send Toker to her.

The butler was not kilted. He was as English as his mistress.

'Toker, tell Mrs Parsall I wish to speak to her. And, Toker,' she added as he neared the door, 'dinner must be postponed until half past eight.'

Not even Toker's impassivity was proof against the slight tremor that shook him, so slight that only the most delicate seismograph would have registered it, but still a perceptible tremor.

'Until half past eight, madam,' he repeated in case his ears had deceived him.

'Yes, and tell Mr Fletcher I should like to speak to him when he comes down.'

'Mr Fletcher is now in the Great Hall, madam.'

'Is Duncan still here?'

'Mr MacDonald is in Mrs Parsall's room, madam.'

'Tell him to come with Mrs Parsall.'

'Very good, madam. Pardon me, madam, but is Ben Nevis aware that dinner has been postponed until half past eight?'

'No; you had better tell him at once.'

This time a definitely sharp tremor ran through Toker's solid shape.

'I will inform Ben Nevis, madam,' he said gloomily.

The Reverend Ninian Fletcher was a venerable clergyman who for the last twelve years had been the private chaplain at the Castle, an unexacting spiritual task to which had been added the somewhat exacting mental task of coaching the sons of Ben Nevis in their holidays.

'Ah, Mr Fletcher, I'm so sorry to disturb you,' said Mrs MacDonald when he came into her room. 'But I need your help.'

'It is always at your service,' said the old Episcopalian divine.

'You have heard about these hikers whom Donald has shut up in the dungeons?'

'I have indeed. May I say that I was a little startled by the news?'

'You couldn't have been more startled by it than I was, Mr Fletcher. However, I am glad to say Donald at once realized that his original plan to keep them shut up for a week on bread and water was not feasible.'

'Dear me, was that his original plan?'

'It was. However, he has now entrusted their release to me.'

'A very wise move, I venture to think.'

'Yes, if it is not too late.'

'Too late?'

'To bring the matter to a pleasant conclusion,' Mrs MacDonald explained. 'Obviously, if these people desire to make themselves unpleasant, Ben Nevis has given them the opportunity. I understand Colonel Lindsay-Wolseley pointed out to my husband that he was exposing himself to all kinds of unpleasantness in the way of actions for damages, but he was in one of his headstrong moods and refused to listen to Colonel Wolseley's advice.'

Mr Fletcher shook his venerable head.

'I gather that Kilwhillie encouraged him,' Mrs MacDonald went on.

'Dear me, I'm sorry to hear that.'

'Yes, it was extremely selfish of Kilwhillie. As you know, Mr Fletcher, nobody is more grateful than I am to Hugh Cameron for his devotion to Donald, but on this occasion I think he made his devotion an excuse to indulge his own Highland intolerance. However, that's beside the point at the moment. Where I want your help is in trying to persuade these people to take the business in good part. I have the keys of the dungeons, but I do not want to unlock the prisoners myself because I do not want to give the impression that there has been the slightest disagreement between myself and Donald. Therefore I am enlisting your help, Mr Fletcher. I want you to do the actual unlocking, or rather as I know the locks are very stiff I'll tell Duncan to do the actual unlocking, but I want you to let the prisoners know that they are free. I'm arranging with Mrs Parsall to give them supper in the old dining-hall, and afterwards the lorry can take them back to the nearest point on the road to their camp.'

'But suppose they refuse to accept your hospitality, Mrs MacDonald? If they are bent on some form of retaliatory action in the shape of a lawsuit against Ben Nevis they might consider it prejudicial to their case to eat, drink, and make merry with an enemy.'

'That is exactly what I fear may happen, and I am relying on your ability to put before them the Christian point of view. I won't venture to suggest what line you take. You will know far better than myself how to present that side. You've always been so tactful about religion and never rammed it down the children's throats ever since you came to live at Glenbogle. I do feel that you are the only person who can hope to adjust this unfortunate affair.'

The chaplain looked a little doubtful.

'I must confess I'm not as confident as I should wish to be of influencing this motley gathering. I fear that all this hiking is closely bound up with the new paganism which is such a distressing feature of contemporary life. The clergyman *quâ* clergyman merely represents to these young people an old-fashioned person wearing too many stuffy clothes. Some of my fellow-clergy have tried to keep pace with modernity by holding special hikers' services at convenient hours. The vicar of a church on the outskirts of London went so far as to conduct a breezy little service every Sunday at a convenient hour in a surplice and black corduroy shorts. He received for a while some publicity in the popular Press as the Hikers' Parson, but I should surmise any success he may have attained owed more to the itch of curiosity than the urge of religion.'

'Oh, I was not suggesting for one moment, Mr Fletcher, that you should try to ram religion down their throats. No, no. As I was trying to explain just now, I'm sure you can rouse their better feelings without the very slightest suggestion of religion. I do feel, however, that even hikers will pay some respect to a clergyman. I don't know if you heard what they were shouting when the lorry drove up with them to the Castle.'

'I heard only a confused noise.'

'Well, I heard what they were calling Donald, and I must say it was very unpleasant and uncomfortable and not a little alarming. By this time after nearly a couple of hours in these dark, damp, grubby dungeons their temper is bound to be even worse, and I feel sure they would be exasperated by the sight of anybody except perhaps a clergyman. I feel a little guilty in leaving you to tackle them without me, but you do understand, don't you, my dread of creating the least suspicion of any difference of opinion between myself and Donald?'

'Perfectly. Well, I'll do my best to adjust matters in the dungeons.'

At this moment Mrs Parsall the housekeeper came in with Duncan.

'Duncan,' Mrs MacDonald said, 'Ben Nevis has decided to release the hikers.'

'I'm very glad, my lady. They'll be more trouble than they're worth, locked up here. It was very annoying the way they spoilt the afternoon on us. But they're after being given a good lesson and I don't think we will be troubled with them again.'

'I hope we shan't indeed,' said Mrs MacDonald without any warmth of conviction. 'And now, Mrs Parsall, I'm afraid I shall have to give you the trouble of arranging for the prisoners to have supper before they go off in the lorry.'

'Very good, ma'am. I shall make the necessary arrangements. Excuse me, ma'am, but Mr Toker was not mistook in giving orders for dinner to be kept back till half past eight?'

'No; I wanted to give Mr Fletcher plenty of time. You will go down to the dungeons, Duncan, with Mr Fletcher, who wishes to say a few words to the prisoners. And after they have had supper you will see that the lorry puts them down at the nearest point to where they are camping.'

'Oh, well, well, he's a very fine gentleman right enough is Ben Nevis,' said the old head-keeper. 'There's few gentlemen would be served as he was served today over Drumcockie and then turn round and treat the culprits like lords. Och, it's wonderful, right enough. A very noble godly gentleman.'

As his ancient henchman followed Mr Fletcher towards the dungeons, the noble and godly gentleman himself was being told by his butler in the very middle of the delicate operation of tying his lace jabot that dinner would not be served until half past eight. The effect of the rush of blood to the head provoked by this announcement was intensified by the fact that under the shock of the news he pulled the knot of the jabot much too tight. The indignant bellow was stifled in his throat and petered out in a low gurgle.

'Can I be of any assistance, sir?' Toker inquired solicitously.

The Chieftain managed to loosen the knot and breathe again.

'Did you say dinner would not be served until half past eight?'

'By Mrs MacDonald's orders, sir,' Toker made haste to add hastily. His master glared at him.

'What are you jigging about like that for, you ninny?'

'I beg pardon, sir. The action was not deliberate. Is there anything I can get you, sir?'

'Yes, you can get out.'

The Chieftain spent some minutes composing his nerves after the shock administered to them by Toker's news about the postponement of dinner for a quarter of an hour by debating with himself which of his doublets he should wear this evening. In the end he chose a tartan one buttoned to the neck with eagles' heads of silver. He looked at himself in the glass. Serenity once more enfolded him as he left his dressing-room and descended to the Great Hall. Outside the massive doors his piper Angus MacQuat stepped forward to ask if there was any special tune he would like this evening.

'No, I leave it to you, Angus.'

'I was thinking if perhaps you would like *Mac 'ic Eachainn's March Against Moy*.'

'Ah, to celebrate our little scuffle in the heather this afternoon?'

'That was my idea, Ben Nevis.'

'Well, Angus, I don't think it's quite fair to put even Macintoshes on a level with hikers.'

'No, perhaps it is a little strong, Ben Nevis.'

'I really think it is, Angus. You'd better give us some Jacobite tunes tonight. Mrs Royde is a very keen Jacobite.'

'Very good, Ben Nevis. Tomorrow night I will be playing my new pibroch.'

'Ah, what's that called?'

'*The Braes of Strathdiddle*.'

'In celebration of our little scuffle in the heather, eh?'

'That is so, Ben Nevis.'

'Capital, Angus. I shall look forward to that. You missed a grand afternoon.'

The Chieftain passed on into the Great Hall, and barked at his assembled guests like an immensely friendly dog.

'Ah, there you all are! Dinner's not till half past. I had to postpone it to give Mr Fletcher a chance to finish a reprimand he is giving to the hikers on my behalf. I'm setting them free after that. They've had their lesson.'

Chapter 5

THE DUNGEONS

'Well, I call this properly chronic, Ethel.'

'You're right. It *is* chronic.'

'It's worse than chronic. It's shocking.'

'It's bloody awful.'

'What language, Elsie!'

'Leave her alone, Mabel. It's nothing to what I'll say in a minute if they don't let us out of this dark hole. So it is bloody awful. Elsie's right.'

A shriek rang out.

'Oh, my god, girls, there's something walking up the inside of my leg.'

Seven shrieks of sympathy shrilled through the murk of the dungeon.

'What are *you* all screaming about? It isn't walking up you, is it?'

Seven shrieks shrilled again.

'Strike a match, one of you. Oh, my god, it's biting my behind now. Oh, whatever is it? Strike a match, I say.'

Trembling fingers fumbled in the pockets of shorts. By the light of two matches simultaneously struck the young woman with fat legs who had asked Ben Nevis to stand still while she focused her camera was revealed with her green corduroy shorts round her ankles.

'Look what it is, somebody,' she adjured, wringing her hands.

A young woman with the thin nose of the born investigator inspected the posterior condition of the appellant and declared it must have been her imagination. There was no sign of snake, or toad, or rat, or bat, or beetle, or mouse.

At this last word another young woman released a shuddering wail which would have made a banshee jealous. The young woman with the thin nose, startled by the sound, threw away the lighted match, which rested for a moment on the behind of the young woman who had thought something was biting her and who now by a scream comparable to the whistle of an express proclaimed her conviction that she had been right.

And that of course set off all the other young women screaming again at one another like sopranos trying to annihilate contraltos in a Mendelssohn oratorio.

It was at this moment that the chaplain and the gamekeeper reached the iron-studded oaken door of the dungeon beneath the North Tower.

'Look at that now,' said Duncan. 'They were singing songs before and now they are screaming. What a lesson to human vanity! What a lesson, Mr Fletcher!'

'We mustn't be too ready to note the effect of human vanity in others, Duncan, in case we fail to detect the effect of it in ourselves.'

This rebuke from Mr Fletcher was inspired partly by the pleasure which he as an Episcopalian clergyman took in putting a Presbyterian elder in his place, partly by his having slipped on one of the damp stones in the passage that led to the dungeon and turned his ankle rather painfully.

'Ay, ay, that's very true, Mr Fletcher. Yes, yes, indeed. We are all as creeping things in the sight of the Lord.'

'I hope those unhappy young women have not been driven mad by terror,' said the chaplain, who was distressed by the sounds on the other side of the door.

Duncan banged on it with the bunch of keys.

'Keep quiet in there unless you want to stay there,' he shouted sternly.

The screaming stopped.

'Oh, my god, girls, it's a man,' cried the young woman who thought she had been bitten. 'Don't let him in till I'm presentable.'

She had just zipped up her shorts when the great lock turned to admit the chaplain and the gamekeeper, the latter carrying a stable-lantern the beams of which illuminated the group of eight young women, but made the vaulted glooms beyond seem more profound.

Mr Fletcher had time to utter only the word 'ladies' when by far the most piercing shriek yet emitted came from the lips of the young woman who thought she had been bitten as with a frantic gesture of horror she unzipped her shorts again. A second later a mouse leapt for freedom. Poor Winifred Gosnay, who was an assistant in one of the great London stores, had not let down her shorts for nothing. Something *had* been walking up the inside of her leg. Something *may* have bitten her behind. And that something actually *was* a mouse.

'Come along, ladies,' said the chaplain in soothing accents. 'You will soon be in more comfortable quarters if you follow me.'

In all his ordained life Mr Fletcher had never been so supremely the shepherd of his flock as when he shepherded a titubation of young women to the great dining-hall of Glenbogle Castle that August evening.

'Supper is being prepared for you, and after supper it has been arranged to drive you back as near as possible to your camp, with the proviso that you will move from the land of MacDonald of Ben Nevis at the earliest possible moment tomorrow. Is that understood?'

The female hikers muttered what sounded like an affirmative, but they were still too much shaken by the memory of that mouse leaping into the lantern-light from Winifred Gosnay's unzipped shorts to express anything except reminiscent shudders.

'I am now going to fetch the gentlemen of your party,' Mr Fletcher went on. 'Ah, here is Mrs Parsall the housekeeper. Mrs Parsall, these are the young ladies whom Ben Nevis has invited to supper.'

Mrs Parsall eyed them coldly. She and Mrs Ablewhite the cook had long ago made up their minds what they would give these shameless half-naked hussies. And it was not supper.

The dungeon beneath the Raven's Tower was a more formidable place of detention than the dungeon under the North Tower. Originally the only access to it was by a trap-door in the floor of what had been the guardroom of the keep. Down this the victims of MacDonald ferocity had been dropped into what was really a large pit, the sloping walls of which left a comparatively small level space at the bottom and thus inspired the name of Mac 'ic Eachainn's Cradle. Such air and light as reached the dungeon came through a few loopholes above the massive sloping walls. At the end of the eighteenth century when the power of the chiefs had been broken and they had degenerated into mere landowners an entrance had been constructed to the Cradle from the stable-yard and it had served for many years as an outhouse, accumulating rubbish all the time. It was the present laird who when putting his estate in order with his wife's dowry cleared out the Cradle, gave it an iron-studded oaken door two inches thick, and entertained his guests with tales of MacDonald prowess, which it would seem had kept Mac 'ic Eachainn's Cradle as full of Macintoshes as a larder of game.

'You'd better put on a coat and hat, Mr Fletcher,' the old gamekeeper advised. 'There's a chill in the night air. Run, Alec, and bring Mr Fletcher's coat and hat,' he told a gillie who was standing by one of the doors at the back of the Castle.

'Oh, we only have to cross the stable-yard,' said the chaplain. 'Come along, Duncan. We can bring them in this way to the dining-hall.'

'If they'll come quietly,' said Duncan.

'Why should they not? The girls came quietly enough.'

'Listen to that, Mr Fletcher.'

Across the yard reverberated a muffled thudding sound.

'What is it?' the chaplain asked. 'It sounds like somebody chopping wood.'

'It will be the hikers banging on the Cradle door,' Duncan replied. 'Och, they did not like it at all when we pushed them into the Cradle. Oh, indeed, no, not at all. They were threatening what they would do when they got out.'

'You're not anticipating trouble are you, Duncan?'

'I'm not anticipating it, but I think we will have trouble with them. They're very fierce, these London people. Wild savage people they are. We had quite a big business to get them into the Cradle.'

'Oh, I think they'll have cooled down by now,' said the chaplain.

'They don't sound very cool at all. They sound very hot. Ah, here's Alec with your hat and coat. You'd better put them on, Mr Fletcher.'

The chaplain surrendered to Duncan's solicitude and they crossed the yard together to the Raven's Tower.

'Did you have a great deal of difficulty in persuading them to go into the dungeon?' the chaplain asked.

'We didn't persuade them at all, Mr Fletcher. We just pushed them in and locked the door upon them. Any kind of persuading would have been wasted upon such trash.'

They had reached the door of Mac 'ic Eachainn's Cradle by now.

'You'd better knock on the door with the keys, Duncan. I'll never make myself heard above this banging.'

Duncan did so. The banging stopped.

'I am speaking on behalf of MacDonald of Ben Nevis,' the chaplain began; but no sooner did the prisoners hear the name of their captor than the banging started again with thrice the vigour.

'We'll have to go inside and speak to them,' he decided. 'My voice is no longer strong enough, I'm afraid, to compete with such a noise. Will you unlock the door, Duncan?'

The old keeper inserted the key and with what was an effort even for his strong fingers turned it.

Of what exactly happened then neither Mr Fletcher nor old Duncan was ever able to give a clear account. The result of whatever did happen was that the chaplain and the gamekeeper found themselves locked up in Mac 'ic Eachainn's Cradle and that the eight hikers were at large.

'Did you get a bang, Mr Fletcher?'

'No, I didn't get a bang, but somebody butted me very heavily in the stomach and knocked my wind out.'

'There you are. I wondered what kind of a queer noise you were making, but I thought it must be your prayers you were saying. They're very different from our prayers these Episcopalian prayers. Quite another kind of worship altogether.'

'Well, passing from the study of comparative religion to the position in which we find ourselves, what do we do now?' Mr Fletcher asked a little irritably. Few men recovering their breath after being winded are able to combine sweetness with dignity. If they can sustain their dignity after making the idiotic noises winded people do make they are lucky.

'We'll just have to wait until they come and let us out again,' Duncan replied.

'Who?'

'The hikers.'

'I'm afraid we'll have to wait a very long time before the hikers let us out. They made on me a strong impression of being out for revenge. I don't suppose they saw I was a clergyman.'

'No, they did not see a thing. They just put their heads down and rushed at us like bulls. Oh, well, we'll just have to wait until somebody does come and let us out.'

'If anybody knows we're here,' said the chaplain gloomily. 'And if anybody has the key.'

'You're looking too much on the dark side of things, Mr Fletcher. When you don't come in for dinner Ben Nevis will send somebody to look for you.'

'What good will that be if he hasn't a key to unlock the door? I think we'll be very lucky indeed if we don't spend the night in this dungeon. Was your lantern broken?'

The chaplain and the gamekeeper were standing at the top of the steps that led down into the dungeon from the outside door. Duncan struck a match, which lit up the bottom of the Cradle dimly enough, but sufficiently to show that his lantern was lying at the bottom of it.

'I'll go down and see if it can be lighted,' he said. 'Have you any matches, Mr Fletcher?'

'No, I haven't any. Why? Haven't you plenty?'

'I have only two left. It's a great pity I didn't get another box. Wait you where you are, Mr Fletcher. I'll go down the steps.' Presently he called up from below. 'The glass is broken all to pieces, but there's a little oil left in it. There you are,' he said when he had used one of his matches to light the wick of the lantern, which smoked a good deal but did at least banish the oppressive blackness of Mac 'ic Eachainn's Cradle.

'This really is not a suitable place in which to shut anybody up,' said the chaplain. 'I wonder where those hikers have gone?'

It was at this moment that they rushed into the Great Hall just as Ben Nevis had noted that the long hand of the clock stood at a minute from half past eight and was wondering what the deuce was keeping his chaplain now.

'Look here, what does this mean?' demanded Mr Sydney Prew, any lack of impressiveness in his own prim voice being supplied by the snarls of the seven younger hikers which provided a menacing accompaniment.

The Chieftain drew himself up to his full height.

'It means that I have decided to release you and I hope the experience will be a lesson not to disturb my birds again, and not to light fires in my heather.'

'And also,' Mrs MacDonald put in, 'that supper is waiting for you in the old dining-hall. Didn't Mr Fletcher make that clear?'

The Secretary of the National Union of Hikers stepped forward, held up his hand to quell the snarling of his seven companions, and thus addressed Ben Nevis:

'If you think, Mr MacDonald, that you can escape the consequences of your fascist behaviour . . .'

Yowls, boohs, and hisses from his followers caused Mr Sydney Prew to raise his hand again.

'I repeat, Mr MacDonald, you cannot escape the consequences of the disgraceful assault you and your fascist . . .' Once again the word was too much for the feelings of the representatives of democracy. Their yowls, boohs, and hisses were redoubled.

'Please, boys,' said Mr Prew, turning round reproachfully, 'please, please! I repeat, Mr MacDonald . . .'

'Well, don't,' the Chieftain bellowed. 'If you call me that any more I'll lock you up again.'

'I repeat, you cannot escape the consequences of the assault you have committed by trying to bribe us with supper. What legal action some members of our party may wish to take against you I do not know, but speaking for the National Union of Hikers as a whole I warn you that we reserve to ourselves the right to take any such reprisals as the Governing Body may judge suitable. We are a great democratic body, Mr MacDonald, and we are not to be bullied out of collective security by fascist insolence.'

At this the yowls, boohs, and hisses of the hikers became so passionate that Chester Royde climbed upon a chair and took down a Lochaber axe from the wall.

'Am I to understand you are threatening me?' the Chieftain demanded, that nose a Caesar might have envied stained with rich Tyrian.

'I am warning you, Mr MacDonald, that you have not heard the last of this,' said Mr Prew. 'And now where are the young ladies of our party?'

'The ladies are at supper, Mr . . . I'm afraid I do not know your name,' Mrs MacDonald boomed amiably.

'My name is Prew, madam. I am the Secretary of the National Union of Hikers.'

'Well, Mr Prew, if you will follow me I will take you to the ladies. The lorry in which you arrived at the Castle is waiting to drive you back, as no doubt Mr Fletcher informed you.'

'One of my rules, Mrs MacDonald, for I presume you are Mrs MacDonald, is never to be rude to a lady, and so you mustn't think me rude when I say that we must flatly decline to eat supper in your house and also to be driven back to our camp in the lorry. We prefer to walk.'

'But you are not going to leave the ladies behind, are you? Of course I shall be happy to put them up at Glenbogle, but . . .'

'Thank you, no. We will wait for the ladies outside. I am sorry to hear they have been persuaded into accepting supper, but that must not be taken to imply the slightest condonation of Mr MacDonald's behaviour.'

'And what about my portable wireless?' the owner of it called out. 'Mr Prew can do what he likes, but I'm suing you over that.'

The future of the portable wireless was left in abeyance, for at that moment Toker flung open the doors of the Great Hall and announced that dinner was served. Almost simultaneously three pipers started off at full blast with the stirring march *Beinn Nibheis Gu Brath* by which from time immemorial the Lord of Ben Nevis had been piped in to dinner.

The hikers looked at one another in dismay. They thought it was a signal for violence of some kind. In a panic they rushed out of the Great

Hall and along the corridor towards the front-door, carrying with them Toker as the Bogle in spate will carry upon its waters the broken branch of a pine. Luckily the table in the entrance hall on which the bonnets of the MacDonalds were always parked gave Toker something to which he could cling and thus escape being swept down the front-door steps and out into the courtyard of the Castle. In fact he was back in the dining-room in time to push in the great chair of his master, who took his seat at the head of the table when the pipes retired to avoid interrupting grace with the odd noises pipes make when a tune expires.

'Dash it, where *is* Mr Fletcher?' the Chieftain asked when from his seat the chaplain did not rise to ask a blessing upon the food.

'Mr Fletcher is probably arranging matters in the old dining-hall,' Mrs MacDonald boomed from her end of the table. 'Won't you say grace yourself, Donald?'

'Oh, very well. For what we are going to receive may the Lord make us truly thankful,' he barked.

The pipers now came in again and began to march slowly round the dining-room to the strains of *Will Ye No' Come Back Again?*, the first of the Jacobite airs Angus MacQuat had chosen for the delectation of Mrs Chester Royde.

'Fine old song, eh?' Ben Nevis said to his honoured guest who was sitting on his right.

'Oh, but of course, it's one of my very very favourite songs,' Carrie declared fervently.

'Yes, I thought you'd like it. I expect he'll give us *Over the Sea to Skye* next.'

Carrie's thoughts were in Glenbristle. Her host's treatment of the hikers had made her a little anxious for those two campers with whom she had spent so delightful an afternoon.

'Tell me, Ben Nevis,' she asked, taking advantage of the pipers being at the end of the room for a moment or two, 'what do you think of Scottish Nationalists?'

The tints of the dying dolphin at their most vivid and most varied would have seemed drab compared with the tints that displayed themselves upon the countenance of the Chieftain when he heard this question. The hats of cardinals, the shirts of Garibaldi's legionaries, the flags of the World Revolution, the ribbons of O.B.E.s, the plumes of flamingoes, the tails of redstarts, the breasts of robins, the skies that warn or delight shepherds according to the time, the tunics of grenadiers, and the tape of the Civil Service mingled and melted, flamed and faltered, and flamed again in his cheeks.

'Scottish Nationalists? I regard Scottish Nationalists as worse than hikers. To me they hardly appear human. They should be stamped out like vermin. But what do *you* want to know about Scottish Nationalists?' he asked, suspicion suddenly dimming his choleric blue eyes.

'Why, I was reading somewhere the other day about their objects, and I wondered if you had interested yourself in the movement at all.'

'Movement? Did you say movement, Mrs Royde? If you call foul subterranean squirming movement, well, I suppose you can call Scottish Nationalism movement. But it's not my idea of movement. I like something healthy and above ground.'

Carrie became pensive. If Ben Nevis was capable of treating sixteen male and female hikers as he had, what was he capable of doing to these two members of the Scottish Brotherhood of Action now camping in Glenbristle? She must warn them tomorrow. She ought to warn them tonight, but that was hardly feasible. She looked across the table at Myrtle, who was evidently not at all interested by Murdoch MacDonald's company next to her. If she took Myrtle into her confidence . . . at that moment Ben Nevis gulped down the rest of his soup and turned to Myrtle.

'I'm sending a cable to my boy Hector tomorrow morning, urging him to get a spot of leave and fly home. I want you to meet him very much. The trouble is I'm not sure whether he's stationed at Tallulahgabad or Bundalpore. I know he expected to be moved from Tallulahgabad to Bundalpore pretty shortly. Do you think the Clanranalds will have moved to Bundalpore yet, Murdoch?'

'Don't know at all,' said the naval Lieutenant.

'If you send it to Tallulahgabad they'll probably forward it on to Bundalpore, Dad,' Iain suggested.

'That's a good idea of yours, Iain. What do you think of that, Murdoch?'

'I think it's quite sound,' the naval Lieutenant allowed cautiously.

'I mean to say, it would be jolly to get old Hector back here for a little stalking, wouldn't it? Well, I'll cable to Tallulahgabad. You approve of that idea of Iain's, Myrtle?'

'Why, surely,' said Myrtle, with what Carrie thought was too obvious a wink at herself.

'You think that's a good idea, Mrs Royde?'

'I think it's a terribly good idea, Ben Nevis. But what I don't think is at all a good idea is for you to call Myrtle Myrtle and me Mrs Royde. What has poor Carrie done?'

'That's very nice of you, Mrs . . . I mean, Carrie,' said the Chieftain, gurgling benignly.

'I was afraid I'd offended you by asking about Scottish Nationalists.'

'What are they?' Murdoch asked.

'Ghastly people,' said Iain. 'I saw two of them hiking up the glen the day before yesterday.'

'You saw two Scottish Nationalists hiking up Glenbogle?' Ben Nevis gasped.

'Well, they were rigged up in reach-me-down kilts and had that awful earnest Highland look,' said Iain. 'Ghastly tartans too, neither of which ought to be allowed outside a music-hall. I'm sure they were Scottish Nationalists.'

'But they weren't proposing to camp in Glenbogle?' Ben Nevis pressed incredulously.

'Couldn't say,' his youngest son replied. 'But if they do, those tartans will scare every bird and stag in the neighbourhood. They'll scare the salmon back to the sea.'

'Do you hear that, MacIsaac? You missed our little scuffle in the heather this afternoon. Here's a chance for you.'

This remark was addressed by Ben Nevis to his Chamberlain, Major Norman MacIsaac, late of the 8th Service Battalion of The Duke of Clarence's Own Clanranald Highlanders (The Inverness-shire Greens). If the White Knight had worn a kilt instead of armour he would have looked much like Major Norman MacIsaac. And the Chamberlain of Ben Nevis had a similar gentle melancholy which most people attributed to the boisterous energy of the Chief he served, but which was his natural disposition. The Chamberlain, to say truth, had been delighted that urgent business in Fort William had kept him off the moors today and therefore relieved him of any responsibility in the matter of that little scuffle in the heather.

'You'd better give orders to keep a sharp look out for these two fellows,' Ben Nevis continued. 'And if they are Scottish Nationalists I'll teach 'em what real Scottish Nationalism means.'

The savage guffaw with which the Chieftain adorned this threat seriously disturbed Carrie, who was convinced that the two kilted figures seen by Iain MacDonald were her fellow-members of the Scottish

Brotherhood of Action. At all costs they must be warned somehow. The pipers were skirling *Over the Sea to Skye* now. It was an appropriate melody for the heroine's mood in which Carrie found herself.

When the pipers' music was finished and they had withdrawn from the dining-room, above what seemed the almost deathly quiet that succeeded, there was heard from the direction of the courtyard on which the windows of the dining-room faced a series of calls resembling the kind of noises made by Red Indians gathering to attack the logwood house of a settler.

'What the deuce is that?' Ben Nevis exclaimed, tossing his head like one of his own stags on Ben Booey challenging a rival on Ben Glass in the misty moonlight of October.

'Cooee! Cooee! Wolla-wolla-wolla-wolla! Oo-ha! Oo-hoo!'

'That's mighty like the war-cry of the Carroways,' said Chester Royde. 'Well, perhaps the Carroway war-cry is more "Oo-ha" than "Oo-hoo". Still, it is mighty like it.'

Toker eyed the guest of honour nervously. He had not yet perfectly recovered from that mad rush which had swept him helplessly along the corridor and but for the bonnet table would have swept him right out of the Castle altogether.

Mrs MacDonald reduced the mysterious sounds to the level of commonplace experience.

'It must be the hikers, Donald, getting their party together before they walk home. Now poor Mr Fletcher will be able to get his dinner.'

'Oo-hoo! Oo-hoo! Gertie! Elsie! Winnie!'

'I never heard such vile sounds,' Ben Nevis declared. 'There you are, MacIsaac. That's the kind of noise these brutes must have been making on Drumcockie to scare the birds like that.'

The Chamberlain eyed the Chieftain a little nervously. He had kept clear of this hikers' business by good luck, and he did not want to be involved in it now, by being asked to go out and disperse the offenders. However, the next 'coo-ee' was less loud, and presently a faint 'wolla-wolla-wolla-wolla' floating back from far down the drive warranted the belief that at last the intruders were definitely bound for their camp.

A few more minutes passed.

'What *is* Mr Fletcher doing?' Ben Nevis asked fretfully. 'Doesn't he *want* any dinner?'

'I do hope he didn't feel bound to eat the supper I arranged for those young women,' Mrs MacDonald boomed anxiously. 'The good man is so very conscientious. He may have felt that his kindly advice would be listened to more attentively if he joined in their cold meat and bread and cheese.'

'I never heard such rank nonsense,' Ben Nevis spluttered. 'Rory, go and tell Mr Fletcher that we're at dinner.'

The gillie retired and presently communicated the result of his errand to Toker.

The butler stepped forward.

'Mrs Parsall, sir, says Mr Fletcher did not return to the dining-hall where the young persons were feeding. It would appear that he and Mr Macdonald busied themselves with the persons in the Raven's Tower, and nobody has seen either Mr Fletcher or Mr Macdonald since that intrusion before dinner.'

'Where are they, then?' Ben Nevis asked.

'Oh dear,' Mrs MacDonald sighed vastly, 'I expect poor Mr Fletcher had difficulty with that nasty little Mr Prew and has been wrestling with him.'

'Nonsense, Trixie. Mr Fletcher's much too old to start wrestling with people at his age,' her husband declared.

'I mean arguing with him, Donald. I do hope he won't feel he has to walk too far. He is so very conscientious.'

Toker stepped forward again.

'I understand from Alec, madam, that Mr Fletcher sent for his hat and coat, and which Alec brought him.'

'Oh dear, oh dear, that's what he must have done. And the poor man's had no dinner. We'd better send Johnnie after him.'

A quarter of an hour later word came that Johnny Macpherson had brought back the Daimler empty. He had overtaken the hikers singing on their way back, but there had been no sign of Mr Fletcher or Duncan.

Ben Nevis had been inclined to discount his wife's alarm about the chaplain, but when he heard that his head-keeper was also missing he himself became alarmed.

'Look here, MacIsaac, we'll have to organize a search-party. And if there's been any dirty work, you'll have to take a few guns and round up these ruffians.'

The Chamberlain sighed. He had known all the while, he told himself, that the luck which had taken him to Fort William would not hold.

Once again Toker stepped forward.

'Excuse me, sir, but Alec reports that it's generally believed in the staff quarters that Mr Fletcher and Mr Macdonald were shut up in the dungeon under the Raven's Tower.'

'Well, why doesn't one of the ninnies go and let them out?'

'That was the intention, sir, but it was frustrated by the absence of the necessary keys.'

'Trixie, I gave you the keys,' said Ben Nevis reproachfully.

'Donald dear, Duncan had the keys.'

'Well, for Heaven's sake, somebody go and find out what is happening,' the Chieftain said irritably. 'This sort of vagueness is wrecking our dinner.'

Another messenger from the back of the Castle brought word that banging on the door of Mac 'ic Eachainn's Cradle and what sounded like the voice of Duncan Macdonald indicated definitely that somebody was shut up in the dungeon. The keys, however, were nowhere to be found.

'They must be found,' bellowed the Lord of Ben Nevis, Glenbogle, Glenbristle, Strathdiddle, Strathdun, Loch Hoch, and Loch Hoo. 'I expect these keys to have been found by the time we've finished dinner. I expect them to be brought to me with the coffee.'

Chapter 6

MAC 'IC EACHAINN'S CRADLE

_____

Alas, when the Chieftain was handed his coffee he was not handed the keys of the dungeons. The most widely accepted theory was that the hikers had carried them off, but when Ben Nevis proposed to dispatch a party to demand the return of them it was pointed out that by this time the keys had probably been flung into the Bogle.

'And we cannot leave poor Mr Fletcher in that horrid place indefinitely,' Mrs MacDonald urged.

'Oh, well, we shall have to break in the door of the Cradle. That's all there is to it,' Ben Nevis ruled.

But it turned out that there was a good deal more than that to it. The lock defied any attempt to force it, and the iron-studded door two inches thick stolidly resisted the repeated assaults of the three heavy-weights that flung themselves against it, now one at a time, now altogether.

'Some door,' declared Chester Royde, rubbing his shoulder.

The two hefty sons of Ben Nevis shook their heads, dazed by the ability of any substance to stand up against them for so long.

'We must try a battering ram,' the Chieftain decided. 'Go and fetch a caber,' he shouted.

A caber was fetched, and the three heavy-weights reinforced by the blacksmith and a couple of other strong men drove it at the door. The noise was considerable, but the result was nil. Ben Nevis was divided between admiration of the door he had installed and annoyance with it for failing to appreciate that one could have too much of a good thing. The caber was replaced by a beam which required eight men to give it any propulsive force but was no more successful in disturbing the door than the caber had been.

Catriona and Mary MacDonald had made one or two attempts to enlist in the battering-parties, but every time their brothers had told them not to get in the way. This had rankled. They were such hefty young women that they had long ago decided to make the best of it and build up their sex-appeal on this very heftiness. Neither ever lost an opportunity to move something or lift something or overthrow something which would have been beyond the strength of the average woman. Both had distinguished themselves in the mêlée with the hikers, particularly Catriona, who had rescued her father from the hiker's staff of the young woman roused to frenzy by his treatment of the mauve-shirted owner of the portable. In fact the successful imprisonment of the female hikers in the dungeon under the North Tower had been largely due to the competent way in which Catriona and Mary had handled them by the backs of their shorts. For this they had received no thanks. Indeed all they had received was a lecture from their mother for taking part in the battle.

Catriona and Mary MacDonald might despise women like Carrie and Myrtle Royde for their appalling femininity and disgusting coquetry, but they recognized bitterly that the sex-appeal of heftiness stood no chance against the odious wiles of small slim women prepared to be shamelessly provocative. Catriona had confessed it puzzled her why such a fuss was made about Myrtle Royde's dark eyes and crimson cheeks, and Mary's imagination was baffled to explain why the greenish eyes and red hair of Carrie Royde should attract so much attention.

'I do think men are extraordinary,' Catriona growled to her sister. 'Just because the two Royde women have come out to watch the proceedings all the men are making the most tremendous business of pretending they're performing feats of superhuman strength.'

'Father's just as bad as any of them,' Mary growled on an even deeper note, for she was just a little bit heftier than her sister.

'He's worse,' Catriona growled, 'because he doesn't lift anything himself but keeps telling everybody else how to lift it.'

'Catriona!'

'What's the matter?'

'I've just remembered something,' Mary twanged in tones that resembled an excited pizzicato on the violoncello.

'What?'

'I've just remembered the trap-door.'

'What trap-door?'

'The trap-door down into the Cradle from the Raven's Tower.'

'But that's been closed for a hundred years or more,' Catriona said.

'I know, but you and I might manage to open it. I expect it will be a pretty hefty job, but I don't see why you and I shouldn't be able to manage it. And if we could it would be a pretty good score,' Mary said, gruffly gloating.

The Chieftain had just ordered an attempt to be made on the door, with a crowbar, and the males one after another were trying their strength, each no doubt hoping he would be the lucky one to force an entrance and win the applause of Carrie and Myrtle Royde.

'Come on, Catriona,' her sister urged. 'If we don't succeed nobody will know and if we do we really will have a hot score.'

The old guardroom of the Raven's Tower was cluttered, not only with the rubbish which had been removed from the Cradle when Ben Nevis fitted it up as a show dungeon some twenty-odd years ago, but with the rubbish which had accumulated in it ever since. The Glenbogle Castle of this date had not heard the broadcast appeal of the Minister of Waste. When it did the contents of the old guardroom would make one of the most notable contributions in the country to the nationwide effort to save its rubbish.

While caber, beam, and crowbar assaulted the door of the Cradle below, up in the old guardroom Catriona and Mary worked strenuously to clear away the rubbish from that part of the floor where they judged the trap-door was likely to be found. They made a good deal of noise, but people outside heard nothing, so much louder were the operations in the yard that Ben Nevis was directing.

'Eureka,' Catriona suddenly growled.

'Well, it's pretty hot work,' her sister answered. 'One's bound to reek a bit.'

'You ass, I mean I've found it.'

'Found what?'

'Good lord, Mary, you are a thickhead. The trap-door, of course.'

'Oh, the trap-door? Oh, stout stuff!' Mary exclaimed.

The joy of flinging sacks about and shifting a chaff-cutter which had been waiting in a West Highland dream for eleven years to be mended had taken possession of her. In the zest of being hefty she had forgotten for a moment why she was being hefty.

'Well, seeing it was your idea to find this trap-door,' Catriona growled, 'you are a bit absent-minded.' She bent down and gave a tug at the iron ring of the trap-door. 'Phew! This blighter *is* going to take some shifting.'

The eyes of Mary lighted up as with a grunt of determination she plunged down to grasp the ring. She knew that the trap-door hoped to prove itself a worthy antagonist of her heftiest heftiness.

'Come up, you brute,' she growled. 'Come up, will you. Get a grip on it, Catriona, you slacker.'

Catriona got a grip on it, and the two sisters tugged and pulled, growling like a couple of sabre-toothed tigresses over the body of a palaeolithic man. The trap-door had forgotten the days when it was opened for captured Macintoshes to be dropped into the safe keeping of Mac 'ic Eachainn's Cradle. Years of idleness beneath gradually accumulating rubbish had sapped its morale. It lacked the resistance of the oaken door put in by Ben Nevis. The combined heftiness of Catriona and Mary MacDonald was too much for it. Five minutes after they had seized its iron ring the trap-door revealed the dungeon, on the floor of which Mr Fletcher and Duncan were sitting, a broken lantern between them, their heads buried between their knees in an attempt to muffle the deafening noise that caber, beam, and crowbar were making in their assault upon the oaken door.

'Mr Fletcher!' Catriona called down triumphantly.

'Duncan!' cried Mary.

Neither of the bowed figures on the floor of the Cradle gave a sign of having heard the voices of their rescuers.

'Yoicks!' Catriona boomed.

'Yoicks!' her sister echoed.

The bowed figures some fifteen feet below remained unresponsive.

'They can't hear us,' Mary said.

'I'm not surprised,' said Catriona. 'I can hardly hear what you're saying in my ear. The noise of that battering is pretty hefty.'

'Wait a jiffy,' Mary growled. She dropped an old sack to attract the attention of the prisoners. Unfortunately it fell on the broken lantern and extinguished it.

'That's torn it,' Catriona observed severely. 'Where's the torch?'

Mary flashed the electric torch down into the dungeon.

'Look up, Mr Fletcher. The Lord has sent an angel to deliver us,' Duncan proclaimed. 'Isn't that wonderful? I was saying to myself like Daniel, "My God hath sent his angel, and hath shut the lions' mouths", and right enough the Lord has sent an angel.'

'It isn't an angel, Duncan,' Mary shouted down. 'It's Catriona and Mary MacDonald.'

'Well, well, it isn't an angel at all, Mr Fletcher. It's Miss Catriona and Miss Mary.'

The venerable chaplain peered up, shading his eyes against the glare of the torch.

'If we let down a rope, do you think you can climb up?' Catriona asked.

'No, I'm afraid that's rather beyond me,' the chaplain replied. 'And anyway, I don't think it's worth while now. That door is bound to give way soon. It can't hold out indefinitely against such battering.'

Catriona and Mary were not at all anxious to lose the honour of having rescued the prisoners and they pressed upon the chaplain the advantage of escaping from the Cradle by means of a rope.

'It'll be quite easy,' Catriona assured him.

'Easy as pie,' Mary declared.

They had found what they thought was a suitable rope and having tied it fast to the iron ring of the trap-door they threw it down into the dungeon.

'Come on, Duncan,' Catriona urged, 'show Mr Fletcher the way. Hand over hand.'

But the old gamekeeper demurred.

'Go on, Duncan, put some beef into it and you'll be up in a jiffy,' Mary promised.

But the old gamekeeper still demurred.

'Look here, I'll show you how easy it is,' Catriona volunteered.

She gripped the rope and dived down through the opening like the heroine of the poem *Curfew shall not ring tonight*.

'Oh, good-oh, Catriona!' Mary commented. 'I'm coming too.'

Whether it was the extra swing her weight gave to the rope or whether it was the removal of that weight from the trapdoor that caused it to rise from the floor and shut itself with a bang might be hard to say. But that is what it did. Catriona was nearly at the bottom when the rope snapped, but even so she winded Mr Fletcher for the second time that evening, only to be winded herself by Mary who had farther to fall.

'I'm awfully sorry, Mr Fletcher,' said Catriona when she had recovered her breath. 'Hope I didn't hurt you. It was the fault of that goof, Mary.'

'No, no, I'm – ah – hah – hah – hah – quite – ah – hah – all right – ah – hah – hah – just a little winded – ah –hah – that's all.'

'I hope you didn't hurt yourself, Miss Mary,' the old keeper inquired anxiously, for Mary was his favourite.

'Mary hurt herself!' Catriona growled indignantly. 'Why, she fell on Mr Fletcher and me.'

'I'm all right,' said Mary. 'But where's the torch? Wow! it's smashed. Strike a light somebody.'

'I've only one match left,' Duncan said.

'You would have,' Catriona growled.

However, that solitary match just managed to light the smoky lantern when it had been released from the sack which had extinguished it.

'The more I think of it the more of an absolute coot you are, Mary,' her sister declared. 'We should have had a tophole score over the others if you hadn't muffed it by barging in with that rope.'

'Never mind,' said the chaplain, who had recovered from the *peine forte et dure* of both sisters being on top of him at once. 'Never mind, you both did your best.'

'If Duncan hadn't funked climbing up the rope,' said Mary, 'it would have been perfectly good-oh. We could have hauled Mr Fletcher up between us.'

'I'm very thankful I did not climb up the rope,' said Duncan. 'I might never have fallen on Mr Fletcher at all, and that would not have been very enjoyable. I wonder what they're doing outside now.'

This speculation was prompted by a lull which had lasted for two or three minutes. The answer came almost at once with a most terrific crash as the oaken door gave way before the impact of a beam twice the size of any yet used and propelled by ten stalwart batterers at the double.

'I knew it could be done,' Ben Nevis was heard proclaiming with a triumphant roar. 'Duncan, are you there? You're all right, I hope? And Mr Fletcher, is he all right?'

The batterers puffing with their supreme effort stood aside to let Mac 'ic Eachainn enter his Cradle, lantern in hand. Macbeth confronted by the three witches on the blasted heath probably looked much less startled than Ben Nevis when he beheld his two hefty daughters in their black silk evening gowns stained with the rust and dust and must of the accumulated rubbish in the old guardroom.

For a moment or two he could only bark wildly in utter bewilderment. Then he found his voice.

'How in the name of all that's . . . in fact how the deuce *did* you get into the Cradle?'

'We came down through the trap-door in the old guardroom,' Catriona growled. 'We'd have had both the prisoners out if the rope hadn't gone phut when we were on it.'

'I should think the rope would go phut,' observed Iain, with a brother's kindly sympathy. 'Any rope would.'

'Less of it from you, fat boy,' Mary rumbled. 'Something had to be done while you Lady Janes were all pecking at that door.'

'Now don't start bickering together,' the patriarch commanded. 'I want to hear how Mr Fletcher and Duncan found themselves in the Cradle.'

'That's a very difficult question to answer, Ben Nevis,' his head-keeper replied. 'But before we knew where we were that's where we were.'

'But where were you?'

'That's what I'm after telling you, Ben Nevis,' said Duncan severely. 'We didn't know where we were till we were where we were. That's how it was, wasn't it, Mr Fletcher?'

'It was certainly all very sudden,' the chaplain agreed. 'Something in the nature of a rush took place when Duncan unlocked the door, but I was unfortunately butted in the wind and that temporarily deprived me of any ability to see what happened.'

'And I had a big bang on the nose,' Duncan added.

'Good lord, I should think you did,' Ben Nevis exclaimed. 'You'd better go in and get Mrs Ablewhite to clap a beefsteak on it. Well, I'm sorry you both got knocked about, but in a way it's just as well because it will give me a chance of bringing a counter-charge against these brutes if they try to sue me for assault.'

The voice of Mrs MacDonald was heard over her husband's shoulder.

'Donald dear, don't you think it will be more comfortable for Mr Fletcher and Duncan if these questions are discussed indoors? Poor Mr Fletcher must be famished. He was expecting dinner over two hours ago when he so kindly offered to attend to the hikers. Come along, Mr Fletcher. Dinner's waiting for you. Catriona! Mary! I'm glad you were able to be of some little assistance to poor Mr Fletcher, but I think you ought to go in now and tidy yourselves. In fact I think the sooner we all go indoors the better. You agree, don't you, Donald?'

The Chieftain led the way back to the Great Hall, where long after the rest of the party had gone off to bed tired out by exercise, excitement, and the strong air of Glenbogle he and the laird of Kilwhillie sat with their whisky, going over the events of this great day.

'By the way, Hugh,' he said as he poured out the *deoch an doruis* or drink at the door to speed Kilwhillie on the road to bed, 'I don't know if you heard Iain saying at dinner that he had seen two Scottish Nationalists in Glenbogle the day before yesterday.'

Kilwhillie tugged at the ends of his long moustache, which by this time of the day met in a droop over his chin.

'No, I didn't hear that,' he said gravely.

'I wouldn't bet much they aren't camping somewhere around,' Ben Nevis went on.

'Oh, they'd hardly have the impudence to do that, Donald.'

'Wouldn't they? Hugh, my boy, these Scottish Nationalists have impudence enough for anything. They're worse than hikers. They're worse than Bolshies. In fact they are Bolshies, only worse, if you see what I mean.'

'Yes, I see what you mean,' said Kilwhillie, disentangling the ends of his moustache which showed signs of twining round one another like two strands of badly-trained honeysuckle. 'Well, we don't want these fellows upsetting people in Inverness-shire. It's difficult enough to keep the rates within reasonable bounds as it is without a lot of Bolshie agitators from Glasgow.'

'Quite,' Ben Nevis agreed. 'Well, I've discovered a way to deal with hikers and I'm not going to be defied by Scottish Nationalists. Look here, you'd better have another jockendorrus.'

'Well, perhaps one more.'

Mac 'ic Eachainn raised his glass solemnly.

'If I find these Scottish Nationalists have been camping on my land, Hugh, I'll tell you what I shall do. I shall have them thrown into the nearest loch.'

'Suppose they were drowned?'

Mac 'ic Eachainn drank down his second *deoch an doruis*.

'Well, that's that, if you see what I mean.'

'Yes, I see what you mean,' Kilwhillie admitted, swallowing his second *deoch an doruis*. 'But I think Beatrice mightn't like it.'

'Why not?'

'Well, she spoke to me after dinner while you were superintending that door business . . .'

'Wait a moment, Hugh. What about another jockendorrus?'

'Well, this really must be the last, Donald.'

'Go on, what did Trixie say?' asked Ben Nevis when he had refilled Kilwhillie's glass.

'She seemed to think I had egged you on to shut up these hikers. She was very cross about it really. She said if that kind of thing happened again her pleasure in our friendship would be destroyed. I was a bit upset. So I'd rather not be brought into this drowning business if you don't mind, Donald. Of course, so far as I'm concerned the more Scottish Nationalists you drown the better I should be pleased. But I'm very fond of Beatrice as you know. And I do think it might upset her if you drowned these fellows.'

'Well of course, if you make it a personal matter, Hugh, I'm not going to do anything to upset you. After all there are other ways of dealing with Scottish Nationalists besides drowning them.'

'Quite, that's what I feel.'

'One more jockendorrus?'

'No really, Donald. It's bed for me.'

'Well, I suppose it's bed for both of us. Don't worry, Hugh. I'll put things right with Trixie. It's a pity women never appreciate loyalty.'

'Oh, I think Beatrice does, Donald, but she said there were times when she put common sense before loyalty.'

'Dreadful!' the Chieftain groaned. 'Well, I'll never understand women if I live to be a hundred.'

On this reflection the twenty-third MacDonald of Ben Nevis switched on as he thought the electric light for the stairway but in point of fact plunged the Great Hall into darkness.

'I wish I'd never given way to Trixie about installing this damned electric light at Glenbogle,' he exclaimed fretfully. 'We were much better off with lamps. The beastly contraption never works properly.'

However, after clicking away for some moments he found the switch for the stairway, and the two lairds went off to bed.

While they had been discussing the future of Scottish Nationalists downstairs, the same topic had been started by Carrie Royde when she went along to her sister-in-law's room for one of those little chats which women find such efficacious sleeping-draughts. Myrtle was already in bed, a great mahogany four-poster, on which Carrie in a pastel rose dressing-gown was sitting with her feet up and her back against one of the posts at the foot. The charming contrast of her red hair with the colour of her dressing-gown was slightly marred by the wallpaper on which life-size flamingoes, whose roseate plumes had been turned by the mists of Glenbogle into a revolting shade of washed-out magenta, were stalking about among greenish yellow tuffets of boggy vegetation or arching their necks apparently to smell the butter-coloured water-lilies that were scattered about the march these antipathetic birds frequented.

'Myrtle, you heard what Ben Nevis said at dinner about Scottish Nationalists?'

'They seemed to worry him a whole lot. But what are Scottish

Nationalists, anyway?' asked Myrtle, who looked as small and merry as Puck in that great mahogany four-poster.

'They believe in the independence of Scotland.'

'Good for them. Give me independence every time. But I don't see why you're worrying, Carrie.'

'You know I'm crazy about Scotland.'

'And how! But what of it? I'm crazy about Scotland myself. So's Chester. That's why he's going to get himself a kilt.'

'Chester's going to get himself a kilt?' Carrie repeated in amazement.

'Oh, don't tell Chester I told you. He wants it to be a surprise for you.'

'It'll be a surprise all right whether I know beforehand or not,' said Carrie, with conviction.

'I don't know. I think Chester'll look kind of cute in a kilt. He's pretty serious about it because when I said "kilts" instead of "kilt" he eyed me as if I was eating peas with a knife. But promise you won't let him know I told you. And don't try to discourage him. After all, it's a compliment to you.'

'I'll wait and see what he does look like in it before I agree to that theory. And oh, Myrtle, before I forget, don't wink at me again across the table like that. I'm sure Iain MacDonald noticed it.'

'Don't worry, my dear. Iain wouldn't notice it if I dropped an eye in the soup. Dumb? Why, there's only one thing dumber than Iain, and that's his brother the Lieutenant.'

'Ben Nevis isn't dumb.'

'You're telling me. Why, Carrie, I think Ben Nevis is the brightest sixty-year-old I've met in all my young life. If Hector's only half as bright as the Monarch of the Glen I'm going to make the Monarch of the Glen my father-in-law. I sure am. I guess I'd make a pretty good Chieftainess. You didn't see Ben Nevis with those hikers, Carrie. He kept picking them up by the collar one after another and shaking them. You missed that. Well, if he's taken a dislike to Scottish Nationalists it's going to be just too bad for the Scottish Nationalists.'

'You surely don't agree with letting your prejudices run away with you, Myrtle?'

'I don't know. I think I'd kind of admire any prejudice that could run away with Ben Nevis.'

'Yes, but if you knew a very nice — two very nice Scottish Nationalists — you wouldn't want Ben Nevis to treat them like these hikers?'

'They'd have to be mighty nice before I got between them and Ben Nevis.'

'But you wouldn't take Iain MacDonald's opinion? And it was Iain who was being so high hat about those Scottish Nationalists he saw. As a matter of fact I know them.'

'You do?' Myrtle exclaimed.

'That is, I met them today in Glenbristle. It was rather romantic really.'

'Tell sister all about it.'

'Well, you know I was terribly anxious to find the exact site of my great-great-grandfather's cottage.'

'I didn't know, but I'm sure you were.'

'He was put out of Glenbristle by the great-grandfather of Ben Nevis.'

'He was, was he? Well, if great-grandpa was anything like great-grandson I bet your relation went out of Glenbristle with a bang.'

'It was he who emigrated to Canada.'

'Uh-huh, that's about where he would land if great-grandpa shook him up the way great-grandson shook up those hikers.'

'Well, I think I've found the site of the old place. There's a family tradition about it. Of course, I can't be absolutely sure, but I felt a very strange unearthly sort of feeling when I came to this place. Some unseen presence seemed to be telling me I had come home. So I sat down on the grass.'

'Didn't the unseen presence offer you a chair?'

'No, please, Myrtle, don't laugh at me. Today was a terribly solemn experience. I sat down on the grass and ate my sandwiches and smoked a cigarette and fell fast asleep. I must have slept for quite two hours.'

'I'll say you did. I never knew you so wide-awake at this hour before.'

'And when I woke up, two young men in kilts were looking down at me. I thought at first they were fairies.'

'So you felt kind of safe and didn't scream for help,' Myrtle teased.

'You have no poetry in you, Myrtle. I mean supernatural beings. And then I realized that they were two perfectly good young men and we talked for a while and they were very interesting about Scottish Nationalism, which is why I asked Ben Nevis about it at dinner. And now here's my problem, Myrtle. These two young men are camping in Glenbristle. In fact they gave me tea at their camp. I must warn them. They know I'm staying with Ben Nevis and if he treats them the way he treated those hikers they'll think I betrayed them. You see the very difficult position I'm in?'

Myrtle nodded, and encouraged by what she thought was the dawn of sympathy in her sister-in-law Carrie became more confidential.

'And that's not the only thing. One of their ideas in coming to Glenbristle was a plan they had to kidnap Ben Nevis.'

'Kidnap Ben Nevis?' Myrtle exclaimed in amazement.

'Yes; but as soon as I said he was a friend of mine they said at once they wouldn't dream of kidnapping him. They'd kidnap somebody else instead.'

'They sound tough guys, your two boy friends.'

'Oh no, it's all political. It isn't kidnapping the way we kidnap in the United States. Oh no, money doesn't come into it. It's a political gesture. Well, what I want you to do, Myrtle, is to say you'd like to go for a walk with me tomorrow morning instead of going out with the guns. I'm afraid if I go off alone again I'll make Ben Nevis suspicious. Will you do this for me, Myrtle?'

'Why, of course I will.'

'Oh, that's lovely of you. But when you see this young man – these young men – I'm sure you'll be just as anxious as I am that nothing should happen to him – to them. Well, I'm not going to keep you awake any longer. Chester'll be wondering where I am.'

'Don't tell him you've heard he's going to get a kilt.'

'Why certainly, I won't tell him, Myrtle. You will come with me tomorrow?'

'Sure.'

'Oh, perhaps I ought to have told you that one of these boys is a poet. Well, honey, I won't keep you any longer. Sweet dreams.'

Carrie blew a kiss to her sister-in-law and went back to her own room.

'What have you been talking about?' her husband asked from a mahogany four-poster even larger than the one which held Myrtle. 'I wanted to tell you something before I went to sleep.'

'What is it, Chester?'

'I've fallen for your country, Carrie. They know how to live up here. I'm going to buy a little place in Scotland.'

'Why, that's lovely news, Chester.'

'Yes, and Kilwhillie's going to show us a lodge of his that he's anxious to sell. Of course, he says he isn't so anxious, but that's hooey.

Knocknacolly it's called. About ten miles from Glenbogle across the hills, but nearer thirty by road.'

'When are we going, Chester?'

'He's going to drive us over tomorrow morning.'

'Tomorrow morning?'

'What's the matter with tomorrow morning?'

'Well, I'd promised to take Myrtle for a walk. I thought you'd be out shooting.'

'You can take Myrtle for a walk any time. We'll be back by the afternoon. Ben Nevis is going to have a drive for some Scottish Nationalists, whatever they are, and throw them into a loch. But he's coming with us in the morning.'

Chapter 7

KNOCKNACOLLY

In spite of having been the last of the party to leave the Great Hall of Glenbogle on the previous night Ben Nevis and Kilwhillie were the first to appear in the dining-room next morning for breakfast. They ladled generous helpings of porridge into their bowls and walked about blowing it.

'Another good day,' Ben Nevis observed enthusiastically.

'Yes, and it looks like lasting.'

'This is the eighth consecutive day without rain. Must be a record for August I should think.'

'We had nine days running without rain in 1911,' Kilwhillie reminded him.

'Did we? Well, if we get a fine day tomorrow that will equal the 1911 record,' Ben Nevis observed, after a scarcely perceptible pause to be sure his calculation was correct.

'Quite.'

'And by Jove, if we don't have rain the day after tomorrow we shall beat it,' he went on.

Delighted with the establishment of this mathematical fact, Ben Nevis stamped across to the side-table and ladled another couple of spoonfuls into his porringer.

'I don't think I'll say too much about this record in front of Royde,' Kilwhillie remarked pensively, 'if you see what I mean.'

'Knocknacolly, eh?' Ben Nevis asked, an expression of tremendous sagacity playing about his florid, weather-beaten countenance.

'Quite. That's why I'm anxious he should see the place as soon as possible. I think places always look better when the sun is shining. Particularly Knocknacolly. It's very good of you, Donald, to come with us this morning.'

'Not a bit, Hugh, not a bit. I mean to say I think I can be helpful, and I do want you to get Knocknacolly off your hands at a fair price. Besides, I think the Roydes will be an asset, what? The more money we can get into Inverness-shire the better for everybody. I'll send a cable to

Hector from the post-office at Kenspeckle. I don't see why he shouldn't be able to get home in ten days from now.'

'I should think he would. Wonderful thing, this flying. I'm really extremely obliged to you, Donald, for coming along with us this morning. If I can sell Knocknacolly at a fair price it will be helpful. But it's rather an interruption to sport.'

'Oh, that's all right, Hugh. Besides, I've given up that idea of throwing those hikers into a loch. I don't want them to cause any friction between you and Trixie. I put things right last night, and she's very pleased I'm going to drive over with you to Knocknacolly instead of rounding up these Scottish Nationalists. By the way, I think we'll take the Daimler. It's more comfortable than your old Austin.'

'If I manage to sell Knocknacolly I'll get a new car,' said Kilwhillie hopefully.

'I've told MacIsaac to arrange for the beaters to get round Glenbristle and Glenbogle this morning and I propose to round up the Scottish Nationalists this afternoon, put them in the lorry, and have them deposited at the railway station in Fort William. It's a pity not to use the dungeons, but Trixie's got this old idea into her head that it'll cause trouble. So I'm humouring her. You've got to humour women, Hugh.'

'Yes, my mother required a lot of humouring during the last ten years of her life,' said Kilwhillie. 'I know what it is.'

'I'm afraid Royde will be disappointed. I told him about throwing any Scottish Nationalists we caught into the nearest loch, and he was very pleased with the idea. What are you going to ask for Knocknacolly?'

'I thought of asking ten thousand and taking eight. Well, as a matter of fact, I'd take seven.'

'Ask fifteen and take twelve.'

'Well, of course if I could get twelve thousand, I could pay off the mortgage on Kilwhillie and have enough to do it up. But what's the use of dreaming?' The Laird of Kilwhillie shook his head sadly.

'Look here, Hugh, you leave this to me . . . by the way, look out, the end of your moustache has got into your porridge . . . that's it, it's out now . . . yes, you leave this to me. I'm going for fifteen. After all, what's fifteen thousand to a man like Royde? His father has over twenty million, and he's the only son. Twenty million pounds is a lot of money, Hugh.'

'Yes, it is a lot of money.'

'I suppose his sister will have at least a couple of million one day. By the way, don't let me forget I have to send that cable to Hector. Oh yes, I'm going for fifteen thousand pounds. After all, if you had twenty millions you wouldn't be worrying about the difference between fifteen thousand pounds and twelve thousand pounds. Look out, Hugh, the end of your moustache has got back into your porridge.'

The Laird of Kilwhillie was trying not to feel optimistic and so kept shaking his head to express a determined defeatism. Hence the erratic behaviour of his moustache.

'The lodge will want a lot doing to it,' he said gloomily.

'Well, that's what these people like, Hugh. Now don't you worry. I'm going for fifteen thousand. And I shall get it.'

Kilwhillie's hopes and fears were presently left to fend for themselves because the rest of the party were coming in to breakfast.

Carrie had already consulted with her sister-in-law about the problem created by this expedition to Knocknacolly, which she had not expected.

'Keep smiling. I'll go along and warn your two beaux that the monarch of the glen's out for their scalps,' Myrtle volunteered.

'It's terribly sweet of you, Myrtle, but suppose Chester wants you to drive over to Knocknacolly too. And even if Chester doesn't, Ben Nevis will be peeved if you don't come, that's a sure thing.'

'Well, the monarch will just have to be peeved,' said Myrtle. 'Now, what do I say to your two beaux?'

'I've written a note warning them to flee. James Buchanan – that's the lawyer – was going anyway on Saturday, but Alan Macmillan – that's the poet – was going to camp on for another few days. But I don't think it's safe for him to stay around here. This is what I've written:

'*Dear Mr Buchanan . . .*'

'That's the lawyer?' Myrtle interrupted.

'Yes.'

'What's the poet done that you don't write to him?'

'Why, I think the lawyer will pay more attention to my warning. Lawyers are kind of practical folk compared with poets.'

'I see,' said Myrtle thoughtfully.

'*Dear Mr Buchanan,*' Carrie went on reading, '*This is to introduce my sister-in-law Miss Myrtle Royde who will explain to you how very necessary it is for you and Mr Macmillan to leave Glenbristle at once.*'

She broke off. 'I thought you could explain better than by my trying to write all about Ben Nevis. They think he's in a rut.'

'Oh, they think he's in a rut, do they?'

'Yes, and you've got to convince them he's not.' Carrie went on reading – '*to leave Glenbristle at once on account of the attitude of the owner towards camping . . .*' She broke off again. 'I think it's wiser to concentrate on the camping side of it. I'm afraid if I make too much of a point about the political side of it they may feel bound to stay and fight it out.' She went on reading: '*It is a great disappointment not to meet you and Mr Macmillan again but I have to drive over with my husband to inspect a property in the neighbourhood. Should we be lucky enough to secure it I need hardly say how glad we shall be to have you camp on our land whenever you feel inclined. Should you decide to make that visit to Canada which we discussed, be sure to write and let me know so that I can give you a few letters of introduction. Mrs Chester Royde Jr, 10 Green House, Park Lane, London, W. 1, is my London address and letters will always be forwarded. But I hope to have an address in Scotland soon, and if you will give Miss Royde your address and Mr Macmillan's I will write and let you know what that is . . .*'

She stopped reading. 'I think that says all I can say in a letter, but I'm relying on you, Myrtle, to impress on them how very fierce Ben Nevis can be. Chester told me his idea was to throw these young men into the nearest loch. Well, I believe he's quite capable of doing it.'

'He certainly is,' Myrtle agreed.

'Then be an angel, Myrtle, and try to get that into their heads.'

'I'll do my best.'

Ben Nevis, as Carrie had expected, was definitely peeved when Myrtle announced her intention of spending a quiet morning by herself instead of driving in the Daimler to Knocknacolly.

'But what will you do with yourself by yourself?' he asked.

'Oh, I'll amuse myself.'

The patriarch eyed his two sons farther down the table. They had just banked up their plates with bacon, eggs, kidneys, and sausages, and were apparently oblivious of anything else. However, he was going to send that cable to Hector and therefore it was a waste of time bothering about Murdoch or Iain. He had given them their chance. They had failed to grasp it.

'Well, I'm sorry you won't come and give your opinion of Knocknacolly, Myrtle. It's the best twelve-head forest in Inverness-shire. The lodge is a bit old-fashioned, but it could easily be turned into a delightful place. You've not done any stalking yet. I'm looking forward to a day on Ben Booey with you soon.'

He turned to Chester Royde.

'What you'll like about Knocknacolly, Royde, is its remoteness, and as for you, Carrie, I think Knocknacolly is going to be the dream of your childhood come true, if I may express myself rather poetically, what?'

'It sounds wonderful, Ben Nevis.'

'Well, it is a wonderful place. I never knew you thought of selling it, Hugh.'

Kilwhillie, who for the last ten years had been thinking almost incessantly of selling Knocknacolly, tried to look startled by his own recklessness.

'Oh, of course, we none of us like parting with land, Donald. Still, when you find the ideal purchaser . . . however, perhaps Royde won't like Knocknacolly.'

'Like it? Of course he'll like it,' Ben Nevis shouted. 'Nobody could help liking Knocknacolly. Ah, by Jove, Hugh, we've had some great days in that forest. Do you remember when . . .' and for the rest of breakfast he talked of the stags he and Kilwhillie had stalked over thirty years. Carrie encouraged him whenever his reminiscences showed signs of flagging. She thought he was much better occupied stalking stags than Scottish Nationalists.

At ten o'clock Johnnie Macpherson drove to the front courtyard with the pre-1914 Daimler, riding in which was like riding in a Victorian boudoir on the back of an elephant. That it still appeared spacious when loaded with Ben Nevis, his two hefty daughters, the Roydes, Kilwhillie, and Johnnie Macpherson the chauffeur was a tribute to life as it was once lived.

Catriona and Mary MacDonald were to desert the party at the entrance of Glenbogle. They wanted the pleasure of what they described as a little jog back to the Castle for lunch by way of the bridle-path across Glenbristle. This meant as a preliminary footing it along five miles of road long out of repair, because Ben Nevis with all his territorial influence had failed as yet to become a member of the Roads Committee of the County Council.

'I can't understand why they don't ask me to be Convener of the Roads Committee,' he used to declare from time to time.

Yet the explanation was simple enough. His fellow-councillors were determined to save the ratepayers the expense of putting the Glenbogle road in good order merely for the benefit of Ben Nevis, his castle, and the cottages of his dependants being all that it served.

'Stop a moment, Johnnie,' he bellowed to his driver when the Daimler reached the turning that crossed the bridge over the Bogle and wound up the Pass of Ballochy. 'What about finding out if these hikers have cleared away from Loch Hoo?' he suggested to his guests.

'If we do that, Donald,' Kilwhillie demurred nervously, 'we may be rather late getting back for lunch.' He was determined that Beatrice MacDonald should not be given the slightest excuse to lecture him again on his encouragement of her husband's autocratic violence.

'Perhaps you're right, Hugh. All right, Johnnie. Drive on. I do want to be back in good time,' he admitted, 'in case my beaters have spotted the whereabouts of these Scottish Nationalists. I told MacIsaac to get a report in by two o'clock, and then after lunch, if there's any prospect of good sport, we'll have a jolly afternoon.'

'Your idea is to throw them into the nearest loch, isn't it?' Chester Royde asked.

'Ah well, I'm afraid I've got a disappointment for you, Royde, over that. Yes, the suggestion seemed to worry my wife, rather. She seemed to think they might be drowned. So I promised her I wouldn't throw them into the loch.'

'That's a pity,' said Chester Royde.

'Yes, it is a pity, but it can't be helped. However, we'll think of something else to do to them.'

'Sure thing.'

'I don't know why you're such a smarty over Scottish Nationalists, Chester Royde,' his wife snapped crossly. 'You don't even know what they are.'

'I certainly don't,' the young financier admitted. 'But if our friend Ben Nevis thinks they ought to be bumped off, that goes with me.'

'They're a kind of tartan Bolshie, if you know what I mean,' the Chieftain explained.

'Communists, eh?' said Royde.

'That sort of thing, only rather worse because they ought to know better. I mean to say they don't come from lower classes. They're agitators. Their great grievance is that Scotland isn't independent of England. Well, of course the idea is ludicrous. If there was the slightest reason for Scotland to be independent, people like Kilwhillie and myself would have sent the fiery cross round long ago and called out the clans.'

'But are there any clans left to call out?' Carrie asked, a noticeable tartness in her tone. 'I thought that people like Kilwhillie and you drove them out of Scotland long ago.'

'Oh, for the love of Mike, Carrie, don't start a political argument,' her husband begged.

'Oh, she's not arguing,' said Ben Nevis. 'That's her Macdonald blood asserting itself. But look here, Carrie, if my great-grandfather hadn't forced your great-great-grandfather to go to Canada you wouldn't be driving to look at Knocknacolly with a view to buying it. You'd still be living in Glenbristle. You haven't seen Glenbristle yet, Royde, have you? Johnnie, you can turn the car at the end of the road in Glenbristle?'

'Oh yes, Ben Nevis.'

'Well, I'll run you up Glenbristle as far as the road goes. It's only about three miles.'

'No, no, please, Ben Nevis,' Carrie begged. 'Chester and I can go there tomorrow or any time. I do think we ought to concentrate on Knocknacolly this morning.'

Kilwhillie's moustache, which had flagged at the proposal to explore Glenbristle, recovered itself as he acknowledged Carrie's firmness with a grateful if slightly melancholy smile.

'All right, Johnnie, keep right on,' said the Chieftain. 'I'm glad you're so interested in Knocknacolly. I won't deny I've set my heart on you two charming people having a place not too far away from Glenbogle. I mean to say, if you take the bridlepaths you'll hardly be ten miles from us. How long do you reckon it takes you to walk to Knocknacolly by bridle-path, Mary?'

'Three hours if it hasn't been raining for a day or two,' she growled.

'About five if it has,' her sister added.

'Which it usually has,' Mary growled.

There was a curious resemblance between the expression of Ben Nevis at that moment and the expression of one of the water-horses mordant that surmounted the pillars of the Castle gates.

'Now don't exaggerate about our rain, Mary,' he said, directing this expression at his daughter. 'People *will* exaggerate about our weather, Royde,' he added. 'What could you want better than today? And this is typical of the West Highlands in August.'

Mary and Catriona turned round and looked at their father in amazement. They had heard him tell tall stories about stags and salmon, about the prowess of the Ben Nevis MacDonalds in clan feuds with the Macintoshes, and about orations he had made at meetings of the County Council; but they had never heard a story the tallness of which came within measurable distance of the one he had just told about West Highland weather in August.

'You'd call today a typical August day, wouldn't you, Hugh?' he went on.

Kilwhillie grabbed his moustache as a drowning man clutches at a straw.

'Oh yes, Donald. I should call this a typical fine August day,' he replied.

Ben Nevis's countenance had reverted to that water-horse mordant expression as he glared at his daughters, defying them to contribute any further to the discussion.

'Well, of course over in America we've always had the idea that it rained a whole lot in Scotland all the time,' said Royde. 'But this is great weather.'

'Mind you, I'm not going to pretend it never rains in the West Highlands,' said Ben Nevis with a generous frankness. 'Oh no, it does rain sometimes. By Jove, Hugh, look at Loch na Craosnaich. I've never seen it so low – this year, I mean,' he added quickly. 'That's where our ancestor Hector of the Great Jaw drowned eleven Macintoshes in the year 1482, Carrie.' He indicated a stretch of water menacingly dark even upon this fine day. 'I call him our ancestor because he's pretty sure to be an ancestor of yours. He had twenty-two sons. One of them, Murdoch Ruadh, was famous for the violent red of his hair, and his descendants known as Clan Vurich lived in Glenbristle. I dare say that jolly hair of yours was inherited from Murdoch Ruadh.'

'Why, that's great, Carrie,' her husband exclaimed. 'That's a name for us to remember some happy day.'

Carrie blushed.

'You'll have to drop a fly on Loch na Craosnaich, Carrie, one of these days. I don't fish much myself nowadays. Too slow for me. But Kilwhillie's a great hand with a rod. Yes, I more or less gave up fishing after I caught that forty-eight pounder in Loch Hoo five years ago. What a battle! He took a Blue and Yellow Flying Dutchman which I used quite by accident, because I'd always used Simpson's Green Boobytrap on Loch Hoo until then. But I hadn't a Boobytrap with me that morning and I used this Blue and Yellow Flying Dutchman which Bertie Bottley was always plaguing me to try. I'd no faith in it at all. None whatever. But I was wrong. Yes, extraordinary thing, I was wrong. Well, to cut a tall story short – ha-ha – this fellow took the Blue and Yellow Flying

Dutchman at five minutes past eleven on a beautiful fishing morning and I played him till three o'clock that afternoon. What a battle! Forty-eight pounds, five ounces and a half. And as clean-run a salmon as ever I saw. Of course I had plenty of other fish after that, but they didn't give me the fights I wanted and so gradually I more or less gave up the rod. Always know when to stop, that's been my motto, ever since I left Harrow.'

Soon after this cautionary tale the entrance to Glenbogle was reached and the Daimler stopped for Catriona and Mary to alight. The two young women gave an unemotional wave over their hefty shoulders and then immediately set out to walk back up the glen at four miles an hour.

'What a dust those two girls of mine are kicking up,' Ben Nevis exclaimed. 'That shows you how dry it is, Hugh. Stop at the post-office in Kenspeckle, Johnnie.'

The small village of Kenspeckle lay about a mile along the main road westward from the entrance to Glenbogle. Ben Nevis strode into the post-office and demanded a form on which to write a cablegram to India. He was supplied by an old lady of about eighty with bright eyes and gold spectacles.

'Wonderful weather we're having, Mrs Macdonald.'

'Oh, it's beautiful weather indeed, Ben Nevis. I don't remember the like of such weather in August since I left school.'

'Where's Willie?'

'Willie's away out, Ben Nevis. He had to see a traveller in Fort Augustus about some biscuits which never reached us.'

'When's he coming back?'

'Och, he'll be coming back some time, Ben Nevis.'

'Well, I'm anxious for this cable to go off as soon as possible.'

'That will be quite all right, Ben Nevis. He'll send it as soon as he comes back from Fort Augustus.'

The Chieftain wrote his cablegram:

Lieutenant Hector MacDonald
Clanranald Highlanders
Tallulahgabad, Punjab

Ask Colonel Rose-Ross as special favour to self to give you month's leave for urgent family business impossible to specify in cablegram stop if leave granted come by plane earliest possible moment.
Ben Nevis

'How much is that, Mrs Macdonald?'

The old lady shook her head.

'I don't know at all, Ben Nevis. Willie will know. But what does that matter? Next time anybody from the glen is passing will be time enough to pay for the telegram. So Master Hector's coming home? Isn't that splendid, now?'

'Yes, we'll all be glad to see him.'

'Indeed, yes. Such a fine young gentleman. Very like yourself, Ben Nevis.'

A compliment from a woman was to Ben Nevis always agreeable whatever her age. He beamed.

'Well, good morning, Mrs Macdonald. And mind Willie sends that cablegram as soon as he comes in.'

'Oh indeed, yes, Ben Nevis. Willie will be wanting to see Master Hector back himself as soon as possible.'

The Chieftain strode from the post-office and climbed back into the Daimler.

'Well, I hope with any luck Hector will be home for the Gathering.'

'The Gathering? What's that?' Chester Royde asked.

'Our little Glenbogle Gathering. We hold it on August 28th this year. Quite a humble affair, of course. We don't compete with Inverness or Oban or Braemar. But we preserve the old spirit.'

'But what's the Gathering for?'

'Oh, tossing the caber and running and dancing and piping. Friendly rivalry and all that sort of thing. It's the only day in the year I encourage trippers. They come in buses. You'll enjoy it, Royde. You'll see a fine display of tartan.'

Chester Royde looked thoughtful. He was wondering if he could get his kilt in time for what sounded like an appropriate occasion for the début of that costume.

About four miles after Kenspeckle the bastions of Glenbore came into sight, and the Daimler turned off from the main road to make up Glenbore a journey similar to the one it had already made down Glenbogle. Kilwhillie had parted some time ago now with most of Glenbore to a rich stockbroker called Dutton, who had pulled down the old Glenbore Lodge and built himself a concrete palace designed by an architect of the modern school. It looked like a frozen cheese lying about in a rockery, and was considered unsuitable to Inverness-shire. So it was, but not more unsuitable than some of the new bridges put up by the Inverness-shire County Council.

'Ghastly looking place, what?' Ben Nevis said as they passed the new Glenbore Lodge. 'Gives me the creeps whenever I see it.'

Kilwhillie was reflecting that the prospective purchaser of Knocknacolly might share Dutton's taste in architecture and therefore refrained from savage criticism.

'Every man to his own taste where a house is concerned,' he observed tolerantly.

'I don't agree with you at all, Hugh,' Ben Nevis argued. 'Nobody has a right to defile one of our glorious Highland glens with a building like that.'

'What I object to much more than his house is his calling himself Dutton of Glenbore,' said Kilwhillie. 'Glenbore was part of Kilwhillie till I sold it and I think it's rather bad form calling himself Glenbore.'

'So if I buy Knocknacolly,' Chester Royde asked, 'I wouldn't be called Knocknacolly?'

Kilwhillie was in a painful quandary. He did not want to risk losing a purchaser for Knocknacolly by denying him the right to use it as a name. At the same time he did feel very strongly about these rich fellows who bought sporting estates in the Highlands and supposed that by doing so they could turn themselves into lairds of long lineage and ancient territorial privileges. He had an equal objection to lairds of long lineage who put a 'The' in front of Macintosh or Macleod or Macneil, always excepting The Chisholm. Kilwhillie in fact was a stickler for tradition, and it says much for his sincerity that he preferred to risk losing a purchaser than to mislead him by letting him suppose that if he bought Knocknacolly he would be justified in expecting to be addressed as Knocknacolly.

'Well, I dare say some people would call you Knocknacolly if they thought you liked it,' said Kilwhillie. 'But I could not undertake to call you Knocknacolly myself.'

'What do you want to call yourself Knocknacolly for, Chester?' his wife asked. 'There's no point in you calling yourself Knocknacolly.'

'I don't want to call myself Knocknacolly,' Chester Royde replied a little huffily. 'Can't I ask a perfectly good question without being accused of wanting to change my name?'

Kilwhillie tried to reassure himself by hanging on to his moustache, but he felt that the prospect of a successful sale had clouded over since they entered Glenbore. Indeed he felt inclined to give up the business altogether and instead of taking the Roydes to Knocknacolly to take them to Kilwhillie House and show them his relics of the 'Fifteen and the 'Forty-five.

Luckily Ben Nevis himself had made up his mind to sell Knocknacolly at a good price, and when Kilwhillie asked if they would not like to turn aside and see his Jacobite relics he condemned the notion as ridiculous.

'You can show our friends Kilwhillie House another day, Hugh. If we're going to be back in Glenbogle for lunch, we have our time cut out.'

Presently the car turned off to the left and began to climb among majestic scenery. Then it dipped down again on a corkscrew descent, crossed a small stream and went on for five miles over as desolate a stretch of level moorland as might be found in all Scotland, at the end of which on a slight elevation surrounded by dense plantations of Scots firs and backed by a savage range of bens stood Knocknacolly Lodge like a stained and faded frontispiece to a novel by Sir Walter Scott.

'Why, I think it's perfectly gorgeous,' Carrie exclaimed. 'It's the house I've prayed for all my life.'

Kilwhillie had received two sharp rebuffs from women in his day. He believed himself asbestos where the female sex was concerned. Yet at that moment he was on the verge of kneeling down in the Daimler and kissing the hem of Carrie's extremely smart skirt.

'Knew you'd like it,' Ben Nevis shouted exultantly. 'It's the best twelve-head forest in Inverness-shire, not to mention quite a pretty little grouse moor on your doorstep as you might say.'

As in most Scottish shooting-lodges the rooms at Knocknacolly tried to make up with quantity for their lack of size and absence of any kind of architectural proportion. The kitchen-quarters were designed to pay out the domestic staff for all the waste and breakages and bad meals of the rest of the year, by making the annual migration to Scotland the equivalent of two months' hard labour in the days before prison reform. But why continue? It is more cheerful to hear Chester Royde assert that Knocknacolly Lodge will want a hell of a lot doing to it inside and out before it remotely resembles anything he calls a house. The mouldering blinds, the dry rot in the attics, the corrugated-iron bothy built along one side, the kennels with their rusty railings, the dead bluebottles on the window-sills, the dead tortoiseshell butterflies on the floors — one knows that all these will vanish if Chester Royde decides to buy Knocknacolly.

But will he?

'I would just adore this place, Chester,' said his wife.

'I knew you'd like it. I am so glad,' Ben Nevis barked. 'And as I say it's the best twelve-head forest in Inverness-shire.'

Kilwhillie said nothing. He just let his moustache nuzzle his hand and comforted himself with its dumb sympathy.

'How much are you asking for it, Kilwhillie?' Chester Royde snapped suddenly.

'Fifteen thousand pounds,' Ben Nevis replied for his friend.

'I'll give you six thousand pounds, Kilwhillie,' Chester Royde said in a voice as hard as the rock of Manhattan.

'I'd hoped to get at least seven thousand,' Kilwhillie murmured.

'That's O.K. by me. I'll give seven thousand,' Chester Royde snapped. 'Do you accept that offer?'

'Why, yes, I'll accept that.'

After all he had always told himself he would take seven thousand for Knocknacolly, and he had taken it.

'You've got a bargain, Royde,' Ben Nevis said. 'You wouldn't have had Knocknacolly from me for seven thousand.'

'No, I guess I wouldn't,' Chester Royde agreed, with a contented smile.

Chapter 8

GLENBRISTLE

The reflections of Miss Myrtle Royde when she set out that morning to Glenbristle were very different from those of her sister-in-law the previous morning. Carrie had been animated by a dreamy interest in the past; Myrtle was inspired entirely by a lively curiosity about the present. She found her sister-in-law's Scottish origin an inadequate explanation of her so evident anxiety about the welfare of these young men she had met, and she was looking forward to ascertaining for herself just how attractive this poet was. With the advantage of three years' sophisticated juniority she was tolerantly amused by Carrie's naïvety in supposing she had covered her tracks by addressing the letter to the lawyer.

When Myrtle appeared in the front courtyard about a quarter of an hour after the Daimler had started for Knocknacolly the trimness of her check cream and brown skirt, the turnery of her legs, the deep carnation of her cheeks, the flash of her dark eyes, and the particularly provocative tilt of her hat combined to quicken faintly the muscle-bound heart of Lieutenant Murdoch MacDonald, R.N., who was receiving from a cocker spaniel the only kind of emotional response by which he was not embarrassed. Myrtle realized at once that he was mustering the words to suggest his company on her walk and anticipated him by waving her stick and hurrying along towards the drive.

It was just after she had turned off into the narrow grass-grown rocky road up Glenbristle that Myrtle saw the coruscation of the Macmillan and Buchanan tartans, and at once decided that the two kilted figures walking towards her were the young men Carrie had sent her to warn against the vengeance of Ben Nevis. If the slightest doubt remained it vanished when she came face to face with Alan Macmillan.

'Pardon me,' she said. 'But I have a letter for you two gentlemen from my sister-in-law, Mrs Royde. At least, I have a letter for Mr Buchanan. Which is Mr Buchanan?' Myrtle asked, trying to look as if she really had not the slightest idea.

A weight descended upon the soul of James Buchanan as he put out his hand for the letter. He told himself he had known all the time that the hundred-dollar bill had been a mistake for a ten-dollar bill. Even that was five times as much as the largest voluntary donation he had yet received for the Scottish Brotherhood of Action.

'Mrs Royde is so very sorry she couldn't give you the warning herself,' Myrtle said as James passed the letter to Alan.

'It's very kind of her,' he said, 'but my friend and I are not at all in awe of people like Mr MacDonald of Ben Nevis.'

'Not at all,' Alan said emphatically, his blue eyes kindled to what Myrtle found an entrancing fire by the flame of poetic action. 'We appreciate very much the trouble Mrs Royde has taken, and the trouble you have taken,' he added with what Myrtle found an entrancingly awkward bow, 'but I think I may say that Ben Nevis has more to fear from us than we from him.'

'A great deal more,' James Buchanan muttered grimly.

'But I don't think you two realize what kind of a man Ben Nevis is,' said Myrtle. 'Will we sit down for a few minutes and discuss the matter? I'm dying to sit down for a few minutes.'

A suitable bank of grass was discovered and the three of them paid homage to Scotland's national pastime by going into committee.

'Now first of all I must make my own position clear,' said Myrtle. 'I'm devoted to Ben Nevis.' She found the scowl on the poet's brow so entrancing that she repeated her assertion with great emphasis for the pleasure of seeing it deepen. 'And Mrs Royde is also devoted to Ben Nevis,' she went on, with a sidelong look to see the effect of that statement on the scowl. Either it was already as deep as he could make it or the announcement of Carrie's devotion had no more effect than the announcement of her own. 'At the same time,' Myrtle continued, 'my sister-in-law is terribly worried because she's afraid you will think she may have said something to Ben Nevis about the plan you told her you had to kidnap him.'

'We gave up that idea as soon as we heard Ben Nevis was a friend of Mistress Royde,' James Buchanan said.

'Well, of course, I don't want to say anything that might sting you into longing to show that you could kidnap Ben Nevis, but . . . oh well, I won't say it. All I want to have you realize is that Ben Nevis is the toughest thing in kilts since Robert Bruce.'

'Bruce didn't wear the kilt,' both young men contradicted simultaneously.

'Well, whatever he wore, I guess he was tough all right. And so's Ben Nevis, believe me. While you and my sister-in-law were having your quiet afternoon together yesterday, I was with him up on the moors, and if you'd seen the way he laid about a camping party and shut them up in the dungeons of his castle you'd know just how tough he is. Well, somebody brought him word that you two were camping out somewhere around on his land, and this afternoon he aims to have you both thrown into the nearest loch. That's what's worrying Mrs Royde. She enjoyed your hospitality yesterday in your camp, and she just can't bear the idea of a watery grave for both of you. And now I've met you both I can't say I'm tickled to death at the notion myself. So put our minds at rest by moving away from Ben Nevis's hunting-grounds, and when I see Mrs Royde at lunch I'll be able to tell her my mission has been successful.'

'Are you seriously suggesting, Miss Royde, that this swollen-headed, Anglicized, degenerate laird will try to throw my friend and me into a loch?' James Buchanan asked.

'It's not a suggestion at all. He certainly will,' Myrtle declared.

'Did you ever hear the like of that, Alan?' James asked.

The question acted like a pitchfork on the bard's shock of fair hair, tossing it in every direction.

Myrtle thought she had never seen hair glint so cunningly.

'But I tell you he will,' she insisted earnestly. 'You didn't see him charge those campers yesterday. I did.'

'A mob of Cockney hikers, I suppose,' said the bard contemptuously.

'I don't know where they came from, but I do know he shook them one after another like so many rats.'

'Let him try to shake me,' said James Buchanan, his round head waving the air like a boxer's. 'I'll pull his lugs for him.'

'His what?' Myrtle asked.

'His ears. Ay, and his nose. Shake me, will he?' James threatened.

'He might shoot you,' said Myrtle. 'He shot a crooner in a portable radio.'

'This is a really great chance for poetic action,' the bard observed, a dreamy smile quickening upon his rowan-red lips.

'It's a great chance for action of any kind, poetic or otherwise,' James Buchanan declared. 'Shake me, will he? Man, I hope fine he just tries. You're sure the ploy is to start this afternoon, Miss Royde, because I have to go back to Glasgow tomorrow and I don't want to miss this shaking?'

'But you forget, Mr Buchanan, that Ben Nevis has keepers and beaters, not to mention his two sons,' Myrtle said.

'So big a Chieftain's sure to have a tail,' Alan Macmillan scoffed. 'Well, maybe he and his tail will be able to throw James and me into the nearest loch. But if they do I promise James and I will come back with a tail of our own and throw him and his sons and his keepers and his beaters into every loch he owns, one after another.'

'You know, I'm crazy about Scotland,' Myrtle declared, gazing into Alan's eyes. 'You're *all* so fierce. It makes Chicago seem kind of slow and sleepy. And you're so much what my idea used to be about poets, Mr Macmillan, until I met two or three of them and found them sissie or highbrow. Well, I suppose if you're set on shooting it out with Ben Nevis nothing I can say or do will change your mind. I don't know what I'm going to tell my sister-in-law when I see her. I guess she's going to call me the world's worst diplomat. She'll be sure that if *she* had given you the warning you'd have listened to her. Perhaps you would,' Myrtle added softly, with a sidelong glance from beneath her long-lashed lids at the poet, whose rose-browned complexion caught a deeper rose as he replied in a carefully indifferent tone that nobody could persuade him to run away from Ben Nevis.

James Buchanan caught Myrtle's sidelong glance, and his brow puckered. Two of them, within twenty-four hours, he reflected. However, this one was not married. He wished he did not have to go back to Glasgow tomorrow. If Alan stayed here in defiance of those 'No Camping' notices, it looked as if things would be amusing.

'Are you rested now, Miss Royde?' he asked. 'Would you like to see our camp?'

'I'd adore to see your camp if it isn't very far,' Myrtle assured them. 'But I have to be back by half past one to lunch. Oh, I know, perhaps I'll be picked up by the car. I'm getting pretty good at walking, but I'm not a world-beater yet.'

'It's about a mile farther up the glen,' she was told.

'I guess I can crawl as far as that.'

Myrtle was right. She did manage to reach the camp, where the two little green tents were pitched on the level sward in the shelter of the granite escarpment.

'I'm devoted to Ben Nevis as I told you, but I can't for the life of me see why he objects to two cunning little green tents like these,' she commented. 'Why, they hardly take up any more room than a couple of lettuces.' She turned to Alan Macmillan. 'Which is yours?'

He showed her and she peeped in to admire the sleeping-bag.

'Is that some of your poetry?' she asked, pointing to an open exercise-book, the manuscript in which was covered with erasures and corrections.

'It's something I'm working at, yes,' the bard admitted unwillingly.

A picture presented itself to Myrtle's mind, the picture of herself living in a little green tent like this and listening some of the time to birdsong and the rest of the time to poetry inspired by herself, a melodious and carefree existence. She looked at her watch, one of the most expensive that ever came out of Tiffany's.

'Oh dear, I'd like to stay, but I suppose I ought to be getting back to Glenbogle if I'm not going to miss that ride back in the car,' she sighed.

'What's the matter, Miss Royde,' the lawyer asked.

'Oh, I don't know. I was just thinking what a false existence we most of us lead. This is real life.'

'It's all right when it's fine,' the bard allowed.

'Yes, I dare say if it's pouring with rain you might feel it was just a little bit too real.' She sighed again. 'It seems a pity you shouldn't be allowed to enjoy this lovely weather. Would your pride be terribly hurt if I were to ask Ben Nevis as a special favour to let you camp here in peace? Mind you, I can't be absolutely sure he'd give you permission, but I've a notion he *would* listen to me.'

'James is going back to Glasgow tomorrow, anyway,' said the bard. 'And I'll accept no favours from a man like Ben Nevis. It's against my political principles.'

'How rigid you are! But what are you going to do if Ben Nevis really does get violent? I mean to say there are only two of you. You couldn't hope to win in a fight. I've seen what he can do with sixteen hikers, and eight of them women. And when Mr Buchanan leaves you tomorrow, what will you do, Mr Macmillan?'

'I am not going to run away from Ben Nevis,' the bard declared. 'I'll not do that for anybody.'

'I'll tell you what you might do, Alan,' said his friend. 'You might move up to that cave on Ben Cruet. They're not likely to find you there.'

'Uaimh na laoigh,' the bard muttered, paying such great attention to the correct pronunciation of the Gaelic that Myrtle thought he was groaning.

'Oh, you're in pain,' she exclaimed with quick sympathy.

The bard looked at her in astonishment.

'No, I'm not.'

'But you groaned as if you were in pain.'

'I wasn't groaning,' said the bard indignantly. 'I was saying the name of the cave in Gaelic. Uaimh na laoigh. The Cave of the Calf.'

'Pardon me. That's where I lag behind my sister-in-law. She knows Gaelic.'

'Not very much,' the bard commented.

'Oh well, of course I can't criticize,' Myrtle said, aware of a slight pleasure in the fact that Carrie did not know very much Gaelic. 'But I think this plan for you to go and live in a cave is very good. Is it terribly far away from where we are now?'

'If you can get a little way up the brae at the back I can show you more or less where it is,' Alan volunteered.

James Buchanan nodded agreement with some reflection of his own.

Scrambling up to a point whence the whereabouts of the cave would be pointed out involved a good deal of help from Alan's hand for Myrtle, who thought it must have been the long walk from Glenbogle Castle which had made her a little stiff.

At last they reached a level grassy ridge from which Alan pointed out a mass of stone some seven or eight hundred feet up the slopes of Ben Cruet on the other side of which was the Cave of the Calf.

'It's quite an easy climb,' he assured Myrtle.

'And I'm getting better and better at climbing every day,' she told him. 'How long do you think you'll camp in that cave?'

'I've only provisions for three days.'

'Only for three days? And then what will you do?'

'I'll have to camp somewhere nearer to where I can buy provisions.'

'And how long will you stay there?'

'I promised my mother I'd be back in Glasgow in another week. She wants to go and stay with some friends in Perth and I said I'd go with her.'

'Why doesn't your father go with her?'

'My father's dead.'

'Oh, I'm sorry. Well, of course you must take your mother to Perth. How long do you think you'll stay there? I'm asking all these questions because I know Mrs Royde will expect me to come back full of the latest correct information about your movements. She took such a very great fancy to you both.'

'I expect we'll be in Perth about a week.'

'And then?'

'Oh, I expect I'll go back to Glasgow.'

'That reminds me. Mrs Royde wants your address and Mr Buchanan's address. She liked Mr Buchanan so very much. She spoke with such deep admiration of his grasp of statistics.'

'I'll give you our addresses when we get back to the tents.'

Myrtle sighed.

'Why do you sigh?' the bard asked.

'I was thinking how sad life was so often. I mean to say, look at us. Ships that pass in the night, and speak each other in passing. Only a look and a . . . and a . . . how does it go on?'

'I'm afraid I don't know.'

'Well, it doesn't matter. You understand what I mean. I'll go back to America at the end of next month by the latest. And you're going to Perth next week. Of course I might see you again while you're living in your cave. But I might not. This may be the last time we ever meet.'

'I hope not,' said the bard, and his eyes were now a melting blue that Myrtle found even more entrancing than when they were lighted by the flame of prospective combat.

'Do you really hope not?'

'Yes, really.'

'Well, of course Mrs Royde and I might come along together either tomorrow or the next day. My sister-in-law's so very romantic. I think she'll be crazy to see your cave. Now, I'm not romantic at all. I suppose that shocks you as a poet?'

'Not in the least,' said the bard. 'I am extremely anti-romantic myself.'

'You are? Well, that's another link between us because I pride myself on being intensely practical. But that isn't quite fair to Carrie – Carrie is my sister-in-law. She is romantic, but she is also intensely practical. Perhaps not quite as practical as me. I'm so practical you could almost call me hard-boiled.'

'Well, being very practical myself,' said the bard, 'I only admire practical women.'

'Didn't I hear your friend Mr Buchanan call you "Alan"?'

'Yes, that's my name.'

'Strange. It has always been a very favourite name of mine. I don't know why at all. I never knew any Alan I had a crush on. I don't remember any Alan in a book I liked very much. And yet I've always been kind of fond of that name. Oh well, we mustn't stay chatting here,

I'll have to get back to Glenbogle. So, I suppose it's good-bye, Mr Macmillan.'

'James and I will walk with you as far as the end of Glenbristle.'

'That's very sweet of you.'

It was even harder for Myrtle to scramble back down to the level where the two little green tents were pitched. She had to hold the bard's hand almost all the way.

'I told Miss Royde we would walk along with her as far as Glenbogle, James,' said the bard.

'And we must walk very quickly,' Myrtle added, 'or I'll miss the car.'

It was already a quarter to one when Myrtle and her escort reached the signpost at the entrance to Glenbristle.

'I'd love to have you walk along with me a bit more of the way, but I think the sight of you both in Glenbogle might stir up trouble,' she said. 'And I do want Mrs Royde and myself to have the pleasure of visiting you in your cave before your provisions run out,' she added to the bard. 'Tell me the name of it again.'

'Uaimh na laoigh.'

'I do think it's the most melancholy sound I ever heard. I'm sure the poor calf it was called after never managed to make such a heart-rending moo when it wanted mother. I'll have lots of fun trying to have Mrs Royde tell me what it means. Will you write it down on the envelope with your address?'

The bard obliged.

'And those three words make a noise like that?' Myrtle asked in awe. She emitted a melodious groan. 'Is that anything at all like it?'

'Ooav na . . .' the bard choked. In his endeavour to make the 'laoigh' sufficiently guttural, the 'gh' broke away from the preceding vowels and entered his windpipe.

'Oh, you haven't sprained your throat?' she asked anxiously.

'No, it's perfectly all right. As a matter of fact "laogh" — that's the nominative — is one of the great test words in Gaelic pronunciation.'

'I'll say it must be. I hope there's a more comfortable word for "veal". Otherwise I think one's table manners wouldn't be considered too good. Well, I suppose we have to part. Good-bye, Mr Buchanan. I won't see you again. Good-bye, Mr Macmillan. Mrs Royde and I will try our hardest to visit you in your cave. If I were you I'd move right up there now just in case Ben Nevis goes on the warpath in Glenbristle.'

'I'll camp up there with you tonight, Alan,' James Buchanan offered.

'I'll take the bridle-path across to Glenbore tomorrow morning and catch the Fort William bus from there. I think it saves sixpence. I'm not sure about that, but I think it does.'

'Oh, I'm so glad you've decided to move too, Mr Buchanan,' Myrtle said. 'That will be such good news for Mrs Royde.'

'Mind you, I'm not moving because I'm afraid of a shaking from Mr MacDonald of Ben Nevis,' James Buchanan announced truculently.

'Surely not, Mr Buchanan. You're moving to oblige Mrs Royde and me, which is most chivalrous of you.'

Myrtle shook hands and set out towards the Castle. The two young men sat down on a bank above the road and watched the trim figure disappear round a bend.

'A nice wee lassie,' James observed. 'Och, I like these American women a lot better than I like Englishwomen. They make you feel at home with them much more quickly. Losh, Alan, there's not many Englishwomen could have made me agree to move up to yon cave because that clown of a laird has been blethering away what he's going to do with campers. I felt it was a bit weak right enough, but och, I hadn't the heart to refuse the wee lassie. You know, I made sure she had come along to say that hundred-dollar bill was a mistake. I was a bit relieved to find she hadn't, I tell you. Twenty pounds is a lot of money for a treasurer to be asked to hand back. I'd been building a good deal on that twenty pounds, Alan. But you'll need to watch your step pretty well.'

'Why?'

'I'm telling you.'

'What are you telling me?'

'I'm just telling you. You'll need to watch your step.'

'Why?'

'I'm telling you, Alan.'

'You're not telling me.'

'You know fine what I mean.'

'I haven't the remotest idea.'

'Ach, get away with you, Alan. Do you mind Annie Duncan?'

'Of course I do.'

'And Jeanie Duncan?'

'Of course.'

'Well, that's what I said, I'm telling you.'

'The circumstances are entirely different.'

'Och ay, the circumstances are different, but the root of the matter is just the same.'

'Neither Annie nor Jeanie was married,' Alan pointed out. 'And they were sisters.'

'Well, I'll admit that you were in a more difficult position with them. Still, though neither of them managed to book you, it started a family row which has lasted ever since. So all I'm telling you is "watch your step". If you start trying to teach yon wee dark-eyed lassie how to pronounce Gaelic you'll be in trouble with the other. And I don't want to lose Sister Carrie's voluntary donations. Besides, she may buy this property up here. She's what the S.B.A. has been looking for.'

'Imphm!' the poet grunted in agreement.

'Imphm!' the lawyer echoed.

Then they lit their pipes and lay back on the grassy bank, staring at the cloudless sky. A quarter of an hour passed in silence, at the end of which time they sat up to look at a car go by in the direction of the Castle.

They did not hear Ben Nevis bellow, 'Scottish Nationalists, by gad!' though the bellow was so loud that those inside the car might have been forgiven for supposing it was heard by the people in the streets of Inverness and Fort William, by the monks of Fort Augustus, by the patients in the Kingussie Sanatorium, and even a faint echo of it by the spinsters and the knitters in the sun on the marina at Oban.

However, the passing of the car stirred them to get up and walk back to their camp in Glenbristle.

'My god!' James exclaimed. 'Somebody has gone off with the tents.'

Alan ran across to where his sleeping-bag was still lying upon the grass at the foot of the rocky escarpment.

'My poems are all right,' he shouted.

'What good are they?' James yelled back indignantly. 'We can't sleep under a blasted exercise-book.'

'We'd better take the rest of our stuff up to the cave right away,' Alan suggested, when his friend reached the scene of the raid.

'But who can have taken the tents?' James demanded.

The answer to that question was given not to the owners of the tents but to the guests of Ben Nevis assembled in the dining-room at the Castle, when at twenty minutes to two Catriona and Mary MacDonald, crimson in the face with the exertions they had made to be back in time for lunch at half past one, came heftily in, and before their father could tell them that they were ten minutes late, like two hunters flinging down the skins of the wild beasts they had slain, flung down on the floor beside him two little green tents.

'Found them in Glenbristle,' Catriona growled.

'We'd taken the bridle-path,' Mary growled.

'Wanted to see if we could put up a record in this dry weather,' Catriona explained.

'We should have done if we hadn't spotted these tents,' said Mary. 'But lugging them with us took the stuffing out of our final spurt.'

'Sorry we're late for lunch, Father,' Catriona growled.

'But we thought you'd like these trophies,' growled Mary.

'These tents must belong to those Scottish Nationalists we saw loafing about by Glenbristle,' said the Chieftain. 'Well, that gives us the beat for this afternoon.'

Carrie and Myrtle were eyeing one another across the table in consternation when into the dining-room there floated from without the sound of choric booing.

'What the deuce is that wild hullabaloo?' Ben Nevis shouted.

Toker hurried to the window.

'Some kind of demonstration appears to be proceeding, sir,' the butler informed him.

'Proceeding where?'

'It doesn't appear to be proceeding anywhere, sir. It's just proceeding in the courtyard. It's some kind of gathering.'

The Chieftain jumped up from the table and looked out of the window. The sight of him swelled the gathering from a pimple to a fiercy carbuncle. The booing doubled and redoubled in volume and above it were heard such derisive epithets as 'Fascist bully', 'Scotch landgrabber', 'Old Bluenose', 'Tartanface', 'Mussolini', and 'MacBlimp', accompanied by arpeggios of shrill and mocking female laughter.

'Donald, Donald,' his wife begged, 'don't expose yourself to this kind of thing. It does no good. Pay no attention and let us get on quietly with our lunch.'

'You infamous riff-raff,' Ben Nevis leant out of the window to bawl at the hikers, who shook their fists at him with cries of 'Fascist hound', 'Fascist crook', 'Dirty Dictator', 'Stinking Blackshirt', and amid catcalls, groans, and hisses, 'We want Mosley!'

The furious Chieftain was now leaning out of the window like Punch in one of his paroxysms, leaning out so far indeed that the anxious Toker was standing by, ready to snatch at his kilt if necessary to save him from diving head foremost into the courtyard.

'Murdoch! Iain!' Mrs MacDonald exhorted. 'Do get your father away from that window. Hugh! Mr Royde! Please use your influence. Mr Fletcher, you know what those dreadful hikers are capable of. Couldn't you most kindly go down into the courtyard and quieten them?'

'Best thing is to turn the hose on them,' Mary growled.

'Mary, I'm astonished at you,' her mother boomed reproachfully. 'After what I said to you and Catriona yesterday evening.'

But above the maternal boom resounded the paternal bellow.

'I defy you, you Bolshie scum! You won't get off so easily next time.'

Mrs MacDonald now rose from the table and went across to lay a soothing arm upon her furious lord.

'Donald, please remember your dignity and do not argue with these people.'

'But you didn't hear what they said to me, Trixie. They said they were going to make me learn the meaning of democracy. They actually had the infernal impudence to threaten me with reprisals.'

The memory of this flooded him with fresh rage, and shaking off his wife's restraining arm he rushed to the window again.

But apparently by now the hikers had said what they had to say. They had hoisted their knapsacks and camping equipment and with bowed backs they were moving off across the courtyard towards the gates.

Few sights offer to the tender-hearted observer so poignant an illustration of man's weary pilgrimage through this vale of tears as that of hikers overloaded with equipment moving from their camping-ground to the nearest railway-station at the end of a holiday. Perhaps the only rival among the spectacles of human misery is that of hikers overloaded with equipment streaming out of a railway-station towards their camping-ground at the beginning of a holiday.

'Poor things,' sighed Mrs MacDonald. 'They do look so tired.'

'Poor things?' her husband echoed wrathfully. 'They'll look a good deal more tired before I've done with them. But come along, let's finish our lunch first.'

'Donald, what are you proposing to do now?'

'I'm going to keep them on the move with the lorry all the way down Glenbogle,' the Chieftain declared, and the expression upon his countenance was the expression of a Caligula gloating over the prospect of some gladiatorial enormity.

'Then do we give a miss this afternoon to these Scottish Nationalists?' Chester Royde asked. The question was not in fact prompted by blood-lust, but by the new owner of Knocknacolly's desire to get a closer view of the Macmillan and Buchanan tartan, the glimpse of which he had caught from the Daimler having inspired him with a greater respect than ever for the possibilities of Highland dress.

'Oh, we can deal with those brutes tomorrow,' said Ben Nevis. 'Or the next day.'

'I hope not the next day,' said Mr Fletcher gently. 'The next day is Sunday.'

Carrie and Myrtle looked at one another. Both of them were thinking what a good day that would be to visit the poet.

Chapter 9

THE CAVE OF THE CALF

Of the way in which Ben Nevis with a motorized column consisting of the lorry, the Daimler, Kilwhillie's seven-year-old Austin, and Murdoch MacDonald's two-seater harried those sixteen hikers for eight miles down Glenbogle the victims shall tell presently. It is enough at this point to say that he returned from the operation in boisterous good-humour and, much to the relief of Carrie and Myrtle, seemed to have forgotten about the Scottish Nationalists in the excitement of planning to shoot the Knocknacolly moors next day.

'Mind you, it's not for the birds you've bought Knocknacolly, Royde. It's for the stalking,' he warned the new proprietor. 'You've not killed your first stag yet. I hope you're going to do that next week. So you mustn't expect the birds we should have had on Drumcockie if they hadn't been scared by those disgusting hikers.'

'There should be plenty of birds,' Kilwhillie put in modestly. 'Of course Knocknacolly is not Clacknaclock and it's not Drumcockie, but you should have some good sport.'

'Ah, but I want to get him after a good stag at the back of Ben Goosey,' said the Chieftain. 'I can't tell you how much I'm looking forward to initiating you into the king of sports, what?'

'I'm looking forward to it myself,' said the young financier.

'I don't want you to go away with the idea that harrying hikers is the only sport we can offer you in the Highlands.'

'My dear Ben Nevis, I wouldn't want to spend a more thoroughly enjoyable time than I spent this afternoon hustling those hoodlums out of Glenbogle. It was great.'

'You haven't seen Knocknacolly yet, Myrtle,' said her host, a genial glow warming his eagle's beak. 'I tell you what. Murdoch shall drive you in his car tomorrow.'

'Oh, that'll be very exciting,' said Myrtle. 'But I don't think I ought to monopolize Murdoch. I know Carrie would like to drive in the two-seater.'

'But I'm not going tomorrow,' said Carrie quickly.

'Carrie!' her sister-in-law exclaimed.

'Well, I've a whole heap of letters to write.'

'So have I,' said Myrtle. 'I believe I ought to stay home too.'

'Oh, Myrtle, you haven't seen Knocknacolly yet.'

'But I'd like to see it with you. I want to hear your plans for it.'

'But I'd like to hear your ideas after you've seen the lodge. Then we can see if your ideas are the same as mine. I think it would be a pity for you not to go tomorrow just because I have a whole heap of letters to write. Besides, I want to work at my Gaelic.'

'Oh, you do?'

'Yes, I really do, Myrtle. When I start something I always like to stick to it.'

'Yes, I know how very persevering you are.'

'Well, now we've bought Knocknacolly I do feel I ought to be able to speak Gaelic. Don't you think I'm right to persevere with my Gaelic, Ben Nevis?'

'I do indeed. Only wish I could speak it as well now as I could when I was a four-year-old,' said the Chieftain. 'I used to rattle it off to my nurse in those days. I've always regretted I didn't keep it up.'

'And I want Chester to learn too,' Carrie went on. 'He's very good at languages.'

'That's right. You mastered Red Indian, didn't you, Royde?' Ben Nevis asked. 'You ought to be able to tackle Gaelic.'

'I picked up a bit of the Carroway language,' Chester admitted modestly.

'Rather like my Gaelic, I suppose. You don't speak it, but you understand it.'

'I understand a word here and there.'

'Oh, I don't understand every word in Gaelic,' Ben Nevis continued. 'But if I know what they're talking about I can follow perfectly what they say. What you want to do is to get hold of a few simple expressions one's always using up here like "Half luke" and "Half ewer", and then when they start talking back you smile and nod and they're awfully pleased.'

'Half luke? What's that mean?'

'Half luke: it's wet. Half ewer: it's cold.'

'Half luke. I must remember that,' said Chester.

'I'll spell it for you, Chester,' said his wife. 'It comes in the first exercise of *Gaelic Without Tears*. T-H-A-E-F-L-I-U-C-H.'

'What's that mean?'

'It's wet.'

'But Ben Nevis said "it's wet" was "half luke".'

'That's what I spelt for you.'

'And you'd have me learn Gaelic?'

'I certainly would, Chester.'

'Well, I've thought of another way of showing my appreciation of Scotland, Carrie.'

'What's that?'

'You'll see presently,' said her husband, a dreamy look in his eyes.

'I believe I'll learn Gaelic,' said Myrtle.

'What do you want to learn Gaelic for?' asked her sister-in-law.

'Goody, why shouldn't I, Carrie?'

'You aren't Scottish.'

'Well, you don't have to be French to learn French,' Myrtle protested.

'No, ma'am, you certainly don't.'

'Oh, if you want to learn Gaelic there's no reason why you shouldn't.'

'I don't think so either,' Myrtle said in a voice that made Carrie more determined than ever that her sister-in-law should go to Knocknacolly tomorrow and that she herself would stay at home to write letters.

But when the Knocknacolly party had left, Carrie felt it was a pity to waste such lovely weather indoors over letters and told her hostess that she thought she'd explore Glenbristle again, and have another picnic lunch by herself.

'Isn't there a cave somewhere near Glenbristle where Prince Charlie hid from the redcoats?' she asked.

'Oh, my dear child, Prince Charlie's cave is away on the other side of Glenbogle half-way up Ben Booey. You'd never find it by yourself even if you could walk as far.'

'I suppose I must have dreamt about this cave near Glenbristle. It seems so familiar somehow. But I have these strange dreams about the past, Mrs MacDonald.'

'Do you, dear?' her hostess boomed placidly. 'You should drink a cup of camomile before you go to sleep. It's an old-fashioned remedy, but these old-fashioned remedies are often the best.'

'But I like dreaming, Mrs MacDonald.'

'I can't say I do. I dislike so much the feeling of not being able to control one's movements, which is such a feature of most dreams.'

When Carrie received her sandwiches from the hands of Toker

she asked him if he knew anything about a cave near Glenbristle.

'I'm afraid I don't, madam, but if you wouldn't mind waiting for a minute I will endeavour to ascertain from one of the gillies if such a cave exists. It is certainly well within the bounds of probability that it does. Excuse me, madam.'

Toker withdrew from the hall in search of information, and when he was gone Carrie caught sight of the two green tents that Catriona and Mary had brought back as trophies yesterday. They were lying neatly folded under the table on which the MacDonalds parked their bonnets. The spirit of the Scottish Brotherhood of Action animated its latest member with the resolution to return the tents to their dispossessed owners. But when she pulled them out from under the table she found it was beyond her power to manage both tents. Even one would not make walking easy. She lacked the heftiness of the MacDonald girls. Just then the butler came back.

'I have made inquiries, madam, about this cave, and it would appear that there is a cave on the lower slopes of Ben Cruet overlooking Glenbristle. I'm afraid I could not venture to make any attempt to pronounce the name of the cave in Gaelic. I have been in the service of Ben Nevis for twelve years, but although I have read all Sir Walter Scott's wonderful novels and take an intense interest in the legendary lore of the Highlands I have no Gaelic.'

'I'm learning Gaelic now, Toker.'

'Are you indeed, madam? May I respectfully express my admiration? You have indeed set yourself a task. But to return to this cave. It would appear that the most convenient way of obtaining access to it from here is via the old bridle-path to Glenbore. When you reach the gate of the drive instead of carrying on along the road down Glenbogle you should bear up the slope, or brae as they call it here, to the left and follow this path. The cave would appear to lie some five miles further along, quite an appreciable walk in fact and by no means any too smooth.'

'I'll take it very easy.'

'Precisely, madam, and the view as you come round the shoulder of Ben Cruet and look down into Glenbristle and across over Glenbogle is said to be exceptionally fine. Probably you will choose this point of vantage to consume your lunch.'

'It sounds the very spot. Oh, and that reminds me, Toker, I thought I'd take one of these tents with me.'

'Pardon my apparent density, madam, but what would be your object in doing that? These are the tents belonging to two campers which Miss Catriona and Miss Mary brought back at lunch yesterday.'

'Why, I thought one of these tents would be so nice to sit on for my lunch.'

'You would not find a plaid more commodious, madam? I will procure a light one for you, if you desire.'

'No, I'd rather have one of these tents. There's no objection to my taking one of them?'

'None whatever, madam. They are at present very much in the position of articles in a lost-property office. I could not say if there would be any probability of your meeting one of the owners, but I should surmise that would be a far stretch even for the proverbially long arm of coincidence.'

'Well, if I did bump into one of the owners I could say I found it,' Carrie suggested.

'That would undoubtedly offer a perfectly feasible explanation, madam. Shall I fold the tent for you as handily as possible?'

'Thank you, Toker, if you will, please.'

The butler set about his task with the gravity of a high priest performing a solemn rite.

'I have made as good a job of it as I could, madam, but I fear it's an awkward bundle, except for the back, which is the method adopted by hikers for what may be called without the least irreverence, I trust, taking up their beds and walking. Are you quite sure, madam, that on second thoughts you would not prefer me to fetch you a plaid?'

'No, I think you've made quite a convenient bundle for me, Toker, thank you.'

'I appreciate the compliment, madam, though I venture to think I hardly deserve it. I hope you will have an agreeable day, madam, and that the cave will repay you for the long and somewhat arduous walk.'

'I'm sure it will.'

Carrie put a loop of the tent round her cromag, swung the cromag over her shoulder, and set out.

'Well, the more I see of Americans, Mrs Parsall, the queerer I think 'em,' Toker presently observed to the housekeeper. 'There's Mrs Royde now. Nothing would please her but she must take a tent to sit on. Gone off with it over her shoulder like a blooming Dick Whittington.'

'Americans?' Mrs Parsall echoed. 'Don't talk to me about Americans, Mr Toker. Good English milk gone sour, that's what Americans are.'

The particular American whose oddity had been the occasion of this observation by the Glenbogle housekeeper had never felt less American than this morning when she was on the way to strengthen the mystical bonds of race that linked her to that attractive young poet. The acquisition of Knocknacolly had changed the outlook a good deal. It meant that for the next two or three years at any rate she and Chester would be coming over to Scotland regularly. It meant that Knocknacolly could become the centre from which the regenerative activities of the Scottish Brotherhood of Action might exercise a benign influence over the whole country. It meant, putting politics on one side, that she might become the patroness of Scottish art. The future was so full of promise that it was some time before Carrie realized what an awkward addition to a walk was provided by a folded tent. She was tempted to deposit it beside the bridle-path and leave it to Alan Macmillan to rescue if he felt inclined. Then she recalled her racial background. Ancestrally she had wandered barefoot along these slopes, her back bent beneath a creel of peats. Was she, a degenerate Macdonald of today, going to falter beneath the weight of a portable tent?

Carrie had been toiling along in laborious progress for about an hour when the repeated changes she had been making in the way she held the tent at last broke down. Toker's careful arrangement of it in a comparatively neat bundle, and the green canvas, after trying to wrap her up in itself, began to drag behind her in an unwieldy train. Once again the temptation to leave the tent beside the path assailed her, but she called upon the spirits of her ancestors and stooped to conquer.

Preoccupied with the task of trying to refold the tent, Carrie did not hear anybody approaching and was much startled when she heard a gruff voice say:

'No camping is allowed here.'

She swung round to see gazing at her over her shoulder a gaunt, unshaven, wall-eyed man in brown tweed with a powerful cromag and a gaunt, matted, wall-eyed retriever.

'I'm not camping,' said Carrie.

'No camping is allowed here,' the gaunt man repeated.

'But I'm not camping,' she insisted.

'No camping is allowed here,' the gaunt man repeated yet again, and as if vexed by the strain that was being put upon his master's speech the wall-eyed dog gave a low growl.

Those who have tried to argue with a wall-eyed man, or for that matter with a wall-eyed dog, will recognize at once the disability under which Carrie laboured. So much does the wall-eye always dominate the other eye on such occasions that every remark is addressed to it, with the result that a despair of establishing rational intercourse asserts itself and one surrenders to the irrational.

'I don't expect you know who I am,' Carrie said, smiling, she felt hopelessly, at the wall-eye.

'No, I don't know who you are,' the gaunt man agreed, and the assertion of his ignorance must have carried with it an indication of hostility, for the dog growled again.

'Tha è blath,' Carrie observed.

'I don't know that name at all,' the gaunt man replied.

'You're not a Gaelic speaker then?'

'Are you a Gaelic speaker?'

'I'm learning to speak it.'

'Were you speaking to me in Gaelic then?'

'Yes, I said "it's warm". Tha è blath.'

'When you are after saying it in English first I know what you are after saying in Gaelic. Yes, it is warm. It's very warm. But camping is not allowed here.'

She was up against that wall-eye again.

'But I told you, I'm not camping here. I'm staying at the Castle. I'm staying with Ben Nevis. I suppose you are one of his keepers?'

'Yes, I am one of the keepers. And you are staying at Glenbogle Castle?'

'I certainly am.'

The wall-eye contemplated the outspread tent for a moment, and then fixed its opaque glance on Carrie.

'If you are staying at Glenbogle Castle, why are you camping here?'

'But I tell you I am not camping here.'

'That is a camping-tent.'

'Yes, that's a camping-tent.'

'If you are not camping here, why do you have a camping-tent?'

Carrie was in a quandary. If she said the tent belonged to a friend to whom she was taking it, this gaunt, wall-eyed man was capable of following her until she reached the cave, and that might make things awkward for Alan Macmillan.

'Well, I don't know if Ben Nevis would approve of one of his guests being questioned like this by one of his keepers, but the reason why I have this tent with me is because I wanted something to sit on while I was eating my lunch.'

The gaunt man shook his head.

'It's not at all what I would be thinking anybody would do,' he said sceptically. Then he doffed his cap and gazed across to the Three Sisters of Glenbogle for counsel. 'Well,' he said at last, turning to Carrie, 'you've put me into a very difficult kind of a situation. I'll just have to walk down to the Castle and receive my instructions. And I'll have to ask you to stay where you are till I am after receiving them. Ben Nevis's orders about campers are very strict. If he was to hear I had let a camper get the better of me, my place would be gone tomorrow. I'm sorry, mistress, to disconvenience you, but if you are a friend of Ben Nevis you'll know the kind of man he is and understand I'm only doing my duty. I'll leave my dog with you. There'll be no harm in him if you stay where you are, but you'll please understand it's his business to see you don't move from where you are.'

With these words the gaunt man said something in Gaelic to his dog and then strode off at a rapid pace along the path leading back to the Castle.

Carrie sat for ten minutes in a fume of indignation under the horribly steady glare of that milky pale-blue eye. The ancestral memories which should have illuminated with a sense of human continuity her present situation at the mercy of a tyrant forsook her. Then she tried to make friends with her gaoler, calling him 'good old fellow' and 'nice old dog'; but no epithet tender or fulsome availed to clarify to the semblance of canine kindness that opaque, remorseless eye.

'Oh well, I may as well eat my sandwiches,' she murmured to herself.

After she had munched away three or four she fancied she discerned a glimmer in that agate which eyed her and flung a sandwich to the dog. It did not even sniff it. It merely growled censoriously. Cerberus was more venal and his three heads less deterrent than this solitary milky wall-eye.

'I'd like to wring your neck, you darned coyote,' Carrie told him.

He settled his nose between his paws and growled a surly defiance.

It says something for Carrie's devotion to an ideal that during the hour and a half which elapsed before the gaunt man came back she had worked through two long exercises in *Gaelic Without Tears*.

'I must apologize, Mistress Royde,' the keeper said, doffing his cap. 'Mr Toker is after telling me that you'll be looking for Uaimh na laoigh. I'll take you there myself.'

'What am I looking for?'

'Uaimh na laoigh. The Cave of the Calf.'

'Wait a minute. I'll have you say that again when I've found the words in my book. I've got it; uamh, cave. What's calf? I've got it. Laogh. Genitive, laoigh. Now say it again, will you?'

The gaunt man did so. Carrie tried to imitate him, and the dog growled fiercely, receiving a blow on the haunches from his master's cromag and a Gaelic oath.

'You're saying it very well, Mistress Royde. It's very difficult to say well.'

'You didn't seem to think much of my Gaelic pronunciation when I said it was warm, and that's a darned sight easier to say than uaimh na laoigh.'

'Will we be going along there now?'

Carrie shook her head.

'Why, no, I don't think I'll go there this afternoon. I'll go right along back to the Castle. You can carry that tent for me,' she added quickly, for it occurred to her that if she left him here the keeper and his dog might go and fix Alan Macmillan with their wall-eyes. 'What's your name?' she asked.

'Neil Maclennan. I hope you'll make a complaint about me to Ben Nevis, mistress.'

'You do?'

'Yes. He'll be hearing then what an eye I'm keeping on me for these hikers and campers and he'll be very pleased. I'm sure of that. Och, yes, he'll be very pleased indeed.'

'Oh, you think he'd like to hear you'd handed over one of his guests to that lovely-looking dog of yours. What's his name?'

'Smeorach.'

Carrie searched the vocabulary of *Gaelic Without Tears*.

'But that means "thrush". That's a bird. What a queer sort of name to give a savage animal like that!'

'Och, he's not at all savage.'

'Oh, he's not?'

'No, no; he's very gentle. Very kind.'

'That shows what very wrong ideas we can get into our heads about animals. But don't worry, Neil, I'll tell Ben Nevis that Smeorach and you together are the most savage things I've seen in this part of the world.'

The gaunt man looked grateful.

'He's a very fine gentleman is Ben Nevis,' he said fervidly.

'He's all that, and then some,' Carrie agreed. 'I suppose you'd lay down your life for him?'

The gaunt man stopped, dropped the tent upon the path, and turned round to Carrie with a puzzled expression.

'Lay down my life for him?' he repeated. 'Was it die for him you were wanting to say?'

'That's right,' Carrie said encouragingly.

'I wouldn't want to die for anybody,' said the gaunt man. 'Och, I don't take to the notion of dying at all. It's very difficult to know what is going to happen. I wouldn't mind death so much at all if I was sure his friend Satan wasn't waiting round the corner just behind him. It's a terrible business that, right enough. The minister was preaching about it last Sunday morning. It was a very powerful sermon. It lasted for all but a quarter of two hours, and when we came out of the church we were just burning with the good man's words as if with the flames of Hell. Big Duncan — that's the head-keeper — he grew so hot that the packet of black-striped balls he keeps in his pocket melted with the heat and when he put his hand in his pocket to find a black-striped ball for his grandson Willie to suck, his hand just stuck inside the bag and he had to give Willie two because he could not pull them apart. Och, no, mistress, I wouldn't be putting myself forward to die for anybody.'

'Doesn't the old clan loyalty survive?' Carrie asked.

'Och, there's no clans left now,' said the gaunt man. 'The clans were finished long ago.'

'And I suppose you think the fairies are finished too?'

'I never saw the fairies myself,' said the gaunt man, picking up the tent and continuing along the path towards the Castle. 'But I wouldn't like to be so positive there are none of them left. Och, I'm not saying there *are* any of them, but there might be.'

Carrie found Toker distressed about the interruption of her walk.

'It was quite all right,' she assured him, 'I was feeling pretty tired when I was made to sit down and behave myself.'

'It's very good of you, madam, to take the unpleasant business so philosophically.'

'And after all he wasn't to know that I wasn't a hiker.'

'I'm afraid I cannot accept your kind excuses for him, madam. It is the business of a gentleman's servant to know these things. It should be second nature, as they say.'

When Myrtle returned from Knocknacolly she was full of what a delightful place could be made of it if the present lodge were pulled down and a modern house built on the site.

'It's a pity our boy friend isn't an architect, Carrie. We might have gotten him a good job to keep him amused till we came back next summer. How did you find him in his cave?'

'I didn't find him.'

'You didn't?' Myrtle exclaimed.

'No; I had all those letters to write.'

'And you wrote them?'

'I certainly did.'

'But Mrs MacDonald said you took your lunch with you.'

'So I did. But I didn't go to the cave. I just sat around and dreamed for awhile and then came back here.'

However, at dinner that night Ben Nevis gave the show away by revealing that one of his keepers had suspected Carrie of being a hiker.

Alone among the audience Toker preserved an expression of restrained disgust. The remainder of the party found the matter comic and laughed uproariously, particularly the victim's husband.

'Say, that's a peach, Ben Nevis,' he declared. 'I'll bet you were mad, Carrie, weren't you?'

'Oh, I didn't mind at all,' she replied. 'I realized he was only doing what he thought was his duty. In fact his greatest anxiety was to have Ben Nevis know what he had done.'

'Hark at that now,' the Chieftain woofed with gusto. 'Well, they may laugh at us up here for our old-fashioned notions of loyalty, discipline, and obedience, but when one finds it I must say it warms the cockles of the heart. Don't you agree with me, Hugh? I say it warms the cockles of the heart.'

'Oh, very much so,' Kilwhillie agreed. The cockles of his own heart were in a responsive condition to warmth that evening because Chester Royde had enjoyed his day with the Knocknacolly grouse so much that he had insisted on adding £500 to the purchase price and this meant the

late owner would be able to buy a new car which ought to last him for
another seven years. He was dreaming now of Royde's first stalk on
Monday and of his killing a stag with such a forest of antlers that he
would insist on adding yet another £500.

The next morning at service in the Castle Chapel Mr Fletcher preached
on the text 'Be thou faithful unto death', while the Chieftain cleared his
throat from time to time in a manner as near to ejaculating 'hear, hear'
as left no doubt of his approval.

'Capital preacher, isn't he?' he said to his guests. 'And what I like
particularly about his sermons is that he never gives one unless I ask him
to. Can't stand this idea some clergymen have that a sermon is always
welcome.'

Carrie and Myrtle had planned to go for a walk together that Sunday
afternoon and visit the cave, for they had both quickly realized that
neither was going to be able to shake off the other. When the time came
for them to start, however, they were discouraged to find that Murdoch
and Iain were proposing to accompany them.

'We heard you wanted to see that cave on Ben Cruet,' said Iain. 'So
as there's nothing for us to do, being Sunday afternoon, Murdoch and
I thought you'd like us to show you just where it is.'

'Oh, that's angelic of you, Iain,' said Myrtle. 'But there's no reason
why you should put yourselves out for Carrie and me. We'll enjoy
exploring the way for ourselves.'

'Yes, indeed,' Carrie added. 'And besides, I think the cave is too far
away for a Sunday afternoon walk. So please, don't bother; we'll just
take a little walk by ourselves.'

'It's no bother,' said Murdoch solemnly.

'And we really have nothing to do this afternoon,' Iain added. 'We'd
enjoy a walk.'

'It's terribly sweet of you both,' Carrie said. 'But Myrtle and I couldn't
think of dragging you out on such a hot afternoon. And it's looking very
much like rain.'

'I like a good tramp in the rain,' Murdoch declared.

'I'm not so fond of rain myself,' said Myrtle. 'I'll tell you what, why
don't you two boys take Carrie for a walk, and I'll stay home and write
some letters?'

'Right-oh,' Iain agreed, without a trace of disappointment in his
reception of the news of Myrtle's defection.

'I don't think I want to get wet just to see a cave,' said Carrie quickly.

'Anyway, I'm not really so anxious to see this cave at all. I just had an idea yesterday that it would make a good object for a walk as I was by myself. And then Myrtle thought the cave sounded kind of cute. And we just thought we'd wander along and perhaps find it. But if it's going to rain I think I'll stay home.'

Murdoch thumped the glass.

'Doubt if it'll rain before the sun goes down,' he decided with nautical knowledgeableness.

'I wouldn't dream of setting my opinion against yours in the matter of weather,' Carrie broke in, 'but I believe it's going to rain this very afternoon. So I think the wisest plan is to give up visiting the cave today and go there some day later in the week. I'm sure I don't know what put this idea of a cave into my head.'

'You may have read about it in my little volume, *Echoes of Glenbogle*,' said the chaplain.

'My, are you a poet too? I mean are you a poet, Mr Fletcher?' Carrie exclaimed.

'I have ventured to commit one or two little indiscretions in verse,' the chaplain confessed.

'And you've written a poem about this cave. Oh, please read it to us, Mr Fletcher,' Carrie begged.

'Oh, do, please, Mr Fletcher,' Myrtle added earnestly. 'I think it'll be so much nicer to hear Mr Fletcher's poem about the cave than walk all that way to see it, don't you, Carrie?'

'I'd just adore to have Mr Fletcher read us his poem.'

The chaplain smiled modestly and going to the bookcase took down the slim volume of his verse from which he began to read:

> 'Hark how the wind from Cruet's icy peak
> Wails through the corries to the glen below,
> The while within a cave a fugitive
> Shivers and shrinks to see the swirling snow.
>
> Through the long week the redcoats, a grim band,
> Glenbogle and Glenbristle for their prey,
> Had searched, and eke Strathdiddle and Strathdun,
> To reach the slopes of Cruet yesterday.
>
> The fugitive had heard their fierce halloos,
> But hidden in a dark and friendly cave,
> Had hitherto escaped their vigilance
> And laughed to think how wildly they would rave,

Did they but guess how near he was to them
And to their brutal and relentless grip.
But ah, they knew it not, and so the band
Passed by and brought a prayer to his lip.

But why, when now the redcoats are away,
Shivers and shrinks he in the swirling snow?
Why doth he hearken to the wild wind's howl
As if it were the howling of the foe?

Alas! it is because his Mary dear,
Mary Macdonald of the nutbrown hair,
Had promised him to come this very night,
And bring provisions to his secret lair.

He gazes from the entrance of the cave
Into the fearsome night of storm without,
And when he cries in anguish, "Mary mine!"
He fancies he can hear an answering shout.

Into that fearsome night the fugitive
Rushes to seek her, but when she is found,
His Mary's lying in a shroud of snow,
A corpse upon Ben Cruet's cruel ground.'

The chaplain closed the volume.

'Is that all?' Myrtle asked.

'That is all.'

'My, I think that's the saddest poem I ever heard. I don't think I could visit the cave this afternoon, could you, Carrie?'

'No, I wouldn't want to visit it right now. But I thought it was called the Cave of the Calf.'

'So it is, Mrs Royde. It was already called the Cave of the Calf when this young Jacobite fugitive had the sad experience which I have tried to express in poetic form.'

'It's a true story?' Carrie asked.

'Perfectly true,' the clergyman replied. 'His name was Alan Macdonald.'

'Alan what?'

'Alan Macdonald.'

'And her name was Mary?'

'Yes, Mary Macdonald. They both came from Glenbristle.'

'And my great-great-great-great-grandfather would likely enough have known them both,' Carrie exclaimed in awe. 'Do you believe in reincarnation, Mr Fletcher?'

'I'm afraid that is not an accepted Christian doctrine.'

'Isn't that too bad? We're very very interested in reincarnation over in the States. Several of my friends are just crazy about reincarnation. A classmate of mine had a revelation after she left college and found she was Catherine de' Medici, or was it Catherine of Aragon? Myrtle, do you remember Katie Van Stiltzkin – Catherine Arkwright that was?'

Myrtle nodded.

'Was it Catherine de' Medici or Catherine of Aragon she was the reincarnation of?'

'I think it was both.'

'Don't be foolish, Myrtle. You can't be the reincarnation of two people at once. That goes right against the whole principle of the thing. However, it doesn't matter about Katie Van Stiltzkin. It just occurred to me that perhaps I was the reincarnation of Mary Macdonald. Certainly when I was sitting up there yesterday afternoon and gazing away across Glenbogle I did feel a kind of hidden presence warning me to be careful.'

'That must have been the keeper's dog,' said Myrtle.

'I'm afraid my sister-in-law's terribly prosaic, Mr Fletcher. But do please read us some more of your poems.'

'I'd like to hear the one about Alan Macdonald again,' said Myrtle. 'I don't know why, but Alan has always been a favourite name of mine.'

'It has?' Carrie asked suspiciously.

'Yes, ever since I can remember,' Myrtle assured her with complete conviction.

Chapter 10

THE MUCKLE HART OF BEN GLASS

It was the custom of Glenbogle for Angus MacQuat or another of the pipers to rouse Ben Nevis every morning at eight by playing beneath his window the ancient *Iomradh Mhic 'ic Eachainn* or *Fame of Mac 'ic Eachainn*, in which the virtue, nobility, valour and generosity of the Chieftain of Ben Nevis were celebrated with what the less imaginative Southerner might have thought a certain amount of exaggeration. The tune, however, had a fine lilt and possessed a persuasive drive to energetic action which the shrilling of an alarm-clock lacks. Even the guest who had not been warned about the significance of this aubade often sprang out of bed to look out of the window and see what was being killed.

On that Monday morning in mid-August the skirling of *Iomradh Mhic 'ic Eachainn* was heard at the top of its power played by two pipers at six o'clock, and when the skirling of the pipers began a housemaid entered and drew the blinds to reveal a sky the grey expanse of which displayed a determination to rain as soon as it could, the kind of sky which makes fishermen stare with distasteful surprise at the fellow-guest in an hotel who remarks that the weather does not look too promising.

'He's getting us out good and early, Carrie,' said her husband. 'Will you go along to the bathroom first or will I?'

'Why, I don't believe I'll come, Chester,' she replied, yawning from the depths of the bedclothes. 'It sounds a kind of a tiring business the way Ben Nevis described it last night at dinner. Besides, I wouldn't want to kill a lovely stag even if I were near enough for a shot at it.'

'I forgot to tell you last night, but we've settled not to go stalking over at Knocknacolly. Ben Nevis wants me to have a shot at some particular stag he's had news of between Ben Booey and Ben Glass.'

'Oh, then I certainly won't come, Chester.'

'The only thing is I told Kilwhillie you'd like to have some time with him at Knocknacolly. I mean to say if we're taking on the place right away I think you want to get wise to the conditions there. After all, we'll have to make quite a few arrangements before we go back to the

States next month. I want to get hold of an architect and have him hustle next winter.'

'I don't see that Kilwhillie will be much use over choosing an architect, Chester. And what about the legal part of it?'

'Why, I thought I'd have our London solicitors put that through.'

'Don't you think it would be better if we employed a Scottish lawyer? Scottish law is quite different from English law, you know.'

'How's it different?'

'I don't know exactly how, but I know it's much better and much cheaper.'

'But do you know any Scottish lawyers?'

'I heard of a young Scottish lawyer the other day who was very highly spoken of. James Buchanan was his name. I have his address in Glasgow. Wouldn't it be a good plan if I asked him to come up here to take your instructions? And he might know of a good architect. I think we ought to employ one of the younger Scottish architects, don't you, Chester?'

'I don't mind how young he is if he doesn't try to make me live in one of those frozen cheeses like we saw on Friday. Gee! That was terrible.'

'I want to have one of the artists of the Scottish Renaissance. I don't suppose you've heard about the Scottish Renaissance.'

'Can't say I have. What's it stand for?'

'The rebirth of the whole country.'

'That's O.K. by me. Only I'd like to use reborn artists who have been weaned if it's all the same to you. But see here, honey, I want you to have all the fun you can get out of this little place. It's yours. Got me?'

'Oh, Chester!'

'Yes, you're to be the owner of Knocknacolly.'

'Chester, how sweet of you!'

'Well, I guess I'll go and dress myself now for this stag-hunt. If you don't want to go over to Knocknacolly with Kilwhillie, you'll have to tell him yourself.'

'All right, Chester. But I'm not going to get up yet awhile.'

'Get up nothing,' said the young financier. 'I wouldn't be jumping around in pyjamas at this time of the morning if I didn't think Ben Nevis would be singing *Kathleen Mavourneen* to me in a minute.'

Carrie dozed off again, but was awakened about seven o'clock by Chester's coming back into the room.

'Say, this deer-stalking seems to be a pretty serious business,' he announced.

'What's the matter, Chester?'

'I've been sent back to put on different clothes.'

'What's the matter with your clothes?'

'That's what I asked Ben Nevis when he took exception to them at breakfast.'

'I think they look very good.'

It is true that her husband looked like an even more brightly-coloured full-page advertisement in *Esquire* than he had on the Twelfth, but Carrie thought men ought to look like that when they were indulging in country sports and pastimes.

'It seems they're too bright,' said Chester. 'Ben Nevis says I'll never get within a mile of a stag dressed like I am.'

'But you're not wearing anything as bright as his kilt.'

'That isn't what he thinks. Oh, he was very nice about it. He blamed it more on the stags than on my clothes. He said stags were exceptionally nervous animals and need to be humoured. It was my pullover which worried him most. He asked if it was made by the Indians.'

'Made by Indians?' Carrie echoed indignantly. 'Why, that's the pullover I gave you last Christmas, Chester. It's a genuine Fair Isle product. I paid thirty dollars for that pullover.'

'Well, Ben Nevis looked at it the way he looked at the shirts of those hikers. But the whole rig-out wasn't his idea of the way anybody ought to be dressed for stalking stags. He said there was a big tradition behind this business of stalking and he wanted me to start in the steps of this tradition right away. Well, what's it matter anyway? I'll be stalking by myself presently in the Knocknacolly forest, and I'll wear what I like there. What I like,' he repeated.

He came back a few minutes later in a suit of darkish green tweed.

'I didn't know you had a suit as quiet as that, Chester,' said his wife.

'I didn't know it myself. That's the advantage of a good valet. He makes it his job to be prepared for emergencies. Well, seeing I'm dressed for a funeral I hope we'll kill a pretty big stag. I'll look kind of foolish if we come home with only a couple of rabbits.'

'When do you think you will be back, Chester?'

'I don't know at all. But there's a look in Ben Nevis's eye which makes me think he intends to kill a stag today even if it involves killing me to do it.'

'Perhaps I'll go over to Knocknacolly with Kilwhillie or perhaps I won't. It looks to me as if we'll have a downpour before long.'

'It doesn't look too good, does it?'

'That'll mean you'll give up stalking and come home?'

'Give it up?' Chester exclaimed. 'Not Ben Nevis. I guess Ben Nevis would be the biggest disappointment to a deluge since old man Noah. Any deluge that thinks it can stand between Ben Nevis and shooting a stag had better start in to think again and remember what it felt like to be a puddle.'

The stalking novice left his wife and went down to join his host.

'Ah, there you are. That's better. I hope you didn't mind my suggesting you toned down your colour scheme, what? I mean to say, I'm a very old hand at this game and I do want to give you some idea of what a grand sport stalking is. You'll hear the young people today running it down. Why? Laziness. Sheer unadulterated laziness. It's those confounded motor-cars. What they want now is to be driven practically to the butts and then have the birds driven to them, with a loader standing by. Then a rich lunch and be driven to the next moor and if they don't kill at least a hundred brace each they think they've had a poor day's sport. Sport? That's not sport. That's nothing but luxury. Of course, fellows like that aren't up to a long day in the hills. But you're different, Royde. You want real sport and I'm going to do my best to let you have some. But you mustn't mind my giving you advice. You've just bought the best twelve-head forest in Inverness-shire, and by gad, you bought it for a song. However, Kilwhillie got twice what he ought to have got from that bounder Dutton for Glenbore, and there's no doubt Knocknacolly Lodge isn't what it was. It never was as a matter of fact, but luckily you can afford to put it in order. I'm hoping to get a cable from my boy Hector today to say he's got his leave. Now, he's just as keen on stalking as I know you're going to be, and I taught him the whole art of it. Because it is an art. You'll hear people talking about painting and poetry and all that sort of thing, but of course if it comes to real art they're not in it with stalking.'

The majestic splendours of the Three Sisters of Glenbogle have been hymned too often to encourage a late comer in the field of Highland romance to venture upon an encore. It is enough to say that by nine o'clock that morning Ben Nevis, Chester Royde, and big Duncan Macdonald were in the midst of them. The sky was heavily overcast, but the rain still held off.

Duncan slowly swept with his glass the craggy and precipitous horizon, the sides of which were green-striped with the course of innumerable burns descending to the great flat where they were standing beside a small black lochan.

'There's a hell of a lot of flies and gnats and midges around here,' Royde remarked.

'Rain on the way,' said Ben Nevis. 'Well, we can do with it. The country's parched.'

'It's not so darned parched as all that,' his guest replied. 'I've been up to my knees half a dozen times already in bog. Blast these midges!'

'They'll get used to you in time,' Ben Nevis assured him.

'Hell, I don't care whether they get used to me. The question is, "will I get used to them?" '

'You're fresh blood,' Ben Nevis explained.

'Oh, I knew I was some kind of a prize-sucker all right. Oi!'

'What's the matter?'

'Why, some flat grey brute of a fly landed on me and planted the needle of his syringe about an inch into my hand. Gosh, the sunnavabitch has drawn blood. What would you say to that now?'

'It must have been a cleg,' Ben Nevis decided. 'You'd better light up a cigar.'

Chester Royde took his host's advice and had just lighted a big Larrañaga Corona when Ben Nevis with a muffled bark bade him throw himself down on the ground. As he seemed inclined to question this order, the Chieftain flung an arm round his shoulder and by falling prone himself fetched his guest down with him.

'Say, what's the big idea?' asked Royde, whose Larrañaga Corona had planted itself between a couple of bog asphodels.

'A stag,' said Ben Nevis.

'Where?'

'Duncan has seen his antlers above Drumstickit, the ridge rising west from Ardoo.'

'Ah, do what? I can't do more than I'm doing with my nose routing about in this god-awful marsh. Still, stalking's stalking and I'll do anything you like.'

'You mustn't mind if I seem a bit ceremonious, Royde,' the Chieftain said. 'We keep very strictly to traditional methods at this sport.'

'Oh, I see. Flinging me down on the ground like that is an old ceremony, is it? They had some queer ceremonies among the Carroways. There was one, I remember, when the Chief put two fingers in the butter and hoicked out a great blob of it which he popped into my mouth before I could stop him. I was just going to spit it out when the fellow who was taking me around the reservation dug me in the ribs and whispered the Chief was paying me the highest compliment a Carroway Chief can pay anybody. He said what I had to do was to swallow the butter, rub my belly, turn up my eyes to express a sort of delirium of delight, and if possible eructate. He said if I could manage even the feeblest little eructation I was a blood-brother of the Carroways for life. But could I contrive even the merest hint of an eructation? No, sir, I could not. I was as dumb as a flute in the window of a music-store. If I'd been told I'd be scalped unless I could produce a suitable response to that blob of butter I could never have arranged . . .'

'Hush, Duncan wants us to crawl along and hear his plan of action,' Ben Nevis interrupted. 'Keep as flat as you can. Now you see why I was so anxious for you to change your clothes.'

'Not half as anxious as I'll be to change them when I've crawled along a bit further like this.'

'We may have to crawl a mile or so like this,' said Ben Nevis.

'A mile?' his guest ejaculated. 'Isn't deer-stalking more of a sport for crocodiles than human beings?'

Presently they reached the spot where Duncan was surveying the ridge running along the horizon from the great black precipices of Ard Dubh.

'It's himself,' he said to Ben Nevis, awe, exultation, and greed mingled in the tone of his voice.

'Not the muckle hart of Ben Glass?'

'It's himself,' Duncan repeated. 'I would know him if the eyes of me did not know anything else at all.'

Ben Nevis turned to his guest.

'You're in luck, I heard he'd been seen feeding between Ben Booey and Ben Glass the last week or so. We've been trying to get that hart for the last five years. It was an old gillie from the Findhorn country first called him the muckle hart. They don't use that word any longer around here.'

'What's it mean?'

'The big hart or stag. You'll never have a finer head if you live as long as Methuselah. Well, I'm glad something warned me to give Knock-nacolly a miss today. Mind you, I never hoped that at your very first stalk you really would have a chance at the muckle hart of Ben Glass, but there you are, beginner's luck, as they say. We're going to have a stiffish stalk, but if you can get a fair shot at him before dusk this is going to be a day you'll never forget.'

'Before dusk?' Royde echoed in accents that verged on consternation. 'We surely aren't going to crawl along on our faces like this for another ten hours?'

'Not all the time,' Ben Nevis replied encouragingly. 'But we have to take advantage of all the cover we can to cross this flat. I don't know whether Duncan proposes to get round to the corrie between Kincanny and Ardoo and climb up Ardoo . . .'

'I told you just now, Ben Nevis, I'll do anything you like,' Royde interrupted with a touch of fretfulness, for a fat gnat had just stung his left eyelid with lustful savagery, and it was swelling rapidly. 'You needn't keep saying, "Ah, do!" '

Ben Nevis laughed boisterously until he was glared at by Duncan, who shook his head in reproof of such noise.

'You'll please to remember, Ben Nevis, that the less noise you are making the nearer we may happen to come to himself.'

'Yes, I apologize, Duncan. I'm setting Mr Royde a very bad example.' Ben Nevis turned to his guest. 'The old man's quite right to remind me not to make too much noise, but I couldn't help being tickled by your thinking I was saying "Ah, do" when I was saying "Ardoo".'

'What's the difference?'

'Ardoo — A-R-D D-U-B-H — means black height. You see those black precipices?'

'And we're scheduled to climb up them?'

'Oh, there are other ways up which offer no problem to the man with a steady head. But Duncan may prefer to make a wider detour and scramble up to the end of Drumstickit — that's the ridge on the other side of which himself is lying down just now. Which side are we going to approach him from, Duncan?'

The old stalker looked at the sky.

'There's no wind. It makes no difference for the wind. He won't get the scent of us one side more than another. I think the rain will begin about eleven o'clock, and when it does it will rain hard, right enough. That will make the climb up by the Ard Dubh a little difficult the way the water will be streaming down.'

'You think we ought to go round and take the long crawl along Drumstickit?' Ben Nevis asked.

'Ay, I believe that will be the best way of it,' Duncan replied. 'It'll be plenty long and plenty wet right enough. But on the Ard Dubh the gentleman might be swept off a ledge and know nothing about it till he was brought up before his Creator.'

'Well, we don't want that to happen, Duncan, even to get a fair shot at the muckle hart of Ben Glass,' his chief told him.

'I feel pretty much the same way about it as you feel, Ben Nevis,' said Chester Royde. 'I know I'll have to meet my Creator one day, but I don't want to butt in on Him when He's busy.'

'The Lord is never too busy to judge a sinner,' Duncan proclaimed sternly.

'Why, I know He holds the biggest one-man job anywhere,' said Royde. 'But that's no reason why I should butt in on Him before I'm expected. I think we'll give "Ah, Do" a miss today. Say, Duncan, if I light up another cigar will that beast over there get a whiff of it?'

'I wouldn't say but what he mightn't, Mr Royde. And we'll have to keep very low for the next two hours before we reach the far end of Drumstickit. You'll hardly be able to keep your mouth out of the moss so as to enjoy a good smoke as it ought to be enjoyed. And I'm not the one to ask a gentleman to waste the gifts the good Lord has given to him. Now you see yon big crag over there to the west of where himself is lying?'

'I see a big grey mass of stone about two miles over to the left. You don't mean that?'

'That's it, right enough. It's you that have very good eyes, Mr Royde.'

'And we're going to crawl on our bellies as far as that mass of stone?' Chester Royde asked incredulously.

'That's the first thing we have to do. I hope we'll reach it just before the rain begins to get really heavy.'

There are many tracts among the mountains of the North which cast a weariness and a disgust upon those who have to tramp across them. The view of the encircling bens may be sublime, but the sublime can become tiresome when exactly the same aspect of it is presented during an hour's plodding over featureless bog furrowed by burns every one of which takes the same dreary course and makes the same monotonous burbling. Such a tract was Achnacallach, the great flat which the stalkers had to cross to reach the westerly shoulder of the ridge known as Drumstickit. To walk across it was a penance; to crawl across it was purgatorial.

'Never mind, Mr Royde, you'll find it easier as you get used to it,' said Duncan, with kindly encouragement.

'I will, will I?' Royde grunted sceptically, raising a fat crimson face already considerably increased in bulk by the attentions of the cloud of gnats and midges which hovered above his head in a satanic aureole.

'Keep your head down, Royde. Keep your head down,' Ben Nevis adjured him. 'It's going to rain pretty hard soon and then you won't be bothered at all by the midges. This flat is called Ackernercallick, which means the field of the old woman.'

'You can't tell me any woman lived to be old in this piece of country,' Royde said emphatically.

'She was a witch,' Ben Nevis recounted. 'That's right, isn't it, Duncan?'

'Ay, she was a bad witch right enough. She would be flying out here by the light of the moon and doing all sorts of devilment on her neighbours.'

'She couldn't have had many neighbours around here,' Royde put in.

'No, no, but she would be flying from here down into Glenbogle and away over down into Strathdiddle and Strathdun to be putting all kinds of illness into the cattle. She lived beside these stones. They call them Carn na Caillich to this day. And it was there that Donald shot her.'

'Take a breather for a moment, Royde, while Duncan finishes his tale,' Ben Nevis advised.

'I'd enjoy my breath more if half the flies around here didn't follow it into my mouth,' said Royde.

'Don't worry about the flies. They'll clear off when it rains. Go on, Duncan, tell Mr Royde the story of Donald Cam.'

'Well, it was this way. Donald Cam was terribly put about by the way this old witch was plaguing all the animals, flying about in the night, and nobody knowing whose byre she would not be lighting on next. The minister in Strathdiddle preached a great sermon against her, och, a very powerful sermon by what they still tell of it. But it was all to no purpose. No purpose at all. The old witch seemed to take a pure delight in spiting the minister's holy words. Now, Donald Cam was a very religious man. Indeed, I believe he was an elder; but if he wasn't an elder he was certainly a deacon. So being full of zeal for the work of the Lord he loaded his gun with a crooked sixpence and two silver buttons that belonged to the King of Scotland, and when the witch was away at her devilment he waited for her by the carn where she lived. Nobody knows to this day what happened exactly, but in the morning they found Donald Cam lying asleep on his back with a dead crane on top of him — heron some call the bird. Och, it was the old witch right enough, because she was never seen again and when they cut the crane open they found the crooked sixpence and the two silver buttons inside. Donald Cam was very pleased they found the buttons, because the King of Scotland gave them to his grandfather, and he would have been missing them sorely from the box where his grandfather put them. Ah, indeed, yes, it shows that the Lord does not turn His face from the godly man who keeps His commandments. And ever since the place has been called Achadh na Caillich. The Field of the Old Woman.'

'But how came this guy Donald to lie there with this bird on top of him?' the American asked.

'It was never rightly known,' Duncan replied. 'Donald himself had a notion that the witch put a spell on him just as he fired. But others said it was the whisky he was after drinking to keep his courage up. Well, if it was the whisky, no man had a better right to it than Donald. There's no man alive today in these parts who would sleep a night in Carn na Caillich, even if he had a bottle of Haig's Gold Cap in each pocket.'

'Would you sleep there yourself, Duncan?' his Chief asked.

'I wouldn't like it, Ben Nevis, and that's the truth I'm telling you. Herself may be dead, but that's not to say the spirit of her will not be flying around still. But we mustn't stay blethering like this. Here comes the rain.'

And indeed there did come the rain with a vengeance.

'Well, this is the first time water wetted my seat first since I used to sit down in puddles when I got tired of walking and wanted my nurse to take me home,' Chester Royde declared. 'Say, Ben Nevis, is that the big idea about the way a kilt is made?'

'What?'

'Why, pleating it all around the behind like that. I'll bet you haven't had a drop of rain through yet.'

'No, I'm all right.'

'Of course you are. I thought at first it was just a picturesque bit of hooey like those feathers the Indians dress you up in when they adopt you into their tribe. War-bonnets they call them. But I'm beginning to grasp the design of the kilt. I see now it's the only wear for up here. These breeches I'm wearing are no manner of use at all against rain like this. I'm just a crawling aquarium. Say, Ben Nevis, you don't think that big stag is going to sit up there much longer in this rain? He's the biggest moron in antlers if he does.'

'Not he. He's enjoying it,' Ben Nevis declared.

'That stag must have the nature of a hippopotamus,' Royde commented.

It was about noon when they reached the cairn and found a dry recess in the stones where they could eat their sandwiches and refresh themselves for a while after the long crawl across Achnacallach.

'Say, do my eyes look kind of funny, Ben Nevis?' his guest asked.

'They do look a little puffy. That's the midges.'

'Well, they don't feel like eyes to me at all. They feel more like a couple of currants somewhere in the middle of a cake. And they're sinking deeper in all the time. I guess I won't be able to see to aim my rifle when the time comes.'

Chester Royde had some reason to inquire anxiously about his eyes, and his host's description of them as a little puffy was far from adequate. There was in fact very little indeed of them now visible because, through the swelling of the lids from the bites, Chester's cheeks, naturally fat, had swelled to nearly twice their size and now threatened to engulf not merely what was left of his eyes but his ears as well.

'It's not raining so heavily now,' Duncan announced after taking a look around the savage landscape.

'You want us to start?' Ben Nevis asked.

'It might be as well,' the old stalker suggested, 'We will have a long crawl along the top of Drumstickit.'

'Not on our bellies?' Royde exclaimed.

'Not all the way. Och, we'll be able to move along perhaps for quite two miles upon our hands and knees, and we'll have good cover from the rocks till we get to the top of Drumstickit.'

'You know, Royde,' said his host enthusiastically, 'I believe you're going to get this fellow this afternoon.'

'You do?' the other countered dubiously. 'Well, I can't say I feel quite so confident about that. In fact I've a hunch I'm not going to get this fellow this afternoon.'

'Oh, you mustn't take up that attitude. You mustn't really,' the Chieftain begged. 'Confidence is half the battle in stalking. What you want to say to yourself all the time as we crawl along Drumstickit is,

"I'm going to get that hart. I'm going to plant my bullet in his shoulder." Now then, forward! We have a long way to go yet.'

There were many moments during that endless crawl along the top of the narrow ridge known as Drumstickit when Chester Royde wondered why he had bought Knocknacolly for the sake of the twelve stags he was supposed to shoot upon its forest every year. There were many moments when he wondered what it was that had so fascinated him about life in the Highlands of Scotland. There was one bitter moment when, in crawling over what looked like a patch of bright short grass, he had sunk into it like the hippopotamus in whose nature he had discovered a kinship with the muckle hart of Ben Glass, and had asked himself what mad impulse had led him to book a state-room for himself and Carrie in the *Ruritania* in which to cross the Atlantic when they might have spent a perfectly good holiday in Vermont.

'Hush, don't make so much noise,' Ben Nevis whispered hoarsely. 'We're getting pretty near now.'

'But my mouth's full of some kind of vegetable matter,' Royde protested. 'I'm only expectorating.'

'You'd better swallow it,' Ben Nevis advised. 'It won't do you any harm. And keep down closer than ever up this rise. We ought to sight him when we get to the top. You're going to have one of the great moments of your life in another few minutes.'

'If I live to see it,' Royde muttered to himself, combing bits of moss off his tongue with his teeth.

But when, drenched to the skin, aching in every bone, and itching acutely, Chester Royde Jr peered over a clump of heather to get his first sight of the muckle hart of Ben Glass there was no sign of him on what was left of Drumstickit before the long ridge was absorbed by the steeps of Ard Dubh. It was idle for Duncan to clap his spyglass to his eye and sweep it round. There was no stag.

'That's extraordinary,' Ben Nevis exclaimed. 'That hart's uncanny. He couldn't have winded us. It must have been sheer instinct which made him move.'

'I never thought he would be such a moron as to sit fooling around here in that rain for us three mutts to shoot him. I guess that stag was wise to us before we ever started crawling across that flat stretch about ten o'clock. It's half past three now. That stag's curled up comfortably somewhere two or three miles from here as dry and warm as I wish I were. Well, what do we do now, Ben Nevis?'

'What do you say, Duncan?' the Chieftain asked.

'I don't know what to say, Ben Nevis, and that's the truth,' Duncan replied disconsolately. 'It's very disappointing right enough. We might go round behind the Ard Dubh and get to the westerly shoulder of Ben Booey where you'll often find them feeding about four o'clock. I'd like Mr Royde to have a chance at a good stag after his disappointment. If we don't find one there, I'm afraid we'll have to give up for today. We'll be a good two hours, and maybe a little more like three before we can get to where the car is waiting, and the rain's coming on hard again.'

'What do you say, Royde? Shall we go round behind Ardoo?'

'Well, I'd hate to have you call me no sportsman, Ben Nevis, but I think I'm going to say "Ah, don't".'

'Well, then we'd better make for the car,' said Ben Nevis regretfully.

'We don't have to crawl on our bellies after that?' Royde asked.

'Ha-ha,' Ben Nevis guffawed. 'I'm afraid you're rather irreverent about the greatest sport in the world. Well, we'd better foot it. And you can light up your cigar now without fear of the consequences.'

'If it will keep alight in this rain. But I don't believe Popocatepetl would keep alight in rain like this,' said Chester Royde.

Even the sanguine spirit of Ben Nevis was damped by the double effect of the disappointment over the stag and this tremendous downpour. He found nothing to say to counteract the moroseness of his guest who, soaked to the skin and with a face that if they had been invented at this date could well have been compared to a barrage balloon, trudged across the dreary flat known as Achnacallach, across which he had crawled that morning accompanied by a cortège of flies, gnats, and midges.

Then suddenly he plucked from his mouth the Larrañaga Corona that was contending with the rain and flung it away, unable to stand the reek of it any longer, so much more now did it resemble a damp leaf from a November bonfire than a Larrañaga Corona.

'You know, I don't believe that guy ever did shoot that witch,' he said to Duncan.

'Och, yes, Mr Royde, the incident was well known at the time all round about Strathdiddle and Glenbogle. I've heard my grandfather tell about it many a time.'

'I believe she's still moving around and up to her tricks. I believe it was her you saw sitting up there on the top of Drumstickit.'

'But it had horns, Mr Royde. I saw them with my spyglass.'

'Hasn't the Devil got horns?'

'Och, never say such things, Mr Royde. You're not telling me it was Satan himself I saw sitting up there on Drumstickit this morning. That's a terrible fancy to put into a man's head.'

'Well, I leave it to you, Duncan. It was either the witch or her master the Devil. You can choose between them.'

'Ach, no, Mr Royde, it was the great stag himself, right enough. I know the antlers on him as well as I know my own two hands. It was unlucky he would take it into his head to go away like that. But never fear, Mr Royde, I'll come for you one morning and we'll go for a stag together. Just you and I. We were too noisy today.'

'You're not saying I'm too noisy, are you?' the Chieftain asked.

The old man stroked his superb beard judicially.

'Och, yes, you're too noisy altogether, Ben Nevis. You've always been the same since you were a bairn. You'd make more noise than twenty buzzards before you were five years old. Screaming about the place, you would be, och, yes, screaming and shrieking and whistling.'

'Well, I don't scream about the place now.'

'No, you don't scream nowadays, Ben Nevis. But you talk twice as loud as anybody else. You can't help it. You don't know you talk so loud.'

'Are you seriously trying to tell me my voice frightened that stag?'

'Ach, I don't know. It's impossible to say what frightened it, but I'd like to take Mr Royde out by himself. He's had a very disappointing day.'

'Yes, I wish we'd gone after those Scottish Nationalists now,' Ben Nevis spluttered.

Then he fell into a moody silence as the rain managed mysteriously to come down harder than ever. They had still two hours of hard walking before they reached the road where the car was waiting for them.

Chapter 11

PEATY WATER

The stalk after the muckle hart of Ben Glass was repeated back in Glenbogle by Carrie and Myrtle Royde, but much more successfully, for they tracked their quarry to his lair before the heavy rain began.

Carrie had been tempted to try to give Myrtle the slip, but on reflection she had decided that in the matter of Alan Macmillan Myrtle held a stronger position as the sister of Chester than she as his wife. After all, she told herself, the fact that the poet was a very attractive young man should not be considered anything more than an agreeable reward for her response to ancestral demands upon her allegiance. The situation had been changed by Chester's acquisition of Knocknacolly and his presentation of it to herself. It would not be fair to Chester or herself to let Myrtle suppose that her plan to make Knocknacolly the centre of a Scottish renaissance was inspired by the *beaux yeux* of Alan Macmillan. And if she gave Myrtle an impression she was trying to sidestep her over Alan Macmillan that was just what she would think.

'Myrtle dear,' she said to her sister-in-law after breakfast, 'I do feel we ought to see Mr Macmillan today if we possibly can. I was talking to Chester this morning and he agrees with me it'll be much better to have a Scottish lawyer do the business about Knocknacolly. So I think Mr Buchanan would be the very one, don't you?'

'Sure.'

'And then we must have an architect, and I expect either he or Mr Macmillan will know of a good young architect. That will mean they can all go and camp out in the lodge, which will make it so much pleasanter. I'm so afraid if we don't see Mr Macmillan before he goes he may not want to come back to this part of the country. And I think it will be wiser not to say we know who took their tents, don't you? I mean, their pride might be upset and they might want to revenge themselves on Ben Nevis. They're so high-spirited.'

'It was you who started off trying to give them back the tents.'

'I know. It was too impulsive of me. I am very impulsive, Myrtle. That's my Celtic blood.'

'Yes, your feminine Celtic blood.'

'But you will come with me this morning, Myrtle? Please do. I want to take Mr Macmillan some provisions, because I'm sure he's run out of them by now.'

'Sure, I'll come with you. But how are we going to get hold of any provisions?'

'Why, I thought if you asked Mrs Parsall the housekeeper to make you up lunch and tea for two, I'd ask Toker to make up lunch and tea for two.'

'Won't that seem a little funny?' Myrtle suggested.

'Oh, they'll just think we each thought the other wasn't going to do it. We can pack everything in my lunch-basket.'

Myrtle looked doubtful.

'I'm positive they'll think it's kind of queer.'

'But they expect Americans to be queer,' Carrie pointed out.

'How about if Murdoch and Iain MacDonald tag on to us the way they did yesterday?' Myrtle asked.

'Oh, I've thought of a splendid plan to get them out of the way. Yes, I'm going to ask them to take the full measurements of Knocknacolly Lodge, and I'm going to ask Kilwhillie to go with them.'

'And what about Catriona and Mary?'

'Oh, they don't like us, Myrtle. They despise us, darling, for being so effeminate.'

Myrtle sat pensive.

'Why so thoughtful all of a sudden?' Carrie asked.

'I was thinking what a man would feel like walking out of church with one of those two and knowing it was no use, he just had to go through with it. I guess it would be easier to marry the Venus of Milo. She's big and she's hard and she'd be pretty cold, but she hasn't any arms.'

'I don't think you ought to think thoughts like that when you're not married.'

'That's the time to think them, angel child. It will be too late afterwards.'

After asking Toker to make up a lunch packet for herself and Myrtle, Carrie found Kilwhillie and the two MacDonalds in the Green Hall.

'Oh, isn't this fine,' she exclaimed. 'Just the very people I wanted. I wonder if you three very charming gentlemen would do me a favour.'

Kilwhillie tugged at his moustache and bowed with what he believed was the kind of courtliness a middle-aged bachelor should show to a young married woman.

'I'm sure we shall be delighted.'

'I was wondering if you would all three go over to Knocknacolly and bring me back the measurements of the Lodge so that I can plan out the alterations we want to make. It would be so very kind and helpful.'

'But I thought I was going to drive *you* over there this morning,' said Kilwhillie, a little ruefully.

'Well, that's just it, but I feel sort of dull and heavy and headachy. I guess it's the weather. So I'm going to be mean and cry off. And that's why I wondered if you'd come to my rescue,' she added, turning the full power of her greenish eyes on Murdoch and Iain.

'I'll do any measuring you want,' the sailor volunteered.

'So will I,' the undergraduate echoed.

'I know I'm asking a lot, but I want the full measurements of every room and the garden and all the outhouses. I expect it'll mean rather a long business. I've just asked Toker to make up a packet of sandwiches for Myrtle and me because we thought you could drop us where the road turns off to Glenbristle. Will I ask him to prepare three packets of sandwiches for you in case you can't get your measuring done before lunch?'

'Oh, don't bother,' said Kilwhillie. 'We'll . . .'

'It's no bother at all,' she interrupted. 'Surely I can do a little thing like that when you're being so kind and helpful. Myrtle and I will be ready for ten o'clock if that's all right for you.'

She hastened lightly from the Great Hall, flashing back a grateful smile for the chivalry with which she had been treated.

'Oh, Toker, I'm so sorry to worry you again, but I wonder if you'd make up another three packets for lunch and tea. Mr Cameron and Lieutenant MacDonald and Mr Iain are going over to Knocknacolly in Mr Cameron's car, and Miss Royde and I are going with them.'

'Quite an expedition, madam.'

'Yes, I do hope the rain will keep off.'

'I fear not, madam. I always dislike adopting a pessimistic attitude, but I never saw a sky look so determined to rain.'

'That's too bad. But never mind, we'll have good shelter. I'll bring down my lunch-basket if you'll put the five packets inside.'

When the butler informed the housekeeper of the additional picnic fare required she told him he must have made a mistake.

'I seldom make mistakes, Mrs Parsall,' he reminded her, with cold dignity.

'Well, what does Miss Royde want two packets for?' she asked. 'Is it a school-treat?'

'Probably Mrs Royde and Miss Royde each thought the other was giving the necessary order.'

'Oh well, I've given Mrs Ablewhite her instructions now. It'll only cause more confusion if I alter them. If there's two packets too many there must just be two packets too many. Mrs Ablewhite will be quite enough annoyed at everybody traipsing out to picnic on a day like this. The whole arrangements for lunch will now have to be altered. Well, I hope it rains good and hard. It will serve 'em right,' Mrs Parsall ejaculated bitterly.

It was half past ten when Kilwhillie pulled up at the corner of the Glenbristle road to let Carrie and Myrtle alight.

'Weighs quite a lot,' Murdoch observed as he deposited the lunch-basket in the road.

'Oh, we'll carry it between us,' said the owner cheerfully.

'You'd better change your mind and come with us to Knocknacolly, Mrs Royde,' Kilwhillie put his head through the window of the car to advise. 'I'm sure we're going to have a drench of rain presently.'

'Oh well, if it does, Myrtle and I will just have to go back home. We can always leave the basket under a rock and have somebody pick it up going past in a car. I'd adore to come with you, but I know if I go for a long drive my headache will start again.'

Kilwhillie's ancient Austin rattled on its way, and the two young women picked up the basket between them.

'My, it does weigh quite a bit,' Myrtle exclaimed.

'I'll say it does,' said Carrie triumphantly. 'There are seven lunches and seven teas in it.'

'Carrie!'

'I told Toker to put in three for our late escort.'

'And they think they'll find their lunch and tea in the car. What'll they do when they find it isn't there?'

'Come home, I guess.'

'Carrie, you're ruthless.'

'You have to be ruthless when you join a cause.'

'What cause have you joined?'

But before Carrie could answer, the red and yellow of the Macmillan tartan flashed upon the grey midge-infested air of the morning, and they saw the bard swinging down through Glenbristle towards them.

'You know, I think he's terribly attractive,' Myrtle sighed. 'I'm not surprised you've fallen for him even though you are married to my brother.'

'I haven't fallen for him in that way,' said Carrie quickly. 'Ours is a political and literary friendship.'

'Just that,' Myrtle murmured in a far-away reflective tone of voice. 'Oh well, I'm not interested at all in politics.'

'Hullo,' the poet exclaimed, with a genuinely glad smile. 'I was afraid I wasn't going to see you both again. Somebody pinched our tents and we moved up to Uaimh na Laoigh last Friday.'

'Isn't that the most melancholy sound you ever heard, Carrie? It's like one of those sad noises you hear out at sea in a fog. Say it again, will you, Mr Poet?'

'I wish I could pronounce Gaelic as well as he does,' Carrie sighed. 'Well, we want to see your cave. And I've got a lot of business to talk. I only wish Mr Buchanan hadn't gone away on Saturday.'

'But he didn't go away,' said the bard. 'He's up in the cave now. He twisted his ankle. We're both going tomorrow morning. I was just off to Kenspeckle to get some food. We're clean out of it.'

'We've brought you some provisions. So you can put that basket on your shoulder and lead the way to your cave. I guess we've saved you getting a terrible drenching. There are spots of rain already, and aren't these flies terrible!'

The bard lifted the basket and they set off along Glenbristle.

'It's a bit of a climb,' he warned them when they reached the spur of Ben Cruet, eight hundred feet up which was the cave.

'I don't believe we'd have dragged that lunch-basket up there,' Carrie said.

'Never,' Myrtle agreed fervidly.

However, they managed to scramble up themselves, though Myrtle had to do without the help of the poet's hand owing to the attention he had to pay to the lunch-basket. The entrance of the cave was reached just as the rain started to come down in earnest.

'Haven't you found a divine place to camp in!' Myrtle exclaimed.

There was indeed some excuse for her rapture. The cave was dry and airy. The view on either side of the hump of stone that marked the entrance was superb, looking down into Glenbristle and away across Glenbogle to the three mighty Sisters – Ben Booey, Ben Gorm, and Ben Glass. While the two young women were extolling it, the husband of one and brother of the other was about half-way across the dreary flat of Achnacallach. Not the most powerful telescope would have revealed him, for between him and the view commanded by the cave lay the ridge of Drumstickit about five miles away as the crow flies, but many more as Chester Royde was crawling. Soon the rain sloping across Glenbogle in great ladders dark as crape obliterated the view, and the two young women turned to the more cheerful sight the interior of the cave presented. The occupants had had time to make divans of dry heather on which they had spread their sleeping-blankets. A convenient venthole at the back of the cave allowed a turf fire to shed a friendly glow of warmth without stifling the inmates. Carrie noticed that the poet's notebook was lying open on his bed. Through the unromantic mind of Myrtle danced a butterfly thought that life in a cave like this with so personable a caveman would be very good. And what mattered the rain without when this cave was lighted within by the radiant tartans of Clan Macmillan and Clan Buchanan?

'It's such a very lovely surprise to find you still here, Mr Buchanan,' Carrie exclaimed.

'I wrenched my ankle like a clown and had to stay here, but I'll be able to get along the bottom of the glen tomorrow if I take it quietly. And then we'll catch the bus to Fort William. The trouble is we've eaten ourselves clean out of food. Did Alan tell you?'

'Fortunately Myrtle and I have brought you enough food to last you till tomorrow. It's mostly sandwiches but there's some tea and some cake, and fourteen hard-boiled eggs, so it'll keep you from starving. You can leave the basket in the cave and we'll fetch it away sometime.'

'It's awful kind of you, Mistress Royde. We're awfully obliged to you. We really are.'

'And now I want to talk to you about a little matter of business,' Carrie began.

Once again James Buchanan experienced that sinking feeling, due not to shortage of victuals but to the dread that he was going to hear the hundred-dollar bill had been a mistake.

'Yes,' Carrie went on, 'I want you to act for me in a business matter.'

James Buchanan gazed at her in something like stupefaction.

'It's over this property which my husband has bought, and which he wants to present to me. I told him I knew of a very clever Scottish lawyer and explained that Scottish law over real estate was quite different from English law, and of course so very much better.'

The gaze of James Buchanan was no longer something like stupefaction: it was stupefaction.

While Carrie was discussing the niceties of legal representation Myrtle and Alan sat on improvised hassocks of heather at the entrance of the cave.

'Did you know there was a terribly sad story about this cave?' she asked. 'Wait a moment, what is it in Gaelic?'

'Uaimh na laoigh.'

'Are you musical, Mr Macmillan?'

'Well, I like music, but I'm no piper.'

'I wasn't thinking of the bagpipes. That's a special kind of music I haven't gotten accustomed to yet. But I am pretty musical myself, and I buy quite a few highbrow phonograph records. I've a Victor recording of a clarinet quintet by Brahms and when I hear you say "Ooav" and what you say after that I could just imagine it was the clarinet on this Victor record. But I was asking you if you knew there was a terribly sad story about this cave.'

'No; I've not heard it.'

'Well, it seems there was once a young fugitive from the redcoats hiding in this cave.'

'Not Prince Charlie?' the poet asked suspiciously.

'No, not Prince Charlie.'

'I'm surprised to hear that. There's hardly a cave in the Highlands in which he isn't supposed to have hidden from the redcoats,' Alan Macmillan scoffed. 'If he'd slept one night in every cave in which he's supposed to have slept he'd have spent three years hiding from the redcoats instead of less than five months.'

'Oh, this really is a true story. His name was Alan Macdonald . . . your name's Alan, isn't it?'

The owner of the name nodded.

'I think I'll call you Alan if you don't mind. It's a name I've always been fond of, and now I've met somebody called Alan it seems a pity to waste the chance of using it. You don't mind, do you?'

'Of course I don't mind,' the poet answered, with a blush.

'That's sweet of you. But if I call you Alan you'll have to call me by my name. I expect you've forgotten what it is, haven't you?'

'Myrtle.'

'Oh, you hadn't forgotten,' she exclaimed, with gentle gratification. 'Isn't that very encouraging!'

She relapsed into a dream from which Alan roused her by asking for the rest of the story.

'Oh yes, the rest of the story,' she said. 'Well, this Alan Macdonald loved a girl in Glenbristle called Myrtle.'

'Myrtle?'

'Did I say Myrtle? Goody, isn't that strange! No, her name was Mary. Fancy me calling her Myrtle! Well, this poor girl set out one night to bring her Alan provisions and she was caught in a blizzard and frozen to death. The chaplain at Glenbogle Castle made a poem about it which he read to us. It was terribly sad. I felt I wanted to cry.'

The more modern poet made a scornful noise.

'I expect it was a ghastly poem.'

'Well, it was an old-fashioned kind of a poem,' Myrtle admitted. 'I mean to say, when he'd finished reading you knew just what had happened.'

'As you would after reading a paragraph of a newspaper,' Alan said derisively. 'I thought you told me you weren't romantic.'

'I'm not romantic. I'm terribly practical. I'm more practical than you are.'

'How do you make that out?'

'Well, while you were sitting around writing poetry, you forgot you'd run out of food, and if it hadn't been for Carrie and me you'd have been walking along Glenbogle now in all this rain to go and fetch it, and your friend Mr Buchanan would have had to wait till about five o'clock this afternoon for his lunch. You ought to write a poem about that.'

'Well, I'll tell you something, Myrtle, I did write a poem about you.'

'You did? Oh, Alan, I'm thrilled to death. Nobody ever wrote a poem about me. I guess the only poets I ever knew were all too sissie. Is it a long poem?'

'No, it's very short.'

'Could you . . . would you say it to me? What's it called?'

'I call it *Peaty Water*.'

The blue eyes of the poet burned as he gazed in front of him and intoned in a voice from which the faintest breath of dramatic expression had been ruthlessly eliminated:

'The heather,
The fading heather,
Is spread like the robe of a dead king
Upon my country,
Upon my dying country.

I do not lament therefore, but laugh
When down through the stale dead purple
Dances the peaty water
Warm with the sharp sun of the high tops,
Prickt by the sun of the high tops,
The prattling peaty dark-brown water,
The warm dark-brown water of life.'

'Yes, go on,' said Myrtle when the poet stopped and looked at her intensely.

'That's all. I'm afraid you'll think it rather old-fashioned. Imagist poetry has not kept its hold upon contemporary expression, but I would justify it by the old-fashioned circumstances in which it was written.'

'But I thought you said you'd written a poem about me?' Myrtle asked in a puzzled voice.

'That poem is about you.'

'Do you mind saying it once again?'

Once more the poet gazed fiercely in front of him from blazing blue eyes and intoned *Peaty Water*.

'I suppose you'll think me just a poor sap, Alan, but I can't see where I come into that poem.'

'You prefer the reverend gentleman's newspaper paragraph in verse about Myrtle Macdonald?'

'Oh, Alan!'

'What?'

'Why, you've said it yourself now. It was Mary Macdonald.'

'I meant Mary,' said the poet with a blush.

'And now you're blushing.'

He blushed more richly, and scowled.

'You mean to say,' he began in tones which his embarrassment rendered ferocious, 'you mean to say you can't perceive the image in that poem?'

'I can see all sorts of images in it, but I can't see my own.'

'The warm dark-brown water of life,' he urged, blushing again.

And then she too blushed, their blushes seeming more vivid because they were flaming against those sombre ladders of rain sloping from the leaden sky to the glen below.

'Say the poem again,' she murmured.

And this time he forgot the rigid principles imbibed from the gospel of Willie Yeats and allowed dramatic expression to enter into his recitation of *Peaty Water*:

> 'The heather,
> The fading heather,
> Is spread like the robe of a dead king
> Upon my country,
> Upon my dying country.
>
> I do not lament therefore, but laugh
> When down through the stale dead purple
> Dances the peaty water
> Warm with the sharp sun of the high tops,
> Prickt by the sun of the high tops,
> The prattling peaty dark-brown water,
> The warm dark-brown water of life.'

Myrtle sighed.

'And you really wrote that about me?'

'I did.'

'It's like a wonderful secret,' she sighed again. 'Say it to Carrie. She'll never guess it.'

Myrtle was right in presuming that her sister-in-law would not connect the poem *Peaty Water* with herself. She listened to it with a rapt expression in her greenish eyes that turned them to beryls.

'I think that's a perfectly wonderful poem, Alan,' she said. 'And the peaty water is S.B.A. of course.'

'S.B.A.?' Myrtle asked, a little sharply, for she had not heard Carrie call him Alan before. 'Who's S.B.A.?'

The other three looked at one another.

'It isn't a person, honeybunch. It's a . . .' Carrie stopped. 'I think she ought to be told, don't you?'

'Certainly,' Alan agreed, with a fervour that won him a flash from Myrtle's dark-brown eyes.

'Och ay,' James Buchanan confirmed. 'Miss Royde is fully entitled to be told.' The treasurer was thinking of more voluntary donations to the fighting fund.

'S.B.A. stands for Scottish Brotherhood of Action,' Carrie revealed. 'It's a secret society aiming at the revival of the national spirit of Scotland.'

'Does it want all that reviving?' Myrtle asked. 'I haven't been here quite a week yet, but I haven't seen much sign of collapse.'

'The country's practically dead, Miss Royde,' James Buchanan assured her earnestly. 'Do you realize the rate at which our industries are being moved south? It's really fearful. When I tell you that in Kilmarnock no less than . . .'

'Don't start giving statistics now, James,' his friend interrupted a little irritably. 'Miss Royde is American. She has no interest in Scottish politics.'

'Oh, but that isn't true, Alan. Since you said your poem and I've learnt that the dark-brown water of life is the image of the Scottish Brotherhood of Action I've become terribly interested in Scottish politics.'

James Buchanan's bullet-head swung round. So she was calling him 'Alan' already, and by the look in the other one's eye the other one wasn't too pleased about it. He would have to warn Alan again. She was a nice wee lassie, but she was not the owner of Knocknacolly, and it was Alan's duty to do nothing that might endanger the latter's interest in the S.B.A.

'Myrtle, how can you say that?' Carrie exclaimed. It was true she had failed to identify her sister-in-law with the dark-brown water of life, but she was under no illusions about her sudden interest in Scottish politics.

'But, Carrie, I am. There's something about the atmosphere here which seems to illuminate my real ego. And I think Chester feels it too. I'm wondering if we haven't perhaps Scotch blood . . .'

'I wish you wouldn't say Scotch blood as if it was broth or whisky,' Carrie interrupted. 'Anyway, Chester never suggested you had Scotch blood. The ancestor he's proud of is that Hungarian great-grandmother of yours.'

'Marka Tiktok. Yes, well, she was a very very exceptional woman and kind of took the shine out of the rest. But there's a lot more great-grandmothers and great-great-grandmothers and the more I think about it the more positive I feel that one of them came from the Highlands.'

'The more you think about anything the more you can think what you want to feel,' Carrie pointed out.

'I don't know why you're so grudging about my Scottish blood.

Chester would be tickled to death to find he had Scottish blood. For all you know, Carrie, that may have been the attraction which brought you two together.'

Myrtle was tempted to suggest herself as a member of the Scottish Brotherhood of Action, but she did not want to ruffle her sister-in-law's red hair by trespassing upon her private romantic property and she refrained. After all, a young man whose attraction Carrie had discovered first had written a poem about herself. She could afford to be generous. And Carrie was very sweet. If Alan wore well and if she herself should decide it was something more than the beginning of a pleasant summer flirtation Carrie would be helpful and understanding. That was certain.

'A curious thing happened after Alan and I went back to our camp in Glenbristle last Friday,' James Buchanan was saying. 'While we were talking to you, Miss Royde . . .'

'As we've all gone so far with Christian names,' Carrie put in, 'I don't see why you have to call Myrtle Miss Royde, James.'

'That's a matter for Miss Royde to decide, Mistress Royde . . . I should say Carrie,' said the lawyer.

'Oh, James, I'd adore to have you call me Myrtle. But go on with your story. What happened when you went back to your camp?'

'We found somebody had walked off with our tents.'

'Good gracious, what did you do?' Myrtle asked.

'There was nothing we could do except take the rest of our equipment up to this cave.'

'Say it, Alan.'

'Uaimh na laoigh.'

Myrtle gave a little laugh of delight deep in her throat as the coo of a dove.

'I'll just have to learn Gaelic,' she cried.

Carrie felt that her hair was brightening to the red in the Macmillan tartan, but she controlled herself admirably and said how much she should enjoy doing exercises in *Gaelic Without Tears* with Myrtle.

'Is Gaelic a good language for love?' Myrtle was asking now.

'The emotional variety is rich – very rich,' Alan informed her.

'What is "I love you"?'

'Tha gaoil agam ort.'

'Oh, another nice clarinet noise? And what's "kiss"?'

'Pog.'

Myrtle blinked.

'I don't think that's quite so good. Do you think that's quite so good, Carrie?'

'I guess no nation thinks any other nation's word for kiss is quite so good,' her sister-in-law replied, with that in her voice which made James Buchanan hastily return to the tale of the vanished tents.

'We thought your friend Mr MacDonald of Ben Nevis must have taken them,' he said darkly. 'I was waiting for him to come along and try to shake me. Ah, I'd have liked fine for him to come along and try to shake me.'

'Oh, I don't think the disappearance of your tents had anything to do with Ben Nevis,' said Carrie. 'I guess a dog must have been nosing around and gone off with them.'

'A dog go off with two canvas tents?' James exclaimed. 'No dog could go off with even one. They're awkward things for a body to carry, leave alone a dog.'

'Oh, they're awkward, are they?' Carrie asked, her greenish eyes innocent as water.

'Alan and I were so sure your wild laird had taken them that if we had not thought it would make it a bit awkward for you we would have gone to the Castle and asked what the blazes he thought he was playing at.'

'Oh, I wouldn't bother to do that,' said Carrie quickly. 'You wouldn't bother to do that, would you, Myrtle?'

'No, indeed I wouldn't,' Myrtle urged. 'He is so very violent, he really is.'

'So you think he'll shake *me?*' James demanded.

'Oh, no, James, I don't think he'd do that, but I wouldn't put it past him to pull a gun on you. I wouldn't really. Besides, if you're going to put through this real estate deal for Carrie, you may have to come to the Castle some time, and you wouldn't want to start off talking business the way they do in a wild west film.'

'Myrtle's right,' Carrie said. 'You'll spoil everything, James, if you start quarrelling with Ben Nevis. My husband won't understand it.'

'Och, that's all right, Carrie. Don't fash yourself about my behaviour. I know when to be professional.'

'I'm sure you do. Well, I'll write to you in Glasgow and give you full instructions.'

'I'll need to know the name of Mr Cameron's lawyer.'

'Yes, I'll find that out. But now there's another thing. Do either you or Alan know of a really good young Scottish architect? I guess we'll pull the lodge to pieces quite a lot, and it would probably mean a good job for him.'

'What about Bob Menzies, James,' Alan asked.

'I was just thinking the very same.'

'Is he young?' Carrie asked.

'No, no. Robert Menzies is about the same age as myself,' said James. 'Twenty-six.'

'Oh my, aren't you old!' Myrtle exclaimed. 'You're not so old as that, Alan?'

'I'm twenty-three.'

'Same age as me,' said Carrie.

'Three years older than I,' Myrtle added.

'And is this Mr Robert Menzies a good architect?' Carrie asked.

'He's very modern,' said Alan.

'Oh dear, will that mean he'll want us to live in a kind of cross between a conservatory and a prison?' Carrie asked anxiously.

'You needn't be afraid he'll suggest any kind of design that will violate the spirit of the place. He's modern, but his modernity is an expression of contemporary Scotland.'

'And he's a member of the Brotherhood,' James added. 'I don't want to make that a reason for giving him the job, but if you wish Knocknacolly to be an expression of the new spirit in Scotland I don't believe you could get a better architect than Robert Menzies. He's an awful nice wee man too. I think you'd like him.'

So finally it was settled that as soon as possible the architect should go and camp at Knocknacolly when, if Carrie and her husband approved of his ideas, he could be entrusted with the job, with James to look after the business side during the winter.

'And perhaps after you've taken your mother to Perth, you'll come and camp at Knocknacolly too?' Carrie asked Alan.

'I don't see what use I'll be,' he demurred.

'But of course you'll be terribly useful,' Myrtle declared. 'Won't he, Carrie?'

'Indeed yes, I should say he would. I'll need your advice, Alan. And I want to get a little runabout, and you could drive it back to Knocknacolly after I'd had a busy day with plans.'

Alan blushed.

'I'm afraid I can't drive a car.'

'What?' Myrtle exclaimed. 'Oh, I'll have to teach you, Alan. I mean Carrie and I will have to teach you. What's the Gaelic for car?'

'They have a synthetic word which I can't remember. But no Gaelic speaker ever uses it. They just say "car".'

'Oh, well, I've learnt one Gaelic word anyway,' said Myrtle. 'And now what about eating a little lunch? James looks terribly hungry.'

So they ate lunch, Carrie and Myrtle very sparingly because they wanted to leave as much as possible for the two young men, and after lunch Alan read a good deal of his poetry, which was not easy to follow: but he looked so attractive on his rostrum of heather that neither Carrie nor Myrtle bothered in the least about the words.

After a time, however, James Buchanan protested.

'I don't see why you want to read poetry as if you were a stirk trying to silence a stirk on the other side of a dyke, Alan. When I read your poetry to myself I can make quite a lot of sense out of it here and there, but when you read it I can't understand one word. It's a daft way of reading.'

'I am reading in the way poetry should be read,' Alan asserted severely.

'Who said so?'

'It's the traditional way of reading poetry.'

'I thought you were so modern.'

'My work is modern.'

'Then why do you read it like an ancient Druid?'

'What do you know about poetry, James?'

'I never will know anything about poetry if I have to listen to you hooting at me like an owl in a tree. Suppose I were to get up in court and hoot at the sheriff like that, what would become of my case?'

'The parallel is ridiculous.'

'Do you or do you not want to make yourself intelligible?'

'It depends what you mean by intelligible.'

'Do you want your poetry to make sense?'

'Poetry is not intended to make sense. You're confusing it with prose.'

'Then prose is sense and poetry is nonsense?'

'If you like.'

'And you're going to spend your life writing nonsense? Losh, no wonder Scotland's going downhill.'

'I think I understand what Alan means,' said Myrtle, remembering the secret of *Peaty Water*.

'That's right, Myrtle. Encourage him. He's been spoilt all his life by encouragement,' James groaned in disgust. 'The only reason he's learning Gaelic is because he wants to add a few more incomprehensible noises to the ones he can make already in English.'

'No, no, James, that isn't fair,' Carrie interposed. 'Alan is learning Gaelic because he knows that the life of a nation is its language.'

And this started another argument, and so with arguments and plans for the future and a few statistics from James and an early tea it was four o'clock, and with the rain seeming to abate Carrie and Myrtle decided they ought to be going back to the Castle.

'My dears, you're drenched,' Mrs MacDonald boomed in dismay when they arrived home. 'Where have you been?'

'We found a cave to shelter in,' said Carrie. 'Mr Fletcher told us about it. And we had a lovely, lazy day. It's only now coming home that we got so wet.'

But when Chester arrived about a quarter past seven it seemed absurd for her or Carrie to talk about being wet.

'Oh, Chester, I've never seen anybody so wet. Did you fall into the river? And oh my, Chester, what have you done to your face? My dear, it's bigger than a pumpkin.'

'I'll tell you when I've had a bath,' he replied.

'Did you kill a stag, Chester?'

'Not yet. But I'm sure going to. I've taken a kind of dislike to stags. You can arrange Knocknacolly as you like, Carrie, but I want one biggish room set apart for me. I aim to cover the walls of it with stags' heads.'

'And is stalking good sport?'

'Stalking isn't a sport at all, Carrie, but killing stags is a duty.'

'Do go and bathe your eyes, Chester.'

'If I can get at them,' he said, moving in the direction of the bathroom.

Downstairs in the Great Hall Ben Nevis, quite as wet as his guest but unmarked by a single midge's bite, was waving a cablegram and shouting to everybody who came in that Hector had been given his leave and hoped to be home by the twenty-eighth.

'My, isn't that splendid!' said Myrtle.

'You'll like him, Myrtle. He takes after me in every way. Voice, figure, features, and general outlook on life. Well, we had rather a disappointing day, but what of it? There are plenty of other days. Fill up your glass, Hugh.'

The Laird of Kilwhillie came over to Carrie.

'We managed to get the measurements you wanted.'

'Oh, isn't that kind of you, Kilwhillie! I really am terribly obliged. And I was so sorry about your lunch. I didn't realize all the lunches were in my basket. What did you do?'

'Oh, it was quite all right. We got a snack at my house.'

'I'm writing off to our lawyer tomorrow. So will you let me have the name of yours? I'm longing to feel Knocknacolly is really mine, and I shall want your advice about so many things.'

Kilwhillie tugged at his moustache, and bowed.

'I will always be at your service, Mrs Royde.'

'Fill up your glass, Hugh, fill up your glass,' the Chieftain exhorted. 'Yes, we had a disappointing day. However, we only just failed to get the finest stag in this part of the country. An historic animal really. The muckle hart of Ben Glass, Hugh.'

'By jove, Donald, the muckle hart himself!'

'Yes, but the beggar slipped us. We had pretty nearly a four-mile crawl on our hands and knees, and some of the time on our tummies.'

'Chester crawled four miles on his tummy?' Carrie exclaimed incredulously.

'Like a good 'un,' Ben Nevis declared with enthusiasm. 'Well, I must go and get into some dry clothes.'

He swallowed one more hefty dram and strode from the hall, his kilt clinging to him like the draperies of a Rhine maiden or Nereid.

The rain that started on that Monday fell heavily and almost incessantly for the next five days and not quite so heavily and somewhat less incessantly for another five days after that. For a time even the hardiest sportsman was deterred from activity, but nevertheless the time passed pleasantly enough. Kilwhillie went back to Kilwhillie House. James Buchanan was put in touch with his lawyers Messrs Macbeth, Macbeth, and Macbean of Inverness, and the meticulous process of selling a landed estate in Scotland was set in motion. Carrie, who had felt guilty over Kilwhillie's lunch, had suggested to her husband he should add another 2,500 dollars to the purchase price of Knocknacolly.

'But I've already added that, Carrie.'

'I know, Chester dear, but I'd feel so much happier if he had what he'd said to himself he would take, and that was eight thousand. That's roughly forty thousand dollars, isn't it?'

'Well, if it pleases you, it's O.K. by me,' said Chester.

'Oh, Chester, you're so big-hearted. But I do think Knocknacolly is worth forty thousand dollars.'

'It certainly is if it's giving you so much pleasure.'

'Oh, it is, Chester. I can't tell you what pleasure it's going to give me. And when the architect comes I'll have him pay particular attention to this room for your stags' heads. Oh, and Chester, I'd like to have a little runabout so that I can run over to Knocknacolly when I feel inclined.'

'A two-seater?'

Carrie hesitated. The temptation was strong.

'No; I think it had better be a four-seater,' she said, conquering it.

'I'm going into Inverness tomorrow. I'll probably find there what you want.'

'Will I come with you, Chester?'

'No, don't you bother, dear. I have a little business to attend to. Oh, by the way, which do you like best, purple or orange?'

'Purple or orange? What for, Chester? Neither suits me. Well, I suppose purple would, but I don't want to think about purple for a few years yet.'

'Why not?'

'It's so ageing.'

'Is that so?' said Chester pensively. 'But I wasn't thinking about a frock for you. I was just asking which colour you like best.'

'Oh, as a colour I like orange – definitely.'

'Yes, I believe I do too.'

'By the way, Chester, I'm arranging for the architect to camp up at Knocknacolly. I want him to soak himself in the atmosphere.'

'He'll do that all right if it goes on raining like this. But if he wants any more soaking I'll take him with me when I start getting my own back on stags. What's his name, again?'

'Robert M-E-N-Z-I-E-S. But it's pronounced "Mingies".'

'For the love of Mike, why?'

'I don't know why, but it is. And I suggested Mr Menzies should have a couple of friends with him. One of them will be Mr Buchanan the lawyer, who wants to get thoroughly conversant with conditions at Knocknacolly, and as he'll have to manage all the business part of it while the alterations are being made after we go back home this fall, I think that's a good idea, don't you?'

'This lawyer of yours can't have much of a business if he can afford to go camping out at Knocknacolly with an architect.'

'But I told you, Chester, he's quite young. I think it's much better to have a clever young lawyer who can give your business more of his personal attention.'

'Where did you get hold of him?'

'I met him in — in Edinburgh when I was waiting there for you to come up from London.'

'Well, it's your house and it's your party. You do what you like. Who's the third in the party?'

'A young Scottish poet called Macmillan.'

'A poet? Holy snakes, are you going to turn Knocknacolly into a National Park? What's the poet going to do?'

'He's going to give me the benefit of his advice.'

'A poet is?'

'Sure.'

'It's lucky your Mr Buchanan has plenty of time on his hands.'

Later Carrie told Myrtle how sweet and understanding Chester had been about her plans for Knocknacolly. She also explained that she had led him to suppose she had met James and Alan in Edinburgh.

'So of course you won't have met them, Myrtle, till I introduce you.'

'Is that a warning?'

'Warning of what?'

'A warning I'll have to be as good as gold and sweet as pie if I ever am to be introduced.'

'Oh, Myrtle, no. You couldn't think I'd be so mean.'

Myrtle looked at her sister-in-law.

'Of course I don't, honey,' she said, laughing softly and patting Carrie's shoulder.

Pleasant indeed and full of happy prospects and activities was Glenbogle in spite of the rain. The Chieftain and his wife were contemplating the leave of their eldest son. The keepers and gillies and workmen were looking forward to the Gathering on 28 August. The children were practising reels and sword-dances for the great annual event with indefatigable zeal. The pipers were hardly ever silent in their resolve to defend the music of Glenbogle against all competitors. Murdoch and Iain MacDonald had proclaimed their intention of tossing the caber and putting the stone for the honour of Glenbogle's muscles against whatever brawny outsiders should venture to challenge their power. Catriona and Mary MacDonald were volunteering to bicycle into Fort William at the slightest excuse to fetch extra yards of ribbons for rosettes. Carrie and Myrtle were driving over to Knocknacolly in the ten-h.p. Austin which Chester had bought in Inverness with the energetic Widow Macdonald who was scrubbing out some of the rooms, and also making expeditions to Fort William for various domestic articles. Chester Royde Jr was much in the company of Kilwhillie, with whom he paid two or three visits to Inverness, the object of which was not divulged. Kilwhillie's moustache under the effect of that unexpected extra £1,000 had to be tugged at continually to prevent its sweeping up like a cow's horns and thus contravening what Kilwhillie considered the suitable habit of growth for a laird's moustache.

The happy inhabitants of Glenbogle were as innocent as once upon a time the inhabitants of Glencoe that down in London an enemy was plotting their ruin.

Chapter 12

OUSE HALL

British democracy has many glories, not the least of which is its ability to produce liberal-minded and progressive peers who instead of sulking about the burden of taxation get in touch with the people and keep in touch with the people. Such a peer was John Henry Charles Bunting, seventh Earl of Buntingdon, also Viscount Ouse and Baron Bunting of Buntingdon, of Ouse Hall, Buntingdon, Beds, and 201 Belgrave Square, sw, the President of the National Union of Hikers. Many readers will be familiar with the photograph of Lord Buntingdon in shorts and shirt holding his hiker's staff, his benevolently domed head hatless, liberty, equality, and fraternity twined in the smile that wreathes his large melon-shaped face of the Rugby not Association type of melon. Underneath this representation one may here read, 'Bachelor peer says everybody should hike', or 'Earl says hiking is shortest cut to true democracy', or 'Hundreds of hikers yesterday acclaimed the Earl of Buntingdon when he presided at the Annual Hikery held in the grounds of Ouse Hall, his picturesque Bedfordshire seat. Lord Buntingdon in thanking the members of the National Union of Hikers for again electing him as their President stressed the moral, mental, and physical value of hiking in preventing Britain from becoming a C3 nation.'

Just about the time on that Monday when Duncan sighted the muckle hart of Ben Glass, Lord Buntingdon came in from a walk round his tortoise enclosures at Ouse Hall – he had the finest collection of tortoises in the world – to receive from his butler a telegram:

Can you possibly come London to preside at very important indignation meeting of N.U.H. at Astrovegetarian Hall, Villiers Street, Strand next Friday at eight? Your presence would be intensely appreciated. Prew ready to come immediately to Ouse Hall if you desire further information

Buckham

'When did this come, Maple?'

'It has just this moment been telephoned through from the post-office, my lord.'

Lord Buntingdon went into the library and wrote his reply:

Percy Buckham, 15 Quilting Gardens, Primrose Hill, NW. If my presence considered absolutely necessary will preside at meeting but shall be glad if Prew will come to Ouse Hall and explain full circumstances stop I shall be glad to put him up tomorrow or Wednesday night stop Please telegraph time of train's arrival
Buntingdon

Such a telegram was typical of that progressive peer. His quick sympathies reacted immediately to the appeal of Percy Buckham, the Acting President of the N.U.H.; but the blood of Whig and Liberal ancestors famous in English politics ran in his veins and with it the caution such an inheritance brought. Hence he answered the appeal, but at the same time was determined to know in advance exactly what his action would let him in for.

Later that day, just when Lord Buntingdon was returning from a second visit to his tortoise enclosures where his progressive mind, ever eager to leap ahead, disciplined itself by the contemplation of nature's Fabians, Maple handed him another telegram:

Grateful thanks for your spirited attitude. Will arrive Buntingdon 7.26 tomorrow evening
Prew

Lord Buntingdon's oval brow became slightly elliptical at the epithet 'spirited'. It had not occurred to him there was anything particularly spirited about his proposed action. It was rather a bore, certainly, going up to London in this hot August weather, but overcoming his own indolence was as much credit as he could take in the circumstances.

'The story you have just told me, Mr Prew, is certainly astonishing,' said Lord Buntingdon when he had listened at dinner the following evening to what the Secretary of the N.U.H. had to say about the adventures of the hikers in Glenbogle. 'Do you suppose this Mr MacDonald is a Fascist?'

'No. Inquiries we have made do not indicate that there is any connection with Fascist activities, Lord Buntingdon. It would seem to be a case of unbridled individualism,' Mr Prew went on primly. 'Indeed, one might almost say demented individualism.'

'I understand his annoyance about the grouse . . . but that does not mean I sympathize with such a deplorable loss of self-control.'

'Oh, I can assure you, Lord Buntingdon, that if he had pointed out we were spoiling his shooting arrangements and asked us to take our tea elsewhere we should have complied with such a request immediately. Oh, but immediately, Lord Buntingdon.'

'Quite, quite. As you know I do not preserve game myself, but consideration is owed to landowners who do.'

'We always impress that on our young people, Lord Buntingdon,' said the Secretary earnestly. 'I always say if you're on private property you must behave as if you were in somebody else's house. But we were given no opportunity to apologize and withdraw. This Mr MacDonald literally charged at us and when I tried to explain what the N.U.H. was he gripped me by the collar and shook and shook and shook and . . .'

'Yes, you've already made that clear,' Lord Buntingdon interrupted. 'Fill up your glass, Mr Prew,' he added, pushing the decanter of port towards his guest.

'Thank you, no, Lord Buntingdon. I find that more than one glass of port tends to aggravate my rheumatism.'

'You suffer from rheumatism, do you?'

'Yes, in the knees, Lord Buntingdon. Ah, well, anno domini, anno domini. One must accept it.'

'You get it in the knees, eh? That's where I get it sometimes. I *have* wondered whether we're wise to wear shorts at our age.'

'Oh, Lord Buntingdon,' the Secretary exclaimed, 'don't say that! My own idea is that if we didn't wear shorts as often as we could we should have much worse rheumatism. I think shorts are the healthiest garments any man can wear, or any woman for that matter.'

'Not *any* woman, Mr Prew. The faintest touch of steatopygy is fatal to the successful wearing of shorts.'

'Yes, I suppose it would be,' the Secretary agreed, wondering what on earth steatopygy was. 'But surely that's a rare complaint?'

'Not so rare as all that among women.'

'I must admit I'm a little ignorant about certain aspects of women, Lord Buntingdon. A bachelor, you know.'

'I'm a bachelor too, don't forget.'

'Yes, indeed, so you are, Lord Buntingdon. Shall I strike a jarring note if I call it a blessed state?'

'I've never regretted it. But then of course I've had so many interests,' the peer went on dreamily. 'The League of Nations, and promoting culture of the soya bean, and basic English, and spelling reform, and hiking, and of course my tortoises.'

'I know, Lord Buntingdon, I know. The variety of your interests is truly phenomenal. Oh, that reminds me, we were approached the other day by the Nudist Ramblers Society asking if we would accept them as an affiliated branch of the N.U.H. The Committee rejected the application.'

'Quite right,' said Lord Buntingdon decidedly.

'I'm glad you endorse our attitude. What we felt was that, although at present the Nudist Ramblers only ramble about over one or two strictly private estates the owners of which have granted their permission, it would not do to create confusion in the mind of the general public between nudists and some of our jolly young people who, revelling as they quite rightly should in their own youthful bodies, wear actually very little in the way of clothes. We did in fact have slight trouble a fortnight ago when two of our most energetic young lady members were asked by the Vicar of Bustard Abbas in Dorset to leave his church. Oh yes, he addressed them from the pulpit in the very coarsest biblical language . . . one would think a clergyman would know better in these days. But I always say if one wants to find old-fashioned bigotry one must look for it in church. The girls were lightly clad, yes. But for the Vicar to complain that his choir broke down in the middle of the Venite through staring at them when they came into the church was a reflection, had he stopped to reflect, not upon the poor girls, but upon the nasty minds of himself and his badly-trained choir. The whole business was most unpleasant. One old woman, an inmate of the Bustard Abbas almshouses, was seized with a form of hysterics and had to be led out of the church in convulsions of laughter, and according to the Vicar continued to laugh ungovernably at intervals for nearly a week, which seems to have exasperated one of the other almswomen into emptying a cup of tea over her. In fact Bustard Abbas appears to be one of those remote and peaceful country villages which is literally seething beneath the outwardly beautiful surface with the rankest and basest animal passions. You'll pardon my strong language, Lord Buntingdon, I hope? And, dear me, I'm wandering from the real question at issue. This degraded medieval superstition which still lingers always rouses my ire.'

'Come along, we'll go into the library and have our coffee,' said Lord Buntingdon soothingly. 'But I'm glad you choked off those nudists. A bachelor's state may be blessed, but we can't be too careful, and I don't want to be associated with nudists. Anyway, I don't like 'em. I came upon a colony of them once in Germany, skating. It was a most unpleasant sight. They looked like chilled meat.'

In the library Mr Sydney Prew returned to the subject which had brought him to Ouse Hall.

'Of course, it was open to me to take out a summons for assault and battery against Ben Nevis.'

'Against Ben Nevis?' Lord Buntingdon gasped, his oval brow suffering another ellipse.

'That is what they call this Mr Macdonald in Inverness-shire.'

'A nickname, do you mean?'

'No, he is known as MacDonald of Ben Nevis.'

'Oh, I see, he's one of those Highland chief fellows. Go on.'

'As I was saying, I could take out a summons against him for assault and battery, and so could young Tom Camidge for shooting his portable wireless set as well as assaulting him personally, and so could all the rest for the assault, and the shutting them up in those dungeons; but Mr Buckham feels that the only lesson to give Mr MacDonald is a lesson that will teach him the power of the National Union of Hikers rather than the power of British justice, which no doubt he knows already.'

'What form does Mr Buckham propose his lesson should take?' Lord Buntingdon asked.

'He wishes the N.U.H. to declare war on Mr MacDonald and make his life a burden to him until he sues for peace.'

'How does Mr Buckham propose to wage war?'

'He wants volunteers from the N.U.H. to camp on Mr MacDonald's land, to pull down the notice-boards, to annoy him in every possible way and possibly even to seize and occupy Glenbogle Castle. He proposes to assume command himself of the operations. The meeting is being held on Friday to rouse the feelings of the Union. Mr Buckham will address the meeting. So will Tom Camidge. His fiancée, too, Miss Winifred Gosnay, will relate the experience of the girls shut up in the dungeon. And finally I shall tell of the way this Highland bully shook and shook and shook . . .'

'Yes, yes,' Lord Buntingdon interrupted, 'that will be what you will tell the meeting.'

'And also I shall relate the really horrible tale of the way we were driven out of Glenbogle by lorries and motor-cars.'

'But what do you want me to do?' Lord Buntington asked, a little dubiously.

'We want you, our much revered and, if I may say so, much loved President to take the chair and lend the weight of your name to what we feel will be one of the most impressive demonstrations of democratic solidarity and determination this country has witnessed for many a long day. I know how strongly you feel on the subject of collective security, and this seems to me, if I may venture to say so, a phenomenal opportunity to display a most convincing example of the advantage of collective security.'

Lord Buntingdon remained silent. He was pondering the motto of his house. *Festina lente*. He was reflecting upon the gait of his tortoises. He was asking himself whether it was wise to involve himself in what amounted to an incitement to the members of the N.U.H. to take the law into their own hands. The Gordon Riots! The Buntingdon Agrarian Outrages? The Buntingdon Raid? A vision passed across his fancy of himself at Madame Tussaud's – of himself in shorts and shirt leaning upon his hiker's staff, with waxen brow and waxen knees and glass eyes, staring at the crowds that read the number attached to him and turned to the catalogue to find out that this was the famous Earl of Buntingdon who had ravaged the Highlands of Scotland with an army of hikers.

'I don't think I ought to take the chair, Mr Prew,' he said at last.

'You don't, Lord Buntingdon? This will be a grievous blow to our Acting President, Mr Buckham. Must we take it you disapprove of the action we plan against Mr MacDonald?'

'By no means, Mr Prew, in my own house. But there is a great difference between commending your energetic proposals in private and commending them upon a public platform. My brother peers already disapprove of me very much. The speeches of few noble lords are received so frigidly as mine. But so far I have not directly attacked the sacred rights of landed property, and as a landed proprietor myself I am in rather a delicate position. You must see that?'

'Yes, I do see that, Lord Buntingdon, but I also see that you are one of democracy's doughtiest champions and I feel that your absence from the platform on Friday next will be a bitter disappointment to our splendid young people who look up to you as a leader.'

'I can assure you, my dear Mr Prew, that I am acutely aware of my responsibility towards these splendid young people, but I confess I am apprehensive of what the Press may make of my open encouragement of what undoubtedly is lawlessness, however much we may recognize that such lawlessness was provoked by the previous lawlessness of Mr MacDonald.'

'But we can exclude the Press,' Mr Prew urged. 'In fact we ought to exclude the Press. It's not a public meeting. Nobody will be admitted who cannot show his or her card of membership. Of course if you decide that you cannot take the chair we must bow to the inevitable, but at the risk of committing a nuisance . . . I should say rather of being a nuisance,' Mr Prew hastily corrected in answer to the surprised expression on Lord Buntingdon's melon-shaped face, 'at the risk, I say, of being too persistent I must beg you to change your mind and agree to take the chair on Friday evening. You have taken the chair on all the momentous occasions in the Union's history. It was you who put to the vote the question of supplying hotels with green signboards painted N.U.H. in white letters under our device of crossed staffs and our motto *Hike On – Hike Ever*. It was you who signed your name at the head of the protest to the Editors of the *Concise Oxford Dictionary* because the word 'hike' was not yet included in their columns. Lord Buntingdon, please, please recall the great Annual Hikery, growing in size and importance every year, which is held in the park of Ouse Hall and try to imagine what it would mean to those splendid young people if their beloved President failed to lead the Hikers' Song.

> ' Hike, hike, hike along the high road,
> Hike, hike, hike along the low,
> Hike across the bens, hike across the fens,
> Hike, hike, hike, never ride a bike,
> And carry with a smile your load,
> Boys and girls, hike, hike, as fast as you like,
> And hike, if you like, as slow.
> Boys and girls, hike together, for it's always hikers' weather,
> And sing the hikers' song as you go.'

Mr Sydney Prew's prim voice did not do justice to the Hikers' Song, but Lord Buntingdon in fancy heard it rolling from the voices of happy young people massed upon the great lawn at Ouse Hall. The spirit that led the first Earl of Buntingdon to whistle James II out of England and himself into an Earldom abode in the seventh Earl of Buntingdon.

'Very well, Mr Prew, I will take the chair on Friday,' he said.

'Oh, huzza!' the Secretary exclaimed with prim enthusiasm. 'I wonder if I may use your telephone, Lord Buntingdon?'

'Certainly.'

'I know Mr Buckham is hanging on to the other end, as the picturesque phrase hath it, hoping to have word with me that you will take the chair on Friday.'

'No Press,' Lord Buntingdon reminded him.

'No Press. Except a great press of young people, I hope,' Mr Prew added archly, as he tripped out of the library to telephone the Acting President.

Mr Percy Buckham has been described in *Boost*, the advertisers' advertiser, as one of the live wires of the wireless world. This paradox meant that Percy Buckham, the managing director of the firm which made the portable wireless-set known all over Great Britain as Buckham's Little Songster, spent a very considerable sum annually on advertising. It is perhaps superfluous to describe him. Who does not know those dark compelling eyes, that out-thrust chin, that masterful mouth and concentrated frown beneath the curly hair of a he-man with the heart of a boy? No matter the pages of what paper you turn you will not find it easy to escape Buckham's talks under the heading *Lend Me Your Ears*. He is as anxious to borrow the ears of readers of the *New Statesman* as those of *Secrets and Flame* that he may return them filled with facts about his Little Songster.

'Buy Buckham's Little Songster and carry the world round with you in one hand.' 'The Four B's of Music — Bach, Beethoven, Brahms, and Buckham.' 'Wouldn't it give you a thrill if Mr Baldwin walked into your room and talked to you? Buckham's Little Songster will bring Mr Baldwin into your room.' 'Have you ever dreamed that the world's great singers sang for you alone? Buckham's Little Songster will make your dream come true.' 'Henry Hall's Band will play hikers up the steepest hill if they carry Buckham's Little Songster in their knapsacks.'

It would be wrong, very wrong, to connect Percy Buckham's interest in the National Union of Hikers with his interest in the Little Songster. He presided as enthusiastically over the hiker without a Little Songster as over the one who never hiked four miles without one. On the other hand, it would be dishonest not to admit that his desire to avenge the treatment of the sixteen members of the N.U.H. was stimulated to the point of fury by the news that Ben Nevis had emptied both barrels of his gun into Tom Camidge's Little Songster.

'Don't prosecute, Tom,' he urged. 'I'll give you another Little

Songster. This has become a personal matter for me. I'm in with you over this up to the hilt. I'm going to show this Highland bully what it means to put Percy Buckham against him. We'll carry the war into the enemy's country, Prew. I hope Lord Buntingdon will support us.'

So on this evening the creator of the Little Songster was waiting anxiously in his house on Primrose Hill for news of this support.

'Hullo! Is that you, Prew? Yes? He *will* take the chair? That's splendid . . . what's that? No Press? But you know I always give the Press their chance. This would be splendid copy for them . . . well, of course, if the old boy's adamant . . . I suppose it will have to be limited to members of the Union. But I think it's a pity to lose the publicity. After all, it is a unique occasion. There's been nothing like it since the sort of thing you read of in history books . . . Oh, I agree it adds very much to the strength of our position if Lord Buntingdon presides over the meeting, and you were quite right to give way over the Press . . . yes, as you say, it isn't as if it was a meeting open to the general public. By the way, Prew, will he be wearing shorts? . . . well, you might ask him, will you? . . .'

Buckham held the receiver to await Lord Buntingdon's decision.

Mrs Buckham, a plump blonde of about thirty-five with china-blue eyes and the winning smile of a successful businessman's wife, smiled encouragingly at her husband.

'You're pleased Lord Buntingdon has agreed to take the chair, Percy?'

'Very pleased,' he rapped out, his chin making passes at the receiver.

Mrs Buckham looked so conventional that it was rather surprising to find her apparently taking for granted her husband's intention to start a civil war. The explanation was that she always attributed any eccentricity of Percy's to its publicity value, and his success in business seemed to her an answer to every criticism.

'Is that you, Prew? What does he say? . . . he thinks it better not to wear shorts? Why? . . . yes, well, perhaps he's right. We'll none of us wear shorts on the platform, then. You'll have to let the speakers know. You'd better come round to my office tomorrow morning. We'll lunch together and discuss any details we've not arranged yet. Thank Lord Buntingdon from me for his assent. Say how much we all appreciate it. Good night, old man.'

Buckham hung up the receiver.

'Funny how timid these lords are, Ethel,' he observed to his wife. 'I don't think if I was the Earl of Buntingdon I should be afraid of the Press.'

'I'm sure you wouldn't, Percy.'

'If this war starts it means washing out that cruise in September, unless you'd like to take Maud Runcible.'

'I'd love to take Maud Runcible.'

'Would you? All right, you'd better arrange it. I hope we get good weather. Are you coming to the meeting on Friday?'

'Do you want me to come, Percy?'

'I shall be making a speech. I think you ought to hear it.'

'Then of course I'll come.'

Chapter 13

THE EXTRAORDINARY MEETING

The Astrovegetarian Hall in Villiers Street, Strand, is one of several such edifices erected in London to house the opinions of the sect or philosophical society or collection of cranks which has subscribed to build a temple of its own. They usually consist of a fairly large central hall with a number of smaller lecture-rooms attached, and the sect or society by letting out these rooms and the main hall itself often derives a handsome return on the investment in the shape of rent.

The Astrovegetarian Society itself used its hall only on certain dates like the Summer and Winter Solstice connected immemorially with the influence of the heavenly bodies upon the fertility of the earth, and such was its broad-mindedness that if a Butchers' Friendly Society had desired to use the hall for some celebration it would have been let to them for the fixed fee.

On this Friday evening in August the lecture-rooms were experiencing the effect of the holiday season, but even so, beside the booking of the main hall for the National Union of Hikers, rooms had been booked for the Society for the Promotion of Non-metallic Gramophone Needles, the Birth Control Crusade (Shock Troops Debating Society), the Root and Branch League, the Friends of Wo Ho Wo, the Edible Fungus Club, and the London Animist Association. It was remarkable with what accuracy the janitor directed the members of these various gatherings to the right room almost before they had time to name their particular objective, for outwardly they all looked much the same mixture of dowdiness and defiance.

Naturally the great majority of those turning into the Astrovegetarian Hall that evening were members of the National Union of Hikers, and by ten minutes to eight the central hall was already full of healthy happy sunburnt young people, with a sprinkling of equally healthy happy sunburnt slightly older people, all singing the Hikers' Song interspersed with some of the favourite songs of the First Great War. It might be said that they made the welkin ring, for the dome of the Astrovegetarian Hall was gilded with planets and stars on a cerulean ground. It was divided into the twelve signs of the zodiac, beneath each one of which was a plaster representation of some prominent vegetable associated with its influence. Nor were the vegetables ruled by the planets uncelebrated. Thus one might behold in coloured plaster the spinach of Saturn, Jupiter's asparagus, the mustard and rhubarb of Mars, the Moon's cabbages, the beans and parsnips of Venus, Mercury's carrots, and the ginger of the Sun. At the back of the platform was a sort of carved reredos on which symbolic figures in flowing draperies stood about in aesthetic attitudes with sheaves and cornucopias.

The last notes of the Hikers' Song had just died away for the sixth time when, much to the relief of the Shock Troops of the Birth Control Crusade debating in Gemini, or more prosaically, and less ominously from their point of view, Room 3, a door at the back of the platform opened and the President, Acting President, Secretary, and Honorary Treasurer of the Union marched in with solemn tread followed by Tom Camidge, whom we last saw defying Ben Nevis in his own stronghold, Winifred Gosnay, his fiancée, whom we last saw zipping up her shorts, and several more of the sixteen hikers attacked on the braes of Strathdiddle and imprisoned in the dungeons of Glenbogle.

Amid a volley of cheers, the echoes of which made one of the Shock Troop debaters in Room 3 get badly mixed up in the defensive tactics he was expounding, Lord Buntingdon rose to address the meeting. If he had been in hiker's garb he would have seemed with his melon-shaped face a fit mate for one of those fruitarian females on the reredos behind him. However, as we know, he had ruled against shorts for the platform party, and his confirmed bachelordom was in no danger.

'Members of the National Union of Hikers, friends (*loud cheers*), our energetic and enthusiastic secretary Mr Sydney Prew (*cheers*) has convened this extraordinary meeting tonight at very short notice in order to deal with what I do not hesitate, I say I do not hesitate to call a most extraordinary situation. In fact I shall not hesitate, I say I shall not hesitate to call it one of the most extraordinary situations I have encountered during thirty years of what I hope I may call public life (*hear, hear*), a life which I have tried to direct along the path of liberal ideas and democratic progress (*applause*). I am not going to anticipate what other speakers better qualified than myself have come here tonight to tell you. I do not consider it the duty of a good chairman to cut the ground, or may I say pull the chair away from under the speakers who follow him (*laughter, a little uncertain at first, but growing louder when the smile upon the face of the President made it clear that the facetiousness was intentional*). I recall the story of a chairman that once took the chair for the late Dean Hole of Rochester, who was to give an audience the benefit of his experience as the most enthusiastic and most knowledgeable amateur rose-grower in the country. This chairman, no doubt a most worthy man, was not endowed with the blessed faculty of knowing when to stop, and in introducing the Dean he allowed himself to ramble on for some three-quarters of an hour, at the end of which time he called upon the Dean himself to give the audience his address. "My address is the Deanery, Rochester," snapped the Very Reverend gentleman, "and I am going there now." (*Loud and prolonged laughter during which Lord Buntingdon reflected what a mercy it was that the chestnuts of his youth were capable of flowering again in his age.*) Well, not wishing Mr Sydney Prew, our most esteemed secretary, to emulate Dean Hole, I have pleasure in calling upon him to address the meeting' (*loud applause, which was renewed when Mr Prew stepped forward on the platform*).

'Mr President, Mr Acting President, girls and boys, I will not, I cannot say "ladies and gentlemen" (*giggles*). Do not misunderstand me, girls and boys, I will not say "ladies and gentlemen", because I cannot bring myself to introduce into the atmosphere of our great democratic pastime the artificial, meaningless, and stuffy epithets of a mercifully decaying and hidebound conventionality. Nobody who has enjoyed the privilege of serving in however humble a capacity under that great champion of progress, our revered President, Lord Buntingdon (*loud cheers*), could bring himself to bow the knee to the household gods of an outworn and discredited social creed. But make no mistake about it, girls and boys, those tawdry household gods are not yet overthrown. Only last week sixteen members of our Union were given literally concrete evidence of their still potent sway over the hearts and heads of some of our fellow-citizens (*shame*). You cry "shame" now, but what will you cry when you hear all the facts?

'A fortnight ago tomorrow sixteen of us entrained at Euston and detrained the following morning at Perth. We had promised ourselves the pleasure of hiking through the romantic Highlands of Scotland as far as Inverness-shire and thence westward by way of Fort William through Glencoe and on to the bonny, bonny banks of Loch Lomond, expecting to entrain again at Glasgow tomorrow night, returning refreshed in mind and body after our fortnight's holiday to our work in London. To our delight – and will my Scottish friends in the audience forgive me if I add to our surprise? – we detrained early in the morning at Perth under a sky of cloudless azure. I shall not take up your time by dwelling on the beauties and absorbing interest of our route, on Birnam wood familiar to students of Macbeth or on the gorge of Killiecrankie where the romantic Dundee met his end. Let it suffice to say that on the night of Wednesday, 11 August, we pitched our camp on the northerly banks of lovely Loch Hoo. Lovely, do I say? Yes, lovely indeed save for one object which defiled the beauty of the scene. That object was a blatant freshly-painted notice-board inscribed with the words with which so many of you are so painfully familiar. No camping. (*Loud cries of "Shame".*) Shame indeed! Shame upon the man who erects such a notice-board and thereby proclaims to the world his anti-social bent and his anti-democratic bias! You who have been privileged to wander carefree adown the pleasances of Ouse Park, have your eyes been revolted by such a notice-board? (*Loud cries of "No".*) Where over the many broad acres owned by your revered President will you find such a notice-board? (*Cries of "Nowhere".*) Nowhere indeed! And why? Because Lord Buntingdon regards his ownership of some eleven thousand acres in Bedfordshire less as ownership than as a sacred trust. (*Loud cheers, during which the owner himself pondered gratefully on the absence of reporters.*) You will not be surprised to hear that we paid no attention to the forbidding notice-board, and you will signify your approval in the usual manner when I tell you that we actually pitched our camp right round this preposterous scarecrow. (*Applause and laughter.*) We had no jugs of wine, but we had jugs of water filled from a babbling stream close at hand. We had loaves of bread, but we had cheese also. And in some cases thou wast – or shall I say wert? – beside me in the wilderness. No matter. For all of us wilderness was Paradise enow. And to add the last touch to our enjoyment we had with us our Little Songster, which under the expert eye of our friend Tom Camidge discoursed sweet music until the whole party, pleasantly tired by the long day's hike in halcyon weather, expressed itself ready for sleep.

'We were so captivated by the site of our camp that on the vote being put to the party it was decided *nem. con.* to prolong our sojourn there for another night and to spend the day in comparative idleness preparatory to a formidable hike of twenty-five miles the following day through some of the most majestic mountain scenery in the British Isles. In the morning we bathed in the clear invigorating waters of Loch Hoo. In the afternoon we decided to wander up the braes of Strathdiddle and take our tea in the bonny purple heather, as the song hath it. The kettles were singing on the spirit-lamps. Note that, please. We were faithful to the rule of the N.U.H. which exhorts members to abstain from lighting fires where the lighting of such fires may cause the faintest risk of damage to the countryside. The kettles, I say, were singing on the spirit-lamps. The Little Songster had just been tuned in to Crooner's Corner, that very popular new feature on which the B.B.C. is so much to be congratulated because by instituting such a feature it shows it is not afraid to stand up for popular taste against the would-be tyranny of musical highbrows. Not that I condemn musical highbrows as such. Far from it. I am something of a musical highbrow myself. I positively revel in Grieg's *Peer Gynt Suite* for instance, but I do not want to ram Grieg's *Peer Gynt Suite* down the throats of those who prefer Bing Crosby or Henry Hall. But I am digressing. Well, there we were in the bonny purple heather doing no harm to anybody or anything, waiting for the kettles to boil and listening to one of Henry Hall's crooners on the Little Songster, when suddenly a line of kilted figures armed with guns appeared on the skyline. When I tell you that these were the first kilts we had seen since we stepped out of the train at Perth five days earlier, and when I remind you that our hearts had recently beaten high at the tale of Killiecrankie and the death of Bonny Dundee, you will understand how excited we were by what seemed a vision of the glamorous past. Those of us who had cameras had hastily trained them upon the advancing line, when suddenly one of the kilted figures charged forward ahead of the rest and in the voice of a bull of Bashan demanded to know what we were doing on his land. I as the senior of the party and Secretary of the N.U.H. stepped forward to explain the scope and objects of the Union, but before I was able to utter more than a few words this Mr MacDonald of Ben Nevis as he calls himself seized the collar of my shirt and shook me — I will not say as a dog shakes a rat because I absolutely refuse to admit the justice of such a comparison. But no matter. He was a bigger man than myself and he did not scruple to take a mean advantage of his strength and size. Then he dropped me in a sudden access of fresh rage and fired both barrels of his gun into Tom Camidge's Little Songster. I shall leave Tom Camidge to tell his own story. It is enough to say now that when he protested at the brutal treatment of his portable wireless-set this bully MacDonald turned on Tom and shook him as violently and brutally as he had shaken me. This naturally roused Miss Winifred

Gosnay, who with great courage like a real Joan of Arc attacked the infuriated landowner with her staff.

'Girls and boys, in that moment for the first time in my life I was tempted to regret that I was a bachelor, so inspiring was the sight of this noble-hearted girl, heedless of all save that the man she loved was in danger, dashing recklessly to his help. The vigour of her attack was such that the minions of Mr MacDonald of Ben Nevis were alarmed. A hefty young woman, who we learnt afterwards was one of his own daughters, gripped Winifred Gosnay by the back of her shorts and flung her on the ground with cowardly ferocity. A moment later and we were all being attacked, and attacked by men armed with guns, mark you, by men prepared, moreover, to use those guns, as was shown when the owner of the land shot Tom Camidge's Little Songster. Well, we put up a great struggle against impossible odds, but at last we were surrounded, disarmed, and forced into a lorry which drove us at high speed to Glenbogle Castle, the residence of this so-called MacDonald of Ben Nevis. You will perhaps laugh when I tell you that his servile dependants fawn upon him by calling him Ben Nevis as if he were in all sooth actually the tallest mountain in the British Isles instead of a common Fascist bully tricked out in a kilt and the unworthy proprietor of some of the finest scenery in the land.

'When we reached the Castle, the male and female members of the party were torn apart, and both were dragged off to separate noisome dungeons. Girls and boys, you may well ask if you are listening to a tale of something that happened during the Wars of the Roses. But you are not. On the evening of yesterday week, 12 August, in this twentieth century of ours, sixteen members of the N.U.H. were incarcerated in dungeons by a kilted Fascist bully. (*A storm of boohs, hisses, and catcalls*.) You are shocked. You may well be shocked. But let me continue. Apparently the wife of this Highland gentleman (*boohs*), the wife, I say, was touched by the plight of those unfortunate girls, some of whose experiences in the dungeon you will presently hear from the lips of Miss Winifred Gosnay, and Mrs MacDonald caused them to be released by the hands of the private chaplain. I do not wish to say a word which can offend the religious susceptibilities of anybody present, but I must declare that a clergyman who accepts the employment of a man like this MacDonald of Ben Nevis degrades his cloth. Beside such a man the turbulent priests of the Middle Ages like Friar Tuck and Thomas à Becket were orderly God-fearing members of society. Not only did Mrs

MacDonald cause the girls to be released, but she also provided them with cold supper. I wish to say all that can be said for the other side; I am no atrocity-monger. Meanwhile, the chaplain and the head-keeper, a bearded giant of a man and the creature of MacDonald, proceeded to release the men of the party, who were incarcerated in a kind of underground bowl. But we were ready for them, yes, we were ready for them, and in a trice it was they who were the prisoners and we who were the freemen.

'Well, to cut the story short, we joined up with the girls and forced our way into the castle lounge where MacDonald and his guests were carousing together. There Tom Camidge and I warned him that he had not heard the last of the matter. I was about to expatiate further on the power of our great Union when MacDonald's pipers sounded the charge and we were driven out of the Castle by his hireling bullies and braves armed with axes. After that we tramped back to our camp and the next day we arrived at the Castle, mustered in the courtyard, and challenged MacDonald to show himself. He did show himself from the safety of a window, and we hurled execrations at him.

'You think I have finished. There is worse to come. We were hiking our way out of Glenbogle when after about three miles we were overtaken by a lorry and three motor-cars filled with fiends in human shape who literally drove us before them for eight miles. Sometimes one or other of us would fall from the road on either side into the grass. Did our tormentors care? No, they laughed. To them it was great sport. To them we were of less importance than their grouse or their stags or their rabbits.

'I have nearly done. We reached the end of Glenbogle literally battered to pieces by these cars and utterly worn out by the speed at which we had been compelled to move along one of the roughest roads in the kingdom. We were quite incapable of hiking another step. So it was decided to take the bus to Fort William, which involved a wait of three hours for half the party who could not be accommodated in the first bus. Then we decided to take the train back to London and bring our case before you. You will hear from our Acting President what action it is proposed to take against the forces of Fascist reaction. Nothing remains for me except to sit down and allow other speakers to take up the case.'

The Secretary resumed his seat amid thunderous applause, and the cheering was redoubled when Lord Buntingdon leaned over and shook him by the hand to congratulate him upon his eloquence and commiserate with him on his ordeal.

Then the President rose and called upon Miss Winifred Gosnay. By this time, however, poor Miss Gosnay was suffering acutely from stage-fright. She had frequently spoken at the Debating Society of the great London store in which she worked, and when she was invited to relate her experiences in the dungeons of Glenbogle she had heedlessly consented. But the sight of that audience of four or five hundred excited hikers was altogether too much for her self-confidence. Perhaps if she had been wearing shorts and grasping her staff she might have managed to summon up the necessary courage, but in her best summer frock and sauciest hat she was paralysed.

The Acting President went across to encourage her to rise, but she shook her head almost hysterically.

'I couldn't, Mr Buckham. I couldn't really. I wouldn't be able to say a word. I'd just make an exhibition of myself. Ask Elsie Vyell. She was in the dungeon too.'

The Acting President beckoned Tom Camidge to try his power of persuasion.

'No, Tom, please. I couldn't really. Don't go on. I'll burst into tears in a minute. I didn't think it would be like this when I said I would.'

Tom Camidge, from the long emotional experience of a two years' engagement to Winifred, advised the Acting President it would be dangerous to press his fiancée further.

Mr Buckham went over to Elsie Vyell and invited her to give the audience an account of what she and her companions had suffered in the dungeon.

'Oh, I couldn't, no, no, I really couldn't, Mr Buckham,' she declared, a nervous giggle striving to free itself from a fog of blushes.

'But Lord Buntingdon is particularly anxious that you should tell the story of the mouse,' Mr Buckham pressed.

Poor Elsie Vyell, torn between the embarrassment of disobliging Lord Buntingdon and of addressing the audience, surrendered and was led to the front of the platform by Mr Buckham.

'I've really nothing to say,' she assured the audience, who by an encouraging cheer made her more nervous than ever, so nervous indeed that the convulsive movement she gave seemed the preliminary to a dive from the platform into the middle of the people in the front seats.

'You're doing splendidly, Miss Vyell,' came the suave voice of the

Honorary Treasurer, who was the officer of the Union seated nearest to her. In private life the Treasurer was Mr Fortescue Wilson, affectionately known as Cutie Wilson to the outlying northern suburb in which he practised as a dentist. 'Don't be afraid. Just speak up.'

Now Miss Vyell lived in the same suburb as Mr Wilson and was a patient of his, and she responded mechanically to the quiet confidence of the voice that bade her 'speak up' as she had often obeyed the same voice bidding her 'open, please'.

'Well, now I'm here,' she started off breathlessly, 'I may as well tell you what happened to Winifred Gosnay in this horrible place where we were all shut up in the dark. It was a sort of coal-cellar, only there was no coal. I was using shocking language (*sympathetic cheers and laughter*) and one of the girls told me to shut up and another girl said what of it and she said what I said was what it was. And then there was a most shocking shriek and Winifred Gosnay called out something was walking up the inside of her leg. Well, of course that started all of us off shrieking and Winifred got a bit annoyed because it wasn't walking up us and then she screamed again because it was biting her, and when we struck a match we couldn't see anything and then the clergyman came with a lantern and let us out and just as he came in Winifred screamed again and a mouse jumped out of her shorts.'

The feminine part of the audience, which was quite half of it, emitted a loud gasp of horror, and stifled shrieks were heard from different parts of the hall. Miss Vyell was dimly aware that any tale of atrocity she could relate after the mouse would be an anticlimax, but she had no notion how to retire from the platform, and stood there, twisting her handkerchief and heaving helplessly.

Once again Mr Fortescue Wilson came to her rescue.

'Thank you, Miss Vyell,' he said in that tone of quiet confidence in which he had often congratulated her upon keeping her mouth open so patiently and at last gave her leave to shut it.

She turned quickly and went back to her seat, and while the auditorium rang with applause he leant over to the table on the platform and poured her out a glass of water which he handed her as he had handed to her so many glasses of water.

'Well done, Miss Vyell,' said Lord Buntingdon benignly, and if Miss Gosnay felt a prick of jealousy it ceased to smart almost at once when her fiancé Tom Camidge began to address the audience. His speech and the two others that succeeded added little to what Mr Prew had already related, and the chairman was beginning to look rather bored. One of the most powerful weapons in the hands of evil is that after a time the basest and most barbaric actions under repetition get accepted as normal occurrences and fail to shock. Moreover, the experience gained from debating such topics as the advantage of collective security at the weekly meetings of this or that local debating society was inadequate to provide the technique required to hold the attention of as large an audience as this. The expressions of indignation grew gradually fainter as successive members related their experience, and it was evident that a more galvanic oratory was required if the National Union of Hikers was to be stimulated into effective action.

Fortunately Mr Percy Buckham was at hand to administer such a stimulus. He possessed, indeed, all the attributes a demagogue requires. His voice was as insistent as a mechanical drill, but the timbre was nevertheless pleasing. He had a chin which gave to his countenance the kind of romantic determination that a cowcatcher gives to the locomotive of a prairie express. He had a forefinger which when pointed at his audience had the admonitory force of a loaded pistol. He was as warm and fluent as the hotwater tap of a hotel bath, as self-confident as an Orangeman contesting a seat in County Down, and as full of catchpenny emotion as an illustrated daily.

'My lord, fellow-members of the great National Union of Hikers, lend me your ears,' Mr Buckham cried, and the meeting came back to life, with cheers and laughter for that phrase which by now was associated in the mind of the general public much more closely with Percy Buckham and his Little Songster than with Mark Antony and his funeral oration.

'I look round me at this magnificent gathering and I ask myself if it is imaginable that the young men and young women who have heard the story they have heard tonight will not exact an eye for an eye and a tooth for a tooth from this proud tyrant who has dared to question their right to freedom. And as I watch your muscles grow taut, your mouths grimly set, and your eyes flash, I know that it is not imaginable. Freedom! Is there any word in this wonderful English language of ours except the word "mother" which can win a comparable response from our hearts? Freedom! Do you remember, some of you, that day in June when a party of us hiked to Runnymede on the anniversary of the signing of the Magna Carta? Do you haply recall the few words I had the privilege of addressing to you on that sacred day in the annals of democracy? Did I not urge you then to give up everything, even life itself, rather than surrender one jot, one tittle, or one iota of your precious freedom? (*Loud and prolonged cheers from the audience, most of whom were chained to office-stools or counters for fifty weeks every year.*) I hear in that noble outburst of spontaneous cheering the answer. No, you will not renounce your freedom, any more than your forefathers would renounce it at Runnymede, at the threat of Castile's dark fleet, at the bidding of James II, or even for the great Duke of Wellington himself.'

This last allusion puzzled the audience, who supposed that the great Duke of Wellington had won a conspicuous victory for freedom by defeating Napoleon at Waterloo. Mr Buckham perceived with the demagogue's quick instinct that his last allusion had missed its mark and hastily reloaded.

'The great Duke of Wellington who, after gloriously freeing Europe from the tyranny of Napoleon Bonaparte, lost touch with the people as he grew older and sought to hamstring the onward strides of democracy by impeding the progress of the Reform Bill. And why did the Duke of Wellington lose touch with the people? Because he lost touch with youth, and a hundred years ago the future of this country of ours was as much in the hands of youth as it is today. Well, perhaps not quite as much, for never in the history of the world has the future depended so much upon youth as it depends today. (*A loud "hear, hear" from Mr Sydney Prew.*) Our energetic secretary agrees with me, I am glad to find. Youth! Is there any word in this sublime English language of ours except the words "freedom" and "mother" which can make our hearts beat so fast? Why does hiking occupy the position it does in the esteem of sagacious men of rank and experience like our President? Because it is essentially a youth movement. Lord Buntingdon in his wisdom knows that it is to youth we must look if we are to weather safely the storms which already threaten our horizon. So it is to you, the youth of Britain, that I appeal now to assert your right to breathe the same air as this proud tyrant, MacDonald of Ben Nevis. I, Percy Buckham of Primrose Hill, speaking as the Acting President of the National Union of Hikers and in the name of all my fellow-members, defy him. I claim the right to breathe the same air as he breathes. I claim the right to hike across the ground he owns. I demand the hospitality of that ground for our sleeping bodies.

'MacDonald of Ben Nevis with two cowardly shots from a double-barrelled gun disabled a portable wireless-set whose merits I have had the honour to proclaim to the world. When MacDonald of Ben Nevis struck at the Little Songster he struck at Buckham of Primrose Hill. (*Cheers and excited laughter*.) Buckham of Primrose Hill will strike back. Buckham of Primrose Hill this night calls for volunteers to carry the war into the enemy's camp, and let me tell him that notice-boards inscribed "No Camping" will avail him nothing to protect that camp. MacDonald of Ben Nevis drove sixteen of you through Glenbogle with lorries and cars filled with his hirelings. Buckham of Primrose Hill with his volunteers will drive MacDonald of Ben Nevis from one end to the other of his own glen. (*Loud cheers*.) MacDonald of Ben Nevis immured sixteen members of the National Union of Hikers in his noisome dungeons. I declare here and now that I, Buckham of Primrose Hill, will lock MacDonald of Ben Nevis into his own dungeon with his own key which is now in my possession.'

And amid rapturous cheering the Acting President of the N.U.H. waved above his curly head the keys of the dungeons which Ben Nevis had expected to be brought him with his coffee that night of the Twelfth of August.

'We shall enlist volunteers tonight. The Secretary will take the names of all who are able and willing to join in this tremendous manifestation of Youth, Freedom, and Democracy against the forces of Reaction and Fascism (*boohs and catcalls*). I know that many of you have already taken your holidays for this year. Those of you who have will regret their inability to share in the fight like the gentlemen who King Harry said would regret being absent from the glorious field of Agincourt. Those of you who have not yet taken your annual holiday will rejoice, I know, to avail yourselves of the opportunity that presents itself to strike a blow for Youth, Freedom, and Democracy. And do not let our young Joan of Arcs hold back. We want the army that marches against MacDonald of Ben Nevis to be truly representative of our great Union. I have myself cancelled my berth for a month's pleasure cruise in the Mediterranean in order that I may devote the whole of my holiday to making this roistering bully bite the dust. (*Loud and long cheers*.) No doubt Mr MacDonald expected our injured members would meekly sue him in a court of law. No doubt he expected to counter-sue for trespass and damage to his property. I venture to prophesy that we shall surprise him by our prompt and resolute action. I do not propose and you will not ask me to give you the details of our campaign. When we can estimate the strength of which we can dispose I shall call a council of war. I hope that within a week the vanguard of our Expeditionary Force can march.

'I have little to add. This is a critical evening in the history of our great Union. I venture to say that upon the response to my call for volunteers the whole future of hiking in this country depends. If we fail our glorious pastime, why then, the sooner we go back to bicycling the better.'

As he uttered this fearful taunt the Acting President of the N.U.H. thrust his forefinger at the audience as you may see it out-thrust in many a paper to demand your attention for the merits of the Little Songster. Then he slowly and gravely lowered his arm and, after bowing to Lord Buntingdon, resumed his seat.

The President rose.

'Fellow members of the N.U.H., after the fiery eloquence of your Acting President you will not be inclined to listen to any words of mine. You are all eager, I know, to register your names with Mr Prew. It may perhaps savour to you of a certain pusillanimity, but I think it is my duty as your President to counsel a certain moderation in any action you take against this Scotch landowner. The reprisals you take should be strictly confined to personal reprisals. They should not include his game or his crops or his fishing. I know Mr Buckham will not consider any such action, but I feel it is my duty to give you this counsel and I am sure you will appreciate the spirit in which it is given. Nothing remains for me except to ask you to accord a very hearty vote of thanks to the speakers who have given us such an enjoyable feast of oratory.'

While Mr Prew sat at a table writing down the names of the volunteers and the dates on which they would be available for active service, Lord Buntingdon took Mr Buckham aside.

'I hope you didn't mind my giving that little caution, Mr Buckham. I know you would frown upon any type of agrarian outrage, but I felt it would help if I expressed myself strongly against it. Let this be a personal struggle with this MacDonald fellow, but don't damage his property.'

'You can rely on me, Lord Buntingdon.'

'That's capital. Well, I think I'll be getting back to Ouse Hall. Will you kindly ask somebody to call my chauffeur?'

Chapter 14

THE GLENBOGLE GATHERING

During the week after that meeting in the Astrovegetarian Hall, of whose weighty decisions not a rumour reached the Chieftain, he was worried by two questions. First whether his son Hector MacDonald, Younger, of Ben Nevis would arrive from India in time for the Glenbogle Gathering on Saturday, 28 August, and secondly whether the sun would shine upon the great occasion.

His mind was put at rest over Hector by receiving a telegram on Thursday to say he would be at Fort William on Friday morning, after which his anxiety was concentrated upon the weather. A dozen times a day he played a tattoo upon the aneroid barometer, and as for Admiral Fitzroy's liquid column, on which the devil's own tattoo would have made no impression, it ran a danger of being petrified into eternal insensitiveness to any atmospheric pressure by the gorgonian glares with which he was continually regarding it.

'I can't understand this infernal weather,' he barked. 'Can you understand this infernal weather, Hugh?'

The Laird of Kilwhillie was again staying in the Castle to support his old friend as always on any great Glenbogle occasion. It might have been expected that after receiving £1,000 more for Knocknacolly than he had agreed to accept he would have been in high spirits, but he was not. The Celtic melancholy in which he was frequently plunged had never appeared so profound. He was almost like a man brooding over some presentiment of disaster, and when addressed seemed to emerge with a start from some dark world of his own horror-haunted imagination.

'I said, "Can you understand this infernal weather, Hugh?" ' Ben Nevis barked more loudly.

'It's the usual weather we get about now.'

'I never heard such nonsense.'

'I cannot recall more than two Gatherings without any rain at all.'

'What a preposterous statement, Hugh! Why, it didn't rain last year.'

'That is one of the Gatherings I was thinking of.'

'I don't know what's the matter with you. Have you had any bad news?'

'No, no,' said the Laird of Kilwhillie, sighing deeply.

'I haven't seen you so gloomy since that champion Belted Galloway cow of yours got bogged and had to be destroyed. You must cheer up. I think the glass has gone up a fraction since morning. We shall probably have a splendid Gathering. Twenty-one coming to lunch, which with ourselves in the Castle will make thirty-four. Royde is keen as mustard on the Gathering.'

Kilwhillie looked even gloomier if possible.

'He is, is he? Did he say why particularly?'

'Well, it'll be a new experience for him, won't it?'

'Oh yes, quite. Yes, a new experience. I hope it won't be very sunny.'

'Why on earth don't you want it to be sunny? I hope the sun will blaze down,' Ben Nevis declared, and rushing across to the aneroid barometer he drummed on it a roll that should have roused Napoleon himself from the tomb.

'Yes, I think the glass really is inclined to go up at last,' he declared.

'Who are coming on Saturday?' Kilwhillie asked.

'Well, the Lindsay-Wolseleys of course, and Bertie Bottley and Jack Fraser and Rawstorne, and oh, well, the usual crowd. Macintosh was coming, but he has some ploy of his own. Lochiel can't come either. Nor can Dunstaffnage. Ross was coming, but he wired me this morning he wouldn't be able to manage it.'

'The Duke, you mean?'

'Yes. Did you mutter "thank god", Hugh?'

'No, I was only clearing my throat.'

'I always thought you liked Ross.'

'So I do,' said Kilwhillie warmly. 'I like him and respect him. I consider him the greatest living authority on Highland dress. You're sure he's not coming?'

'No; I told you he wired me this morning. He has to open a sale of work at Strathpeffer. He'd promised and couldn't get out of it. What a strange fellow you are, Hugh. A minute ago you were in a state of utter gloom, and now you're humming to yourself.'

'I often do that, Donald. I caught the habit from my dear old mother. She used to hum over her patience, and then I used to hum.'

'I never heard you hum before,' said Ben Nevis, a little suspiciously. At that moment Chester Royde came into the Great Hall, and the Chieftain's attention was diverted from Kilwhillie's humming.

'Hullo, Royde. The glass has gone up a fraction since this morning. I believe we shall get it fine on Saturday.'

'That's corking,' said the American guest enthusiastically. 'But I give you fair warning, Ben Nevis, I'm going to enjoy myself, wet or fine.'

Presently he drew near to Kilwhillie and said in a low voice:

'It's arrived. It's up in my dressing-room now.'

'Oh, that's splendid,' Kilwhillie gulped.

'Some time today or tomorrow I'd be mighty glad if you'd come along up to my room. I'd like to dress myself from top to toe and have you give me the O.K. for Saturday.'

'Of course, I'll be delighted.' Kilwhillie gulped again.

'What are you two plotting over there?' their host barked genially.

But at that moment a piece of blue sky about the size of the flag over the Cambridge University Boathouse appeared in the sky, and he went charging out into the courtyard to gloat up at it.

'I'm afraid it is going to be fine on Saturday,' Kilwhillie murmured to himself.

'Afraid it is going to be fine?' Chester Royde exclaimed.

'Did I say that, Royde? I meant I'm afraid it's *not* going to be fine.'

'Well, I don't give a darn either way, Kilwhillie. I guess this orange kilt of mine will look fine if it's a second deluge.'

'Orange kilt?' Kilwhillie gasped. 'But you decided on a purple one.'

'Oh, I'm having a purple one as well, but it's the orange one they've sent along from Inverness. I told the tailor if he couldn't get both of them made in time to put all his work into finishing the orange one.'

'And he has?'

'He certainly has. It's a peach. Say, why don't you come up and have a look at it?'

'I think I'll wait till you have it on,' said Kilwhillie in the voice of a man under sentence of death.

'But don't breathe a word to Carrie about it. I aim to give her a little surprise on Saturday morning.'

'I don't think you'll miss,' Kilwhillie commented, with a touch of the sardonic in his tone.

The morning of Friday was the nicest since the rain started on the day Chester Royde went stalking. Ben Nevis, excited by the prospect of a really brilliant day for the Gathering and the arrival of his eldest son, went barking all over the place with such persistency that his guests retreated to some of the more remote rooms in the Castle, unable to deal with the noise so early in the day.

Carrie and Myrtle retired to the room in the North Tower, to discuss whether or not to send word to Alan Macmillan to bring the architect from Knocknacolly and come to the Gathering, or whether to wait until James Buchanan arrived with the deeds early next week, before presenting them all at Glenbogle.

'I wouldn't like it if Ben Nevis was rude to Alan,' said Carrie.

'Indeed, no, nor would I,' her sister-in-law affirmed.

'And perhaps as they're arriving tomorrow,' Carrie went on, 'they might find the walk from Knocknacolly a bit tiring.'

'I believe they would. I think we'll drive over to Knocknacolly in your funny little runabout on Sunday,' said Myrtle. 'I think that will be more fun. Besides, there's no need for Chester to meet them till James Buchanan comes. And if this architect turns out to be a nice boy we can have a party of our own.'

Carrie agreed a little dubiously. She had a notion that Myrtle intended to start her right off on architecture.

At that moment the noise of what they had supposed was the barking of Ben Nevis reached even this remote room. In point of fact it was the sound of Old Ben Nevis and Young Ben Nevis barking at one another, for Hector had just driven up to the Castle.

The Chieftain had not exaggerated when he said his eldest son was his second self. To be sure, Hector was neither so florid nor so weatherbeaten as his father, and though his nose was the authentic eagle's beak of Mac 'ic Eachainn it lacked as yet the rich deep hues of amaranth and damson which could flood his father's. He was slimmer too, naturally, and was indeed a fine figure of a young man; but he had the same choleric blue eyes, and already even at twenty-five the same rumbustious voice.

Carrie observed, a little gladly it may be added, that her sister-in-law was obviously agreeably surprised by Hector MacDonald, Younger, of Ben Nevis.

'He's had a good trip. You had a good trip, Hector, didn't you?' Ben Nevis bellowed.

'Absolutely tophole,' Hector bellowed back. 'The Colonel wasn't too keen on giving me leave. I won't be able to take more than the inside of a week.'

'Oh, well, one can do a lot in a week. Now would you like some more breakfast?'

'No, thanks, I had a very good breakfast in the train. But I think I'll go and get out of these clothes, and have a bath.'

'That's the stuff.'

And as Hector MacDonald, Younger, of Ben Nevis strode off towards his room, Angus MacQuat piped before him *Mac 'ic Eachainn's Return to Glenbogle*.

On the morning of 28 August Carrie awoke to the agreeable thought that Ben Nevis had been granted his desire and that it was a gloriously fine day. As a matter of fact it was a fine day, but the rich glow that filled the room was caused not by the sun but by her own husband, who was standing at the foot of the bed wearing a kilt that was not so much orange as flame-coloured, a doublet of amber tweed, and a heavily-brassed leather sporran.

'Chester! That's why you asked me whether I liked orange or purple best. But why didn't you wear my tartan – the Ben Nevis Macdonald?'

'Listen, sweetheart, I went into the whole business of tartans with Kilwhillie, and he ruled right out the idea of wearing a wife's tartan. By what I could make out those who know about these things calculate no man can do anything much dirtier than sport his wife's tartan. Kilwhillie classed a man who sported his wife's tartan with cattle-rustlers and kidnappers and communists. He wanted me to have a grey kilt, but I said "nothing doing". And then he admitted that some guy in the eighteenth century used to wear a purple kilt. And that was my first idea. In fact there's a purple kilt being made for me right now in Inverness. But you remember those Scottish Nationalists who got Ben Nevis's goat?'

'I remember a whole lot of foolish talk about Scottish Nationalists, yes.'

'All right, honey, don't you get peeved now. But one of those Scottish Nationalists was wearing a red and yellow kilt which took my eye as we drove past in the car. And I said to myself right then I'd have an orange kilt.'

'A red and yellow kilt? That sounds like the Macmillan tartan. Mr Macmillan, the young poet I told you about, wears a red and yellow kilt. Or at least he did when I met him in Edinburgh. By the way, I'm expecting him and Mr Menzies, the architect, to reach Knocknacolly today, and I thought Myrtle and I would drive over tomorrow and see how they're getting along.'

'That's fine. But you haven't said what you think of my costume?'

'Why, Chester, I think you look a perfectly good Highlander.'

'Are you pleased I've shown my appreciation of your ancestral territory like this?'

'Chester, you've been just as sweet as you could be about my country.'

'I was a bit worried at first I'd look too fat in a kilt, but the tailor told me he'd far sooner make a kilt for a figure like mine than for one of those thin fellows. Wilton was a bit obstructive about it.' Wilton was Chester Royde's English valet.

'He was?'

'Yes; I think he was annoyed because I dressed myself yesterday afternoon and asked Kilwhillie to look me over.'

'And Kilwhillie said it was all right?'

'I don't think he's tickled to death by the orange kilt. He said it was brighter than he thought it would be. He said he'd have advised a saffron kilt, the kind some of the Irish use, if he'd known I was going all out on orange. He put me wise, too, about the sporran.'

'How?'

'Why, I thought it would be more convenient to wear it on one side like a trouser pocket. But it seems that for a fellow to wear his sporran on one side tells against him pretty heavily in Highland society. I suppose I'll soon get used to walking about like a kangaroo with a pouch in front of me, but I still think the place for a pocket is on the side. I asked him if there was any objection to me carrying an extra sporran on the hip, but that suggestion upset him a lot. He wouldn't hear of it. Still, there's no question about it, Carrie. The kilt's pretty comfortable.'

Chester Royde took a turn round the room to demonstrate the ease with which he could carry the unfamiliar garment.

'You look very comfortable,' his wife assured him.

Chester stopped suddenly and gazed at her gravely.

'Say, Carrie, what do you suppose I'm wearing underneath this kilt?'

'Why, I don't know, Chester. Little panties?'

'Little panties nothing. I'm not wearing a darned thing underneath except the tails of my shirt.'

'Didn't the tailor send them?'

'Nobody wears anything underneath a kilt.'

'Chester, I don't believe it.'

'Well, would I be such a mutt as to go about like a nood statue hung around with a curtain unless it was what they were all doing?'

'Chester, you *must* have made a mistake.'

'No mistake at all. The tailor told me some folk wore tartan trews when they were going to a dance. They're the kind of panties old maids used to wear. But when I consulted Kilwhillie he said he wouldn't agree even to that. He said if I'd made up my mind to wear the kilt I must wear the kilt properly, or he'd take no responsibility in the matter.'

'He's taken on a much bigger responsibility as it is,' Carrie declared.

'Aw, don't worry. I'm not going to fall down on this business.'

'I hope not. If you start falling down the sooner you go back to your own clothes the better.'

'You're not nervous about me, are you, Carrie?'

'Well, I rather wish you hadn't told me about wearing nothing underneath. I feel a bit nervous even about Ben Nevis now. But, look here, you're dressed or as much dressed as you can be. You'd better go on down to breakfast and let me get dressed.'

'It isn't breakfast-time yet.'

'What time is it?'

Chester looked at his watch.

'Twenty-five after seven.'

'What?' Carrie gasped indignantly. 'And you're up and dressed already?'

'I wanted to dress myself before Wilton came up. It gives me a kind of kick to keep him in the background over this kilt business. I don't think he thought I was serious when I said I was going to wear it today.'

'What are you going to do till breakfast?'

'I'm going outside to practise walking about by myself.'

Just after eight o'clock when Angus MacQuat was playing the customary aubade beneath the window of his chief, for the first time in twenty years he played a false note in the middle of *Iomradh Mhic 'ic Eachainn*. It was caused by suddenly catching sight of Chester Royde coming round the corner of the North Tower.

Ben Nevis rushed to the window to let his piper know his mistake had not escaped his ears and received his first sight of Chester Royde.

'My god, Trixie,' he turned to shout at his wife, 'there's a Scottish Nationalist in the courtyard.'

'Well, you can't do anything about it in your pyjamas, Donald,' she boomed placidly from the four-poster.

The Chieftain rushed to the window again to demonstrate that he could do something about it and this time recognized his cherished guest.

'Hullo, Royde,' he bellowed down, 'this is a very sporting effort on your part. By Jove, it is! All right, Angus, you needn't go on playing.'

The piper saluted and retired. Just before he vanished round the Castle walls he threw a backward glance over his shoulder, and then with a puzzled shake of the head proceeded on his way to his porridge.

'I can't quite make out what that tartan is,' Ben Nevis was calling down.

'It isn't a tartan at all,' Royde replied. 'Kilwhillie advised me to steer clear of tartans. This is his idea of a good substitoot.'

'Do you know what I thought you were at first? I thought you were a Scottish Nationalist. I did, upon my soul. Well, I must say it was jolly nice of you, Royde, to think of this way of paying a little tribute to the Gathering. And by Jove, what a day, eh?'

'Some day.'

'I knew it was going to be fine. We always get fine weather for our Gathering. Last year it was lovely. Well, I must go and get dressed myself. See you presently at breakfast.'

Back in his room Ben Nevis turned to his wife. 'I can't understand why Hugh advised Royde to get an orange kilt, Trixie.'

'An orange kilt?' Mrs MacDonald boomed in equable astonishment.

'Well, it's really more a kind of orange-scarlet. I cannot understand why Hugh chose such a bright colour. He hates bright colours. That Erracht Cameron tartan he wears is pretty full, but even so he always buries a new kilt for two years in a bog before he'll put it on. I really can't understand it. Well, we've got an absolutely glorious day for our dear old Glenbogle Gathering, Trixie.'

'I'm so glad, dear.'

'And I think that pretty little Royde girl took quite a fancy to Hector, didn't you? I noticed her smiling at him a lot last night at dinner.'

'Well, it would be a very wonderful match for her if Hector did take a fancy to *her*,' said Hector's mother.

'I wish that silly Colonel of his had given him more leave. But Rose-Ross always was a silly fellow. Talking of Ross I wish the Duke was coming today. I'd have quite liked to hear what he had to say to Hugh when I told him Hugh advised Royde to get that orange-scarlet kilt.'

However, any speculations in which Ben Nevis was tempted to

indulge about Chester Royde's kilt or his son's ability in the time at his disposal to secure the hand of Myrtle Royde were soon ousted from his mind by the claims of the Glenbogle Gathering upon his attention. Those familiar with the West Highlands and the slight inclination in that part of the world towards the romantic timelessness which is prosaically called unpunctuality will appreciate what a struggle the Chieftain had every year to begin the Games not more than two hours after the printed announcements hung up even as far as in the shops of Fort William advertised that they would begin. This was ten o'clock, but the remoteness of Glenbogle made it difficult to muster many spectators from outside the glen by that time. Therefore, naturally, those who lived in and round about the Castle took it for granted that not many would have arrived before eleven o'clock at the earliest and usually started to get ready themselves at that hour. Since the introduction of summer time the tendency had been to get ready even later than that because, as they argued, it was not really eleven o'clock but only ten o'clock. They were still devoted to Mr Lloyd George on account of old-age pensions, but their devotion did not extend to according what was called Lloyd George's time an equality with God's time.

The combination of Harrow and Cambridge with his own natural impetuosity had given Ben Nevis that passion for punctuality of which we have already had a taste in his irritation when dinner was postponed on the night of the Twelfth of August; and if the march headed by himself and his pipers to Achnabo, the field where the Gathering was held, did not leave the courtyard of the Castle by half past eleven and thus allow the games to start before noon he grew fierce.

The exhilarating prospect of a cloudless day and the presence of his eldest son made him more than usually anxious this year to reach the field as soon as possible and more than usually boisterous over the preliminary marshalling.

'You're rather late, Wolseley . . . glad to see you, Mrs Wolseley . . . we're just forming up in the courtyard . . . the ladies are going on ahead . . . ah, there you are, Bertie . . . you'd better take up your place . . . if any of the visiting pipers who are competing want to join you, Angus, you'd better get them lined up . . . ah, Rawstorne, where's Jack Fraser? . . . has anybody seen Jack Fraser? . . . oh, there you are, Jack, you're rather late . . . Hugh! Hugh! Hugh! . . . where the deuce is Kilwhillie? . . . ah, there you are, Hugh . . . look here. I want you to march on the right of Royde . . . I'm going to put him on my right . . .

Hector will be on my left . . . I want nothing but kilts in the front line . . . Wolseley, will you and Bottley muster the second line round you . . . now, we'll give the ladies another five minutes . . . Angus! Angus! Angus! . . . where the deuce is Angus MacQuat? . . . ah, there you are, Angus . . . now, you know what you have to play us down with . . . *Mac 'ic Eachainn's March to Sheriffmuir* until we approach the field, and then break into *Clan Donald is Here* . . . Catriona! Mary!! . . . Good lord, haven't you started down to the field yet? . . . Where's your mother? . . . Trixie! Trixie!!! . . . I'm sorry, Trixie, I didn't see you were just behind me . . . but do make the ladies move along . . . Mrs Wolseley and Mrs Rawstorne and Lady Bottley went on five minutes ago . . . oh, you're waiting for Carrie and Myrtle . . . ah, there they are . . . come along, young ladies. We can't begin our march until you're on the field . . .'

At last the group of thirty or so friends, relations, and dependants privileged to accompany Mac 'ic Eachainn on this glorious occasion was marshalled and waited only the command of Ben Nevis to march. He donned the high bonnet with the two eagle's feathers of a chieftain in which Raeburn had painted his great-grandfather, and which he wore only on the day of the Glenbogle Gathering.

'Now, are you all ready?' he bellowed. 'Very well then, on we go!'

The skirling of ten pipers rent the air as they stepped out to the tune of *Mac 'ic Eachainn's March to Sheriffmuir*, followed by the honoured guests, every man with a cromag nearly as tall as a window-pole.

'Enjoying this, Royde?' Ben Nevis asked.

'Why, I should say I am,' replied his guest, who had added to the brilliancy of his appearance by carrying an orange plaid over his shoulder. In fact to a casual glance it might have seemed for a moment that the right side of Ben Nevis was in eruption.

But not even that rumbustious voice could compete with ten pipers blowing full blast three or four yards in front of it, and the Chieftain was silent until he had taken his seat on the mound which overlooked the arena.

Then he observed as he had observed at the beginning of every Glenbogle Gathering for the last twenty-five years:

'Not so many here yet as there ought to be.'

There never had been and there never would be enough people with faith that games advertised to begin at ten o'clock would begin much before one o'clock. In any case except to piping experts the earlier part of the proceedings was a little dull, consisting as it did of the same example of *ceòl mór* – the classical music of the bagpipe – played by twelve pipers in turn on a wooden platform before which sat the judges with notebooks and pencils, marking the faults and merits of each performer's grace-notes, slides, and doublings. Kilwhillie was one of the judges; Colonel Lindsay-Wolseley was another; the third was a former pipe-major of the Clanranalds called Farquhar Macphail. It was noticeable that both Kilwhillie and the Colonel always ascertained his opinion of each performance first, and then after the very faintest camouflage of expert hesitation proceeded to agree with it. If Pipe-major Macphail had been a cynic he might have lured Kilwhillie or the Colonel into expressing a positive opinion of some performance before he gave his; but Pipe-major Macphail was not a cynic. Through twenty-one years' service with The Duke of Clarence's Own Clanranald Highlanders (The Inverness-shire Greens) he had preserved a simple belief in human nature.

'You're not looking quite so well this beautiful morning, Kilwhillie,' he observed in an interval of silence while one of the competitors was intent upon his tuning slides. 'No, sir, you're not looking so well as usual.'

'I'm quite all right, Pipe-major,' said the Laird, giving a listless tug at his moustache. He could not explain that a light remark of his lifelong friend and neighbour Ben Nevis was weighing very heavily upon his mind. Pipe-major Macphail was not to know that Ben Nevis had said he could not understand why he had advised Chester Royde to choose an orange kilt, and then he added, 'You'll have Ross on your trail, Hugh, when he hears about it.'

Kilwhillie was not inclined to hero-worship, but the Duke of Ross he had long worshipped not for his rank but for his infallible judgement on any question connected with Highland dress, jewellery, use, custom, lore, genealogy, and coat-armour.

And as if in answer to his unspoken thoughts Colonel Lindsay-Wolseley asked him at this moment why he had allowed that American fellow to rig himself out in that extraordinary get-up.

'It's not my business, Wolseley,' Kilwhillie snapped. 'I'm not his tailor.'

'No, no, of course not,' said the Colonel soothingly. He had never heard Kilwhillie bite like this at a remark. 'I just thought with a great authority like you at hand he'd have taken the chance of a little good advice. I wish the Duke had been able to come today. I can just imagine what he would have said.'

The Colonel chuckled to himself, and then concentrated on the eleventh performance of the pibroch chosen for the competition.

Kilwhillie hunched himself moodily in his chair. On many a previous morning when Glenbogle gathered he had sat wrapped in his plaid while the rain poured down, listening much more cheerfully to the same composition played over and over again.

In another part of the field the competition for putting the stone was proceeding, to describe which would be even more tedious than to watch it.

This, indeed, was the hour of the Glenbogle Gathering, when those who were wandering round the field asked themselves why they had arrived only two hours late. The friends from Fort Augustus or Fort William they were expecting to meet and with whom they were hoping to enjoy a fruitful gossip had not yet arrived. Even from Kenspeckle only one busload had been delivered as yet.

Myrtle Royde, catching the prevailing mood, was thinking how pleasant it would be if among the spectators the red and yellow of the Macmillan tartan, brighter even than that tango kilt Chester was wearing, should suddenly flicker into view, when a voice barked in her ear:

'Enjoying yourself? You're looking very thoughtful.'

She turned to see Young Ben Nevis smiling down at her.

'I was wondering just exactly what they were doing with that stone.'

'Putting it.'

'Putting it where?'

'As far as they can. Iain's ahead now with his second put. I think myself he'll win, though old Murdoch usually fetches up a bit of extra beef for his third put.'

'I can't pretend to be terribly excited, Lootenant.'

Young Ben Nevis blinked. His father had pressed upon him the immense advantage it would be to consider Myrtle Royde as a prospective twenty-fourth Lady of Ben Nevis, but like his brother Murdoch before him he was a little startled to be addressed as Lieutenant with the pronunciation 'Lootenant'.

'I say, don't call me that,' he begged.

'Well, what do I call you? Ben Nevis Junior sounds kind of awkward to me.'

'Couldn't you manage "Hector"?'

'Why, I dare say I wouldn't find it terribly difficult, Hector.'

'That's topping. Look here, you'll give me the first eightsome tonight?'

'The first what?'

'The first eightsome reel.'

Myrtle still looked blank.

'It's a dance.'

'But I don't know how to dance it.'

'I'll teach you before dinner. You'll learn it in no time. I think we'll manage one or two sixteensomes tonight. But we shan't get a thirty-twosome. Not enough of us.'

'Isn't that too bad? Tell me, Hector, what do you think of my brother in his kilt? I think he looks cute, don't you?'

'Yes, but I don't know why Hugh Cameron made him get an orange kilt.'

'I'd call that colour more of a tango than an orange.'

'Personally I should have advised him to get a grey one.'

'But Chester's crazy on colour.'

'Oh, great put, Murdoch! Bravo!' young Ben Nevis barked. 'I thought old Murdoch would call up some extra beef for the third round. He's a good foot beyond Iain now. Oh, good one, Kenny!'

'Who are you cheering now?'

'That's Kenny Macdonald, our blacksmith. He's an inch or two better than Murdoch, I fancy. Yes, I thought so.'

A light crepitation of applause from the few who were watching the putting was audible above the piping.

'Now it's Iain's last put. Oh, jolly good, Iain! Jolly good indeed!' the eldest brother exclaimed. 'Did you see that last put, Dad?' he shouted across the field to the Chieftain enthroned on the mound.

'Jolly good!' the Chieftain bellowed back.

The two or three competitors left failed to come within a couple of feet of Iain, who emerged from the contest as the winner amid general enthusiasm.

'We'll probably go back to the Castle now for lunch,' said Hector.

'That'll be more exciting, won't it?' Myrtle suggested.

'Oh, putting the stone's pretty exciting,' Hector insisted.

'Is it?' Myrtle asked doubtfully. 'Well, I wasn't terribly thrilled by it. It's about the least exciting thing I've seen since I came to Glenbogle.'

Far different was the scene on the field of Achnabo when Ben Nevis and his guests returned to it after lunch. Omnibuses and cars from Fort William and Fort Augustus, and even from lordly Inverness itself, had discharged their sightseers. The battered Fords and Morrises and Austins of many a village and clachan had brought gossips old and young, male and female. Former pupils were asking former schoolmasters and schoolmistresses if they recognized them. Shepherds were discussing gloomily the latest low level to which the price of wool had sunk. Crofters were exchanging tales about the misdeeds of the Department of Agriculture. Farmers were shaking their heads over the prospects for store-cattle at the next sales. Tea was being swilled in half a dozen tents and insides were being plastered with slices of chalkwhite Glasgow bread. Towards one tent with the Committee's cardboard sign a procession of slightly surreptitious figures, all with the same expression of elaborate purposelessness, was ever wending, and from the same tent another procession of figures whose tongues sometimes peeped from pursed satisfied lips but whose eyes had the innocent look of children beholding life for the first time was ever emerging. It is a remarkable tribute to the enduring influence of John Knox's ethics that in a country where enough whisky had been distilled and drunk during the four centuries of Presbyterianism to flavour every loch in Scotland, natives who take one dram of it at a public festivity like the Glenbogle Gathering should still be able to romanticize the little indulgence with the flavour of mortal sin.

Within the rope ring that enclosed the arena the change was not less remarkable. Runners were tearing round amid the excited exhortations of their supporters to win or lose races. Massive figures in kilts and vests whose muscles stood out like bumps in the mattresses of remote Highland inns were tossing the caber and throwing the hammer. And on that platform, where for three seemingly endless hours piper after piper had marched up and down playing the same example of *ceòl mór*, half a dozen little girls whose velvet doublets jingled with medals were dancing reels and strathspeys and jigs and as they leapt higher and higher displaying beneath their kilts a lather of frilly underclothes. Laughter and chatter and cheers resounded upon the sunny air, and in all that merry throng only Kilwhillie and Colonel Lindsay-Wolseley and seven pipers looked sad, the seven pipers because they had not won a prize, Kilwhillie and the Colonel because the piping had only just finished and they had not yet lunched.

'You're not one of the judges for the dancing, Hugh?' the Chieftain asked.

'I think Wolseley and I have done enough judging for the present,' Kilwhillie answered reproachfully. 'We haven't had any lunch yet, and there will be another hour or two later with the piping.'

'You'd better toddle back to the Castle. Toker will look after you. Who won in the Coalmore?'

'Angus.'

'Oh, he did, did he? That's good news.' He looked across to where Mrs MacDonald was sitting on the mound, almost as massive a female shape as the great statue of Liberty. 'Trixie! Trixie!' She looked up and acknowledged his hail with her parasol. 'Angus has won the Coalmore!'

Mrs MacDonald tried to express gratification over the result of the *ceòl mór*, which was difficult partly on account of the distance between her and her husband, but chiefly because she had been the recipient of this announcement at about this time of the afternoon in every one of the last fourteen years. True, she was carrying a parasol this year instead of an umbrella for the first time.

'Hullo,' said Ben Nevis, 'that's a big busload of hikers from Fort William.'

A number of young men in khaki shorts and the usual polychrome of shirts were alighting from an omnibus which had just driven up to the field of the Gathering.

'You're not going to order a general attack, I hope,' said Colonel Wolseley with a smile.

The Chieftain guffawed genially.

'Not today Wolseley. Glenbogle is Liberty Hall today, what? Delighted to welcome everybody here to our Gathering. Even hikers. But look here, Wolseley. You and Hugh really must go and get some lunch.'

The Laird of Kilwhillie was drawing one half of his moustache across his mouth in a manner that suggested he should eat part of it as an hors d'oeuvre if he and the Colonel did not soon sit down to a substantial meal.

They set out for the Castle, and Ben Nevis wandered patriarchally about the field. This was perhaps the hour in all his year he most enjoyed, this opportunity to meet the old friends of a lifetime, farmers and tradesmen, crofters, shepherds, schoolmasters, and gillies. The enjoyment of his patriarchal promenade was much enhanced today by the perfection of the weather. The wrinkled faces of Donaldinas and Kennethinas, of Kirsties, Morags, Floras, Peggies, and Ealaisaids usually smiled up at him from beneath dripping umbrellas. On this superb afternoon whatever moisture bedabbled them was caused not by rain but by the warmth of the blazing sun.

'Hullo, how are you, Jemima?'

'I'm feeling fine, thank you, sir. And how is yourself, Ben Nevis?'

'Grand, Jemima. Splendid Gathering, isn't it?'

'Beautiful, Ben Nevis. There never was a better, I'm sure.'

'Have you had a talk with Hector yet? He's back from India.'

'No, I haven't had a talk with Master Hector yet. From India? Fancy that now. It's very warm in India, they say.'

'Jolly warm in Glenbogle today, what?'

'Och, indeed, yes, it is warm right enough.'

'And how's the bottuck?'

Jemima managed to grasp that he was inquiring after the *bodach* or old man, and answered solemnly, 'My father's fine. He has the rheumatism sometimes. But och, he'll be ninety-five next week, and that's a great age for a man like my father.'

'Well, tell old Rory I was asking after him, Jemima.'

'I will indeed. It's himself that will be pleased when he hears Ben Nevis was asking for him.'

'I don't suppose I'll ever see ninety-five, Jemima, what?'

'Och, it's you that will be seeing more than ninety-five, Ben Nevis. Och, yes, indeed, and perhaps a hundred whatever.'

Ben Nevis took a snuff-box from his pocket and offered it to old Jemima Macdonald, the widow of a former shepherd of his. She took a hefty pinch of which she expressed keen appreciation, and the Chieftain bellowed a greeting to an old man with a beard of snow over a face like the ruins of Petra, 'rose-red and half as old as time'.

'Hullo, how are you, Alasdair?'

'Ah, well, well, well, what a beautiful day, Ben Nevis, and what a beautiful Gathering!'

'Yes, it's one of the best I ever remember. I was sorry Sandy didn't manage to do better with the caber.'

This was the grandson of the old gentleman.

'Och, he was tossing like a clown. Just like a clown. Nothing more. It's better not to be speaking about it. You're looking very well, Ben Nevis.'

'I'm feeling very well, Alasdair. Did you hear about our little affray up at Drumcockie on the Twelfth?'

'Yes, yes, indeed, we were all hearing about it. Terrible people, those hikers. Worse than the Chermans, I believe. But some people like them.'

'They do?'

'Och, yes, there's my neighbour, Mrs Macfarlane who lives three miles away up Strathdun just where the road comes into it. She's daft for hikers. Bed and breakfast and eggs and milk and teas. They're round her like bees in the heather.'

'Good god! But she hasn't one of my crofts?'

'No, no, she has one of the Department holdings.'

'There you are, Alasdair. There's Government interference for you. Poking their noses into the Highlands, and the only result is hikers. Well, I'm going to devote myself to stamping out hikers in Inverness-shire. I only wish I could stamp them out all over the Highlands, but we get no kind of co-operation from Argyll in this sort of thing. Of course, the truth is they're all so many Mrs Macfarlanes in Argyll. They batten on them, the County Council included. I'm glad to see you at the Gathering and looking so well, Alasdair. Have you talked to young Hector yet?'

'Och, yes, I had a word with him. Fancy flying all the way from India. What a time we live in! Where will we be flying next?'

'You and I will be flying to Heaven, I hope.'

'Not in an airioplane, Ben Nevis. No, no. It might break down and we would be finding ourselves in the wrong places.'

'Well, take care of yourself, Alasdair. I may be over in Strathdun soon, and I'll look in and have a crack. How's the old lady?'

'Och, the *cailleach*'s very well, but she would never admit it. She's like all the women that way.'

Ben Nevis waved a patriarchal arm and passed on to chat with another crony. If anything was lacking to make his day a success it was supplied when after an hour of such gossip he noticed that Hector was sitting by Myrtle on the mound and apparently keeping her very well entertained. A glow of pride suffused his being. Murdoch and Iain might be able to toss the caber, throw the hammer, and put the stone, but it was his eldest son and successor who knew what was really vital to preserve the glories of Mac 'ic Eachainn's line. A great lad, Hector MacDonald, Younger, of Ben Nevis. The Chieftain was roused from such fond patriarchal reflections by the voice of Chester Royde at his elbow.

'Ben Nevis, have you noticed the head guy among that bunch of hikers?'

'I haven't been looking at them. I welcome the brutes to Glenbogle on the day of the Gathering, but I can't bring myself to look at them. If I look at a hiker for more than a minute I get a curious kind of buzzing in the top of my head.'

'Chance the buzzing for once and take a look at him,' Royde urged.

'Do you mean the fellow with the chin?'

'That's the guy I mean.'

'His face is familiar to me somehow. Was he among that crowd we dealt with on the Twelfth?'

Chester Royde shook his head.

'I can't recognize any of them from that bunch of hoodlums. This is a new gang. They've been staring at me quite a lot. Particularly that stiff with the chin. Now what are they staring at me for?'

'I expect it's your kilt.'

'Hell, there are plenty of other folk around in kilts. I don't see what they want to pick on me for as a close-up.'

'A close-up?'

'Yes, that guy with the chin, which invites punching, keeps nodding in my direction, and then one of these hikers strolls along and stares me up and down as if he wanted to be sure of knowing me again. If I hit one of them, would that spoil your notion of a happy day?'

'I sympathize with you, Royde. But I'd rather you didn't hit any of these brutes this afternoon. I mean to say, Glenbogle is Liberty Hall today. Highland hospitality and all that sort of thing, don't you know? It's a tradition with us in Glenbogle. In the old days we even welcomed Macintoshes who came to the Gathering, and normally of course we cut the throat of any Macintosh at sight.'

'I don't want to break up tradition, Ben Nevis, but if that guy with Cape Cod tacked on to the lower part of his face sends any more of his young friends to stare me up and down I don't believe I'll be able to keep from hitting him.'

'Look here, Royde, the prize-giving will start in another few minutes. You don't want to wait for that. It takes about an hour with the speeches, and it'll be very hot in the tent. Why don't you stroll along back to the

Castle and have a drink? I'd suggest your going into the Committee tent, but it's full of flies and you hate flies.'

'I went into the Committee tent, Major MacIsaac kindly offered me a highball. But every time I looked up one of these hikers was peeping in at me around the flap.'

'I never heard anything so outrageous,' the Chieftain declared warmly. 'I tell you this, Royde, if a single hiker dares show himself in Glenbogle after today I'll have him thrown into the Bogle.'

'He won't find me standing by with a hook to fish him out,' the indignant Royde vowed.

'That fellow's face is curiously familiar to me,' said Ben Nevis, looking again at the man with the chin, who it is hardly necessary to say was Percy Buckham himself. 'I've seen him somewhere. But where, that's the question?' Just then another old crony who had not yet had a chance of a gossip came up, and when Ben Nevis looked round again Chester Royde had wandered off.

During the prize-giving Mrs MacDonald and her two daughters, who stood on either side to hand her the prizes for presentation to the embarrassed winners, must have lost between them not less than seven pounds of weight, so furiously hot was the inside of the tent, crowded with people who had not won prizes and through whose serried ranks those who had won prizes were compelled to fight their way to get within reach of Mrs MacDonald's gracious hand. After this the Chieftain made his annual speech and was dug in the back by his daughter Catriona because he began as usual, 'Fellow clansmen and clanswomen, and all my good friends, in spite of the weather . . . I mean thanks to the glorious weather, I think we can say that of the very many great Gatherings this dear old glen of ours has seen, the Glenbogle Gathering this year has surpassed all its predecessors . . .' But there is no need to continue, for such speeches whether made by the Squire at a flower-show in Hampshire or by the Highland Chieftain upon his native heath are all essentially the same.

'Well, Carrie,' the Chieftain asked when they were all back in the Great Hall and he had just drunk a highball as high as Ben Booey itself and a great deal more yellow, 'well, Carrie, how did you enjoy your first Glenbogle Gathering?'

'Oh, it was marvellous, Ben Nevis.'

'Where's the MacRoyde?' asked the Chieftain, whose wit had been stimulated by that majestic highball.

'I don't know. I haven't seen him for a long while.'

But it was not until Carrie went up to dress for dinner, and found no sign of Chester in his dressing-room and Wilton, his man, with what she called that British look on his face, that she began to wonder if anything had happened to him.

'Where's Mr Royde, Wilton?'

'I don't know, madam. Is he not downstairs?'

'I haven't seen him since before we left the field.'

'I'll go downstairs, madam, and make some inquiries.'

Presently the valet came back to inform his mistress that nobody had seen Mr Royde.

'It's mighty queer, Wilton.'

'It is indeed, madam.'

Carrie went along to her room to dress, but when dinner-time came and she joined the rest of the house-party in the Great Hall there was no Chester.

Chapter 15

THE FIRST PRISONER

The disappearance of Chester Royde cast a gloom over what should have been as festive an evening as Glenbogle Castle had ever known. Hector had found Myrtle an apt pupil in the eightsome reel which they had practised together in the library for half an hour before dinner, but what sister could have the heart to dance reels when her only brother had vanished?

Ben Nevis expressed the mood of all the guests when he said that after a very quick dinner they must send out search-parties.

'My theory is the poor chap's sprained his ankle,' he declared, in a tone that Einstein might have used to announce his Theory of Relativity.

'But, Ben Nevis, why should he have sprained his ankle?' Carrie asked.

'He may have been a bit confused by his kilt. It was the first time he'd worn a kilt, remember. Of course, he *may* have broken a leg.'

'But if he'd sprained his ankle or broken his leg,' Carrie argued, 'surely he'd have been able to call for help. There were so many people about.'

'But he may have wandered off into the hills.'

'What would he do that for?' Myrtle objected. 'He hasn't gone wandering off up into the hills any other day.'

'Ah, but he wasn't wearing the kilt,' Ben Nevis pointed out sagaciously. 'I'm sure it was the feeling of freedom the kilt gives a man that made him walk further than he meant. We'll find him all right. He can't have walked very far.'

'I saw him leave the field round about half past five,' said Kilwhillie, without adding that the sight of that orange kilt moving off the field had removed a weight from his mind.

'I know,' said Ben Nevis, 'he was annoyed by those hikers. They would keep coming up and staring at him. It was I who advised him to go back to the Castle. He wanted to hit one of them, but I explained that on the day of the Gathering, Glenbogle was Liberty Hall and that I even gave a welcome to hikers. He understood my point of view perfectly and said he wouldn't hit any of them.'

'Perhaps one of them followed him off the field and he did hit him,' suggested Catriona.

'Oh no, Catriona,' Carrie said positively. 'If Chester gave his word to your father that he wouldn't hit one of them, you can be sure he wouldn't. Chester never breaks his word, does he, Myrtle?'

'Only in Wall Street. Never in private life, of course,' Myrtle replied.

'Ah, well, business is different,' said Ben Nevis. 'Breaking your word is what business really means.'

'Hullo, Dad, you're getting very cynical,' Hector barked affectionately.

'What I was going to say,' Catriona managed to interpose, 'was that if Mr Royde had hit one of the hikers the others might have set on him.'

'Don't believe it. Don't believe it,' the Chieftain scoffed. 'Don't believe hikers would have the courage to set on anybody. Look at the miserable resistance they offered to us the other day on Drumcockie.'

'I must say I think you were very lucky, Ben Nevis, not to be involved in any unpleasant legal business,' said Colonel Lindsay-Wolseley, who was one of those who had stayed on to dinner at the Castle.

'Never thought they would attempt any legal tom-foolery with me,' the Chieftain replied. 'Shouldn't have minded if they had, but I knew they wouldn't. I'll tell you what, Wolseley, you missed a jolly fine bit of sport by going off like that.'

'I still think you were lucky,' the Colonel maintained.

Ben Nevis exhaled contempt for the initiative of hikers in a great gusty ejaculation, and turning presently to Kilwhillie he expressed his unalterable opinion that of all the many obstinate men he had met in his life Lindsay-Wolseley was without doubt the most obstinate.

'I suppose it's all that time he spent on the North-west Frontier. Hope they won't send the Clanranalds to Peshawar. I don't want Hector to grow obstinate and be unable to see anything except what lies straight in front of his nose.'

Kilwhillie might have commented that with such a nose even so restricted an outlook would be wider than that of many.

'As a matter of fact absolutely between ourselves,' his old friend continued, 'if things go as I rather think they will go I shall advise Hector to chuck the Army.'

He looked across fondly to where his eldest son was trying to convince Myrtle that her brother might have taken it into his head to drive down the glen in one of the omnibuses for the sake of the walk back and misjudged the distance.

Just then Toker came in to announce dinner, which the host said must be eaten as quickly as possible, and with a view to securing speed he hushed the pipers and stopped Mr Fletcher from saying grace, after which he began to arrange plans for the various search-parties that were to set out the moment the meal was over. He had already given orders that all his tenants and dependants who were being entertained at the Castle were to start looking for the missing guest immediately.

It was a pity her master could not hear what Mrs Ablewhite had to say about him to Mrs Parsall.

'Six good days it's taken me to prepare for this evening, and now just because that Mr Royde isn't back in time for dinner He must want to charge through my dinner like a bull in a china-shop. Disgusting isn't the word for it. What *are* you doing with those peas, Flora? For goodness' sake, girl, go away and do nothing if you can't do something better than anything. Well, really, Mrs Parsall, these Highland girls are enough to try the patience of an angel in heaven. Tell Mr Toker, Alec, it's not a bit of good him fidgeting and fretting me. No dish can be served quicker than what it can be served. Consideration, Mrs Parsall? He doesn't know the meaning of the word. After that lunch I had to prepare for thirty-four! And now dinner's shovelled into them quicker than anyone could shovel coal into a range! Maggie, if you're going to stand gaping like that, go and gape outside of my kitchen, girl. Why doesn't Mrs MacDonald stop Him, Mrs Parsall? But it's always the same at every one of these blessed Gatherings. They just go to His head.'

In the dining-room Ben Nevis was hoping that Carrie did not feel it was heartless of them all to be enjoying their dinner while she and for that matter all of them were so anxious to be off in search of her husband. Had anybody been watching Toker at that moment he would have noticed that at the word 'enjoying' his face contracted like the face of one who had bitten recklessly at a chocolate under the impression that it was filled with fondant and found too late from an exposed nerve that it was filled with caramel.

'Iain, you're through with your fish. I wish you'd go round to the back and muster the first party. The moon's already up. You won't want more than one or two lanterns to give Royde a chance of sighting you and giving a shout. I suggest you cross by the bridge and comb the other side of the river. And look here, Murdoch. I think you'd better take a party with pitchforks and see if by any chance he's in trouble with the bull.'

'Oh, Ben Nevis!' Carrie gasped.

'I don't think he is for a moment,' he assured her. 'But it just occurred to me he might have crossed over the Bogle to get away from being stared at and wandered into the bull's field. Ordinarily that shorthorn is as decent and docile a beast as you'd meet anywhere, but your husband's plaid may have excited him. Of course, it wasn't red, but the bull may have thought it was red, if you see what I mean. Don't you think that's possible, Hugh?'

'Very possible indeed,' the Laird of Kilwhillie agreed with conviction.

'Don't listen to Donald, my dear,' the hostess boomed reassuringly. 'If there had been any unpleasantness with the bull, people on this side of the river would be sure to have seen. Donald dear!'

'What is it now, Trixie?'

'Don't let yourself get too excited, will you? You're making Carrie and Myrtle nervous.'

At this moment Catriona and Mary rose from the table simultaneously.

'Mary and I are feeling as fit as be blowed. We propose to foot it to the entrance of the glen and then beat both banks of the Bogle all the way back.'

'Catriona,' her mother protested, 'you won't be home till five or six in the morning if you do that.'

'That's all right, Mother,' Mary growled. 'We'll take some grub with us.'

'Good girls, good girls,' their father applauded. 'Don't worry, Trixie. It's a thoroughly sound scheme. When on earth is the next course coming, Toker?' ·

The butler approached his master's chair and murmured some words in his ear. 'Well, why does she let herself get fussed? I don't let myself get fussed.'

At this moment one of the gillies made a sign to Toker from the doorway that he wished to speak to him.

Mrs MacDonald seemed oblivious of what Sir Hubert Bottley on her right was saying to her. She was watching Toker. Her mighty bosom heaved slowly like the Atlantic at the approach of a storm. She was wondering if the request of Catriona and Mary for grub to carry with them to Glenbogle had been that last straw to break the camel's back of Mrs Ablewhite's endurance, and if Toker was to be the bearer of an ultimatum. She saw him receive a note from the hands of the gillie, and after a momentary hesitation bring this letter to the Chieftain. She saw her husband tear open this letter and read it, and as he read she saw his countenance illuminated by a crimson fluorescence, his nose darken to the purple of a Himalayan potato, his ears smoulder, his eyes grow globular and luminous, his left hand grasp a handful of air and squeeze it into a vacuum.

'Something's happened to Chester!' Carrie exclaimed.

'Ben Nevis, what is it?' Myrtle cried. 'Oh, tell us the worst.'

'Donald!' his wife boomed, and tolled him back to his sole self.

The Chieftain threw the letter across the table to Kilwhillie.

'Read it, Hugh. I shall burst if I try to read it myself.'

Kilwhillie took his spectacle-case from the pocket of his mulberry-velvet doublet, put on his glasses and pored upon the letter.

'Not to yourself, Hugh,' the Chieftain bellowed. 'Read it aloud.'

And in the fashionably unemotional voice of a barrister reading a love-letter in a breach of promise suit Kilwhillie read:

> NATIONAL UNION OF HIKERS,
> 702, GOWER STREET,
> WC2

'Sir,

This is to notify you that by a unanimous vote of the Union taken at an extraordinary general meeting convened on 20 August at the Astrovegetarian Hall, Villiers Street, Strand, the President of the Union, the Rt Hon. the Earl of Buntingdon occupying the chair, the outrageous action taken by you on 12 August last against sixteen members of the Union including the Secretary, Mr Sydney Prew, was declared an intolerable infringement of democratic privilege. In the opinion of the meeting any redress through legal channels was found inadequate and by another unanimous vote it was resolved to set in motion against you the full powers of the Union for offensive action on a level with your own.

Misled by the apparent success of fascist methods in Foreign Affairs you have attempted to imitate such methods in England . . .'

'England!' Ben Nevis exploded. 'The ruffian thinks Glenbogle is in England! Do you hear that, Hugh?'

Kilwhillie decided to treat this question as purely rhetorical, and went on reading . . .

'but you will find that when a great democratic institution decides to take offensive action it can act with greater vigour, effect, speed, and ruthlessness than any dictator. The war declared upon you, MacDonald of Ben Nevis, by the National Union of Hikers, began this afternoon when one of your accomplices in the dastardly aggression committed by you against the collective security of the aforesaid Union was seized by the Union's armed forces. To him will be meted out the same treatment as was meted out by you to sixteen members of the Union.'

'They've kidnapped Chester!' Carrie cried.

'Well, what would you say to that?' Myrtle asked. 'Oh, pardon me, Kilwhillie, you want to finish reading. Carrie and I interrupted you.'

'Furthermore the same treatment will be meted out to every one of your accomplices including yourself. You have asked for war, MacDonald of Ben Nevis, and you shall have war, ruthless war until you sue humbly for peace. The National Union of Hikers will then decide the terms upon which its members will grant you peace.

PERCY BUCKHAM,
Acting President.'

'There you are, you see, Ben Nevis,' said Colonel Wolseley, shaking his head. 'This is what comes of taking the law into your own hands.'

'What do you mean, Lindsay-Wolseley?'

The Colonel recognized by being addressed with both his surnames that his host was angry, but in his position as Convener of the Police Committee of the County Council he felt bound to express his opinion even if such frankness should lead to a temporary breach between Ben Nevis and himself.

'I mean exactly what I say,' he replied. 'Your action on the Twelfth was responsible for what amounts to a threat of plunging this part of Inverness-shire into anarchy.'

'Are you seriously trying to argue with me, Lindsay-Wolseley, that this impudent epistle is on the same level as my drastic but completely justifiable attempt to solve the hiker problem in the Highlands once and for all? I never heard a more preposterous comparison.'

'What is the difference?' the Colonel pressed.

'The difference is that I had a perfect right to give a lesson to those hikers trespassing on my land,' Ben Nevis declared angrily.

'That way lies anarchy,' the Colonel retorted.

'Look here, Lindsay-Wolseley, I don't often lose my temper, but if a guest at my own table is to sit there and call me a Bolshevist I warn you I may not be able to keep my temper.'

'My dear Ben Nevis, you are the very last person in this world to whom I would apply such an epithet. What I said was that if you arrogate to yourself the right to take the law into your own hands you are inviting other people to do the same, the result of which will be anarchy.'

'I suppose you'll argue next I have no right to take immediate steps to rescue my guest from the hands of these detestable Cockney brigands? I suppose you expect me to notify that beetroot-headed police constable at Kenspeckle and ask him to do it for me?'

'Constable MacGillivray is one of the best fellows we have in the County Police,' said the Colonel warmly. 'I take strong exception to your describing him as beetroot-headed.'

'He is beetroot-headed. His face is the colour and shape of a beetroot, and any brains he has are the brains of a beetroot.'

'Surely I'm in a better position to assess his qualities than you? In fact I have so high an opinion of MacGillivray that I've just pressed for his promotion to Sergeant, promotion which he thoroughly deserves.'

Ben Nevis snorted.

'You might as well press for the promotion of a beetroot, Lindsay-Wolseley. Anyway, I'm not going to notify MacGillivray that one of my guests has been carried off by hikers. I know exactly the sort of silly expression he'd have on his beetroot-face after riding up from Kenspeckle on that bicycle of his.'

'Well, what are you going to do, Ben Nevis?' the Colonel asked.

'I'm going to beat the glen for hikers all tonight and tomorrow . . .'

'Don't forget tomorrow's Sunday, Ben Nevis,' put in the chaplain, who, though no Sabbatarian himself, knew what a tremendous sermon any beating of the glens and straths and bens of Mac 'ic Eachainn's country would evoke from the Reverend Alexander Munro of the United Free Church in Strathdun.

'Look at that now, Lindsay-Wolseley. And yet you can bring yourself to sympathize with brutes who deliberately take a mean advantage of my being handicapped by a pompous little ass of a minister like Munro. Anyway, the question of Sunday doesn't arise yet. Sufficient for the day is the evil thereof, what? We'll beat Glenbogle and Glenbristle for hikers tonight. And the sooner we start the better. Look here, Toker, I think we'll cut out the rest of the dinner. I'm sure everybody's had enough. You've all had enough, haven't you? We'll all have to change into proper clothes for the beating of the glens. Hector, you'd better drive Myrtle in that curious contraption of Murdoch's he calls a car. Where's Angus? Oh, look here, Angus. I'm sorry to upset the pipers' evening after the splendid way they upheld the honour of Glenbogle today, but I want them to go and play in different parts of the glen and to listen carefully about every five minutes.'

'What would they listen for, Ben Nevis?' his piper asked.

'Why, to hear if they hear anybody shouting for help. Don't you realize Mr Royde has been carried off by hikers?'

'What would they be doing that for, Ben Nevis?'

'I can't waste any more valuable time explaining the whys and wherefores of this business.'

'Very good, Ben Nevis,' said his piper, retiring with a puzzled expression on his long lean face.

'Now, look here, Wolseley, I refuse to quarrel with you over this wretched business. Two old friends and all that sort of thing. But I don't want . . . what's the name of that bounder who wrote to me, Hugh? . . . Buckham? . . . yes, well, as I was saying, Wolseley, I don't want to involve you if I catch this fellow Buckham and decide to have him thrown into Loch na Craosnaich. I mean to say if he were drowned or anything, you might have to resign your seat on the County Council. So I think you and Mrs Wolseley ought to go home.'

The rest of the guests who had been invited to the dinner and the dance hastily said they thought they should be going. The prospect of being summoned before the Procurator-Fiscal's deputy lacked attraction.

'I feel terribly bad about spoiling the lovely time we were having,' Carrie told her host when the last of the guests' cars had gone sweeping down the drive.

'My dear young lady, what have you done to spoil it?'

'I feel that perhaps if Chester hadn't taken to wearing the kilt all of a sudden like that this wouldn't have happened.'

'Not a bit of it! Don't you worry your pretty little head any more, except of course about poor old Chester. The extraordinary thing to me is that a man like Colonel Lindsay-Wolseley, who's spent half his life chasing Afghans and all that sort of thing about the hills of the North-west Frontier, wouldn't insist on leading one of the search-parties. But they're all the same, these old soldiers. Their livers get congested, I think. What Wolseley likes is bringing up petty points at a Council meeting. That's his idea of excitement nowadays. Awful, isn't it? I hope

Hector'll soon find the right girl and get married. He's been in the Army just about long enough. In fact between you and me, Carrie, I wish he and Myrtle would make a match of it.'

'Oh, you think they'd suit one another?' Carrie asked, with a touch of dubiety in her tone.

'Don't you?'

'Well, Myrtle is a girl who'll choose for herself, that's sure.'

'I'm very glad to hear it. I mean to say a young fellow like Hector wants to feel he's been chosen, not just picked out of a drawer like a handkerchief. But look here, I must get along and change. Will you join my rescue-party?'

Carrie hesitated.

'Don't you think I'd be wiser to stay home?' she suggested. 'If I weren't home when Chester came back with his rescuers he'd feel he'd have to go out again and look for me.'

Mrs MacDonald coming along at that moment overheard this remark of Carrie's, which she acclaimed as profoundly sensible. She was not given to making demands on the sympathy of her guests, but a brief interview she had just had with Mrs Ablewhite, during which she had not received the support she might have expected from Mrs Parsall, had left her with a desire to confide in another woman.

So when the various noises connected with the dispatch of the search-parties by Ben Nevis had died away in a medley of shouting, piping, whistling and tooting, Mrs MacDonald asked Carrie to come and sit with her in that room that was for ever England in spite of still being called the Yellow Drawing-room. There she spoke to Carrie of the temperamental peculiarities of Mrs Parsall and Mrs Ablewhite and even of Toker. And in her turn Carrie talked to Mrs MacDonald about Wilton's British oddities and the French excitability of her own maid Célestine.

'But still I have so much to be thankful for, Carrie. It's only very rarely that Mrs Ablewhite gets quite beyond herself as she was when I went down to see her after dinner this evening. And there's no doubt she had taken a great deal of trouble about our dinner tonight. However, I think everything will be all right when she and Mrs Parsall and Toker have had a night's rest.'

'I was telling Ben Nevis a while back how much I felt to blame.'

'My dear child, you? What possible blame can attach to you? I think you've been most considerate in not making any fuss about your poor husband. I have the greatest admiration for your courage. No, no, it's my dear Donald who's entirely responsible for the little uncomfortableness. He lets himself get too excited. Just like a child indeed. If I could only get him to drink a cup of camomile tea every night. But he won't. He says he'd sooner pour hot-water on the clippings of the lawn-mower and drink that. I'm afraid Hugh Cameron is a bad influence.'

'Kilwhillie? Oh, surely not, Mrs MacDonald?'

'Yes, yes. And the tragedy of it is that at one time there was nobody I welcomed more gladly to the Castle. I used to say Donald never slept so soundly and so peacefully as when Hughie Cameron had dined at Glenbogle. But of late he has seemed to take a delight in egging Donald on. I blame him entirely for that first affray with the hikers.'

'Well, it's true it was Kilwhillie who persuaded Chester to get an orange kilt. I know Chester was intending to get a purple one.'

Mrs MacDonald shook her head.

'Dear, dear, dear! And Hugh Cameron used to be so quiet in every way – quiet in his tastes and quiet in his habits. But he's never been the same since he saw the Loch Ness Monster last spring. He's never really recovered from the excitement of it. I do hope he won't egg Donald on to do anything desperate tonight if by chance they come into contact with the hikers.'

Mrs MacDonald and Carrie sat on talking until Carrie felt that a sameness was creeping into the conversation. She told her hostess she was going up to the room in the North Tower, the windows of which afforded the widest view of any in the Castle.

'I'm going to play Sister Anne for a little while, Mrs MacDonald, up in the tower-room.'

'You'll probably find Mr Fletcher up there. That's his favourite haunt.'

'Maybe we'll hear some news of Chester soon.'

Mrs MacDonald patted Carrie's shoulder.

'Don't fret too much, my dear. I feel convinced that nothing serious has happened to Mr Royde.'

With the sweet sad smile of the young matron in some fragrant old-fashioned tale of the knightly days of yore, Carrie left the Yellow Drawing-room.

Mrs Macdonald had been right. The Reverend Ninian Fletcher was in the tower-room, reading in a grandfather's chair beside a glowing peat fire.

'Ah, Mrs Royde, this is a welcome and unexpected visit.'

'I came up here, Mr Fletcher, because I thought I might see something down in the glen.'

'Let me pull the curtains,' the chaplain suggested.

They stood for a while gazing out upon the moonlit scene, but there was no sign of so much as a lantern. Carrie asked the chaplain if he would mind the night-air from an open casement, and receiving his assurance that he slept every night with his window wide open she leaned out and listened.

'What was that?' she asked when a melancholy hoot was heard. 'Isn't that Chester's voice calling for help?'

But Mr Fletcher assured her it was an owl, and a moment later the great white bird itself swept past the casement on silent wings.

'Goody, that scared me,' Carrie exclaimed, and she hastily shut the casement. 'It was like a ghost.'

'They are uncanny birds,' the chaplain agreed. 'Better come and sit by the fire. I'm sure we shall soon be getting news of your husband.'

'I hope so, Mr Fletcher. But of course you yourself had a nasty experience with those hikers, didn't you?'

'It was rather unpleasant, but at any rate Mr Royde is not in Mac 'ic Eachainn's Cradle.'

'What makes you say that?'

'Because the door is still off its hinges, and from what I know of this part of the world likely to remain off its hinges for a long, long time to come. Doors that are broken in the West Highlands don't get mended so quickly as all that,' the old chaplain chuckled.

'Mr Fletcher, I wish you'd read me some more of your poetry. I think there's nothing so soothing as poetry when one's feeling anxious the way I'm feeling about my poor husband right now. I do wish we could have some news of him.'

The chaplain went to the bookcase and came back with *Echoes of Glenbogle*. Turning over the pages, he chose a poem and began to read it, explaining that the verses were spoken alternately by a daughter and her mother:

> ' "O where is my Ronald, my bonny young Ronald,
> O where have they hidden my Ronald so true?
> 'Tis a week since he bade me farewell in the gloaming,
> A week since he kissed me a tender adieu."

"Oh, ask not, sweet Flora, where Ronald is hidden,
'Tis better the tidings thou never should'st hear,
Thy Ronald slain foully by one of Clan Chattan,
Fares home to Glenbogle this morn on his bier."

"My Ronald slain foully by one of Clan Chattan?
Now tell me, oh, tell me, which one did the deed?
Was it Iain, the Red Macintosh of Loch Stuffie,
The foulest of all of Clan Chattan's foul breed?"

"Yes, Flora, sweet Flora, 'twas Iain of Loch Stuffie,
Who stabbed with his sgian thy Ronald's true heart,
For jealous was Iain of thy love for young Ronald
And made up his mind two fond lovers to part."

"Oh, mother, dear mother, I hear the pipes wailing,
Oh, mother, dear mother, the coffin is here,
Why didst thou not . . ." '

'Oh, please, Mr Fletcher,' Carrie interrupted. 'I really don't think I can listen to any more of that poem. It's a little bit too appropriate.'

'But this happened more than two hundred years ago,' the chaplain explained with a reassuring smile, 'though they do say that the ghost of Ronald MacDonald still haunts the spot where Iain Roy Macintosh murdered him. Flora, who was a daughter of the MacDonald of Ben Nevis of that time, killed herself, as I tell in the rest of the poem. Shall I go on?'

'No, please, I'd rather you didn't, Mr Fletcher. It's so terribly realistic.'

'But I've tried to preserve a happy mean between romance and extreme realism. What I forgot to tell you was that this was Flora's bower and it's said that her ghost is sometimes seen making its way from the tower to keep a tryst with the ghost of her murdered lover.'

'Oh, please, Mr Fletcher . . .' Carrie was protesting again when she stopped abruptly and cried:

'Hark! That's not an owl.'

'No, no,' the chaplain agreed, 'that's definitely a deeper note than an owl's, and more persistent.'

Persistent was perhaps rather lacking in colour as an epithet for the almost continuous howling that seemed to come through the floor of what had been the ill-fated Flora's bower of long ago.

'That *is* Chester's voice,' Carrie declared, after listening intently for a while. 'It's the noise he used to make when he was a cheer-leader at

Yale. I didn't know him in those days, but I heard him howl like that for the Carroway Indians in Canada and they said it made their traditional war-cry sound kind of tame. Hugging Bear, the Carroway Chief, asked Chester if he'd mind terribly if they used it as a new war-cry for the tribe and Chester said it was O.K. by him so long as they didn't come and do it at New Haven during the match against Harvard.' She listened again. 'Oh, yes, that's Chester sure enough, but where is he?'

She ran across to the window and flung open a casement. 'You can't hear it so well from here,' she said. 'It must be somewhere inside the tower.'

'I wonder,' said the chaplain, 'I wonder if the noise can possibly be coming from the dungeon where the young women hikers were shut up.'

'I never saw that dungeon. Where is it?'

'Immediately underneath where we are now, though there are two rooms in between. If that noise is Mr Royde, he must have exceptionally powerful lungs.'

'Oh, he has,' said Carrie eagerly. 'You wouldn't think it to hear him speak ordinarily, but Chester has one of the biggest voices anywhere. I suppose that's why he was a cheer-leader at college. Oh, Mr Fletcher, do let's go and let the poor boy out.'

'But that's the problem,' the chaplain replied. 'The keys of the dungeon have been missing ever since the night of the Twelfth. Ah, wait a moment. I'm on the track of the solution. The hikers carried off the keys with them. Dear me, dear me, what an exceedingly cunning revenge.'

'Revenge?' Carrie cried. 'Oh, they haven't done anything horrible to Chester? They haven't cut off his nose or blinded him or anything like that?'

'He would never be able to make a noise like that unless he were in possession of all his faculties,' the chaplain declared emphatically.

'But how are we going to get him out?' Carrie fussed. 'It's nearly eleven o'clock and he must have been shut up since this afternoon. I can't think how nobody heard him calling.'

At this point the howling from below took on a fresh intensity of sound.

'Mr Fletcher, Mr Fletcher, we must get him out. Oh, dear, why did everybody go off to look for him in the glen when he was here in the

Castle all the while? Think what a terribly long business it was to get you out of the other dungeon. What *are* we going to do?'

The chaplain smiled benignly.

'We are going to release Mr Royde in a very few moments,' he announced.

'But we'll never break in the door.'

'We're not going to break in the door; we're going to use the secret passage.'

The chaplain went across to a cabinet set in the wall. He turned a handle to open what was in reality a door and disclosed the narrow stone stairs of Gothic romance.

'I'm afraid you'll find the descent will mean sweeping off a good deal of dust and cobwebs,' said Mr Fletcher. 'But I dare say you won't mind that in such a good cause.'

'Oh no, of course I won't, Mr Fletcher. Oh, listen to poor Chester now.'

With the door at the head of the stairs open and a channel to conduct the sound the noise was certainly impressive.

'Come along then. I have a taper here which I use for my sealing-wax. I don't think we need a lantern.'

They went slowly down some eighty steps in a spiral that was by no means adequately illuminated by the chaplain's taper until they reached a door, the rusty bolts of which took some time to pull back. However, at last they pushed it open to enter a vaulted cellar that reverberated with the din of Chester Royde's shouts.

From this cellar they passed through into another and beheld the captive sitting on a packing case, throwing back his head from time to time to produce a still louder yell.

'Chester! It's Carrie,' his wife cried, running across the cobbled floor to embrace him. 'Chester, why didn't you call out before?'

'Why didn't I call out before?' the captive echoed indignantly. 'How the hell . . .'

'Chester, please. Mr Fletcher's with us.'

'Oh, I'm not so easily shocked as that, Mrs Royde,' the chaplain put in.

'How could I call out before, Carrie, when I was gagged?'

'Gagged?'

'Sure, I was gagged. I'd be gagged now if a mouse hadn't run up the inside of my kilt and made me give such a jump that the darned gag bust. I understand now why women can't stand the idea of mice. I used to laugh at them, but that was before I took to the kilt.'

'Oh, Chester, your hands are tied behind your back.'

'Sure, they're tied behind my back. You don't think I wouldn't have beaten hell out of that door if they hadn't been. My ankles are tied too.'

The chaplain produced a penknife, and Carrie cut the cords round her husband's wrists. Then she knelt down and severed those that bound his ankles.

'Gee, that certainly feels good,' he declared.

'And now tell us what happened,' Carrie begged.

'Wouldn't Mr Royde tell his story more comfortably by a good fire?' the chaplain suggested.

'Why, yes, how wise you are, Mr Fletcher,' Carrie agreed.

At this moment Mrs Parsall had just entered the Yellow Drawing-room to inform Mrs MacDonald that the emotional tension in that part of the Castle she ruled, which had only just been allayed, was now more acute than ever because Flora MacInnes and Maggie Macphee had come running along from their bedroom into the housekeeper's room, screaming that one of the Castle ghosts had chased them with a horrible roaring noise.

'And that's set Mrs Ablewhite off again, ma'am. She's withdrawn the withdrawal of the month's notice she gave me after Mr Toker brought word that dinner was over before the *crème brûlée* she'd made was served. And that's how matters stand. As soon as I tell Florrie and Maggie to go back to their rooms they just sit down on the floor and scream. And they've nothing on but their nightdresses and bare feet.'

'Dear me, Mrs Parsall, I'm afraid you're having a very difficult time with the staff,' Mrs MacDonald sighed. 'Which room are Florrie and Maggie in?'

'They sleep in the room off the passage that leads to the door down into the dungeon under the North Tower. That's the trouble. It seems that the body of a hunchbacked pedlar who'd been murdered and robbed in the glen was hidden in this dungeon a hundred years ago or more, and the silly girls think it's this hunchback that's after them, though as I said to them whatever did they think he'd want to chase them for even if it was his ghost and which of course is nonsensical. But I do not want Mrs Ablewhite to leave us, ma'am, and if she gets ghosts on top of all her other worries, that's what she will do.'

'I wonder if some camomile tea . . .' Mrs MacDonald began.

'You'll excuse me, ma'am,' the housekeeper interrupted impatiently, 'but things have gone beyond anything camomile tea can do. I dislike causing you trouble, ma'am, but the only thing is for you to come down to my room and try and alleviorate matters a little.'

Mrs MacDonald rose with a sigh.

'Very well, Mrs Parsall. I'll see what I can do. It would be sad if Mrs Ablewhite left us.'

'It would indeed, ma'am. Mrs Ablewhite has her faults. We all of us have if it comes to that, but take her all in all we should find it very hard to replace her.'

The Lady of Ben Nevis and her housekeeper were on the way to the latter's room when down the stairs from the corridor leading to the room in the North Tower appeared Carrie and Mr Fletcher, both of whom were covered with cobwebs, and Chester Royde.

'Mr Royde! You've been found!' Mrs MacDonald boomed.

'Mr Fletcher and I found him,' Carrie said proudly. 'The hikers had shut him up in the dungeon, and we heard him shouting for help.'

'There's your ghost, Mrs Parsall. I think you can put matters right now.' Mrs MacDonald sighed with relief. 'And ask Mrs Ablewhite to be kind enough to send up some dinner for Mr Royde, and particularly some of her always delicious *crème brûlée*. He must be famished. Unless of course you think it wiser to arrange something for Mr Royde without consulting Mrs Ablewhite.'

'Oh no, ma'am, Mrs Ablewhite will be gratified to think there's somebody in the Castle with an appetite.'

In the Yellow Drawing-room Chester Royde recounted his adventure:

'I'd noticed these hikers following me around on the field, and it got my goat, but Ben Nevis asked me to remember it was a special occasion and not to take any notice. So after a while I walked back to the Castle. Everything was pretty quiet. I went into the Great Hall and poured myself out a highball. And then I felt I'd let myself be annoyed unnecessarily by these hikers and I decided I'd stroll back to the field. Well, I went out, and the next thing I knew was my head was in a sack and I was being run along as if I was a bad man being run out of a mining-camp. I think I know who the guy was that got his hand around the back of my neck, and believe me, I'm gunning for him till I get him, and if I don't change the shape of that chin of his into something the nose above it won't recognize I'll resign my blood-brotherhood with the Carroway Indians.

'Well, they tied me up and gagged me and left me sitting in that dungeon, and if a mouse hadn't run up inside my kilt and made me jump and bust the gag I'd be sitting in that dungeon now.'

'Dreadful!' Mrs MacDonald boomed dolorously.

'That's what happened to one of the young women hikers,' said Mr Fletcher. 'There must be quite an appreciable number of mice in that dungeon.'

'You've never had a mouse run up your leg, Mr Fletcher?' the released captive inquired.

'No, I can't say I ever have,' the chaplain replied. 'On one occasion many years ago when I was taking duty for the Bishop of South-east Europe at Taormina a scorpion got into my tooth-glass, which was very unpleasant, but . . .'

'Well, I always did like cats,' said Chester. 'But when I go back to the States I'm going to found the Chester Royde Home for stray cats. And, Carrie, it'll be some Home.'

Chapter 16

BUCKHAM'S CAMPAIGN

———

Ben Nevis allowed himself to be dissuaded next day from attacking the hikers, apparently in deference to the Sabbath, actually because it was not yet known where their camp was, and he felt disinclined to indulge in vain reconnaissance after the long day of the Gathering and the restless night of searching for his kidnapped guest.

'I do often get a little irritated by our Highland Sunday,' he admitted, 'but there's something to be said for it after a day like yesterday. All the same, if they want to have a quiet day once a week I wish they wouldn't drag religion into it. Religion always makes for bitterness. Don't you agree with me, Mr Fletcher?'

'It should not,' said the chaplain, a gentle deprecation in his voice.

'Oh, I'm not suggesting that's the whole object of religion, though, by Jove, after arguing at council meetings with one or two of those ministers from the West, I might be excused if I did think so. No, all I mean is I think religion should be kept out of ordinary life. But I'll always maintain religion's the finest thing in the world in its proper place. I've always maintained that, haven't I, Trixie?'

'Always, Donald,' his wife replied, with such a glance at the chaplain as the soft pedal of a piano might give did a soft pedal possess eyes.

Not that Mr Fletcher required the warning. He had not lived at Glenbogle for more than ten years to start arguing with Ben Nevis now.

'What about coming for a drive with me in Murdoch's car, Myrtle?' Hector MacDonald asked. 'You don't mind lending me your car, Murdoch?'

'Not a bit,' Murdoch replied, with the yawn of a watch-keeping lieutenant who hears with relief eight bells sound. He intended to doze away this Sabbath afternoon. 'You may sight some of those hiker blokes. Visibility is good.'

'That's a jolly fine notion of yours, Hector,' his father declared enthusiastically. 'Jolly fine. And tomorrow we'll get a move on.'

'I'd adore to come with you, Hector,' said Myrtle, 'but I promised Carrie I'd go with her to Knocknacolly and meet the new architect. And didn't you tell me, Carrie, there was a young poet or painter you wanted me to meet?'

'That's all right,' her brother put in. 'I'll go along with Carrie. You can meet these folks another time.'

'But, Chester, wouldn't you rather rest? You must be feeling terribly weary after yesterday,' his wife urged.

Chester Royde shook his head.

'No, no, I'll come along with you. I want to talk over one or two ideas of mine with the architect.'

Carrie with the lightest shrug of a shoulder signalled to her sister-in-law that she did not want to discourage Chester's interest in Knocknacolly, that sooner or later he would have to meet the young men, and that she considered it wiser for Myrtle to give way.

'You realize, don't you, that Mr Buchanan the lawyer hasn't arrived yet at Knocknacolly?' she asked when with Chester beside her instead of Myrtle she set off down Glenbogle that Sunday afternoon.

'I know, dear, but it's the architect I want to see, not the lawyer.'

'Can you move over a little to the left, Chester? I always feel cramped sitting on the wrong side of an automobile the way they do over here.'

'If I move any further along to the left the bulge on this side of your little runabout won't be any too easy to push in again.'

'I guess it must be your kilt, Chester.'

'What must be my kilt?'

'You never used to take up so much room before. I think you'd better drive.'

So they changed places, and Carrie felt safer, though no more comfortable.

'I wonder why the British build their automobiles for sardines instead of human beings,' Chester speculated as they turned round into Glenmore.

'Never mind, it won't be so long now before we reach Knocknacolly,' said Carrie.

It may be remembered that she and her sister-in-law had tried to cheer up with bright hangings one of the rooms of the Lodge for the visit of the Scottish Brotherhood of Action. With those hangings and with the lustral energy of the Widow Macdonald they had faintly lightened the gloom of that edifice in the baronial style which several years of emptiness and neglect had deepened. Nothing, however, they had been able to achieve in this direction was comparable to the effect achieved by the Macmillan and the Menzies tartan, the red and white of which was perhaps even more startling than the Buchanan polychrome.

Carrie need not have worried about the impression the young poet would make upon her unpoetical husband. After all, it was the brief glimpse Chester Royde had already caught of the Macmillan red and yellow from the window of the Daimler speeding up Glenbogle which had inspired the orange kilt he was now wearing. He stepped forward and shook the poet cordially by the hand.

'Mr Macmillan, I'm pleased to meet you,' he declared with a genuine warmth when Carrie had introduced the poet.

Nor was he less cordial when Robert Menzies, a swarthy little man with fine features, was presented to him.

'My sister-in-law was hoping to have the pleasure of meeting you this afternoon, Mr Menzies, and you too, Mr Macmillan, but she'd promised to go for a drive with our host's eldest son who's back on leave from India and so she couldn't manage to come along with Mr Royde and myself,' said Carrie.

It was useless to pretend. Alan's eyes were not quite so blue when he heard that Myrtle was not coming. She turned to the architect.

'Mr Royde is anxious to discuss our ideas for transforming or rebuilding Knocknacolly Lodge, Mr Menzies.'

'If you'll come in, Mrs Royde, I have a few rough sketches I'd like to show you.'

Indoors it was useless to pretend. Instead of coming indoors with them to share in the discussion of the sketches Alan lingered behind and was studying the Austin from which he had been expecting to see Myrtle alight. Carrie allowed herself one sigh, and then concentrated upon the architecture of the new Knocknacolly shooting-lodge.

'There were one or two things you specially wanted to ask Mr Menzies, Chester.'

'Only one thing,' he said. 'I wanted to ask Mr Menzies if he'd ever designed a dungeon from which a contortionist couldn't escape until the man who put him there let him go.'

'No, I can't say I ever have, Mr Royde.'

'Get busy Mr Menzies and design one. That dungeon and a biggish room to hang up stags' heads in are all I want. Mrs Royde'll let you know what she wants.'

'A dungeon, Chester?' his wife exclaimed.

'I want Mr Menzies to design me the finest dungeon that was ever built. I want a dungeon that'll make Sing Sing look like a bandbox,' said Chester Royde sternly.

'A dungeon rather suggests you would like to carry on the tradition of the earlier Scottish architecture before it was so much influenced by the French alliance,' said the architect. 'I have as a matter of fact a sketch here of a building which would certainly suit the scene here and yet is as modern as some of the latest work of the functional school. The only thing is that it would mean pulling down the present residence altogether.'

'Let's have a look at this sketch,' said Chester.

Robert Menzies produced from his portfolio a watercolour of a severe and massive keep defying the surrounding bens.

'That is the way it will appear from the north,' he explained. Then he produced another sketch. 'And this is how it will appear from the south.'

This aspect showed as much glass as the other aspect showed of stone.

'In summer all these windows would slide back like this,' the architect went on, and produced another sketch which transformed the southerly, south-westerly, and south-easterly aspects of the keep into tiers of loggias.

'I haven't worked out the details,' he continued. 'So much depends on the number of rooms you want, but my aim would be to expand vertically rather than horizontally, in the way that New York itself has expanded. Referring back to that dungeon, I think you will see the strength of any dungeon in a building like this. However, I'm afraid I'm wasting your time with a fantasy, for of course I realize that a place like this is not practical.'

'Why not?' Chester Royde snapped.

'It would cost too much to build.'

'How much?'

Robert Menzies shook his head.

'I could not say exactly. So much would depend on the size and the number of rooms.'

'Well, I'd want to be able to entertain about a dozen guests,' said Chester Royde. 'And I'd want a big central hall and a library and a big dining-room and a room for Mrs Royde and a room for my stags' heads, and say sixteen bedrooms.'

'That would mean at least four lifts.'

'Four what?'

'Four elevators,' Carrie put in.

'I wonder why you British folk can't use simple ordinary English for simple ordinary everyday appliances,' said Chester Royde. 'Well, I've given you a rough idea of what we'd want. Give me a rough idea of what it would cost.'

'Certainly not a penny less than forty thousand pounds,' said the architect. 'Transport would be tremendous up here. Oh, I'm afraid my idea is just fantastic.'

'Why?' Chester Royde snapped again.

'Well, the cost.'

'Don't bother about the cost. If you can satisfy me you have a proposition that will give me value for my money I'm not worrying about the cost. How long will it take to build?'

'At least eighteen months, and even to get it finished in that time would increase the cost.'

'How do you like this house, Carrie?' her husband asked.

'I think it might be wonderful,' she answered a little vaguely, for she was thinking about Alan's obvious disappointment over Myrtle.

'See here, Mr Menzies. You get to work on a more detailed proposition on the lines indicated, and if Mrs Royde and I approve your design you can obtain an estimate from a builder. I don't want to go beyond three hundred thousand dollars.'

'That's about sixty thousand pounds,' the architect murmured in a voice that sounded like the voice of one in dreamland.

'Just about,' Chester Royde agreed.

Robert Menzies passed a hand across his brow. He had an idea that it was damp. It was.

'I'll get to work on the plans right away, Mr Royde,' he said hoarsely, for the moisture on his brow had escaped there from his throat.

'That's fine,' said Chester Royde. Then he turned to his wife. 'I guess we don't want to talk about this old lodge. It just wants pulling down as soon as possible.'

The architect suggested showing a few more of his sketches, but Royde dismissed the notion.

'No, you concentrate on this little place you have in your mind. I believe it's going to be good. I've taken a fancy to it already. And mind, Mr Menzies, that dungeon must be the toughest thing in dungeons ever built.'

Alan Macmillan came into the room and Carrie told him that she and Myrtle would be up soon; but he was obviously still too much disappointed by Myrtle's failure to reach Knocknacolly today on account of her date with Young Ben Nevis to respond to so vague a date as 'soon'.

'What's the matter with you, Alan?' asked Robert Menzies when the Roydes had left.

'Oh, just a feeling that life is a blind alley, that's all,' Alan replied morosely.

'Blind alley?' Robert Menzies echoed. 'If I get the job to build this keep . . .' he broke off. 'No, I will not believe it's going to happen. Man, do you realize that if it did happen I'd make perhaps three thousand pounds? Three thousand pounds! It's a fantastic sum of money. But no, no. I just will not believe it's going to happen. I wish Mrs Royde had seemed a little more interested. That's what's worrying me. But her husband's keen, I believe. That's a strange kilt he's wearing. What did you make of it?'

'I didn't notice it.'

'You didn't what?'

'I didn't notice it.'

'Gosh, Alan, no wonder you think life's a blind alley!' Robert Menzies exclaimed in amazement. 'We'll have James with us on Tuesday or Wednesday. If I get this keep to build and James gets the business side to look after . . . Alan, it's just incredible. It's like something in a fairy-story. Well, when James told me about that donation of twenty pounds to the S.B.A. I was really staggered, but that was only a beginning. He and I may get anywhere with a start like this. Oh, boy, America's a great country.'

'I wish you'd get on with your plans and abstain from platitudinous ejaculation,' Alan observed severely.

If Robert Menzies had heard what Carrie was saying to her husband on the way back to Glenbogle in the Austin he would have felt that the likelihood of his plans for the keep being accepted were indeed incredible, for she was asking Chester if he did not think he was making Knocknacolly a much bigger proposition than they had originally intended.

'It's sweet of you, Chester, but I never wanted you to spend so much money on it as that.'

'I thought you were aiming to make Knocknacolly the centre of this Scottish rebirth?'

'Yes, Chester, I *had* thought of doing that.'

'If you're going to have a centre you want it to look like a centre, and

I guess that building will look like a centre. Anyway, I want a stronghold up here. We can rent a place next summer when we come over, but the year after that I aim to spend three months killing off what stags I don't kill next year and shutting up every hiker I can catch in that new dungeon.'

'You'll have forgotten all about hikers by then.'

'Never,' he declared. 'I'll never forget about hikers till I've shut up that guy with the chin in a dungeon alive with mice.'

'But, Chester, I don't want mice at Knocknacolly.'

'If this Scottish architect of yours builds that dungeon as I want it built not even a mouse will be able to get out of it.'

Carrie would have shuddered if there had been room to shudder beside Chester in her runabout, but there was no room for more than the faintest twitch of disgust, and even that was not easy.

'Tell me, Chester,' she said presently, 'how did you like the poet?'

'He didn't say a great deal. I thought poets always had a mouthful to say. But I liked that tartan of his.'

'He was unusually quiet this afternoon. I guess he must have been thinking about a poem.'

'Maybe he was. I don't know what way that takes anybody, but I suppose poetry's something like crossword puzzles, and they keep people quiet except when they're asking fool questions of other people to get themselves out of a dictionary jam.'

When the car reached Kenspeckle a party of hikers bowed down by camping equipment were alighting from a Fort William omnibus. Among them was Mr Sydney Prew.

'Why, there's that spider-legged guy Ben Nevis shook up on the Twelfth!' Chester exclaimed, pulling up and jumping out of the car without sticking long enough in the door for Carrie to tug at his doublet and beseech him to do nothing rash.

The hikers looked apprehensive. Loaded as they were with camping equipment, they were incapable of defending themselves against what they supposed was the Highland chieftain on whom they had declared war.

The Secretary of the N.U.H. allayed their anxiety and came forward primly to meet Chester Royde.

'Can I give you any information?' he asked. He did not recognize Chester as one of those who had attacked him on the Twelfth.

'No, you can't; but I can give you some information,' said Chester truculently. 'I can inform you that you're safer away from this part of Scotland. There's a war on up here, and you may get hurt.'

'Oh, indeed?' asked Mr Prew perkily. 'And may one inquire if you are one of the enemy?'

He remembered that the reinforcements he was bringing to the Acting President were not in a position to offer fight at the moment, but he did not suppose that this orange-kilted Fascist bully would venture to attack twelve of them. Moreover, he noticed from the corner of his eye that Constable MacGillivray was within hail.

'I had the pleasure of helping to run you out of Glenbogle just over a fortnight ago,' said Chester. 'And I'll have great pleasure in repeating the operation. Only, I'll make you hurry twice as fast next time.'

The Secretary turned to his detachment.

'Boys, this is one of them,' he said. 'I recognize him now.' Then he turned to Chester again. 'I do not know your name, Mr Mac . . .'

'Mr Mac nothing!'

'Mr MacNothing.'

'My name's Royde, not MacNothing,' Chester shouted wrathfully.

'As you please, Mr Royde. The boys here and myself are not impressed by either name. However, I have no leisure to bandy words with you on the King's highway. And now, boys, off we go. We have a long trek before us yet and we want to pitch our camp before the shades of night fall fast.'

If Chester had been a good intelligence officer he would have waited to see what direction Sydney Prew and his reinforcements took, for thus he would have made a valuable reconnaissance for the defenders of Glenbogle. However, with the figure of Constable MacGillivray to deter him from throwing Mr Prew into Loch Ness, he had only one way in which to relieve his feelings and that was to squeeze himself back into the Austin and drive on to Glenbogle as fast as possible.

Meanwhile, Mr Prew and eleven heavily-loaded young men trudged on towards the headquarters camp of the N.U.H. forces, which was situated in one of the corries of mighty Ben Booey. It had been dark for a good two hours when the reinforcements reached their destination.

'You're very late, Mr Prew,' said the General Officer Commanding sternly.

'We may have missed the shortest route,' his Chief of Staff admitted. 'Still, I expect we shall muddle through in the time-honoured way to victory.'

Percy Buckham drew himself up proudly.

'There has been no muddling through so far, Mr Prew. Yesterday afternoon we locked up Mr MacDonald of Ben Nevis in one of his own dungeons. A very brilliant little operation for a commencement.'

'Oh, huzza, Mr Buckham, huzza, huzza!' cried Mr Prew as loudly as the exertion of the climb a third of the way up Ben Booey would allow him.

'Yes, we snaffled him with a sack. I recognized him by his orange kilt.'

'Orange kilt?' Mr Prew echoed. 'That couldn't have been MacDonald, Mr Buckham; that must have been somebody called Royde. I was parleying with him anon. An American, if one may judge by his accent. But what of it? As I said, we shall muddle through in the time-honoured way to victory.'

Half an hour later the Chief of Staff was summoned to the General's tent to hear his plan of action. In ordinary circumstances a camp of over fifty male and female hikers would have been resounding with favourite choruses lustily shouted round the camp fire, but the leader had insisted that his force should remember it was on active service in hostile country and behave accordingly. Sentries had been posted; in the tents the lanterns were masked; the low murmur of conversation was audible only when drawing near to one of them.

'Come in, Mr Prew,' the leader rapped out in a militaristic tone of voice. Whether as command or invitation it was unnecessary, for Mr Prew tripped over one of the ropes at the moment it was uttered and dived into the tent with such velocity that he might have dived right through it if the occupier had not been sitting cross-legged in the way.

'I'm so sorry, Mr Buckham. I don't know how I came to do that. I must have tripped, I think.'

'I think so too,' the leader said sarcastically. 'Well, before you turn in I want you to get at any rate the rough outline of my plan of action.'

'The rough outline? Quite. The details of course can be elaborated later.'

'Quite,' Mr Buckham agreed.

'Quite,' Mr Prew echoed.

'Have you your map with you?'

'I have, yes. At least I think I have. Ah yes, I have.'

'Your elbow went into my eye then, Mr Prew.'

'I am so sorry.'

'All right. I'll get my own map out.'

It was now Mr Buckham's turn to excavate the hip-pocket of his shorts, but when he and his Chief of Staff tried simultaneously to open their maps the stability of the tent was threatened, and in the end they had to sit cross-legged side by side and study the same map like two pre-Atatürk Turks poring over the Koran.

'This is roughly where we are now,' said Mr Buckham, obliterating Ben Booey with that thumb which always delighted palmists by an almost morbid display of the characteristics associated with self-will.

'Quite.'

'The present concentration is fifty-two – thirty-six men and sixteen women. I understand we may expect another twenty-nine, of which seventeen are men, on Saturday and Sunday. Next week therefore will see us at our maximum strength, and I propose to make an attempt to seize and occupy Glenbogle Castle on Tuesday, 7 September. Meanwhile, harassing operations over a wide extent of country will be carried on throughout this week by the force at my disposal, for which purpose it will be broken up into six columns each consisting of six men and two women.'

'But that leaves four women unaccounted for.'

'They will be used as a mobile reserve. *La donna è mobile*,' Mr Buckham hummed.

'Quite,' said Mr Prew, wondering what on earth his Commander-in-Chief was talking about. 'And these harassing operations, what will they entail?'

'Uprooting of all notices of "No Camping". Menacing warnings posted up on buildings. Weird noises in the vicinity of the Castle at night. Seizure of hostages whenever and wherever possible. The columns will operate from camps on Ben Gorm, Ben Glass, Ben Cruet, in the country above Strathdun and Strathdiddle, and from where we are now, which will be my headquarters. The commanders of columns will see I receive a daily report of the damage inflicted on the enemy. I will give instructions for the principal operation on Monday, 6 September, when the whole of the present force together with the reinforcements expected next Saturday and Sunday will be concentrated where we are now. I think that's all perfectly clear?'

'Oh, clear as daylight,' said Mr Prew.

'You're sure the man in the orange kilt we captured yesterday was not MacDonald?'

'Oh, definitely, Mr Buckham.'

'A pity. Never mind, we'll shut him up in one of his own dungeons when we seize the Castle next week.'

'Quite.'

'You sound sleepy, Mr Prew.'

'Perhaps a trifle. Yes, well, we had quite a trek up here from Kenspeckle. I think unless you have anything more to discuss, Mr Buckham, I'll be off to my own tent and turn in.'

Mr Prew was half-way through another yawn when the face of one of the sentries, a solemn narrow-headed young man called Arthur Blencoe, appeared in the opening of the tent.

'Hullo, Blencoe, something suspicious on the move?' asked his leader.

'I wanted to know if those shaggy bullocks round here are apt to be at all fierce at night, Mr Buckham.'

'I don't suppose so. Why?'

'Well, there's about forty of them nosing about the camp,' said the sentry. 'They've got horns on them like mammoths. I mean to say it may be all right, but I wouldn't care to interfere with them without I knew they were really all right.'

'I sympathize with you, Arthur,' said Mr Prew. 'I should be inclined to let them alone.'

'They're not doing any harm?' Mr Buckham asked.

'No, they're just nosing about round the tents, and snorting occasionally,' Arthur Blencoe replied.

'I think I'd leave them alone if I were you, Blencoe,' his leader advised. 'They're curious about the tents, that's all it is. They'll move along presently, I expect.'

'The moon's pretty bright now,' said Arthur Blencoe. 'And I thought one or two of them looked at me a bit hard.'

'Only curiosity,' his leader assured him.

'Yes, I agree with Mr Buckham,' said Mr Prew. 'Just curiosity.'

'It may be,' said Arthur Blencoe, doubtfully.

'I think you're prefectly safe to go back to your post,' his leader told him.

'Oh, definitely,' Mr Prew agreed. 'You're not turning in just yet, are you, Mr Buckham?'

'Not for another half-hour.'

'I thought I'd stay and talk over one or two little arrangements. My sleepiness has vanished all of a sudden. No, no, Arthur, I wouldn't worry my head at all about those bullocks. After all, they are only bullocks, you must remember.'

Mr Prew's reassurances were sharply interrupted by a wild shriek the echoes of which among the crags and precipices of Ben Booey were drowned by a louder shriek that made Mr Buckham's chin quiver like blancmange.

A moment later the ground was shaken by the thunder of hooves and Arthur Blencoe wriggled into the tent like a crocodile taking cover in the Nile.

'Something must have frightened them to stampede like that,' said Mr Buckham in a voice which lacked a little of its wonted incisiveness.

Mr Prew peeped out cautiously.

'Yes, they've stampeded right away from the camp. I remember now reading somewhere that these Highland cattle are very easily scared. But what caused the shriek?'

By now the camp was a-buzz, and figures were crawling out of the tents into the moonlight on every side.

'We must investigate,' Mr Buckham decided, his chin back to its old jut, his voice as vibrant as ever again. 'If you and Mr Prew will move, Blencoe, I'll be able to move myself.'

In the furthest corner of the camp a knot of hikers had gathered. The leader walked quickly towards it, and asked what was the matter.

'Oh, Mr Buckham, it's Gladys and Mabel Woodmonger,' a young woman babbled excitedly. 'A bull put his head into their tent and blew on Gladys's face and when she screamed he caught his horns in the tent and went off with it. I looked out when I heard the scream and the bull charged right past me waving the tent on his horns, and all the other bulls went galloping off like mad things.'

'Is that all?' the leader commented with the icy indifference of a dictator who hears that the purge he ordered has been carried out. 'Well, you'd better get back to your tents.'

'But Gladys and Mabel Woodmonger haven't got a tent, Mr Buckham. The bull took it away with him.'

'They must squeeze in somewhere else. Now, Blencoe, you'd better get back to your post.'

And this was the man whom, away across the glen in his castle, the Lord of Ben Nevis, Glenbogle, Glenbristle, Strathdiddle, Strathdun, Loch Hoch, and Loch Hoo thought light-heartedly he could expel from his demesne like a stray cat from a backyard.

Chapter 17

FISHING

During the next two or three days nothing occurred to precipitate a direct clash with the forces of the hikers. Reports came in of 'No Camping' notice-boards being thrown down or defaced, but none of the Glenbogle keepers or gillies caught more than an occasional glimpse of the elusive invaders. The Castle garrison lost Murdoch MacDonald, who had to rejoin his ship, his leave being over. However, as nobody in the Castle was aware of Buckham's proposal to attack, seize, and occupy it, nobody was particularly worried by the departure of Murdoch and his bulging muscles.

Ben Nevis was annoyed by the news about the notice-boards, but he contented himself with giving orders to destroy any camping equipment found on his land and to hale before his judgement-seat every hiker caught trespassing.

This judgement-seat (*Cathair-breitheanais Mhic 'ic Eachainn*) was a prostrate megalith upon a grassy mound overlooking the Bogle about half a mile down the glen.

'From time immemorial Mac 'ic Eachainn has sat here to give judgement,' the Chieftain proclaimed solemnly to his guests. 'Cahav-rayanishvickickyackan we call it in the Gaelic.'

'That must have frightened bad men out of this part of the country before there was any need of a posse,' observed Chester Royde. 'You might click that out again, will you?'

'Cahavrayanishvickickyackan.'

'You know, Carrie,' her husband said gravely, 'the more I hear of Gaelic the more it reminds me of the Carroway language. That sounds very like "pleased to meet you" in Carroway. It sounds a bit like ducks in a marsh too, but then so does "pleased to meet you" in Carroway.'

'How is it spelt, Ben Nevis?' Carrie asked. She was sure such a word was right outside the scope of *Gaelic Without Tears*. Indeed, it was a cataract in itself.

'Ah, I'm afraid I can't spell it for you,' said Ben Nevis. 'As a matter of fact very few people can spell in Gaelic, and I always believe those who say they can only get away with it because nobody else can, if you see what I mean. No, I picked up my Gaelic by ear from my nurse. I used to rattle it off when I was four years old.'

'I've got it,' Chester exclaimed.

'Got what?'

'What that word reminded me of. It's not ducks. It's a machine-gun. Say it once again, will you?'

'Cahavrayanishvickickyackan.'

'Yes, it's just the noise a machine-gun makes in action. And you picked up that word by ear, Ben Nevis, when you were four years old?'

'I did indeed. And my nurse used to sit up there with me and tell me stories about my ancestors. I always remember what an impression Hector MacDonald, the fourth of Ben Nevis, made on me. He had a tusk.'

'A tusk?' Chester Royde exclaimed.

'Yes, as big as a walrus according to clan tradition. Well, this Hector of the Tusk as they called him was an absolute terror on the judgement-seat. He thought nothing of hanging or spearing or drowning or burning twenty or thirty felons in a day. And he had one very curious habit. When he'd condemned some felon to death he used to nick the back of his head with this tusk. I suppose the idea was to prevent confusion. I mean to say, there was nobody in those days to write down who'd been condemned and who hadn't. But of course once these felons had been nicked with Hector's tusk they were marked down for execution. The nick this tusk made was known as Mac 'ic Eachainn's kiss. Pockvickicky-ackan in Gaelic. And the extraordinary thing is that to this day up in Strathdiddle if anybody gets a scar the people will say, "Hullo, I see Mac 'ic Eachainn's been kissing you." Of course after the Forty-five, when the hereditary jurisdictions were abolished, the judgement-seat was never used. But I thought it would be the appropriate place to try any hikers we catch.'

'Pity you haven't got a tusk like your ancestor, Ben Nevis,' said Chester Royde. 'I'd give a thousand dollars to see you nick a square inch out of that hobo's chin.'

'Hector of the Tusk must have been an ancestor of yours too, Carrie,' Ben Nevis reminded her.

Three weeks ago Carrie would have been thrilled by the thought of having such an ancestor, but just now her mind was concentrated upon the present. It had been made clear during her last visit to Knocknacolly that Alan Macmillan was in love with Myrtle. If it had been a case of which of the two of them he fancied for a summertime flirtation she would have been jealous at his choice of Myrtle, but if he had really fallen in love jealousy was out of the question, and she intended to show herself worthy of her membership of the Scottish Brotherhood of Action by doing all she could to help him. Having made up her mind accordingly, she was not well pleased to notice the amount of attention Myrtle was allowing Young Ben Nevis to pay her. It was obvious she was not in the least in love with him and her own Macdonald blood did not urge her to do anything to help in bringing about such a match. On the other hand, she fancied Myrtle might easily fall in love with Alan Macmillan, and if she did she was determined to promote that match. She would persuade Chester to give Myrtle the Keep of Knocknacolly as a wedding-present and she and Alan could preside there together over the accouchement of Scotland's rebirth. Carrie felt as noble as Sydney Carton when on the Wednesday of that week she asked Myrtle to come with her to Knocknacolly and fetch James Buchanan with the deeds.

'I can't, Carrie. I've promised Hector to go fishing with him.'

'Fishing for what? Compliments?'

'No, fishing for fishes.'

'You haven't seen Alan Macmillan since he came back,' Carrie remarked, eyeing her sister-in-law keenly.

'I know, but Hector's going back to India on Friday.'

'And you want to see if you can make him propose to you before he goes, just for the pleasure of refusing him?'

'You know, angel child, there are moments when I wish my dearly beloved brother had never met you,' said Myrtle.

'Oh, you do?'

'I certainly do.'

'Myrtle! Myrtle!' sounded the loud bark of Young Ben Nevis. 'Oh, there you are! Look here, we ought to be starting. I'm going to use a Redwinged Biffer this afternoon.'

'What's that? A new cocktail?'

Hector guffawed merrily.

'No, no; it's the best fly for Loch Hoch. Always use Redwinged Biffers there. But I'll take two or three Blue Spankers as well, because if they won't look at a Redwinged Biffer, that's the time to try 'em either with a Blue Spanker or a Smith's Zigzag Nonpareil. Iain! Iain!'

'What is it?'

'Have you got any Zigzag Nonpareils? Myrtle and I are tootling over to Loch Hoch, and I haven't one left.'

'Here you are,' growled Mary, detaching a couple of gaudy flies and handing them to her brother.

'Oh, that's very sporting of you, Muggins. Thanks awfully. Are you ready, Myrtle?'

'I'm ready.'

'Hullo, going off fishing with Hector?' Ben Nevis woofed, when he met them in the entrance-hall. 'Hope you'll have good sport. What flies are you taking, Hector?'

His eldest son told him, and the Chieftain shook his head.

'If you're wise you'll take some Yellow Munks — medium and large. When you get a day early in September clouding over about eleven o'clock after a bright morning, Yellow Munks are the flies for Loch Hoch. That was always my experience when I fished regularly.'

'You prefer Yellow Munks to Speckled Champions?' Hector asked.

'Oh, every time, my dear boy, every time. If I couldn't make 'em look at Yellow Munks I'd try 'em with Forktailed Violets before Speckled Champions any day, or for that matter Brown Nixies.'

'If you suggest any more bugs to Hector, he'll want a beehive to carry them around,' Myrtle said.

'Bugs?' Ben Nevis echoed in astonishment. 'You never fish with bugs.'

'Well, what are we going to do with these rainbow-coloured bugs if the fish won't eat them?'

'These aren't bugs. These are flies,' Ben Nevis said.

'We call them bugs at home.'

'*Do* you?' Ben Nevis exclaimed in amazement, and as his eldest son and Myrtle got into the two-seater he shook his head in what was evidently a sudden apprehensiveness about the future. Then he recalled the Chester Royde millions, and his brow cleared like Ben Cruet's peak emerging from the wrack of a passing storm.

When Carrie reached Knocknacolly she found James Buchanan waiting for her, dressed in a dark grey suit and wearing a dark grey hat.

'James,' she cried, 'where's your kilt?'

'A kilt is not the right way to dress for a matter of business. I have all the papers for Mr Royde to sign.'

'But my husband will be terribly disappointed if you don't wear your kilt. I tried to tell him what the colours were in the Buchanan tartan; but after red, yellow, dark blue, light blue, dark green, light green, purple, and puce I couldn't remember any more. I told my husband there were quite a lot more colours in it, and he was very very interested. I said it was really brighter than the Macmillan tartan and he said he couldn't believe that was possible. Oh, how d'ye do, Mr Menzies? I'm glad to see *you* haven't left off the kilt to work at your plans. How are you getting along?'

'I'll be able to give you quite a good idea of what I'm trying to do by the end of the week, Mrs Royde.'

'I'm so glad. We're both of us so keenly interested.'

The fantastic sum of £3,000 once more became credible to Robert Menzies. His dark eyes glittered.

'I was just telling Mr Buchanan I thought it was a pity to put off his kilt the way he has.'

'Och, no, Mrs Royde,' said James obstinately. 'I always draw a sharp distinction between business and pleasure. I wouldn't feel comfortable arranging a matter of business in the kilt, I really wouldn't.'

'Where's Alan?'

James looked round.

'He was here a minute ago. Where did Alan go to, Robert?'

'I don't know where he went. Will I give him a shout?'

'Oh, that would be kind, Mr Menzies,' said Carrie.

The architect went off to look for the poet, and Carrie turned to the lawyer.

'James, you just have to put on your kilt. I know what I'm talking about. I know my husband. You don't. I want you to make an impression on him. And listen, James, I want Alan to come with us because, when you and my husband and Mr Hugh Cameron of Kilwhillie go to Inverness to settle up everything at Kilwhillie's lawyers, I want Alan to go for a ride with me.'

'I'm sorry to disoblige you, Mistress Royde . . .' the lawyer began.

'There you are, you see, James. You can't believe you're a member of the S.B.A. when you're dressed in those town clothes. You turn all stiff and awkward.'

'Mistress Royde,' the lawyer went on, 'you've been kinder to me than enough. You've been kind to all three of us. I'm grateful to you. I hope you'll believe that. Very grateful. But all the gratitude I feel could not make me go to the office of Macbeth, Macbeth, and Macbean in the kilt.'

'But Kilwhillie and my husband will be wearing kilts,' Carrie argued.

'They're clients, Mistress Royde. Clients are in a different position. I'm a lawyer. Macbeth, Macbeth, and Macbean are lawyers. And they would consider it a very grave breach of legal etiquette if I were to assist at a matter like this, wearing the kilt. It would . . . it would . . . well, I just cannot do it, Mistress Royde, even to oblige you.'

Poor James was evidently suffering so acutely that Carrie had not the heart to plague him longer.

'Very well, James, if you feel as strongly as that about it, you must do as you like, but it's going to be a disappointment to my husband.'

James grinned his relief, and recovered his dignity by asking Alan in his gruffest voice what he was at keeping Mistress Royde waiting like this.

'Waiting for what?' the poet asked, assuming a rival dignity.

'Did you not ken she's taking you for a ride?'

'I never heard anything about a ride,' the poet protested.

'Oh yes, Alan, we arranged that last time I came to Knocknacolly.'

'I must have forgotten,' he said.

'You're getting awful absent-minded these days, Alan,' said his friend severely. 'It's a good job Robert and I don't go about with our heads in the clouds the way you do.'

'I'm very sorry, Mrs Royde,' said the poet. 'But I really hadn't understood you expected me to go for a drive with you today. How is Miss Royde?'

Carrie shook her head.

'James, I guess you've put the Scottish Brotherhood of Action into town clothes as well as yourself. Myrtle's very well, Alan. Come on, we ought to be moving. It's too bad leaving Mr Menzies behind. But I know he wants to work at his plans.'

'Och, he's back at work on them already,' said James. 'He's just living in a dream. Though if he'd arranged to go for a drive with a lady he wouldn't have forgotten it,' James added severely. 'Imphm! I'm telling you, Alan.'

When the Austin reached the gates of Glenbogle Castle Carrie was inspired by the two water-horses mordant on their pillars to park Alan and the car by a clump of pines and walk up the drive with James. Her original intention had been to bring Alan back to lunch, but she decided it would be more fun to picnic with him tête-à-tête, and in view of her proposed self-abnegation she considered that she was entitled to the pleasure of such a tête-à-tête.

'I'll come back for you when I've introduced James to my husband. He'll be having lunch at the Castle, before they drive to Inverness.'

'And you're not going to be there?' asked James, aghast at the prospect before him.

'No, I want you business men to get together,' said Carrie firmly.

To her surprise she found Chester had doffed the kilt and was back in one of his rural costumes from the full-page colour advertisements of *Esquire*.

'Why, Chester, Mr Buchanan wouldn't wear his lovely rainbow of a kilt and now you're not wearing yours.'

'Well, it was Kilwhillie. According to him there's a prejudice in Inverness against anybody they don't know wearing a kilt. There's some kind of a Ku Klux Klan of a Kilt Society, it appears, which takes action against outsiders. I couldn't understand what it was all about, but he set off on such a rigmarole I got tired of it and changed. Do you know anything about this kilt society, Mr Buchanan?'

'All kilt societies are ridiculous exhibitions of snobbishness, Mr Royde,' James Buchanan declared.

'Well, what about beating up this particular one some day?' Chester asked.

'It's what it requires,' said James sternly.

'I'm glad to hear you agree with me,' Chester said. 'I guess if you and I and your two friends at Knocknacolly went into Inverness in our kilts we'd make that bum society look pretty foolish.'

'Och ay, and it would give the *Inverness Courier* something to write about for a change,' said James.

Carrie saw with pleasure that Chester liked her young lawyer, and she slipped away to extract a picnic lunch for two from Toker.

She and Alan ate it together up at the Pass of Ballochy, looking down from a green knoll upon the silver stretch of Loch Hoch and over the wide level of Strathdun. They talked of the Scottish rebirth of which the Keep of Knocknacolly was to be the centre; they talked of the accident of Carrie's walking up Glenbristle that day not yet quite three weeks ago; they talked of Carrie's progress in Gaelic.

'I found out a strange thing the other day. Do you know what roid means? R-O-I-D.'

Carrie said she had no idea.

'I looked up roid in my dictionary.'

'Oh, you did? R-O-I-D without an E, you said?'

'Yes.'

'I wonder what made you look up such a word?'

'It just came into my head.'

'I see. And what does it mean?'

'That's the extraordinary thing. It means "bog-myrtle".'

A slow blush flowed into the poet's face and to shake off his embarrassment he ran down the slope to gather some sprigs of a miniature shrub that was growing in profusion in the moist ground below.

'Crush the leaves. They smell very sweet.'

'Alan, they smell delicious.'

'Do you remember that poem of mine, *Peaty Water?*'

'I certainly do.'

'I've added to it slightly. This is how it goes now.

> 'The sweet breath of bog-myrtle
> Blows on the wind,
> And green grow they still,
> The leaves of the bog-myrtle.
> But the heather,
> The fading heather,
> Is spread like the robe of a dead king
> Upon my country.
> Upon my dying country.
> I do not lament, therefore, but laugh
> When down through the stale dead purple
> Dances the peaty water,
> Warm with the sharp sun of the high tops,
> Prickt by the sun of the high tops,
> The prattling peaty dark-brown water,
> The warm dark-brown water of life
> Whose sweet breath blows on the wind,
> Bringing bog-myrtle.'

'Yes, you certainly have made it very much clearer now. I'm wondering how I ever thought the water of life was the S.B.A.,' Carrie murmured half to herself. 'We'll go on soon, will we, and explore around Loch Hoch?'

Not long before Carrie and Alan reached the loch Hector MacDonald had decided that the day must be redeemed from failure by landing a bigger catch than any its water could provide. He and Myrtle had been rowed up and down by a gillie for four hours without persuading a single fish to pay the slightest attention to Redwinged Biffers, Blue Spankers, Zigzag Nonpareils, or Yellow Munks. It was after three o'clock, and Hector had had to give up all hope of catching the trout he had promised to cook for Myrtle's lunch.

'Most extraordinary thing. I've never known Yellow Munks to fail even when every other fly's been a wash-out. I expect you're feeling hungry, aren't you?'

'I believe I could toy with two or three crumbs,' Myrtle admitted.

'Well, what about landing on Ellenanie?'

'Is she good company?'

'Is who good company?'

'Ellen.'

'Ellen who?'

'I don't know, Hector. She's your friend, not mine. You suggested landing on her.'

He guffawed genially.

'Oh, Ellananie! That's that island over there. I thought it would be a good place for lunch.'

'Any place sounds good to me with lunch tacked on to it,' said Myrtle. 'If we don't eat soon I'll start nibbling at those bugs the fish refused.'

Hector turned to the gillie.

'All right, Lachy, put us ashore on Ellenanie and come back for us in about half an hour.' He turned to Myrtle again. 'There's one fly I haven't tried yet. Hopkinson's Belted Pinkhead.'

'Why don't you try a garden-worm, Hector? I used to catch lots of little fishes with garden-worms in our lake at home.'

'I'm afraid that wouldn't be considered very sporting, would it, Lachy?'

Lachlan Macdonald looked at Myrtle as if she were another Lucrezia Borgia, and shook his head in stern disapproval.

'You rather shocked poor Lachy,' Hector told her when they had landed on the little island, which consisted of about half a rood of lush grass with a bosket of rowans and elders in the middle.

'He'll get over it,' Myrtle prophesied confidently. 'My, those sandwiches certainly look good.'

They both munched away in silence for a while until hunger had been assuaged.

'I don't believe I care a great lot for fishing,' said Myrtle at last. 'I think putting the stone and fishing are kind of slow.'

'I think fishing is very like life, if you see what I mean.'

'Elucidate,' she bade.

'Well, I mean to say, some people go through life and catch a basketful and others don't catch anything.'

'You're some philosopher, aren't you?'

'Oh, I wouldn't go as far as that,' said Hector modestly. 'I mean to say we don't get any time for that sort of thing in the Army. But I think a good deal to myself. It's awfully hot in India and sometimes I can't sleep and then I start thinking.'

'What do you think about?'

'Oh, I don't think about anything in particular. You know? I just think.'

'But you must think about something.'

'I don't, really. Unless of course there's something to think about. I mean like what we'd have made if my partner had redoubled in some hand at contract. Do you play much contract?'

'Never.'

'You are an extraordinary girl, Myrtle. You must find it awfully dull sometimes, don't you?'

'No; I've kept myself awake all right so far.'

'Did you ever think about marrying?'

Myrtle looked quickly at Hector MacDonald, but a second later she looked even more quickly beyond him across the water to where a red-and-yellow kilt was walking with Carrie beside the banks of Loch Hoch.

'Think about marrying?' she echoed. 'Do you mean marrying anybody in particular?'

'As a matter of fact, that's just what I did mean,' said Hector, snapping at the hook of the interrogation mark much more greedily than the trout of Loch Hoch had snapped at any of his flies. 'I mean to say, could you think about marrying me?'

'Why, Hector, I don't believe I could,' she answered, still following over Hector's shoulder the progress of that red-and-yellow kilt beside the banks of Loch Hoch.

'I just asked the question,' Hector said. 'I mean to say if you can't think about marrying me it's not much use my suggesting we might get married. Or is it?'

'No, Hector, I'm afraid it isn't. After all, we are such very good friends, and I think it would be sad to spoil a friendship by getting married.'

'Yes, I see what you mean. And you feel sure it would spoil it?'

'Oh yes, Hector, I certainly do.'

'I'd chuck the Army, of course, if we got married. As a matter of fact I am pretty bored with it. Our Colonel's rather a trying fellow. He's worrying about another war all the time.'

'Oh, I don't believe we will have another war.'

'No, that's what worries him,' said Hector. 'But as I say, if we got married I'd chuck the Army.'

'Oh, Hector, look! There's Carrie!'

'So it is. But what on earth's that walking with her?'

'Surely it's somebody in a kilt. Oo-hoo! Oo-hoo! O Carrie! She's walking away from us. Carrie! Isn't it silly of her not to hear me and turn around,' Myrtle exclaimed petulantly.

'I don't know what she's got with her, but it doesn't matter to us, does it?'

'Of course it does, Hector. Carrie! O Carrie! I'm sure she's looking for me. I hope nothing's happened to Chester. She just won't turn around. She is very silly sometimes. Where's Lachy? It's surely time he came back for us.'

'I told him half an hour.'

'I'm sure we've been on this island more than half an hour. I really do think Carrie can be thoroughly stupid when she chooses.'

'We'll row after them when Lachy comes back.'

'I don't know why we didn't eat our lunch on the banks.'

'I thought you'd prefer the island.'

'But islands are so inconvenient, Hector. When you're on an island you can't get off it. And I'm sure Carrie's looking for me.'

By the time Lachlan Macdonald arrived with the boat, Carrie was a mile away along the banks of Loch Hoch, and the red-and-yellow of Alan's kilt seemed no larger than a bandana handkerchief.

'It's all right, Myrtle,' said Hector. 'The Austin is still there. She's evidently only gone for a stroll with whatever it is she's strolling with. Shall we have a shot with Hopkinson's Belted Pinkhead while we're waiting for her to come back?'

Myrtle danced with impatience.

'I don't want to fish any more, Hector. I'm tired of fishing. It's a bromide sport anyway. You stay here and fling your imitation bugs about. I'm going to walk along and meet Carrie.'

Any mortification Hector felt at being thus deserted was forgotten when on Hopkinson's Belted Pinkhead he caught a couple of pounders and a two-pounder in quick succession.

'There you are, Lachy,' he roared in triumph. 'I knew that was the fly for them.'

'Oh yes, she's a good fly, right enough, Master Hector. A pity we didn't try her earlier when the young lady was with us.'

'Yes, it was a pity, but you can never tell with trout.'

'No, trout are very fanciful, right enough. Very like the women themselves, Master Hector.'

'Tell me, Lachy, how are you getting on since you married? Do you like married life?'

'Well, there's a great deal to be said for marriage in one way, Master Hector; but there's a great deal to be said against it. Och, yes, you might call it a position for a man betwixt and between happiness and misery. That's what I would call married life.'

'Myrtle darling,' her sister-in-law cried when she met them beside the loch. 'Where *did* you spring from?'

'Didn't you hear me calling to you, Carrie?'

'Was that you calling? What do you say to that, Alan? Alan and I thought it was birds.'

'You're both of you pretty dumb if you thought that was birds. I guess parrots don't fly around wild in these parts. Do you mean to say you couldn't hear me call "Carrie!"?'

'But Alan and I weren't expecting you down here, were we, Alan?'

The poet's promise of obedience extracted from him by Carrie before they left the Pass of Ballochy had been severely strained by the command not to pay any attention to Myrtle's voice. He did not think it was fair of her to demand such testimony. His lips moved, but it was his eyes that spoke.

'Listen, honey,' murmured Carrie, 'wouldn't you like to drive Alan back to Knocknacolly in my funny little runabout? You remember that poem he read us about peaty water? Well, he's added one or two more lines to it and even if you didn't understand it before I guess you'll understand it now.'

'What about Hector?' Myrtle asked.

'Hector shall drive me home.'

Carrie reached him just as Lachlan was unhooking another two-pounder from his line. He had noticed that somebody was approaching along the bank, but the concentration required for the two-pounder had not allowed him to notice the substitution of Carrie for her sister-in-law.

'If you hadn't gone off, Myrtle, you'd have seen what a Belted Pinkhead can do,' he shouted exultantly, as he watched the victim's convulsions upon the bank.

'Well, I've been called lots of names,' said Carrie, 'but I've never been called that before.'

'Good lord, it's you! Where's Myrtle?'

'She's kindly offered to drive a friend of our architect back to Knocknacolly. A Mr Macmillan.'

'Oh, that's what that was! I couldn't think what it was.'

'What what was?'

'That tartan. But the Macmillan tartan's notorious. It was always said they invented it to frighten Campbell of Inverneil. But of course nothing could frighten Campbell of Inverneil or any other Campbell off somebody else's land.'

'So I'm going to plead for a lift in your two-seater, Hector.'

'That's topping.'

'My, what lovely fishes!'

'Got 'em all on a Belted Pinkhead,' said Hector, gazing at the four trout with fatherly pride. 'Young Somerled MacDonald of Ours will be no end bucked when I tell him about it. He always swears by Hopkinson's Belted Pinkhead. We had a terrific discussion about that fly and the Redwinged Biffer one night in the mess at Tallulahgabad. Well, I'll be seeing Somerled again pretty soon now. Off back to India the day after tomorrow. All right, Lachy, you can put the fish in the car. I shan't do any more today. Good lad, that,' he observed as the gillie went off with the catch. 'Got married last year.'

Hector made a noise like a whale spouting which Carrie recognized as a sigh.

'Why that sigh, Hector?'

'Took rather a knock this afternoon. What is it old Kipling says? Can't remember, I'm afraid. But I know he wrote some jolly good lines about the way a fellow feels when he's taken a knock over a girl.'

'Poor Hector! And was Myrtle the girl?'

'Yes. I asked her to marry me just before you buzzed along. I led a heart, but she hadn't got one in her hand and trumped it with a small club, or in other words said she thought friendship was better than marriage. It'll be a blow to the old man. He was convinced that Myrtle and I were made for one another.' He spouted again. 'Oh, well, such is life! Very like fishing, as I said to Myrtle. One fellow catches a basketful and the other fellow catches nothing. Still, that Belted Pinkhead taught me a lesson. I may cast one over the right girl one day, what?'

'I'm sure you will, Hector. And I don't really think you and Myrtle were suited to one another.'

'You don't?'

'No, I think you require a softer, gentler kind of a girl. Myrtle is hard as nails.'

'By jove, I believe you're right, Carrie. You know, she actually wanted me to fish with a worm. I must admit that did give me a bit of a bump. Yes, I believe you're right, Carrie. I don't believe we should ever have seen eye to eye over sport. And that would have created a rift in time.'

'It would have created a chasm,' said Carrie decidedly.

'And married people can't afford to do that over really important things like sport,' Hector observed gravely. 'I mean to say you can differ about things like religion because everybody's got a right to their own religion and anyway one doesn't talk about religion in public. But fishing for trout with worms – and garden-worms at that!' He spouted again, but this time it savoured less of a sigh for what he had lost than an exhalation of relief at what he had escaped.

That night Carrie went along to Myrtle's room in her pastel-rose dressing-gown and sat on the bed with her back against one of the mahogany posts.

'Well, did you find out you were right?' she asked her sister-in-law.

'Right how?'

'Right in thinking he was your property?' said Carrie.

'I believe I'll marry him if he asks me.'

'Well, if he doesn't ask you himself I'll ask you on his account,' said Carrie. 'He's probably afraid of your money. Did he read you the poem?'

'He read me a lot of poems.'

'And all about little you?'

Myrtle nodded.

'What's it feel like to have poetry written about you?' Carrie asked, her voice touched by wistfulness.

'It's lots of fun, Carrie.'

'He'll have to ask you pretty quick, honey, because now you've refused

Hector I don't think we ought to stay on at Glenbogle indefinitely. Anyway, we ought to be nearer Knocknacolly. I suggested to Chester we should furnish some rooms at the Lodge and camp out there till we go home at the end of the month, but Chester's afraid what Wilton will say, and he doesn't want to lose him. However, I guess we'll manage. We can send Wilton down to London.'

'You'll have to make it clear to Alan that money doesn't matter,' Myrtle said. 'What's money anyway?'

'Just nothing at all, honey, when there's as much of it as you and I have.'

Chapter 18

THE PRINCE'S CAVE

Ben Nevis felt depressed for nearly five minutes when his eldest son told him that he had been refused by Myrtle Royde; but that sanguine disposition was incapable of protracted gloom and by the time Hector left on Friday for India he was as rumbustious as ever, having been particularly elated by the news that two of his gillies with Neil Maclennan had destroyed a small encampment on one of the spurs of Ben Cruet and that Smeorach, Neil's wall-eyed dog, had bitten the leg of the hiker left in charge.

'I hope it was a really good bite, Neil?' he asked eagerly.

'Oh yes, it was a good bite, right enough, Ben Nevis.'

'Not just a scrape?'

'No, no; it was more than a scrape.'

'Good! I'll teach these brutes to threaten me,' the Chieftain boasted in his pride.

'That guy's chin would be worth biting,' Chester Royde observed pensively. 'I reckon he's the leader of the whole gang.'

'By Jove, that reminds me,' Ben Nevis exclaimed. 'Old Duncan sent word last night that this fellow with the chin is camping in one of the corries of Ben Booey. What do you say, Royde? Shall we try and bag the brute?'

'Fine. Nothing would suit me better,' Chester Royde declared.

'We'll have to do some stalking to get our quarry.'

'Stalking?' Chester repeated suspiciously. 'Do you mean crawl along for miles on our bellies the way we did after that darned stag?'

'Oh, not quite such a tussle as that,' Ben Nevis said. 'You wouldn't put a hiker on a level with a noble beast like the muckle hart of Ben Glass. No, my idea was to approach the camp fairly cautiously and march them all back to Glenbogle in front of our guns. If this fellow with the chin is the leader and we bag him, that will put an end to the nuisance.'

'How?'

'Why, we'll keep him a prisoner here till every hiker has cleared off my land. But I shan't shut him up in a dungeon this time. I shall shut him up in the Raven's Nest at the top of the Raven's Tower.'

'A nest sounds a lot too comfortable for that guy with the chin,' Chester Royde objected.

'Oh, it's not really a nest. It's a little room at the top of the tower where the watchman used to keep a look-out for marauding Macintoshes once upon a time.'

All that night derisive boohs and catcalls round the Castle indicated that the hikers were growing bolder, as well they might with the reinforcements due to reach them in the course of the next two days.

This act of defiance made Ben Nevis more than ever determined to strike a decisive blow at the enemy's heart, and besides Chester Royde and old Duncan, Iain and a couple of gillies were brought in to strengthen his force. Kilwhillie had gone home two or three days before.

'I'm a little doubtful about that kilt of yours, Royde,' Ben Nevis said when the punitive expedition was mustering after breakfast that Saturday. 'I'm afraid it'll give us away long before we reach the Black Corrie where these brutes are camping.'

'Well, my purple kilt came along from Inverness yesterday, I'll put that on.'

'Oh, that's much better,' Ben Nevis decided when he saw it. 'You'll look like a patch of heather, what?'

Duncan was waiting for them where the bridle-path that led to the fastnesses of the Three Sisters of Glenbogle joined the road.

'I did not bring the ponies, Ben Nevis,' he explained. 'It's no more than four miles from here to the Black Corrie.'

'You'd better come back for us at one o'clock, Johnnie,' Ben Nevis said to his chauffeur. 'And tell Archie MacColl to bring the lorry for our prisoners.'

Johnnie Macpherson touched his cap and after turning the Daimler with some difficulty drove off.

'Now look here, Iain,' he said to his youngest son, 'I want you and Lachy and Roddy to work round to the other side of the corrie and cut off the retreat of any of the hikers who get away from us. How many do you think there are in this camp, Duncan?'

'It was Roddy who saw them on Thursday. How many, Roddy, did you see?'

'I would say there were six of them,' the gillie replied.

'Did they speak to you?'

'There was a fellow with a huge great chin on him asked me was we having trouble at the Castle. "What trouble would we be having at the Castle?" I said. And he just laughed.'

'Come on, Ben Nevis,' Chester Royde urged. 'What are we waiting for?'

After the stampede of the bullocks Percy Buckham had moved his headquarters to the Black Corrie and it was there that he was concentrating his forces for the attack he had planned on Glenbogle Castle. The small columns which had been operating during the week against notice-boards of 'No Camping' had by now all reached the Black Corrie, the only loss suffered having been the destruction of the equipment of one column on Ben Cruet by Neil Maclennan and the bit taken out of the leg of Hiker Charles Cudlipp, who had been left on guard. Instead of the force of half a dozen strong reconnoitred by Roddy Maclean, there were now thirty-six hikers with one casualty and sixteen hikeresses, two of whom – Margery Pidcock and Gladys Woodmonger – were casualties, the former having been stung on the upper slopes of her thigh by two wild bees and the latter's nerve not having yet recovered from being suddenly awakened by a bullock blowing on her face. Moreover, seventeen hikers and twelve hikeresses were expected to join the party in the course of today and tomorrow.

'Frankly, I don't see what can stand against us, Mr Prew,' said Percy Buckham, fixing his Chief-of-Staff with two eyes that resembled animated essence of beef.

'No, indeed, Mr Buckham. I cannot see myself.'

'What is it, Miss Butterworth?'

A plump young woman in dark crimson corduroy shorts which matched her countenance was standing all of a tremble like a wine jelly before the leader's tent.

'Please, Mr Buckham,' she panted. 'Arthur Blencoe has signalled he can see the enemy approaching.'

Percy Buckham leapt to his feet and blew his whistle. Hikers and hikeresses hurried from every direction to gather round and hear his orders.

'Hiker Williamson!' he rapped out.

'Here I am, Mr Buckham.'

'Take six men and debouch from the entrance of the corrie.'

'Very good, Mr Buckham.'

'And when you've debouched, don't forget to deploy.'

'I won't, Mr Buckham.'

'Hiker Hughes, get in touch with Hiker Blencoe. Hiker Rosebotham, get your men up to the ridge. Hiker Hickey, take your column over to the left above the corrie and nip any attempt by the enemy at an enveloping movement in the bud. Mr Prew, muster the mobile reserve and keep in touch with me.'

'Where are you going, Mr Buckham?' asked Mr Prew, who was a little annoyed to find himself left in charge of the mobile reserve, a female corps.

'I am leading the attack with the main body. And mind, Mr Prew, if you have to debouch with the mobile reserve, don't forget to deploy immediately.'

From the top of the corrie the hikers' leader surveyed with his glasses the advance of the Glenbogle forces a mile away. He observed Iain MacDonald and the two gillies detach themselves and move across to their right with the evident intention of preparing the enveloping movement he planned to nip in the bud. At the same time he saw Ben Nevis, Chester Royde, and Duncan move left towards the entrance of the Black Corrie. With Napoleonic rapidity he decided upon his tactics. He dispatched two more columns to support Hiker Hickey, and brought the rest of his force down again into the corrie.

'Now, take cover,' he commanded, 'and when I blow my whistle, attack and disarm the enemy.'

'But suppose they fire at us?' Mr Prew asked. 'They have guns, and once Fascism starts it's not easy to predict where it will stop.'

'That's the whole point of collective security, and I think you'll admit that my disposition of the force under my command has achieved the maximum collective security. Frankly, I don't believe they *will* fire their guns. Except perhaps in the air. But we shall not be frightened.'

'Oh no,' Mr Prew declared, with a certain lack of conviction in his negative.

As a matter of fact when Ben Nevis, Chester Royde, and Duncan on hands and knees crawled up the rough brae that led to the entrance of the great hollow known as the Black Corrie and the hikers yelling the motto of the N.U.H. as a war-cry — *Hike On, Hike Ever* — swept down upon them from their ambush on either side, Ben Nevis did discharge both barrels into the air, and to judge by the screams of the mobile reserve with deadly effect. However, that was all he was able to do before he and his companions were overwhelmed by the weight of numbers and tied up in tents.

On the heights above the corrie the day went equally badly for Glenbogle, for though Iain MacDonald tossed two or three of the hikers farther than he had tossed the caber at the games a week ago, he, Lachy, and Roddy were borne down by the superior forces of the enemy. The victory of the hikers was rapid and complete.

And while the prisoners tied up in tents lay waiting for Buckham's decision about their disposal, along the path that led from the other side into the rocky fastnesses of the Three Sisters of Glenbogle there was heard the grand refrain of the Hikers' Song upon the lips of the first body of reinforcements tramping in from Kenspeckle, where they had been deposited by the omnibus from Fort William that met the London train.

Mention has been made of the cave on Ben Booey in which Prince Charles Edward, according to local tradition, spent several nights hidden from the redcoats. Uaimh na Phrionnsa or the Prince's Cave was in every way a much more striking piece of natural architecture than the Calf's Cave on Ben Cruet. The view was superb from the rocky terrace in front that ended in an almost sheer precipice of four hundred feet and if Percy Buckham had chosen the view with the express purpose of enraging his enemy he could not have been more devilishly successful, comprising as it did Glenbogle Castle lying among its pines six miles away across the glen and beyond Ben Cruet, in the remoter background, mighty Ben Nevis itself, the Lord of which was impotent in the hands of hikers. It was to the Prince's Cave that Percy Buckham consigned his captives that September day when the sons of Hector suffered the most humiliating defeat in all their long and bellicose history.

At first the prisoners had refused to move from the corrie, but a threat to carry them to the cave tied up in tents persuaded them to give way on this point. On their arrival their arms and legs were bound with ropes, and they were sitting thus too much dejected to talk when Percy Buckham came along with a paper, and addressed Ben Nevis:

'I will read you out a letter, which I have composed. If you will sign this letter I will give orders for your release, and hostilities can terminate. If you refuse to sign I shall have no option but to keep you prisoners here while I proceed with my original plan to seize and occupy Glenbogle Castle.'

As a cat chatters at a sparrow beyond the range of his spring, so did

Ben Nevis chatter at Percy Buckham when he heard this insolent threat. And even as the sparrow safely out of reach pays no attention to the chattering of the cat, so did Percy Buckham ignore the chattering of Ben Nevis.

'Here is the letter I propose you shall sign,' he began. 'Dear Mr Buckham . . .' he broke off. 'I am Percy Buckham, the Acting President of the National Union of Hikers.'

'One of these days you'll wish you weren't Percy Buckham,' Chester Royde warned him.

'Don't bandy words with this blackguard. Keep cool, Royde, like me,' urged Ben Nevis, whose face was bubbling like molten lava in the crater of a volcano.

'Dear Mr Buckham' [the leader of the hikers went on reading] 'I have first of all to express my very sincere regret for my outrageous behaviour on the 12th ult., when I assaulted and imprisoned in my dungeons sixteen members of the National Union of Hikers, including Mr Sydney Prew the Secretary. I must also express my sincere regret for wantonly firing into the portable radio-cabinet known as the Little Songster which belongs to Mr Thomas Camidge and I hope Mr Camidge will be good enough to overlook my loss of self-control and accept a new Little Songster to replace the one I destroyed.

'In expressing my regret I desire at the same time to offer my humble apologies to the National Union of Hikers, and in particular to the President the Earl of Buntingdon, the Secretary Mr Sydney Prew, the Honorary Treasurer Mr Fortescue Wilson, and your good self. In order that the extent of my regret and the sincerity of my apologies may be appreciated I have decided to take down all the objectionable notices prohibiting camping on my land and I desire here and now to extend a hearty invitation to all members of the N.U.H. to camp whenever and wherever they like on my land. I have instructed my tenants and employees to afford them every facility they require in the matter of obtaining water and to supply them with milk, eggs, fruit, and vegetables at a reasonable price.

'In the hope that you will persuade the National Union of Hikers to accept my apologies and collaborate in future with me in promoting true democratic feeling,

I remain,

Yours very truly,

'I think you'll agree with me, Mr MacDonald, that considering your behaviour on 12 August you are being let off very lightly. I have a fountain-pen here. If you will sign this letter I will set you and your party free and you can avoid the unpleasantness of having Glenbogle Castle seized and occupied by my forces.'

Turner himself would have been baffled to depict the changing hues upon the Chieftain's countenance while Percy Buckham was reading out this letter.

'Give me that piece of paper,' he choked.

They unbound his arms and taking the letter he tore it into fragments. Then his mouth opened to breathe in the inspiration that would provide him with the epithet to annihilate the hikers' leader. None of sufficient explosive force was granted to him.

'So that is your reply to my generous offer, Mr MacDonald. Perhaps after a night in this cave you will be feeling in a more reasonable state of mind. And that brings me to another matter. I will leave your arms free if you will give me your parole that you will not attempt to escape. In any case I will have your legs untied, for the approaches to the cave are well guarded.'

But the Highland pride of Ben Nevis would not allow him to give his parole to a man like Percy Buckham. So he and Chester Royde and old Duncan were left trussed up in the Prince's Cave. Iain and the two gillies were taken down to the camp, for Buckham did not want to maintain too large a guard up at the cave because if by chance one of them should get out of his ropes and set the others free he was doubtful of the guard's ability to hold all the six.

'I feel quite sure we shall soon be rescued,' said Ben Nevis when he and Chester Royde and Duncan were by themselves. 'There'll be a hue and cry for us down in the glen when we don't come back. You think we shall soon be rescued, don't you, Donald?'

The old keeper shook his head.

'It rests with the Lord, Ben Nevis. If it please the Lord to set us free we will be set free.'

'When Johnnie Macpherson finds we don't come back at one o'clock, he'll wait about for an hour or two, and then he'll go back to the Castle and give the alarm.'

'Och, Johnnie Macpherson will go back to the Castle right enough,' Duncan agreed. 'But what will be the use of that? He won't be able to tell where we are. We might be anywhere. We might be nowhere at all. Who is to say?'

'What makes me so mad,' said Chester Royde, 'is to think that this is the second time that guy with the chin has made a fool of me. It's humiliating.'

The afternoon wore away. About five o'clock the prisoners were unbound and given tea.

'It makes my gorge rise to eat their food,' said Ben Nevis. 'But I suppose we can't starve.'

'It's very good tea,' Duncan observed. 'I wouldn't have believed such people as these hikers could make such good tea as this.'

'All tea tastes alike to me,' said Chester Royde. 'And it's not any too good to taste either.'

After the meal they were roped up again and sat in gloomy silence for an hour.

Suddenly Duncan muttered something in Gaelic, and the others looked. At the entrance of the cave a magnificent stag was gazing at them.

'It's himself,' Duncan gasped.

'The muckle hart,' Ben Nevis whispered hoarsely.

'The muckle hart himself,' Duncan confirmed. 'Look at the antlers on him.'

'Do you mean to tell me that beast staring at us is the beast we stalked in the rain?' Chester Royde asked.

'The very same, Mr Royde.'

'There's not another stag within a twenty-mile radius with a head like that,' Ben Nevis declared.

'Well, I don't know,' said Chester Royde. 'It seems to me I'm the stooge for man and beast in this part of the world. Get away, you brute. Booh! Bang!'

The stag threw up his mighty head, and seemed to sniff at the sound. Then he tossed his antlers, shook his flanks, lolloped away from the cave with a contemptuous lack of urgency.

'Duncan, I believe that stag was laughing at us,' Ben Nevis said.

'That was the very thing I was thinking myself,' the old keeper agreed. 'He'll be on his way back to Ben Glass now with the hinds. He'll be blowing to them all the way he mocked us.'

'If I could stick that stag's horns on that stiff's chin or alternatively stick that stiff's chin on that stag's horns I won't worry what kind of a mess Franklin D. Roosevelt makes of Wall Street,' Chester Royde declared.

Chapter 19

BOG-MYRTLE!

It was too late when Johnnie Macpherson returned with the empty
Daimler to make any effective attempt to rescue the six prisoners of the
hikers that day. He and Archie MacColl, the driver of the lorry, had
spent one of those afternoons so dear to the hearts of West Highlanders,
an afternoon of cigarettes and gossip, completely unaware that the
situation called for the slightest initiative on their part. It was not until
a certain emptiness reminded Johnnie Macpherson the hour for his tea
had passed that he wondered what could be keeping Ben Nevis.

'My goodness, Archie,' he exclaimed, 'it's a quarter to six by the new
time.'

'A quarter to six?' Archie MacColl echoed, shaking his round red
freckled face. 'Look at that now. And I promised Coinneach Mór' (this
was Kenny Macdonald the blacksmith) 'I'd fetch that broken gate for
him this afternoon so as he could get to work upon it on Monday
morning.'

'What gate is that?'

'The gate into the bull's field. It's been broken since last October, and
it's a big nuisance untying it and tying it up again all the time.'

'Och, it's waited so long now it can wait till Monday just as well.'

'Och yes,' Archie agreed. 'Just as well.'

'I'd promised to have a look at Mrs Parsall's wireless for her this
afternoon,' Johnnie announced.

'Is it broken?'

'Och, I don't know if it's a valve or if the high tension is wrong, but
it hasn't been working for nearly three weeks now. She's on at me to look
at it every time she sees me. "What about my wireless, Johnnie, what
about my wireless?" Och, I got tired hearing about her wireless. So I
told her I'd look at it this afternoon, but och, a man can't do everything
at once. But that's the way with women. They think a man has nothing
to do except be mending a lot of nonsense for them.'

'That's true right enough. But they can't help themselves. No, no.
They're just made that way.'

'Ay, that's just about what it is, Archie. Just made that way, and that's all there is to it. I wonder what's keeping Ben Nevis. One o'clock we were to be here, and it's nearly six o'clock now.'

'He may have walked back by the other side of Ben Booey,' Archie speculated.

'Ay, he may have. I never thought of that. Perhaps we would be better to go back to the Castle and find out if there's any news of him.'

The absence of Ben Nevis made all at the Castle realize how much they depended on him in an emergency like this. They recalled the vigour with which he had organized search-parties for his missing guest only a week ago. All that Mrs MacDonald could suggest was that after he had had his tea Johnnie Macpherson should drive back to where he had spent the afternoon waiting for his master. Mrs MacDonald was determined to believe a sprained ankle was the explanation of the mystery.

'But, Mother, they can't all six of them have sprained ankles,' Catriona protested. 'I think they've been captured by the hikers.'

'I'm certain of it,' Mary growled.

Carrie and Myrtle supported this theory, and even Mr Fletcher, who had spent so many years in avoiding any difference of opinion either with Ben Nevis or his wife, felt bound to question the probability of the sprained ankle theory.

'Oh dear,' Mrs MacDonald soughed, 'I wish Hughie Cameron was here.' All recent criticism of Kilwhillie was forgotten in this anxious hour.

At midnight Johnnie Macpherson came back with worse news than ever. Miss Catriona and Miss Mary had set off together along the path towards Ben Booey and had not been seen since they got out of the Daimler about half past eight.

'But why did you let them go, Johnnie?' Mrs MacDonald boomed reproachfully.

'How was I to stop them, madam?' he asked. 'They just jumped out of the car when we reached the head of the path and were away.'

'The hikers must have captured them too,' Carrie declared.

Carrie was right. The hikers had captured Catriona and Mary. The gallant and hefty girls had marched boldly into the Black Corrie, and though they had put up a magnificent fight against the mobile reserve they had finally been overwhelmed by twenty young women fighting for the honour of their sex under the eyes of their male companions. Back to back Catriona and Mary had fought, but as fast as they unzipped the shorts of their assailants others took their places, and though five were unzipped with such heftiness that they had to retire from the contest, the rest were able to zip themselves up again quickly enough to fling themselves all together against Catriona and Mary and finally to drag them down to the ground. When Johnnie Macpherson reached Glenbogle with the news of their disappearance the two gallant and hefty girls were lying in a tent, bound securely with ropes.

'What *are* we to do?' Mrs MacDonald boomed desolately.

'We'll have to wait till Monday now and see what can be done,' Johnnie Macpherson said.

'Wait till Monday?'

'Tomorrow's the Sabbath,' he reminded her. 'We might get one or two to have a look for them tomorrow, but och, we won't get many. The Minister has been fierce about Sabbath-breaking for the last four Sundays.'

'But surely when Ben Nevis himself may be in danger there will be plenty of volunteers,' said Mrs MacDonald.

Johnnie Macpherson shook his head.

'It's a pity Major MacIsaac went away for his holiday after the Gathering,' he said. 'He might have persuaded some of them, but they'll never listen to me. And Big Duncan, he might have persuaded them, but himself is missing. So's Lachy Macdonald. So's Roddy Maclean. Archie MacColl would go right enough, being an Episcopalian from Appin, but what would Archie and me do by ourselves? They're saying in the bothy there are five or six hundred hikers camping in the Black Corrie.'

'And Catriona and Mary are in the hands of these people,' Mrs MacDonald moaned.

In spite of her own anxiety about Chester, Carrie could not help winking at Myrtle, who could not contain an explosion of merriment which she apologized for as a sneeze.

'I think we may safely assume they will come to no grievous harm, Mrs MacDonald,' said the chaplain. 'The intention is probably to use them to bargain with.'

This notion was too much altogether for Myrtle, who was seized with such spasms of pent-up laughter that she was driven into crawling under the table on all-fours to look for an imaginary ruby supposed to have fallen out of her bracelet.

'Well, I know what I'm going to do tomorrow morning,' said Carrie. 'I'm going to drive to Knocknacolly and consult Chester's lawyer, Mr Buchanan.'

'Oh, and I'll come with you, Carrie,' said her sister-in-law, emerging from beneath the table. 'That's a wonderful idea.'

So on Sunday morning, rather later than they'd intended because Mr Fletcher took advantage of the Chieftain's absence to give a longer sermon than usual, they arrived at Knocknacolly at the moment when Robert Menzies was making an omelette and his two companions were pointing out his mistakes, standing one at each elbow.

'For God's sake, you silly pair of clowns, stop your blethering, and let me make the damned omelette my own way,' the architect was shouting as Carrie and Myrtle walked into the room, that room which they had taken so much trouble to make pleasant and cosy for the three young men and which now after a week of exclusively male attention was as richly squalid as a Hogarth garret.

'Oh, you're making an omelette,' Carrie exclaimed. 'I'm terribly good at omelettes.'

'So am I,' said Myrtle eagerly. 'The secret of a good omelette is always to . . .'

But Robert's omelette was too far advanced by now to be interfered with and there were not enough eggs left to show him how it ought to have been made.

'Anyway, what's more important than omelettes is the problem of Glenbogle,' Carrie said, and she related what had happened yesterday. 'Once upon a time, Alan, you and James had a plan to kidnap Ben Nevis. Now you've got to think out a plan to unkidnap him and my poor husband,' she went on.

'If we could get a few of the S.B.A. to Glenbogle,' said James, 'we'd soon deal with these Cockney hikers, would we not?'

The poet and the architect warmly agreed.

'Well, why don't you get the S.B.A.?' asked Carrie.

'Oh yes, why don't you?' said Myrtle.

James Buchanan looked worried.

'It's really a question of finance,' he admitted at last. 'Two or three of them could manage right enough, but most of them are students and they haven't really got the money to come all the way up here at a moment's notice.'

'If that's all you're worrying about, James, you needn't worry any more. I suppose I have a right to call on the members of the Brotherhood for action at my expense. Now see here, I'm pretty practical over matters like this. My notion would be for you to go and collect as many as you can and hire automobiles to rush them up to Glenbogle as soon as possible. How many do you think you could collect?'

'I think we might collect a couple of dozen, don't you, Robert? But I don't suppose we could get them together before Tuesday at the earliest.'

'Well, let's make it Tuesday afternoon at the Castle with as many as you can get. Twenty-four aren't very many against five or six hundred but twenty-four will be better than nobody.'

'Five or six hundred?' James gasped.

'That's what they say. They're camped on Ben Booey,' Carrie said.

'I don't believe it's possible,' James declared. 'Fifty or sixty perhaps. But five or six hundred! It's a ridiculous figure.'

'Camped on Ben Booey, are they?' Alan put in. 'I'll bet they have Ben Nevis and Mr Royde shut up in that cave they say Prince Charlie hid in, which of course is nonsense.'

'Why should it be nonsense?' Robert Menzies demanded sternly. He was a fiery Jacobite, and resented a slight even on a cave hallowed by the Prince's name.

'Och, away with you, Robert, I'm not going to argue about Prince Charlie, just now,' Alan told him.

'Who started the argument, Alan?'

'No argument *has* started. What's the use of arguing about Prince Charlie when we have to deal with the present? You may be a good architect, Robert, but you're frightfully unpractical. You've no conception of poetic action.'

'He certainly is a good architect,' Carrie interposed. 'I've been looking at his last sketch for the new house, and it's quite lovely.'

'Do you like it, Mrs Royde? I'm awfully pleased.'

Robert Menzies had not had the advantage of meeting Carrie in the romantic circumstances in which his two friends had met her that day in Glenbristle. So far he had been able to behold her only as a possible patroness. He had fancied she was not particularly impressed by his plans for Knocknacolly. Her sudden compliment to his work made him her slave. Carrie wanted the help of the S.B.A., and Robert Menzies made up his mind there and then that she should have it.

'You and Alan and I had better get along down to Glasgow tomorrow morning, James. We'll need all of two days to collect our fellows,' he said.

'Wouldn't it be as well if one of us stayed here?' Alan asked.

And thus it was decided that Alan should be the one to stay.

'It's a pity in a way Robert and I can't catch the train from Fort William this afternoon,' said James presently. 'We'll have all our work cut out to collect enough of the S.B.A. and be back by Tuesday.'

And thus it was decided that Carrie should drive the lawyer and the architect into Fort William, returning later to fetch the poet and Myrtle to Glenbogle.

'How far away we seem from the rest of the world up here,' Myrtle exclaimed when she and Alan were sitting on the tangled lawn of Knocknacolly Lodge that looked out across the wide level moor to the mountains all round.

'But it's only seeming, that's the worst of it,' Alan muttered. 'And at this moment it's the world that's worrying me.'

'But why do you let it worry you?' she asked. 'I don't let anything worry me. Of course, I don't like to think of poor old Chester in the hands of those hikers; but it doesn't worry me, because I know nothing really serious will happen to him.'

'I suppose it wouldn't worry you in the least to know I love you?' he inquired gloomily.

'No, it wouldn't worry me,' she murmured gently, casting a quick sidelong glance at that rose-browned face gazing across the moor to where its enemy the world was lurking on the other side of the mountains. 'Why should it worry me?' she added still more gently.

'Why indeed?' the poet asked, with Byronic scorn for the feminine wiles he despised even as he succumbed to them.

'It seems to worry you a lot,' she said.

'Well, it isn't exactly soothing to fall madly in love with a girl utterly beyond one's reach.'

'It doesn't seem to me I'm so far beyond your reach. I couldn't sit much closer to you unless I sat on your knee, and I can't sit on your knee because you're resting your head on your knee and making faces at the poor old world.'

'You needn't jeer at me.'

'Oh, Alan, I never thought you were quite so dumb. When I met you first I thought you were shy, but that didn't bother me because I liked your shyness. And when you read me that poem about the dark-brown water of life . . .' She sighed. 'And when you read me that poem with what you added about bog-myrtle . . .' she sighed again, and was silent.

'*You* have nothing to sigh about,' he observed severely.

'I don't think you've any right to say that about me.'

'Why not?'

'Because I don't think you know enough about me, Alan.'

'I'll never have the chance to learn much more.'

'It'll be your own fault if you don't. You could learn pretty well all about me by asking one little question?'

'And what is that wonderful question?'

'Oh, you can look after the question, Alan. It's my job to look after the answer.'

'There's only one question I want to ask you,' he declared sombrely.

'Hadn't you better ask it?'

'Do you think you could ever love *me*?'

'Alan,' she cried, 'you really are too dumb. I thought you were going to ask me to marry you. It's no good asking *unnecessary* questions. That's just wasting time.'

'How can I ask you to marry me?' he demanded indignantly.

'I should think it would be pretty easy even in Gaelic.'

'How can I ask you to marry me? You rich and me poor!'

'Well, that's a whole lot better than both of us being poor,' she pointed out.

And then suddenly the present tripped up the future and nothing mattered except the joy of being together on this tangled lawn, with the wide level moor before them and the blue mountains beyond. They were still sitting there when Carrie came back from Fort William. Her greenish eyes looked quickly at the pair of them and brightened.

'So that's settled at last,' she said.

Myrtle nodded.

'Carrie darling, I wonder how you understood so well,' she murmured.

'I just guessed somehow. Of course I *am* three years older than you,' Carrie reminded her.

'I'm glad you're my sister-in-law,' Myrtle exclaimed. 'For lots of reasons,' she added softly.

Carrie smiled. With those four words Myrtle had repaid her own generosity in like measure.

'It's all very well for you two to be so pleased about everything,' said the poet. 'But what kind of a clown will I feel when I tell Mr Royde?'

'Oh, don't call Chester Mr Royde,' the wife and sister expostulated with one voice.

'Never mind about what I call him,' said Alan glumly. 'What kind of a clown will I feel when I tell him about me and his sister?'

'But Chester liked your tartan so much,' said Carrie.

'Yes, he adored your kilt,' Myrtle added.

'You're not going to marry my kilt. You're going to marry what's inside the kilt.'

Myrtle laughed, and the poet blushed.

'You know fine what I mean,' he muttered like an embarrassed schoolboy.

'Oh, I've got the most wonderful idea,' Carrie ejaculated suddenly. 'Oh, it's the most wonderful idea anybody ever heard! Listen. I know what Alan must do to impress Chester. Somehow or other he must rescue him from the hikers. Oh, it'll be just like one of those books men enjoy reading. Chester coming forward and shaking Alan by the hand and telling him he'll never forget the way he rescued him against fearful odds. And Alan will blush and say it was nothing, but anyway he'd go through worse than that to rescue the brother of Myrtle Royde. And then Chester'll look kind of surprised for a moment and then it'll dawn on him what's happened and he'll squeeze Alan's hand in a brotherly grip and say he only wished he had two sisters so as he could give them both to his rescuer.'

'What would he want to give Alan two sisters for?' Myrtle asked indignantly. 'He isn't a Mormon.'

'I really am serious about rescuing Chester from the hikers,' Carrie insisted. 'Didn't you say you thought he might be in the Prince's Cave on Ben Booey?'

'Yes, Uaimh na Phrionnsa,' said Alan.

Myrtle threw her arms round him and kissed him. 'Oh, Alan, I do love you when you talk Gaelic. Now say the name of the other cave.'

He obliged, and she kissed him again.

'Well, if you have a hunch that the hikers have shut Chester and Ben Nevis and the rest in Uaimh na Phrionnsa . . .'

'No, no, Carrie, you can't do it. I'm sorry, darling, but you don't get that kind of gurgle like the last drop of water running out of a bath.'

'Alan, what do you think?' Carrie went on. 'Wouldn't it be worth while to see if your hunch is right?'

'I'll climb up where the ground drops down in front,' said Alan. 'I did it the year before last.'

But when in the road that branched off from Glenbogle on the farther side of Ben Booey from the Castle he pointed to what at two miles away appeared the sheer precipice in front of the Prince's Cave, Myrtle declared she'd rather leave Chester there as long as Rip Van Winkle than that Alan should attempt such a climb.

'It's not really at all difficult,' he assured her. 'You can't see the way up from here.'

And before Myrtle could argue any more he jumped out of the car, telling them to wait with it, and set off at a rapid pace up the spur of the mighty ben towards the precipice before the cave.

'If anything happens to him Carrie, I'll never forgive you,' Myrtle declared almost tearfully.

'Nothing will happen to him, honeybunch, and think what a story we'll have to tell Chester if he *is* in that cave, and after all Chester Royde Senior and Mrs Chester Royde Senior have to be considered. You'll want a bit of help from Chester when you go home and announce you're going to marry a wild Highlander with an empty sporran.'

It happened that, just as the poet scrambled over the top of the precipice in front of the cave, Percy Buckham was telling his prisoners that when darkness came they would have to move to new quarters on the other side of the glen.

'I want to give you the pleasure, Mr MacDonald, of seeing with your own eyes my forces march into Glenbogle Castle, pull down that flag of yours with half the Zoo on it, and hoist the crossed staffs of the N.U.H. The escort will arrive in an hour.'

Buckham turned his back on the prisoners and marching out of the cave came face to face with Alan Macmillan.

'Who are you?' he demanded.

And Alan hit out, catching Percy Buckham fairly on the chin.

'Oh, boy, what a K.O.!' shouted Chester Royde exultantly as Percy Buckham went down on his back.

The congratulations Alan received upon his masterly blow were more than his pugilistic skill deserved. Anybody who hit Percy Buckham was almost bound to hit his chin.

With his *sgian dubh* the poet cut the bonds of the captives, and urged a speedy retreat before Buckham could raise the alarm. There were two hikers on guard further along the narrow path leading round from the cave, but unlike Professor Moriarty they were not prepared to risk a struggle so near the edge of that precipice and scrambled away in the other direction crying 'Wolla-wolla-wolla!' to summon help from the camp.

An hour later the prisoners had reached the Austin.

'I'll drive you back to the Castle,' Carrie volunteered. 'Myrtle and Alan will have to walk.'

Perhaps their sufferings in the cave had reduced their bulk. Otherwise it is difficult to know how Ben Nevis, Chester Royde and big Duncan Macdonald all managed to get into that little Austin.

'What did Chester say to you, Alan?' Myrtle asked.

'He was pleased about my hitting that fellow on the chin.'

'What did he say when you told him about you and me?'

'I didn't tell him about you and me.'

'Alan, you really can be terribly dumb, darling. Never mind. I guess Carrie'll tell him all about you and me. Oh, what's that sweet scent on the air?'

'Bog-myrtle,' he told her.

'And you and I are wandering along together in the scent of it,' she sighed happily.

> 'The warm dark-brown water of life
> Whose sweet breath blows in the wind
> Bringing bog-myrtle,'

he whispered.

And they stood there in the gloaming, lost in a long kiss.

Chapter 20

BEN NEVIS FOR EVER

It was undoubtedly a shock to Ben Nevis when he found that he had been rescued from the cave by a Scottish Nationalist, that the said Scottish Nationalist was engaged to the girl he had fetched his eldest son back from India to marry, and finally that the defence of Glenbogle Castle itself must depend on a body of Scottish Nationalists now being mustered in Glasgow.

'But, Donald, if you feel as strongly about these people as you do, why don't you call in the help of the police?' his wife asked.

'My dear Trixie, do you seriously think I'll give Lindsay-Wolseley such an opportunity of scoring off me? I can't say I like the idea of what amounts to an alliance with Scottish Nationalists. It's as if the British Government were to listen to those pestilential Labour fellows and make an alliance with the Bolshies. But sometimes a situation calls for desperate measures, and we must remember that Iain, Mary, and Catriona are still in the hands of these foul hikers, not to mention Lachy Macdonald and Roddy Maclean.'

'It's really lamentable,' Mrs MacDonald boomed plaintively. 'I still think it would be advisable to get into communication with the police.'

'Trixie, you know what a reasonable man I am. Now please don't make me angry by talking any more about the police. I'd sooner Glenbogle were burnt to the ground than give Lindsay-Wolseley a chance of saying to me "I told you so." '

'He seems quite a pleasant young man, this Mr Macmillan,' said Mrs MacDonald, steering the conversation away from Colonel Lindsay-Wolseley.

'I don't object to him personally at all,' Ben Nevis admitted. 'And I really was very glad that he turned up when he did. I was on the point of bursting, I think. It's a fearful strain having to sit and listen to the bragging of a bounder like this Buckham creature . . . Good god!'

'Donald, what is the matter now?'

She might well ask. Lady Macbeth called upon to calm her husband when the ghost of Banquo sat down in his place at dinner may have been confronted by such an expression of incredulous horror.

'Donald dear, what *is* the matter?'

For answer Ben Nevis pointed with his finger at a page of the *Scotsman* upon his knee.

Mrs MacDonald leant over to see what in that austere newspaper could have thus convulsed her husband's countenance.

She saw looking round the corner of a wireless cabinet a face. She saw a finger pointed, it seemed, at her personally. She read in large letters LEND ME YOUR EARS. She read on:

Friends,

The other day I overheard my secretary say to a client, 'Mr Buckham will be away on his holiday next week,' and my heart leapt like a schoolboy's at the sound of the magic word. Some of you will be away on your holidays next week. Don't forget to take your Little Songster with you. The good weather I hope you'll enjoy will seem all the better if set fair to music, and if by some unlucky chance it should rain the Little Songster will make you never mind a bit about the weather. Cheerio, folks. Have a good time, and good listening!

PERCY BUCKHAM.

'That's why his face was vaguely familiar to me,' Ben Nevis roared. 'I must have seen it in an advertisement. But I'm astonished at a paper like the *Scotsman* printing an advertisement like this. I shall write a letter of protest. Oh, well, I knew as soon as they started a page of photographs and a crossword puzzle the *Scotsman* was going to the dogs like everything in this modern world. Fancy opening my *Scotsman* and seeing that bounder's face glaring at me round one of those ghastly wireless contraptions.'

'Well, turn over the page, Donald. Don't keep looking at this man's face if it irritates you.'

At that moment Toker brought word that Neil Maclennan wanted to speak to Ben Nevis. The Chieftain came back presently, looking grave. It appeared from Neil Maclennan's information that the Castle was now entirely surrounded by hikers.

Ben Nevis took out his watch.

'Ten minutes to five. Come along, Trixie, let's go and have some tea.'

Chester and Carrie and Myrtle were in the Great Hall with Alan Macmillan.

'We're surrounded,' the Chieftain announced as nonchalantly as

Leonidas addressing his Spartans the day before Thermopylae. 'What's the earliest you expect your people, Macmillan?'

'I'm afraid they won't be here before tomorrow afternoon,' the poet replied.

'Well, we must hold out somehow,' said the Chieftain. 'By the way I've found who this fellow Buckham is. He's an advertisement. Mary, go and get the *Scotsman*.'

'Donald, you're forgetting,' his wife boomed tragically. 'Our poor Mary isn't here.'

'Oh no, nor she is. Oh well, we must hope for the best,' said the stricken father.

'I'll get your paper for you, Ben Nevis,' Myrtle volunteered. 'If I'm going to marry over here I guess I'd better begin to practise being a good little wife by British standards.'

'I'll get it, sir,' said Alan. 'Is it in the library?'

'Yes, that's where it is. Thanks very much,' said the Chieftain, and when Alan was out of the room he looked benevolently at Myrtle.

'I rather like this young man of yours, Myrtle. He has good manners.'

'He has a darned good punch with his left,' said Chester.

'He writes lovely poetry,' Carrie added.

'Oh well, of course I don't know anything about that, I'm afraid,' Ben Nevis barked. 'I'm not great at reading at all, as a matter of fact. I mean to say, you start a book and then you put it down, and then when you pick it up again you can't find where you left off. I remember once I read a book twice, and I hadn't any idea I'd already just read this book till I came on a fly I'd squashed in it. Now think what a waste of time that was. Reading a book I'd already read! Heart-breaking, what?'

Alan Macmillan came back with the *Scotsman*, and with him came Kilwhillie.

'Ah, Hugh, you've got here,' his old friend bellowed. 'Did you see any hikers?'

'Did I see any hikers? The place is alive with them,' said Kilwhillie. 'They tried to stop my car.'

'Good lord, what brutes! Well, I think they'll attack us tonight.'

'You really do? Hadn't you better get in touch with the police?'

'Hugh! I never thought I'd live to hear advice like that from a Cameron. Do you think I want to spend the rest of my life watching Wolseley grinning at me down that yellow nose of his?'

'What are you going to do, then?'

'I'm going to fight the brutes. As a matter of fact we hope to be reinforced by some . . . by some keen young fellows from Glasgow.' He could not bring himself to confess to Kilwhillie he had made an alliance with Scottish Nationalists.

'From Glasgow?' Kilwhillie echoed in amazement.

'Highlandmen, of course. By the way, have you met Miss Royde's fiancé, Mr Macmillan?'

Kilwhillie shook hands with Alan, looking dazed. Glenbogle had taken on the quality of a dream-place since he left it hardly a week ago.

'I thought of using boiling water from the windows of the first floor,' Ben Nevis mentioned casually.

'Boiling water? What for?'

'For the hikers, Hugh, of course. What else would I use boiling water for? The girls can pour it over the brutes when they try to force their way in. I'd like to use boiling oil, but I doubt if we've got enough oil to boil. Have we got enough oil to boil, Trixie?'

'Certainly not, Donald,' the Lady of Ben Nevis replied firmly.

However, the attack on the Castle did not develop as quickly as Ben Nevis expected, though the enemy all through dinner were very noisy, one particularly objectionable feature being the repeated singing of the Hikers' Song in the courtyard.

'I can't stand this much longer,' Ben Nevis declared at last. 'I shall have to do something.'

'Excuse me, sir,' said Toker, 'but the blacksmith, the cowman, the carpenter, and two or three of the gillies attempted a counter-attack a few minutes ago, and it was not quite as successful as could be wished.'

'What happened?'

'Mrs Parsall and two of the maids are tying up their wounds, which consist of minor injuries inflicted by those long sticks with which the enemy is armed. It would seem that a very determined effort was made to capture Kenneth Macdonald and it was while our side were pulling him by the arms and the enemy were pulling him by the legs that the injuries were inflicted by these sticks.'

'The cowardly brutes,' Ben Nevis exclaimed.

'In point of fact, sir, it was the young women hikers who used the sticks so recklessly. The men fought more cleanly, if I may use the expression.'

The offensive noises continued for two or three hours after dinner and Chester Royde, basing his forecast on his researches into Indian warfare, held strongly to the opinion that an attempt would be made to rush the Castle just before dawn. The Chieftain gave orders that the garrison was to be on the alert all night, the various guards relieving one another at intervals of two hours. He himself did not rest, but stalked about the Castle, encouraging everybody to stand firm for the honour and safety of Glenbogle, like a composite of Macbeth, King Henry V, and the ghost of Hamlet's father, a truly impressive Shakespearean shape.

About half past four loud feminine shrieks were heard coming from the courtyard, and by the dim light of a decrescent moon and the first grey of dawn two massive figures were visible hurrying towards the south postern where Chester Royde was in command of the guard. He seized the pail of soapy water which Ben Nevis had been persuaded to substitute for boiling water, and told Toker who was with him on duty to fling open the postern so that he could make a sally and soak the attackers.

'Hold your fire, sir,' Toker begged. Through the casement beside the postern he had recognized the massive figures. 'Hold your fire, please, sir. I'm going to open the door. It's Miss Catriona and Miss Mary.'

The butler's eyes had not deceived him. Through the open postern the hefty daughters of the house dashed panting and as it closed behind them each threw down upon the floor a wriggling squealing hikeress.

'Got away from the Cave of the Calf on Ben Cruet,' Catriona growled. 'And bagged those two squawkers by the edge of the larches.'

'Well, I do congratulate you girls,' said Chester, looking at the two captives in green corduroy shorts who were sitting up by now and scowling at their assailants.

'We had to dash for it good-oh,' Mary said. 'The Castle's going to be attacked. We overheard them talking about it.'

'They're all around us already,' said Chester. 'Your father's in command. You'd better go along and report with your prisoners.'

'Get up, you little blighter,' Catriona growled at her prisoner, a small dark young woman. 'And if you try to bite me again I'll give you a jolly good welting.'

'And that goes for you, you little tick,' Mary growled at hers.

'I'm not going to get up before I get a safety-pin,' said Mary's captive, a towzled fluffy girl called Edith Bassett.

'What do you want a safety-pin for, you little squirt?' Mary growled contemptuously.

'Never mind what I want it for, you. I'm not going to get up for anybody till I have a safety-pin,' said Edith Bassett.

'Where are we going to put these two?' Catriona asked.

'I know where they ought to be put,' Mary replied cryptically.

'Oh, you do, do you?' said Edith Bassett. 'I know where you ought to be put — isn't that right, Minnie?'

'Yes, and be careful to pull it,' said Minnie.

The hefty sisters were not prepared to be jeered at by these two little Cockneys. They bent down and picking up Edith Bassett and Minnie Rogers, put them under their arms and walked off. It was at once apparent why Edith Bassett had demanded a safety-pin.

'Very strong young ladies, sir,' Toker commented. 'I never did think these hikers would contrive to keep Miss Catriona and Miss Mary long in durance vile, as they say. And I made so bold as to express that opinion to Mrs MacDonald when she was inclined to take it to heart so much after they were kidnapped by the hikers. Hullo, sir, look out! I think there's some more excitement coming our way. Yes, indeed, sir, by the living jingo, it's Mr Iain, or I'm a footman. Pardon my excitement, sir, but nobody except Mr Iain could do it like that.'

Chester Royde looked out through the casement and by the glimmer of the dawn beheld a burly kilted form tossing hikers about. And then just as half-a-dozen more hikers sneaking up from behind seemed on the point of recapturing him, another kilted form dashed across the courtyard to the rescue and engaged them with his fists.

'Gee, that poet has a lovely punch,' cried Chester Royde as he charged from the postern into the fray.

A minute later Iain MacDonald was safe within the Castle.

'Capital bit of work,' the Chieftain pronounced. 'You hit one of those brutes pretty hard, Macmillan. I don't think you've met my youngest boy, Iain. This is Myrtle's fiancé, Iain.'

Iain for one brief instant looked as much surprised as an undergraduate ever allows himself to look, but quickly recovered his normal imperturbability, and nobody could have supposed that he had spent much of the past sixty-six hours rolled up in a tent and tied with the ropes of it and that he had returned home to find one of his father's guests engaged to what unless it had been Glenbogle Castle he would have vowed was a Scottish Nationalist.

'How many hikers do you reckon there are, Iain?' his father asked.

'Not far off a hundred.'

'Oh, is that all? Kenny Macdonald was putting them at over seven hundred last night.'

'He would,' said Iain.

'And what's happened to Lachy and Roddy?'

'They're probably still rolled up in tents.'

'Well, you'd better lie down for a few hours and get a bit of rest. We'll wake you if there's an alarm.'

'I'm all right, Dad. I've done enough lying down rolled up in that tent to last me for some time,' said Iain.

'You'd better go up and see your mother, girls,' Ben Nevis said to his hefty daughters, who had just come back from handing over Edith Bassett and Minnie Rogers to the grim guardianship of Mrs Parsall and Mrs Ablewhite, both of whom were drinking tea in the housekeeper's room, an occupation in which they had been almost continuously engaged all night.

'Won't she be asleep?' Catriona suggested.

'No, no, I don't think so. Every time I've been up to see her she's been awake,' said her father. This was not to be wondered at. A visit from Ben Nevis in his present martial mood was only a little quieter than a visit by a squadron of heavy dragoons.

While the garrison of Glenbogle was waiting for zero hour early on that Tuesday morning, the seventh Earl of Buntingdon was turning over restlessly in an L.N.E.R. sleeper, bound for Fort William, and wondering whether he had been wise to respond to Percy Buckham's impassioned appeal to preside at the surrender of Glenbogle Castle to the N.U.H. He switched on the light above his bed, sat up, and took out the telegram which had reached him at Ouse Hall just after lunch on Monday:

After a brilliant little operation in which every unit greatly distinguished itself have honour to inform you MacDonald MacDonald's son American guest headkeeper and two underkeepers were captured on Saturday morning and are now held prisoners stop on Saturday evening MacDonald's two daughters also captured stop am satisfied of ability to seize and occupy Glenbogle Castle on Tuesday and consider it vital to dignity of proceedings you should be present in person to receive MacDonald's apology and accept Magna Charta for N.U.H. from his hands stop have demanded removal of all no camping notices freedom camp anywhere on MacDonald's land and recognized market price for all produce purchased from his tenants stop confident MacDonald will accept terms and give apology demanded stop our casualties so far extremely light only damage being to small quantity of camping equipment and one leg bitten by dog stop secretary and self earnestly hope you will endeavour join us Tuesday for successful accomplishment of expedition's objective as your presence will lend dignity to lesson administered and rouse enthusiasm among members of union who have fought so gallantly in this campaign stop felt your presence at great democratic triumph will serve as notable rebuke to fascist influence everywhere lamentably on increase stop personally realize I am asking great deal but have complete confidence in your generous response stop suggest your wearing of hiking uniform would be intensely appreciated and will send two of our boys to meet train Fort William Tuesday morning with car and bring you to Glenbogle stop unable to receive answer as we are surrounding castle tonight with view to entry tomorrow when you arrive stop salute from every loyal hiker in the field

    Buckham

'A very long and expensive and rather repetitive telegram,' Lord Buntingdon murmured to himself. 'I wonder if I am wise in falling in with it. Buckham has always been prone to excessive optimism.'

Lord Buntingdon experienced one of those sudden waves of home-sickness which sweep over the traveller at moments of discomfort. The sleeping-compartment was stuffy, and the application to the top of his head of a draught set in motion by a switch and directed by a metal slide merely agitated the stuffiness without providing fresh air. He wondered why he had been so weak as to forsake the ample tranquillity of Ouse Hall for this constricted rumbling cell. He thought of his tortoises, whose leisurely approach to life had so often checked his more violent progressive impulses to disobey the motto of the Buntingdons, *Festina lente*. However, in spite of these doubts before sunrise, when full morning arrived and the sleeping-car attendant brought him a cup of tea and informed him breakfast would be served half an hour hence, Lord Buntingdon packed away his civilian clothes and put on the uniform in which he had so often been photographed at the Annual Hikery held in the grounds of Ouse Hall.

The other breakfasters could not understand why the stewards paid so much deference to this elderly hiker with a melon-shaped face. They did not know he was an earl.

Then somebody suggested it was Lord Baden-Powell, and though it would have been hard to find two people less alike, as everybody in the saloon wanted to say he had travelled up from King's Cross with Baden-Powell the will to believe asserted itself and the lack of resemblance was ignored. And when the elderly hiker alighted at Fort William and was met on the platform by two younger hikers, who presented arms to him with their staffs, nobody remained in doubt but that the hero of

Mafeking had shared their paste called cream, their mess of fuller's earth called porridge, their varnished chips of driftwood called kippers, their tea called coffee or their coffee called tea, and all those other luxurious and costly imitations of food that make up breakfast in a contemporary British train.

'Mr Buckham expects the Castle will be in our hands, sir, by the time our car reaches Glenbogle,' Hiker Barlow informed the President of the N.U.H.

'All going well, eh, Barlow?'

'Yes, sir, except that Mr Buckham was rather badly mauled on Sunday night by six of MacDonald's Fascist bullies.'

'Dear me, I'm sorry to hear that. How did it happen?'

'He was trying to prevent the escape of MacDonald himself whom we had taken prisoner, but he was outnumbered. Luckily it was only his chin that was rather bruised. He's leading the assault in person at eleven.'

'And that should be over by the time we reach Glenbogle?' Lord Buntingdon asked, with a touch of anxiety in his tone.

'Oh yes, sir,' Hiker Barlow confidently declared. 'We shall see our flag floating over the Castle when we drive up.'

There lingered upon the melon-shaped countenance of Lord Buntingdon a trace of that dubiety about the future which had affected his fancy before sunrise, but he shook off presentiment and followed his hiker escort to the waiting car hired for the great occasion.

Away in Glenbogle Mr Buckham, the bruise upon his chin a tartan of leaden blue and livid green and lurid yellow, was addressing his forces on the verge of the assault.

'Now don't forget,' he wound up, 'the girls will form a mobile reserve ready to throw their full weight into any gap made in the Castle defences by the men. Do your best, all of you, so that when your President arrives he will greet an N.U.H. victorious all along the line. I am leading the main assault on the front door. Hiker Williamson will command the feint against the back of the castle. Hiker Rosebotham and Hiker Hickey will lead the assaults against the side doors. Mr Prew will command the mobile reserve and give the order when it is to advance. Now then, boys and girls, three cheers for collective security and the freedom of the road!'

Three times did the fifty male hikers fling themselves against the doors of Glenbogle Castle to be drenched from above by pail after pail of soapy water, one of which wielded by Carrie accompanied its contents and temporarily extinguished Buckham himself and thereby perhaps saved the Castle from being rushed at the third and most vicious assault by diverting the attention of some of the hikers to extricating their leader from the bucket over his head. Up in the room in the North Tower the Lady of Ben Nevis and the chaplain were the only two inactive members of the garrison, and should they be called inactive whose prayers for the defenders never ceased as the tide of battle ebbed and flowed? Once during that third assault the south postern was forced, but Alan Macmillan, his blue eyes burning with this supreme expression of poetic action, flung Hiker Hickey head over heels back into the courtyard, while Chester Royde, Butting Moose of the Carroways, rammed another hiker in the midriff, so that he lay gurgling for breath upon the gravel.

The repulse of that third assault was followed by a lull. The defenders gathered to consult. Reports were unanimous about the strain upon the doors and the unlikelihood of their holding out much longer.

'We'll use the Lochaber axes,' Ben Nevis proclaimed. 'Get them down from the walls.'

Now, the long-handled Lochaber axe is a formidable weapon, and even Chester Royde, who after the Chieftain himself was the member of the garrison most intoxicated by the fighting spirit, looked doubtful about the effect of using it against the hikers. Fortunately, however, something happened to make it unnecessary to disturb the merely decorative existence in which the Lochaber axes had spent nearly two centuries. That something was the sound of the pipes still a long way off, but coming nearer all the time.

'These must be your Scottish . . . your fellows from Glasgow, Carrie,' said Ben Nevis.

And then suddenly his brow clouded and the veins in his eagle's beak seemed to run with ink as he cupped an ear to listen.

'Kilwhillie! Macmillan! Iain!' he gasped. 'Am I going mad or are those pipers playing *The Campbells are Coming?*'

The Cameron, the Macmillan, and the young MacDonald scowled in unison.

'What on earth are James Buchanan and Robert Menzies thinking of?' the poet exclaimed angrily.

'Angus! Angus!' Ben Nevis bellowed. 'Tell the pipers to play *Clan Donald is Here* full blast. Full blast, do you hear, Angus? The Campbells are coming, are they? Great Scott, I'd sooner hear in my country that ghastly song those hiker brutes were singing last night.'

When the strains of *Clan Donald is Here* died down there was no answering skirl from without, and at that moment the full force of the hikers charged for the front door.

'It'll never hold, never!' Toker was heard to declare. 'No door could,' he added loyally.

And sure enough at that moment it cracked; but even as it cracked, into the courtyard charged the kilted members of the Scottish Brotherhood of Action, like a tartan catalogue come to life.

'Outside, and at 'em!' shouted Ben Nevis when the front door gave way.

'Where's that guy with the chin?' cried Chester Royde, following Ben Nevis as another Chester once followed Marmion.

But at the last moment he was baulked of his heart's desire. He was almost in reach of Percy Buckham when Percy Buckham waved a white handkerchief.

'The yellow-livered coyote,' Chester gasped in utter disgust. 'He's thrown in the towel.'

But it was not respect for his own skin or his own chin which had made a poltroon of Percy Buckham. It was the sight of the Earl of Buntingdon in the hands of the kilted horde whose arrival had snatched victory from his grasp. The person of the President of the N.U.H. was more precious than even its honour.

'It was a mistake, Mr Buckham, to send me that telegram,' said Lord Buntingdon when they were driving back to Fort William that afternoon after peace had been signed.

'As it turned out, yes, it was a mistake, Lord Buntingdon. I frankly admit it. But the arrival of those six cars packed with what I understand are all members of a Scottish terrorist society was not foreseen by anybody. Without them you would have reached the Castle at the moment when our fourth assault was successful and you would have received from the hands of MacDonald our Magna Charta. Who would have dreamed you would be captured on the road with your guard of honour?'

'Well, well, it can't be helped, Mr Buckham. And at any rate we did obtain from Mr MacDonald a promise that the whole business should be kept out of the Press.'

'Yes, in consideration of a document signed by you, Prew, and myself accepting full responsibility for that outrage on 12 August, compensation to MacDonald's employees for wrongful imprisonment, and what is worst of all a solemn pledge that no member of the N.U.H. will ever camp again on the land of MacDonald or this Mr Cameron's land or the land of that most objectionable Yankee.'

'Still, I do comfort myself with the thought that the whole business will be kept out of the Press,' Lord Buntingdon repeated gratefully. 'I hope your chin isn't hurting you very much.'

'Oh, no, it's nothing and I console myself with the thought that it took half a dozen of them even to do that amount of damage.'

'A curious type, that Highland chief,' Lord Buntingdon observed pensively. 'I'm glad we don't get that kind of thing in Bedfordshire. A man like that would be a great nuisance on the Bench. Well, well, I shan't be sorry to get back to my tortoises. By the way, are we expected to wait for the members to reach Fort William?'

'Oh no, Prew has been left in charge of the return to London.'

The President and the Acting President relapsed into silence as the car turned out of Glenbogle.

Back in the Castle the victory was celebrated with such a feast as Mrs Ablewhite, protesting all the time to Mrs Parsall that it was impossible, loved to provide.

The members of the Scottish Brotherhood of Action left for Glasgow about midnight, all now as firmly convinced that there was something to be said for Highland chieftains of long authentic lineage still in possession of their land, as the Chieftain himself was now inclined to admit that there was something to be said for young men who desired the glory and grandeur of Scotland. In reaching this opinion he was much encouraged by the performance on the pipes of *Mac 'ic Eachainn's March to Sheriffmuir* by Colin Campbell, the student who had been responsible for desecrating the air of Glenbogle with *The Campbells are Coming*. To sit in his own Great Hall and hear a Campbell piping that tune to a MacDonald was compensation for many historical events which had taken the wrong course.

James Buchanan and Robert Menzies did not go back to Glasgow with the rest of the Brotherhood. They, like Alan Macmillan, were guests of Ben Nevis. The plans for the Keep of Knocknacolly were approved by Chester Royde, and the lawyers and the architect were bidden to go ahead with the work.

'Well,' said Kilwhillie to Ben Nevis, 'I never expected to see a cross between the Tower of London and the Crystal Palace at Knocknacolly.'

'You never expected to see the Loch Ness Monster, Hugh, but you did.'

'That's true, Donald,' said Kilwhillie, pouring himself out a second powerful *deoch an doruis*.

Chester and Carrie decided it would be politic for Myrtle to go back with them at the end of the month and prepare Mr and Mrs Chester Royde Senior for Alan's arrival a month or two later.

'Well, I want to be married in November,' Myrtle insisted. 'So you'd better be ready to sail a week or two later, Alan. And your mother must see the colouring of the trees in our fall.'

'Well, when you all come back next year,' said Ben Nevis, 'you won't find any hikers in Glenbogle. And next Twelfth I'll give you the finest sport you ever had, Royde, on Drumcockie.' He raised his glass.

'Slahnjervaw!' he bellowed.

And none had so little of the Gaelic as not to recognize that one who could now truly be called the Monarch of the Glen was wishing them 'slainte mhór' or 'good health'.

The last word may be spoken by Mr Fletcher in the following little poem which he read aloud after dinner that September night:

> 'Last August the Twelfth on the moor of Drumcockie,
> You conquered, Ben Nevis, a barbarous foe;
> You eluded his claws on the braes of Ben Booey
> And at last in Glenbogle itself laid him low.

> 'Though hikers may camp in the rest of the country,
> Not a tent shall be seen where Ben Nevis is lord:
> Ben Booey, Ben Gorm, Ben Glass, and Ben Cruet
> Will never bow down to that pestilent horde.

> 'Salute Mac 'ic Eachainn, the brave and the mighty,
> The Chief who has routed the Sassenach crew,
> The lord of Ben Nevis, Glenbogle, Glenbristle,
> Strathdiddle, Strathdun, Loch Hoch, and Loch Hoo.'

'You couldn't write a poem like that, Alan,' said Myrtle.

'No, I couldn't,' Alan agreed.

'Marvellous, isn't it?' Ben Nevis glowed. 'I simply don't know how it's done. I don't really.'

WHISKY GALORE

AUTHOR'S NOTE

By a strange coincidence the s.s. *Cabinet Minister* was wrecked off Little Todday two years after the s.s. *Politician* with a similar cargo was wrecked off Eriskay; but the coincidence stops there, for the rest is pure fiction.

To all my dear friends in Barra in grateful memory of much kindness and much laughter through many happy years

CONTENTS

Chapter 1

THE SERGEANT-MAJOR'S RETURN

From the bridge of the *Island Queen*, which three times a week made the voyage between Obaig and the outer islands of the Hebrides, Captain Donald MacKechnie gazed across a smooth expanse of grey sea to where the rugged outline of Great Todday stood out dark against a mass of deepening cloud in which a dull red gash showed that the sun was setting behind it. Captain MacKechnie muttered an order in Gaelic to the steersman, and the mailboat changed her course to round the south-west point of the island that was her next port of call. Presently the low green land and white beaches of Little Todday appeared west of the larger island and the mailboat made a sweep to enter the Coolish, the strait of water two miles wide which separated the two Toddays from each other.

It was a Saturday afternoon toward the end of February in the year 1943, and this was the first time for a week that the mailboat had been able to call at Snorvig, the little harbour in Great Todday which served the two islands.

'And there's some tirty weather coming,' Captain MacKechnie piped in that high-pitched voice of his, with a baleful glance from his bright eyes at the heavy sky louring over the Atlantic Ocean beyond Little Todday.

At this moment the trim soldierly figure of Sergeant-major Alfred Ernest Odd appeared in the doorway of the bridge-house.

'Room in here for a little one?' he asked, with a grin of welcome.

'Well, well,' the skipper exclaimed in astonishment, 'if it isn't Sarchant Odd! Man, where have you been all these months? And where have you been since we left Obaig this morning?'

'I was having a jolly good lay down. What a journey! Stood up in the corridor all the way from Devonshire the day before yesterday. Stood up in the corridor all the way from Euston up to Glasgow the night before last. Stood up in the corridor for the first half of the journey to Fort Augustus where I had to see Colonel Lindsay-Wolseley. He very kindly got me to Obaig in time for the boat and which meant leaving Tummie at three o'clock this morning in the Colonel's car, and as soon as ever I got on board the dear old *Island Queen* I got the steward to find me a bunk and I slept right through the day.'

'You've had a long churney right enough, Sarchant. Teffonshire? That's a place I neffer was in. It's a crate place for cream, I believe.'

'It may have been a great place for cream before this war, but we didn't see much cream where I've been since I got back from Africa,' said the Sergeant-major. 'No, give me good old Scotland before Devonshire any day of the week – except perhaps Sunday,' he added quickly.

'Ah, but the Sabbath's not what it was,' Captain MacKechnie insisted firmly. 'When I was a poy, man, it *wass* a tay. My word, what a tay, too, what a tay! I remember my mother once sat down on the cat, because you'll understand the plinds were pulled down in our house every Sabbath and she didn't chust see where she was sitting. The cat let out a great *sgiamh* and I let out a huge laugh, and did my father take the skin off me next day? Man, I was sitting down on proken glass for a week afterwards. My father was Kilwhillie's head stalker.'

'What, Captain Hugh Cameron of Kilwhillie?'

'Not the present laird. His father. A fine figure of a man with a monster of a peard praking below his nose like a wave on the Skerryvore. Well, well, well, it's nice to see you again, Sarchant. You've been away from us a long while now.'

'Nearly eighteen months,' said the Sergeant-major in disgusted tones. 'But that's the way in the army. As soon as anybody's got a job that suits him and he suits it, shift him. I was getting along to rights as P.S.I. with Colonel Lindsay-Wolseley's . . .'

'What's P.S.I. at all?' the skipper interjected. 'Man, the alphabet's gone mad like the rest of the world since this war.'

'Permanent Sergeant Instructor with Colonel Lindsay-Wolseley's Home Guard battalion. Yes, I've been away eighteen months too long. However, the Colonel's got me back at last, and he very kindly gave me the week-end to come over and have a look at my young lady in Little Todday. I was reckoning to get married last autumn year, and then biff! Transferred to a special job in Devonshire, and that tore it. The old man kicked up at the idea of her going so far away, and Peggy thought she couldn't leave her dad, and so that was that for the moment.'

'It was pretty annoying for you, I believe.'

'Annoying? It was enough to drive a man off his rocker. But that wasn't the worst of it. Last April instead of getting married as I hoped, biff, again! And it's West Africa, with not enough embarkation leave to risk coming up to the Islands. Then I got back in January only to find myself down in Devonshire again. Did I create? Well, to cut a long rotten story short, I'm back at last, and I'm going to get married as soon as ever it can be managed.'

'You waited a fair time, Sarchant, before you thought about getting married at all,' Captain MacKechnie pointed out, with a shrewd smile. 'Very wise, too.'

'Very wise once upon a time,' the Sergeant-major agreed. 'But I was forty-five last month. And I can't afford to wait much longer. Here, I mustn't talk to the man at the wheel.' He had noticed that the skipper's eyes were turning away from the topic of marriage toward the Snorvig pier thronged as usual with the inhabitants of the two Toddays, though it was already on the edge of dusk. 'Joseph Macroon will probably come over himself for the mail as the weather's so calm.'

'Ay, it's calm enough now, but there's plenty tirty weather away out there in the west. It'll plow as hard as effer by morning.'

'So long for the present, Captain. I dare say I'll be seeing you up at the hotel before we cross over to Kiltod.'

'I don't believe I'll be going up to the hotel this evening at all,' the skipper replied, his usually bright eyes clouded and curiously remote.

'But Joseph will expect to have a crack with you, especially as you have had to miss two runs this week.'

'Ay, it's a pity right enough, but I want to be ketting along up to Nobost. Well, well, I'm clad to see you pack, Sarchant, in what used to be the land of the free before this plutty war.'

Sergeant-major Odd left the bridge and went below to the promenade deck, where he walked up and down the port side looking across to the diminutive harbour of Kiltod and the small cluster of houses beyond, in one of which the girl he had hoped to marry so many months ago was waiting for him. Oh, well, he was back again now. Not like some of those poor chaps in Africar and Burmar and Indiar and what not who hadn't managed to get married all those months ago and didn't know when they would now.

'Good evening, Sergeant-major.'

He swung round to see the stocky form of the Snorvig bank agent.

'Hullo, Mr Thomson, you're looking well. I am glad to see you,' he declared, shaking Andrew Thomson's hand so fervidly that the bank agent's dark complexion grew darker with embarrassment. He was a man to whom words came with difficulty, and he had been walking behind Sergeant-major Odd twice up and down the length of the deck before he had managed to summon up the necessary resolution to break into speech with a greeting.

'You've been away quite a long while, Sergeant-major,' said the bank agent; but the Sergeant-major knew Andrew Thomson's manner and did not suppose that the scowl which accompanied this observation was meant to convey that it was a pity he had ever come back.

'Yes, but I'm glad to say Colonel Wolseley has got me back again at last.'

'Imphm? Is that so?'

'And how's G Company getting on? I suppose you're all as smart as guardsmen by now.'

The bank agent made a determined effort to smile at this pleasantry and in consequence his scowl became absolutely ferocious.

'Not quite yet,' he gulped. 'As a matter of fact, Captain Waggett has been having a lot of difficulty lately in getting the men together for drill. There were only two at the last parade – that is, there were only Captain Waggett and myself.'

The Sergeant-major clicked his tongue.

'Still, as long as they keep up their shooting . . .' he began.

'They're not,' said the bank agent, who was also G Company's sergeant-major. 'The turn-out for shooting practice has been very poor all this month.'

'I expect they'll be more keen as the spring comes along.'

'It's not the weather,' Andrew Thomson observed gloomily. 'There's another reason.' And then to prevent his companion's asking what that was he added hastily, 'I took Mrs Thomson over to Edinburgh on Friday. She's to stay with Mrs Pringle – that's her mother – imphm . . .' speech evaporated in a dusky blush.

'And you thought you'd have a little run around on your own, eh? Ah, well, I shall be married myself this spring if all goes according, so I mustn't talk.'

'I intended to return on Tuesday, Sergeant-major,' Andrew Thomson assured him gravely, 'but the weather held the mailboat up on Tuesday and again on Thursday.'

'A good thing I didn't arrange to come over earlier in the week,' said the Sergeant-major. 'I'd have gone bats hanging around at Obaig. Hullo, we're just getting in. I'll see you up at the hotel before I cross over to Kiltod.'

'I'll have to attend to the correspondence, Sergeant-major. There'll be three days' mail, and the head office will be wondering what's happened. I'm afraid you'll find it kind of dull up at the hotel just now.'

'I won't find it dull. I'm looking forward to seeing a lot of old friends and having a jolly good Jock and Doris, as you call it, to celebrate getting back to the two tightest little islands in the world.'

The bank agent smiled sardonically.

'They're not very tight just now, Sergeant-major,' he said, and went off quickly to find his bag.

Sergeant-major Odd puzzled for a moment over this remark, and then with a sudden thought that perhaps his beloved Peggy might have come over from Little Todday to welcome him on the pier he hurried off round to starboard. The pier was crowded with familiar figures, among them Peggy's father in his knitted red cap; but Peggy herself was not there.

'You're a proper mug, Fred,' he murmured to himself. 'As if the poor girl would want to see you for the first time after nearly eighteen months with everybody staring at her!'

A minute or two later he was hurrying down the gang-plank to greet his future father-in-law.

The movements of the postmaster and leading merchant of Kiltod seemed less quick than he remembered them, and his grey moustache usually so trim was slightly ragged. If Sergeant-major Odd had not been so acutely conscious of the twenty years' difference between his own age and that of his prospective wife he would have said that Joseph Macroon had grown appreciably older during these last eighteen months. There was, too, in the way he shook hands with him a kind of absent-mindedness as if he was hardly aware of the Sergeant-major's presence. And as he wished him *'failte do'n dùthaich'* (welcome to the country), he was not looking at the returned wanderer but at Roderick MacRurie, the owner of the hotel, who was working his great bulk up the gang-plank in search of the purser.

'How's Roderick?' the Sergeant-major asked.

'Ach, he's not well at all at all, Sarchant. He's had a terrible time, poor soul.'

'I'm sorry to hear that. And how's . . . how's everything on Little Todday?'

'Terrible. Just as bad there as here. Terrible.'

'Nothing wrong with Peggy?'

'What would be wrong with Peggy or Kate Anne?' their father demanded contemptuously. 'Smoking away, the pair of them, like two peats. It's a pity the Government doesn't run out of cigarettes.'

Joseph took a battered clay pipe out of his pocket, lit it with a noise like a rotary pump, drew two deep gurgling puffs at the closely packed twist, removed the pipe from his mouth, spat gloomily between his legs, and replaced the pipe in his pocket.

Several of Sergeant-major Odd's old acquaintances had been greeting him, and one of them, a man with a nose and a chin like a lobster's claw, said something to Joseph in Gaelic.

'I don't know, Airchie, but there's nothing to be seen of Captain MacKechnie, and if they'd brought it he'd have come ashore by now.'

'Ay, I believe he would,' agreed Archie MacRurie, generally known as the Biffer, a fisherman of prowess about fifty years old. 'Ay, he'd have been ashore by now right enough if it had been on board.'

'Look at Roderick now,' Joseph exclaimed. 'You can see it isn't there by the way the man's shoulders have died on him. Ah, *duine bochd*, it's me that's sorry for the poor soul. Ah well, Sarchant, we'll be getting down to the *Morning Star*,' he said, thrusting his hands into the pockets of his greatcoat.

'You'd better come up to the hotel and have a dram with me first while you're waiting for the mails to be sorted,' the Sergeant-major suggested.

His two companions looked at him quickly to see if he was laughing at them. Then, perceiving that the invitation had been given in earnest, their manners forbade them to tell him how futile it was lest he should suppose they had suspected him of a deliberate meanness in giving it. Joseph Macroon sighed deeply.

'What is the use of waiting for the mail? Just a lot of letters for nothing,' he declared. 'We'll be getting them Monday morning.'

Sergeant-major Odd was only too happy not to wait for the sorting of the mail. He had expected to be kept at least another hour or more away from the sight of his Peggy. As Joseph Macroon and he moved across the pier to the steps at the foot of which the *Morning Star* was moored, Roderick MacRurie came down the gang-plank.

'Any news, Roderick?' the postmaster of Little Todday asked.

'Not a single bottle. *A Chruitheir*, this is a terrible war, Iosaiph, right enough. Do you remember that Sunday night the day the war started? Nobody in the islands could mind such a storm of rain. Water? I never saw so much water come down Ben Sticla. My best cow was drowned like a kitten that night. It wass a sign, Iosaiph, it wass a sign right enough of what wass coming to us. Water! Chust nothing but water! My brother Simon said we would have to pay for it by going to war on the Sabbath. I didn't take any notice at the time because an elder has to talk like that, you'll understand. But he was right.'

'But what exactly has happened? How does water come into it?' the Sergeant-major asked.

'Because there hasn't been a trop of whisky in the two islands for twelve days,' Roderick MacRurie replied. 'And I was handing it out for a month before that like my own blood, we were that short.'

'And we'll have Lent on us in a fortnight next Wednesday,' said Joseph Macroon, who as a Catholic of Little Todday was not prepared to allow the Protestants of Great Todday a monopoly of religious emotion. 'Fancy the Government running out of whisky just before Lent. What a Government!'

'Do you think Winston Churchill knows they've run out of whisky?' Roderick asked.

'I don't believe he will,' Joseph replied.

'It's a pity he wouldn't be saying something about it on the wireless,' Roderick observed sagely, for he was a profound admirer of the Prime Minister's oratory. 'You never know what these Governments will be doing next. Before we know where we are there'll be no peer either. We're running terribly low.'

The passage of time since last he had visited Little Todday was brought home to the Sergeant-major by his first sight of Joseph's youngest son, Kenny, who was now a lanky stripling of sixteen in charge of his father's motor-boat and always threatening when he was denied anything he wanted for the engine to be off to sea. This evening the *Morning Star* was on her best behaviour and chugged across the Coolish without stopping once. The water was as smooth as a tarnished silver plate and there was still a glimmer of twilight when they reached the tiny harbour on the top of the tide.

'Captain Waggett hasn't managed the perfect black-out at the end of a perfect day yet?' the Sergeant-major observed with a grin when he saw the light from Joseph Macroon's shop streaming across the road leading up from the harbour.

'Ach, they haven't drawn the curtains. Plenty time,' said the Chief Warden of Kiltod. 'Plenty time,' he murmured to himself remotely.

The Sergeant-major felt that he was indeed back in the islands when he heard those two words, and that of course gave him the keenest pleasure. All the same in view of what he hoped to settle about his own future during this precious week-end, he was chary of accepting the dictum too easily.

'Time flies, you know,' he reminded his host. Then in the lighted door of the post-office he saw tall and slim as ever his Peggy, and a moment later he was holding her hands and looking into her deep-blue slanting eyes.

Chapter 2

THE WAKE

The gathering in the bar of the Snorvig Hotel on that February evening was so exceptionally gloomy an occasion for Great or Little Todday and the host Roderick MacRurie was so unlike his usual expansive self that it is only fair to give a picture of the islands in happier times and by the kind permission of Mr Hector Hamish Mackay, the well-known topographer of the Hebrides, to quote what he says about the two islands in his book, *Faerie Lands Forlorn*:

And so after sailing for the whole of a fine summer's day along the magical coasts of Tìr nan Òg the gallant *Osprey* reached Snorvig, the picturesque little port of Great Todday (Todaidh Mór) where we dropped anchor and soon afterwards went ashore to enjoy the hospitality of the Snorvig Hotel and the tales of 'mine host', Roderick MacRurie, the 'uncrowned king' of the island. After a lordly spread, of which a magnificent lobster was the *pièce de résistance*, we sat outside on a terrace of shingle to pore spellbound over a scene of natural beauty which is nowhere surpassed in all the wondrous West.

Down below we could hear the voices of children playing among the various merchandise lying all over the quay and pier until Iain Dubh, the piermaster, should find time to put it away in the store – sweet Gaelic voices that seemed to reach us like the 'horns of elfland faintly blowing'.

Mr MacRurie, with a grave shake of his impressive head, assured us that the Snorvig children were getting out of hand. Only last week two of them had ridden into the sea a motor-bicycle just arrived from the mainland for the schoolmaster at Bobanish on the other side of the island.

Soon, however, all discussion of modern youth was hushed by the splendour of the sunset beyond Little Todday (Todaidh Beag) which was turning the mighty Atlantic to a sheet of molten gold. Kiltod, the diminutive port of Little Todday, lies opposite Snorvig from which it is separated by a strait of water two miles wide. Little Todday is not so very much inferior in superficial area to its sister island and probably earned its qualifying adjective by the comparative lowness and flatness of the vivid green machair land framed by long white sandy beaches, which contrasts with the more rugged aspect of Great Todday. Here the soil is peaty and the shores are rockbound, while three of its hills, of which Ben Sticla (1400 feet) is the most conspicuous, rise above a thousand feet. The contrast in appearance between the two islands is so remarkable that we are not surprised to learn the inhabitants of both have preserved for hundreds of years an equally remarkable independence of one another, and differ considerably not merely in character but even in religion, Great Todday being Protestant and Little Todday Catholic.

Both of the islands were formerly under the protection of St Tod who is said to have sailed there from Donegal on a log, his monkish habit providing the sail, his arm uplifted in benediction the mast. He built a church at Kiltod the foundations of which beside a holy well are still discernible close to the port. My grief! Nowadays even on Little Todday the old tales of the saint are passing from the memory, and the store of legend has been sadly depleted.

In our time the two islands display no more than a friendly rivalry, but in the old period of clan feuds the MacRuries of Great Todday were always raiding the cattle of their neighbours, and the Macroons of Little Todday were not less adept at making inroads upon the MacRurie sheep. Authorities disagree about the comparative antiquity of the two clans. The Macroons claim to be descended from a seal-woman who loved an exiled son of Clan Donald and bore him seven sons every one of whom brought himself back a mortal bride from the mainland. The MacRuries on the other hand claim to be descended from an exiled Maclean called Ruairidh Ruadh, reputed to have stood seven feet six inches without his brogues. This Ruairidh Ruadh was a noted pirate who stole at least one wife from almost every island in the west. The fact that there is no legend of his having stolen a Macroon wife is held by those who support the claim of the MacRuries to greater antiquity to prove that the Macroons had not yet appeared upon the scene.

We shall not venture an opinion on this vexed question. The air is too soft and balmy upon this June evening for genealogical controversy. Let us lean back in our deck-chairs and watch the great sun go dipping down into the sea behind Little Todday. Is that St Brendan's floating isle we see upon the Western horizon? Forsooth, on such a night it were easy to conjure up that elusive morsel of geography. And now behind us the full moon clears the craggy summit of Ben Sticla and swims south past Ben Pucka to shed a honey-coloured radiance over the calm water of the Coolish, as the strait between the two Toddays is called. Why, oh why, the lover of Eden's language asks, must the fair Gaelic word Caolas be debased by map-makers to Coolish, so much more suggestive of municipal baths than of these 'perilous seas'? Alas, such sacrilege is all too sadly prevalent throughout Scotland. We turn our gaze once more to rest spellbound upon the beauty of earth and sea and sky and to let our imagination carry us back out of the materialistic present into the haunted past.

We see again Ruairidh Ruadh's dark galley creep out from Snorvig and sweep with measured strokes northward up the Coolish on rapine bent. We see again the seal-beaked galley of the Macroons off Tràigh nam Marbh – the Strand of the

Dead – and we hear the voices of the rowers lamenting their own dead Chief as they bear his body to the burial-place of the Macroons on the little neighbouring isle of Poppay. Alas, for these degenerate days, although Poppay is still a breeding ground for the grey Atlantic seals, the Macroons no longer use it as a burial-ground.

But, hark! What is that melodious moaning we hear in the west? It is the singing of the seals on Poppay and Pillay, the twin small isles that guard the extremities of Little Todday, their fantastic shapes standing out dark against the blood-stained western sky. Would that the present scribe possessed the musical genius of Mrs Kennedy Fraser that he might set down in due notation that melodious moaning!

And now in the entrance of the hotel we notice our host beckoning to us. With one last lingering look at the unearthly beauty of this Hebridean twilight we turn to answer the summons. In our host's snuggery the glasses reflect with opalescent gleams the flicker of a welcome fire of peats, and as we raise the *uisge beatha* to our lips with a devout *'slàinte mhath, slàinte mhór'* we feel that we are indeed privileged visitors to Tìr nan Òg, and rejoicing in our own renewed youth we give thanks to the beneficent fortune which has brought us once more to the two lovely Toddays, there to dream away a few enchanted days on the edge of the world.

Tempora mutantur. This evening an almost silent group of elderly or old or very old men sat on the wooden benches round the bar and eyed the glasses of beer on the tables in front of them without relish. Beer does not taste like itself unless it is chasing a dram of neat whisky down the gullet, preferably two drams. To add to the prevailing depression, on account of a shortage of paraffin only two of the six lamps hanging from the ceiling were alight.

'Did you hear any word of Donald in the post, Airchie?' the Biffer was asked by Angus MacCormac, a big crofter with an immense grey moustache who had driven in with the lorry from Garryboo, in the extreme north of the island. Donald was the eldest of Archie MacRurie's four sons now serving their country in the Mercantile Marine.

'Not a word, not a word,' he sighed.

'Och, he'll be a prisoner of war,' put in Sammy MacCodrum, another Garryboo crofter, a small man with sparse hair and a nose on him even larger and beakier than the Biffer's own.

'Ay, maybe he will and maybe not,' said the father gloomily. 'His mother's made up her mind the lad's drowned.'

'Where wass his ship sunk?' Sammy asked.

'By what we can reckon it must have been off the Irish coast.'

'Look at that now,' Sammy commented. 'So near and yet so far, as they say.'

'That's the worst of it,' said the father. 'If he'd been torpedoed away out it might have been long enough before we heard if he was safe, but being so near we ought to have heard by now if he's a prisoner of war.'

Heads all round were shaken dejectedly. There was indeed nothing in the atmosphere of the bar that evening to encourage an easy optimism.

It was at this moment that Captain Alec MacPhee, the patriarch of Snorvig, now in his ninetieth year, rose from his seat and taking his glass to the bar-counter asked his host to fill it up again.

'I'm sorry, Captain MacPhee, but unless the peer comes by Monday's poat the peer will be where the whisky is, and that's nowhere at all,' said the big hotel-keeper.

The ancient mariner, who was sailing the Seven Seas before the Franco-Prussian war, emitted such a tremendous gasp of amazement that his great white beard shivered like a grove of aspens.

'A *Thighearna bheannaichte*,' he exhaled, 'what are you telling me, Roderick?'

'I'm telling you you've had two pints of peer already this evening, Captain MacPhee, and no man can have more.'

The ancient mariner turned on his heels and walked out of the bar without another word. Outside, they heard the shingle of the terrace crunched by his resolute footsteps. There was neither moon nor star to light him on his way home; but an inward blaze of indignation illuminated the road down the hill to his house, which stood back from the main road round the island in a small garden, of which the principal feature was an enormous clam-shell from the Great Barrier Reef, mounted on a small cairn. His own snug sitting-room was a museum of his long adventurous life. The walls were covered with paintings and faded photographs of the ships in which he had sailed, with assegais and clubs and blowpipes, with bits of china and bits of armour, while over the mantelpiece hung a glass case in which two green pigeons from Fernando Po eyed perpetually an emerald bird of paradise from New Guinea.

Into this room the Captain strode upon that dark February evening and struck the Burmese gong with which he was wont to summon his great-grandniece Flora, a pretty, amiable flibbertigibbet of a girl, who at this date was looking after him until she could get to Glasgow and become a tram-conductress.

An hour later Dr Maclaren came into the bar, where by now the frequenters were all sitting in front of empty glasses.

'Did the Captain seem all right when he left here?' Dr Maclaren asked sharply.

He was told what had happened.

'Well, the shock has killed him,' the Doctor announced. 'And I'm not surprised. For the last fifteen years to my knowledge he drank his three drams of whisky and three pints of beer every night of his life and on such a tonic he might have lived to a hundred. He's had not a drop of whisky for twelve days, and before that only one dram a night for nearly a month. And now tonight he wasn't able to get his third pint of beer. Well, it's killed him.'

Dr Maclaren's usually jovial florid face was lined with bad temper. He was a man who liked his dram, and he was beginning to feel the effects of no whisky on himself.

'I've sent Flora along to her mother,' he went on. 'I suppose some of you will be sitting up with the body tonight.'

'Ay, we'll see about the *caithris* right enough,' one of the men in the bar assured him. 'Don't you worry yourself for that, Doctor.'

When the women had laid out the body in the bedroom on the other side of the passage, some seven or eight male representatives of Great Todday gathered in the Captain's sitting-room to watch the night away and keep the dead man company.

Roderick MacRurie sat in the Captain's own armchair, and his presence was a tribute to the sorrow he felt for that failure of his hospitality which had shocked the old mariner out of this world into the next. In the armchair on the other side of the hearth, where a well-laid fire of peats was glowing, sat the Biffer. Round the table were Angus MacCormac, Sammy MacCodrum, Alec Mackinnon, the headmaster of Snorvig School, and two or three more. They were joined presently by Norman Macleod, the attractive young schoolmaster of Watasett, a village at the head of Loch Sleeport near the south-west point of the island.

'I tried to persuade George Campbell to stay with us for a while,' he told the company. 'But he went back in the lorry to Garryboo. He and my sister Catriona fixed things this afternoon and they'll be married at the beginning of the summer holidays.'

'Ah, well, Catriona will make him a good wife,' Roderick MacRurie declared amid general agreement. 'There isn't a better cook in Todaidh

Mòr.' He paused. 'Does Mistress Campbell know Chorge is to be marrying himself so soon?'

'George is going to tell his mother tonight,' said Norman. 'Och, I'm glad for Catriona's sake, for I'll be away in the R.A.F. any time now. I've had my papers.'

'Did you have a good dram to drink their health?' Angus MacCormac asked.

'Where would I have a dram in this drought of whisky?' retorted Norman Macleod, with an indignant toss of his long wavy hair.

Sammy MacCodrum shook his head.

'Chorge will neffer be having the courage to tell Mistress Campbell he's going to be married on her. Neffer!' he declared. 'Not unless he'd trunk a tram the size of Loch Sleeport itself, and then I believe it would turn to water inside of his *stamac* when he saw his mother gazing at him.'

Further discussion of the Garryboo schoolmaster's chances of escaping from bachelorhood was interrupted by the entrance of Mrs Farquhar Maclean, the Captain's great-niece and the mother of Flora, with tea, scones, and oatcakes to sustain the watchers. She was a plump bustling woman of about forty whose husband was away at sea.

'Ah, Morag, *eudail*, the Captain went terrible quick,' Big Roderick sighed.

'Och, it was better that way,' said Mrs Maclean. 'He lived a terrible long time before he went at all, and I'm sure himself would have wanted to go quick. The *bodach* was always so quick about everything. Our Flora got as thin as bone the way she would be jumping when he always put his head round the door so quick.' She surveyed the table. 'There's plenty more tea and scones in the kitchen, and you'll just be helping yourselves when I go back home.'

'*Tapadh leat, tapadh leat, a Mhorag*,' said Big Roderick. '*Oidhche mhath*.' The others murmured their thanks and good nights, and when Mrs Maclean had left them to their vigil they started to pour themselves out cups of tea.

'Ah well, well,' Roderick muttered with a deep sigh, 'it's not for us to crumple at what the Lord provides for us.'

'I believe the Captain would have grumbled if he was sitting up here with us this night,' said the Biffer. 'Och, I've often seen him drink a cup of tea right enough, but he would never be looking at it so lovingly before he drank it the way he would be looking at a dram.'

'That's right,' Angus MacCormac agreed. 'It was a pleasure to see the way he would be looking at a dram before he put it to his mouth. You'd almost be thinking you were going to drink it yourself.'

'Ay,' the Biffer agreed in turn, 'there was a relish in the man's eyes which made you warm toward another dram yourself. *A Chruithear*, many's the time I've called for one myself just because the Captain had enjoyed his own so much. When do you think you'll be seeing whisky again, Roderick?'

'How would I know, Archie?' the hotel-keeper replied sombrely. 'Wasn't the Minister's wife asking me that very question this afternoon?'

'The Minister's wife?' exclaimed Alec Mackinnon, his thin body bending over the table like a tall black note of interrogation.

Norman Macleod threw back his head and laughed loudly.

'*Ist, ist*, Mr Macleod,' the hotel-keeper rebuked, 'don't be laughing, please. Mistress Morrison was wanting some whisky for the Minister's cold. My brother Simon went up to the Manse to see him this evening, and he says the poor soul has no more voice in him than a bit of dead grass in the wind.'

'What kind of a stuffed pird is that at all?' the high-pitched voice of Sammy MacCodrum broke in suddenly to ask. He had been staring for some time at the emerald bird of paradise between the two green pigeons over the mantelpiece. 'I never saw a pird with a tail on him like that.'

'That's a bird of paradise, Sammy,' the Snorvig headmaster informed him.

'A pird of baratice,' Sammy echoed in amazement. 'How was the Captain after shooting a pird of baratice and him on earth? You're making a fun and a choke of me, Mr Mackinnon, and this is no time to be making funs and chokes of people whateffer.'

'No, no, Mr Mackinnon's not joking, Sammy,' Norman Macleod assured him earnestly. 'Captain MacPhee shot it in a balloon.'

'Don't you believe him, Sammy,' said Alec Mackinnon. 'The Captain brought it back with him from New Guinea. And those two green pigeons came from West Africa.'

'Ah, well, well, well, fancy a man who's travelled about all over the world like the Captain having to stand before his Creator chust for the want of a pint of peer.'

Sammy MacCodrum shook his head in a bewilderment of ironic and melancholy reflection.

'It wassn't the want of a pint of peer that killed the Captain, *a*

Shomhairle,' said the hotel-keeper. 'Ach, yess, it was a shock right enough when I had to tell him he could not be having his third pint, but if his constitution had not been weakened so powerfully for want of whisky chust at the time of year when a man needs it most, himself would be sitting where I'm sitting now in his own armchair. *A dhuine dhuine*, we are all miserable worrums in the eyes of the Lord. He chust stamps on us when He has a mind to. Did anybody bring the Book? Maybe Mr Mackinnon would read us the death of Moses in sight of the Promised Land flowing with milk and honey.'

'But the poor old Captain never had a glimpse of the Promised Land,' Norman Macleod pointed out. 'There wasn't a drop of whisky in sight.'

'Angus, will you see if the Captain has his Bible there,' said Roderick, with a reproachful glance at the flippant young schoolmaster.

Angus MacCormac searched the Captain's bookshelf. 'The China Pilot, the West Africa Pi-lot, the Pacific Pi-lot,' he read out. 'Och, there's nothing but Pi-lots.'

Roderick clicked his tongue. 'The poor Captain! There's only one Pilot for the voyage he's making now. Maybe it's beside his bed.'

'And it's not for us to be taking it from him if it is,' the Biffer declared firmly. 'He was a good man, and he was a very patriotic man. I remember fine when we had no weapons for the Home Guard and we all thought the Germans would be on top of us at any minute, and the Captain brought those assegais hanging up there down to the police-station, ay, and he handed his own shot-gun over to Constable Macrae at the same time.'

'Sarchant Odd wasn't too pleased at all this evening when he heard we hadn't been keeping our shooting up to the mark,' said Angus MacCormac.

'It would be the Panker who wass telling him that. He didn't see Mr Wackett on the pier,' Sammy MacCodrum put in.

'I'll bet Waggett hasn't run out of his whisky,' Norman Macleod chuckled.

'You oughtn't to say a thing like that, Mr Macleod,' the Snorvig schoolmaster urged, 'unless you have positive proof.'

Paul Waggett was the retired stockbroker who had bought Snorvig House and rented the shooting of the two islands from the Department of Agriculture. He commanded the Home Guard Company recruited from the Toddays and in the opinion of the islanders never allowed himself to run out of creature comforts.

And indeed Norman Macleod was right. When the watchers down in the Captain's house were preparing for their long vigil with the support of tea, up at Snorvig House Paul Waggett was pouring himself out a carefully measured dram, which he handed to his wife.

'If you'll add sugar and hot water, old lady, I'll drink it when I'm in bed. I rather think I caught a germ at the Manse this afternoon. Mr Morrison really ought to keep that cold of his to himself.'

'I know, dear, I think it's so selfish the way people scatter colds all over the place. I do hope you've caught it in time.'

'You mean "not caught" it, Dolly,' said her husband with that superior smile which sent his sharp nose up in the air.

'Yes, of course, dear, how silly of me!'

'I think if I drink a double ration of hot grog I may fend it off. That's the beauty of only drinking whisky on rare occasions. One gets the benefit of it when one does drink it.'

Mrs Waggett who had been hearing this observation reiterated over nearly twenty-five years of connubiality tried to look as if she had heard it now for the first time.

'You're worried because there are no lemons,' said her husband kindly. 'Don't worry, old lady. *À la guerre comme à la guerre*, as the French used to say in the last war.' He stressed the word 'last' severely. The French collapse in 1940 was a favourite theme of his for a display of prosy superficiality.

And his wife who knew it hurried off to boil the kettle.

'You go on, dear, and get quickly into bed. I'll bring your whisky up to you.'

When a few minutes later she arrived in the bedroom with a steaming glass of heavily-sugared whisky, Paul Waggett was lying back in pillowed luxury.

'Now sip this, Paul, while I'm getting ready for bed, and then I'll take the glass away. You won't want it left beside you.'

When Mrs Waggett returned in a dressing-gown her husband was leaning back with an expression of profound satisfaction.

'I think that ought to defeat my cold,' he announced with evident admiration of his own cunning. 'Mrs Morrison was complaining this afternoon that she couldn't get any whisky for the Minister.'

'We still have another bottle,' Mrs Waggett reminded him.

'I know, but if every time people run out of whisky we are going to be called upon to supply it we shall be in the same position as them.

They must learn not to be improvident. Improvidence is the besetting sin of the Islands. If they had all the whisky in Scotland, do you think they would be able to keep it? No, no, they'd drink it as fast as they could. Just as fast as they could,' he repeated dreamily.

'But poor Mrs Morrison never expected not to be able to get whisky from Roderick MacRurie when it was wanted for medical reasons,' Mrs Waggett ventured to point out. 'The Minister never keeps it in the house.'

'That's exactly what I mean by improvidence,' her husband insisted. 'Look at Captain MacPhee. Maclaren tells me that it was being suddenly cut off from whisky which killed him. Of course, Maclaren always exaggerates. Yet no doubt the old man was inconvenienced. Now, you'd think somebody like him who has had the command of ships would have taken care not to run out of whisky if it was so important to his comfort. But no, he was just as improvident as that silly niece of his who was supposed to be looking after him. It's in the blood. And it's even getting hold of a man like Sergeant-major Odd. I'd no idea he was coming over this evening. I must say I'm rather surprised he didn't come up to Snorvig House before he crossed over to Little Todday.'

'Oh, well, Paul, I expect he was anxious to see Peggy Macroon. He's been away a long time.'

'Yes, that's why it's so strange he didn't come up here as soon as he got off the boat. I noticed before he left us to go to that job in Devonshire that this West Highland casualness was getting hold of him.'

'I wonder if he and Peggy Macroon will be getting married soon,' Mrs Waggett said.

'I'm afraid I'm more anxious to know if he will be able to smarten up my men. They're getting terribly slack.'

'It *is* disheartening for you, Paul, after all the trouble you've taken with them.'

'When duty calls we don't consider our personal feelings, Dolly. Where's the book I was reading? I hope you haven't taken it downstairs.'

'What's it called?'

'*Death in the Jampot*. It's a Crime Club volume.'

'Oh dear, I believe I did take it downstairs. Silly of me. I thought you'd finished it,' said Mrs Waggett.

Her husband shook his head.

'Don't you start going native, old lady.'

She removed the empty glass and went off in search of the book. It was quickly found.

'Is it a good story?' she asked solicitously as she presented it to him.

'Not quite enough action for me, but it's not too bad.'

Mrs Waggett doffed her dressing-gown, got into bed and composed herself for sleep. Her husband read a few pages of *Death in the Jampot*; but the agreeable fumes of the hot grog made him too drowsy to spot even the most obvious clue, and he was not long in following Mrs Waggett's example.

Chapter 3

A QUESTION OF MARRIAGE

The Sergeant-major found Joseph Macroon in a mood of pessimism about the prospect of marriage. When the two daughters of the household had retired to bed with a paternal reminder that the barrel of paraffin was almost empty, that they must not be late for early Mass, and that the saying of their prayers did not require a lamp, the postmaster took his guest into the little room at the back of the shop and expressed an opinion that there was enough coal on the fire to last as long as they would be wanting to sit up.

'I was hoping we might settle the date when me and Peggy get safely married, Mr Macroon,' the Sergeant-major suggested after he had seated himself in one of the armchairs on either side of the hearth.

'Ah, yes, well, we'll be talking about that when summer's over,' Joseph replied, his eyes wandering round the room, his tone vague. 'Och, that'll be quite time enough,' he added on a firmer note.

'I don't agree with you there, Mr Macroon.'

'We'll see better then the way the war is going. These Chaps are terrible. I believe they're worse than the Chermans,' said Joseph.

'Oh, they're regular bastards. No mistake about that. All the same, I don't see what they've got to do with me and Peggy getting married.'

'No, no,' Joseph murmured ambiguously. 'Will you have a bottle of ginger-ale, Sarchant?'

'No, thanks, I don't think I'll have anything.'

'You won't get anything,' Joseph assured him. 'Do you know when I last had a dram? Twelve days ago, and Lent begins the week after next.'

'Don't you ever drink whisky in Lent?'

'Och, I drink whisky any time of the year. I don't drink so much of it that I must give it up in Lent.'

'Then what difference will Lent make?' the Sergeant-major asked in perplexity.

'Man, we always allow ourselves a few extra drams before Lent begins. You're not a Catholic. You don't understand what a solemn sort of a time Lent is. And it's very long.'

'We have Lent in the Church of England,' said the Sergeant-major. Joseph Macroon looked doubtful.

'At least, I'm pretty sure I remember having to give up sugar in Lent when I was a nipper.'

'Look at that now,' Joseph exclaimed in astonishment. 'Well, well, well, I never thought that the English ever denied themselves anything. Isn't that strange, now? Ay, ay, you live and learn. That's very true. When do you think this terrible war will be over, Sarchant?'

'Oh, it may go on for another three years with the Jerries, and I daresay you could add another year or more to finish off the Japs. That's why I'm anxious not to waste any more time in getting married. You see, if the war does stop sooner than we expect my job at Fort Augustus will stop too. That'll mean me going to live down in Nottingham to look after my mother's shop. And I want you to have as long as possible to get used to the idear of Peggy living so far away. Fort Augustus is much nearer her old home than what Nottingham will be. And by the time she and me have been living for a couple of years at Fort Augustus you'll hardly notice it if she goes a bit further off. Colonel Lindsay-Wolseley's very kindly offered me a furnished cottage at Tummie for ten bob a week. It's a gift. He's a fine gentleman.'

'Och, he's a fine gentleman right enough,' Joseph agreed. 'We've never had a disagreeable word at the Council meetings. And I believe he'll support us when the question of the new school for Kiltod comes up again at the March meeting.'

'I'm sure he will,' the Sergeant-major declared fervidly.

'The present school is not fit for children at all. It is not fit for chickens. "How many water-closets have you?" one of these wise men from the East as Ben Nevis calls them was asking me at the last meeting. General Mackenzie of Mam. "How many water-closets, General? The whole island is a water-closet," I said. The General was a bit taken aback when I told him that. Och, I believe we'll get our school right enough.'

But Joseph's optimism was all too brief. A moment later he was sighing. 'And yet I don't know so much at all. They want all the rates for themselves in Inverness. They're terribly greedy for themselves on the other side of the county. So many Mackenzies there, and the air just gives them an appetite.'

'But what about me and Peggy getting married?' Sergeant-major Odd pressed. 'Don't you think just before Easter would be a good time?'

'Just before Easter? What are you saying, man?' Joseph exclaimed in horror. 'You have some very peculiar thoughts, Sarchant.'

'Well, just after Easter? Anyway, before April's out?'

'Ah, we'd better talk about it when the summer's over. I don't know at all why you're in such a hurry.'

'If you'd been wanting to marry a girl for nearly two years you'd be in a hurry, Mr Macroon. And I'm getting on, remember.'

'Och, you're not so old as all that, Sarchant. I'm sixty-three myself. Two of my daughters are away married long ago. Peigi Mhór's away married down in Glasgow and Peigi Bhàn's away married in Obaig.'

'I know that,' said the Sergeant-major, trying not to seem impatient.

'And they tell me Peigi Bheag's going with one of the school-teachers in Barra, and talking of getting married to him, Neil MacNeil. Och, he's not a bad fellow, with huge great glasses on him. Ah, well, the fire's going very black. You'll be wanting to be away to your bed, Sarchant, I believe. You must be pretty tired. You're sure you won't have a bottle of ginger-ale?'

'No, thanks, Mr Macroon.'

'Or a bottle of lemonade?'

The Sergeant-major shook his head.

'I don't blame you,' said the postmaster sadly. 'That's another thing. How can we have a wedding when there's no whisky?'

'There's bound to be plenty of whisky by the end of April,' the Sergeant-major argued.

'It's easy to see you've been out of the country,' Joseph Macroon told his guest. 'There hasn't been plenty whisky for a year and more. It wasn't so bad on Todaidh Beag while that barrel of rum lasted, but it didn't last long at all. There were too many in the secret. We were all hoping for another barrel when the *Jamaica Maid* went down last winter off Barra Head; but if she had any barrels aboard they did not come ashore here or on Todaidh Mór. No, no, nothing but what they call grapefruits, and they were just an amusement for the children.'

'Yes, I expect they enjoyed eating them.'

'Och, they didn't eat them at all. They threw them at one another. Tràigh Swish was alive with them. We never thought they were fruits at all till Mr MacIver the School Inspector came over and told us what they were. But by then what was left of them was all rotten.'

Joseph Macroon rose from his chair, pulled his knitted red cap over his ears, and moved toward the door where he stood listening.

'The wind's getting up again, right enough,' he said. 'You'll find a lamp in your room, Sarchant.'

'And you'll think over what we were talking about,' the Sergeant-major asked.

'I don't think about it at all,' his host replied. 'What's the use of thinking about whisky when there's not a nip to be thinking about?'

'I mean about me and Peggy getting married after Easter?' the Sergeant-major pressed.

'It's too late to be talking about a big subject like that tonight.'

'What about if Peggy's called up?'

'She won't be called up. She's indispensable to the post-office.'

'What about Kate Anne?'

'She's indispensable to the croft. She's an agricultural worker. Hark the way it's blowing. We'll have a dirty night, Sarchant.'

'A very dirty night,' Sergeant-major Odd agreed gloomily.

And as he lay for a long while awake on a mattress that was hard even by the standards of hardness to which many years of military service had accustomed him, the heart of Sergeant-major Odd was weighed down by a heavier depression than that now playing havoc with the Atlantic. The higher the wind rose, the lower his spirits sank. 'The next time I come to Little Todday,' he vowed to himself, 'I'll put a bottle of whisky in my haversack, whatever it costs. That's one sure thing. Whatever it costs! If I'd only have known in time I'd have brought a bottle with me even if I'd have had to pinch one. Her father would have been another man if I'd have been able to produce a dram for him tonight. He'd have taken quite a different view of the matter. That's the worst of these fathers without wives of their own. All they think about is turning their daughters into slaves. Indispensable! Isn't she more indispensable to me than what she is to the post-office? Post-office! With a post three times a week. Why, it's comical.'

Then for a while the mattress seemed to grow softer and the wind to blow more gently as he thought of his Peggy asleep in the room next to him. She'd been a bit shy, of course. Well, any girl would be shy after all those months. Still, she'd been glad to see him. She knew now all right that he loved her. Come to think of it, she'd never kissed him quite so . . . well, quite so much as if she liked kissing him. If only this wind would drop they'd be able to walk over to Try Swish tomorrow afternoon, and sit where they'd sat on that Sunday afternoon at the end of April nearly two years ago, that Sunday afternoon when he'd asked her to marry him. She thought then that a man couldn't fall in love with a girl he'd only known for a few days. Well, she knew now all right that a man could. Next April. That's when it had got to be. Whisky or no whisky. All the same, it was going to be hard to persuade Peggy to defy the old man, and insist on getting married whether he liked it or not. They were a bit old-fashioned out here in the Islands. They paid a lot more attention to what their fathers said than what they did anywhere else nowadays. Sergeant-major Odd's thoughts travelled into the future. 'And quite right too,' he murmured to himself. 'I think a father ought to have a bit of authority at home. Within reason, of course, within reason.' Just then a louder gust than any yet swept round the house, and away to the west the gale was booming. 'Blowing big guns,' the Sergeant-major muttered. How long was the First Army going to be held up in Tunis? Things were going a bit slow there. Of course, the war wouldn't really last another three or four years. Or would it? Well, the war wasn't going to stop him marrying Peggy. Suppose they called her up? Well, she might get directed to work close by.

'I know what I'll do,' the Sergeant-major told himself. 'I'll pop across tomorrow evening and ask Father Macalister's advice. Perhaps he'll talk to the old man. And on Monday I'll have to go over to Great Todday and talk to Captain Waggett about G Company. This whisky business is upsetting them over there pretty badly from what I can make out. Well, you can't blame the poor chaps. Fancy coming in to a parade on a night like this all the way from Garryboo or Bobanish and then when you go into the hotel to have one afterwards you can't have one. No wonder they've been slacking off. Wouldn't it be fine if next time I came over from the mainland I could bring a case of whisky along with me! I'll lay there'd be a good turn-out of every blinking section in the two islands. Don't be soppy, Fred,' he adjured himself scornfully. 'Where are *you* going to find a case of whisky? Be your age, you silly b — r, and go to sleep.'

The foolish body obeyed the wiser mind, and Sergeant-major Alfred Ernest Odd presently fell asleep.

Next day the weather was fiercer than ever. Huge brooms of rain swept the green carpet of Little Todday almost continuously. The huddled sheep were too soggy to browse. The stirks and ponies drooped. The gulls gave up flying and dotted the grass like white stones. No dogs barked. The plan to walk the four miles across to the long white beach of Tràigh Swish on the west coast of the island was beyond the power of the Sergeant-major's romantic determination to carry out on that Sunday afternoon. And when Peggy and he were left alone together in the sitting-room after dinner the wind rattled the door so often that he grew tired of jumping apart from Peggy at every false alarm.

'I think I'll go up and see Father Macalister, Peggy darling,' he said when the wind had interrupted what looked like being the longest kiss she had given him yet.

'I'm sure Father James would like to see you, Fred. Kirstag told me this morning he was asking for you.'

'I'll go right away,' the Sergeant-major declared firmly.

He went to fetch his greatcoat from the porch.

'Coupons!' he exclaimed.

'They're terrible, these coupons,' Peggy grumbled as she helped him into his coat. 'Even if we could be married, Fred, I wouldn't have any coupons for you.'

'Oh, I wasn't wanting your coupons, Peggy darling, I was thinking that if there were coupons for whisky I'd give mine up to your father.'

'You'd do no such thing,' she pouted. 'You'd give them to me for my clothes. Who wants whisky?'

'Your father does. And I'm going to try and get hold of some for him. Don't you want to be married in April?'

He held her to him. She was almost as tall as himself.

'Don't you want to be, Peggy?' he repeated.

'You're holding me awfully tight,' she protested in words.

'I'm always going to hold you tight,' he murmured.

Then a savage gust of wind rattled every door in the house, and they hastily drew apart.

'Ach, be off with you now up to Father James,' she urged him, smoothing her ruffled dark-brown hair.

A couple of minutes later the Sergeant-major was knocking at the door of the Chapel House, which was opened for him by Kirstag MacMaster, Father Macalister's housekeeper, a neat pippin of a woman whose life was devoted to a perpetual struggle to keep the priest's cosy sitting-room as tidy as the rest of the house.

'Will I be disturbing Father Macalister?' the visitor asked.

'Not at all. Not at all. He's just at saying his Office and he'll be very glad to put it aside for a while,' the housekeeper insisted. 'What weather we're having, Sergeant.'

'Dreadful, isn't it! How is his reverence?'

'Och, he's fine and middling, but his wireless isn't working and that fidgets him a bit. He's been very restless for the last few days. He was expecting a new battery yesterday, but it didn't come with the boat. He was very disappointed.'

She opened the door of the priest's room.

'Here's Sergeant Odd to see you, Father,' she announced.

The portly priest shut his breviary with a bang and jumped up with astonishing alacrity for a man of his bulk from the deep armchair in which he had been plunged beside a blazing fire.

'Great sticks alive, Sergeant, I'm glad to see you. Welcome back to Paradise,' he exclaimed in that rich voice whose warm *vibrato* had made so many visitors feel truly welcome to his hearth. 'How are you, my boy?'

'Oh, I'm in the pink. And how are you, Father?'

The bulky priest exhaled a deep sigh.

'Holding on, Sergeant, just holding on. Ach, I'm like my wireless. I've no battery. Ah, well, I suppose you've heard of the rotten condition of the state of Denmark?'

'It's very serious, isn't it?'

'It is very serious,' the priest avowed. 'We were always proud of our hospitality and it touches our noble and beautiful island pride. Look at me now. Here's an old friend back from barbarous places like Africa and Devonshire, and I haven't a sensation to offer him, not so much as a wee snifter. I've nothing but my own chair. Sit down in it, Sergeant.'

'No, really, Father Macalister, I'll take this one,' said the Sergeant-major, turning to the smaller armchair on the other side of the fire.

'You'll do nothing of the kind, my boy,' his host declared sonorously. 'You're in my parish and you'll sit where the parish priest tells you to sit. You may be a heretic in matters of faith, but you'll not be a heretic in matters of behaviour.'

Sergeant-major Odd took the deep armchair but with less assurance of comfort than his host expected.

'Put your backside where your backside ought to be,' he commanded. 'It's not a fence you're sitting on. It's a chair. That's more the style,' he added when his guest was well ensconced. Then he went to a cupboard from which he took a bottle and filled two glasses with what looked like a mixture of port and brown sherry.

'It's not the real Mackay,' he commented, as he offered his guest one glass and took the other for himself. 'A *dhuine, dhuine*, no, indeed. Still, it's a little better than Joseph's ginger-ale and much better than his lemonade.' The priest raised his glass. *'Ceud mìle fàilte agus slàinte mhór!'* Then he drained it in honour of his guest and put it down with a wry face. 'Ah, well,' he sighed deeply, 'we're in a pretty bad way.'

'What wine is it exactly, Father?'

'It's altar wine, my boy. It's the best I can offer. Indeed, it's all I can offer.'

'I think it's very nice,' said the Sergeant-major.

'Ah, well, it's drinkable,' Father Macalister allowed. 'But only just, by Jingo,' he added quickly. 'And when are you going to marry Peigi Ealasaid?'

'I'd marry Peggy Yallasich tomorrow, if I could, but I can't get the old man up to the scratch,' the Sergeant-major replied gloomily. 'And Peggy won't go against her father. Quite rightly, of course. I tried to pin him down to a date last night, but every time he'd try and talk about something else.'

'He's pretty good at that, is Joseph,' the priest observed.

'In the end I held out for Easter week, and he held out for not talking about a wedding till summer was over. That's all very fine, but I was forty-five last month. I'll be getting on for forty-six by autumn. Colonel Lindsay-Wolseley has promised me a lovely little furnished cottage so long as I'm with him as Sergeant-instructor. I've had to wait nearly two years as it is, through me getting sent down to Devonshire like that and then out to West Africa. If the war comes to an end I've got a good home for Peggy in Nottingham. What's your advice, Father Macalister?'

'My advice is to roll right over them and marry her at Easter. She's a lovely beautiful girl. And she's a good girl. Roll right over them, my boy,' said the priest firmly.

'Yes, that's all very fine, Father, but it's jolly difficult to roll over somebody like my future father-in-law to be. He isn't there when you start in rolling. He's as slippery as an eel.'

The priest shook his head in reflective agreement.

'Ay, Joseph can be slippery right enough,' he agreed. 'But don't you worry yourself, Sergeant. I'll speak to him. I'll tell him he's got to have the wedding at Easter. And if he won't agree, by Jove, *I'll* roll right over him myself.'

'I'm awfully grateful, Father Macalister, I am really. You were so kind when it all started. If you remember the idea was to get married in the autumn of '41. Well, that idea went down the drain with me being transferred so sudden. Well, perhaps you'll remember I told you then that of course I'd promise all the children would be brought up as Catholics the same as their mother. Well, I've been thinking over things a bit and – er – I didn't want to say this before I knew you were still in favour of me marrying Peggy, if you know what I mean, and – er . . .' The Sergeant-major gulped in embarrassment. Then words deserted him.

'You'd better have another glass of wine,' the priest advised.

'No, really, Father, thank you, it's not that . . . I mean to say, what I'm trying to say is a bit awkward. You see, I wouldn't like you to think I was trying to curry favour, if you get my meaning, but the fact is I really have been thinking things over, and my idea was that perhaps if I became a Catholic myself it 'ud make things better at home. I mean to say, anybody doesn't want his kids to look upon him as something different to what they are themselves, and so I thought perhaps . . . I mean to say, well, there it is.'

'Ay, ay, just as you say, Sergeant. There it is. And it's a mighty big It. You'll want instruction. Being a Sergeant-instructor yourself, you'll know what a lot of instruction is required.'

'That's a fact.'

'And so I'll write to Father MacIntyre at Drumsticket and ask him to supply the needful.'

'I'm afraid he'll find me pretty ignorant.'

'Never mind, Sergeant. The less you know the easier for him.'

'And there's another thing, Father Macalister,' the Sergeant-major continued. 'I wonder if it could be kept quiet till it's settled about the wedding? I mean to say, I wouldn't like the old man to think I was trying to get round him by becoming a Catholic. Peggy wouldn't like that. She'd think it was done for the purpose.'

'Don't you worry yourself about that, Sergeant. We'll not say a word.'

'What I thought was when the wedding was all fixed up I'd tell Peggy first.'

'That's the spirit, *a bhalaich*. Oh, well, well, it's really a disaster that we can't celebrate the occasion in the glorious traditional way.'

It was at this moment that Kirstag came in to say that Duncan Macroon had called.

'Let him come right in, Kirsty,' Father Macalister told her, and then he added, turning to the Sergeant-major,

'Duncan Bàn is the very man we want. You leave it to me. Duncan is our man.'

Duncan Macroon was the crofter and poet who commanded the Little Todday platoon of G company. Sergeant-major Odd's experience of him in that position made him a little doubtful whether Duncan Bàn was their man, but he had no time to express his doubts, for Duncan Bàn himself with his fair tumbled hair and glowing countenance and eyes as blue as the kingfisher's wing was already in the room as the priest spoke.

'Yes, yes, I'm your man, Father James,' he declared, beaming. 'Hullo, Sarchant. I'm glad to find you here. You didn't give us much of your time after Mass this morning. She's a fine girl though. When is the wedding to be?'

'Just the question we've been discussing, Duncan,' said the priest, 'and we've decided to have it in the week after Easter.'

'Very good,' said Duncan.

'But we must have the *rèiteach* before Lent,' Father Macalister went on, 'and you'll have to speak for the Sergeant, Duncan.'

'What's a rayjack?' Sergeant-major Odd asked nervously.

'The *rèiteach* is the betrothal,' Father Macalister told him. 'It's a great occasion. The future bridegroom's friend tells the future bride's father what a glorious splendid magnificent fellow she is going to marry and the father says what a beautiful lovely capable daughter he is parting with, and everybody drinks the health of the happy couple and the father and the . . .'

'Wait a minute, Father James,' Duncan Bàn interrupted. 'How are we going to drink to all these healths when there's not a drop of whisky in the whole of Todaidh Beag and Todaidh Mór?'

'There's not a drop today, Duncan, but that doesn't say there won't be a drop next week. The *Island Queen* will be in on Tuesday.'

'Not if it's blowing like this, Father. There's a huge great sea running in on the west just now,' Duncan insisted.

'Quick come, quick go. The wind got up in a moment and it will drop just as suddenly,' the priest declared with the authoritativeness of an archbishop.

'I hope the boat *will* come,' said the Sergeant-major. 'I told the Colonel I'd be back for certain by Wednesday.'

'Suppose the boat comes but the whisky doesn't, Father James?' Duncan asked. 'What *rèiteach* can anybody be having? It's against nature to have a *rèiteach* with tea and ginger-ale and lemonade. Even if there was plenty of beer it would still be against nature.'

'The fairies will bring up the whisky, Duncan,' Father James assured him solemnly.

'There's nobody else will bring it nowadays, *a Mhaighstir Seumas*, and that's one sure thing,' Duncan declared.

'*Rèiteach* or no *rèiteach*,' said Father James, 'the Sergeant will marry Peigi Iosaiph on the Wednesday after Easter. That's April 28th. And what you have to do, Duncan, is to tell everybody the date and I'll tell everybody the date, and, by the holy crows, that will *be* the date!'

'Yes, but what if Joseph Macroon refuses?' the Sergeant-major asked.

'He won't refuse,' the priest declared in his profoundest bass.

'Ah, the rascal, he daren't refuse,' said Duncan Bàn. 'Not if Mhaighstir Seumas and I are working hand in glove together . . .'

'And the fairies,' Father James added.

'Ay, the darling craytures,' Duncan chuckled.

'You'll start composing a good song for the wedding, Duncan,' the priest warned him.

'Don't you worry, Father. I'll compose a beauty — a regular beauty,' the crofter poet promised with enthusiasm. 'But I hope we *shall* soon have a little inspiration. No fiddler can fiddle his best without a bit of resin for his bow.'

Chapter 4

ALSO A QUESTION OF MARRIAGE

Sergeant-major Odd was not the only man that week-end who was finding his matrimonial future obscured by the threat of parental opposition. George Campbell was faced by a still more unfavourable prospect. George Campbell was the headmaster of the school at Garryboo, a crofting township some four miles away from Snorvig in the north-west corner of Great Todday.

The low rocky promontory of Garryboo afforded a landing only when the tide was fairly high and the Atlantic absolutely calm, a combination so rare that none of the crofters went in for fishing, preferring to gain their livelihood from the wide and gentle slope of good grazing and arable ground which extended as far as the road that ran round the island, on the other side of which a great stretch of level bog below the rocky bastions of Ben Bustival furnished peat in plenty. Garryboo with its houses dotted about at different angles on the green machair was the only part of Great Todday which resembled the landscape of Little Todday, and the people there were regarded by the rest of the island as only a little less barbaric than the papist inhabitants of Little Todday itself. The people of Garryboo, on the other hand, regarded with contemptuous pity the fierce agricultural struggle of their neighbours in Great Todday with rock and heather and sour peaty soil. They were happy to be considered behind the times so long as their stirks fetched prices at the Obaig sales as high as the well-nourished cattle from Little Todday.

In spite of Garryboo's reputed lag in the matter of progress, in spite of the fact that the girls of Garryboo carried less lipstick than the girls of Snorvig, more impermanent waves than those of Watasett and fewer silk stockings than those of Bobanish, Garryboo possessed the only fairly new school in the two Toddays, a building which claimed to be as modern as any in a Glasgow suburb. No doubt, if it had been erected in a Glasgow suburb, the wind and rain and salty air of the Outer Hebrides would not have made the roughcast walls look like cracked egg-shells only eight years after it had been erected. Jerry-building is a wasteful experiment beside the Atlantic.

The greater part of the school was taken up with two large classrooms, but the main building was extended to include a house for the headmaster, the flimsy shoddiness of which was made more obvious by the heavy mahogany furniture of the headmaster's mother, who presided as heavily as her furniture over the domestic life of her only son. Mrs Campbell, a large majestic old woman, with icy pale blue eyes and a deep husky voice, was the widow of the last factor of Great Todday before the Department of Agriculture acquired the island from Sir Robert Smith-Cockin, a magnate of Victorian industrialism. She had produced her only offspring late in life and still regarded him as a child of ten in spite of the fact that he was thirty-five years old and a headmaster. George Campbell himself was a small shy man who, until the formation of the Home Guard, had scarcely ever been seen in public except when he appeared on the platform of the Snorvig Hall to sing Gaelic songs in an agreeable light tenor at charitable functions patronized by the Minister. In spite of his mother's opposition to his command of the Garryboo section, George Campbell had found his duties in the Home Guard an opportunity to escape some of the maternal vigilance, with the result that he had fallen in love with Catriona Macleod, the sister of the Watasett headmaster, who kept house for him in the cosy old schoolhouse over nine miles away at the south end of the island.

On the afternoon of that Saturday which saw the arrival of Sergeant-major Odd, but not of the whisky, George Campbell, to his great astonishment, had succeeded in proposing marriage to Catriona and to his much greater astonishment his hand had been accepted. She was pretty. She was a splendid cook. She was for an islander an economical housekeeper. George Campbell was overwhelmed by his success. When he sat down to tea with Catriona and her brother Norman that evening to watch her deft housewifely fingers and to blush in the sparkling warmth of her eyes as she ministered to him with tea and scones and buttered eggs, George Campbell wished that he was on the platform of Snorvig Hall so that he might sing those oft-sung Gaelic love-songs with a fervour he had never dreamed of attempting hitherto.

'Och, it couldn't have happened at a better time,' Norman declared heartily. 'I'll be getting my notice to report for service in the air on the ground any time now, and I was a bit worried what Catriona would do. She didn't like the idea of looking after the old people on the croft at Knockdown for the rest of the war. Ach, they're reasonable craytures right enough, but the nicest old people can be a bit of a tie. Anyway, at Garryboo she won't be three miles away from them.'

When Norman Macleod made this observation about old people the pancake in George Campbell's hand which had been seeming as light as sea-foam suddenly became as heavy as a dictionary.

'Yes, old people can be a little difficult sometimes,' he agreed.

'I wonder what your mother will say, George, when you tell her you're going to be married,' Catriona speculated. 'I hope she won't be hating the idea too much.'

George gulped down a piece of pancake which felt like swallowing a nutmeg grater.

'Oh, I'm sure she won't,' he muttered.

'I think you'll have a bit of a fight, Georgie boy,' said Norman. 'Mind you, I'm not saying she'll object to Catriona in particular. I think she just won't fancy the notion of your getting married at all. She's had it too much her own way all these years.'

'She doesn't realize that I'm thirty-five,' said George gloomily.

'Boy, boy, she doesn't realize you're weaned,' Norman laughed. 'Perhaps when she sees a baby of your own clinging on to Catriona she'll let *you* go.'

His sister tossed her head.

'What a chick to talk about me like that!' she protested.

'No cheek at all about it,' her brother retorted. 'And I hope you'll ask Captain Waggett to be the godfather. Ah, well, he won't have to worry next summer about my poaching. If I poach as much as an egg in the R.A.F. I'll be lucky.'

George had no heart to laugh even at jokes about Captain Paul Waggett. Within a short while, an all too short while, he would be trying to break the news to his mother that he was going to marry Catriona Macleod. He shuddered.

'I'll tell you what, George,' said Norman, 'if you're going to tackle the old lady tonight you ought to tap the steward first. There should be plenty of whisky tonight. It was expected on Tuesday and this is the first trip the *Island Queen* has been able to make this week. If I'd known you and Catriona were going to get married on me I wouldn't have finished that bottle of Stag's Breath we had for the New Year.'

'You'd have kept anything in a bottle of whisky for two months?' his sister exclaimed. 'Ah, well, it's you that have a nerve to pretend such a thing, Norman.'

'I don't enjoy whisky – really,' George Campbell protested, 'I hardly ever touch it.'

'That's the trouble with you,' his colleague told him. 'If you'd fortified yourself as regularly as I have you'd not be giving twopence about telling your mother you're going to be married. What is it gives me the necessary sagacity to outwit the Inspector? Whisky. What is it that helps me to know just where to put down the net in Loch Sleeport for Waggett's sea-trout? Whisky. What makes me a good shot at a grouse or a snipe? Whisky. What is it makes Maclaren such a hell of a good doctor? Whisky. Love makes the world go round? Not at all. Whisky makes it go round twice as fast. That's why I'm the most revolutionary crayture in the whole of Todaidh Mór.'

'Will you listen to him blowing,' his sister jeered.

'Well, whisky agrees with you,' George argued. 'It wouldn't agree with me.'

'George, you're going to have two powerful drams with me in Snorvig before you go home this evening, and when you come back to dinner with us after church tomorrow you're going to tell us what date you've fixed with Mistress Campbell for the wedding.'

However, when Norman Macleod and George Campbell reached Snorvig, there was no whisky, and they were greeted instead with the news of Captain MacPhee's death from shock.

'Och, well, Doctor dear, we'll all be dead if this drought continues,' Norman Macleod said. 'And don't be looking at me so fierce. You're missing the noble stuff just as much as I am myself.'

'Will you be going down to the *caithris* tonight, Norman?' Doctor Maclaren asked.

'I will indeed. The old man was the finest liar I ever listened to in my life.' Then turning to George Campbell he added, 'You'd better come along with me, George. You'll never face the music tonight.'

George Campbell thought the music might be even more difficult to face if he did not arrive home till morning. The Garryboo lorry was waiting; he climbed up beside the driver.

'I'll be seeing you tomorrow, George,' Norman Macleod called after him. 'Maybe somewhere or other I'll find a dram to celebrate the occasion.'

'You're some optimist, Norman,' the Doctor jeered. 'But I suppose a Red like you has got to be an optimist to believe in his wild dreams for the future. What are you and George Campbell hoping to celebrate?'

'He and my sister Catriona have just come to terms.'

'Good God,' the Doctor exclaimed, 'how on earth did George Campbell muster up the courage to ask her? He's a lucky man, though. She's the best cook in the two islands. You'll miss her.'

'I'll be away in the R.A.F.'

'Ah, yes, I forgot. Don't you go preaching your communism there.' The Doctor took a meditative pinch of snuff. 'So George Campbell is going to marry your sister. I wonder what the old lady will say.'

'I expect George is wondering just that in Donald Ian's lorry,' said Norman Macleod with a grin. 'But see here, Doctor, why don't you join us at dinner after church? Maybe I was a bit optimistic about the dram, but we'll have a good meal and a good crack afterwards.'

'That'll suit me,' said the Doctor.

Norman Macleod was right. George Campbell *was* wondering what the old lady would say, as he sat pensively beside Donald Ian Gillespie in the cab of the lorry, which was roaring up the road below Snorvig House on second speed and provoking a lecture from Captain Waggett to his wife on the bad driving of everybody in Great Todday except himself.

'Very sad about the Captain, Mr Campbell,' said Donald Ian when the lorry was clear of Snorvig and passing the upward sweep of the moorland between Ben Sticla and Ben Bustival.

'Very sad,' the schoolmaster agreed.

'Ay, ay,' Donald Ian sighed, easing himself in his seat and peering forward into the murk, 'we all come to it. First we get born, then we get married, and then we get dead. You'll have to think about getting married yourself soon, Mr Campbell. Your mother must be a tidy bit over seventy now.'

'She's seventy-five.'

'Look at that now. Och, well, she's pretty active right enough. Still, you ought to be getting married.'

If George Campbell had had even one dram he might have told Donald Ian that he was going to marry Catriona Macleod; but without the encouragement of a dram he felt too shy, and they drove on in a silence which was not broken until Donald Ian bade him good night where the road down to the school branched off to the left from the main road.

When the headmaster of Garryboo reached the door of his house he found it locked. He struck a match and looked at his watch before he tapped. It was just a quarter to ten.

'What a time to come back, George!' Mrs Campbell growled when she opened the door. 'Where have you been?'

'The lorry was a little late in leaving Snorvig,' the headmaster of Garryboo muttered as he followed his mother into the sitting-room where she leant down to pick up the bible and spectacles she had deposited on her chair and resumed her seat, the bible and spectacles now upon her knee. 'Why didn't you come back with the six o'clock lorry?' she asked sternly.

'The mails weren't sorted. In fact they weren't ready in time for the nine o'clock lorry. Captain MacPhee died suddenly this evening.'

Mrs Campbell gave a contemptuous grunt which sounded rather like 'Serve him right'. Then she shook her head.

'Well, it's not for us to speak against those who have passed on, and I'm told that he took to reading his bible last year, but what good it could do him after spending every night drinking up at that bar I wouldn't care to say. You haven't been up at the bar tonight, have you, George?' the old lady asked sharply.

'Good gracious me, no, mother. What made you ask that?'

'You're looking guilty, George. You're not looking me straight in the face. George, you've been drinking.'

'I have not been drinking,' he declared with the courageous indignation of unassailable innocence. 'I couldn't have been drinking. There's not a drop of whisky in the whole island.'

'What do you mean, not a drop of whisky in the whole island? It's swimming in it. It always has been swimming in it. Your father spent all his life trying to get the licence taken away from the hotel. He knew it was the only way to get any work out of the people.'

'There's no whisky now,' George insisted. 'There's a shortage on account of the war.'

'The Lord is merciful indeed. What a lesson for us! We go to war on the Sabbath day, but He returns good for evil and leads us out of temptation. Well, if you've not been drinking, what have you been doing all this time, George? Where did you have your tea?'

'I went along to see Norman Macleod at Watasett.'

'Fine company you're keeping. That good-for-nothing Radical! I don't know what the Education authority is thinking of, letting a rascal like that corrupt the minds of children,' said Mrs Campbell wrathfully.

'He's been called up. He's going into the Air Force.'

'The best place for him. He's never had both feet on the ground since he could walk. His mother always spoilt him disgracefully. She spoilt all her children. Was that sister of his — Cairistiona, isn't it? — was she there?'

'Catriona gave us tea,' said George.

'A rattleplate of a girl, just like her mother before her. Permanent wave, indeed! Permanent wickedness more like. I am not one to criticize our Minister, as you know, but he has been sadly weak about all this lipstick and permanent waves and cigarette smoking.'

'Catriona looks after her brother very well,' George ventured to remind the old lady.

'What do you know about being looked after? Don't talk so wildly, George. You've had nobody but your mother to look after you. You'll learn the difference if you're ever so foolish as to marry one of these modern girls.' Mrs Campbell pronounced it 'modderan' as if with the scornful rolling of the 'r' she could drum them out into ignominy.

George tried to conjure up the brightness of Catriona's dark-brown eyes when she had turned to look at him with 'yes' upon her lips, the quick movements of her as she laid the table for tea, and the light touch of her fingers on his hand as she pressed him to have another pancake. Alas, the vision of Catriona eluded him. All he could see was his mother sitting upright in the high-backed mahogany armchair and piercing him with those hard, sharp, light-blue eyes. How could he tell her tonight that this afternoon he had asked Catriona to marry him and that she had said 'yes'?

'Well, it's time we were going to bed,' his mother announced. 'High time, indeed, with the Sahbbath close upon us. I was thinking I'd take advantage of the calmer weather to go to church myself.'

It was accepted in Garryboo that the old lady had the right to commandeer a place in any of the traps driving into Snorvig on Sunday morning, a privilege of which in fine weather she seldom failed to take advantage.

'I'm told the Minister has a terrible cold on him,' said George whose plan to have dinner with Catriona and her brother was threatened by his mother's intention.

'Why would that keep me from worshipping the Lord?' Mrs Campbell demanded.

'You'll get a sermon from Simon MacRurie, and you don't like that at all,' her son pointed out.

The suggestion of opposition made the old lady determined to break it down.

'I'll go to church tomorrow morning, George, sairmon or no sairmon,' she declared.

As the old lady spoke, the first uneasy heralds of the coming gale moaned round the gimcrack house.

'The wind's rising again,' said her son.

And on Sunday morning even Mrs Campbell's resolution was baffled.

'You'd better stay at home yourself, George,' she advised. 'We'll worship the Lord in our own home.'

This meant for George remaining on his knees while his mother indulged herself in long extempore prayers. He preferred to worship in the comparative comfort of church where nobody knelt for fear of being suspected of popery, the interest of presbyterianism once upon a time having been to deprive the kirk itself of any peculiar sanctity.

'I'll walk in to church, mother, if you don't mind. I'm needing the exercise. Miss Ross will come in to you.'

Miss Ross was the assistant schoolteacher at Garryboo – a carroty wisp of a young woman with a nose like a pointer whom Mrs Campbell was considering as a possible daughter-in-law, her influence over Miss Ross being already paramount.

'Dinner will be ready at half past two. Be sure now and be back in good time,' Mrs Campbell warned her son as he bent his head and plunged out into the wind and rain.

On the way up to the main road George stopped at the house of Angus MacCormac where Miss Ross lodged.

'You're never going to walk in to Snorvig on such a morning, Mr Campbell?' exclaimed Mrs MacCormac. 'Himself has just come back from the *caithris* as wet as a dog. I'm just after making him go out and mop his moustache. It was dripping all over my clean tablecloth. Yes, indeed, I'll tell Miss Ross your mother would be glad to see her.'

To his relief George Campbell had no company for most of the long walk to Snorvig in the teeth of the gale. Apart from his shyness he was preoccupied at once with the immediate and the distant future. The engagement to Catriona could not be kept from his mother indefinitely. The tussle between them must take place sooner or later. He would have to confess to Catriona that he had not yet broken the news to his mother. Suppose his cowardice should provoke her into taking back the promise she had made him yesterday? Yet everybody in Great Todday knew how difficult his mother could be. He would explain to Catriona that he must be the judge of the best moment to make his announcement. He would explain that his long absence yesterday had put her in a bad mood and that he had thought it wiser to postpone the occasion. Perhaps after all it would be tactful to go home to dinner at half past two instead of going on to Watasett after church. But if he was not going to dine with Catriona and her brother he might just as well have stayed at home this morning. The figure of his mother appeared to his fancy as grim and forbidding as Ben Bustival itself when he contemplated turning round; he decided to go on.

The attendance at church was sparse that morning, but that did not persuade Simon MacRurie to shorten his prayers or his sermon. The chief elder, who was also the leading merchant of Snorvig, liked nothing, apart from money, so well as the sound of his own voice. The absence of the Minister was his opportunity, and he took such good advantage of it that it was close on two o'clock when the congregation was released after as tough a couple of hours as any member of it could remember. Even Roderick's loyalty as a brother was strained.

'Och, I was pretty tired after sitting up all night with the poor Captain, and I couldn't get a wink of sleep in church what with the noise of the wind and the way Simon was trying to get the petter of it. And no sooner was Simon quiet than Donald Post must be starting. It was like a couple of pulls pellowing at one another over a fence. And not a tram in the whole of Todaidh Mór, Toctor, chust when I'm feeling chock full of emptiness for want of the smallest sensation as Father Macalister says. Och, poor soul, I'm sure he's feeling the pinch over in Todaidh Beag. He's a man who likes to trink a lot in motteration.'

'Seriously, Roderick, when *do* you think we shall have some more whisky?' Doctor Maclaren asked glumly.

'Toctor, don't be putting rittles to me without any answer. Hullo, Mr Campbell, so you're going to be married. You've chosen a fine curl. You'll enchoy fine being married to her. Och, with a wife of your own it'll be more cheerful for you at Garryboo. You're a long way from the centre of things out there.'

'Come on, George, get into the car. I'm taking you along to Watasett now,' said the Doctor.

George looked surprised.

'I'm asked to dinner too, and I never lose a chance of eating a dinner cooked by Catriona,' he was told.

Fate had decided at any rate one of the questions which had been perplexing George Campbell's mind during that wind-swept, rain-washed trudge to church. He took his seat beside the Doctor in the Morris Minor, and a quarter of an hour later the dreich aspect of Loch Sleeport was forgotten in the cosy sitting-room of the schoolhouse.

'Well, isn't this splendid?' said Norman, twinkling at his guests with satisfaction. 'And wouldn't it be better still if there were three full glasses in our hands?'

'Don't talk about it,' said the Doctor. 'There aren't. And that's that. I smell something good in the kitchen.'

'Golden plover,' Norman proclaimed. 'We won't be getting so many more now before autumn. Well, George, did Mistress Campbell skelp you last night when you told her the news?'

George Campbell blushed.

'As a matter of fact, Norman, I didn't tell her after all, last night. She was a little annoyed, because she'd expected me back by the earlier lorry. And I don't suppose your people have been told yet,' he added hopefully.

'They have not. The Doctor's going to run Catriona and me up to Knockdown this afternoon. He has to go and see old Hector MacRurie, who's pretty poorly.'

'We'll go round by the west side, and then I can drop you at Garryboo, George.'

'Thanks very much, Doctor,' said George Campbell without enthusiasm. The nine-mile walk from Watasett to Garryboo in this weather would not be pleasant, but at least it would postpone the moment for a full two and a half hours.

'Dinner's ready,' Catriona was calling.

And when they went into the dining-room on the table there was a bottle of claret.

'Oh, well, well, well!' Norman exclaimed. 'Doctor, you're a darling!'

'It's the last,' said Doctor Maclaren. 'And I hope we didn't shake it up too much. I kept it in the inside pocket of my overcoat.'

Presently he raised his glass to Catriona and George:

'I didn't have the pleasure of bringing either of you into the world, but I hope I'll have the pleasure of bringing a few of your children into the world. George, you're a lucky man: you're going to marry one of my favourite lassies in the island. I'm not so sure that she isn't the pick of the whole bunch. Dash it, George, I don't know how you managed to pick her. And I'm not casting reflections on your own worthiness by that remark. No, no, George, I was merely animadverting on your modesty. Well, here's to you both, and may you both be happy and prosperous and, except for an occasional little incident such as I alluded to at the beginning of my speech, may you never see me across the threshold of your house in my professional capacity, though if I'm asked, and I hope I'll be asked pretty often, may I cross it many a time as a friend! And, George, you'll have to learn to be as good a poacher as your future brother-in-law, the MacLenin of MacLenin. First catch your hare, wrote the famous Mrs Beeton in what so far as we know was an unique ebullition of humour. And I repeat her advice to you, George. It's no earthly use marrying a good cook like Catriona if you don't keep her supplied with the necessary material to display her skill, and when, as I've no doubt they will, your neighbours in Garryboo collect the wherewithal for a handsome wedding present, I hope you'll devote a reasonable proportion of it to procuring for yourself a really good gun.'

'Ah, well, Doctor,' Norman Macleod declared, 'it's a pity you were not in the Cabinet before this war started. You have such a fine appreciation of the need to arm for any emergency.'

George Campbell was excused from making a speech in reply to the Doctor's toast, and the company turned their attention to the food.

'Well,' said the Doctor, as he laid down his knife and fork, 'when I eat a grouse I think there's no bird like it and when I eat a woodcock I think there's no bird like it, but dash it, I believe a golden plover cooked to the very moment is the best of the lot.'

'A pheasant's pretty good,' Norman reminded his guest. 'I wish Captain Waggett had a few pheasants on Todaidh Mór. He wouldn't have very many.'

After dinner when the Doctor and Norman Macleod moved to the sitting-room George Campbell remained behind with Catriona for the alleged purpose of helping her clear away.

'I hope you don't despise me, Catriona, for not telling my mother last night about you and me. But, you know, I simply couldn't bring myself to do it.'

She laughed lightly.

'I'm just wondering what she's going to say to me when we meet.'

'I think once she's taken it out of me,' George replied, 'she may be all right with you. After all, she'll have to live with you.'

'Yes, I suppose she will,' Catriona assented, with a hint of a sigh.

'Well, where else could she live? She's too old to live by herself now.

Anyway, I'm sure she'll grow to love you as a daughter,' he assured her solemnly.

Catriona's eyes sparkled with mirth.

'Not as a daughter, George. I might find that just a little bit too much like going to school again.'

It was about five o'clock when they dropped George Campbell at the road down to the school at Garryboo and drove on round the north side of the island, past the great aquiline headland of Sròn Ruairidh thrusting itself defiantly into the stormy sea, to Knockdown, the remote little cluster of thatched houses in one of which lived Dr Maclaren's patient, in another John Macleod, generally known as Iain Thormaid, and his wife.

John Macleod was a fine figure of a man with iron-grey hair and a trim dark beard, his wife small and merry with rich brown hair as yet scarcely dusted with grey.

'And so you want to marry George Campbell, Catriona,' said her father. 'Well, well, it's your business, *a nighinn*. And what does Mrs Campbell say to that?'

'George hasn't told her yet. He's telling her now,' Catriona replied.

'Ay, the poor chap is going through it just at this very moment,' said Norman. 'Unless he's run away from the music again,' he chuckled.

'And who would blame the poor *truaghan* if he did run away from it?' Mrs Macleod laughed.

'She's a warrior right enough,' her husband agreed. 'I mind fine when she first came to the island from Mull with the factor, before George was born. They lived where the Doctor lives now. Ay, she went to war the moment she set foot on the pier, and she's been at war ever since.'

'Well, I won't pretend I'm not disappointed you're not coming to live with us when Norman goes to the R.A.F.,' said Mrs Macleod. 'But we want you to be happy.'

'I'll be with you for quite a while, *a mhammi*,' said her daughter. Sitting here in the sunny kitchen of so many childish memories, Catriona felt a sudden dread of the inhospitable newness of the school at Garryboo. She reproached herself for having imagined that she would not be content at home.

'When do you think you will be getting married?' her mother asked.

'We were thinking we'd be married in the summer holidays, if George's mother doesn't make it too difficult.'

And as Catriona said that, Mrs Campbell *was* making it extremely difficult for poor George, who had just reached the schoolhouse and was being greeted by his mother with the information that she knew all.

'I was going to tell you last night,' he stammered, 'but you seemed so anxious to go to bed.'

'The bed I have made for myself and on which I must lie,' Mrs Campbell said in tones that Isaiah himself might have envied. 'This comes of spoiling my only child.'

'Of spoiling me?' George exclaimed in amazement.

'Spare the rod . . .'

'You never did,' he put in.

'And spoil the child,' his mother concluded, ignoring the interruption. 'And now in my old age I am reaping as I have sown. To think that I would be hearing from others that my own son is going to be married!'

'Who told you?'

'Who told me? Jemima Ross told me.'

'It was none of her business.'

'None of her business, indeed? When that great good-for-nothing Angus MacCormac came back this morning from Snorvig with that other rascal Samuel MacCodrum and blared the story all over Garryboo that the factor's son was going to marry Catriona Iain Thormaid?'

George's heart sank. When his mother referred to him as the factor's son he was back in knickerbockers.

'I only knew it myself yesterday afternoon,' he explained apologetically.

'Do you mean to stand there, George, and tell me that you'd not been thinking about that girl until yesterday afternoon?'

'I'd thought about her, yes.'

'Then why was I kept in the dark about your thoughts?' Mrs Campbell demanded sternly.

'What would have been the use of upsetting you until I knew what Catriona's feelings were?' George asked, and realized too late what an opening he had given his mother.

'So you knew it would upset me, and your mother's feelings didn't matter,' she commented bitterly.

'I mean upset you by the uncertainty,' he said, trying to recover the ground he had lost.

But Mrs Campbell was now in too strong a position.

'You knew it would upset me, and yet you went on, thinking only of yourself. You wanted to marry that girl, and if it meant breaking your old mother's heart you were set on having your own way. But you always were set on having your own way, George. How many times as a child did I catch you among the black currants, though you knew I wanted all the black currants there were for my jam? I used to try so hard to make you think less of your own desires, but no, black currants you wanted, and black currants you would have.'

'Catriona is a very nice girl,' George ventured to assert mildly.

'Perhaps you'll allow your mother to know better than you what a nice girl is. Your father had as much trouble with her father, Iain Thormaid, as with any crofter in Great Todday. He was the moving spirit behind the rascals who raided Knockdown and spoilt the best shooting in the island. And when Sir Robert gave orders to burn down the bothies they'd been running up for themselves on land that wasn't theirs, wasn't it John Macleod who loosed the Garryboo bull on your father and the Sheriff's men? No wonder his son grew up to be one of these good-for-nothing socialists who are just a set of thieves breaking the Tenth Commandment every hour of the day.'

'We must move with the times, mother. A lot of good people are socialists nowadays.'

'Sahtan has made you pretty glib, son. Will there be any times to move with in eternity?'

'You're bringing religion into it now, mother,' George protested feebly. 'And I don't see what religion has got to do with my wanting to marry Catriona.'

The old lady stiffened herself in her chair triumphantly.

'That's very true, George. You're just pushing religion right aside for the sake of what some people would call a pretty face. Well, I'm not going to interfere in the matter. I'll go and live in Glasgow with your aunt Ina.'

'But you hate Glasgow, mother,' her son objected.

'Never mind if I do. The Lord chastiseth those whom He loves, and who am I to set myself up against my Lord?'

'Surely you can try the experiment of living here with Catriona? She expects you to be living here.'

'I'm much obliged to her ladyship, but I've never lived anywhere on sufferance yet and I am not going to begin at my age,' Mrs Campbell snapped.

'People will think it so strange if you go away to Glasgow, mother.'

The old lady's cold blue eyes glittered for a moment and then turned again to ice.

'You might have thought more of what other people would think when you started to deceive your mother by going with Catriona Macleod.'

'But, apart from disapproving of her because you think her brother Norman is a socialist, you don't dislike Catriona herself, do you?' he asked anxiously.

'I don't like girls who go gallivanting over to Obaig for these permanent waves. Does she smoke?'

'I believe she smokes a cigarette occasionally.'

'Do you ever see me smoke a cigarette?'

'You don't like smoking. You don't like me to smoke,' George reminded her.

'Did the Apostle Paul smoke?' the old lady demanded.

'There wasn't any tobacco in his day. It hadn't been discovered.'

'If Sahtan had put tobacco in the hands of men, wouldn't the Apostle Paul have preached against smoking as a sin?'

'Well, if I bring Catriona to tea next Saturday will you be nice to her, mother?' George asked, in a desperate effort to get away from that old enemy of his childhood, the Apostle Paul.

Mrs Campbell looked at her son. She scented victory.

'The day you bring Catriona Macleod to this house I leave it and go to Glasgow,' she declared in a triumphant glow of self-righteousness.

George's eyes wavered wretchedly under his mother's icy regard. He longed for the strength of mind to tell her that he intended to bring Catriona to tea on Saturday and that if his mother did not like the idea the boat would be leaving for the mainland that afternoon. It was no use. The strength of mind was not there.

'Well, of course, if that's how you feel about it, I can't bring her,' he said, turning away in dejection.

The consciousness of victory flickered in Mrs Campbell's eyes the way a little blue flame will run across a peat and vanish almost simultaneously.

'That is for you to decide, George. And now you'd better go and feed the hens. I was too much upset by what Jemima Ross told me to feed them myself this afternoon.'

Chapter 5

A RUN ROUND GREAT TODAY

Sergeant-major Odd, fortified by his visit to Father Macalister, did not resume the discussion with Joseph Macroon about the date of his marriage that Sunday evening. Instead, he talked with so much apparently inside information about the length of time the war was likely to last that Joseph was driven to bed in a gloom and left the sitting-room to Peggy and himself.

'It's going to be all right, Peggy darling,' he assured her. 'It's going to be All Sir Garnet as my old dad used to say. Father Macalister is going to tackle your dad. He and Duncan Macroon are going to tell everybody it's all fixed up for the Wednesday after Easter. So you'd better start seeing about your clothes. What I thought was we'd go off next day and take my old mother back to Nottingham . . .'

'Your mother?' Peggy exclaimed apprehensively.

'Well, I thought she and me would arrive by the boat on Tuesday. Of course we'd have to stay in some other house. I dare say Duncan Macroon would put us up. Then you and me and her might go over to the Snorvig Hotel after the wedding and catch Thursday's boat. We could travel back to Tummie over the week-end and I'd be back on duty by the Tuesday and you'd be lording it over our little cottage.'

'You're very sure of yourself, Fred,' she told him.

'Well, it was going to see Father Macalister. He understood everything so well. What a man, eh?'

'I hope your mother will like me.'

'Like you? She's going to love you. Well, I mean to say her one idea for the last twenty years ever since Dad went has been for me to settle down, and now thanks to you I'm going to at last. No, I'm not worrying about Ma.'

'I wish you weren't a Protestant, Fred,' his Peggy sighed.

The Sergeant-major grinned.

'Well, I am, and there it is.'

She sighed again.

'Yes, there it is, I suppose.'

The Sergeant-major was on the point of revealing his intention, but at that moment Kate Anne put her head round the door and said she was off to bed; the interruption saved his secret.

The wind had abated by morning, but Peggy was busy with the accumulation of the mails from last week; and the Sergeant-major decided it would be tactful to cross over to Snorvig and pay a visit to the company commander.

The prophylactic of hot grog on two successive nights had been effective in defeating the attempt by the Minister's germs to invade Captain Paul Waggett's head.

'No need to ask how you are, sir,' his visitor told him. 'Anyone can see you're in the pink.'

'Yes, I'm very well. Shall we go into my den, Sergeant-major? I think Mrs Waggett wants to do some household chores in the lounge. We've no maid at the moment, but a new one's coming in a day or two.'

'I don't think I was ever in this room before,' said the Sergeant-major when they entered the den, much of the floor-space of which was occupied by Paddy, Captain Waggett's overgrown Irish setter that was more like an auburn-haired St Bernard.

'No, I only made up my mind to have a den last year when Mrs Gorringe, Mrs Waggett's sister, stayed with us all last summer. She had a nervous breakdown.'

'I'm sorry to hear that.'

'Evacuees,' said Captain Waggett simply.

'That's one thing you've been spared, sir, in Great Todday.'

'Yes, the people here don't realize how well off they are,' Captain Waggett observed loftily.

'Except for whisky, sir,' the Sergeant-major reminded him.

'Entirely their own fault. They shouldn't drink it all up. I have no sympathy whatever with them. Paddy!'

The huge dog thumped the floor with his tail.

'Get up, old man, and let Sergeant-major Odd get to his chair.'

'I can step over him, sir,' said the Sergeant-major a little too optimistically, for as he stepped Paddy did get up, and for a moment or two Captain Waggett's den had never seemed quite so much like the genuine article. When the confusion had subsided, the owner of the den pointed out its beauties and its conveniences.

'Those photographs are mostly of little shoots friends and I used to take in the days before I bought Snorvig House. That's Huckleberry in

Essex.' He pointed to a stubble field across which a party of sportsmen were advancing behind dogs in the September sunshine of 1933. 'Best partridge shoot within reach of London. The tall man on the left of the line is Mr Blundell, the senior partner of the firm of chartered accountants to which I used to belong.' He continued to point out for his visitor's benefit the interesting details of the framed photographs. 'But I always say, Sergeant-major, that I wouldn't exchange any of these places for my own little shooting and fishing in the two Toddays. People in London thought I was mad when I came to live up here, but I've never regretted it. Never once. And I think I can feel that I'm of some use to the Islands. Of course, if the people would listen more to what I tell them, I could be of even more use; but they're very unresponsive to new ideas, except of course the claptrap talked by these Labour fellows. They're responsive enough to that. I see you're looking at my books, Sergeant-major. I have rather a good collection of Crime Club yarns. Did you ever read *Murder on the Escalator*? Or *Death on the Centre Court*? No? Both full of action. I must have plenty of action. You've read *The Garrotted Announcer*? You haven't? Oh, well, when you come over to do a spot of training, I'll lend it to you. It's interesting, quite apart from the story, for the inside view it gives of life in the B.B.C.'

'Talking of training, sir, how's G Company going along?' the Sergeant-major managed to inquire.

'I'm very disappointed,' the company commander admitted sadly. 'The attendance at parades has been growing steadily less for a year now, but just lately it has been appalling. Sergeant-major Thomson has been very conscientious, but then one expects a bank agent to be conscientious. I'm really most disappointed, after all the trouble I've taken to build up the Home Guard in the two Toddays. And then there was the unpleasantness of that Nelson bomber which made a forced landing on Little Todday.'

'What was that, sir? You must remember I've been away nearly eighteen months now.'

'Well, last October a Nelson made a forced landing on the machair about half-way between Tràigh Swish and Kiltod and as requested by R.A.F. Obaig I arranged for the plane to be guarded until the salvage squad arrived. Nobody has ever been able to find out exactly what did happen, but when the salvage squad did arrive there was practically nothing left of the plane.'

The Sergeant-major clicked his tongue.

'How did Lieutenant Macroon account for such a condition?' he asked.

'Fortunately for Lieutenant Macroon he was on the mainland at the time, but when I asked him to make a report he amazed me very much by saying that after inquiring into the matter he had come to the conclusion that the fairies were the culprits. And of course Joseph Macroon made a lot of capital out of it over that new school he's agitating for. He said the schoolchildren must have done all the mischief and that there'd be no keeping them in order until Kiltod had a new school. Why a leaky roof should make children pillage a plane I don't pretend to understand. But what amazed me most of all was to get rather a sharp letter from Colonel Wolseley to say that it wasn't part of the duties of the Home Guard to assume any responsibility for crashed planes and that he did not want to be involved in a lot of unnecessary correspondence with the R.A.F.'

'I see the Colonel's point of view, sir,' the Sergeant-major said.

'Well, of course I should never dream of criticizing my Commanding Officer, Sergeant-major; but I can't help thinking that Colonel Wolseley is inclined to leave too much to the police just because he's Convener of the Police Committee in the County Council. Constable Macrae actually suggested that I had butted in over his head.'

'And what about the shooting, sir?' put in Sergeant-major Odd, who did not want to find himself committed to any expression of opinion about what had evidently been a lively controversy while it lasted.

'They've been very slack about that too. I offered a cup for competition.'

'I remember that, sir. It was won by the Little Todday platoon in 1941.'

'Well, last year it was won by Snorvig, but the Little Todday people said the markers had altered the targets and they wouldn't give up the cup. It's still on Little Todday. And last week when I put up a notice in the Hall that the cup would be shot for again this August somebody wrote across it, "Will there be plenty whisky in the cup?" It really is rather discouraging, especially when I think what a job I had to get hold of the cup, on which by the way I had to pay luxury tax. I took that up with the Territorial Association, but I got no satisfaction. Still, when one remembers what the Germans have done all over Europe, one mustn't grouse about things like that.'

'That's right, sir. And I'm sure we can work up the keenness again. Of course, I don't know what the Colonel's plans are for me. I understand he wants me to go to Glenbogle on Wednesday for a few days. Major Macdonald of Ben Nevis has got very keen on grenades, and the Colonel made a bit of a point of me going over there before any damage was done, and after I've been to Glenbogle Sir Hubert Bottley wants me up at Cloy for a day or two, but if you was to write to the Colonel right away I'm sure he'd let you have me for a week after that. Say tomorrow fortnight. I think the whisky and beer situation ought to be easier by then.'

Captain Waggett looked at the Sergeant-major in surprise. He hoped that his head had not been affected by the equatorial sun of Africa.

'I meant to say, sir, I think they're all feeling the effect of the shortage. It's bound to make for what they call war weariness. From what I can make out they haven't been without whisky for thousands of years. It's like depriving them of the very air they breathe.'

'They drink far too much whisky when they can get it,' said Captain Waggett austerely.

'And I wouldn't say that, sir, either. Put it this way. A fish doesn't drink water all the time, but you take a fish out of water, and where is the poor animal? Lost. It's the same with the people here. They don't want to drink whisky all the time, but they want to feel it's there.'

'Well, I'll write to Colonel Wolseley and ask for your services here as soon as he can spare you, but I'm afraid, whisky or no whisky, you'll find it a hard job to work up any enthusiasm, Sergeant-major. I'm very fond of the Todday folk, but it's no use shutting one's eyes to the fact that they lack staying-power. Where there was a chance that the Germans would try and invade us they were keen enough; but, now the danger of immediate invasion has faded, all that keenness has vanished. They're not sporting. They don't enjoy doing things just for the sake of doing them. That's where the English are superior to every other nation in the world. They play the game for the sake of the game. Other nations play games just for the sake of winning them. I tried to introduce football on Great Todday. I presented a ball each to the schools at Snorvig, Bobanish, Watasett, and Garryboo. Naturally, I was the referee, and I had to give a foul against one of the Garryboo team. It was more than a foul. It was an assault. What happened? Young Willie Macennan, the captain of Garryboo, deliberately dribbled the ball to the touch-line and kicked it into the sea!'

Sergeant-major Odd turned his head away and coughed.

'Excuse me, sir, something was tickling my throat.'

He did not add that it was a hastily strangled laugh.

'However, Sergeant-major, if you feel that you can pull the men together and get them to take their training seriously, nobody will be happier than I shall be. I'll write to Colonel Wolseley by tomorrow's post.'

'I shall do my best, sir, to buck things up.'

'I'm sure you will, Sergeant-major. Of course, being without a regular P.S.I. all this time has been a great handicap. We've had one or two itinerant Instructors, but they were inclined to bark at the men too much. And that's no use.'

'No use at all in the Islands, sir.'

'By the way, what about your marriage with Joseph Macroon's daughter? When is that to come off?'

'The idear is for us to get married just after Easter, sir, if all goes according. I don't think they can shift me all of a sudden again, touch wood.'

'Well, I'm sure I wish you all happiness, Sergeant-major, but I wish you could persuade your future father-in-law to be a little more strict about the black-out in Little Todday. The whole of Kiltod was a blaze of light one night the week before last. It was better last week.'

'I think there's a shortage of paraffin just now,' said the Sergeant-major. 'And, with all the lighthouses and all the harbour-lights in the Islands going strong, the people can't understand the point of the black-out.'

'Same old story,' Captain Waggett commented sadly. 'No idea of discipline. Can't people understand that the whole point of the black-out is to show the determination of the British people to win the war? And anyway an order is an order surely?'

'Quite, sir, but it is a bit refreshing to find people who think more of what you might call a common-sense order. Perhaps it's having spent all my life in the army makes me feel that. Still, you're undoubtedly right, sir, and I'll say a word in Joseph Macroon's ear.'

Sergeant-major Odd thought it prudent to avoid the slightest appearance of sympathizing too much with the views of Little Todday about the black-out. He was anxious that Captain Waggett should regard him as indispensable to the recovery of discipline.

'I think it would be rather a good idea if I were to run you round the island in the car,' Captain Waggett suggested. 'I'd like them all to see that you're back with us again.'

'Just as you like, sir,' said the Sergeant-major.

'Are you afraid of catching cold?' he was asked.

'We shan't catch cold in your car, sir. And anyway, I think it looks like turning into a really fine day at last.'

'I wasn't thinking about the weather. I was thinking that perhaps it would be a good thing if you called on the Minister, and he's got a very bad cold.'

Captain Waggett himself did not get out of the Austin when they pulled up outside the door of the Manse.

'You'll get away from Mr Morrison more easily if I don't come in,' he explained.

The Sergeant-major found the Reverend Angus Morrison hunched up by a coal fire in the study, a black and yellow Dress Macleod plaid round his shoulders.

'How nice of you to call, Sergeant-major Odd,' said Mrs Morrison, a rather pretty, nervously ladylike young woman from Kelvinside. 'The Minister has a really terrible cold. He can hardly speak, and tomorrow he has to bury poor Captain MacPhee. So sad, wasn't it?'

'Yes, a fine old type. Now don't you get up, Mr Morrison, please,' the Sergeant-major urged, for the little Minister's gallant attempt to welcome his caller had produced a spasm of coughing.

'I can't think where I got this cold,' he gasped when the spasm had exhausted itself. 'I'm sure we're all very glad to welcome you back to Great Todday, Sergeant-major Odd. They've missed you in the Home Guard. I'm afraid they've been inclined to rest upon their laurels too much. You've travelled a long way they tell me since we saw you last, Sergeant-major Odd.'

'I was out in West Africa, sir, yes.'

'You'll have seen something of our missions out there. You've been greatly privileged, Sergeant-major Odd.'

'I'm afraid I was too busy with military duties to see very much of any missions, Mr Morrison. But I know there are a lot of missionaries out there.'

'I would have liked very much to be a chaplain to the Forces,' the little Minister wheezed wistfully. 'A great experience, Sergeant-major Odd. Yes, indeed. A great experience right enough. But with a wife and a baby I did not feel my domestic responsibilities would have justified me in taking such a step. And they tell me you're going to get married yourself. I'm sure I wish you every happiness.'

'Yes, Peggy Macroon and me are hoping to be married just after Easter.'

'I don't know her well,' put in Mrs Morrison, 'but I've always thought she was a very nice girl.'

'You'll be Church of England yourself, Sergeant-major Odd?' the Minister asked.

'That's right, sir.'

'Ah, well, I have a great respect for Father Macalister,' the Minister said. 'He's a great hand at teasing, though. I remember I once said to him, "Ah, well, *a Mhaighstir Seumas*," – for of course we were talking in the Gaelic to one another – "ah, well," I said, "we're all labourers in the same vineyard." And I remember Father Macalister said – I thought it was rather witty, though it was against myself – "Ay," he said, "we're all labourers in the same vineyard, Mr Morrison, but it was we who planted the grapes." '

The little Minister's chuckle was swept away in another spasm of coughing, and the Sergeant-major rose to take his leave.

'I hope to find you quite your active self again when I come back presently for a bit of training. Captain Waggett and me are just having a run round the island this morning. We're going to call on Mr Campbell at Garryboo first.'

'You'll have to congratulate him, Sergeant-major Odd,' said Mrs Morrison. 'He's just become engaged to Norman Macleod's sister Catriona.'

'Well, Captain Waggett was complaining about the falling off in the shooting,' said the Sergeant-major. 'But there doesn't seem much wrong with Cupid's shooting in these parts, that's a fact. He's a proper marksman in the two Toddays.'

The Sergeant-major saluted and withdrew.

'I'm sorry you told him about George Campbell and Catriona Macleod, Janet,' the little Minister said to his wife when their visitor was gone.

'Why, Angus?'

'Old Bean Eachainn Uilleim was in this morning to see me about her pension, and she was telling me that Mistress Campbell is not taking it at all too well. I won't be able to do anything with her until I get my voice back. I'll want all the voice I've got. And then I must try to make her see reason.' The little Minister gave a bronchial sigh and pulled the black and yellow plaid closer round his shoulders.

The Austin was passing Captain MacPhee's trim garden where the giant clam-shell from the Great Barrier Reef in front of the darkened house seemed like Captain MacPhee's coffin.

'I'm sorry I didn't see the old man again,' said the Sergeant-major. 'He had some wonderful yarns about the old windjammer days.'

'But he became absolutely reckless towards the end,' Captain Waggett said. 'I got up a Brains Trust last December, and somehow an argument started about Jonah and the whale. I pointed out that anybody with the most elementary knowledge of natural history knew that a whale couldn't swallow anything larger than a sardine, and Captain MacPhee said I was talking nonsense. So I said, "Surely you're not going to tell me that you were ever swallowed by a whale, Captain MacPhee?" And what d'ye think his answer was?'

'Not that he had been?' the Sergeant-major asked.

'No, he didn't go as far as that, but he said he knew a man who had been. And the audience actually clapped. I said, "Well, Captain MacPhee, the whale may have swallowed your friend, but I'm afraid I can't swallow your story." And, you know, the audience never saw my joke. They just sat like a lot of dummies. Oh, well, the old man's gone now, so one mustn't be too critical, but I confess I was really staggered at the time.'

'I must remember that one next time somebody at Fort Augustus tells me he saw the Loch Ness monster cross the road with a sheep in his mouth.'

'Yes, but what I find so annoying, Sergeant-major, is that people who believe a lot of nonsense about the Loch Ness monster laugh when you tell them that Hitler may still invade us. In my opinion people like that deserve to be invaded.'

Sergeant-major Odd, looking across the Coolish to Little Todday as the car drove northward and wondering whether he would be back in time to walk with Peggy over to Tràigh Swish that afternoon, found it easier for his enjoyment of the drive to agree with everything Captain Waggett said.

George Campbell was in school when his mother admitted them.

'You remember Sergeant-major Odd, Mrs Campbell,' Captain Waggett smirked. 'He's just back from Africa, and we shall have the benefit of his advice again.'

'Advice?' asked Mrs Campbell. 'What about?'

'Our training in the Home Guard.'

The old lady grunted.

'I dare say the Sergeant was better occupied in Africa. I'm sure I hope so.'

'Your hens are looking very well, Mrs Campbell,' said Captain Waggett.

'They *are* very well,' she told him.

'I suppose they've started to lay now?'

'They wouldn't be alive if they hadn't,' Mrs Campbell rapped out.

'We've been rather short of eggs in Snorvig,' Captain Waggett murmured hopefully.

'I quite believe it,' said the old lady.

At this moment George Campbell came in from the school to greet the visitors.

'I've just heard from the Minister that we have to congratulate you, Mr Campbell,' said the Sergeant-major, shaking George warmly by the hand.

'Congratulate him on what?' the old lady demanded.

'On his approaching marriage,' said the Sergeant-major.

'The Minister told you that George was going to be married?'

'Yes, just now.'

'I'll be seeing the Minister in a day or two,' Mrs Campbell said balefully, and with this she walked out of the room.

'And when's the happy day, Mr Campbell?' the Sergeant-major asked.

'I don't quite know yet,' George replied, following his mother's exit with his eyes.

'I suppose you're waiting for the whisky ship to come home the same as everyone else,' the Sergeant-major laughed. 'From what I can make out it isn't lawful wedlock here without there's whisky.'

George Campbell smiled feebly, and Captain Waggett who deprecated so much attention being paid to Venus brought the subject round to Mars. Five minutes later, the schoolmaster of Garryboo said he really must be getting back into the classroom.

'Any message for your intended, Mr Campbell?' the Sergeant-major asked. 'We shall be calling at Watasett on our way back to Snorvig.'

'No, thank you, there's no message,' said George, looking nervously in the direction of the door, for he heard his mother's footsteps.

'Well, I hope we'll see you over on Little Todday when Peggy Macroon and me get married after Easter,' said Sergeant-major Odd cordially.

'Are you a Roman Catholic, Sergeant Odd?' asked Mrs Campbell, who had re-entered the room in time to hear this invitation.

'No, m'm, I'm not,' he told her.

'And you're proposing to marry a Roman Catholic? A man of your age?' the old lady demanded sternly.

'We must be getting along, Mrs Campbell,' Captain Waggett hastily intervened. 'Sergeant-major Odd and I have to see quite a few people this morning.'

When they were back in the car the Sergeant-major expressed a strong desire to bring his mother to Great Todday in order to give Mrs Campbell an opportunity of hearing what a decent, sensible, and kindly old woman thought of such a fossilized terror.

'And she'd tell her too, sir. Not half she wouldn't. The way that old Tartar glared at me!'

'She's very bigoted of course,' Captain Waggett said. 'I've had a lot of trouble with her. Don't you remember when we had that invasion exercise on a Sunday and she locked Sergeant Campbell up in his room the day before to prevent him from taking part in it?'

'It's hardly credible that there are such people nowadays. Well, it makes anyone feel glad they didn't live once upon a time, and that's a fact. I'd sooner be up against one Hitler than a world full of Mrs Campbells.'

The car drove on past Knockdown and turned south along the east coast of the island, below the steeps of Ben Sticla, until it came to Bobanish, a sizeable village at the head of Loch Bob, the largest of the island's sea lochs. Here they called upon Captain Waggett's second-in-command, Lieutenant John Beaton, the local schoolmaster. Like his colleague at Garryboo John Beaton was in school, but they were warmly welcomed by his wife in the gabled schoolhouse by the door of which the veronica was already in bloom.

'Welcome back to the Islands, Sergeant,' exclaimed trim and dainty little Mrs Beaton, her bright bird's eyes sparkling with pleasure. 'Yes, indeed, I'm sure John has missed you all these months. And so you've found yourself a wife in Little Todday. Bravo, it's you that's a wise man. I'm a Great Todday woman myself, but a Little Todday woman is the next best, and I've no doubt you'll be saying to yourself that she is the best. What a pity we can't offer you a dram!'

'I never drink anything before lunch, Mrs Beaton,' Captain Waggett assured her.

'Ach, it's not you I'm worrying about, Mr Waggett. It's for Sergeant Odd.'

'That's all right, Mrs Beaton,' said the Sergeant-major. 'When there's a spirit like you about there's no other spirit needed.'

'Get along with you, Sergeant. We never had to teach you the blarney. You had enough for yourself, even if you are a Sassunnach. I'm sure it was the way you won Peigi Iosaiph, and a lovely girl she is too. Such lovely eyes. They tell me you're to be married after Easter.'

'Talk about radiolocation,' the Sergeant-major exclaimed. 'It's slow compared with the way news travels on the two Toddays.'

'But, Mr Waggett,' Mrs Beacon went on in a flutter of excitement, 'have you heard the news about George Campbell and Catriona Macleod?'

'We've just come from Garryboo,' said Captain Waggett. 'We found Mrs Campbell in a very gloomy mood. Very gloomy. I don't think she's at all pleased.'

'I'm sure she won't be. Nothing will please her till she finds herself in Heaven and everybody else in the other place. Then she'll be happy. I'm really sorry for poor Catriona, for she's one of the nicest girls on the island, and she'll make George Campbell a splendid wife. And how's Mrs Waggett? I hope the hens are laying well.'

'Not too well, I'm afraid,' said the henwife's husband.

'Ah, well, ours are doing just splendid. But wait you now, I'll go and tell himself you're here.'

Mrs Beaton bustled away to fetch her husband, while the two visitors waited in the sitting room. Scilly White narcissi filled the air with sweetness from pots in the window. The low February sun streamed in through the panes. The door of the cuckoo-clock hanging on the wall beside the fireplace flew open and the wooden bird proclaimed noon.

'This is more like what I call home, sir,' the Sergeant-major observed.

And then John Beaton himself came in, a burly Skyeman in his mid forties with a high complexion and sandy hair.

After the greetings and the congratulations on his approaching marriage, which the Sergeant-major was by now accepting as congratulations on a *fait accompli* in spite of the fact that Joseph Macroon's approval of the date for the wedding had not yet been obtained, the three men came down to the sterner business of war.

'I'm worried about the growing slackness of the Home Guard, Mr Beaton,' said the commander of G Company. 'I'm considering the advisability of prosecuting one or two of the worst shirkers.'

'I don't believe that would do any good at all,' his second-in-command argued. 'Indeed I am quite sure it would do a great deal of harm. You'll put their backs up, Captain.'

'Well, something must be done to make them realize that they are under military discipline.'

'I'm afraid there's not much anyone can do, Captain,' the schoolmaster insisted. 'You'll never make the people in the Islands do anything they think is a waste of time.'

'They waste a lot of time in talk,' Captain Waggett snapped.

'Ah, well, Captain, they don't think that such a waste of time. And anyway they'd consider they were wasting their own time. What they dislike is having their time wasted for them by other people.'

'Are the people of the two Toddays going to claim that they know more about what must be done to win the war than the Prime Minister?' Captain Waggett inquired in lofty disgust.

'We would none of us be so presumptuous as that, Captain,' his second-in-command assured him. 'But I think we all of us feel that Home Guard work should not be allowed to interfere too much with really vital jobs. We must remember, Mr Waggett, that both islands have made a great contribution to the war by sending so many of their men to fight the battle of the Atlantic in the Merchant Navy, and indeed, where would the country be now without the Merchant Navy?' John Beaton continued, cracking his finger-joints in the way he did when emotion was rising in his burly frame.

'I'm sure nobody realizes better than Captain Waggett how much the two Toddays have done to keep the Win in Winston and take the Hit out of Hitler,' the Sergeant-major put in, with a lenitive smile.

'Naturally I realize the contribution made by the two Toddays to the Mercantile Marine,' said Paul Waggett huffily. 'But all the food and munitions in the world wouldn't help us if our country was overrun by the Huns.'

'That's true enough, Captain,' John Beaton admitted, 'but the people here feel that, if at this stage of the war the Germans are strong enough to overrun us, there's nothing they can do to stop them.'

'I call that rank defeatism,' Captain Waggett said severely. 'And I must say I'm surprised by your attitude, Mr Beaton. It comes as a painful shock to me.'

Sergeant-major Odd was winking at John Beaton as fast as a heliograph behind Captain Waggett's back; but the choler of the man with a high complexion and sandy hair was beyond the sedative power of winks.

'I take exception to that remark, Mr Waggett. I consider it uncalled for and very injurious to my position. I really don't know what you'll be saying next.'

'I'm sure Captain Waggett wasn't meaning to cast any reflections, Mr Beaton,' said Sergeant-major Odd soothingly. 'Nobody knows better than Captain Waggett what a lot of hard work you've put in over Home Guard correspondence. This is just a little misunderstanding.'

'I am very willing to resign from my position in the Home Guard, Mr Waggett,' the schoolmaster declared, a crimson spot flaming now on both of his cheekbones. 'I had no desire to take on so much responsibility outside my own work. But when you talk about prosecuting men for not attending parades it is my duty to tell you that you would be making a great mistake.'

The last thing that Captain Waggett wanted was to have to deal with the Home Guard correspondence himself, and if John Beaton were to resign there was nobody else in the island to whom he could hand it over. He decided to be propitiatory.

'I'm sorry if I hurt your feelings by that remark about defeatism, Mr Beaton. I didn't intend it to be derogatory. If you think that prosecuting a few shirkers won't effect anything I'm content to abide by your judgement. All I'm anxious about is that Sergeant-major Odd shouldn't take up his duties again only to find that there's nothing for him to do.'

'Sergeant-major Odd was always well liked by the people, Captain, and if he can convince them that they are not wasting their time I'm sure he'll find good support,' said John Beaton.

'Nothing could be fairer than that, could it, sir?' the Sergeant-major urged. 'I'm sure if Colonel Wolseley lets you have my services for a few days presently Lieutenant Beaton and me will fix up a scheme of training for the spring and summer that won't tread on anybody's corns.'

The schoolmaster's choler had subsided under the Sergeant-major's good nature combined with the gratification of having wrung from Captain Waggett the nearest approach to an apology anybody in the islands had hitherto achieved.

'Well, we must be going on now to see Sergeant Macleod at Watasett,' said the commanding officer.

As they passed out to get into the car Mrs Beaton whispered to him:
'I put half a dozen eggs for Mrs Waggett on the seat at the back. I

wish I could have put some butter with them, but our cow's dry just now.'

And while Mrs Beaton was saying this to Captain Waggett her husband was saying to the Sergeant-major:

'I'm really mortified that there is simply not a dram in the house. But you know the state of affairs, Sergeant. It's unprocurable. Nobody in the island can remember anything like it.'

'It may come by tomorrow's boat,' the Sergeant-major said cheerfully.

'It may, it may. But we've been saying that now for a fortnight. And even if it does come I'm sure Roderick will not have a bottle to spare. He'll want every drop for the bar. Ah, well, *beannachd leibh, beannachd leibh*. Good-bye, Sergeant. We'll be seeing you again, soon.'

The car drove on southward, making a wide curve round the base of Ben Pucka, to reach the head of Loch Sleeport.

'Lieutenant Beaton was in a very strange mood,' his Commanding Officer observed to the Sergeant-major.

'He was a bit worried, sir, by your talk of prosecuting men for non-attendance at parades.'

'Well, what am I to do, Sergeant-major? I don't want to prosecute anybody. But something must be done to bring home to these people that there's a war on.'

'I think this drought of whisky has taught them that, sir. And seriously, sir, I don't believe prosecutions would do a bit of good. I don't think they're easy to drive out here, though nobody could wish for a better lot of fellows to lead.'

'I don't want to prosecute, Sergeant-major. It's no pleasure to me. I could have prosecuted a lot of people for poaching, but I never have. Unfortunately, the command of the Home Guard here isn't my private affair. I'm the representative of the country's will to victory, and, however painful it may be to my personal feelings, I may have to ask the Colonel to prosecute. This is total war. We are fighting to preserve England – I mean Britain – and I have to do my bit, as we used to say in the last war. What surprises me is that Lieutenant Beaton didn't seem able to grasp my point of view. He's quite an intelligent man.'

'Ah well, he gets a bit het up sometimes. Anyone with a ginger top always does. Once the fine weather comes on and they get down to shooting I'm sure everything will go well.'

'There's another problem. Who's going to be the section commander at Watasett when Sergeant Macleod goes?'

'I expect Sergeant Macleod will have his eye on somebody, sir.'

'Of course he'll have his eye on somebody, Sergeant-major. But he'll have it on the wrong person. Well, there's one thing, perhaps when he leaves Watasett I shall get an opportunity of catching some of my own sea-trout.'

The car was now in sight of the township of Watasett, the houses of which were clustered along either side of the winding inlet of Loch Sleeport. This had once been the harbourage of a dozen fishing-boats before the destructive activity of trawlers had made fishing profitless.

The discussion between Norman Macleod and the commander of G Company about the best man in Watasett to select for promotion to section commander lasted for about twenty minutes, during which time the class Norman Macleod had temporarily deserted was at work writing a composition on the theme, 'Why I am proud of Great Todday'. Half-way through the examination of the claims of two MacRuries, a Maclean, a Macmillan and a Fraser to the position Sergeant-major Odd slipped away to have a chat with Catriona.

'Well, Miss Macleod, so you and me are going to take the plunge together,' he said. 'Now see here, I've just come from Garryboo, and your intended isn't looking so happy as any young fellow ought to look when he's just got engaged to a girl like you. And the trouble is your future mar-in-law. Well, when I tell you she actually had the nerve to try and tell me off because I was going to marry a Catholic you'll understand what she'll be capable of saying to her own son.'

'Did she say that to you, Sarchant? What a chick!' exclaimed Catriona.

'It *was* a cheek. If it hadn't been I didn't want to make things worse for your young man I'd have walked into her properly. But what I want to say is this. Peggy and me are going to have what you call a rayjack.'

'A what?'

'Raychack . . . rayjack . . . what you have before the wedding; I know whisky comes into it. And, of course, that may mean we may have to wait a bit.'

'Ach, a *rèiteach*!'

'That's what I said, didn't I? Only perhaps I forgot the cough at the end. Well, if you have trouble with that old rhinoceros . . . asking the poor animal's pardon . . . you drag your young man over to our rayjack, and if he doesn't rayjack some common sense into that old Tartar when he gets home that night, well, George Campbell isn't the man I took him for when I heard you and him were going to be married. That's all I wanted to say. I think you're in for a bit of trouble, but don't you worry. I've had a bit of trouble with my future par-in-law, and the only thing to do is what Father Macalister said . . . roll right over them.'

The discussion about the future leader of the Watasett section was still undecided when Sergeant-major Odd went back into the sitting-room.

'Well, I'm afraid we'll have to postpone the decision, Sergeant Macleod. Mrs Waggett will be expecting me back for lunch.'

'Ach, we none of us want to postpone our food, Mr Waggett,' said Norman Macleod. 'But apart from that, I believe postponement is one of the great pleasures of existence.'

'Not of marriage, Mr Macleod,' said the Sergeant-major.

'Ah, well, I've postponed the need of any further postponement in that matter, Sergeant, by postponing the notion altogether,' the young schoolmaster grinned.

'Don't you be too sure of yourself. You don't know what may happen when you get into the R.A.F.'

'I'm not worrying. Cupid rhymes with stupid for me.'

'You're asking for trouble, you are,' the Sergeant-major warned him.

'I'm afraid we really *must* be getting along,' said Captain Waggett, who disliked badinage except on a public platform when he could gently chaff an audience. 'Didn't you tell me Joseph Macroon was going to meet you at the pier at half past twelve? It's twenty to one already.'

Captain Waggett and the Sergeant-major got into the car. Norman Macleod went back to his class.

'Well, let me have a look at what you've been writing,' he told them.

He picked up the first composition by a juvenile MacRurie, and read out:

'I am proud of Great Todday because it is bigger than Little Todday. We have cows and sheeps in Great Todday. The Island Queen comes to Snorvig three times every week but it did not come last week because the wether was too bad. and when there is no wisky we are all very sad.'

Captain Waggett dropped the Sergeant-major by the road down to the pier, but when he reached it there was no sign of the *Morning Star*.

'Are you looking for Joseph Macroon?' Constable Macrae sauntered up to inquire. 'He was asking for you half an hour ago, but he said he had to go back to Kiltod.'

'Well, I've done something I never managed to do yet in these islands, Constable.'

'What was that, Sergeant?'

'I've managed to be late for a boat crossing the Coolish.'

The Constable smiled. He was from the mainland and therefore under the delusion that the islanders were more unpunctual than his own people away in Kintail.

'Ay, it's pretty difficult to be late anywhere in the Toddays,' he agreed. 'Wait a minute, though, Sergeant, there's the *Kittiwake* out there. The Biffer will take you over. He's feeling fine this morning. He's had a letter that his son Donald is safe in Ireland.'

In response to shouts from the pier the Biffer, much to the relief of the Sergeant-major who was seeing his walk with Peggy that afternoon washed out, brought the *Kittiwake* alongside.

'Will you take the Sergeant over to Kiltod, Airchie?' Constable Macrae shouted down to him.

'Sure, I'll take him. Come along, Sergeant,' and when the Sergeant-major was aboard he turned to him, 'I've had some good news, Sergeant. My boy Donald who was torpedoed is all safe and sound. Ay, he came ashore on some island off Donegal, and the weather was so bad they couldn't put him over to the mainland. He got on fine, though. He said they managed to understand one another in the Gaelic very well after a bit.'

'You must be feeling pretty good, Corporal.'

'Och, I'm feeling right on top of the whole world this morning, Sergeant. I was just away to see if my lobster-pots had all been broken to pieces by the terrible weather we've been having. What a morning for a good dram! I believe I'd stay on top of the world for a week if I could have a really good dram. That was a funny way of Joseph to behave going away like a shot out of a gun, and you not there. What kind of hospitality is that at all? Ach, I believe he's in a bit of a stew because you'll be taking Peigi Ealasaid away from him so soon. They tell me the wedding is to be just after Easter. I was asking Joseph, and he was off in the *Morning Star* like a shot out of a gun. Ach, he's feeling the shortage of whisky. We're all feeling it, Sergeant. Never mind. Good things will come again, and we'll have whisky galore. *Uisge beatha gu leòir!*'

While the Biffer was taking the Sergeant-major over to Kiltod, Captain Waggett was occupying the time before his wife brought in lunch by writing to Captain Quiblick, the Security Intelligence Officer responsible for No. 14 Protected Area:

Snorvig House
Great Todday
SECRET
Western Isles
February 22nd, 1943

Dear Captain Quiblick,

I feel I ought to let you know that there seems to be a wave of defeatism in this island at present. It has affected the Home Guard to some extent, and I think it might be worth your while to investigate the phenomenon which, I confess, baffles me completely. Possibly you might care to notify your opposite number, Captain Lomax-Smith, at Obaig in case he would like to make investigations on Little Todday. I need hardly say that I am entirely at your disposal if you decide to pursue the matter. With kind regards,

Yours sincerely,

Paul Waggett, Capt. H.G.

Captain P. St John Quiblick,
Security Intelligence Corps,
No. 14 Protected Area,
Nobost Lodge,
Nobost, Mid Uist

This letter the commander of G Company enclosed in an envelope marked SECRET in red ink, and the envelope thus inscribed he enclosed in a registered envelope.

'What's the matter, Paul? You look worried,' said his wife.

'Oh, it's nothing much, old lady. But one can't help worrying sometimes over one's responsibilities.'

He sighed patriotically.

Chapter 6

THE TWO TRAVELLERS

A small consignment of whisky did arrive by the boat on Tuesday; but as John Beaton had foreseen it was all required by Roderick MacRurie for the bar, and it was in such short supply that nobody was served with more than one dram in two days. This naturally led to arguments. Everybody was convinced that he had had his dram the day before yesterday, never yesterday. On top of that those who came in from remoter districts and particularly those who had crossed over from Little Todday complained that the people of Snorvig itself were getting preferential treatment. Finally, although the whisky situation had been faintly, very faintly relieved, the beer situation deteriorated rapidly, and within a week after Sergeant-major Odd had gone back to the mainland nobody was being allowed more than a pint a day.

'And the way things are going,' Big Roderick told his customers, 'you'll be lucky to have half a pint very soon.'

On Saturday, February 27th, not a barrel of beer arrived with the *Island Queen*, and that evening Ruairidh Mór cut the allowance to half a pint a day.

In the corner of the bar on that Saturday night sat a thin young man with a neo-Caroline moustache. If his nose had been a little shorter and his chin a little longer he would not have been bad-looking. He was sporting plus-fours of the barrage-balloon type, from the umber convolutions of which his ankles emerged like chicken-bones. Nobody had paid much attention to him on the pier that afternoon, and carrying his own bag he had walked up to the hotel where he had registered as William Anthony Brown, Tweed Merchant. When dark fell he had proceeded cautiously to Snorvig House, the adverb meaning that every ten yards he had turned sharply round and listened for the sound of footsteps following him.

'Can I speak to Captain Waggett?' he inquired when the door was opened by a small girl in a cap and apron.

'Captain Waggett doesn't live here,' said the small girl, panting with shyness. 'This is the Manse.'

'And he turned round just like a flash,' the small girl told Mrs Morrison afterwards.

Mr Brown turned round three times more before he emerged from the drive that led up to the Manse, so fearful was he of being followed. A hundred yards along the road he came to the stone pillars on either side of the gate of the Snorvig House drive. The door was opened to him by another small girl in a cap and apron. It was the first time Kennethina Macdonald had been called upon to answer the front-door bell, for she had only joined the Waggett household on leaving school two days previously.

'Can I speak to Captain Waggett?' Mr Brown inquired again.

'I don't know,' Kennethina whispered, her chubby face shimmering with embarrassment.

'Will you say Mr Brown would like to speak to him?' Kennethina seemed, and indeed was, on the verge of bursting into tears.

'I don't know who you are at all,' she managed to gasp tremulously.

'I'm Mr Brown, and I want to speak to Captain Waggett.'

Luckily Mrs Waggett had heard the bell ring and, doubtful of Kennethina's aplomb yet in dealing with callers, came along to see who it was.

'Is Captain Waggett expecting you?' she asked.

'I think so,' said Mr Brown, in such a mysterious tone of voice that Mrs Waggett's fancy began to race round all sorts of dire possibilities from assassination to blackmail.

'Run and tell the master that a gentleman wants to speak to him,' she said to Kennethina.

Kennethina looked puzzled. Then her face cleared.

'Will I go along to the Manse the way I am now, or will I put my hat and coat on?' she asked.

'Captain Waggett, Ina, not the Minister.'

When Kennethina had gone off to the den, Mrs Waggett decided to assume that Mr Brown had no fell purpose.

'Such a shortage of girls nowadays, Mr Brown. And Captain Waggett and I always encourage them to join up,' she said with a bright smile which covered her face with what stucco experts call hair-cracks.

'Quite,' said Mr Brown sagaciously.

A minute or two later Mr Brown was closeted with Captain Waggett in the den.

'Didn't you get Major Quiblick's letter notifying you of my arrival?' he asked.

'I was just going to open my post when you called.' Paul Waggett looked at the letters and selected a registered one from which he drew a heavily sealed envelope stamped VERY SECRET. He broke the seal and read:

VERY SECRET

Security Intelligence Corps
No. 14 Protected Area
Nobost Lodge
Nobost, Mid-Uist
25/2/43

Dear Captain Waggett,

I am much obliged for your letter of the 22nd inst. I am taking steps accordingly. Last week No. 13 Protected Area was incorporated with No. 14 P.A. and therefore I am now the S.I.C. officer in charge of both with the rank of Major. This means that it will no longer be necessary to apply for a permit to travel between Great Todday and Little Todday. It also means that I am now responsible for all security intelligence on both islands.

Lieut. W. A. Boggust will arrive at Snorvig on Saturday the 27th inst., to investigate the matter to which you called my attention in your letter of the 22nd inst. He will travel under the name of W. A. Brown, and his apparent object will be to enquire into the tweed industry on both islands. I am sure you will give him any help in your power to fulfil his mission satisfactorily. I have instructed Lieut. Boggust to contact you on his arrival provided that he can do so without calling attention to himself. You can rely absolutely on his discretion.

Yours sincerely,
P. St John Quiblick
Major S.I.C.

'You have a very interesting job, Mr Boggust,' said Captain Waggett.

'Brown, Brown, please, sir. I think it's always best to preserve one's cover all the time.'

'Well, of course, we're quite safe in my den.'

'Oh, I know that, sir. But I'm tremendously thorough. I only think of myself now as Brown. Now, sir, will you put me in the picture here? I understand from Major Quiblick that defeatism in these islands is rampant.'

'I wouldn't go so far as to use the word "rampant". I should prefer to say it was rife.'

'Quite, quite,' the Intelligence officer quacked in comprehension of the nice distinction.

'I'd better call you "Mr Brown", hadn't I? I mean to say if you really were a tweed merchant I shouldn't call you "Brown", should I?'

'Quite, quite. And I shouldn't call you "sir", should I?' Mr Brown suggested.

'No, quite,' Captain Waggett agreed. 'Well, now, what exactly do you want to know, Mr Brown?'

'What can you tell me, Captain Waggett?'

'Well, I think you should form your own impressions.'

'Quite. But what would be the best way of putting myself in the picture?'

'I'd suggest that after your tea — they give you tea up at the hotel — of course, I'd be delighted to give you dinner, but I think that might make you rather conspicuous — yes, after you've had your tea I'd go in the bar if I were you and just listen to the conversation. I think you'll realize then what I mean by this wave of defeatism.'

'Quite. And what about tomorrow, sir? I mean what about tomorrow?'

'What do you mean, what about tomorrow?'

'I mean would it be possible for us to meet somewhere without being too conspicuous?'

'It's not easy. Not at all easy,' said Captain Waggett after a moment's reflection. 'You see it's Sunday tomorrow. If it were Monday you could go round the island looking for lengths of tweed, but you couldn't do that on Sunday.'

'What about Little Todday? That's a Catholic island, isn't it? They wouldn't pay any attention to Sunday there, would they?'

'No, but there's no tweed woven on Little Todday, and anyway unless you'd made arrangements with one of the Little Todday boatmen you wouldn't get across. The people here won't use their boats on Sunday.'

'There seems to be very little intercourse between the two islands,' said Mr Brown. 'I was looking up our card-index of permits issued and I couldn't find that we'd had one application for a permit to travel between the two islands.'

'How long have you been at Nobust?' Captain Waggett asked.

'Only a fortnight, sir. I mean only a fortnight. I was transferred there from Number 22.'

'Number 22 Protected Area? Where's that?'

'No, no, Number 22 is our headquarters in London.'

'Quite, quite,' Captain Waggett quacked hastily. 'Well, you've been out in the Islands such a short time that you probably don't realize the calm way in which the people flaunt every rule and regulation. I did my best when the order was first made over eighteen months ago about permits between the two Toddays to get it enforced. But I had no support from anybody, with the result that it was a dead letter from the start. People just went backwards and forwards over the Coolish as if they were crossing the road.'

'Extraordinary!' Mr Brown exclaimed. 'Don't they realize that there's a war on?'

'That's the question I often ask myself,' Captain Waggett replied sadly. 'You'll be able to answer it for yourself after an evening in the hotel bar. Do you know they actually listen to the news on the Irish wireless?'

'Amazing! Is the reception better?'

'They'd sooner tune in to the atmospherics from Athlone than the best reception from the B.B.C. And mind you that's just as true of Great Todday as it is of a Catholic island like Little Todday. Of course, they listen regularly to the German wireless.'

Lieutenant Boggust stroked his neo-Caroline moustache.

'Staggering!' he murmured. 'Personally I'd make it a penal offence to listen to enemy wireless. I mean to say we can learn a lot from the Germans.'

'Oh, I agree with you every time. I mean to say you've got to hand it to the Germans. They are thorough.'

'Absolutely,' Lieutenant Boggust affirmed enthusiastically. Then he reverted to his cover.

'Well, I'd better be going back to the hotel. And you think it would be much wiser if we didn't meet tomorrow?'

'Much wiser,' said Captain Waggett. 'Come round and see me here on Monday evening, and I'll fill up any gaps in your investigation.'

Mr Brown found his way back to the hotel without meeting anybody. That was satisfactory at any rate. After he had eaten a couple of herrings and drunk the strongest cup of tea he had ever drunk in his life the Security Intelligence officer adjourned to the bar where for some time he sat in a corner listening to the conversation.

'Will you be seeing Donald before he gets another ship?' somebody was asking the Biffer.

'I don't believe we will. Och, he enjoyed himself fine in Ireland. He's in Glasgow now. The *cailleach* had a letter from Johnny yesterday morning. From Liverpool he was writing, and he's away off to Australia again.'

Mr Brown made a note in his pocket-book. This was careless talk. He must find out who this man was.

'You had a tram yesterday, Angus,' the host was saying to Angus MacCormac, who had just moved to the bar to request a whisky.

'I had a dram yesterday?' exclaimed the big crofter, grasping his huge moustache as if it was the only solid thing in a dissolving world. 'How could I have had a dram yesterday when I was working all day at home?'

'You had a tram yesterday,' Ruairidh Mór repeated firmly. Angus MacCormac appealed to his friend Sammy MacCodrum, who himself had just been served.

'Was I working at home yesterday?'

'I believe you were,' Sammy told him.

'I'm not after saying you weren't working at home,' said Roderick. 'What I'm after saying is that you came in with Donald Ian in the lorry and was in the bar till nine o'clock.'

'That was Thursday.'

'You were in the bar on Thurssday too. And we had the same argument about Wednesday.'

'Ah, well, well, well, well,' Angus declared, apparently overwhelmed by the revelation of the depths to which human nature could sink. 'Did anybody ever hear the like of that now? You've got a bigger imagination than Captain Waggett. He's for ever seeing Germans who aren't there at all and you're seeing whiskies that aren't there at all.'

Mr Brown made another note.

'He's talking very big again about the Home Guard is Wackett,' said one of the Snorvig fishermen. 'Just a lot of nonsense.'

'Ay, it's a nonsense now right enough,' the Biffer agreed. 'But it wasn't such a nonsense when Hitler was almost on top of us.'

'It was nonsense from the start,' the fishermen argued. 'What use would Wackett have been against Hitler? What use would any of you have been if it comes to that? If the Government can't win this war, how would the Home Guard win it?'

'I believe they're doing pretty well in Africa just now,' somebody else said.

'Ay, that's what they say. But who's to believe them?' the fisherman asked.

There was a murmur of agreement from the company in whom half a pint of beer and a dram here and there had induced a sceptical attitude towards the whole of existence.

'I think you can rely on the B.B.C.,' Mr Brown put in from his corner.

'The P.P.C. chust say what the Government tell them to say,' Sammy MacCodrum maintained. 'And efen if it was all true what they were saying who would want to be hearing such foices? Och, I listen to the news in Gaelic when they have it, and you get a bit more sense from them then, but who wants to listen to the news in these days? Chust nothing but war.'

'Well, until the war is over we mustn't think about anything except winning it,' said Mr Brown.

'We can think about winning it without hearing about it all the time,' Sammy MacCodrum argued. 'Here we are with half a pint of beer for the whole evening and a poor kind of tram three times a week if we're lucky. That's what the war has done for us. If we're winning the war, why doesn't the Government give us our own whisky?'

'We're exporting it to America to help pay for our war expenditure,' Mr Brown tried to explain.

'Ay, and when these Americans have drunk all our whisky, it'll be they who've won the war not ourselves,' put in the fisherman, who by this time was a suspect in Mr Brown's notebook.

The Security Intelligence officer slept badly that night. The hotel bed was hard. The herrings combined with the strong tea to promote sharp indigestion. He said to himself that Waggett had underestimated the defeatism of the island by calling it rife. It was in fact rampant.

It was pouring with rain on Sunday morning, and when Mr Brown looked out of the windows of the coffee-room after breakfast he felt that this rampant defeatism if unjustifiable was at least intelligible. The only other guest of the hotel in the hotel was a large elderly commercial traveller with a white walrus moustache from Inverness who was bemoaning the patriotism which had called him forth from retirement to allow a younger man to serve the country in the armed forces.

'I don't know why I did it, Mr Brown . . . the name *is* Brown, I believe?'

'Yes, yes, that is my name.'

'Yes, I thought I wasn't mistaken. Well, as I was saying, I really don't know why I did it. I have a nice wee house in Rose Terrace, Inverness . . . do you know Inverness at all, Mr Brown?'

'No, I don't know it at all.'

'It's a fine city. Very fine. The air is beautiful. Yes, I made up my mind I was going to do nothing but read a little, and walk along to the library, and play a bit of bowls on a summer evening . . . do you play bowls, Mr Brown?'

'No, I don't.'

'It's a wonderful game. You can go on playing it for ever, and you'll never get to the end of it.'

'I can quite believe it,' said Mr Brown.

'However, as they say, man proposes and God disposes. I felt the call of duty, and here I am; but as I tell my firm, what's the use of travelling nowadays when we really have nothing to sell? I could have got any amount of orders for our Dreadnought Sheep Dip. Do you know our Dreadnought Sheep Dip?'

'No, I don't.'

'I'm surprised at that. A tweed merchant like yourself has a stake in our Dreadnought Sheep Dip. I estimate that Duthie's Dreadnought Sheep Dip has saved us tons of wool, yes literally tons. But as I was saying, what's the use of me singing its praises now? If you wanted just a couple of gallons of it I couldn't guarantee delivery in this summer. Yes, it's a wearisome journey up through the Islands in war time. And I find so many of my friends have passed on. Here's my card, Mr Brown.'

Mr Brown accepted it rather ungraciously.

'Ay, Macintosh is my name,' said the traveller, with a touch of complacency.

Mr Brown felt inclined to say that it was a very good name to have on such a morning, but having heard that the Celts lacked humour he decided to refrain.

'I believe I can boast that ten years ago no traveller was better known in the Highlands and Islands than Charlie Macintosh. Oh, and they still remember me, Mr Brown. Oh, yes, I was up in Harris last month. Terrible weather we had.'

'Worse than this?'

'Oh, much worse. This is nothing.'

'Good God!' Mr Brown ejaculated.

'Yes, I was up in Harris . . . you know Harris of course?'

'No, I don't.'

'Man, you a tweed merchant, and you don't know Harris!'

'I know the tweed of course,' said Mr Brown irritably. 'But I've never been to Harris itself. This is my first visit to Scotland.'

'Ay, I thought you were from England by the way you talked. It's very noticeable to us in Inverness the queer way the English speak their own language.'

'We might think it equally queer the way you speak our language,' Mr Brown retorted sarcastically.

Mr Macintosh chuckled.

'Ah, that won't do, Mr Brown. Everybody knows that the purest English spoken anywhere is spoken in Inverness.'

'The Americans and the Australians might say the same. That wouldn't make it true.'

'Ah, but everybody admits that the English spoken in Inverness is the purest spoken English,' Mr Macintosh insisted.

'Who's everybody? Everybody in Inverness, I suppose?' Mr Brown asked indignantly.

'No, no, no, other people too. It's an established fact. You'll probably find it in the *Encyclopaedia Britannica*.'

'I very much doubt that. Indeed, I'll go so far as to say I don't believe it.'

'That's a pretty risky thing to say,' Mr Macintosh observed. 'Still, I don't suppose I can have the pleasure of proving you're wrong. We're not likely to find the *Encyclopaedia Britannica* on Great Todday. Unless Mr Waggett has it. Do you know Mr Waggett?'

Mr Brown hesitated. Had this bore noticed him enter or leave Snorvig House last night?

'A friend of mine in London told me to look him up if I found myself on Great Todday,' he answered ambiguously.

'I haven't met the man myself, but the Todday people seem to consider him a bit of a windbag,' said the traveller.

'The people here have a lot of extraordinary opinions,' Mr Brown snapped. 'I was amazed last night in the bar to hear the freedom with which they were criticizing the Government. They don't realize what would happen to them in Germany if they talked like that.'

'But isn't that just what we're fighting for?'

'I don't follow you.'

'To prevent any of us realizing what would happen to us in Germany if we opened our mouths a bit wide.'

'There is a war on, you know, Mr Macintosh.'

'Indeed, and I do know it. I'd be sitting in front of the fire in my wee house in Rose Terrace if there wasn't a war on,' the traveller said. 'You are exempt, I take it?'

'Yes, oh, yes, I was . . . er . . . indispensable.'

How little people appreciated the price paid by a good Intelligence officer in doing his duty, Mr Brown reflected in admiration of his own self-restraint in allowing this old bore to assume that he had escaped uniform.

'I don't believe you'll be able to do much business here, Mr Brown,' said the traveller. 'This rule they've made about giving up coupons for yarn has discouraged the tweed making.'

'As far as I can make out every rule that's made annoys the people here. The only rule they seem to keep is not to do anything at all on Sunday.'

'Ah, well, you'll feel all the fresher for it yourself on Monday morning.'

'After sitting about in this dreary coffee-room looking at that?' asked Mr Brown, pointing to the drench of rain.

'Oh, it is as well for it to rain itself out today when there's nothing doing anyway, and then maybe it'll be a fine day tomorrow. I was thinking we might share the hire of a car round the island. I expect you'll have a list of people you're wanting to call on about these tweeds.'

'As a matter of fact I was thinking of crossing over to Little Todday tomorrow morning,' said Mr Brown quickly, for the prospect of touring the island with this bore of a traveller affected him as unpleasantly as the prospect of being shut up in a room with a bluebottle he was unable to squash.

'You'll find no tweed on Little Todday, Mr Brown.'

'No, I dare say not, but I should like to see what the island is like. I'm making a sort of a holiday of this business trip.'

'Well, I'll be going over to Little Todday on Tuesday morning, and we might share the hire of Archie MacRurie's boat. Do you know him?'

'Isn't he the fellow with two sons at sea?'

'Four sons at sea. Oh, he's a great chap is the Biffer, as they call him.'

'I thought he was talking rather indiscreetly last night about shipping movements. For instance, he let out that one of his sons was sailing for Australia this week from Liverpool. That's exactly what the enemy wants to know.'

'I'm sure the Biffer wouldn't want to say anything to put his own sons' lives in danger,' Mr Macintosh averred warmly.

'That's just it. I'm not saying it's deliberate. It's what we call careless talk.'

'Well, if we take him over to Kiltod on Tuesday, you'll be able to warn him, Mr Brown.'

'Thanks very much, but I think I'll stick to my original timetable. As I say, I'm not expecting to do much business here.'

'Please yourself, Mr Brown. But they're not afraid to charge for motor-boats and cars, you know.'

However, Mr Brown, whose expenses were not his own affair, regarded with equanimity the likelihood of being overcharged.

'I think I'll go for a short walk in spite of the rain,' he told his fellow-guest.

'Well, I wouldn't mind a breath of air myself,' Mr Macintosh admitted.

Mr Brown's skill as Intelligence officer in throwing his pursuers off the trail was useless against the determined adhesiveness of Mr Macintosh, in whose company he had to spend the whole of that wet Sunday besides being given for his evening meal an even stronger cup of tea than yesterday to accompany some tough and desiccated cold mutton.

'I wonder if this is the heel or the sole,' he observed gloomily. 'I think it's too tough for the sole.'

'I think it's the leg,' said Mr Macintosh, apparently oblivious that his fellow-guest had been speaking sardonically.

Mr Brown got up from the table and rang the poached-egg bell beside the fireplace.

'Can I have some whisky, please?' he asked when Annag, one of the two daughters of Roderick who was helping to keep the home fires burning, came in.

'Whisky!' she exclaimed. If he had asked her for arsenic she could not have seemed more shocked. 'You're after having all the whisky you can be having till tomorrow.'

'But I haven't had any today.'

'You had your whisky yesterday evening.'

'There's a shortage, Mr Brown,' the traveller put in. 'We're rationed to one small whisky every other day.'

'Oh, very well,' said Mr Brown, who after the way he had been sticking up for rules and regulations did not feel justified in suggesting that an exception should be made in his favour. 'Very well, bring me half a pint of ale, please.'

'You had your half pint with your dinner, Mr Brown.'

'Do you mean to say I can't have another half pint now?' he asked fretfully.

'No, my father's very sorry, but he can't be serving anybody with more than half a pint for the day,' Annag informed him.

Mr Brown shook his head, and as she went out of the coffee-room shuddered and poured himself out another cup of tea.

When the meal was finished he rose from the table with aching jaws and asked Mr Macintosh if he played cribbage.

'I noticed some of them were playing last night in the bar. It's not a bad game.'

'Oh, I play a good game of cribbage,' the traveller boasted. 'But they wouldn't like at all to see us playing on a Sunday, and indeed, I wouldn't care to do it myself.'

On one thing Mr Brown was determined. He would listen to no more of his fellow-guest's foully boring conversation. He sat down in one of the worn leather armchairs beside the fire and buried his head in the *People's Journal*, which was the only printed fodder he could find except Murray's Railway Guide for June 1939, and even if that had been readable it was much too small to shut out the sight of Mr Macintosh's large face and white walrus moustache and moist pale-blue eyes. Indeed the *People's Journal* was only just wide enough.

'You're sure you won't change your mind, Mr Brown, and make the round of Great Todday with me tomorrow morning?' the traveller inquired after Mr Brown had been reading the *People's Journal* for about twenty minutes.

'I can't. I've asked Mr MacRurie to arrange with the man who owns the boat,' Mr Brown replied, without lowering his paper.

'Oh, well, then, if you'll excuse me, Mr Brown, I think I'll go down to the pier-house for a *cèilidh* with my clansman, John Macintosh.'

Mr Brown was suddenly seized by a longing for chocolate. No whisky. No beer. That ghastly tea embittering his inside demanded chocolate to assuage its acrid ferment.

'I wonder if you could get hold of a packet for me?'

'A packet of what, Mr Brown?' the traveller asked in perplexity.

'A packet of Caley's chocolate.'

'I doubt if John Macintosh will have any chocolate. He's the piermaster. Iain Dubh they call him. Black John. He's not a merchant.'

'But you said you were going to get some Caley's from him.'

Light dawned on Mr Macintosh.

'I said I was going for a *céilidh* with him. A *céilidh* is what we call a visit in Gaelic.'

'Oh, well, in that case, please don't let me detain you,' said Mr Brown sombrely.

When he found himself alone the Security Intelligence officer laid down the *People's Journal* with relief. He thought he had never read a paper with such an immense amount of news about nothing. His indigestion grew worse. He had an impression that damp squibs were going off in his inside. He rang the bell again.

'I wonder if you have any Sodamint in the house,' he asked Annag when she answered it.

'I believe we have just one bottle of soda-water left,' she said. 'Will that be what you're wanting?'

'No, not soda-water. Sodamint. Tablets.'

'Tablets? Aspirin?' she asked hopefully.

'No, I'm afraid aspirin would be no use. Never mind,' he said, and noticing for the first time that Annag was really rather a pretty girl he stroked his neo-Caroline moustache and adjusted the folds of his umber plus-fours.

Annag, however, hurried from the room to avoid any more incomprehensible demands upon her hospitality.

'Extraordinarily primitive people,' Mr Brown murmured to himself. He was thinking of that strange old woman in the shop at Nobust last week who when he had asked her if she kept toilet-paper had replied with a slightly puzzled but equally propitiatory smile, 'No, no, I'm afraid we haven't that kind of paper just now, but we have emery paper if that would do as well for you.'

Mr Brown told himself that he really must have something to read.

'If I ring and ask that girl she'll probably bring me in the family Bible,' he muttered to himself.

Then he noticed a small cupboard he had not yet tried. He opened it and found beside two cruets a novel by Annie S. Swan. He settled down to read. An hour later he heard the voice of Mr Macintosh back from his visit. He hurried off to bed, taking the book with him.

Chapter 7

THE CROCK OF GOLD

Just about the same time as Mr Brown went off to bed in the Snorvig Hotel with that novel by Annie S. Swan, over on Little Todday, Hugh Macroon, a stocky clean-shaven crofter with a bald domed head in which was set a pair of quick shrewd eyes, rose slowly from the long wooden seat at right angles to the range in the kitchen where he had been indulging in an agreeable *céilidh* for an hour.

'Ah, well, *matà. Feumaidh mi falbh.* I'll be going along, Jockey.'

'I believe the rain will have stopped,' said his host, John Stewart, known as Jockey, a round sandy little crofter whose cattle, the best in the island, had been providing an hour of absorbing conversation for the two crofters. 'I'll come along for a bit of the way with you.'

Outside they saw that the machair was now lapped in clouded watery moonlight and that the rain, as Jockey had guessed, had indeed stopped.

'I wonder would we take a bit of a walk up to Bàgh Mhic Ròin,' Hugh Macroon suggested.

'It would give us a bit of air right enough,' Jockey agreed.

Inasmuch as both men had walked three miles each way to Mass in the morning and another three miles to Benediction in the late afternoon, it might have been thought that they had had enough air that Sunday.

Bàgh Mhic Ròin or Macroon's Bay was an inlet on the north-west coast of the island, where according to legend the seal-woman had first met the exiled son of Clan Donald who was to make her his bride and become the progenitor of the clan. It was about a mile equidistant from the crofts of both Hugh and Jockey, and opening directly to the Atlantic it provided as rich a store of flotsam as anywhere in Little Todday.

'I was thinking that with the set of the tide and the calm sea we might be taking a look at what's moving,' said Hugh.

'Ay, quite a good idea,' Jockey agreed.

Presently, as the two men trudged northward over the drenched machair, the clouds thinned for the moon to shine through and illuminate the raindrops clinging to the grass. They did not talk. The topic of the cattle had been exhausted at the *céilidh*.

After nearly twenty minutes of silent progress they reached the head of the bay and stood on a sandy bluff scanning the grey water, with their backs still to the moon. Some five hundred yards out to the north-west the fantastic craggy shape of Pillay rose from the sea, the cliffs rising to a couple of hundred feet but seeming higher beside the expanse of Little Todday's gently undulating low land.

'*Seall, Uisdein*,' Jockey exclaimed in sudden excitement, 'what is that black thing floating in?'

'Man, that's the Gobha,' said Hugh.

The Gobha or Blacksmith was a dark rock off the east side of Pillay right opposite the mouth of Macroon's Bay.

'Where are you looking?' Jockey exclaimed, his voice rising almost to a treble in his excitement. 'I don't mean out there. Here man, here, half-way in to the bay, and the tide will be making in another hour.'

'Ay, I see it now,' said Hugh. 'But the tide won't be making for two hours. You're after forgetting about summer time.'

'*A Dhia*,' Jockey expostulated, 'what do they want to jicker about with the clock for? It wass bad enough when we had summer time in summer the way the cows wass putting themselves against it, but summer time in winter is chust laughing at Almighty God. Ay, chust that.'

'Would it be a barrel, Jockey?' Hugh asked in that slow voice of his, after his gaze had been concentrated on the floating object for a couple of minutes.

'Ach, we can't see yet awhile. I wouldn't say it wassn't a parrel. It might be a parrel from the *Chamaica Maid*.'

'It might be grapefruits,' said Hugh cautiously.

'*A Dhia, Dhia*, don't be saying that, Hugh. The crapefruits wass never in poxes. Chust lying on the *traìgh*. Crapefruits *chaca*!'

Hugh Macroon once more contemplated for a while the dark object in the grey water of the little bay.

'That's never a barrel, Jockey,' he decided at last. 'That's a box. The last box I had was lard.'

'*A Dhia*, who wants lart?' Jockey Stewart demanded indignantly.

'The women were pretty pleased about it,' said Hugh. 'It was good lard.'

'Ay, maybe it wass, but who wants to be putting himself out for lart? I like my own putter petter,' Jockey scoffed. 'She's ferry teep in the water,' he said a moment or two later. 'She's not full of emptiness whateffer is in her.'

'Ay, there's something in her right enough,' his companion agreed.

Four hours later the two crofters dragged up the sandy bank a black iron-bound chest on which was painted in white lettering:

The Manager
City and Suburban Bank
Lombard Street
London, E.C.
England

'Ah, well, I don't think she will be whisky, Jockey,' said Hugh Macroon.

'No, I don't think she will be,' his partner agreed regretfully.

'It's too heffy for whisky altogether. It's terrible heffy.'

'Look at all the iron that's round it. That would make her heavy enough if she wasn't heavy at all. The Manager, City and Suburban Bank,' Hugh Macroon read out slowly. 'I wonder if it could be gold,' he added after a long pause pregnant with speculation.

'Cold?' Jockey Stewart exclaimed shrilly.

'*Nach ist thu*,' his partner growled. 'Do you want everybody in the island to hear you screeching about it? If it isn't gold, it must be something pretty valuable, I believe. Who would be sending a box like this to a bank if it was just nothing at all?'

'Ach, it must be cold right enough,' Jockey declared. 'This is petter than that Chinese paper which came ashore by Ard Swish.'

A consignment of Chinese notes printed in England had been lost by enemy action a couple of years back, one of the cases of which had reached Little Todday.

'Now what do we do with it, that's the big question?' Hugh Macroon asked pensively.

'We'll take it back to your place or my place and open it right away,' Jockey told him.

'Ay, and let the whole island know we had something by the noise we'd be making,' Hugh jeered. 'No, no, we'll hide it tonight in your rick and you'll send word tomorrow morning will I come along to give you a hand with your plough because it's broken. Then if there's a lot of hammering they'll be thinking it's your plough.'

'Ferry good, ferry good, Hugh,' Jockey applauded. 'Ah, well, it's you that's smart right enough.'

'And now the sooner we get it to your rick the better. It'll be pretty near four o'clock before we get it safely stowed away. I wish it would cloud over again. The moon's as bright as day. She is a bit of a nuisance right enough.'

'Ach, I don't believe anybody will be about at this time of the night.'

'I wouldn't say Willie Munro wouldn't be about. He's always up early enough, seeing what there is moving while other people are still in their beds,' said Hugh.

Willie Munro was the only Protestant in Little Todday and therefore suspected by the rest of the island of an unbridled individualism of thought and action. The fact that he had been appointed a coast-watcher at the beginning of the war only added to the disrepute he enjoyed among his neighbours.

'Och, Willie, who minds about Willie?' John Stewart scoffed.

'I don't care nothing about Willie,' Hugh Macroon affirmed stoutly with the help of two negatives. 'All the same, if there's gold inside this case I'd just as soon that Willie didn't see it at all. So come along.'

Between them the two men lifted the black chest, which had no handles, and proceeded like a couple of crabs for a hundred yards. Then Jockey put his foot in a rabbit-burrow, and fell full length on the wet grass.

'*Ist*, man, you're making more noise than a lorry,' Hugh said crossly, as Jockey gurgled and gasped to recover the breath knocked out of him by the black chest. 'I never heard such a noise in my life.'

'The pox kicked me in the *stamac* like a horse,' Jockey explained. 'A *Dhia*, there was no life left in me at all. Never mind. On we go.'

He lifted his end of the box again, and Hugh suggested it might be easier if they took it in turns to walk backwards.

'Ay, and if I wass walking packwards and put my foot in another hole the pox would be more on top of me than effer. No, no, Hugh, we'll carry it chust the way we are.'

Two hundred yards further on Hugh whispered, '*Ist*,' and they stopped.

'Are you after hearing something?' Jockey murmured.

'I thought I saw something move, away there beyond the *sìthein*.'

The *sìthein* was one of the many rounded knolls which broke the level of the machair all over the island, but it had a certain renown as the one in which fairy music had been heard not so long ago.

'What were you seeing?' Jockey whispered.

'Just a kind of quick movement.'

'A rappit?'

'It was a bigger movement than a rabbit.'

The two men peered into the moonshine, listening. A curlew fluted far away. There was no other sound.

'Ach, I don't think it was anybody,' said Hugh, and the black chest was lifted again.

At last they reached Jockey Stewart's croft, which lay due south of Macroon's Bay, and the chest was carried to the rick in a corner of the field behind the little house. Enough hay was pulled out to make a hiding-place for the black chest, which was then carefully covered again.

'Ah, well, I'm sweating,' said Hugh.

'Ay, it's thirsty work right enough,' his partner agreed.

Then both of them sighed for the unattainable.

'Well, well, *matà oidhche mhath leat*,' Hugh said, turning toward his own croft.

'It's nearer to morning now,' said Jockey. 'I'll send Lachie or Florag along after school to say will you come and help me mend my plough. A *dhuine, dhuine*, if it iss cold that's in it I'll go to Obaig on Tuesday and find two pottles of whisky in this plack market they talk so much about in the papers. It'll have to be pretty plack if I can't see two pottles of whisky in it, ay, and perhaps more, by Chinko,' he added fervidly.

Hugh Macroon walked across to his croft and retired to bed without waking his wife. Jockey on the other hand when he went up to the bedroom felt too much excited by the thought of the gold that might be in the black chest to be able to get quietly into bed. Bean Yockey's vast bulk – she was the largest woman in the island – tranquilly sleeping filled him with a longing to wake her in order to talk about his plans for the future of the croft with the money that was going to be his. He had no intention of revealing the secret of the black chest, but he could talk about his plans without doing that. At the same time he could not quite bring himself to the point of prodding his wife in the back and expatiating forthwith upon his dreams of wealth. He decided to wake her strategically. To this end, after undressing, he knelt by the head of the bed and began to say his prayers at the top of that high piercing voice of his. Half-way through the *Paternoster* the bed quivered as Bean

Yockey stirred in her sleep. At the first *Ave* Bean Yockey moaned faintly. As the second *Ave* finished she turned over. In the middle of the third *Ave* she sat up in bed and gazed about her in affright.

'A *Mhuire mhàthair!* For the love of God, John, what is the matter?' she gasped. 'Have you hurt yourself?'

'*Ist*, woman, I'm at saying my prayers.'

His strategy having been successful, Jockey began the interrupted third *Ave* again and after crossing himself with exaggerated formality rose to his feet. His wife asked what time it was.

'Nearly fife o'clock,' she was told.

'John, have you been drinking?' she asked.

'Trinking?' he echoed indignantly. 'What would I be trinking?'

'God knows,' his wife replied devoutly. 'If you could be drinking that oil you could be drinking anything.'

The oil alluded to was a bottle of the finest vegetable oil used for delicate machinery which her husband had found two or three months ago on the *tràigh*, and which, after he had added some wood alcohol to it, he had defiantly declared to be as good as drambuie.

'Ah, well, *a Chairistiona*, not a trop of anything am I after trinking tonight,' he assured her.

'Where have you been then?'

'Nowhere at all. Chust nowhere at all. I was thinking I would go to Obaig on Tuesday and buy myself two cowss. Apperteen-Angus. Ay, and I wass thinking I would build a punkalow for towrists. We'll be having towrists like flice when the war's ofer. And I wass thinking I would . . .'

'It's a pity you weren't thinking you would go to your bed like a man with a little sense,' Bean Yockey interrupted sharply, 'instead of waking people out of their sleep, shouting like a great clown and then pretending it was your prayers you were saying. I'm sure I don't know what's come over you, man. What will the children be thinking if they hear their father talking the way a tinker would be ashamed to talk? Come to bed and stop your nonsense.'

'You titn't let me finish what I was coing to say. I wass thinking I would buy you a new coat. Is that nonsense?' Jockey demanded. Then feeling that he had extinguished his wife he extinguished the lamp as well and got into bed.

It was not one of Jockey's children who came round after school to ask for Hugh Macroon's help with the plough. It was Jockey himself who at nine o'clock was asking Bean Uisdein where her husband was.

'He's still in his bed,' said Mrs Hugh Macroon, a neat prim little woman of fifty, already grey.

'I'll go up if you please, Mrs Macroon,' said the crofter.

'It's not bad news for us?' Bean Uisdein asked in sudden alarm.

'Ay, it's terrible news,' said Jockey.

'It's not about Michael?'

Michael was her eldest son, a corporal in the Clanranalds fighting in North Africa.

'No, no, it's worse than that.'

'He's been killed!'

'Not at all. It's worse than that, I'm telling you. Chust let me see Hugh, if you please. It's not a family matter at all. It's a tissaster.'

Bean Uisdein stood aside for Jockey to go up to the bedroom. She longed to follow him lest indeed he should be bringing bad tidings of Michael, or of Anthony, her second boy, who was at sea. However, she had made it a rule of her married life never to be inquisitive about masculine affairs and she held herself in hand.

It was not easy to disconcert Hugh Macroon. Lying back in his bed that morning, he looked as calm as a monk who had long since learned to despise mortal fretfulness. The bald domed head upon the pillow was like a rock against which life's waves must beat in vain.

Yet, when Jockey announced that the black chest had vanished from the rick in which he and Hugh had hidden it hardly four hours ago, Hugh sat up in bed as suddenly as Bean Yockey had sat up at the sound of her husband's third *Ave.*

'Gone? The box is gone?' he repeated.

'Chust nothing but hay,' Jockey groaned.

'You must have looked in the wrong place,' his friend insisted.

'Wrong place? There's no place at all in the rick now, the way I'm after pulling it about. The missus sent Florag helter-skelter to Kiltod to fetch Dr Maclaren with the *Morning Star.*'

'How's the doctor going to find it?'

'She thinks I've gone daft. Och, it's a long story. I'll tell you some other time. The main point for us is to find out which pukkers have taken away our cold.'

'And it'll be pretty difficult,' said Hugh glumly. 'We can't go shouting about the island that we've lost a box of gold. We'd have the constable over in a twinkle. Ay, and before we knew where we were we'd be up before the *siorram* at Loch Fladdy and go to prisson, which wouldn't matter if we had the gold; but while we were in prisson the blaggarsts who've stolen our gold would be laughing at us. No, no, we'll just have to hold our tongues and open our eyes.'

'I opened my ice so wide this morning when I couldn't find our pox they nearly fell out,' said Jockey. 'Och, I wonder who it could have peen.'

'Didn't you hear a sound of anything?'

'I titn't hear a sount of nothing. I was snoring like a pick and talking away in my sleep, the missus said.'

'What were you talking about?' Hugh sternly demanded.

'Ay, I asked her that, and she told me I was talking about the Pearl Harper Hotel.'

'What kind of an hotel is that?'

'Och, how do I know what kind of an hotel one finds in one's sleep. I was shouting out, "No room in the Pearl Harper Hotel!" '

'No wonder your missus thought you were daft. What else did you talk about?' Hugh asked.

'Otters.'

'Otters? Why would you be talking about otters?'

'How would I know why I would be talking about otters? If I knew why I would be talking about otters in my sleep I wouldn't be talking about otters at all,' Jockey expostulated.

'You didn't say anything about the gold?' Hugh pressed.

'If I did, the *cailleach* never said a word about it.'

'Well, I'll get up and dress myself,' said Hugh. 'And then I think we'll be walking over to Kiltod.'

They reached the port and metropolis of Little Todday just as the Biffer was steering the *Kittiwake* with Mr Brown into the little harbour.

'The *Morning Star*'s not at her moorings,' Hugh observed. 'Joseph must have sent her for the Doctor after all.'

'Get away with you, man, Choseph wouldn't be doing such a thing chust on a word from the missus.'

'Still, it's queer right enough that the *Morning Star*'s away so early on a Monday morning. Joseph will have heard how you were pulling about your rick this morning,' said Hugh, his shrewd eyes glinting under puckered brows. 'Who's yon Rhode Island Red?'

The question referred to Mr Brown, whose plus-fours fluffing out above such thin ankles as he disembarked from the *Kittiwake* made the comparison to that particular breed of fowls a happy one.

'Ach, he will be one of those fellows from the Department of Agriculture. They all wear these bluss-fours,' Jockey replied.

'He might be an exciseman,' said Hugh suspiciously. 'Come to that, I wouldn't say he mightn't be a detective.'

'A detective? *A Dhia*, what's a detective going to be looking for in Todaidh Beag?'

'He might have heard about the gold?'

'How would he know the cold had come ashore here?'

'He might be making inquiries all the way up the islands,' said Hugh Macroon.

Just then Mr Brown approached them from the quay.

'Good morning,' he said, with synthetic geniality. 'It's a fine morning after yesterday's downpour. Do you happen to know anybody in Little Todday by the name of Macroon?'

The two crofters gazed at him in amazement for an instant. They were accustomed to silly questions from visitors, but this was so silly that they could not help believing that it was prompted by an ignorance assumed to cover a cunning purpose directed against the island and its inhabitants.

'Which Macroon would you be wanting?' Hugh asked.

'Mr Joseph Macroon. He has a shop in Kiltod, I believe.'

Hugh Macroon took his pipe out of his mouth and used it as a pointer to the post-office a few yards away.

'I'm interested in tweed,' Mr Brown continued. 'Do either of you know where any tweed is being woven in the islands?'

'Tweet?' Jockey exclaimed at the top of his high voice. 'There's no tweet being made in Little Todday. The Covernment want coupons for yarn. Who's going to be wearing himself out making tweet when the Covernment does a stupid thing like that?'

'May I inquire your name?' the visitor asked.

'Perhaps you'd like to have a look at my identity cart?' Jockey suggested.

'No, no, thank you,' said Mr Brown quickly. 'That's none of my business. My name is Brown.'

'Well, my name is Stewart. Chon Stewart,' said Jockey.

'I'm very pleased to meet you, Mr Stewart.' Mr Brown looked

inquiringly at Hugh, who did not volunteer his name, but stared hard at the stranger, puffing away at his pipe.

'Chust a Chessie,' Jockey commented when Mr Brown had entered Joseph's shop.

'Ay, he may be just a Jessie,' said Hugh. 'But I believe he's up to no good.'

The two men walked along the quay to greet the Biffer.

'What's that *dreathan-donn* you had perched in your boat, Airchie?' Hugh asked, reducing the Biffer's passenger from a Rhode Island Red to a brown wren.

'*A Chruithear*,' exclaimed the Biffer, spitting over the side of the *Kittiwake*. 'He was preaching me a sairmon about careless talk all the way over the Coolish. I don't know what to make of him at all. He was asking whether he would get any chocolate at Joseph Macroon's shop.'

'Och, he'll be one of these snoobers from the Ministry of Food,' said Jockey. 'We had one of them round last autumn, moaning and croaning that he was starfing and pecking for shooker and tea and putter and cham and when the merchants took pity on the poor *truaghan* and let him have what he wanted without his ration card they wass all threatened to be prosecuted from Inverness. Ach, I don't like such tirty cames at all.'

He spat over one side of the quay. Hugh Macroon spat over the other side. The Biffer spat over the side of his boat.

'Ah, well, he won't get much out of Iosaiph,' said Hugh Macroon. 'Have you had much in along the shore on Todaidh Mór, Airchie, after these gales?'

'Not a great deal at all. I had some tins of what they call sweet corn. *A Chruithear*, I never tasted such stuff. We gave it to the hens. They liked it fine. Hens are queer right enough, what they'll be eating. Ach, it's whisky we're wanting, not sweet corn.'

'*Seadh gu dearbh*. Yes, indeed,' said Hugh, like the sound of a great Amen.

He had been right in supposing that Mr Brown would find it difficult to get anything out of Joseph Macroon. Joseph was in a mood that morning when it was even more difficult to pin him down to anything definite than on the night the Sergeant-major tried to pin him down about the marriage of his daughter. He had noticed Mr Brown making his way along to the post-office and had immediately decided that he was utterly uninterested in the newcomer's past, present or future.

So when Mr Brown by way of opening the conversation asked if he had any chocolate Joseph repeated the word as if he had never heard it before.

'Chocolate? Ah, chocolate. No, no, there's no chocolate.'

'It's in short supply, is it?'

'No supply at all.'

Mr Brown went on to explain that he was interested in tweed.

'Ah, beautiful stuff,' Joseph sighed in a rapture of his own. 'When will we see it again? You won't find a drop of it in Little Todday.'

'A drop of tweed is a new expression to me,' said Mr Brown.

'Ay,' Joseph murmured remotely.

Then he began to hum to himself, a sure sign of Joseph's intense preoccupation, after which he stopped abruptly and muttered 'Ay, ay, ay,' to that other self with whom he had been communing.

'Brown is my name,' said the visitor, stroking his moustache. Beyond the counter he had caught a glimpse of a most attractive girl in the little room behind.

'Ah, Brown, Brown,' Joseph repeated. 'That will be a well-known name in England?'

'It's fairly common, yes.'

'Ay, Ernest Brown, Secretary for Scotland. I wrote to him the other day about the new school we're wanting in Kiltod. Have you met Father Macalister, Mr Brown?'

'No, this is my first visit to Little Todday.'

'Ah, you'll have to meet him. I'll take you along now. He lives close by.'

Almost before he was aware of it Mr Brown found himself following Joseph Macroon's red knitted cap towards the Chapel House.

'Ay, I told you he wouldn't get nothing out of Iosaiph,' Hugh Macroon observed to John Stewart.

'A *Dhia*, he was pretty quick unloading that cargo,' Jockey exclaimed, when almost as soon as he had entered the priest's house Joseph was hurrying back to his own shop.

Indeed, all that Joseph had said was:

'Here's Mr Brown, Father. And you'll please excuse me, Father, for I'm rather busy this morning.'

Father James Macalister by no means conformed to Mr Brown's conception of what priests looked like, and he conformed still less to his notions of how they behaved.

'Sit right down, Mr Brown,' he was bidden in a profound bass. 'I don't know who you are. But I suppose Joseph wants to get rid of you. *Am bheil Gàidhlig agaibh?*'

Mr Brown looked as bewildered as he felt.

'Ah, well, well, you evidently don't understand our lovely and glorious language. What a pity!' The sigh that followed this ejaculation was so loud and so deep that Mr Brown was on the point of asking the priest if he had rheumatism, when he went on. 'And what brings you to Little Todday, Mr Brown?'

'I thought I'd like to see it.'

'Good shooting!'

'And then I was wondering if I would find any tweed here. I'm a tweed merchant.'

'Are you really now?' the priest exclaimed with such sonority that for a moment Lieutenant Boggust of the Security Intelligence Corps was afraid that he was like a joint of meat from which the cover has been taken.

'Oh, yes,' he said nervously, 'I do quite a lot of business.'

'You won't do much business on Little Todday,' the priest assured him.

'So I understand from Mr Macroon. I suppose the war has affected everything in the island.'

'Och, we're standing up to Hitler in our own way. We've a very fine Home Guard.'

'Men very keen, eh? That's good to hear.'

'Ay, it's a pity we can't send them out to North Africa, and then we might get a move on there.'

'Oh, I think things are moving pretty well out there as they are.'

'Perhaps they are. Perhaps they are. I'm still waiting for a wireless battery. Did Celtic win on Saturday?'

'I'm afraid I don't listen to the football results, padre.'

'Ah well, if you don't speak Gaelic, Mr Brown, you speak Spanish really beautifully.'

'No, I don't speak Spanish either.'

'Don't you really now? Ah well, I thought you did. But then I make these peculiar mistakes sometimes.' The priest exhaled another of those loud and deep sighs. He was finding Mr Brown a little too much of a good thing so soon after his breakfast.

'I'm afraid I'm interrupting your work, padre,' said the visitor.

'Ah well, a parish priest is kept pretty well occupied,' Father

Macalister admitted, and when his guest had departed he settled down again in his armchair and went on with the Wild West thriller which Mr Brown's visit had interrupted.

Mr Brown himself found the people of Little Todday extraordinarily stupid. Dullness, not defeatism, seemed their characteristic. At whatever house he called he was received with stares and sheepish monosyllables. He wondered whether to attribute this stupidity to Catholicism or inbreeding, and decided finally that it must be a mixture of both.

'One would almost think that the word had gone round to say nothing to me,' he said to himself.

And indeed that is just what the word had gone round to say. Theories about what his real object was in coming to Little Todday were many and various, but on one thing all were agreed: he was certainly not a tweed merchant. On the other hand if that seems to reflect on the efficiency of the Security Intelligence Corps in disguising itself it must be said at once that nobody suspected he was a Security Intelligence officer. He was credited with being a snooper from the Ministry of Food, a snooper from the Ministry of Shipping, and generally with being a snooper from the Government. It was speculated whether he was a coastguard in disguise, a deserter from the army, or a detective looking for a deserter from the army. Curiously perhaps, in only one house was he confidently declared to be a German spy. Optimism led some people to believe he was an exciseman because a visit from an exciseman would mean that the Government was expecting spirits to come ashore, and many a man who had been discouraged by grapefruit from beachcombing resolved to be about betimes on the chance that a barrel of rum would be sighted again.

In justice to the usual hospitality of the islanders which was denied to Mr Brown it must be borne in mind that there was hardly a house on Little Todday which did not contain a certain amount of undeclared treasure trove from the sea — turpentine, cheese, lard, tinned asparagus, salt (very salt) butter, tyres, pit props, paper, tomato juice, machine oil, lifebelts, in fact almost everything that could be thought of except spirituous liquors. And besides the treasure trove from the sea there was hardly a house which had not a bit of that Nelson whose forced landing had caused so much anxiety to Captain Waggett. Naturally the people of Little Todday did not want to entertain a guest who might report against them. So when Mr Brown arrived back at the Snorvig Hotel that afternoon he was tired and hungry, and when Mr Macintosh inquired what he had thought of the island he answered crossly that he thought it contained the dullest people he had met since he arrived in Scotland.

'You surprise me, Mr Brown. Did you come across my old friend, Father Macalister?'

'I thought him a most eccentric sort of person. He's not at all my idea of a priest,' Mr Brown snapped. 'And as for that fellow Macroon you made such a point of my seeing I thought him half-witted.'

'You're wrong there, Mr Brown,' the traveller insisted. 'Oh, you're very far out there. Joseph Macroon is as able a merchant as is anywhere in the Islands.'

Mr Brown shrugged his shoulders disdainfully and asked his fellow-guest if he knew what there was for dinner.

'Or rather tea I suppose it should be called,' he added.

'I don't know at all, Mr Brown,' the traveller replied. 'But it'll likely be mutton.'

Lieutenant Boggust was thankful that tomorrow he would be himself again at Nobost, leaving behind him Mr Brown and, he hoped, his indigestion for ever.

'I wonder what's keeping Hugh Macroon and John Stewart hanging about all day in Kiltod,' Joseph Macroon said to Peggy at dusk.

'They were asking where Kenny was a while ago,' she told him.

What exactly was keeping Hugh Macroon and John Stewart hanging about in Kiltod was a strong suspicion (and well Joseph knew it) that wherever the black chest was now it would reach the big shed at the back of Joseph Macroon's house some time in the course of the night. From the start Hugh had made up his mind that the man most likely to have removed the chest from Jockey's rick was the man who lived on the next croft, and that was Willie Munro. If that was so, Hugh argued, Willie Munro as a coast-watcher would be frightened to break open the chest himself. If it had been whisky or rum, as no doubt he had hoped it was when he must have seen them hiding it, that would have been a different matter. He would just have buried it and drunk the contents at his leisure. But if when he saw it he suspected that it contained gold, he would require help if it was to be safely negotiated. The man he would turn to would be Joseph Macroon, who was the only man on the island able to handle such a business. Indeed, Hugh himself had been puzzled to know how he and Jockey were going to deal with the gold when they opened the chest, particularly as Jockey, good man as he was with cattle, was not conspicuously sensible about anything else. His suspicion that the chest would reach Joseph was confirmed when he heard that Willie Munro had come in to Kiltod that morning at eight o'clock and that he had gone off with Kenny in the *Morning Star* shortly before nine, since when neither of them had been seen.

Not long after Joseph made that remark to Peggy, Hugh, who had been worrying himself all day to think out a plan for recovering the chest if he did succeed in tracking it to Joseph, said to Jockey:

'I believe we'll go and see Father James. I didn't like the look of that fellow who was in and out of every house all day. I'd sooner Joseph had it than the Government.'

'Choseph?' Jockey piped. 'I'd rather put it back in the sea than let him or that pukker Willie Munro have as much as one colden pound. But come along, Hugh. We'll see what Father Chames has to say about it all.'

Father Macalister listened to the tale of the night's find with a grave face.

'Ay, ay, you found a crock of gold,' he said, when Hugh had finished, 'and the fairies took it away from you. Isn't that awful? And you think it will be in Joseph's shed by dark? Ah well, I daresay that's not a bad guess. But look here, my boys, if it is gold, it's a pretty serious matter not to declare it. It'll puzzle even Joseph to get away with that one. You leave it to me. I'll tackle Joseph. You go home, and come and see me tomorrow evening and I'll give you the latest intelligence. I wish I could promise you a good dram . . .' he exhaled one of his tremendous sighs '. . . but who knows? We've kept the Faith, and Almighty God won't forget us. No, no, no. The Israelites were in a pretty poor way when the manna fell from Heaven. You remember that peculiar business, Hugh?'

'Ay, Father, though I never understood what kind of stuff it was at all.'

'I don't think anybody does, my boy, but when it falls on Todaidh Beag I believe it will taste and smell very like *uisge beatha*.'

'The water of life,' Jockey piped. 'It's a pewtiful name right enough, Father Chames.'

'Oh, by Chinko, yes, Chockey, it's really pewtiful,' Father Macalister declared with a magnificent guffaw.

At 1 a.m. Joseph Macroon, wearing his red knitted cap and looking more than ever like a troll at his traditional business, was hammering away at the black chest in the great shed at the back of his house which was heaped high with the lumber of a lifetime. He had already wrenched up all but one of the iron bands when there was a loud knocking on the bolted door.

'A *Thighearna*, who is that?' quaked Willie Munro, a little swarthy man with a yellowish complexion.

'*Co tha'n sud?*' Joseph asked sharply. 'Who is it?'

'Winston Churchill,' a tremendous voice without proclaimed.

'A *Dhia*, it's Father James,' exclaimed Joseph irritably. 'What can he be wanting at this hour of the night? What are you wanting?' he shouted.

'The crock of gold,' Father Macalister boomed in response.

'It's no use trying to deceive that man,' Joseph muttered. 'He has a nose on him like a blind man.' He went across to the door and unbolted it. The parish priest strode in.

'You'd better finish your work,' he said. 'And you'd better be getting back home,' he added, turning to Willie Munro. 'You're not a member of my flock, thank God, so I just won't tell you what I think of a chap who plays a dirty trick on his neighbour like yours.'

Willie Munro hesitated for a moment, and then hurried out into the night.

Joseph wrenched off the final bar and levered up the lid of the black chest with a chisel.

When Father Macalister saw what the contents were he laughed and laughed and laughed until Joseph thought that the lumber of a lifetime would come clattering down upon them. The priest stamped about the shed, slapping his thighs and wheezing and coughing and laughing.

'Ay, it's pretty comical right enough,' Joseph allowed, without a smile on his own face.

This sent Father James off into another spasm of mirth until at last he sat down on a packing-case and mopped his eyes.

'And what will I do with it, Father?'

'Send it to Mr Brown,' the priest replied.

And then he started to laugh again uncontrollably.

On the following afternoon when Mr Brown went into his cabin on the *Island Queen* to return to Nobost he found in the middle of it a black chest tied with rope. He read the address printed in white letters and rang for the Steward.

'This has been put in my cabin by mistake.'

'No, sir, it's for you,' the Steward said. 'You'll see your name on the label.'

And sure enough on the label was written *Mr Brown, Tweed Merchant, c/o S.S. Island Queen.*

'But who brought it on board?' Mr Brown asked.

'I don't really know, sir,' said the Steward.

Lieutenant Boggust was too good an Intelligence officer to betray mystification in the presence of a ship's steward.

'I think I know what it is,' he said. 'It's tweed.'

On the way up to Nobost Mr Brown was tempted to undo the chest and see what was inside, but he was reverting so rapidly now to Lieutenant Boggust that he thought it would be more dignified to refrain. Besides, it would be interesting for Quiblick to be present when the chest was opened. After all it might be anything.

So the black chest reached Nobost Lodge intact so far as Lieutenant Boggust was concerned.

'Hullo, Boggust, had a fruitful journey?' his chief asked. Major Quiblick was in uniform, a lantern-jawed man with the expression of a professional palmist, who had become a major so recently that he was still as proud of his crown as a king.

'I think so, sir. I'll get out a full report for you tomorrow. You'll probably want to strafe one or two people in both islands.'

'What on earth's that black box?' his chief asked. Lieutenant Boggust told him of the way it had arrived.

'We'd better open it,' said the Major. 'What do you suppose it is?'

'I haven't a notion, unless it's tweed.'

'Tweed?'

'My cover, sir.'

'Oh, yes, quite.'

Lieutenant Boggust unroped the black chest and opened the lid.

'Good God, what on earth is it?' the Major exclaimed.

'It looks like some kind of vase, sir.'

'It looks to me more like an urn,' said the Major.

Lieutenant Boggust lifted the vessel out of the heavy box. It *was* a metal urn.

'What's that label round it say?'

Lieutenant Boggust read:

The ashes of Mr H. J. Smith who was cremated at Toronto, December 10th,

1942. Forwarded to the Manager, City and Suburban Bank, Lombard Street, London, Eng., in accordance with instructions received.

'Well, I'm da . . .' but the Major stopped himself in time and saluted the urn with solemn respect. 'Why on earth was this sent to you?' he asked his subaltern.

'I really can't imagine, sir,' Lieutenant Boggust replied.

'I'm not in the picture either,' said Major Quiblick. 'Do you think it's a joke?'

'I think it's more likely to be a mistake, sir.'

'We'd better send it on to the consignee,' the Major decided.

'I couldn't agree more, sir,' said his subaltern fervidly.

Chapter 8

THE DROUGHT

March came in on Monday like a very wet lamb that year, but by the end of the week the two Toddays, except for a begrudged and often acrimoniously contested half-pint of beer a day for the individual drinker, were more dry than they had been yet. Except in a securely locked cupboard in Snorvig House there was not a single drop of whisky in either of the islands, and the only thoroughly happy creature, Catholic or Protestant, was Mrs Campbell. She thrived on the discomfort of her neighbours, the discomfiture of the young woman who had dared to aspire to her son's hand, and the distress of that son himself.

That George was weak nobody denied, but there was not a man in Garryboo or that matter in all Todaidh Mór who was prepared to brag that he would never allow any woman to treat him as Mrs Campbell was treating her son.

'Ach, I don't know at all what we're all coming to, Sammy,' observed Angus MacCormac. 'I'm almost afraid to light up a pipe, the hair on my face is that dry.'

And indeed as he brushed that haycock of a moustache away from his lips it did seem to be shrinking.

'Ay, he ought to put his foot down right enough,' Sammy MacCodrum declared. 'But the Minister himself is afraid to put his foot down to yon woman. She was after coming out of the Manse yesterday with a face on her as fierce as a pollisman. "Och," I said to Macrae, "if you had a face on you like Mrs Campbell, constable, you'd scare all the Snorvig stiffs into law and order chust by looking out of your own door." '

'Ay, I believe he would,' Angus agreed, puffing away at his pipe, which was making noises like a geyser about to erupt.

'And it's time they wass scared,' Sammy went on. 'Did you hear the latest?'

'Breaking into the store and taking away the potatoes the Government sent for us to live on when the invasion comes?' Angus asked.

'Ach, who cares about patatas? No, no, throwing class all over the road and puncturing all the tyres. *A Chruthadair*, as if it wassn't bad enough to be seeing nothing but empty class in the hotel par!'

'I believe the situation will have taken the heart out of Macrae,' Angus MacCormac said gravely.

'It's after taking the heart out of all of us except Hitler and Copples and Mistress Campbell. They're chust enchoying themselfs.'

'Ay, I believe they will be.'

The two friends shook their heads gloomily. In the distance they could hear the voices of their wives summoning them for some domestic task. The low state of their morale made even procrastination savourless. They turned their faces meekly towards tyranny and obeyed the summons.

At Watasett Catriona was inclined to criticize George's feeble surrender to his mother's intransigence.

'It's all very well to say he can't help himself, Norman,' she complained to her brother. 'If he can't help himself, how is he ever going to be able to help me?'

'Ach, it'll be all right when you're married,' Norman argued.

'And if he hasn't the pluck to ask me to tea at his own house, how will he ever find the pluck to marry me?' Catriona asked indignantly. 'I believe I'll just write and tell him it was all a mistake. He can marry Jemima Ross.'

'If I could only get outside a couple of really good drams I'd go along and tackle the old lady myself,' her brother avowed.

'Thank you for nothing,' said his sister tartly. 'It's not me that is going to be married on the strength of my brother's long tongue when he's carrying a big load of whisky.'

'Say that again for God's sake. A big load of whisky! Lassie, you're just speaking the purest poetry.'

'Ach, be done with your nonsense. I've no patience with you,' Catriona exclaimed, and she flounced off to her kitchen. 'Just as soft as dough, that's what men are,' she grumbled to herself as she wielded the rolling-pin.

Not long after this conversation Dr Maclaren called in the Watasett schoolhouse on the way up to have a look at a couple of patients he had in Knockdown.

'Ah, well, I'm sorry for you, Catriona, because George is being so feeble, and I'm sorry for your brother because he can't enjoy a dram with various old friends before he goes into uniform, and I'm sorry for Big Roderick who's being driven nearly off his head by having to say "no" to so many customers, and I'm sorry for all the poor folk on Little Todday facing the grim prospect of Lent without any ammunition, and I'm sorry for John Beaton on whom I simply won't look in nowadays because he suffers so much from an enforced inhospitality, and I'm more than sorry for Father James and myself because both of us really require fortifying; but I'm sorriest of all for old Hector MacRurie who has made up his mind that he will shortly have to face his Maker without a dram inside him to sustain him through the ordeal. It makes me feel I'm no kind of a doctor at all when I visit the old man and can give him nothing better for his rheumatics than some confounded extract of coal tar.'

Hector MacRurie was a white-haired crofter who had fought in the Boer War with the Lovat Scouts and was now looked after by a middle-aged unmarried daughter, his wife having died the previous year. Dr Maclaren found the old man in a more than usually pessimistic mood that afternoon when he went upstairs to his room in the little house at Knockdown. Hector was sitting up in bed, gazing out of the small window at the fog drifting in from the sea and slowly obliterating the rocky moorland between his croft and the cliff's edge eastward.

'No boat today, Hector,' said the doctor. 'There's a lot of fog about. So if there's any whisky on board we shan't see it till Monday at the earliest.'

'Ay, ay, it's the Sabbath tomorrow,' the old man muttered. 'The *Queen* would never be crossing the Minch on the Sabbath. And I believe it will be thicker yet, Doctor.'

'How are you feeling today?'

'Och, I don't feel like anything at all, Doctor. Bones, that's all. Ay, ay, just bones, and most of them aching at that.'

'I've brought you a few ounces of twist, Hector.'

'*Móran taing*, Doctor. It is very kind of you. *Móran taing*. Thank you very much. But my pipe has gone. Just fell to pieces on me. I sent Mairead down to John MacLean's shop. Nothing doing. Not a pipe to be got. And John says he doesn't know when he'll be having another pipe, they're that hard to come by. Och, well, well, I don't believe the world has been in such a terrible mess since the Lord sent the Flood.'

The old man looked across to where on the wall hung a steel engraving, spotted and stained appropriately with damp, of the last pair of animals entering the Ark.

'Come, come, we can't have you cut off smoking as well as everything else,' the doctor exclaimed. 'Here's a pipe of mine. It's what they call a Lovat which is just the shape for you.'

'Och, I couldn't be robbing you of your own pipe, Doctor. You're too kind altogether.'

'Come on, Hector, take this pipe and fill it. Have you never heard of doctor's orders?'

The old man protested for a few moments, but there was no resisting Dr Maclaren's orders. Soon he was rubbing the twist in his furrowed palms, and a minute later he was puffing away at the pipe.

'Ah well, it's yourself, Doctor, that is a doctor right enough,' the old man declared. 'So this is a Lovat pipe, is it? Isn't that beautiful, now? Och, we had some grand times with the Scouts in the old days. The old days, ay, and they are pretty old days,' he sighed. 'Ay, it was South Africa then. Now it's North Africa. I suppose there's no news of Ben Nevis paying us another visit on Todaidh Mór, Doctor?'

'I've not heard of any.'

'I had a fine crack with him about the old days in the Scouts when he came over with the Home Guard. That was before the *cailleach* went ahead of me. He gave me the biggest dram I ever had in all my life that day. Och, I seemed to float in the air all the way back from Snorvig to Knockdown. "My goodness," the *cailleach* said when I got home, "you're looking wild, Eachainn." "Ay, woman," I said, "and I'm feeling pretty wild. I'm after having the biggest dram I ever had in my life with Ben Nevis, and I hadn't seen the man for forty years." Well, I'd like to have one more really good dram, Doctor, before I join the *cailleach*. Glenbogle's Pride, that was what the whisky was called. His butler told me. Ah, well, it was wonderful stuff right enough.'

'I've a good mind to write to Ben Nevis and tell him an old friend is sighing his heart away for another dram of that whisky,' the Doctor declared.

'No, no, Doctor. I wouldn't have you do that for anything. Och, he's a fine gentleman, the finest gentleman in Scotland, is Ben Nevis, but I wouldn't like to be accepting a bottle of his whisky if somebody was asking him for it.'

Dr Maclaren saw that the old man's pride had been wounded by his suggestion and he did not press it.

'Well, Hector, you know best, but I'm sure Ben Nevis would be only too glad to hear he could be of use to an old friend.'

'Och, it's not that I'm dependent on a dram, as you know yourself, Doctor. It's just the idea that you can't have one. We've never been used to that all our lives. And I don't believe I'll be here at all much longer.'

'Nonsense,' the Doctor interjected. 'You've many years to live yet. You'll be about again by early summer.'

'Ah, well, I know better, Doctor, and by that I don't mean any disrespect to yourself as a doctor. Ay, I'm looking at life the way I'm looking at my croft just now and seeing how the fog is creeping in from the sea and covering it up and turning it into just nothing at all.'

The old man gazed out of the window at the view that was gradually being annihilated.

'You're not the only one in Great Todday who's looking at life like that just now, Hector,' the Doctor assured him earnestly. 'No, nor in Little Todday either. We're all watching it fade away from us. But that won't last any more than the fog will last. Whisky will come again and the sun will shine again. And I'll promise you this, Hector. The first bottle of whisky I put my hands on, I'm going to jump straight into my car and I'm coming along with it to Knockdown. And I'm going to sit right where I'm sitting now and Mairead's going to bring up two glasses — not two wee dram glasses . . . no, no, I'm telling you . . . a couple of tumblers you'd ordinarily see filled up with beer . . . and, Hector, I'm going to fill each of them right up with whisky and you and I are going to look each other in the eyes, the two old friends that we are, and I can hear the words chiming in my mind like a noble peal of bells. *Slàinte mhath, slàinte mhór*. And then the two of us are going to drain our glasses to the last golden heart-warming drop.'

'*A Chruithear bheannaichte!*' the old man gasped reverently. 'What a beautiful dream, Doctor!'

Then a twinge of rheumatism made his face contract with pain.

'But it is only a dream,' he added sadly.

'It's a dream that's coming true,' Dr Maclaren averred.

'My goodness, Doctor, if it does, you'll have to be careful not to drive back to Snorvig over the top of Ben Sticla. Ay, you may be floating yourself the way I was when Ben Nevis gave me that great dram yon time, but your car won't be floating and you'll have to be a bit careful. And indeed, I believe you'd be wise to be soon on the road now. It's thickening all the time.'

'Right, I'll be leaving you now. I believe you're feeling better already.'

'Och, I'm feeling the better for seeing you, right enough,' the old man admitted. 'He'd be a queer kind of a crayture who wouldn't be the better for seeing you, Doctor. And thank you again for the pipe and the tobacco. Ay, I'll admit I was feeling pretty far down the drain when my old pipe went to pieces on me. Och, I was just saying to myself, "*Eachainn, a bhalaich*, you may as well go to pieces yourself now." And then you were after coming along.'

The old man held out his gnarled fist. Dr Maclaren grasped it.

'We're going to get that great dram, Hector,' he said. 'I feel it in my bones.'

'Is that so? I wish my bones would be feeling that kind of a feeling instead of what they will be feeling, the rascals,' the old man observed, a twinkle in his eyes as welcome to the Doctor as the sight of the stars to a steersman whose ship was wrapped in such a fog as was now drifting in from the sea.

'Ah, you're laughing at me now,' said Dr Maclaren. 'But you'll be laughing with me when I bring that bottle along.'

'Ach, I believe you'll have to distil it yourself, Doctor, in a *poit dhubh*. Oh, I've had a *poit dhubh* myself and made the stuff. It was a grand sight on a fine summer's morning to see the way the thin blue smoke of it would be stealing into the sky so quiet.'

'Did the exciseman ever catch you out?'

The old man gave a contemptuous ejaculation.

'Not he! He had a long nose on him right enough, but it wasn't long enough to find that wee lochan on Ben Bustival beside which I had my *poit dhubh*. Ay, he was a smart fellow all the same. A *Leodhasach*, he was . . . Alec Macaulay was his name, and he was as black as my own *poit dhubh*. Ay, he was that. He went over to Easter Ross when he left the Islands and I never heard what became of him after.'

'We're not much troubled by the present man, Ferguson.'

'I never set eyes on him yet,' said Hector.

'He's from Aberdeen.'

'Ay, they think themselves pretty smart over there,' Hector chuckled. 'But och, what's the good of talking? We're all keeping the law nowadays. Ay, ration cards and coupons and identity cards and filling up forms instead of glasses. Och, I won't be so sorry at all to be leaving it.'

'You'll feel differently when I arrive with that bottle,' Dr Maclaren declared. 'And now I really must be getting back.'

'Ay, indeed you must, Doctor. My goodness, I hope you'll be all right on the road. It's pretty rough between here and Bobanish. I believe the County Council thinks we're just a lot of savages at this end of the island.'

'I'll take the road by the west,' said the Doctor. 'It'll be tricky going along by Loch Bob in this fog, and it may be clearer on the other side. Besides, the surface will be much better once I'm past Garryboo.'

Dr Maclaren's hope of getting out of the fog on the west side was not fulfilled. Indeed, it was thicker there if anything. Not so much as a rooftop in Garryboo itself was visible from the road. Visibility was hardly as much as twenty yards and he drove very slowly, hooting almost continuously to protect himself as far as possible against the recklessness of one or two of the lorry drivers. He was glad when he reached home safely.

'It's about the worst fog I ever remember in the Islands,' he said to Mrs Wishart, his grim but extremely competent middle-aged house-keeper from Fife.

Mrs Wishart pursed her tight lips. She took an equally low view of the weather and the people of the two Toddays, and she was not prepared to accept the worst behaviour by either as anything but an everyday occurrence.

'It's always rain or wind or mist out here,' she complained acidly.

'Ah now, come, Mrs Wishart, we very very seldom get fog. You'll get much more fog in the Kingdom of Fife. Any messages while I was out?'

'Not one.'

'Thank God for that! We'll have no boat this evening. I doubt if we'll get a boat till Tuesday.'

'I'm not worrying about that, Doctor. Indeed, if I was to worry myself every time the boat did not come I'd be in my grave by now.'

At that moment the sound of the *Island Queen*'s siren in the Coolish betrayed Dr Maclaren's prophecy about her non-arrival.

'By Jove, I may get a dram tonight, after all,' he exclaimed. 'Really, Captain MacKechnie's a great seaman. Who'd have expected him in this fog?'

There was a full gathering at the bar that evening in the hope that Roderick's stock would have been replenished; but those who left their firesides to visit the hotel were disappointed. Half a pint of beer a head had to be eked out until closing time.

To make up for the lack of whisky on such a frore foggy night, some of Roderick's customers and Roderick himself had received letters from Major Quiblick which certainly had a warming influence.

'What's this at all?' exclaimed Ruairidh Mór himself, scanning through his spectacles a letter in a buff envelope O.H.M.S. 'Who is this Major Quibalick?'

He began to read it aloud:

'Teer Sir,

I have to notify you that I have received a most unfavourable report about the atmosphere of the Snorvig Hotel . . .'

Roderick broke off in wrath.

'Atmosphere? There was neffer a finer atmosphere in the whole of the Islands. *Mac an diabhoil*, does he think that he knows more than the finest ladies and chentlemen in the country what iss a good atmosphere? Wassn't the Tuke of Ross himself after shaking me by the hand and conkratulating me on the air in the Snorvig Hotel? "It is petter than my own castle, Mr MacRurie," says the Tuke to me.'

'Let's hear what else my bold major says,' said the Biffer. 'I'm after having a letter from the man myself.'

Roderick continued:

'I am informed that the conversation there is often unduly critical of the conduct of the war by those who carry upon their shoulders a great weight of responsibility. I earnestly hope that in future you will exercise your influence as landlord to check such criticism to the best of your ability. We must all remember that we are fighting for our existence against a skilful and ruthless enemy and that nothing will encourage him so much as to suppose that the people of Great Britain are losing confidence in their leaders.

I am sure that you will take whatever steps you consider appropriate to improve the atmosphere of the Snorvig Hotel and so avoid putting me under the unpleasant necessity of taking further action.'

'And he signs himself P. Saint John Quibalick, Major Sick,' Roderick added.

'Sick?' somebody repeated.

'Ay, S.I.C. And Saint John!' Roderick gasped. 'Look at that now for a piece of impudence. Joseph Macroon himself would neffer be signing himself Saint John.'

'S.I.C. means Security Intelligence Corpse,' the Biffer translated. 'It's written the same on his letter to me.'

'No intelligence at all,' Roderick scoffed. 'Chust a lot of nonsense. What is the clown after saying to you, Airchie?'

The Biffer began to read his letter:

Dear Sir,

I have to notify you that I have received a report that on at least three occasions recently you indulged in careless talk about the movements of shipping viz. . . .'

'What kind of ship is that? Viz?' asked the Snorvig fisherman who on a former occasion questioned Captain Waggett's ability to defeat Hitler on his own. Alan Galbraith was his name, but he was always known as Drooby, a nickname the origin of which none could tell except Drooby himself, and he never would. He was a big, brawny, red-faced man, and his own boat, a Zulu, was called the *Flying Fish*.

'I don't believe it's a ship at all,' said the Biffer. 'It's one of those words these Government fellows write when they want to get anybody in a bit of a muddle about how they have to fill up a form. Where was I? Ay, *the movements of shipping viz. on the 27th ult.* . . .'

'What's an ult?' asked Drooby.

'That's another kind of a viz. Och, I'll never be finished reading my letter, Drooby, if you keep on asking so many questions. You ought to belong to the Government yourself. *Viz. on the 27th ult., on the 28th ult., and on the 1st inst.*'

Drooby shook his head.

'Och, it's easy to see he means last Saturday, Sunday, and Monday,' said the Biffer.

'Why can't he say Saturday, Sunday, and Monday, if that's what he means?' Drooby asked.

'Because that's the way these fellows have to write. Ult. means February.'

'You were after saying just now it meant Saturday,' Drooby pointed out sceptically.

'Let the man read his letter, Alan,' said Roderick. 'You and your ult. and your viz. It's the right way when you're sending an official communication. You get plenty such letters when you're on the County Council. Och, I don't pay any attention to them. Go on, Airchie.'

The Biffer resumed the reading of his letter from Major Quiblick:

'I realize that you did not intend to do any harm, but in mentioning that your son was sailing from a certain port at a certain time for a certain destination you might have been giving valuable assistance to enemy agents who are always on the . . .'

The Biffer hesitated and frowned. 'Do you ever have this one on the Council, Roderick,' he broke off to ask, 'Quy vyve?'

'Quy vyve?' the master of the house repeated. 'No, I never heard that one before. Ay, that's a new one to me, right enough.'

The Biffer continued:

'On the qui vive for information about the movement of shipping which can be communicated to enemy submarines. I hope that in future you will keep a close check on your tongue, and if no further reports are received of indulgence by you in careless talk I shall be spared the unpleasant necessity of taking further action.'

'Oh, well, well, did anybody ever hear the like of such nonsense? But I know who it was. It was that fellow Brown who was staying in the hotel over last week-end. I took him over to Kiltod.'

'The tweed merchant?' asked Roderick.

'Tweed merchant. All the tweed he ever bought he put round his own backside,' the Biffer scoffed. 'Ah, well, they knew better how to deal with that fellow in Todaidh Beag. Not a word could he get out of them, no, and not a bite of food or so much as a glass of milk. Let the rascal come back here again and I'll throw him off the end of the pier. Mr Brown? He'll be all the colours of the rainbow before I've finished with him.'

'Wait a bit now, Airchie,' Roderick advised cautiously. 'You want to go a bit slow with these fellows from the Government.'

'I'll go as slow or as quick as I've a mind to go, Roderick, Government or no Government. Careless talk! Ay, he'll talk a bit careless when I've knocked all his teeth out on him. Aren't you after having a letter, Drooby? You were opening your mouth pretty wide about the Home Guard when this Brown was in the bar last Saturday.'

'I wasn't in at the post-office,' said Drooby. 'But if I'll have a letter on Monday morning I'll throw him off the end of the pier myself.'

At this moment Captain Paul Waggett entered the bar, so unusual an occurrence that a silence fell upon the gathering, and the frequenters in their surprise drank up their glasses of beer nearly an hour before they meant to.

'Good evening, everybody,' said Captain Waggett graciously. 'The fog's still very thick. It looks as if the *Island Queen* will be here over

Sunday. I had quite a job to find my way up to the hotel, Roderick. In fact I nearly went to the Manse instead.'

'You would have found chust as much to drink there as you'll find here, Mr Wackett,' said the host.

'Yes, I'm sorry to hear supplies are so short. I'm afraid I can't offer to stand a round.' He smiled his condescending smile to which nobody responded because nobody thought there was anything to smile at. 'Still,' he went on, 'we must remember that every drop of whisky we don't drink is helping to pay for the war.'

'So is every drop we drink, the way it's taxed,' said Drooby. 'And I'd sooner pay for the war by drinking whisky, tax and all, than by not drinking it.'

This statement evoked a murmur of agreement from the gathering.

'Ah, but the point is that by not drinking whisky the whisky goes to America,' Paul Waggett explained, 'which means that the Americans are helping to pay for the war, whereas if we drink it ourselves they don't.'

'Do they drink our beer too, these Americans?' Drooby asked.

'No, no, that's a question of barley. We have to remember the food situation.'

'Och, we have to remember too much altogether,' Drooby muttered.

'But we must not grumble,' Captain Waggett insisted. 'That's one of the reasons why I've come up to the bar this evening. I've had a letter from Major Quiblick of the Society Intelligence Corps at Nobost to say he's had information that there is a lot of criticism of the country's war effort in the two Toddays.'

'Och, a lot of us are after having letters from Major Quibalick, Mr Wackett,' said Roderick. 'I've had one myself. Ay, some people have nothing petter to do than to write a lot of letters.'

'But it really won't do to let people get an impression that there is any defeatism here,' Captain Waggett urged. 'However, if Major Quiblick has written directly to some of you, I shan't say any more about that. Only, I do hope you realize that the Government have very strong powers in time of war — very strong powers indeed. I mean to say you wouldn't like it if it was decided to evacuate all the people from the two Toddays to the mainland.'

'What are you saying, Captain Waggett?' exclaimed the Biffer.

'I'm not saying that the Government will decide to do that. I'm simply reminding you all that if they did decide to they could. But we'll say no more about that. What really brought me along this evening is to ask if any of you know anything about an urn with ashes of somebody who was cremated in Canada?'

Every man present stared at Paul Waggett in bewilderment. One or two irreverent spirits had already put forward the theory that since he became the commander of the Home Guard on the two Toddays the owner of Snorvig House was showing signs of going off his head. The awkward silence was broken by the entrance of Andrew Thomson, the bank agent, who advanced to the counter, and claimed from the host his allotted half-pint.

'You'll be interested in this, Mr Thomson,' said Captain Waggett. 'It appears that an urn with the ashes of somebody who was cremated in Canada and addressed to the Manager of the City and Suburban Bank, Lombard Street, was sent to Major Quiblick at Nobost from Snorvig.'

'I know nothing about any urn, Captain Waggett,' the banker replied, scowling with embarrassment at suddenly finding himself the centre of interest. Luckily for him, Captain MacKechnie now entered the bar and diverted public attention.

'Do you know, Captain MacKechnie, that an urn containing the ashes of somebody who was cremated in Canada was left in a cabin of the *Island Queen* last Tuesday?'

'What?' Captain MacKechnie squeaked. 'Ach, the fock has got into your head, Mr Wackett. Who'd be putting anybody's ashes in my ship?'

'That's just the point,' said Paul Waggett. 'Who did? It's a serious matter. After all, as Major Quiblick points out, it might have been a time-bomb.'

'Major Quiblick is a clown. Ach, he pesters the life out of me at Nobost. He's chust a clown,' Captain MacKechnie declared.

'I don't think you ought to say that, Captain MacKechnie,' said Paul Waggett stiffly. 'You can't call the officer in charge of Security Intelligence for a Protected Area a clown.'

'Ah, but I will,' said Captain MacKechnie. 'What cappin was this firework found in?'

'In the cabin of Mr Brown, a tweed merchant, who spent last week-end at the Snorvig Hotel,' said Captain Waggett.

'Tweet mairchant? Not at all,' the skipper of the *Island Queen* squeaked. 'He's one of those pocket Hitlers at Nobost Lotch. I know him fine. It's a good thing for him there's a fock. He'd have heard the rough site of my tongue if we'd gone on to Nobost tonight.'

'Well, you'll have to settle that with Major Quiblick, himself,' said Captain Waggett, in what he hoped was an impressive tone of voice. 'He asked me to make inquiries this end. Somebody in Snorvig must have put these ashes in Mr Brown's cabin.'

'His real name isn't Brown. His name is Lieutenant Pokkust. Didn't I pring him to Nobost about a month ago, and didn't he come up on the pridge and nearly drive me daft with the questions he was asking?'

Captain Waggett made a mental note to draw Major Quiblick's attention to the indiscretion of his subaltern if an opportunity afforded itself.

'Well,' he said, 'I hope that if anybody here does obtain any information about this urn he will let me know at once so that I can send a report to the appropriate authorities. I mean to say, we don't want unnecessary mysteries. Secrecy, of course, is all-important as you know, but mystery is not. Well, I'll say good-night. Do you think you'll get away in time to be back at Snorvig on Tuesday, Captain MacKechnie?'

'I wouldn't care to give you an answer about that in weather like this, Mr Wackett. We were lucky to make the island at all today. It came round us so quick.'

'I only asked because I'm expecting Sergeant-major Odd by Tuesday's boat,' said Captain Waggett. 'I had a telegram from Fort Augustus to say we could have his services for a week. I'm sure you'll all be pleased to hear that,' he added, turning to the Home Guards present.

'Ay, that's good news, Captain,' the Biffer agreed.

'Imphm,' murmured the Banker.

'He's a really fine chap is the Sergeant,' said the Biffer. 'He's no tweed merchant. Och, we'll all be glad to have him with us for a while.'

'Imphm,' murmured the Banker.

When Captain Waggett had withdrawn, the company in the bar began to speculate about the urn.

'What size of a thing would it be at all?' somebody asked.

'Och, it's pretty large,' said somebody else. 'They use them for tea when there's too many people for a teapot.'

'I wouldn't care at all to see my ashes in a teapot,' another said.

'Now I come to think of it,' said the Biffer, 'I saw Kenny Iosaiph and another Kiltod fellow carrying a sort of a black box up the gangway of the *Queen*.'

'If those ashes were after coming from Joseph Macroon,' Captain MacKechnie declared, 'you'll never know where they came from.'

There was a buzz of agreement.

'Ay,' said the Biffer pensively, 'that's right. It might be they were after finding the box and when they found it wasn't what they were hoping it might be . . .' He broke off. 'Och, well, well, I'd like to have seen Joseph's face when he found it was ashes instead of whisky. Ach, well, boys, we'll never be knowing. Never. There's not a man on Todaidh Beag will let us have the laugh at him next time we give him a dram.'

'It'll be long enough before we give anybody a dram,' Drooby prophesied sombrely.

And the frequenters of the bar passed out into the clammy darkness of the fog that night like ghosts from a happier age.

Chapter 9

THE *CABINET MINISTER*

> 'Now where we are I cannot tell
> But I wish I could hear the Inchcape Bell.'

There is no need to waste sympathy on Sir Ralph the Rover as he paced the deck, because he himself some years earlier had cut the bell from the Inchcape Rock merely to annoy the good old Abbot of Aberbrothock who had placed it there for the benefit of mariners. We can, however, commiserate with Captain Buncher who on that Sabbath morning in March paced the deck of the s.s. *Cabinet Minister*, outward bound to New York, when he expressed a passionate desire to hear the bell which warned mariners against the Skerrydoo, an unpleasant black reef awash at half tide to which ships proceeding down the Minch gave a wide berth. The reason why Captain Buncher could not hear the bell buoy of the Skerrydoo was that he was ten miles away from it and that in his anxiety to avoid it in the dense fog he had taken the *Cabinet Minister* into the Sound of Todday and thus right off his course.

The people coming out of church at Kiltod heard the siren of the *Cabinet Minister* sounding away to the north just as the people going into church at Snorvig heard it sounding to the north-west.

'That's queer right enough,' said Drooby to the Biffer, the expression of piety considered suitable for entering church lost for a moment in an expression of the liveliest curiosity.

'Sounding from the west,' the Biffer observed.

'Some ship's finding herself in trouble,' said Drooby. 'She's no business to be out there at all.'

Then the animation of curiosity which had been lightening their countenances died away to be succeeded by an expression of severely introverted piety as they turned into church and proceeded toward their accustomed seats.

Over on Little Todday the congregation, gathered in groups outside the towerless church of Our Lady Star of the Sea and St Tod, listened to the sound of the siren with as much attention as they had paid to the brief but eloquent sermon of Father Macalister whose view of Lent's rapid approach had perhaps never seemed quite so profoundly affected by the solemnity of the season.

'He was pretty fierce this morning Alan,' said one of his flock.

'*A Dhia*, what'll he be giving us on Wednesday?'

'Ay, he was fierce right enough,' agreed Alan Macdonald, a long, lean crofter with a trim square beard, as he slowly rolled some twist between his palms preparatory to filling a pipe. 'What do you make of that ship's siren, Hugh?'

Hugh Macroon, who was also preparing his after Mass pipe, stopped to listen more intently.

'I believe she's coming nearer.'

'Och, she's coming nearer all the time,' declared John Stewart positively.

'Will she be in the Coolish?' somebody asked.

'I believe she's more to the north,' said somebody else.

'I believe she'll be pretty near Bàgh Mhic Ròin,' said Hugh Macroon slowly.

A silence fell upon the group, not a man in which did not know the story of the black chest but not a man in which would have considered for one moment alluding to it.

'Ay, I believe you're right, Hugh,' said John Stewart. 'Ah, well, you and me had better be moving along towards home.'

The congregation was dispersing into the fog by the various tracks across the wet machair which led to the houses scattered all over the island. Presently Hugh Macroon and John Stewart could have fancied themselves the only people left in all Little Todday as they trudged northward. Their wives and families had driven on ahead.

'I'm not after hearing her blow for some time,' said John Stewart presently.

'I didn't hear nothing,' Hugh added in these deliberate tones of his which seemed to lend such weighty support of, or offer equally weighty opposition to, other people's assertions.

'There she goes again,' Jockey exclaimed.

'That's not a ship,' said Hugh. 'That's a stirk or a heefer.'

'Ay, ay, it would be a heefer right enough,' Jockey agreed as the melancholy mooing sounded somewhere in the distance of that silver-grey annihilation of figure and form, of sea and land.

They walked on for half an hour in silence, each preoccupied with the same dream which neither of them thought it would be decorous to put into words. At last they came to where the track forked to their respective crofts.

'I dare say dinner will not be ready for a while yet,' said Hugh.

'Och, it'll be a long while yet,' Jockey agreed.

'It's pretty quiet,' said Hugh.

'Ay, it's pretty quiet right enough,' Jockey agreed.

'She might have run into clearer weather,' Hugh suggested.

'Ay, she might, but it's kind of queer that she stopped hooting so sudden,' Jockey commented.

'Ay, it's queer right enough,' Hugh agreed. 'Maybe it wouldn't be a bad notion to walk on a bit and see if we could get a sight of her from the head of the *bàgh*.'

'*Ceart gu leoir*. Right you are, Hugh. Ay, we'll walk along to the head of the *bàgh*, and tinner will be chust about ready by the time we reach home.'

They had walked on for another twenty minutes when Hugh suddenly gripped Jockey's wet sleeve.

'*Eisd!*'

Both men stood still. From ahead of them through the viewless air there came thinly, remotely, but unmistakably the sound of someone hallooing at intervals.

'That's never a *Todach* shouting like that,' Hugh declared.

'Neffer!' Jockey agreed. 'Come on, let's hurry. I believe she iss. I was after thinking she wass all the way from church.'

At that moment the figure of a man running toward them along the track materialized from the fog. It was Willie Munro.

'There's a big steamer on the Gobha,' he gasped in excitement. 'I'm away to Kiltod to send word over to Snorvig.'

'What for?' Hugh Macroon asked.

'It's me that's the coast-watcher. The supervisor will want to send word to Nobost for the lifeboat.'

'Man, you're daft,' said Hugh contemptuously. 'What lifeboat could come from Nobost in such a fog? And the sea as smooth as glass. If they want to come ashore they don't want no lifeboat. Wass it you that was shouting just now?'

'I was never shouting.'

'Very well then,' said Hugh, 'I believe some of them will be ashore now. You'd have done better to wait where you were. Come on, Jockey. We'll be getting down to the *bàgh*.'

'Och, well, I'll be getting along to Kiltod,' said Willie Munro. He hurried on his way.

'Ay, he's cunning is Willie,' Hugh observed when he and Jockey had moved on. 'But he's a bit of a fool. Oh well, I don't believe this big steamer will be full of ashes.'

'*A Dhia*, I hope not,' Jockey exclaimed.

'She might be full of nothing,' Hugh suggested. 'If she's outward bound.'

'She would neffer be setting a course through the Sound of Todday if she wass outward bound,' Jockey pointed out. 'No, no, she's homeward bound. *A Dhia*, she might be from Chamaica with plenty rum aboard. Parcels and parcels of it.'

'Stop your dreaming, Jockey,' Hugh Macroon advised. 'We were after dreaming of gold and it turned to ashes. If we go dreaming of rum it'll end up in grapefruits.'

A minute or two later two strangers emerged from the fog.

One of them was tall and lanky with red hair. The other was short and plump and also had red hair.

'Can you tell us where we are, mate?' the short seaman asked in the accent of Clydeside.

'You're on Little Todday,' John Stewart replied.

'Where in hell's that?' asked the lanky seaman in the same accent as his companion.

'I don't know at all where it is in hell,' said Hugh Macroon slowly. 'But I can tell you where it is on earth.' And this he proceeded to do.

'And you don't think she'll float off at high water?' asked the short seaman whose name was Robbie Baird.

'I'm pretty sure she won't,' said Hugh.

'What did I tell you, Robbie?' exclaimed his companion. 'Och ay, the old *Minister* will make a job for the salvage and that's about all she will do. Anyway, Fritz won't get her now.'

'Och, I'm not so sure myself she winna float,' Robbie Baird insisted.

'All richt, all richt. I'm not arguing aboot it,' Sandy Swan replied with a touch of impatience. Then he turned to the crofters.

'Look, will you two fellows come back on board with Robbie Baird and myself? The old man had better get word from strangers what's coming to him. He'll think he's gone plain daft when he hears where he is '

'What port were you making for?' Jockey asked.

'New York.'

'Outward pound?' Jockey exclaimed in shrill amazement. 'How were you coming round the north end of Little Todday, and you outward pound?'

'Put the blame on the *Cabinet Minister*'s cargo,' Robbie Baird chuckled. 'The old ship was absolutely fou'.'

'There's cargo in her, is there?' Hugh asked. 'There's not much cargo outward bound these days.'

'Cargo in her?' Robbie Baird exclaimed with a wink. 'I'm telling you. There's fifty thousand cases of whisky in the auld *Cabinet Minister*,' he added with a triumphant toss of the head.

'What?' Jockey shrilled like a questing falcon.

Even the imperturbableness of Hugh Macroon was shaken by this news. He gulped twice.

'Fifty sousant cases of whisky?' Jockey lisped. He was never perfectly at ease with 'th' and emotion now deprived him of any power even to attempt the combination of letters. 'She must be a huge crate ship.'

'Four thousand tons. Blue Limpet Line.'

'Fifty sousant! Fifty sousant!' Jockey murmured in awe. 'And twelf pottles in effery case? Oh, well, well, Clory be to Cod and to His Plessed Mother and to All the Holy Saints,' he ejaculated as he crossed himself in a devout rapture of humble human gratitude. '*Uisdein, eudail* wasn't it Mhaighstir Seumas who was saying we'd kept the Faith in Todaidh Beag and Almighty God would not be forketting us?'

The two red-haired Clydesiders grinned at the round sandy-haired Hebridean.

'Here's tae us,' said Robbie Baird, raising an imaginary glass.

The captain's cutter had been made fast to a rock, halfway up Macroon's Bay.

'You were pretty lucky to come in here,' Hugh commented. 'You might have lost yourselves.'

'The fog lifted for a while after we struck. That's why the old man sent us ashore. Then it came down thicker than ever, and we started to shout.'

'Ay, we heard you,' Hugh told them.

Now the fog lifted again, and presently the *Cabinet Minister* was visible.

'*A Dhia*, she's lying terribly crooket,' Jockey exclaimed.

'Och ay, the first big sea's likely to break her back,' Sandy Swan prophesied confidently.

'And there's a big sea running between Pillay and Todday when the tide's making and the wind is easterly,' Hugh observed thoughtfully.

'Ay, and you get a pick sea when the tide iss tropping and the wind is sou-west,' Jockey added.

'Och, you get a big sea whichever way the wind is or the tide either,' said Hugh. 'You'd better not be staying aboard any longer than you have to. You're in luck, too, because the mailboat got into Snorvig yesterday afternoon and couldn't leave again. I don't know if she'll go back to Obaig tonight if the fog clears right away. They're very strict about Sunday over in Great Todday. They're all Protestants there and we're all Catholics here; but still, I believe she will be going back tonight. The coast-watcher must have sighted you when the fog lifted for a bit. We were after meeting him on the way to Kiltod to get word to the Supervisor. But even if they won't send over for you from Snorvig on Sunday we'll get you across the Coolish.'

'Ay, and we'll get some carts over to the head of the pay and you'll be aple to take wiss you what you've a mind to,' Jockey added.

'You'd better tell the skipper all that,' Robbie Baird advised.

'Och, yess, we'll tell him right enough,' Jockey assured the two sailors. 'It wouldn't be ferry nice at all if the wind got up after this fock and you still on the Gobha.'

'Och, aye, it would be a bit gory,' Robbie Baird chuckled.

'It iss not *gobhar*. It iss *gobha*,' said Jockey. '*Gobha* iss a blacksmiss. *Gobhar* is a coat.'

'A coat, eh?' Robbie Baird nodded.

'No, not a coat. A coat.'

'A goat,' Hugh put in to help the seaman.

'Ah, a goat,' Robbie Baird repeated. 'And the name of this rock we're on is the Blacksmith, eh? Well, it's black all richt. All the same, goat widna hae been a bad name for the b——r the way he butted into us.'

The *Cabinet Minister* had been going dead slow when she struck the Gobha, but she was well on top of the submerged reef which extended for twenty yards on either side of the black fragment of basalt which thrust itself up out of the water. Two hundred yards ahead rose the dark cliffs on the eastern face of Pillay whitened by the droppings of the seafowl that nested upon their ledges.

The steamer was heeling over at enough of an angle to make the Captain's cabin seem as perilous a place in which to remain too long as the two crofters were anxious to persuade him it was.

'So that's where I am, is it?' said Captain Buncher, putting his finger on the chart. 'And you say there's no chance of floating off on the top of the tide?'

Hugh Macroon shook his domed head, and when Hugh did that onlookers were apt to be impressed. Captain Buncher, a small man with a small grizzled beard, a high complexion, and hair as dark as the rock on which his ship had struck, *was* impressed.

'But there's no need for you people to be bringing carts and wagons to this bay. We can row round in the ship's lifeboats to Snorvig. You say the mailboat is there now?'

'Ay, but she might not go back to Obaig till tomorrow morning, being Sunday,' Hugh replied. 'But you'll find good accommodation at the hotel. At least pretty good. There's very little beer just now. And no whisky at all.'

'No whisky, eh?'

'There's not been as much whisky as you'd get in a poorhouse for two months and more.'

'That's bad,' Captain Buncher clicked. He rang the bell, and when the steward came he bade him bring glasses. Then he went to a locker and produced a bottle of Stag's Breath, a brand which had been particularly favoured by the inhabitants of the two Toddays in the good old days of plenty.

'Stack's Press,' murmured Jockey, transfixed by the beauty of the sight before his eyes and under his nose and hardly a couple of feet away from his mouth.

'Help yourselves,' Captain Buncher commanded when the steward had brought the glasses. 'But no, that's not fair. I'll help you.'

'And, poys,' Jockey told them later that famous Sunday before Lent, 'it *wass* a help. It wass reeally powerful. Ay, and the man helped us twice. Neffer plinked an eye. Chust poured it out as if he was a *cailleach* pouring you out a cup o' tay. And mind you, the man's heart must have been sore inside of him, the way his ship was lying there on the Gobha. But he neffer plinked an eye. Chust poured it out.'

When Hugh and Jockey were raising to their lips that second glass Captain Buncher suddenly remarked: ·

'The glass is high and steady.'

'Ay, it's high right enough,' Jockey agreed. 'But it's not so steady as it wass the first time, Captain.'

Captain Buncher laughed.

'I was thinking, I might leave a couple of my chaps on board till the salvage people took over.'

'You know best, Captain,' Hugh Macroon allowed with grave courtesy. 'But you couldn't have a worse place than you are except when it's calm as it is just now, and when there's anything of a ground swell it's tricky right enough to get ashore at all.'

'Yes, well, I expect you're right, my friend. If she becomes a total loss there'll be no lives lost with her. Well, I'm much obliged to you for your help. Baird and Swan will put you ashore in the cutter, and then I think we'll make for Snorvig in the lifeboats. You don't think the mailboat will leave before evening, that is provided the fog doesn't come back, and she's able to leave at all?'

'Och, she'll never move on a Sunday afternoon,' Hugh assured him. 'Anyway, Jockey and me will go in to Kiltod and send word you'll be round before sunset. And you'll not be forgetting there's not a drop of whisky in Snorvig?'

'I won't forget,' Captain Buncher replied, with a smile. 'And as there isn't a drop of whisky in your island either, perhaps you'd like to take a bottle each with you ashore. Good-bye, and thanks very much for your help.'

When the two red-headed Clydesiders put Hugh and Jockey ashore inside Bàgh Mhic Ròin each pulled out his bottle of Stag's Breath to offer the seamen a dram.

'No, no, mates, we'll not rob you,' said Sandy Swan.

'It is not robbing us at all,' said Hugh in whom the two potent drinks he had had in Captain Buncher's cabin had induced that extreme deliberation of utterance which was the recognized sign that Hugh Macroon had had a hefty one. 'No, it is not robbing us. It is giving us pleasure to be able to offer a dram to a friend. Isn't that right, Jockey?'

'Right? Sure, it's right. It's a pleshure we've not been after having for munce, *a chàirdean*,' Jockey insisted, unfastening the stopper of his bottle.

The seamen saw that the islemen would be chagrined by their refusal.

So each took a short swig from Jockey's bottle, and having wished and been wished good health and good luck they sheered off and pulled back to the *Cabinet Minister*.

The two crofters sat on an outcrop of rock and watched, now the cutter, now the two bottles of Stag's Breath. The sun like a great silver plate was visible again through the ever-lessening fog, and larger patches of pale-blue sky were spreading above them.

'Oh, well, who would have thought when we were walking to Mass this morning that we would be sitting here like this before two o'clock?' said Hugh. 'We'll just have a bite to eat and then we'll get the cart and drive along to Kiltod. I want to give my bottle to Father James.'

'Och, I want to give him my pottle,' Jockey protested.

'We've all had a dram out of yours. Och, one's enough for him just now,' Hugh decided firmly. 'A Dhia, there's six hundred thousand bottles where this came from.'

'Tha gu dearbh, Uisdein. Tha gu dearbh,' Jockey agreed, in his voice a boundless content. *'Uisge beatha gu leòir, taing a Dhia.* We'll chust be saying three Hail Marys, Hugh.'

'Ay,' the other agreed, 'for favours received.'

The two crofters knelt down, and mingling with the murmur of their prayers was the lapping of the tide along the green banks of Bàgh Mhic Ròin and a rock pipit's frail fluttering song.

Chapter 10

WHISKY GALORE

The strict Sabbatarianism of Scotland has been the target for a good deal of satire. Some have not hesitated to suggest that it encourages among its devotees a Pharisaical observance of the letter of the Divine Law without any corresponding observance of its spirit. Scoffers are invited to contemplate the behaviour of the people of Great Todday on that Sunday in March when the s.s. *Cabinet Minister* became a wreck a few hundred yards from Little Todday.

Not one man was willing to break the Sabbath by crossing the Coolish to investigate that wreck: if cynics demand a lower motive, let it be said that not one man was brave enough to flout public opinion by doing so. The weather was fine. The sea was dead calm. Captain Buncher and the whole of his crew were going off with the *Island Queen* when she left for Obaig at dusk. There was for the moment nobody with authority over the wreck. Excise and salvage had not yet appeared upon the scene. The supervisor of the coast-watchers was John Macintosh the piermaster at Snorvig, known as Iain Dubh, but his only job was to notify the head of the coastguards at Portrose eighty miles away that a ship had been wrecked or to summon the lifeboat from Nobost if a ship was in danger of being wrecked. After that his responsibility ceased. Constable Macrae was charged with the invigilation of crashed aircraft and with notifying Rear-Admiral, Portrose, if he saw an enemy submarine. Wrecks were not his pigeons.

Captain Paul Waggett was profoundly convinced that the war would not be over until he had been granted authority to deal in the manner he considered appropriate with crashed aircraft, enemy submarines and wrecks, but this authority he had not yet been able to acquire. He was not even allowed to put Home Guards in charge of the stores of food locked up in the now disused old school at Snorvig as emergency rations for the island in the event of invasion. Most of these stores had been removed by what Captain Waggett declared he had no hesitation in calling common thieves, and this was just as well, because the rest of them had gone bad in the course of over two years.

It was obvious to the people of Great Todday that for once in a way there was no time like the present, but the present being the Sabbath their principles would not allow them to take advantage of it. Tribute must be paid to the staunchness of those principles. Mental agony is hardly too strong a term to describe what many of the people of Great Todday went through on that Sabbath evening when they thought of the people of Little Todday not merely breaking the Sabbath but encouraged to do so by the tenets of their religion.

The Biffer was one of those who suffered most acutely. He had seen the lifeboats of the *Cabinet Minister* coming round into the Coolish. He had been down on the pier when they landed. He had been almost the first man in Snorvig to know what cargo the wrecked ship was carrying. For the rest of that afternoon he was jumping up and going to the door of his house built not far from the water's edge on the rocky point that protected the harbour from the north. At last even his large placid wife protested.

'Will you not be sitting quiet for more than one minute, Airchie?'

'I'm keeping a sharp look-out on the weather,' he replied. 'If it came on to blow when the sun goes down she might break in two before morning the way they tell me she will be lying on the Gobha.'

'The weather won't change one way or the other because you're for ever jumping up and running to the door,' his wife observed. 'For goodness' sake be still for a moment. It's the only quiet time I have in all the week.'

'I might take the *Kittiwake* round the north side of Todaidh Beag and have a look at her,' Airchie suggested. 'No one could call that breaking the Sabbath.'

'Couldn't they?' said his wife, shaking her head in compassion for such self-deception. 'You know as well as I do, Airchie, what everybody would say when they saw you out there in the Coolish on a Sabbath afternoon. Indeed, what would yourself be saying if you saw Alan Galbraith out there just now?'

'If I saw Drooby out there I'd be out there myself pretty quick,' the Biffer replied emphatically.

'And a fine sight you'd be giving the neighbours, the pair of you.'

'Och, well, he isn't there.'

'No, indeed, I hope he has more sense, and if he hasn't the sense himself Bean Ailein will have the sense. Goodness me, you're like a child, Airchie. Let the ship bide till Monday.'

'Do you think they'll let the ship bide till Monday on Little Todday? Och, Ealasaid, you're talking very grand about my sense. But where is your own sense, woman?'

'If the poor *papanaich* on Todaidh Beag don't know better than to break the Sabbath, is it you that's wanting them to lead you by that great nose of yours into breaking it with them?'

'I'm not so sure if it would be breaking the Sabbath just to have a bit of a look round,' the Biffer ventured to speculate.

'Are you not? Ah well, I'm not going to argue with you, Airchie. We'll have been married twenty-five years next July, and if I'd argued with you every time you were wrong I don't know where we'd have been today. No, indeed. You'll just go your own way, and if you want to be breaking the Sabbath you'll be breaking it.'

Such recognition of his obstinacy took all the relish out of being obstinate. That had always been Ealasaid's method with him. He felt almost inclined to be aggrieved by her reasonableness.

'I believe I'll go along and see what's doing on the *Queen*. Maybe Captain MacKechnie won't be leaving till tomorrow. He may be afraid of what everybody will say if he goes to Obaig tonight.'

The sarcasm was lost on his wife. She was sitting placidly back in her chair, her hands folded in her lap, her eyes closed.

The Biffer found Drooby standing on the pier in contemplation of the *Island Queen*, aboard which there was no sign of life.

'Is she going tonight?' he asked.

'Ay, six o'clock, the Captain said. They're all up at the hotel now,' Drooby replied. 'They brought a tidy bit of stuff with them in the boats. It's all safe aboard now.'

'What will they do with the boats?' the Biffer asked.

'Och, the salvage men will have them.'

'I was thinking, Alan, I'd go along in the *Kittiwake* after twelve o'clock and see what's doing over yonder.'

'Not a bad idea,' Drooby observed.

'Will you be going along yourself with the *Flying Fish*?'

'I don't believe I will. Two of the crew went home yesterday till tomorrow. I wouldn't be able to get hold of them tonight. And anyway I wouldn't want to take the *Flying Fish* round there. Iain Dubh and me are not very good friends just now. He made a proper mess of that last lot of whitefish I sent over to Obaig.'

'Ay, I heard about that.'

'We lost a lot of money over him being so obstinate the way he was. Ay, and nothing would give him more pleasure than to be reporting me to the Navy up at Portrose if he thought I was doing anything on the side with the *Flying Fish*!'

'Would you like to come along with me tonight in the *Kittiwake*?' the Biffer asked. 'Just you and me, and young Jimmy to stand by while we get aboard?'

'*Ceart gu leoir*. Right you are, I'll come along with you, Airchie.'

'It would be a pity to let them have all that whisky over yonder.'

Drooby shook his head.

'They'll never get it all, Airchie. There's thousands and thousands and thousands of bottles in the *Cabinet Minister*. Some say there are fifty thousand cases. Others say it's fifteen thousand cases. Whichever it is, it's a lot of whisky. And it's wonderful stuff too. Not a drop under proof, they tell me. That's the kind of whisky you and me drank before the last war. And we didn't pay twenty-five shillings a bottle for it in those days.'

'Were you having a crack with some of the crew?'

'Ay, and I had a couple of drams too,' said Drooby.

'Ach, I thought you were looking a bit pleased with yourself, Alan, when I came on the pier.'

'Ay, it's only when you haven't had a good dram for a long while that you're knowing how important it is not to go without it.'

A golden decrescent moon was hanging in a clear blue sky below Ben Sticla and Ben Pucka when Drooby, the Biffer, and the Biffer's youngest boy Jimmy went chugging up the Coolish in the *Kittiwake* soon after midnight. The strait was glassy calm, and even when they rounded the north-easterly point of Little Todday the Atlantic itself was almost without perceptible motion.

'I believe this weather will hold for a few days yet,' said the Biffer.

'Unless it comes on thick again,' Drooby qualified.

'Ay, it might do that.'

The *Kittiwake* was now approaching the entrance of Macroon's Bay, and a minute or two later the 4,000-ton steamer loomed before them in the tempered moonshine.

Presently they were hailed by a sizeable fishing-boat.

'Who are you?'

'That's the Dot,' said Drooby.

Donald Macroon, generally known as the Dot, owned the largest of the Little Todday craft; it was called the *St Tod*, except by Father Macalister who always called it the *St Dot*.

'Hullo, hullo,' the Biffer shouted back. 'This is Airchie MacRurie and Alan Galbraith in the *Kittiwake*.'

He slowed down the engine and presently drew alongside the *St Tod*.

'You've been a very long time coming,' said the Dot, a small, swarthy, and usually taciturn fisherman. Tonight he was, for him, voluble.

'Ay, we had to wait till the Sabbath was over,' the Biffer explained.

The Dot laughed.

'Ay, that's what we were thinking. Never mind, boys, there's enough for everybody from the Butt of Lewis to Barra Head. You'd better have a dram right away now before you get on board. How many crans did you catch last week, Alan?'

'We had nine.'

'Och, well, *a bhalaich*,' said the Dot, 'there's thousands of crans of whisky on board of her. There's more bottles of whisky on board of her than the biggest catch of herring you ever made in your life, Alan. But have a dram with me before you go aboard.'

The Dot thrust a bottle of Islay Dew at the Biffer.

'Don't spare it, *a bhalaich*, you couldn't drink it all if you lived for ever.'

'*Slàinte mhór*,' said the Biffer, and then took a deep swig. '*A Chruithear*,' he commented reverently, 'that's beautiful stuff.' He wiped his mouth and passed the bottle to Drooby.

'Oh, well, well,' said Drooby when he too had drunk deep, 'that stuff would put heart into anybody.'

'When were they saying in Snorvig that the salvage men were coming?' asked the Dot.

'They might be here with Tuesday's boat,' the Biffer told him.

'Och, well, we must do our best to make their job as easy for them as we can,' the Dot chuckled. 'You'd better get on board and help yourselves. We've shifted quite a lot of it. I've been backward and forward loaded with cases a dozen times already, but you wouldn't see what we're after taking, there's so many thousands of cases.'

'You're pretty lucky over here,' said the Biffer. 'It won't be so easy to land it on the other side.'

'You'd better take back a good load with you tonight,' the Dot advised. 'You needn't worry to pick and choose. It's all beautiful stuff. We've rigged a rope-ladder to get down into the hold. It took a bit of doing, too. Still, so long as the weather keeps good for a bit, we ought to get a tidy few cases out of her the way she's lying now. Take another dram before you go, boys. It's pretty hard work coming up with those cases from the hold.'

'Well, I've known the Dot for forty years and more, Drooby,' the Biffer told his friend as they took the *Kittiwake* alongside the wreck. 'But I never heard him say so much in all those years as I heard him say tonight.'

'Nor I either,' said Drooby. 'Mostly it's just *"tha"* or *"chan 'eil"* and a big spit and you've heard all he has to tell you. Islay Dew,' he added reflectively. 'I hope we'll hit on a case of that.'

Many romantic pages have been written about the sunken Spanish galleon in the bay of Tobermory. That 4000-ton steamship on the rocks of Little Todday provided more practical romance in three and a half hours than the Tobermory galleon has provided in three and a half centuries. Doubloons, ducats, and ducatoons, moidores, pieces of eight, sequins, guineas, rose and angel nobles, what are these to vaunt above the liquid gold carried by the *Cabinet Minister*? It may be doubted if such a representative collection of various whiskies has ever been assembled before. In one wooden case of twelve bottles you might have found half a dozen different brands in half a dozen different shapes. Beside the famous names known all over the world by ruthless and persistent advertising for many years, there were many blends of the finest quality, less famous perhaps but not less delicious. There were Highland Gold and Highland Heart, Tartan Milk and Tartan Perfection, Bluebell, Northern Light, Preston Pans, Queen of the Glens, Chief's Choice, and Prince's Choice, Islay Dew, Silver Whistle, Salmon's Leap, Stag's Breath, Stalker's Joy, Bonnie Doon, Auld Stuarts, King's Own, Trusty Friend, Old Cateran, Scottish Envoy, Norval, Bard's Bounty, Fingal's Cave, Deirdre's Farewell, Lion Rampant, Road to the Isles, Pipe Major, Moorland Gold and Moorland Cream, Thistle Cream, Shinty, Blended Heather, Glen Gloming, Mountain Tarn, Cromag, All the Year Round, Clan MacTavish and Clan MacNab, Annie Laurie, Over the Border, and Cabarféidh. There were spherical bottles and dimpled bottles and square bottles and oblong bottles and flagon-shaped bottles and high-waisted bottles and ordinary bottles, and the glass of every bottle was stamped with a notice which made it clear that whisky like this was intended to be drunk in the United States of America and not by the natives of the land where it was distilled, matured and blended.

'Ah, well, Jockey,' said Hugh Macroon when he and John Stewart were coming back with the last boat load of the *St Tod*, 'we were after thinking we had found plenty gold last Sunday and it turned to ashes; but it was a sign right enough that a better kind of gold was on its way.'

The grey of dawn was glimmering above the bens of Todaidh Mór, and the high decrescent moon, silver now, was floating merrily upon her back across the deep starry sky toward the west.

'I believe I never worked so hard and enchoyed myself so much in all my life,' Jockey averred.

Over on Great Todday, Drooby and the Biffer were conveying a dozen cases of whisky up the rocky path to the Biffer's house while Jimmy kept watch against any sign of curiosity from the pier house and the police station.

'It's a good beginning, Drooby,' the Biffer said when the cases were stowed away at the back of his shed under a heap of old nets. 'But we mustn't be wasting tomorrow night. There's the weather to think about and the salvage, and I'm sure Ferguson will be along from Nobost, and there's the pollis. Och, you'd better take the *Flying Fish* over and get a big load aboard.'

'I'll do that right enough,' Drooby vowed. 'I'm just wondering where will be the best place to store it.'

'There's the old curing-shed down by your place.'

'Ay, there's that; but, if it got about that the stuff was there, some of my bold fellows who never put foot or hand to bring it across might be helping themselves.'

'That's right enough,' the Biffer agreed. 'How would it be to take the stuff up Loch Sleeport? There's a fine big loft in Watasett School. We used to climb up there when we were children.'

'Not a bad idea, Airchie. And Norman Macleod would likely come along with us tomorrow night. There's bound to be a lot of them over from Todaidh Mór tomorrow. Well, I'll just take half a dozen bottles along with me now.'

'Ay, we'll open a case and I'll take the other half-dozen into the house,' said the Biffer.

'I believe a dram would do us both good just now,' Drooby suggested. 'It'll keep the cold air out of our *stamacs*. Is there any Islay Dew in that case?'

The Biffer looked at the bottles.

'No, this is Lion Rampant and Tartan Perfection. We'll try Lion Rampant.'

'Well, I don't believe anything could be better than that,' Drooby decided, putting down the bottle with a sigh. 'Still, we might as well try Tartan Perfection. Ah, well, I don't know which is best,' he declared after the second dram. 'I'll take another dram of Lion Rampant just to make sure. And now I'm not sure, after all,' he said.

'And I'm not so sure,' the Biffer echoed. 'We'd better try Tartan Perfection again.'

'Ay, it's a pity not to know which really is the best,' Drooby agreed. 'I don't know what's the matter with me, Airchie, but I'm feeling much better.'

'Ay, I'm feeling much better myself, Alan. Och, I don't believe the war will last for ever at all. *Slàinte mhath!*'

'*Slàinte mhór!*' Drooby wished in return. 'I don't believe anybody could find out which was best. Well,' he went on, 'some people say they're close in Little Todday. I wouldn't say that, Airchie.'

'I wouldn't say that myself,' the Biffer agreed. He poured himself out another dram, but whether it was Lion Rampant or Tartan Perfection he was hardly aware. 'I wouldn't say it at all. *Slàinte mhór* to all friends on Little Todday.'

'*Slàinte mhór!*' Drooby echoed, with a hiccup like the castanets at the beginning of a cachucha. 'They never grudged us a bottle. "Help yourselves, boys," that was the spirit. I'll never see a Little Todday man go without a dram so long as there's whisky in the country. Never.'

'Never,' the Biffer echoed. 'What about a song, Alan?'

Drooby rose to his feet and, swaying to the combined effect of the whisky and the tune, delivered *Mo Nighean Donn* (My Nutbrown Maid) in the very resonant but slightly raucous tenor that hardly suited his bulk, to which a profound bass would have been more appropriate.

'*Glè mhath! Glè mhath*. Very good, Drooby,' the Biffer applauded. 'Let's have another.'

Drooby had started *Mo Rùn Geal Dìleas* (My Faithful Fair One) even more resonantly when Jimmy appeared in the doorway of the shed.

'*Istibh!*' the boy warned them sharply. 'Are you wanting to wake up everybody in Snorvig?'

'I don't want to wake up nobody,' his father replied with dignity. 'I'm feeling pretty sleepy myself. Is Iain Dubh about?'

'There's nobody about, but it's getting light,' Jimmy pointed out.

'Ay, I'd better be making my way back home,' said Drooby.

'You'd better see that there's nobody about, Jimmy,' his father told him.

The boy went off again.

'Only two of my boys left in the home, Alan,' the Biffer went on sentimentally. 'Four of them serving in the Mairchant Navy.'

Drooby poured out another dram.

'*Slàinte mhór* to the Merchant Navy,' and his toast was followed by a hiccup that rivalled the performance of a xylophone. He then planted bottles in all his pockets and proclaimed his intention of going home immediately in case his wife should be worrying where he was.

'You'd better have a *deoch an doruis* before you go, Alan,' the Biffer advised.

'Ay, I believe you're right, Airchie. I'm just beginning to feel a little tired out. Och, we did a hefty night's work. Up and down, up and down.'

Drooby swallowed the *deoch an doruis*; but it took him no further than the heap of nets on which he was sitting, and leaning back, all his bottles chinking, he fell asleep at the same moment as the Biffer tipped backwards off the lobster-pot on which he was sitting and lay on the cork-strewn floor.

Ten minutes later Jimmy looked in to say that no time was to be lost if Alan Galbraith wanted to get home without being observed. He eyed the two sleepers with a grin. Then he pulled a tarpaulin over them and went off to his own bed.

Chapter 11

THE SERGEANT-MAJOR BACK AGAIN

We have seen that Bean a' Bhiffer was a placid woman. She merely smiled when her youngest son informed her where his father was sleeping.

'You'd better go and tell Bean Ailein or she'll be asking after Drooby.'

'Well, and I was just beginning to wonder what had become of him,' said Bean Ailein, a bright, bustling little woman. 'He's asleep in your father's shed, is he? Och, he'd better stay there till he wakes up. I'm sure he'll be out again tonight,' she laughed.

'There'll be a lot of them out tonight,' said Jimmy.

Just before one o'clock that Monday, Mrs Wishart came in to inform Dr Maclaren that Archie MacRurie and Alan Galbraith wanted to see him.

'Hullo, what's the matter with them?' he exclaimed.

'There's strong smell of liquor in the hall,' Mrs Wishart said severely. 'I noticed it the moment I opened the front door. I asked them why they didn't go round to the surgery and they said they'd come to see you about business.'

'A strong smell of liquor?' the Doctor chuckled. 'Already?'

'Terrible,' his housekeeper sniffed. 'Worse than any bar.'

'You don't mean to tell me you ever frequented bars, Mrs Wishart.'

'I used to accompany Mr Wishart sometimes when we were first married. It was a duty,' she replied mournfully.

'Well, show them in here,' the Doctor told her.

'Don't forget your lunch will be on the table at one sharp,' Mrs Wishart reminded him as she withdrew.

'And what can I do for you both?' Dr Maclaren asked when Drooby and the Biffer were in his sitting-room.

Drooby pulled open his jacket and thrust a huge hand into a pocket. The Biffer did the same.

'Lion Rampant,' said Drooby, putting an oblong bottle on the table.

'Tartan Perfection,' said the Biffer, putting a bottle with shoulders like a Victorian miss beside it.

'Just for a start,' said Drooby.

'You'll be getting a case pretty soon,' the Biffer promised.

'It's really kind of you chaps to think of me,' the Doctor exclaimed.
'I appreciate the thought. You know old Hector MacRurie over at
Knockdown?'

'Sure, I know him,' said the Biffer. 'His grandfather and my great-
grandfather were second cousins. He was in the Home Guard for the
first year, but he had to give it up on account of his legs.'

'As soon as I've had my lunch I'm going to take one of these bottles
up to him.' The Doctor picked up Lion Rampant and read the export
stamp in the glass.

'Ninety-nine per cent proof,' he ejaculated reverently.

'And Tartan Perfection is the same,' the Biffer assured him.

'Dash it, I've asked a lot of patients to say ninety-nine,' Dr Maclaren
laughed. 'But I never expected to say it myself with such relish. Oh, this
is the real Mackay!'

'Ay, it's good stuff, right enough,' Drooby said. 'We tried it ourselves
when we got back this morning. And, Doctor, there's thousands of
bottles in the *Cabinet Minister*. Every kind of whisky anybody could
think of. I'm not surprised those Americans have come into the war. I
believe we'd have won the war without them by now if they hadn't drunk
all our whisky.'

'And the Germans like whisky themselves,' the Biffer added. 'I
remember the first time Donald was torpedoed – he's been torpedoed
three times – that was in 1940 – the captain of the U-boat asked them
if they had any whisky aboard the lifeboat. "Just one bottle," says they.
"All right," says he, "hand it over, and take these three bottles of gin
instead." That shows you what the Germans think of our whisky.'

'I suppose they're doing well on Little Todday, aren't they?' the
Doctor asked.

'They're doing wonderful,' the Biffer replied. 'And I'm glad they are.
They couldn't have treated me and Drooby better if we'd been born and
bred on the island. "Plenty more where that comes from, boys." That
was the slogan.'

'Did you see Father Macalister?'

'No, no. We didn't get across till after twelve o'clock. But they say
he was pretty pleased.'

'I hope you'll get plenty of the stuff safely put away before too many
officials make things difficult. I hear Mr Waggett is talking of putting

the Home Guard on to guard the wreck. That'll cramp your style, Biffer.'

'I joined the Home Guard to keep Hitler out of Todaidh Mór. I'm a sniper, Doctor, not a snooper. Och, Sergeant Odd is coming on Tuesday. I don't believe he'll want to waste his time doing the work of the pollis and the excise-man.'

When Corporal Archie MacRurie was making this observation to Dr Maclaren in Great Todday, over at Tummie the Sergeant-major himself was reading a telegram from Duncan Bàn:

Rèiteach arranged for Tuesday evening everybody very pleased don't worry yourself about the wherewithal all in good order here very strong reinforcements arriving all the time will be on pier looking for you tomorrow tingaloori till then
Duncan

'Did you ever hear of a rayjack, sir?' the Sergeant-major asked his Commanding Officer later on that afternoon.

Colonel Lindsay-Wolseley looked up from the desk where he was wading through the correspondence of his slightly harassed adjutant, George Grant.

'Never. What kind of an instrument is it, Sergeant-major?'

'It's not an instrument, sir. It's a way they have out here of announcing an engagement. It's a kind of party. I know whisky comes into it a good deal.'

'I thought they had no whisky in the Islands.'

'They didn't have, not when I was there a fortnight ago, sir, but I've had a telegram from Lieutenant Macroon which sounds as if the drought had broken. You'll excuse me bothering you with my private affairs, but it's all right is it, sir, about your cottage?'

'I'll be glad for you to have it whenever you want it, Sergeant-major.'

'I'm very much obliged, sir. This rayjack makes it look as if I'll be wanting it in Easter Week. I mean to say it's a rayjack for Peggy Macroon and me tomorrow night.'

The Colonel offered his hand in congratulation.

'That's capital, Sergeant-major. I wish I could come to the — what's it called?'

'Rayjack, sir. I did know how to spell it, but I've forgotten, and you can look through one of these Garlic dictionaries for an hour and not find what you want. Talk about a missing word competition!'

'Well, I'm no hand at the Gaelic myself. Perhaps Captain Grant can tell us. Do you know how to spell "rayjack", George?' he asked the adjutant who had just come into the room.

'I never heard of the place, Colonel.'

'It's not a place, George. It's a ceremony. Sergeant-major Odd is engaged to be married.'

'Oh, really. Congratulations, Sergeant-major. I wish you joy,' said the adjutant.

'I think the excitement must have gone to my head, sir,' said the Sergeant-major. 'I've got the word here in a telegram from Little Todday. R-E-I-T-E-A-C-H.'

'And you think you've got the right pronunciation?' the Colonel asked, with a smile.

'That's what they call it on Little Todday, sir.'

'George, you and I will have to persuade Ben Nevis to give us lessons in Gaelic. By the way, how did you find Major MacDonald, Sergeant-major?'

'Oh, he was very much up and doing, sir. He's anxious to get hold of some more Sten guns for C Company.'

'I dare say he is,' said the Colonel drily. 'But I'm afraid there aren't any to spare.'

A fortnight ago Sergeant-major Odd had slept almost all the way to Snorvig. He was in no mood for sleep when he boarded the *Island Queen* at Obaig on Shrove Tuesday.

'Flat as a pancake, they say,' he murmured to himself as he walked up the gangplank. 'Well, I don't feel very flat this morning and that's a fact.'

The Sergeant-major took an early opportunity of going up on the bridge to have a chat with Captain MacKechnie.

'Ah, there you are, Sarchant. They told me you were aboard. You're looking petter than when you arrived. Well, what do you think about the *Cappinet Minister*?'

'I think they're all much of a muchness if you ask me. Except Winnie of course.'

'Och, I'm not talking about politics. I'm talking about the ship.'

'What ship?'

'Didn't you hear the news from Little Todday?'

'I didn't hear anything about any ship.'

'Och, fine doings. She struck the Gobha between Pillay and Todday on the morning of the Sabbath in the fock. Ay, high and try with fifteen thousand cases of whisky. We took the crew pack with us to Obaig the same evening. Och, it wass a terrible fock. I thought I was lost myself.'

That phrase about reinforcements in Duncan Macroon's telegram came back to the Sergeant-major's mind. So he had guessed right about the ending of the drought.

'Who's in charge of the wreck?' he asked.

'Och, I believe the *Todaich* from both sides of the Coolish will be in charge chust now. I was expecting to see Ferguson on board at Obaig coming over with the *Island Queen*, but not a sign of him. And not a sign of any salvage fellow either. Ah well, we crumple sometimes about the slowness of these officials, but there are times when one's pretty clad that they are so slow.'

'Who's Ferguson? I don't remember him.'

'The Exciseman at Nobost. One of these wise men of the East from Aberdeen. He thinks himself pretty smart. Ay, and he'll have to be pretty smart if he's going to check up on every case in the *Cappinet Minister*. Och, but he's not a bad fellow at all.'

'Was the Captain very much upset?'

'Och, no Captain likes to lose his ship, but if she had to be lost it was petter to lose her like that for the benefit of the *Todaich* than to be sunk in the middle of the Atlantic and let Dafy Chones put all that whisky in his locker. Yess, yess, inteet!'

'I'm very interested in what you're telling me, Captain MacKechnie.'

'Ay, it iss very interesting.'

'It means that my rayjack looks like being a success.'

'What's that at all? Is it some kind of a new weapon?'

'No, it's the party to celebrate two people getting engaged to be married.'

'Ach, a *rèiteach*,' Captain MacKechnie squeaked. 'So you're going to have a *rèiteach*, are you? You and Peigi Iosaiph, eh? You've picked a good one, Sarchant. She's a fine curl. When are you going to be married?'

'Easter Week if all goes according.'

'Ferry good, ferry good inteet. Ach, we'd petter go along to my cappin.'

The skipper of the *Island Queen* led the way out of the wheelhouse and took a look round on the bridge.

'Ah, well, well, who'd have thought last Saturday that we'd be seeing weather like this? It's too fine for the season, Sarchant. We'll pay for it next month, I believe. But come along below and we'll tap the steward.'

In his little cabin Captain MacKechnie took from a locker an almost spherical bottle of whisky.

'King's Own,' he said. 'Captain Puncher gave me a pottle on Sunday evening. In fact he gave me two or three. So don't be afraid of having a good tram. This is good stuff. They send it round the world for a year in a sherry cask before they put it into these queer-looking pottles. Och, I don't suppose the voyage does the whisky any good, but it doesn't seem to do it any harm either.'

Captain MacKechnie poured out drams for himself and the Sergeant-major, and then raised his glass for a toast.

'Here's long life to you, Sarchant, and may you have a full quiffer. *Sonas!* Do you know what *sonas* means?'

The Sergeant-major had to admit that he did not.

'*Sonas* means happiness. It's a much petter word for happiness, don't you think so yourself, Sarchant? *Sonas!* But the Gaelic is a much better lankwitch than Inklish. Do you know this? There's said to be four hundred ways of saying "yess" and "no" in Gaelic. Look at that now. Think of the convenience of such a lankwitch. Have another dram.'

'I don't think I will, thanks very much, Skipper. I've got a bit of an evening in front of me.'

'Ay, you'll have that right enough. And now I'll tell you a pit of a good choke, Sarchant. You know fine what a time they've been having over the shortage of whisky and peer in the two Toddays. Och, I hardly dared bring the *Island Queen* alongside I was so unpopular. Well, now that there's plenty whisky I'm pringing enough whisky and peer with me today to have put everything right. And I'm chust wondering what Big Roderick is going to say about the competition. Joseph Macroon tried many a time to get a licence at Kiltod, but Roderick was always one too many for him. Ach, your future father-in-law knows a thing or two, Sarchant, but Ruairidh Mór knows a thing or three. He won't like the idea of the *Cappinet Minister* as an hotel. It'll be interesting to see chust how he goes to work. Well, well, I'd better go back to the pridge. I'll be seeing you later, eh?'

The pier was crowded with people to welcome the mailboat on that calm, glittering afternoon which was more like May than March.

Like a sunbeam himself, Duncan Bàn was dancing about under the influence of poetry, whisky, and the prospect of unstinted hospitality.

'How are you, Sarchant? Ah, well, isn't this splendid now?' he bubbled as he grasped the arrival's hand and pumped it up and down.

'The *Morning Star* is waiting by the steps. Will we cross right away and send her back for the mail, or would you rather wait till they've collected it?'

'I think I ought to go up and report my arrival to Captain Waggett,' the Sergeant-major suggested.

'Right you are. I have a few messages I want to take round. Och, I'll tell you what. I'll get a hold of a car and bring it up to Snorvig House and then we can invite a few of your Todaidh Mór friends to the *rèiteach*. I thought you'd like to have Norman Macleod and his sister Catriona, and John Beaton and his wife, and George Campbell . . .'

'And his mother?' the Sergeant-major put in with a grin.

'*A Dhia*, no. It's not Ash Wednesday till tomorrow. Have you heard the story of the ashes yet?'

The Sergeant-major shook his head.

'That's a good one, but you ought to get Father James to tell you that one. Who else is there we ought to ask? We ought to have Doctor Maclaren. He's a darling of a man. Och, we'll think of one or two more. It's a great occasion. You and I are having something to eat with Father James first and when it's all over you're coming back to stay at my place. I thought you'd like to have a Home Guard parade tomorrow as it's a bit of a melancholy holiday. All right, Sarchant, you go along up and see Captain Waggett. I've got to fetch a bag up from the steps. Do you want to ask Captain Waggett and Mrs Waggett to the *rèiteach*?'

'I suppose it would be polite,' the Sergeant-major replied without enthusiasm.

'Ay, it might be a little bit too polite,' Duncan Bàn commented.

'Do you think I ought to ask them?'

'Well, you'll just see how you feel when you see him.'

'Yes, we'll leave it open,' said Sergeant-major Odd.

As he turned round to look back at the view of the harbour from the steps of Snorvig House he saw Duncan Bàn disappearing into the bank with a large and apparently very heavy kitbag.

'How are you, Sergeant-major? Very glad to see you back to Snorvig,' said Captain Waggett, who was in one of those graciously languorous moods in which he seemed to bask in the warmth of his own effortless superiority. 'Come into my den. I forget if I showed you my den the last time you were here.'

'Yes, sir, you did ask me in. Very snug, too.'

'Of course I intend to put in electric light after the war. I'd do it now, but I don't think it's fair to the country to take people away from the war effort. Well, what are your plans for this week you're spending with G Company?' the commanding officer inquired when they were settled down in the den.

'Well, sir, tonight if you don't mind I think I'd like to cross over to Little Todday, and then tomorrow being Ash Wednesday, and which is more or less of a holiday for them there . . .'

'They're always having holidays on Little Todday,' Captain Waggett interrupted with austere disapproval. 'However, it's part of their religion, so I suppose we mustn't criticize. What were you going to say about Ash Wednesday?'

'Well, I thought it would be a good opportunity to give the Little Todday platoon a bit of an exercise with some shooting practice. But it's just what you say, sir?'

'You'd get back here by Thursday morning?'

'That was my notion, sir.'

'Approved,' said Captain Waggett loftily. The War Office itself seemed to be speaking. 'Where are you going to stay in Snorvig?'

'Miss MacRurie — Miss Flora MacRurie is going to put me up. I was always very comfortable there,' said the Sergeant-major. 'Er — do you know what a rayjack is, sir?'

'Something to do with radiolocation, I suppose.'

'No, sir, it's a Gaelic word. It's when you announce your engagement. Well, there's going to be a rayjack tonight for me and Peggy — Peggy Macroon. It's to be in her father's house.'

'I hope you'll see that Joseph doesn't forget he's the warden for Kiltod, Sergeant-major. It's very discouraging when I look across the Coolish and see a blaze of light coming from the post-office.'

'I was wondering if you and Mrs Waggett would care to come to the party, sir?'

'It's very kind of you, Sergeant-major. I don't know whether Mrs Waggett will feel up to it. She's at the Manse just now. She and Mrs Morrison are getting up a jumble sale for the Red Cross. May we leave it open? Transport may be a problem. I suppose you've heard about this wreck off Pillay?'

'Captain MacKechnie was telling me about it on the way across, sir. Quite a goldmine, according to him.'

'It's a heavy responsibility for me, Sergeant-major,' said Captain Waggett, with a deep sigh.

'For you, sir?'

'You see, I feel I ought to arrange for the wreck to be guarded by the Home Guard until the salvage men arrive. But I ask myself whether I can trust my own men. That's a fearful thing for an officer to have to ask himself after nearly three years in command of a company.'

'If you'll excuse me, sir, I don't see what responsibility you have for this wreck. I mean to say a wreck is right outside our beat. Why, Major MacDonald of Ben Nevis might as well assume the responsibility of guarding the Loch Ness monster. And in fact that's what he did want to do, only Colonel Wolseley put his foot down and said the Loch Ness monster wasn't the Home Guard's pigeon.'

'Well, I can't accept any comparison between the Loch Ness monster and this ship wrecked off Pillay. The Loch Ness monster isn't full of whisky.'

'You'd think it was, sir, if you believed some of the tales they tell about it round Fort Augustus.'

Captain Waggett frowned slightly. He hoped Sergeant-major Odd was not trying to be flippant.

'The point is, Sergeant-major, that unless this wreck is properly guarded some of the cargo may be tampered with.'

'I wouldn't be at all surprised if it was, sir. You could hardly blame the people here if they did do a spot of tampering.'

'Which, don't forget, is robbing the Revenue.'

'Yes, I suppose it is, sir, if you put it that way. All the same, if I was you I'd wait for instructions first before I started in to protect the Revenue. The authorities know that the *Cabinet Minister* has been wrecked and it's up to them to call on your services if they require them.'

'Oh, of course, I shall get no thanks,' said Captain Waggett virtuously. 'But I'm not looking for gratitude. I'm thinking solely of what is right. And it can't be right to put temptation in the way of the people here by leaving that wreck without a soul in charge of it. We had a very curious incident last week which the Security Intelligence wallahs at Nobost took up with me. An urn with the ashes of somebody who had been cremated in Canada came ashore apparently on Little Todday, and the box was put in the cabin of Lieutenant Boggust who was conducting an investigation here.'

'What was he investigating, sir?'

'A report of the defeatist atmosphere in the two Toddays which reached them at Nobost.'

'Defeatist atmosphere?' the Sergeant-major exclaimed. 'Who do they think is going to defeat them?'

'The Germans, I suppose.'

'That was just the shortage of whisky, sir. There was a good deal of grumbling about that when I was over a fortnight back. These chaps in Security Intelligence must have something to investigate. It's what they're for, in a manner of speaking.'

'They were very much upset about this urn. In fact Major Quiblick wrote me a personal letter about it. He also said that Lieutenant Boggust had reported a lot of careless talk. If they were talking carelessly when there wasn't a drop of whisky in the island what kind of talk will they indulge in if they get hold of any of that whisky?'

'Well, sir, if you'll pardon my plain speaking, I think if they mean to get hold of any whisky it won't make any difference who's in charge, and I don't believe the Home Guard or anybody else will stop them. In fact it would be putting temptation in the way of the Home Guard.'

'That's why I'm feeling so depressed, Sergeant-major. After all my work to make G Company a crack unit, I feel I can't really trust my own men.'

'I wouldn't trust the Brigade of Guards to look after that ship, sir. No, not if the old Duke of Wellington himself was in command of 'em. Well, sir, I mustn't keep you any longer. If you and Mrs Waggett look in on us this evening we shall be very proud to welcome you.'

'Thank you, Sergeant-major. We shall come if it can be managed.'

When the Sergeant-major reached the road he found Duncan Bàn waiting for him in the most disreputable of the island cars. It looked not unlike a dustbin on wheels and belonged to a Watasett man, Calum MacKillop, more familiarly known as the Gooch — why, not even the Gooch himself was able to say.

'We must be back at the pier by six o'clock,' said Duncan Bàn. 'So I got hold of the Gooch because he's a fast driver.'

'Ay,' the Gooch admitted with a complacent grin, 'I can drive pretty fast.'

As the car shot northward by the west side Sergeant-major Odd reflected with gratitude that all the island lorries and cars were probably in Snorvig at this hour of the afternoon.

'What have you got in that kitbag?' the Sergeant-major asked.

'That's a pretty easy conundrum to answer,' Duncan replied. He pulled open the bag and showed it half full of bottles. 'It's not as heavy as it was. I unloaded half the contents on old friends in Snorvig.'

Just then the Gooch jammed on the brake to avoid a dozen black-face sheep which had decided to cross the road in front of them. The bottles in the kitbag clinked at the narrow escape, but Duncan went on imperturbably.

'Ay, I gave three bottles of Moorland Cream to Iain Dubh. Nothing like a bit of bribery and corruption for these rasscals. Oh yes, he's an accessory after the fact now, right enough.'

'Captain Waggett passed the remark to me that he thought the Home Guard should be put in charge of the wreck,' said the Sergeant-major.

'There'd be a big turn-out for that parade,' said Duncan. 'And we could practise our shooting with the empty bottles afterwards. Did you ask Waggett to the *rèiteach*?'

'I asked him and his missus, and he said they might come. He seemed doubtful about transport.'

'What a pity. If we'd known in time we could have sent for the royal barge. Did you ever try crossing the Coolish in this Rolls-Royce of yours, Calum?'

The driver looked round in amazement.

'What are you saying, man? She never would be able to cross the Coolish.'

'Why don't you offer to take Mr and Mrs Waggett over this evening?' Duncan pressed gravely.

'Och, I wouldn't be trying such a thing, Mr Macroon. This car was never built for going on the water. Och, you're after making a fun,' said the Gooch, suddenly aware of the twinkle in Duncan Bàn's kingfisher-blue eyes. 'I might have known it was a fun,' he added, as he accelerated to restore the dignity of himself and the car.

At Garryboo, while Duncan Bàn visited one or two houses with bottles of whisky, Sergeant-major Odd went along to the schoolhouse.

'Didn't you see my son in Snorvig?' Mrs Campbell asked suspiciously. 'He went in with the lorry immediately after school.'

'I must have missed him, mum,' said the Sergeant-major. 'I came to ask him if he would come to our rayjack tonight at Kiltod?'

'If that's some nonsense with the Home Guard, George won't be able to come,' said his mother.

'No, it's a rayjack.'

'I don't know what you're talking about, Sergeant. But whatever it is George can't come,' the old lady answered emphatically.

'It's the announcement of my engagement to Peggy Macroon,' the Sergeant-major explained.

'A *rèiteach*? A *rèiteach* in Little Todday, with all that liquor they're talking about? Certainly not. George won't be able to come.'

'I'm not going to argue the point, Mrs Campbell . . .'

'I wouldn't think so indeed,' she broke in sternly.

'I say I'm not going to argue the point, but it'll be a bit of a jollification and I thought . . .'

'Jollification? Did the Lord send us into the world for jollification as you call it? No, no, Sergeant, my son will not be at any jollification tonight,' the old lady declared confidently.

Mrs Campbell was too confident. When Duncan Bàn and Sergeant-major Odd reached the schoolhouse at Watasett, Duncan's kitbag empty by now except for a bottle of Heather Blend and two bottles of Cabarféidh, they found George Campbell there. He had been having a difficult half-hour with Catriona who had told him that he must choose between her and his mother. She could not continue any longer in the ridiculous position of being engaged to somebody who was afraid to let her meet his mother. It was idle for George to say that his mother would have behaved in the same way to any girl he intended to marry. If that was true, George looked likely to remain a bachelor for the rest of his life.

'I'm sorry, George, but if you don't love me enough to stop your mother from interfering between us it's better for us to break it off. When Norman goes into the R.A.F., I'll volunteer for the A.T.S.'

This was the ultimatum she had just delivered when Sergeant-major Odd and Duncan Bàn arrived at the schoolhouse.

'Come to your *rèiteach*, Sergeant Odd?' Catriona exclaimed. 'Why, surely we will.'

It was perhaps less a tribute to the Sergeant-major's Gaelic pronunciation than to Catriona's state of mind that she understood him immediately.

'Drooby was along yesterday. He's bringing the *Flying Fish* up Loch Sleeport tonight,' Norman Macleod murmured, a twinkle in his eyes.

'I was hoping you'd come too, Mr Campbell,' the Sergeant-major said, turning to George, 'but Mrs Campbell didn't seem to think you'd be able to manage it.'

Catriona looked sharply at George.

'Oh, you went to see my mother, did you?' George asked.

'Yes, I called in special to give you the invite.'

'And she said I wouldn't come?' George repeated.

'That's right.'

'Well, I will come,' George gulped.

'Come along, Sergeant,' said Duncan Bàn, 'we must be getting down to the pier.'

'You'll have a dram first,' said Norman. 'Man, you can't give a fellow three bottles of the real Mackay and then refuse to take a dram with him.'

But the Sergeant-major was firm.

'No, we mustn't keep the boat waiting. Peggy will be wondering where I am. We've got a long evening before us, and we'll be seeing you all on the other side.'

When they were going across the Coolish in the *Morning Star* Duncan asked his companion if he'd noticed anything at the Schoolhouse in Watasett.

'Nothing particular, no.'

'It's my opinion that perhaps we changed the whole course of a man's life by calling in there when we did,' said Duncan.

'What d'ye mean?'

'Did you not notice the look Catriona gave George Campbell when you said that about the old lady's not thinking George would be able to come tonight? If George had listened to the echo of his mother's voice at that moment he was finished. Ay, just completely on the scrap-heap. Ah, well, poor George, he saved himself in the nick of time.'

Duncan Macroon went on up to Father Macalister's house to announce their arrival while the Sergeant-major turned into the post-office to greet Peggy. He found she had already gone up to her room to start the preparations for her toilet, but her father was about.

'This was a very pleasant surprise you gave me, Mr Macroon.'

Joseph was just turning over in his mind the problem of the best place to store twenty-five cases of 'Minnie' as the *Cabinet Minister*'s cargo was now called affectionately by everybody on Little Todday. That pet name would become famous far beyond Little Todday. Indeed, although 'all too rarely com'st thou, spirit of delight', you may still be offered a dram of the famous Minnie as far away from Little Todday as Glasgow.

For the present, Joseph was saying to himself, they would have to go in the shed, but his fancy was playing with the idea of burying them on Poppay, Pillay's companion isle on the south side of Little Todday. One advantage of Poppay was its reputation as a rendezvous for ghosts or *bòcain* on account of its having been the burial place of the Macroons in ancient days. On the other hand, tourists enjoyed digging about in Poppay for relics.

'How are you, Sarchant? Glad to see you. Are you staying with us in Kiltod?' he inquired vaguely, his mind still on the cases of Minnie.

'I'm staying with Duncan Macroon tonight. Yes, it was a very pleasant surprise.'

'What was that?'

'The rayjack.'

'A *Dhia*, I was forgetting about the business,' Joseph exclaimed. 'What else could I do? Father James and Duncan Bàn between them arranged it on me over my head. Ach, well, never mind; we'll be able to offer people a decent dram. That reminds me, Sergeant. Did you say anything to Colonel Wolseley about the new school in Kiltod?'

'I didn't as a matter of fact. I thought he might think I was butting into what didn't concern me.'

'I'm very glad you didn't. I don't believe we want a new school so much just now. I believe we want a new road. Ay, I think we ought to have a road running from Bàgh Mhic Ròin right across the island to Tràigh nam Marbh.' The latter was the sandy beach at the south end of Little Todday on which once upon a time the bodies of dead Macroons were embarked to be ferried over to Poppay. 'Yes, I believe we want a road more than we want a school. I'll bring it up at the Council meeting later on this month. Ay, ay, we want a road on which a lorry can run.'

'But you used to have a lorry on the road to Try Swish, didn't you, and found it didn't pay?'

'Ay, but if we had the two roads the situation would be easier altogether.'

'You know best, Mr Macroon, but I should have thought the traffic just now was a bit exceptional, and by the time you get a road surely it'll have quietened down for a long while. Well, I'll be getting along to Father James. I'll be seeing you presently, eh?'

Joseph gave a gesture of vague agreement and went out to the shed in order to choose the best corner for those twenty-five cases of Minnie pending their ultimate concealment elsewhere.

Peggy who had laid the foundations of her toilet came downstairs to greet him.

'Peggy darling,' he told her as he held her to him, 'this is the biggest day in my life. No, and that's not right. The day I met you first was just as big, and the biggest day of all will be when we're married.'

'We're not married yet, Fred. You'll see if my father doesn't make it just as difficult as he can.'

'Well, I'm feeling right on top of the world today, and something tells me we're going to be married on the Wednesday in Easter Week.'

'I know fine who told you,' she murmured. 'It was just Minnie who told you?'

The Sergeant-major chuckled.

'I did have a dram with Captain MacKechnie coming over, and I had another with Lieutenant Beaton and Lieutenant Macroon when we looked in at Bobanish to invite him and Mrs Beaton over to the rayjack.'

'*Rèiteach*,' she corrected.

'Raychack, I mean. And we asked Sergeant Macleod and Catriona and Sergeant Campbell and Sergeant Thomson and Mr Mackinnon, the Snorvig schoolmaster, and Captain and Mrs Waggett.'

'*A Mhuire mhàthair*,' she exclaimed. 'What made you be asking them for? They're so snop.'

'I daresay they won't come.'

'So stiff and stuck up,' she pouted.

'Still, it was only tactful, Peggy darling. I mean to say it wouldn't do for Captain Waggett to think I was making a convenience of him just to get over here and see you.'

'Indeed, it's a queer kind of a *rèiteach* anyway,' Peggy said. 'Father James and Duncan Bàn going all over the island inviting people, and my father never inviting a soul. I'm sure I hope everything will be all right.'

'All right? It's going to be super. Give me a kiss, Peggy Machree. That's a good one, isn't it?' he beamed. 'I got that one off a gramophone record.'

'I suppose you mean *mo chridhe*.'

'Peg o' my heart, eh?'

And he held her so close that she began to fear for the foundations of her toilet and sent him off to Father Macalister.

'Come in, Sergeant. Come in, my boy. Oh well, this is really a glorious moment,' the burly priest declared in his most hospitable bass.

'Sit right down. You're going to have a snifter before Kirsty tells us the food is on the table. Now then, which will it be?'

Father Macalister pointed to the ten bottles of Minnie, each a different brand, upon the top of one of his bookcases.

'I leave it to you, Father.'

'Then it's going to be Prince's Choice. Oh, a real beauty.'

The drams were poured out and drunk with genuine reverence.

'Oh well, Sergeant, I've really suffered lately because I could not offer my friends even the most minute sensation. Och, indeed, yes. Never mind. Almighty God has been very good to us. You'll have seen Father MacIntyre by now, Sergeant?'

'Yes, Father.'

'Good enough, my boy. And Duncan has written a great song for tonight. Oh, really good. It's a pity you can't follow our noble and glorious language.'

'I was a bit rushed with it, Father,' Duncan Bàn explained apologetically.

'Ay, but the Pierian spring was in full spate, my boy. The fountain did not fail. *Gradus ad Parnassum!*'

'They were pretty erratic steps, Father,' Duncan laughed. 'I was walking up and down the Tràigh, and it was a pretty curly kind of a track.'

Kirsty came in to say that the food was on the table.

'Come along, boys, and eat as much as you can,' said Father James. 'We've a hefty evening before us.'

Chapter 12

THE *RÈITEACH*

The lavishness with which Father Macalister and Duncan Bàn had flung
out invitations to the *rèiteach* of Sergeant-major Odd and Peggy Macroon
had made the host's house too small for the entertainment of the guests,
and so it was held in the parish hall, one of those erections of corrugated
iron and matchboarding with a platform at one end which are familiar
objects of the countryside from Caithness to Cornwall. The food problem
caused by the war made anything like a feast out of the question at such
short notice, but the knowledge that there was whisky galore more than
compensated for the absence of the muscular fowls which were usually
the main dish of such an occasion. There was a lack of young men in the
prime of life, for the great majority of the young men of the island were
sailing the seven seas in ships of the Mercantile Marine. The question of
winding up with a dance had been mooted, but Peggy and Kate Anne
had declared that this would mean abandoning the evening to boys and
girls in their 'teens, while the rest of the company sat on the hard bench
which ran right round the hall against the walls and allowed the very
young to take control of the proceedings. Speeches, songs and piping
were declared likely to make the evening more enjoyable for everybody
than dancing.

A trestle table had been set on the platform, at which Joseph Macroon
presided patriarchally over a few relations and special friends. On his
right was Father Macalister. On his left was Peggy, the convention
being that he was not allowing her to be betrothed to her suitor until he
had been persuaded by the eloquence of the suitor's advocate. Duncan
Bàn, the advocate appointed, sat at the other end of the table with
Sergeant-major Odd, the suitor, on his right. On Duncan Bàn's left was
Dr Maclaren who had come over with Catriona and Norman Macleod,
George Campbell, Andrew Thomson, and Alec Mackinnon in the *Flying
Fish*, which after depositing them at Kiltod had proceeded round to
Bàgh Mhic Ròin on business that was itself a pleasure. Others at the
special table were the headmaster of the Kiltod school, Andrew Chisholm
and his wife, Michael Macroon, a schoolmaster from the west side of the

island and a nephew of the host, two or three girl friends and contemporaries of Peggy and Kate Anne, and two or three middle-aged aunts and elderly great-aunts.

The company had just settled down to the scones, bannocks, girdle-cakes, pancakes, and oatcakes which mixed with tea would provide a solid basis for the whisky, when Captain and Mrs Paul Waggett entered the hall. Mrs Waggett had by no means welcomed the prospect of crossing the Coolish in the Biffer's *Kittiwake* even upon so calm and clear an evening, but her husband had stressed the importance which everybody would attach to their patronage and she had, as always, surrendered. She was looking a little more like a battered nursery doll than usual because she had just discovered that the *Kittiwake*'s engine had deposited a large patch of oil on her squirrel coat.

'A *Dhia*,' muttered Joseph, 'here's Wackett! What's brought him over?' Then he rose from his chair and stepped down into the body of the hall to welcome the newcomers almost effusively. '*Thig a stigh*, Mr Waggett. Come right in please. Very glad to see you, Mrs Waggett.'

'Come right in to the body of the kirk, Colonel,' Father Macalister boomed.

If there was one thing Captain Waggett disliked it was being called 'Colonel' by Father Macalister. He disliked it so much that he never hesitated to attribute what he considered a breach of good manners to the fact that the priest of Little Todday must have had a drop too much. Mrs Waggett, who now heard her husband greeted as 'Colonel' for the first time, looked anxious.

'It's quite all right, Dolly, he's just being funny in his own rather primitive way,' he whispered reassuringly. 'Good evening, Mr Macroon. Good evening, everybody,' he went on, smiling his *haut ton* smile.

'Come up to the table, Mrs Waggett,' Joseph invited. 'Will you give Mrs Waggett your chair, Mairead, and you'll give Mr Waggett yours, Morag.' The two contemporaries of Peggy and Kate Anne to the annoyance of their friends and themselves were banished from the special table to make room for these two unwelcome guests. Nor was Captain Waggett himself pleased because he thought that by taking the places of Morag and Mairead he and his wife were not being treated with so much ceremony as they were entitled to.

For a time the evening was heavy going; but presently the whisky began to go round, and it was wonderful to see the effect of even one dram, particularly on the old ladies, who all looked at the glasses as if they had not the least idea what was in them and who on being told to drink up turned to their neighbours, giggling and waving away temptation until they felt they had protested enough, when they took their drams like seasoned warriors and immediately afterwards all began to talk at once, interspersing the chatter with jocund squeals and much laughter.

It was now time for Duncan Bàn to make his speech on behalf of Sergeant-major Odd. He opened with a few conventional compliments in English about the soldier who had come back from the wars to the girl with whom he had fallen in love and extolled the military virtues of his friend in whom, when he was married to her, Peggy Iosaiph would find domestic virtues not less notable.

The orator stopped abruptly at this point.

'Ach, ladies and gentlemen,' he resumed, 'it's no use at all for me to be talking to you in a language which isn't my own language at all.'

'Hear, hear!' Father Macalister declaimed sonorously.

'I'm just making a ringmarole of it,' Duncan apologized.

'Ay, ay, going round and round in a ringmarole,' the priest gurgled. 'You'd better speak in the language of Eden, my boy.'

So Duncan Bàn addressed the company in Gaelic and to judge by the shrieks of merriment he was making a good job of it. The Sergeant-major wondered what on earth Duncan Bàn was saying about him when people kept turning round to gaze at him and grin. He tried asking Dr Maclaren once or twice, but all the Doctor would say was what a pity he couldn't understand what Duncan was saying because it was so good, and English would only spoil the flavour of it anyway. Then suddenly everybody began to look at Peggy, who was blushing hotly, and the Sergeant-major had to sit and look vacant, though he was sure he ought to be looking knowing.

At last Duncan Bàn's speech came to an end amid loud applause led by Father James, and Joseph rose to make his reply.

'Reverend father, ladies and gentlemen,' he began, 'it is a great occasion for me to offer the hospitality for which our island is so famous. I have always tried as the representative of Little Todday on the Inverness County Council to keep the flag flying. We want a new school.'

'Hear, hear!' ejaculated Andrew Chisholm, who was a very dark little man with burning eyes.

'My friend the Sgoileir Dubh says "hear, hear!" He can feel sure that I will take every opportunity to bring the question of a new school for

Kiltod before the Council. But a school is not all that we want. No, indeed. We want a new road running from the north to the south of the island like the road I was able to persuade the Council to make from east to west. I'm sure you'll all agree with me that a road from Bàgh Mhic Ròin to Tràigh nam Marbh would be a benefit to the whole community. Well, I don't believe I have anything more to say, except to make you all welcome and wish you . . .'

At this moment Peggy pulled her father's coat, and looking round to see what she wanted he suddenly remembered why she was sitting by him.

'Carried away by the great enthusiasm which always takes a hold of me when I begin to speak of the island we all love I never said a word about my own daughter. My friend and fellow clansman, Duncan Macroon, has spoken about our friend Sarchant Odd, and we all agree that if a stranger is to come and take away one of our island beauties – and she is a beauty right enough, she's very like her father – why, then we'd as soon that a fine fellow like the Sarchant would do it as anyone. Well, ladies and gentlemen, Peigi Ealasaid is a good girl and I ought to know, for I have had five girls to teach me. And she's a good daughter. But daughters are not wives. I'm sure there isn't a man here who would want to be giving his wife away and keeping his daughter. Well, seeing that wives are so much better than daughters I don't believe I ought to stand in the way of letting my own daughter become a wife.'

There was loud applause at this.

'And so I'm not going to stand in the way of the pair of them coming to an understanding about the future and we'll drink their health in this beautiful whisky which arrived in the very nick of time.'

After the health of the engaged couple had been drunk Father Macalister rose to his feet.

'I'll just say in that unfamiliar tongue for the benefit of the Sergeant, who has the misfortune not to speak or even to understand our glorious language, that we welcome him to the finest island in the world. He has chosen a lovely and beautiful girl and he has been lucky enough to find that she chose him. Sergeant Odd is not a Macroon himself, but I'm not a Macroon myself either, and so he need not feel too much cast down by the failure of his ancestors. And I'm going to remind all Macroons present tonight that they wouldn't be here at all if once upon a time a stranger had not come to Todaidh Beag and chosen a seal-woman for his bride, and we are told that the seven sons of this stranger who came to Todaidh Beag once upon a time went off to the mainland when they grew up and came back, each of them, with a bride from there, which goes to show that there were Macroons on Todaidh Beag before ever there were MacRuries on Todaidh Mòr, because nobody would go to the mainland for a bride if he could find one in an island close at hand.'

After the applause evoked by this triumphant demonstration of the greater antiquity of the Macroons the priest went on more gravely for a few moments.

'And now I'm going to reveal a secret. Some of you may be wondering why I am such a keen supporter of a mixed marriage. I'll tell you why. It's because Sergeant Odd confided in me his desire to become a Catholic, and by the time he and Peigi Ealasaid Nic Ròin kneel at the altar to be made man and wife on the Wednesday in Easter Week . . .'

'Och, you're galloping ahead too fast, Father James,' Joseph broke in to protest. 'The date of the wedding is not settled yet.'

'But it is settled, Joseph. I settled it myself,' declared the parish priest amid rapturous applause.

'As I was going to say, when the County Councillor for Todaidh Beag interrupted me, when I marry them on the Wednesday in Easter Week it will not be a mixed marriage at all. And now if you poor unfortunate people who can only speak the tongue of the Sassunnach will excuse me I'll say the rest of what I have to say in a more impressive way.'

When Father Macalister sat down after what was evidently an extremely lively discourse in Gaelic the Sergeant-major was called upon for a speech.

'Father Macalister and all friends, I thank you very much for the kind way in which you have drunk the health of Peggy and – er – myself. I took a fancy to Little Todday the moment I set foot on it nearly two years ago and I think I must have realized I was going to find here the girl who I'd been looking for all my life. You'll hear a lot of people say there's no such a thing as love at first sight. Isn't there? I know there is. Owing to circumstances over which I had no control I was away from you all for a long time, but here I am again. I'm a lucky man if ever there was one. I don't think there's anything more to say except thank you very much one and all for your kindness to yours truly.'

The Sergeant-major was about to sit down when Father Macalister ejaculated in a reproachful tone.

'Great sticks alive, Sergeant, you've forgotten all we arranged.'

'You've forgotten the ring,' Duncan reminded him.

The Sergeant-major wrung his hand.

'Tut-tut,' he clicked. 'Nice example to show the Home Guard, I don't think.'

And then he began to search the pockets of his battledress, innumerable as the laughters of the sea, for the engagement ring he had bought for Peggy — the two small sapphires on a gold circlet with which he intended to symbolize her eyes. The bridegroom searching frantically for the wedding-ring at the altar steps is a spavined hack of humour. The Sergeant-major's behaviour was essentially the same except that instead of the whispered advice of the best man to try this or that pocket he received advice from all the people at the table on the platform except Peggy, who tried to look as if she didn't know what all the fuss was about. In the end the ring was found, appropriately in the pocket over his heart.

'Put it on her finger, Sergeant,' advised Father Macalister, who after three or four drams of a whisky called All the Year Round was sitting like old Saturn himself exhaling wisdom and benignity upon the air of the Golden Age.

The Sergeant-major placed the sapphire ring on the third finger of Peggy's left hand and leaning over kissed her upon the lips to the accompaniment of tremendous applause. He then led her away from the seat next to her father and brought her to sit by himself at the other end of the table.

'Now what about a *pìobaireachd*?' Father Macalister asked. 'Come along, Andrew, and give us a real rouser.'

The Sgoileir Dubh was about to obey these orders when Captain Waggett rose to his feet.

'Excuse me, Father Macalister, but before Mr Chisholm gives us a tune on the pipes I should like to say just a few words.'

'Certainly, Colonel, as many as you like,' the priest assured him, with deep dithyrambic emphasis.

'I don't know why Father Macalister gives me a rank to which I'm not entitled,' Captain Waggett began with a hint of peevishness in his voice. 'I am a simple captain.'

'Simple Simon met a pieman,' the priest intoned.

'Father Macalister will have his little joke,' said the speechmaker.

'He will indeed,' the priest asserted with an almost portentous nod, followed by a profound sigh.

Mrs Waggett, who felt that her husband was being treated with a deplorable lack of courtesy, tapped the table to admonish everybody.

'Well, ladies and gentlemen, it is my pleasant duty to propose the health of my friend Mr Joseph Macroon, the father of the young lady whose engagement to our good friend Sergeant-major Odd we are celebrating this evening. He has entertained us lavishly and I am sure we all wish to express our grateful thanks for such hospitality. And now I hope you'll none of you take it amiss if I utter a word of warning, and in doing so I am not going to beat about the bush. I don't like beating about the bush, and ever since I came to live among you at Snorvig "far from the maddening crowd" as they say . . .' Father Macalister breathed out an immense sigh at this misquotation but refrained from comment, '. . . I've always tried to avoid beating about the bush.'

'Quite right, Mr Waggett,' said the priest, 'there's usually very little in a bush when you have beaten it.'

'Every man here knows that a steamer of the Blue Limpet Line called the *Cabinet Minister* has been wrecked off the island of Pillay and that the greater part of the cargo of the *Cabinet Minister* consists of whisky.'

A burst of loud applause greeted this statement.

'I want to ask you to beware of considering that this cargo belongs to you. No, it belongs to the Government. This whisky was being exported to America in order to do its bit towards lightening the grievous burden of the war against aggression. The war is now costing us about fourteen million pounds a day . . .'

Father Macalister rose.

'Really now, Mr Waggett, I don't think this is the suitable occasion for a political speech.'

'I'm not making a political speech, Father Macalister. I'm only trying in my own humble way to show the other side of the picture. I want the people of the two Toddays to realize that the cargo of the *Cabinet Minister* is the property of the Government and that if they help themselves to Government property the penalties are very heavy. Major Quiblick of the Security Intelligence Corps at Nobost has already reported most unfavourably on the general attitude in these islands towards the war, and I expect most stringent measures will be taken if the people here give the Authorities the least excuse for action.'

Captain Waggett sat down in a puzzled silence, and Dr Maclaren jumped up.

'I think myself it's time we all paid a little attention to the business before us, and the business before us tonight is to enjoy ourselves. If the Government are concerned about what happens to the cargo of the

Cabinet Minister it's up to them to take the necessary steps accordingly. I think we can safely leave it to them, my friends.'

'I don't agree with you at all, Doctor Maclaren,' said Captain Waggett.

'Well, Mr Waggett, you and I have disagreed so often on so many different questions that I don't think the world will come to an end if we disagree once more. Anyway, in spite of the Government, I'm raising my glass to Sergeant-major Odd and Peggy Macroon, and I hope I'll be invited to the wedding, and now I'm not going to stand in the way of the piper any longer. *Suas am pìobaire!*'

Andrew Chisholm was given a great ovation when he tucked the bag of his pipe under his arm and began the fearsome process of tuning up. Feeling that the gathering required a tune to set their feet tapping he began with *The Road to the Isles*, and as the little dark man marched up and down the middle of the hall he was not unlike a black cock displaying his virtuosity for the admiration of the grey-hen he was wooing. *The Road to the Isles* was followed by a reel and a strathspey. Then old Michael Stewart, an uncle of Jockey, sang a *port a beul*, which means literally mouth music and is usually a comic narrative delivered at some speed, with a lilt to it that used to serve dancers for a pipe or a fiddle once upon a time. It is a dying art and only to be heard in perfection from old men and old women. Michael Stewart was wildly applauded, and after he had put away another dram he sang another *port a beul* with such verve that four old ladies took the floor and executed a Scots reel to the loud delight of the onlookers.

'Now, Duncan, you'll give us your song,' Father Macalister proclaimed. 'Och, it's a great pity you won't be able to follow this, Sergeant. It's really a beauty.'

By this time Duncan Bàn's fair hair was tousled, his face vividly flushed, his blue eyes bright as ever but faintly out of focus for his immediate listeners and concentrated upon some vision beyond the hall. The song, delivered in a nasal tenor, was evidently full of personal allusions, the Sergeant-major decided, because the people were continually looking at him and Peggy; and once or twice when she clutched his arm and murmured, 'Oh well, what a chick!' or '*A Mhuire Mhuire,* what will he be saying next?' he tried to get a translation from her, but every time she merely said '*Ist, ist,*' and waggled a forefinger to rebuke his interruption. The Sergeant-major promised himself that when he and Duncan Bàn got home after the rayjack he would make him translate the song for him right through before he went to bed.

And so the evening went on its way with songs and piping, occasional reels, much chatter, and an ever-increasing volume of laughter, which reached its maximum when the Banker who had been sitting monosyllabic for three hours suddenly rose from his chair and going down into the hall solemnly began a Highland fling, for which the company in an ecstasy of appreciation provided the music with a *port a beul* in unison.

'And now Captain Waggett will sing *The British Grenadiers*,' Father James announced.

'No, no, Father Macalister, I never sing.'

'There's no such word as "never" in your language or ours on a beautiful occasion like this. Come along, my boy, and sing *The British Grenadiers*.'

'No, really, Father Macalister, I'm afraid I have no parlour tricks.'

'Parlour tricks?' the priest repeated in a richly wrathful bass. 'Music and love will come from the West until the day of the seven whirlwinds,' he quoted sonorously. 'And he calls them parlour tricks. You'll give us *The British Grenadiers*, or by all the holy crows I'll disband the Home Guard. Come along now, we respect your modesty and we honour you for it, but you can't indulge in your modesty to the detriment of a glorious and beautiful occasion like this. We *must* have *The British Grenadiers*.'

'But my husband doesn't sing,' Mrs Waggett tried to explain, growing pink with indignation.

'Then the sooner he starts the better, Mrs Waggett.'

Luckily — for Mrs Waggett was beginning to get really angry — Drooby and the Biffer appeared in the entrance of the hall just then to say that the boats were waiting.

'*Thig a stigh, a Dhrooby. Thig a stigh, a Bhiffer*,' the parish priest bombilated like a great bee, 'you've got to drink the health of the happy couple. And then I'll be leaving you. It's not yet midnight by Almighty God's time, but I think Lent is close enough at hand to make it advisable to break up the party.'

So, after Drooby and the Biffer had drunk the health of the Sergeant-major and his Peggy, the guests from Great Todday gathered to make their way down to the quay and the guests from Little Todday gathered to take their various tracks across the machair under a moonless sky full of stars. Duncan Bàn expressed a firm resolve to see the Great Todday guests safely aboard before going home himself, and thus gave the

Sergeant-major an opportunity to have a few words with Peggy before he went home with Duncan. Her father had gone off to have a look at his shed and make sure that nobody had taken advantage of the merry evening to carry off any of the cases of Minnie stored away there until a more secure hiding-place could be found.

'Do you like your ring?' he asked when she was looking at it by the glow of the peat fire in the little room at the back of the shop.

'Who wouldn't be liking such a lovely ring?' She turned to him suddenly. 'Fred, you never told me you were going to be a Catholic.'

'I didn't want you to think I was just doing it to make your dad agree to us getting married. Are you pleased, sweetheart?'

'Och, Fred, I am really happy.'

'I'm getting instruction from Father MacIntyre at Drumsticket which is about ten miles this side of Fort Augustus. I run over on my motor-bike two evenings a week. And there isn't half a lot to learn.'

'We'll go to Mass tomorrow,' she said.

'Rather! Funny thing, isn't it? If anybody had have told me two years ago that I'd be buzzing in and out of church like a bluebottle and sitting down learning a catechism like a kid in a Sunday school I'd have said "sez you". And talk about soppy reading! You know, a book can't be too soppy for me nowadays. Did you notice George Campbell tonight?'

'He was looking all the while at Catriona.'

'Goggling at her, I know. And he had quite a few drams. So did Norman Macleod. I hope they won't fall into the harbour when they're going aboard. There's one sure thing; if they do, Lieutenant Macroon won't be able to do much about hauling them out. In fact he was so top heavy I don't think I ought to have let him go down to the harbour with them. I wouldn't have, only I did want a few minutes with you, Peggy darling.'

'Och, it's Duncan Bàn you're talking about,' she exclaimed, her brow clearing suddenly. 'For goodness' sake don't be calling him Lieutenant Macroon. He hates anybody to laugh at him.'

'I'm not laughing at him. That's what I've got to call him so long as I'm a Sergeant-instructor.'

'You're talking like Mr Waggett. *A Mhuire, Mhuire*, what nonsense he was talking, poor soul! I felt quite sorry for him, and Father James was just encouraging him and then putting his hand up to his mouth and laughing away to himself. And then trying to make him sing! It was really too bad.'

'Well, we owe a lot to Father James, you and me do, ducks. Think of it. Next month we're going to be married. Next month!'

'Don't be too sure. My father can be terribly thrawn when he likes.'

'Thrawn! Do you remember when you told me I was thrawn, and I thought it was Garlic and asked you what it meant? And do you remember when you thought I didn't know the Garlic for kiss and I did and I kissed you for the first time? That was the end of April 1941, and at the end of April 1943 we shall be married. No wonder I've gone in for soppy reading! Lovely weather it was too, if you remember. I hope we'll have lovely weather like that at the end of next month.'

'Was your mother angry when she heard you were going to be a Catholic?'

'Angry? Not she! I tell you, she's been trying to get me to settle down for over twenty-five years, and now I've done it properly. No, Ma's highly delighted, Mar is. She's going to think no end of you, Peggy.'

'I'll be terribly shy when I see her.'

'No, you won't. Not a bit, you won't. I mean to say, she's so homely and jolly. I wish she could have been with us tonight. Here, I wonder what's happened to Lieutenant Macroon.'

'Goodness me, Fred, you can't be calling him that. You're making a fool of the man when you call him that.'

'I hope he hasn't fallen into the harbour.'

'Are you getting so tired of being with me?' she asked demurely.

He caught her to him.

'All the soppy reading in the world won't tell me what I'd like to say to you, Peg of my heart. I loved you the first moment I saw you and I'll go on loving you till the end.'

'A ghràidh,' she murmured, raising her lips to his.

'Gry? That's a new one on me. What's it mean?'

'That's a secret for me,' she trilled.

The voice of Duncan Bàn was heard without.

'Hullo, hullo, where are you all?'

His flushed face appeared in the doorway.

'Oh, eudail, what a set out at the quay. Everybody holding up everybody else. And the Kittiwake has hardly a couple of inches of freeboard she's that loaded up with Minnie. I tried to persuade Drooby to take the Waggetts. Nothing doing. "I wouldn't take him, Duncan," he says to me, "not if the Flying Fish was Noah's Ark herself." Oh well, I had to laugh. So the Captain and his missus are sitting up each of 'em on a couple of cases of Minnie in the stern of the *Kittiwake* and I don't believe the tiller will move twelve inches to port or starboard. It's a real comedy. "You'll have to steer her with your nose, Airchie," I said to the Biffer. Poor old Waggett, he was looking a bit nervous. "Och," I said, "You'll be all right, Captain. You won't drift farther than Mid Uist on a night like this unless you might be drifting to West Uist or East Uist." "Ay, he'll be able to see the Security Intelligence Corpse," says the Biffer, who you'll understand had had a hefty one, and didn't mind what he said at all. Anyway, away they went and God knows if they'll ever reach Snorvig tonight.'

'Why wouldn't Alan Galbraith take them?' the Sergeant-major asked.

'Och, he had a huge load of Minnie in the *Flying Fish*, and he was taking her to Loch Sleeport. I believe he and Norman Macleod will have found a safe place in Watasett to hide the stuff away. He wouldn't want Waggett to know about that. And indeed, it's as well he wouldn't be knowing after that sermon we had from him this evening. He'll be up to mischief. Och, he doesn't really mean any harm. Somebody must have told him once that he was a clever boy and he's grown up on the strength of it. Dr Maclaren's the one for Waggett. Did you hear what he said to me when Waggett was preaching that sermon? Och, well, he made me laugh right enough. "Duncan," he says, "if you *pitheid* yatters much longer I'll tell him to stick out his tongue and have a look at it."

'He put away a tidy few drams did the Doctor. He said to me, "Duncan," he said, "if Waggett's figures are right, this evening we must have drunk what would pay the cost of the war for about one thousandth part of a second." Oh well, the Doctor enjoyed himself right enough. Ay, ay, he was as red as a geranium in a pot. And the Banker! I don't know what Mrs Thomson will be saying to him when he gets home. He was telling Alec Mackinnon a really long story about the first job he ever had at Corstorphine, and Alec Mackinnon sat looking at him the way anybody would look if a statue of St Joseph started talking to him. And did you see George Campbell? There's breakers ahead for him when he gets back to Garryboo tonight and has to tell his mother where he's been. Yon woman's a pure terror. She got me a fierce skelping once when she was the factor's wife and caught me at her currants when my grandmother sent me down to Snorvig to pay the feu of the croft.'

'Do you think he and Catriona Macleod will ever be married?' Peggy asked.

'I wouldn't care to give an opinion,' Duncan replied. 'Norman was telling me that George has been pretty feeble. Still, George was asking me if I knew where you got that ring for Peggy, and you'd do the man a kindness if you let him know.'

'I hope he won't be giving Catriona one just like mine,' said Peggy apprehensively.

'That's all right,' her affianced told her. 'There wasn't another one like it in the shop in Inverness where I bought it.'

'Catriona has brown eyes. I think rubies would suit her better,' Peggy decided. 'But look, you and Duncan ought to be going along, Fred. The second Mass is at ten.'

It was about three miles to Duncan Bàn's croft, almost due west from Kiltod but a little to the north of the metalled road which Joseph Macroon had secured from the County Council about a couple of years before the outbreak of war. It ran right across the island to the long sandy beach called Tràigh Swish, of which Hector Hamish Mackay has written in *Faerie Lands Forlorn*:

Many and fair are the long white beaches that stretch beside the western shores of the islands at the edge of the mighty Atlantic, but none is fairer than lovely Tràigh Swish of Little Todday. Philologists differ about the origin of the name. So let us fly backwards out of the prosaic present upon 'the viewless wings of poesy' and accept the derivation from Suis, a Norse princess of long ago who, legend relates, flung herself into the ocean from that grey rock which marks the southern boundary of the strand. Alas, her love for a young bard of Todaidh Beag, as Little Todday is called in the old sweet speech of the Gael, was foredoomed.

And while we are back in the faerie days of yester year let us ponder awhile that grey rock which marks the northern boundary of Tràigh Swish. Does it seem to resemble the outline of a great seal and justify its name – Carraig an Ròin? Some relate indeed that it is no mere likeness of a seal but the petrified shape of the seal-woman herself from whom the Macroons sprang. Who shall say? Upon this magical morning of spring when the short sweet turf of the machair is starred with multitudinous primroses, the morning-stars of the Hebridean flora as they have been called, we yield our imagination to the influence of the season and are willing to believe anything. We stand entranced midway along Tràigh Swish and watch the placid ocean break gently upon the sand to dabble it with tender kisses. We listen to the sea-birds calling to one another as they wing their way to their nesting grounds on the two guardian isles of Poppay and Pillay. We gaze at the calm expanse of the Atlantic and try to forget its winter fury of which the heaped-up tangle along the base of the dunes reminds us. We are at one with nature. We have the freedom of Tìr nan Òg – the Land of Youth.

It was on the green turf above this beach that Sergeant-major Odd had first declared his love to Peggy just on two years ago, and it was on this beach that Duncan Bàn found his chief source of poetic inspiration. Duncan had not been at all grateful to Joseph for his metalled road, particularly when he put a lorry on it. Nobody liked that lorry. It frightened the ponies in the carts and disturbed the cattle, and everybody on the island had been pleased when Joseph sold the noisy monster to Simon MacRurie in Snorvig.

'We'll have to put a stop to this notion Joseph has taken for a road from Bàgh Mhic Ròin to Tràigh nam Marbh. Does the man think we will be spending the rest of our lives unloading cases of whisky and carting them away to a safe place? I never knew a crayture like Joseph for getting an idea into his head and keeping it there till it goes bad on him. Poor old Andy Chisholm saw his new school fading from him like a morning dream.'

The starry walk back to Duncan's croft had given him a fresh thirst by the time they reached this thatched house, one of the few left on the island. It was built in a hollow of the machair sheltered from the worst of the Atlantic blasts by a grassy ridge which ran between two knolls. Here Duncan Bàn had lived alone since his grandmother's death, his mother having died when he was a baby and his father having been drowned at sea when he was a small boy. He had been a student at Glasgow University, and a promising student too. However, when a girl jilted him and almost at the same time he had found himself the owner of the croft he had left the University without taking a degree and chosen this solitary life with a particularly intelligent dog called Luath, a couple of cows, some fowls, and a good Gaelic library. He had inherited some £2,000, the income from which allowed him to indulge from time to time in bouts of deep drinking, when one neighbour or another would look after his cows and his fowls until he had recovered. He wrote good Gaelic poetry, of which a collection had been going to be published for some ten years but was always being postponed because Duncan was dissatisfied with what he had written and thought that if another year was allowed to pass the collection would be a better one.

'Welcome to Tigh nam Bàrd, Sarchant,' he said as he lighted the lamp and pointed to an armchair in the little room off the kitchen. 'I'll soon have the fire in good order, and we'd better have a dram before we take ourselves to bed.'

'A very small one for me,' said the Sergeant-major.

'This is one I don't think you've tried yet. Bard's Bounty. And you're going to drink it in Tigh nam Bàrd – the House of the Bard. The word has gone round that every bottle of Minnie with that name on it rolls right along here. It's not often that a bard gets his due in these days, but by Jingo, he is going to get it from the good ship *Cabinet Minister*.'

Duncan Bàn poured out a hefty dram for his guest and a hefty one for himself.

'Here, you've given me too much,' the Sergeant-major protested.

'Not at all. Not at all. Free and easy, my boy. That's the way when there's whisky galore. Ah well, *slàinte mhath, slàinte mhór*.'

He raised his glass.

'Slahnjervah, slahnjervaw,' said the Sergeant-major, raising his.

'Ay, it was a grand evening right enough,' said Duncan. 'I've never enjoyed myself better. And the Great Todday contingent enjoyed themselves fine.'

'I wish you'd do something for me, Lieutenant Macroon,' Sergeant-major Odd began.

'I'll give you such a terrible bang on the head with this bottle if you call me that, you won't know which island you're on. My name is Duncan, and Duncan is what you'll call me or the end of the evening won't be as enjoyable as the beginning, and that's a fair warning. A man toils hard to write a song for your *rèiteach* and you call him Lieutenant Macroon for his trouble.'

'It was about that song I wanted you to do something for me, Duncan.'

'That's more like it.'

'I want you to translate it into English for me,' said the Sergeant-major earnestly.

'Och, it sounds like nothing at all in English,' the author protested.

'Never mind, I'll get the general sense of it.'

'*Ceart gu leoir*. I'll do my best for you when I've had another dram. And you'd better have another yourself.'

'No, no, I won't really. I'm full up.'

'You may be full up, but you're not overflowing, and when Almighty God sends His bounty to the bard He expects his gratitude to be overflowing. So you'll just drink up another, or not a word will I be translating for you.'

'But look here – isn't it tomorrow now?'

'And if it is just tomorrow now, what does it matter? Och, I don't think very much at all of Father MacIntyre at Drumsticket if he's after instructing you that you can't drink a dram in Lent. We deny ourselves voluntarily. Voluntarily. And that's a pretty long word for me to be saying in English by now. I'm not going to Communion tomorrow. We'll go along quietly to the ten o'clock Mass and we'll get a cross of ashes on our foreheads. "Dust thou art," the priest will be saying, "and to dust thou shalt return." And, man, it's myself that will be feeling I really am dust, with the mouth on me I'll have by tomorrow morning, because I have a date with a fairy woman on the Tràigh when you'll be in your bed and she and I will be drinking Bard's Bounty together till the bens of Todaidh Mór are dark against the dawn. Now come along, fill up your glass and I'll try to give you an idea of my song, though it'll be a pretty poor idea.'

The Sergeant-major, seeing that he would get nothing out of the bard unless he accepted his bounty, allowed his glass to be replenished.

Duncan found the piece of paper on which the Gaelic version was written out and began:

'From over the sea a warrior came to our green and sunny island as long ago there came a son of Donald who was banished . . .' he broke off. 'Och, that's just all about an old tale of this MacDonald who came here and found the seal-woman and she put love upon him and they had quite a family. It goes on for two or three verses, but it all happened a long time ago, and I'm sure you won't want to be hearing all that ringmarole tonight. And then I sing about a girl with lips like the rowan and a neck like a swan and eyes as blue as the sea and then I say how she's like a seal-woman . . .'

'That's Peggy, of course?' said the Sergeant-major, who was wondering if it was being compared to a seal-woman which had made Peggy exclaim at Duncan's cheekiness.

'Yes, yes, that's Peigi. And then I say that she must have seven sons like the seal-woman because seven is an *odd* number. Och, there's a whole lot more, but you want to hear it in the Gaelic.'

'I wonder you never married yourself, Duncan,' said the Sergeant-major, who was so happy that he wanted the rest of the world to be as happy as himself.

'Ah, well, the *cailin* I wanted to marry married somebody else,' said Duncan. 'And that was that.'

'Don't you ever feel lonelified?'

'Ay, I was feeling pretty lonely when Minnie came along in the nick of time to cheer me up. But, my word, she's a good companion. And now you ought to be going to your bed, Sarchant.'

'What's Fred done, Lieutenant Macroon?'

Duncan laughed.

'That's one to you, *a Fhred*.'

'A red?' the Sergeant-major exclaimed.

'I'm giving it to you in the Gaelic. You always aspirate in the vocative, and the F becomes mute; but if you want to speak to Peggy, you'd say "*a Pheigi*".'

'That's what it is, is it? I thought Fecky was some sort of a nickname she had. I really must get down to it after I've mugged up this catechism and learn a lot of Gaelic, even if I sprain my jore in doing it. Are you coming up to bed yourself?'

'No, I'm going to take Minnie for a walk on the Tràigh.'

'You are? Hadn't you better come to bed? Don't forget we arranged we'd have a parade tomorrow and a bit of shooting practice.'

'Don't you be worrying about me, boy. I will be quite all right tomorrow.'

'Well, I suppose you know best what you can do,' said the Sergeant-major, 'but I'd have said bed was what you wanted.'

However, he realized it would be useless to argue with Duncan Bàn, who after seeing that his guest had all he wanted vanished into the starshine with the bottle of Bard's Bounty.

Duncan arrived at Mass next morning in a state of such confused piety that when he knelt to receive the ashen cross upon his brow he put out his tongue under the impression that he was going to be given the Host.

'Dust thou art and to dust thou shalt return,' said the parish priest in Latin. Duncan, his eyes closed, kept his tongue out.

'And when I put some ashes on his tongue to bring him round to his senses,' said Father Macalister afterwards, 'I don't believe Duncan was aware of it at all, his mouth was so much like the inside of an ashbin itself.'

Nevertheless, when it came to shooting that afternoon, Duncan Bàn Macroon scored more bull's-eyes than any man in the Little Todday platoon.

Chapter 13

MRS CAMPBELL'S DEFEAT

_____

'I really don't know what's going to happen to the two islands,' Captain Waggett in the *Kittiwake* said sadly to his wife as across the Coolish came the sound of a ragged but extremely hearty chorus from the deck of the *Flying Fish*. The raggedness was due to the fact that half the singers were singing *An t'eilean Muileach* – the Island of Mull, and the other half *Maighdeanan na h'airidh* – Maids of the Shieling.

Captain Waggett had taken advantage of the Biffer's being occupied with the engine to make this observation.

'I think the warning you gave them tonight ought to do good,' Mrs Waggett assured him hopefully.

'I don't think any of them will pay the slightest attention to it,' her husband replied. 'There's nobody with the faintest sense of responsibility, and the non-Toddayites are just as bad as the Toddayites. I must say when Thomson the Banker started making a fool of himself by dancing that fling I was shocked.'

'I'm afraid it's going to be rather a shock for poor Mrs Thomson when her husband gets home tonight,' said Mrs Waggett.

'I've never seen him give a sign of being the worse for drink,' her husband went on. 'If there was one man in Snorvig I would have said would always know how to keep himself in hand it would have been Thomson. Before we know where we are we shall hear that the Minister has been tippling.'

'Oh, Paul, what a frightful idea!'

'Well, it hasn't happened yet; but something will have to be done to stop this stuff being handed about like water. Here we are fighting a war for our very existence as a nation, and the one idea of the people here is to get hold of whisky which doesn't belong to them. And I hear that the *Island Queen*'s brought a plentiful supply of whisky and beer this afternoon. I'm going to talk to Roderick MacRurie about it tomorrow. He may see things in a reasonable light if he thinks his pocket will be touched.'

'I thought Sergeant-major Odd behaved very well, this evening,' said Mrs Waggett.

'I've no complaint to make against him. Of course, he was flattered by our turning up. That's what annoys me. You and I take the trouble to cross the Coolish in order to enter into the spirit of the island life, and all the thanks we get from Father Macalister is to call me "Colonel", which he knows I dislike, and then badger me to sing, which he knows I never do. These Roman priests have far too much power. Of course, he'd had too much to drink tonight. Something will have to be done about this wreck. I'm going to telegraph to Ferguson the Exciseman at Nobost tomorrow and say I think his presence here is urgently required.'

'Wouldn't the people resent that, dear?'

'I don't care if they do. I'm not going to sacrifice duty to cheap popularity.'

'No, of course you wouldn't, Paul. But you could send Mr Ferguson a letter. It would be less conspicuous.'

'A letter wouldn't reach him till Friday morning, and the matter is urgent. Do you know that at this very moment we're sitting on cases of whisky taken off this wreck? Look what a position that puts me in. The officer commanding the Home Guard in the two Toddays sitting on cases of whisky rifled from a wreck. It would be funny if it weren't so serious.'

At this moment the owner of the *Kittiwake* looked up from his argument with the engine.

'Keep her a bit more to starboard, Captain. The tide's running northerly and we don't want to find ourselves the other side of Snorvig. I don't know what's wrong with the engine. She's not putting her back into it at all. I believe somebody's been putting Minnie in my petrol tank.'

'I can't keep as much to starboard as I should,' Captain Waggett explained, 'because the tiller has not enough play between these cases, which I suppose contain whisky,' he added severely.

'Ay, that's Minnie right enough,' the Biffer said. 'We're loaded pretty deep. I wouldn't move about too much. We've hardly three inches of freeboard.'

'I hope there's no danger,' Mrs Waggett said tremulously.

'Oh, you're safe enough if you sit quiet, Mistress Waggett,' the Biffer assured her. 'The only thing is if the tide takes us past Snorvig we may have to go in to Garryboo. There'll be a bit of a ground swell, but we'll get ashore quite easily.'

'Go on to Garryboo?' Captain Waggett gasped. 'But how will Mrs Waggett and I get home from there?'

'You'll have to ring up for a car to come out and fetch you. You can telephone from the schoolhouse. It's awkward for you right enough, but och, these things happen and it's no use worrying yourself beforehand. Keep her as much to starboard as you can, and maybe we'll not miss the harbour at all.'

'You know, Dolly, sometimes the people here make me feel as if I was in a lunatic asylum,' Captain Waggett ejaculated in exasperation. He could give vent to his feelings because the Biffer was absorbed again by the behaviour of the engine. 'Snorvig? Garryboo? What does it matter where we go? And I suppose if we fail to make the point at Garryboo it won't worry Archie MacRurie. We'll get somewhere.

'It'll be rather awkward for you with all this whisky on board if we find ourselves at Nobost,' he told the Biffer when he left off messing with the engine for a moment.

'Och, that wouldn't worry me. There were two boats from Mid Uist taking the stuff away tonight. They'll be coming over from all the islands, perhaps over from Obaig and Mallan and Portrose before the week's out. The fiery cross has gone round everywhere.'

'Complete demoralization, that's what it is,' Captain Waggett said to his wife. 'Utter and complete demoralization!'

The *Flying Fish* with her choral passengers had steered southward for Loch Sleeport, and her powerful engine had soon taken them out of earshot of the little *Kittiwake*.

During the singing the Banker had been inclined to dance another fling, but the rest of the party were sufficiently sober to insist that the deck of a zulu under way was not the safest of platforms, and he had seated himself on a coil of rope to conduct the singing, the Gaelic words being beyond him. The crew of the *Flying Fish* had taken enough refreshment in the course of loading her with cases of Minnie to join in the choruses themselves. Drooby himself was at the wheel. Presently the impulse to sing exhausted itself, and the passengers sat about the deck in the starshine.

'I'll drive you back to Garryboo, George, if you like,' Dr Maclaren volunteered. 'My car's at Watasett!'

'Thank you, Doctor. That's very kind of you,' said George Campbell who in his mind accepted the Doctor's offer as a sign that the resolve he had made at the *rèiteach* would be accomplished. He turned to Catriona, who was sitting by him on a case of Minnie. 'I'm going to have it out with my mother once and for all tonight,' he told her.

'You've promised me that before, George,' she reminded him.

'Yes, but I feel much more sure of myself tonight. I suppose it was seeing other people so happy at the prospect of being married soon.'

'And a few drams to make yourself believe you're a brave man after all,' Catriona added.

'I may have had too much to drink,' said George gravely. 'I don't really know. I've never had too much to drink in my life.'

'Ask Norman,' Catriona advised. 'He knows the symptoms well. Norman,' she called across to her brother. 'George wants to know if he's tipsy.'

'You're after having had quite a few drams, George,' said Norman.

'I had four.'

'Is that all? Man, I believe I had a dozen, and hefty ones at that.'

'Yes, but you're used to whisky. I'm not.'

'How do you feel? Is your head swimming?'

'I feel grand. I felt when we came out of the hall that I was swimming down to the harbour instead of walking, but that feeling has gone away. I feel more clear-headed than usual and better able to express myself,' George declared.

'I certainly never heard you talk so free and easy in all the years I've known you,' Norman assured him.

'I was just telling Catriona that I intended to have it out with my mother once and for all tonight.'

'Good enough, *a bhalaich*. But won't the old lady be in her bed?'

'If she is I will get her out of it,' George proclaimed with real resolution in his tone.

'You'll want to be sure, my bold George, that this furious condition you're in will last as far as Garryboo,' Norman warned him. 'Speaking as one with a considerable amount of experience in these matters, I'm telling you you'll have to beware of the reaction. You may be feeling as bold as a lion just now, but by the time you get home your courage may have evaporated and you'll be as timid as a mouse when you face up to Mistress Campbell.'

'Of course he will be,' said Catriona scornfully.

'There's a saying, you know, pot-valiant,' Norman went on. 'You'll have to beware the pot isn't empty by the time you reach home.'

'Doctor Maclaren has very kindly offered to drive me back to Garryboo from Watasett.'

'Then I'll tell you what we'll do. We'll prime you with another dram and that ought to bring you into the ring in the pink of condition. Stand up a minute, George, and let's see how you hold yourself.'

George Campbell did so.

'Ay, you're standing steady enough on your pins,' Norman admitted. 'Not a doubt of it. He's standing pretty steady, eh, Mr Mackinnon?'

'He certainly is,' said the tall thin headmaster of Snorvig school. 'Did you enjoy yourself this evening, Mr Campbell?'

'Oh, I enjoyed myself very much indeed. Very much indeed I enjoyed myself,' said George earnestly.

'I think we all did. Was Mr Chisholm telling you about the tooth-paste, Mr Macleod?'

Extreme formality was always a sign that Alec Mackinnon was carrying a good load.

'No, I heard nothing about tooth-paste. Sit down, George. You don't have to be standing all the way back.'

'Well, it would appear that there's a certain amount of mixed cargo in the *Cabinet Minister*, and among other things some boxes of tooth-paste in tubes, and Mr Chisholm was saying the children were using them as squirts. He said the Kiltod school smelt like a chemist's shop, tooth-paste everywhere.'

'If any of the little devils start squirting tooth-paste at Watasett I'll spread it between a couple of pieces of bread and make them eat it,' Norman Macleod vowed.

The two schoolmasters moved to another part of the wreck, leaving Catriona and George to themselves.

'I know you think I won't have it out with my mother tonight,' he said to her. 'But I'm absolutely determined. I realize that my whole future happiness is at stake. You've every right to jeer at me, Catriona, but you won't have to jeer at me any more. I'm going to tell my mother, that you and I are going to be married at Easter . . .'

'At Easter?' Catriona exclaimed. 'A *Thighearna*, how will I have enough coupons to be marrying at Easter?'

'I thought we'd go and get married in Glasgow,' said George. 'I know Sergeant-major and Peggy Macroon are going to be married in Little

Todday, but the Sergeant-major doesn't belong to the place and he's an older man and they wouldn't be playing the tricks on him they might be playing on me. So if you don't mind, Catriona, I'd rather we were married in Glasgow.'

'Och, I'd rather be married in Glasgow myself,' said Catriona quickly, 'but I'll want just as many coupons in Glasgow as here, and we'll have to wait till the summer holidays.'

'No, we're going to be married at Easter,' George declared firmly. 'I've made up my mind.'

Catriona could not withhold a glance of admiration for this new and resolute George Campbell.

'Och, it's just the whisky that's talking,' she said.

'I admit that I probably wouldn't have been able to talk like this without the drams I had this evening, but when the effect of them passes off I'm not going back to being my mother's slave. If I find I'm in any danger I will take a few more drams.'

'You'll not become a drinker if you're going to marry me,' Catriona told him.

'I may have to until we're safely married,' George replied. 'So that's another reason for us to be married at Easter. Then I'll settle down.'

'Did anyone ever hear the like of the way you're talking, George?'

'Would you rather I just went on havering?' he asked.

'No, I don't believe I would,' she said softly.

'You could stay with your mother's sister in Glasgow before the wedding,' George went on. 'And I'll stay at an hotel. I've never stayed at an hotel by myself. It'll be quite an adventure.'

The *Flying Fish* was rounding Ard Slee, and even the trifling motion of her progress against the tide in the Coolish vanished as she glided up Loch Sleeport to Watasett.

'Not too much noise, boys,' Norman Macleod warned. 'We don't want everybody in the place to know there's quite so much of the stuff.'

Dr Maclaren's car was pretty full, with George Campbell, Alec Mackinnon, Andrew Thomson, and four cases of Minnie. Just before they started Norman Macleod came along to the door with a bottle of Annie Laurie and some glasses.

'A *deoch an doruis*,' he said.

'Not for me, Norman,' Dr Maclaren replied. 'I have to drive these chaps home.'

'Not for me, thank you very much, Mr Macleod,' said Alec Mackinnon. 'I'm just exactly right.'

'Not for me, Mr Macleod,' said the Banker, who did not feel that his forthcoming encounter with Mrs Thomson would be sweetened by the breath of Annie Laurie. He put a peppermint in his mouth instead.

'George?' Norman Macleod asked.

'Thank you, yes, I'll have just one more.'

'You've nine miles to drive,' said Norman pensively. 'You'll be home in about half an hour. I think this is about the right dose.'

He poured three fingers of Annie Laurie and handed the glass to George, who drank it down with the aplomb of young Lochinvar, waved to Catriona and settled down in the seat beside Dr Maclaren with a look on his face of what was known in Wardour Street English as derring-do.

The Banker and Alec Mackinnon were dropped in Snorvig, each with his case of Minnie, and the Doctor drove on towards Garryboo with George.

'I feel I'm imposing on your kindness, Doctor,' the latter said.

'Not at all. You wouldn't expect me to leave a man to walk the better part of four miles at past one in the morning with a case of whisky after such a party as we've just been enjoying.'

'All the same I'm very grateful, Doctor, I really am,' said George earnestly. 'I wonder if Captain Waggett is back yet.'

'They'll have been home half an hour ago,' the Doctor replied.

'I did enjoy myself at the *rèiteach*. Usually I feel terribly shy when I go to a party like that, but it was all so homely. I think Father Macalister is a wonderful man.'

'He is a wonderful man. I never met a better.'

'Catriona and I decided tonight to get married at Easter ourselves,' George went on.

'You did, did you? What's the old lady going to say to that?'

'I don't care what she says. She can say what she likes. It won't have the slightest effect on me one way or the other. One way or the other,' George repeated firmly.

'Is that so? George, I think you're more than a little tight.'

'I may be. I don't care. I thought that drink made me muddled. Well, I never felt less muddled in my life. I see quite clearly that the time has come for me to put my foot down, and I am going to put my foot down tonight, Doctor. Mind you, I knew I was treating Catriona badly by not insisting on my mother's inviting her to tea as soon as she heard we were engaged, but I just hadn't the strength of mind to assert myself. And then suddenly tonight at the *rèiteach* I saw that I was risking the whole of my future happiness and I made up my mind that I must do something about it. Either my mother is going to behave sensibly and decently to Catriona or I'm going to turn her out of the schoolhouse.'

'George, I think you must really be very tight.'

'I may be. I don't know. I've never been tight before.'

'The test will come when you're sober again.'

'If I find that being sober means being shy and feeble and unable to stand up to my mother I shall get tight again, Doctor. I've got this case of whisky that Alan Galbraith gave me.'

'You'll have to watch out you don't become the slave of drink, George. I very nearly let that happen to me, and I only just pulled myself out of it. Indeed, a lot of people don't think I've pulled myself out of it yet.'

'If Catriona and I are married at Easter, I won't need drink to give me confidence in myself. I'll have her.'

'Yes,' said the Doctor, with half a sigh. 'You're lucky, George Campbell. Yes, yes, you're a very lucky chap.'

'I know fine I am,' George agreed solemnly.

They drove on in silence after that, and soon enough the car approached the point where the road to Garryboo branched off from the main road.

'Don't you bother to take me right down to the house, Doctor. I'll walk from here. The road's very rough.'

'You can't lug that case of whisky all that way. Besides, I rather want to wake up your mother.'

'Don't you worry, Doctor. She won't be asleep. She'll know where I've been because the Sergeant was along this afternoon and she told him I wouldn't be at the *rèiteach*. It was when I heard she'd said that that I suddenly made up my mind I'd go. I had a feeling that the whole of my future life depended upon what answer I gave him.'

'I wouldn't say you were wrong, George.'

The car turned off to go bumping over the quarter of a mile or so of road for which the people of Garryboo held Roderick MacRurie personally responsible. They had even gone so far as to threaten to put up a rival candidate for the County Council at the next election, and by appealing to regional passions they stood a good chance of putting him in by making it a fight between Snorvig and the rest of the island.

Outside the schoolhouse Dr Maclaren sounded his horn several times.

'Just in case the old lady isn't awake,' he said to George. 'I think you're in the right mood to tackle her tonight. *Oidhche mhath*. Good night.'

He swung the car round on the grassy stretch in front of the school, and with one loud final blast such as knights used to give outside castles Dr Maclaren shot off back up the bumpy road on his way home.

Norman Macleod had timed the effect of that *deoch an doruis* to a nicety. While George Campbell waited outside the schoolhouse for his mother to come and open the door, which, as he expected, he found locked, he felt absolutely calm, absolutely determined, absolutely certain that what he intended to say (and if necessary do) was right. The sound of his mother's padded tread advancing along the passage on the other side of the gimcrack door had once upon a time made him gulp with nervousness and mop his forehead with a handkerchief. Once the sound of that padded tread would have made a man-eating tiger's tread seem as harmless in comparison as the pitterpat of childish footsteps. Once the sight of that black quilted dressing-gown had been as awe-inspiring as the last Empress of China at the height of her ruthless power. Now thanks to two drams of Pipe Major, two drams of Fingal's Cave, and three fingers of Annie Laurie the padded tread and the black quilted dressing-gown were like childish fears and fantasies which have been outlived.

'And what have you to say for yourself?' demanded the old lady when she opened the door.

'I have a great deal to say when I come in,' her son replied. 'But I'm not going to start a conversation out here. And will you please go back into the sitting-room, mother, while I take this case of whisky along to the dining-room? I don't want you to tear your dressing-gown on it, and if you stand there that's what may happen.'

'Case of whisky?' Mrs Campbell exclaimed. 'Did you say case of whisky?'

'Yes, yes,' said George impatiently. 'Don't pretend you're getting deaf.'

'George, you're drunk.'

'It's possible I am,' he admitted. 'If I am, it's nobody's business except my own. Anyway, will you make a cup of tea? There are a few things I want to talk over with you and we'll both be the better for a cup of tea.'

'I will certainly not start making tea at this hour of the night,' Mrs Campbell replied. 'Do you know what the time is?'

'It must be after half-past one.'

'It is a quarter to two,' Mrs Campbell answered in a doomsday voice.

'Yes, I daresay it will be,' her son said with an almost elaborate casualness. 'You'd better go in the sitting-room. I want to open a bottle of whisky and get myself a dram.'

'You'll do no such thing, George,' the old lady declared grimly.

'Won't I? Ah, but I will. If you're not going to make a cup of tea, I must have a dram.'

'If I make a cup of tea, George, will you not open a bottle of the liquor?'

'As long as I have something to drink I don't mind,' he answered, and almost chuckled aloud, for this was the first time his mother had ever bargained with him. He knew now that she was beaten before the battle began.

When Mrs Campbell came into the sitting-room with tea George noticed that she had brought a cup for herself. This he regarded as fresh evidence that she was losing her self-confidence.

The peat-fire in the sitting-room had been smoored, but it was soon stirred into life, and the mother and son sat down opposite one another on either side of it, she straight as a statue in her high-backed mahogany chair; he lolling as far as it was possible to loll in the old leather armchair of his father the factor. He lolled purposely because ever since he had inherited the right to sit in that armchair his mother had been accustomed to bid him sharply not to loll, and he was anxious now to disregard her injunctions by lolling more defiantly. Perhaps instinct warned her not to risk a rebuff. At any rate, she said nothing about lolling.

'I'm waiting, George, for an explanation of your behaviour in coming home at a quarter to two,' she said, after they had sipped their tea for a while in silence.

'It's a very simple explanation, mother,' he replied. 'I've been to the rèiteach of Sergeant Odd and Peggy Macroon at Kiltod.'

'After I told Sergeant Odd that you couldn't possibly go?' she demanded.

'You were answering for yourself, mother. You weren't answering for me. I saw the Sergeant-major myself at Watasett, and he told me you'd said I couldn't be going which . . .' George paused. 'Which,' he repeated with emphasis, 'made me absolutely determined to go.'

'And I suppose Catriona Macleod went with you?' Mrs Campbell asked bitterly.

'Surely. We were quite a party. Her brother, Doctor Maclaren . . .'

'Was there any chance of getting liquor that *he* ever missed?' she exclaimed scornfully.

'Now don't be talking against Doctor Maclaren, mother. He drove me home tonight.'

'So that was he, was it, blaring away outside the house. The man's without any shame at all.'

'If you mean to stay on the island, you'd better keep the right side of him, mother. You never know when you won't be needing his services,' said her son.

'If I stay on in the island? Is there any question of my not staying on?'

'That's for you to choose. Catriona and I are going to be married next month, and she's not terribly impressed with the notion of yourself as her mother-in-law. And indeed I don't blame her. I think you'd be wise to make yourself as agreeable as you can.'

'Have you gone mad, George?' the old lady gasped.

'Not at all,' her son replied. 'I've gone sane. I think I may have been a bit mad all these years, the way I've let you order me around and treat me as if I was still a child, but that's over now. Yes, I think I must have been a bit mad,' he went on reflectively. 'When I think of the time when we had that Home Guard exercise on a Sunday and you locked me up in my bedroom and I was actually soft enough to let you do it!'

'So the Sahbbath has become Sunday has it since you took to visiting your papist friends on Little Todday?'

'Oh, for goodness' sake, mother, don't be talking such nonsense. Are you really so ignorant as to suppose that only Roman Catholics say Sunday?'

'I think we'd better resume this talk tomorrow when you're sober.'

'We'll resume it all right,' her son told her, 'because I'm going to give you a night to think over what I have to tell you before you go up to bed. All my life it's been you who've ruled it. When I was small you terrorized me, and my father who had a kindly side to him hadn't the pluck to interfere. I suppose you'd terrorized him from the moment you married him . . . no, don't interrupt. You've talked enough. I'm doing the talking now.'

Mrs Campbell passed a hand across her brow as if she was testing it for an escape of brains which had left her incapable of grasping what was going on around her.

'Don't worry yourself,' said her son, 'this is real. This is not a bad dream. This is George Campbell, your son, speaking his mind.'

'And forgetting the Fifth Commandment,' the old lady reminded him, mustering her voice to repeat it.

'I don't want to hear that Commandment again,' said George, holding up his hand. 'You've dinned it into my ears since I was three years old.'

'Blasphemy now!'

'Och, please don't be stupid, mother. You don't help your case by being stupid. I'm not going to give you a catalogue of all the miseries you made me suffer as a child, and I am not going to give you a catalogue of what you've made me put up with, first of all when I was an assistant-teacher at Snorvig school and even more since you came here to keep house for me. You wouldn't be in bed before dawn once I started. All I want to get into your head tonight is that it won't ever happen again. I don't want to turn you out of the house, but that's what I will do unless in future you do what I say in all matters that affect me.'

'I must wait for my own son to speak to me as I've never been spoken to in all my life,' Mrs Campbell bemoaned.

'It would have been much better for you if I'd spoken earlier. I wish I had. Unfortunately your pride has never been curbed, and you've reached an age now, mother, when pride's the worst ticket to take for the next world. You've read your Bible an awful lot, but I wonder if you've ever read a verse of it with an eye on yourself instead of on other people. Now, don't look so angry. It's only that pride of yours which is making you angry. It was your pride which made you think you could break up matters between Catriona and me. You said to me when I first told you I was going to marry her that if I did you'd go and live with Aunt Ina in Glasgow, and I like a fool thought I had to appease you. You were Hitler. I was Chamberlain. What I ought to have told you was to go off right away and live in Glasgow because Catriona and I would be much happier here without you. All the same, you are my mother, and I feel I ought to give you a chance to pull yourself together and end your days where you've lived so long. So if you write a note to Catriona to invite her to come back with me after church on Sunday and spend the rest of the day here, and if when she comes you welcome her as a daughter, and if you give her all your coupons, I'll try to persuade Catriona that when we get married next month and she comes to live at Garryboo you'll keep your own place in the house and won't attempt to take hers. But if you'd rather not put your pride in your pocket, why, then I think you'd better telegraph to Aunt Ina that you'll be crossing to Obaig by Saturday's boat and will arrive in Glasgow that night.'

'Have you forgotten that the furniture in this house is all mine?' Mrs Campbell demanded in what she fancied was a menacing tone of voice, but which was in fact not much more than a croak.

'All but two or three pieces of my own,' said George. 'No, I've not forgotten that, and I'll have all your furniture sent down to the pier. I don't know when it will reach Glasgow, but I would think that when it does it won't look very much like furniture at all.'

'And where will you get furniture?' Mrs Campbell asked. 'Furniture is an expensive business these days.'

'I know that, but Norman Macleod will be leaving Watasett for some time when he goes into the R.A.F. and he'll be able to lend us enough to get on with for the present. Don't count on our being unable to manage. We shall manage all right, somehow. I believe I'll find people pretty anxious to help. I've had to make a good many excuses for you, mother, in Great Todday, and I know how nearly everybody in the island feels about you. You won't get any sympathy – even from Jemima Ross.'

'If you bring that Macleod girl to this house,' Mrs Campbell was beginning when her son rose from his chair and cut her short.

'I told you to go to bed and think it over. If you want to make your choice now, make it, but don't turn round and say I never gave you a chance to stay where you are,' her son said firmly. 'And I'll tell you this,' he went on. 'I wouldn't give you that chance if I didn't blame myself a bit.'

'Ah!' his mother put in.

'For not having told you before what a proud domineering old *cailleach* you are.'

Mrs Campbell was searching for a piece of scripture to cite for her own purpose, which was to annihilate this rebellious son of hers, when a knock on the front door made both him and her momentarily oblivious of what had passed between them in their astonishment at such a sound at such an hour.

'Who on earth can that be?' George exclaimed.

The knocking was repeated.

'You'd better go to the door and see who it is,' his mother told him.

'It may be survivors from a torpedoed ship,' he speculated.

In the first two years of the war a good many survivors had reached Great Todday and knocked in the night on the doors of houses near the sea. None had arrived for more than a twelve-month now, which to the islanders was the surest sign of victory in the Battle of the Atlantic.

'It's to be hoped it isn't more whisky,' said Mrs Campbell in gloomy disgust.

Chapter 14

CAPTAIN WAGGETT'S ADVENTURE

When what can now be called the master of the house opened the door he began to think that a second stage of drunkenness had succeeded the phase of truth and resolution, that phase of imaginary visions such as pink mice of which he had read in teetotal tracts handed to him by his mother.

'Mr and Mrs Waggett!' he exclaimed, half expecting to see both dissolve into nothingness as he spoke.

'I'm sorry to get you out of bed at this time, Sergeant Campbell, but I wanted to ask if you would let me use your telephone. Mrs Waggett and I have had rather an unpleasant adventure.'

'Come in, Mr Waggett – er – Captain Waggett. My mother and I were just having a cup of tea. I'm sure you'd like a cup of tea, Mrs Waggett.'

'Oh, I'd love a cup of tea,' she gushed gratefully. George Campbell led the way to the sitting-room.

'Here's Mr and Mrs Waggett, mother. And Mrs Waggett would like a cup of tea.'

The old lady rose from her mahogany chair, looking slightly dazed, as much by her son's inviting a visitor to have a cup of tea without waiting for her to give the invitation as by the unexpected arrival of Mr and Mrs Waggett in Garryboo after two o'clock in the morning.

'Would you prefer a dram, Captain?' George asked.

Captain Waggett would greatly have preferred a dram at that moment, but in his present mood of waging war against the cargo of the *Cabinet Minister* he felt he ought not to accept this offer and said he would prefer tea.

'Quite right, Mr Waggett, I'm glad to hear it,' Mrs Campbell applauded sombrely.

'All right, mother,' said her son. 'But don't keep Mr and Mrs Waggett waiting.'

The old lady went off to the kitchen, looking not unlike Lady Macbeth in the sleep-walking scene.

'I'd better telephone before I tell you what happened,' said Captain Waggett.

'I hope you get an answer at this time of night, Captain.'

'They're on duty all night at the post-office,' Captain Waggett reminded him loftily. 'I spoke to Donald MacRurie about that. I explained to him that the whole point of having a telephone is that it must be answered at any hour. Any hour,' he repeated.

After he had been ringing for ten minutes a sleepy small voice at the other end asked:

'Who is it?'

'This is Captain Waggett speaking.'

'Who is it, please?'

'Captain Waggett. I'm at the schoolhouse in Garryboo.'

'Do you want the Doctor's house, Mr Campbell?'

'This isn't Mr Campbell. This is Captain Waggett.'

'Who?'

'Captain Waggett of Snorvig House.'

'This is the post-office.'

'I know it's the post-office. Who is it speaking? Is that you, Mrs MacRurie?'

'Mrs MacRurie's in her bed.'

'Where's Mr MacRurie?'

'Is it Mr MacRurie at the hotel you're wanting? Or is it Mr Simon MacRurie the merchant.'

'No, no, no. Mr Donald MacRurie the postmaster.'

'He's in his bed too. Who is it speaking, please?'

'Captain Waggett. W for what . . .'

'I want to know who's speaking, please?'

'Captain Waggett. W for Wind. A for Accident. G for George. G for George again. E for Empty. T for Tommy, and then T for Tommy again.'

'Will I wake Mr MacRurie?'

'There's no need to wake Mr MacRurie. Have you understood who I am?'

'We can't be sending any telegrams till the morning.'

'I don't want to send a telegram. I want a car. Do you know who's speaking?'

'No.'

'But I spelt my name.'

'I'm sorry, I thought it was a telegram you were sending.'

'No, no, no. This is Captain Waggett. Mr Waggett.'

'Oh, it's Mr Waggett?'

'Yes, I'm at the schoolhouse in Garryboo. And I want you to ring up Donald Ian . . .'

'Donald Ian's lorry is at the pier. It's broken down.'

'Yes, but I want him to come for me in a car.'

'They were after carrying him home to bed two hours back or more.'

'Did he have an accident?'

There was a faint giggle at the other end of the telephone.

'No, he was asleep in the telephone kiosk. I think it was Minnie.'

'Who's she?'

Again there was a faint giggle.

'You're just laughing at me, Mr Waggett.'

'I'm not laughing at all. Mrs Waggett and I are stranded at Garryboo, and I must get hold of a car.'

'I'm sure I don't know where you'll get a car now.'

'Is Calum MacKillop on the phone?'

'Who?'

'Calum MacKillop. The Gooch.'

'No, he hasn't the telephone at all.'

'Is John MacPhail on the phone?'

'He has the telephone, yes.'

'Well, please put me through to him.'

Five minutes passed.

'I can't get any reply.'

'Who else on the phone has a car?'

'I really don't know.'

Captain Waggett put his hand on the receiver and called on George Campbell for help.

'Who is this stupid girl they have on night duty at the post-office now?' he asked irritably.

'I expect it will be Mrs Donald MacRurie's niece, Murdina Galbraith,' said George.

'I wish you'd speak to her and try to find out where I can get hold of a car.'

George Campbell took the receiver from Captain Waggett, but by the time he announced himself the telephone had been cut off.

'I wonder what would happen if the Germans had landed in Garryboo,'

Captain Waggett sighed. 'I do wish I could implant the most elementary rudiments of responsibility in the people here,' he added fretfully.

'Will I speak to her, Captain Waggett?' George Campbell asked when Garryboo was again in communication with Snorvig.

'She may be a little more intelligent in Gaelic,' said Captain Waggett. 'Apparently Donald Ian is drunk and the Gooch isn't on the phone and John MacPhail isn't answering.'

Sergeant Campbell was no more successful than his company commander.

'I'm sorry, Captain Waggett, but I'm afraid there's no chance of getting a car for you,' he said at last. 'The only thing to do is to get hold of Angus MacCormac or somebody who has a pony and trap and see if he'll drive you and Mrs Waggett into Snorvig. There's Murdo MacCodrum's lorry of course, but Murdo's apt to be a bit difficult. He's never really got over that time when we had the Home Guard exercise for putting all the motor vehicles on the island out of action.'

'Very petty,' Captain Waggett commented with disapproval. 'Very petty indeed. I wonder what Murdo MacCodrum would have done if the Germans had taken his car. A lot of compensation he would have got from them.'

'And we also queried his charges for transport once or twice. In fact, he says we still owe him two pounds. He was over at Bobanish only the other day seeing Mr Beaton about it.'

'Hopelessly unpatriotic of course,' Captain Waggett commented scathingly. 'Well, I suppose a pony and trap is the only solution. Will you go along to Angus MacCormac, or shall I?'

'It might be as well for me to go. Mother, will you look after Mr and Mrs Waggett while I go along and wake Angus MacCormac?' said George. 'What actually did happen, Captain?'

'Well, it seems that while Archie MacRurie was down in the hold of the *Cabinet Minister* somebody put whisky in his petrol tank with the result that the engine of the *Kittiwake* was running very badly.'

'I would think so indeed,' Mrs Campbell interposed. 'The engine just as drunk as its owner! Disgraceful!'

'Of course that may merely have been an excuse for being unable to manage his boat properly,' Captain Waggett went on.

'Yes, indeed,' Mrs Campbell agreed. 'Sahtan will always find an excuse for those who serve him well.'

'I was at the tiller,' Captain Waggett resumed, 'but there was no room to give it full play, and with the tide taking us up the Coolish all the while we couldn't keep the bow of the boat enough to starboard. The reason why I was so cramped at the tiller was that Corporal MacRurie had loaded up the *Kittiwake* with cases of whisky. Well, to cut a long story short, we failed to make Snorvig harbour and had to steer close inshore up to Garryboo Head.'

'And where's Airchie MacRurie now, Captain?' George Campbell asked.

'I suppose he's down at the landing-place. I was so angry that I left him. If it comes on to blow he'll lose his boat, cargo and all, and I'm bound to say it would serve him right if he did.'

'Don't worry yourself, Mr Waggett. He'll lose nothing,' said Mrs Campbell. 'Sahtan looks after his own.'

'It was really rather nerve-racking,' Mrs Waggett put in.

'I'm sure it was,' Mrs Campbell agreed. 'But that set of MacRuries were always a disgrace to the whole island. Donald Angus MacRurie, Airchie's father, was always brawling and bragging about the place. The old minister used to say he was a thorn in his side. And Airchie himself was the most mischievous boy in Snorvig. A regular young rascal if ever there was one. Just one of Sahtan's favourites.'

'You might remember, mother, that Airchie MacRurie has four sons in the Merchant Navy,' George said in rebuke of his mother. 'And I don't know how you'd be drinking that tea you're drinking now without the Merchant Navy.'

Captain Waggett looked at the headmaster of Garryboo in astonishment. He had never heard him, or indeed anyone else, speak like that to Mrs Campbell. He ascribed such self-confidence to the gradual effect of the training he himself had given George in the Home Guard and the authority he had acquired as sergeant in command of the Garryboo section.

'Well, I'd better be getting along to Angus MacCormac, Captain,' said the rebel. 'I'm sure you'll be anxious to get back home after your unpleasant experience. My mother will look after you while I'm away.'

When George Campbell reached Angus MacCormac's house the sitting-room was lighted up, and on being admitted by Angus he found Sammy MacCodrum and the Biffer in the sitting-room with a bottle of the favourite Stag's Breath on the table.

'Very glad to see you, Mr Campbell,' said the Biffer cordially. 'Angus and Sammy and myself are just having a little refreshment. You'll join us in a dram?'

George swallowed like a veteran the dram offered to him.

'By Chinko, Mr Campbell, you put that tram away ferry well,' Sammy MacCodrum exclaimed in admiration. 'I neffer knew you could put a tram away so well.'

'Slàinte,' said Angus, putting away a dram himself with equal dexterity, afterwards wringing out a few drops from his big moustache with his hand and absorbing them noisily.

'Mr Waggett was wondering if you would drive him and Mrs Waggett to Snorvig,' said George Campbell. 'He can't get a car anywhere.'

'Och, I'll take him back in the *Kittiwake*,' said the Biffer. 'Sammy here is going to get some petrol from his brother Murdo. I'm leaving most of the Minnie here. That was my idea in coming to Garryboo. Captain Waggett was plaguing the life out of me to take him over to Kiltod this evening.'

'And you meant to come here all the time?' George asked with a smile.

'I had a big cargo to deliver at Garryboo. Fifteen cases at £2 a case,' said the Biffer. 'Three of them going along to Knockdown. The Doctor bought a case for old Eachann Shimidh.' This was Hector MacRurie, the son of Simon.

'He's a grand fellow is the Doctor,' George declared.

'Och, he's a darling of a man,' the Biffer agreed.

'There never wass a petter man,' Sammy echoed. '*Slàinte* to the Doctor.' He drained his glass.

'Ay, and he's a good man at his job,' Angus MacCormac added. 'I don't believe anybody would find a better man not if he went to Glasgow.'

'You wouldn't find as good a man,' the Biffer asseverated. 'Is Waggett at your place now?' he asked, turning to George Campbell.

'Yes, my mother's giving them tea.'

'Is Mistress Campbell up and doing at this time of night?' exclaimed Angus MacCormac.

'She is. I was telling her that Catriona Macleod and I were going to be married next month,' said George with an elaborate nonchalance.

The two Garryboo crofters stared at him in amazement.

'By Chinko,' exclaimed Sammy, 'we must have another round on that.'

The glasses were filled again; the health and happiness of George and his future wife were drunk with enthusiasm.

'That'll be a bit of a shock for somebody in this house,' observed Angus, looking up at the ceiling.

'Does the teacher sleep chust over head?' Sammy asked.

'Ay, that's where she sleeps,' said the owner of the house.

'Och, well, I hope the news will give her a nasty sort of a tream,' said Sammy with enthusiasm. 'I wasn't after complaining to you, Mr Campbell, but she's really fishus. She strapped Annag last week till the child's hand was plack and plue. Ay, and she shook her like a tuster for no reason at all.'

'Well, I ought to be going back to let Mr Waggett know where he stands,' said George who was not anxious to be involved in a discussion of Jemima Ross's demerits as a teacher. 'What time will I say you'll be ready for him, Airchie?'

'If he gets down to the boat by three o'clock I won't be keeping him very long at all,' the Biffer replied.

'You don't think you could take him in your trap, Angus?' George asked.

'No, no, no. We have to get all this Minnie stowed away. That'll keep Sammy and me busy for another two hours.'

'Tell him he'll be back in Snorvig in no time,' said the Biffer. 'The tide will have turned by the time we start.'

So George Campbell went back to the schoolhouse to break the news to Captain Waggett that he would have to return, as he had arrived, by sea.

'Well, well, well, well, well,' Angus MacCormac ejaculated when he was gone, 'what's after happening to George Campbell? I never saw such a change in any man. Did you see the way he took his dram? Just a real warrior. And mind you, he's going right back to herself.'

'Ay, it's a pity the factor isn't alive,' said Sammy. 'I believe he't have been proud of Chorge in his heart, though he would neffer have had the pluck to say so to herself.'

'It's wonderful right enough what a woman can make of a man,' the Biffer observed.

'I'm not so sure it was Catriona Iain Thormaid,' Angus opined, stroking his moustache as if it was a judge's wig. 'There was plenty talk about him and Catriona getting married next summer, but if anybody was saying a word about it to the factor's wife she came down like a hammer on such talk. And Miss Ross up there was telling the missus that Mistress Campbell refused to have Catriona in the house. It was something stronger than Catriona which changed George Campbell. Did you ever see him take two drams the way he took those two drams just now, Sammy?'

'Neffer.'

'There you are now.'

'Ay, ay, it wass Minnie right enough,' Sammy declared.

'There was plenty Minnie at Peigi Iosaiph's *rèiteach*,' the Biffer said. 'Boys, they were swimming in it. "*Thig a stigh, a Bhiffer*," says Father James to me, and he gave me a huge dram with his own hands. "That'll keep the *Kittiwake* afloat, Airchie," he says. No, no, I reckon Mistress Campbell found she wasn't able to sink George tonight, though he may be a bit unseaworthy by tomorrow morning. Well, if I'm going to take the Captain and his missus back to Snorvig we'd better be getting the rest of the Minnie up, and if you can get that petrol from Murdo, Sammy, I'll be much obliged to you.'

It was exactly a quarter to four when the Waggetts embarked again in the *Kittiwake* after waiting three-quarters of an hour for the owner.

'It was rather a pity you didn't arrange to call for us at the schoolhouse on your way down,' said Captain Waggett in dudgeon.

'Ay, it would have been better right enough,' the Biffer agreed cheerfully. 'But Sammy MacCodrum had to get some petrol from his brother. Never mind, Captain, we won't be long now. The tide's running strongly with us, and you'll have more room for yourselves now the cargo has been unloaded.'

'Have you left all that whisky at Garryboo?' Captain Waggett asked sternly.

'Ay, I left most of the cases there, but we've still some left.'

'Look here, Archie, I do think you're playing rather a dangerous game,' Captain Waggett told him.

'In what way, dangerous, Captain?'

'I don't pose as an authority on the law, but I feel pretty sure that the sheriff could put you in prison for what you've been doing tonight.'

'If the *siorram* put me to prison he'd be sending plenty others to prison with me.'

'Yes, but you ought to set an example,' Captain Waggett pointed out in a tone of kindly patronage. 'After all you are a Corporal in the Home Guard, and as such you have a special responsibility.'

'But, if we didn't unload the whisky here ourselves, there'd be plenty more from all about would be unloading it,' the Biffer argued. 'They're round the ship already like flies on a sunny window. If the Government are so much worried about what happens to the wreck, why don't they put somebody in charge? We've had a spell of fine weather since she went on the Gobha in that fog on the Sabbath, but the fine weather won't last for ever, and if there came a heavy sea she might break in half the way she's lying now. We'd all feel pretty foolish if we left all that whisky for the fishes.'

'That's not the point, Archie. A burglar doesn't get off more lightly if the house he breaks into is empty.'

'I don't see why anybody would want to break into an empty house.'

'I mean empty of people,' said Captain Waggett.

'And anyway I don't know why you're worrying your head about what happens,' the Biffer went on. 'You're not in charge of the *Cabinet Minister*.'

Captain Waggett was silent. Feeling as he did that he ought to be in charge of the *Cabinet Minister* he did not like being reminded that he was not.

It was well after five o'clock when the Waggetts reached Snorvig House. The thin decrescent moon was floating clear of Ben Pucka.

'Oh look, Paul dear,' said Mrs Waggett wearily, 'there's the new moon. I must turn my money over.'

'That's not the new moon, old lady. We only see the new moon just before it's setting. That moon is nearly a month old.'

Mrs Waggett was only too glad to be relieved of the ceremonial of superstition, and she smiled gratefully.

'Shall I make you some hot grog, Paul?' she suggested.

'Thank you. I would like one,' he told her.

'Or would you rather go straight to bed?' she added hopefully. 'You must be frightfully tired.'

'I am tired, Dolly, but I'm going to write one or two letters before I go to bed.'

'Paul!'

'I must get them off my mind. I should only lie awake worrying about my responsibility. You must have realized tonight that both islands are on the verge of a complete moral collapse.'

'Yes, but surely there's nothing you can do about it at this hour,' she protested. 'Won't the letters wait till tomorrow? The post doesn't go till Thursday.'

Captain Waggett smiled compassionately at his wife's weakness.

'You know my rule, Dolly. Do it now. I'll be in the den. You'd better make yourself some grog too.'

When Mrs Waggett brought him the whisky, sugar, lemon, and hot water her husband looked at it reverently.

'I suppose this is the only whisky in the island on which duty has been paid,' he said. 'And now you go off to bed, old lady. I shan't be long over these letters.'

The first letter was to the Security Intelligence Corps in Nobost:

March 10th, 1943

Dear Major Quiblick,

You have probably been informed by now of the wreck of the s.s. Cabinet Minister (Blue Limpet Line) on the rock called the Gobha (pronounced Gaw) off Pillay, but you may not have been informed that up till now nobody has been put in charge of it with the result that the people of both Great and Little Todday are 'recovering' as much as they can of the cargo, which I hear is anything between fifteen and fifty thousand cases of whisky consigned to New York.

I should be quite willing to make arrangements to put the Home Guard here in charge of the wreck, but I do not want a repetition of the unpleasantness caused by my attempt to prevent a Nelson bomber which made a forced landing on Little Todday last year from being looted, and I can take no steps about this ship without being expressly authorized to do so.

I don't have to point out to you how much the danger of careless talk about which you were so rightly concerned will be increased by what amounts to a flood of 'free for all' whisky let loose in the two Toddays. Of course, I'm not in a position to know just how dangerous careless talk here can be and so I hope you will not think I am trying to butt in. I thought that it was my duty to let you know that I was at a gathering tonight in Little Todday at which approximately nobody except my wife and myself was absolutely sober.

Yours sincerely,
Paul Waggett

The second letter was to Mr Thomas Ferguson the Exciseman at Nobost:

Dear Mr Ferguson,

I am far from wishing to intrude, but I think it is my duty to inform you that the s.s. Cabinet Minister is without a guard of any kind and that everybody is helping themselves to whisky from the cargo. I am credibly informed that yesterday evening two large fishing boats from Loch Stew – probably from Nobost itself – and another from West Uist went off loaded. As Commanding Officer of the Home Guard on the two Toddays I shall be glad to offer my co-operation if there is anything I can do to help you. Of course you may be arriving here by the Thursday boat as also may the salvage party. Meanwhile, hundreds of bottles of whisky on which no duty has been paid are already in circulation. As a taxpayer I feel some resentment at seeing the country's revenue being poured down the drain like this.

Yours truly,
Paul Waggett, Capt,
O.C. G Company
8th Bn. Inv. H.G.

The last letter was to his own commanding officer:

Lt.-Colonel A. Lindsay-Wolseley, D.S.O.,
H.Q. 8th Bn. Inv. H.G.,
Fort Augustus.   March 10th, 1943

Dear Colonel,

You may not have heard that the s.s. Cabinet Minister (Blue Limpet Line) with a cargo of 50,000 cases of whisky consigned to New York has been wrecked off Little Todday. Nobody is in charge and the cargo has been steadily pillaged since the ship struck last Sunday. Do you wish me to assume control of a situation which is rapidly deteriorating all the time? Please telegraph instructions.

Yours sincerely,
Paul Waggett
O.C. G Co.
8th Bn. Inv. H.G.

With the steady tread of the village blacksmith Captain Waggett left his den for a well-earned night's repose.

Chapter 15

NOBOST LODGE

It is beyond the scope of this simple tale to make any attempt to clarify the obscure motives which animate the business of salvage. They present a problem which might puzzle the most expert psychologist. The four representatives of the salvage company were preoccupied with the best method to save the ship itself: the cargo was apparently in theory already lost. Therefore the first thing which had to be done was to dump the cargo of the *Cabinet Minister* into the sea together with the coal out of her bunkers and the ship's furniture. If a curious observer asked why the coal could not be sold to anybody prepared to carry it away the answer was that such a transaction would complicate matters too much from the point of view of the insurance. If the same curious observer asked why the cases of whisky could not be transferred to a salvage ship and sold in due course to a thirsty public on the mainland, the answer was that the whole matter was such a complicacy of insurance, Inland Revenue, Board of Trade regulations, and Lease-Lend, that it was far more simple to dump the whisky in the sea.

So the four representatives of the salvage company were boarded and lodged in various houses in Little Todday and worked steadily every day at emptying the *Cabinet Minister*. They could hardly be expected to watch by night to see that nobody continued their job. For about a fortnight the cargo of the *Cabinet Minister* went into the sea by day and over the sea by night Boats came from every island in the Outer and Inner Hebrides to help in lightening the task of the salvage men. A few came from ports on the mainland. Then the weather broke, and after a series of gales the *Cabinet Minister* broke in half which spared the salvage men the wearisome job of emptying the coal into the sea. It was then decided to postpone further operations until May, when an attempt was to be made to tow to a mainland harbour the half of the *Cabinet Minister* that was left. The cases of whisky in that half were much more difficult to reach in the changed condition of the wreck, but that did not worry the people of the two Toddays who by now had hidden away as much as they could safely hide.

Captain Waggett's letters had not been successful in stirring up authority in any shape to take action. Major Quiblick wrote to say that a wreck was not the pigeon of the Security Intelligence Corps. Tom Ferguson the Exciseman had merely acknowledged the receipt of Captain Waggett's letter of the 10th inst., and Colonel Lindsay-Wolseley had telegraphed that the Home Guard must avoid meddling in matters which did not concern it.

'Well, I've done what I can,' Captain Waggett told Sergeant-major Odd when the latter came up to the den to report his imminent return to the mainland after his week in the Islands. 'If Colonel Wolseley says anything to you you'd better try to put him in the picture here. What was the shooting like at Garryboo yesterday?'

'Very encouraging, sir. Very encouraging indeed. Sergeant Campbell was in particularly good form. They'll be strong candidates for your cup next August.'

'Of course, the Home Guard has made a new man of Sergeant Campbell. It seems to have given him real self-confidence at last.'

'Yes, sir,' the Sergeant-major assented, a slightly remote expression in his eye. 'And in fact he's getting married next month.'

'So are you, aren't you?'

'Yes, sir. The date we're hoping for is Wednesday, April 28th; but Mr Macroon is being a bit hard to pin down to it, if you know what I mean.'

'It's very difficult to pin Joseph Macroon down to anything.'

'He hasn't actually said "no" to Easter Week, but he keeps on talking as if it was to be in October, and which of course is a bit annoying for Peggy and I, especially after the raychack. The trouble is she's too useful to him just now. Oh, I think he'll come round all right. I'll take a run in to Inverness when he comes over for the Council Meeting, and try and get it all firmly fixed. He'd counted on putting up the salvage chaps, but they're lodging with people nearer to where the wreck is, and I think that was a bit of a disappointment.'

'When do you expect you'll be able to get over to us again, Sergeant-major?'

'That depends on what the Colonel says, sir. If I'm to get a week's leave for my marriage at the end of April, I expect he won't want me to spend any more time over here for the present. And I really think you'll find the men'll be more keen now. There's a very different spirit now to what there was when I first came back.'

'I hope you're right, Sergeant-major,' said Captain Waggett with obvious pessimism.

'Might I pass a remark, sir?'

'By all means,' the Sergeant-major was told graciously.

'It's none of my business, sir, in one way, and yet in another way it is, being naturally keen to get the best out of the men. I think there's a feeling that you're against them getting the stuff out of the wreck, and as it's now been laid down that the Home Guard has no responsibility for wrecks, I think it might be as well, sir, if you closed your eyes to anything they might be doing. Their point is that if it's all going to be dumped overboard, they have a right to it.'

'I'm afraid I can't accept that view, Sergeant-major. The people here have no right at all to suppose that they know better than the Authorities what ought to be done with this whisky. And I'm rather surprised to find you defending such a deplorable lack of discipline.'

'I'm not saying that the people here are right, sir. I'm simply trying to give you their point of view.'

'Which is another word for anarchy,' Captain Waggett commented sternly. 'Complete anarchy!'

The Sergeant-major was silent. He felt he had given the officer commanding some good advice about the handling of his company. If he did not choose to heed it he himself was not prepared to say any more about the matter.

'I ought to be going down to the boat soon, sir. Are there any orders or messages? I won't forget to speak to Captain Grant about the Sten guns, but they're being a bit close with them at Fort Augustus.'

'Keeping them all for the Loch Ness monster, I suppose,' Captain Waggett commented, with what he hoped was withering sarcasm. 'However, if they go on drinking whisky here at the rate they're drinking it now we shall have a Loch Sleeport monster presently.'

'Funny you should say that, sir. As a matter of fact one of the Bobanish chaps was telling me only yesterday that what they call a Yak Ooshker had been seen in Loch Skinny.'

'A Yak Ooshker? What on earth's that?'

'A sort of long-haired horse that lives in lochs, and by what I can make out a very fierce animal too. I was in calling on old Hector MacRurie at Knockdown later on that evening and he wouldn't have it at all that there's no such thing as a water-horse. He said his father Simon often talked about one of these Yak Ooshkers which chased a man his grandfather knew half-way up to the top of Ben Bustival, and if he hadn't have hid in that cave where you arranged to store ammunition for the gorilla fighting he'd have been eaten alive.'

'I'm afraid old Hector's famous for tall stories,' Captain Waggett sniffed. 'By the way, how is he? I heard he was very ill.'

'He seems to have got much better all of a sudden just recently, sir. You wouldn't have said there was anything the matter with him last night. He told me some rare good yarns about the South African War.'

'You mustn't miss the boat, Sergeant-major,' Captain Waggett reminded him. He was bored by other people's stories.

'No, sir, I'll be getting along.'

The Sergeant-major saluted and retired.

Captain Waggett's own strict sense of discipline might have been tried to the point of criticizing the conduct of his Commanding Officer, twenty-four hours later, if he had seen Sergeant-major Odd lay on the Adjutant's desk at Fort Augustus two almost spherical dark-green bottles labelled King's Own.

'The Little Todday platoon was anxious for you and the Colonel to accept these, sir.'

'I say that's a very sporting effort, Sergeant-major,' Captain Grant exclaimed.

'I don't know this brand,' Colonel Wolseley said, stroking one of the bottles almost affectionately.

'I think you'll find it to your liking, sir,' the Sergeant-major declared confidently.

'I'm really very much obliged to the good folk in Little Todday,' the Colonel said. 'I take it that this . . . er . . .'

'Yes, sir.'

'Quite,' said the Colonel quickly.

'Quite,' the Adjutant echoed.

'Thank you, sir,' said the Sergeant-major. 'Excuse me, sir, but if you liked the idea I think I could get both you and Captain Grant a case next time I go over. They're charging two pounds a case for them now, but I wouldn't say the price wouldn't go up to three pounds presently. And that's not unreasonable.'

'Not unreasonable at all,' the Colonel agreed. 'What do you say, George?'

'Not much black market about that, sir,' he laughed.

'We can manage that, I think, Sergeant-major,' the Colonel decided.

'I won't guarantee it'll be King's Own, but it's all top-notch stuff, sir. There's nothing below ninety-eight or ninety-nine under proof.'

'Good God,' the Colonel ejaculated.

'Marvellous,' the Adjutant murmured dreamily.

The Sergeant-major withdrew.

'What a capital chap he is,' said the Colonel. 'And a first-class Instructor.'

'Oh, absolutely,' the Adjutant agreed. 'I must get him to tell us the whole story of this wreck.'

'If Ben Nevis hears about it, he'll be wanting to invade the two Toddays again,' the Colonel chuckled. 'Still, I think we'd better keep quiet about this whisky, George.'

'Oh, every time, sir.'

'I don't fancy poor Waggett would approve at all. I wonder why some fellahs go looking for trouble.'

'I think it makes them feel important, sir,' said the Adjutant.

'I suppose so. Some fellahs feel important when they've got a toothache,' Colonel Wolseley observed.

It was nearly three weeks after the Sergeant-major had left the Islands that Roderick MacRurie paid a visit to Captain Waggett on his return from the County Council meetings.

'Come into my den, Roderick.'

'Your ten, Mr Wackett? What's that at all?'

'Haven't you been into my den yet? I found I wanted a place where I could get together with myself and do a spot of reading and a bit of quiet thinking.'

'Och, well, well, it's snock right enough,' Roderick declared when he had been greeted by Paddy and taken the comfortable armchair offered him.

'A man wants a place he can call his own,' said Captain Waggett, the full weight of philosophy in his tone.

'*Seadh gu dearbh*. Ay, a man wants that right enough. Look at me, Mr Wackett. Chust at the peck and call of efferypotty. And no thanks at all from anypotty. Och, I don't believe I'll stand for the Council next time. Crumple, crumple, crumple, that's chust all it iss. I believe I'll sell the hotel and go and live in Glaschu.'

'That sounds rather a revolutionary step.'

'I'm chust about fed up with it all. You know what a commotion they keep on with at Garryboo to put their road in order for them? Well, on the way across in the boat I said to Choseph, "Look, Choseph," I said, "if I give you good support for the new school you're wanting at Kiltod will you be giving me good support for the Garryboo road?" And what do you think he was after saying? "Och," he says, "*a Ruairidh*, I don't believe we want the new school at all chust now. I think we want a road from Bàgh Mhic Ròin to Tràigh nam Marbh." I was really stackered for the moment. And then I got a bit angry. "If you think the rates will give you a road chust to be selling whisky at three pounds a case you'll find yourself in trupple," I said to him. He gave me a rather peculiar look, but he knew fine I wasn't chust speaking to hear myself talking, and we heard nothing more about that road. He wass back to his school when the meetings began. But he was so annoyed with me for what I said that he stood up and opposed a grant for the Garryboo road.'

'Did you oppose a grant for the new school?' Captain Waggett asked.

'I certainly did after the way Choseph spoke against the Garryboo road. And so the road and the school are both put back till Chune. Well, the way I look at it, Mr Wackett, is thiss. We can't afford to be quarrelling among ourselfs in the Islands, and so long as there's whisky it means quarrels. Would you believe me, Mr Wackett, I've not sold hardly a drop in the bar since this Minnie was going around efferywhere. No, they chust fill themselfs up with whisky outside and then come to the par for peer to chase it down. And, mind you, I've plenty whisky now.'

'I can assure you, Roderick, I did my best to get the Authorities to take action, but they've paid no attention to me whatever.'

'Ay, I know you were trying to wake them up at Nobost. That's why I thought I'd come around and have a quiet talk with you. Something really must be done. Ach, it wasn't too bad at first when they were chust helping themselfs to what they could trink, but now it hass become a reckular business. Ay, selling it at three pounds a case already, and before long it will be at five pounds and perhaps more. I know if I wass to try and buy a few cases myself they'd be asking me five pounds at the ferry least.'

'What do you suggest should be done?' Captain Waggett asked.

'There's only one thing we can do. Ferguson must come over here and make an example of one or two. I don't know at all what Macrae's thinking about.'

'Oh, as usual he shuts his eyes,' said Captain Waggett bitterly.

'Ay, he shuts his ice all right, but he doesn't shut his mouth,'

Roderick complained. 'That's open pretty wide all the time chust now. No, no, Macrae won't do a thing unless he's made to.'

'Colonel Lindsay-Wolseley is Convener of the Police Committee. I might get him to speak to the Chief Constable,' Captain Waggett suggested.

'Ach, I don't believe the Colonel would say a word. He had a bottle of Minnie himself.'

'Colonel Wolseley had a bottle of contraband whisky?' Captain Waggett gasped. 'Where on earth did he get it?'

'Why, I suppose Sarchant Odd would be taking him back one.'

'Most extraordinary,' Captain Waggett exclaimed. 'I simply don't know where I am nowadays.'

'Well, to come back to what we were saying, Mr Wackett. Couldn't you be writing a letter to this Major Quibalick? He seems a pretty interfering kind of a chap.'

'I've already written one.'

'Ay, I know you have.'

'How did you know?'

'Somebody was after telling me. Donald MacRurie himself likely enough.'

'A postmaster has no right to tell people who are sending letters to whom,' said Captain Waggett indignantly.

'Och, we don't pother about little things like that in Snorvig. We leave that sort of thing to folk on the mainland to pother their heads about. Couldn't you be writing Major Quibalick another letter? He wrote me a pretty fierce letter about the atmosphere in the hotel.'

'I'll write to him again, but I haven't much hope that he'll be paying any attention. Anyway, I think Ferguson would be more effective.'

'I'll write to Ferguson myself. He'd be over quick enough if I wass to start selling Minnie in the bar. But perhaps you'll write again yourself to Ferguson. If he hears from the pair of us that they're selling the stuff he may do something about it.'

'And now that the salvage people have gone away till May,' Captain Waggett added, 'what is left of the ship is not guarded at all. Of course, this is exactly the moment when I should be asked to arrange for the Home Guard to take over, but apparently that's frowned upon. Well, I don't suppose it will do any good, but I'll write.'

However, Captain Waggett's pessimism was not justified, although it must be added that it was not entirely his second letter to Major

Quiblick which set in motion the machinery of Security Intelligence. The day before it reached Nobost Lodge, Major Quiblick, Lieutenant Boggust, two staff-sergeants, four stenographers, and one of the two corporals attached to the headquarters of the Security Intelligence Corps for what was now Number 14 Protected Area incorporating Number 13 Protected Area had been perturbed by the disappearance of Ruskin, the other corporal, a sturdy, burly rosy-cheeked young warrior of the East Anglia Light Infantry whose indispensable services Major Quiblick had managed to retain for over three years in spite of the most vicious and determined efforts to transfer Corporal Ruskin to various centres of Intelligence overseas.

'I'm worried about Corporal Ruskin,' Major Quiblick had said to his subaltern. 'We must have the Island combed.'

So Mid Uist had been combed, but by late afternoon not a tooth had emerged with Corporal Ruskin himself impaled upon it, or even with any news of Corporal Ruskin.

At dusk, when Major Quiblick and Lieutenant Boggust were walking along the road beside Loch Stew to discuss with the police-sergeant in Nobost the mysterious business, they saw vanishing round the corner of a large byre four men carrying with solemn tread a khaki-clad body.

'My God,' Boggust exclaimed, 'that must have been Corporal Ruskin, sir.'

'Steady, Boggust,' Major Quiblick hissed, 'don't make a sound. Have you got your pistol with you?'

'No, sir; but my stick is loaded.'

'That's all right. You know where to hit a man?'

'On the head, I take it.'

'No, no, behind the knees. Then jump on him and sit on his head.'

'I see, sir.'

Lieutenant Boggust's heart was beating fast not with nervousness but with the exhilaration of at last tackling a real secret service job in the traditional style. So far he had been rather disappointed by the whole business of hush-hush, so much inferior was it to what he had been led to expect by the writers of spy stories. Only the face and figure and manner of his own chief had come up to that standard set by his reading.

As they crept round the corner of the byre nobody was in sight, but when they drew near to the entrance they could hear the murmur of voices within.

'They're speaking in Gaelic,' the Subaltern whispered.

'By Jove, if we were as thorough as the Huns we shouldn't allow Gaelic to be spoken,' Major Quiblick muttered. 'However, they'll speak English fast enough when they see me.'

With this the lantern-jawed Chief Security Intelligence Officer of Number 14 Protected Area sprang forward like a black panther into the dark byre and, landing in the middle of an archipelago of cowpats, demanded to know what all this was about.

The four men who were looking at the body of Corporal Ruskin lying motionless upon the straw where they had just laid it turned their eyes on the two Intelligence officers.

'Och, he'll sleep it off where he is,' one of them said.

'Ay, he'll be quite comfortable like that till the morning,' observed another.

'Minnie was a bit too much for him,' chuckled a third, with a sympathetic grin.

'Minnie?' Major Quiblick repeated. Under his breath he bade his subaltern make a note of that name.

'He was pretty lively last night,' said the first man who had spoken. 'But he started again when he woke up and Bean Phadruig Ruaidh was after saying he could not be sleeping on her kitchen table no more, and so we brought him in here.'

'Whose house was he in?' the Major asked sharply.

'Mrs Macdonald's.'

As there were quite five hundred Mrs Macdonalds in the three Uists, this did not go far towards elucidating where Corporal Ruskin had spent the night.

'Mrs Patrick Macdonald. Her husband's away out in India with the Clanranalds. Padruig Ruadh we call him.'

'Make a note of that name, too,' Major Quiblick told his subaltern. Then he went across to where Corporal Ruskin was lying on his back, the top button of the blouse of his battledress undone, his rosy cheeks a vivid aniline cerise, snoring in a steady ground bass mostly but from time to time in a sudden burst of mounting arpeggios.

'Corporal Ruskin!' his Commanding Officer barked.

The Corporal went on snoring.

'Shake him, Boggust,' the Major ordered.

The Subaltern bent over and prodded Corporal Ruskin several times.

'Minnie,' the Corporal muttered, and then suddenly emitted such a terrific arpeggio of snores that Lieutenant Boggust involuntarily jumped back as if the prostrate form was on the point of exploding.

'I'm afraid he's right out, sir,' he said to his chief. 'What do you think we'd better do about it?'

'He'd better stay where he is for the present,' Major Quiblick decided. 'I don't think he's capable of careless talk in his present condition, but I'm wondering what he said to this woman Minnie Macdonald before he passed out. Who does this place belong to?' he asked the bearers of the corpse.

'It belongs to me,' said a small red-haired crofter.

'What's your name?'

'Patrick Macdonald.'

'I thought you said Patrick Macdonald was out in India with the Clanranalds,' Major Quiblick checked him sternly.

'That's my brother.'

'Look here, my man, don't try to be funny with me,' Major Quiblick snapped.

'He iss my brother,' the small red-haired crofter insisted.

'That's right enough,' another of the crofters put in. 'This is Padruig Og, and his brother is Padruig Ruadh.'

'We'll have to go into the whole matter when we get back to the Lodge,' the Major told his Subaltern. 'We can settle then what to do with Ruskin. All right,' he said to the bearers, 'you can leave the – er – you can leave the Corporal here. I'll probably send somebody to fetch him.'

'You'd better be sending more than one,' the owner of the byre advised. 'He weighs very heavy.'

'Well, I'm much obliged to you. Good evening,' said Major Quiblick, and then he and Lieutenant Boggust steered their way through the archipelago of cowpats out of the byre.

'You'd better clean your right boot on the grass, sir,' Lieutenant Boggust advised his chief when they were outside.

'What? Oh yes, I see. Thanks. You know, I'm worried about this business, Boggust,' said Major Quiblick. 'Anyway, I'm glad we've found out who Minnie is. I wonder if we ever gave her a Milperm.'

Milperm, it should be explained, had nothing to do with hairdressing. It was an affectionate abbreviation of Military Permit, the talisman with which the inhabitants of a protected area were able to move into it, out of it, and about it. It was also the telegraphic address of the Military

Permit Offices in various parts of Scotland, England, Wales, and Northern Ireland, whose grand objective was to immobilize as much of the population as possible.

Back at the Lodge, Major Quiblick sent first of all for the other corporal.

'Sir?'

'Corporal Beard, I have discovered where Corporal Ruskin is.'

Corporal Beard looked a little worried. He had been to Mrs Patrick Macdonald's house during the comb-out and made an unsuccessful attempt to get Corporal Ruskin back to the Lodge.

'He is in a byre on the left of the road half-way between here and Nobost.'

'Is that so, sir?'

'So when it's dark I want you to take the car along, get Corporal Ruskin round somehow and put him to bed. I will see him tomorrow morning.'

'Is he under the influence, sir?' Corporal Beard asked, assuming hopefully an expression of cherubic innocence.

'He's utterly drunk and incapable,' the Commanding Officer replied.

'Tut-tut. I'm sorry to hear that, sir. It's not like Corporal Ruskin at all.'

'You have your orders, Corporal,' his Commanding Officer rapped out to cut the testimonial short.

Corporal Beard clicked his heels.

'Ask Miss Pippit to come to my room.'

Corporal Beard retired.

Presently an earnest-looking young woman wearing spectacles wrought out of one of the more exotic forms of plastics came in.

'I'm so sorry, Major Quiblick,' she said breathlessly, 'but Miss Pippit has just gone for a walk with Miss Aynhoe. I wondered if I could do anything.'

'I want you to look through the card index, Miss Cuffins, and see if we have issued a Milperm to a Mrs Patrick Macdonald whose Christian name is probably Minnie.'

'You'd like her card if I can find it, Major Quiblick?'

'Certainly.'

Ten minutes later Miss Cuffins returned.

'I have three Mrs Patrick Macdonalds here, but none of them seems to be called Minnie,' she informed her Chief. 'One living in West Uist to whom we have issued three Milperms to travel to Mid Uist is called Flora,' Miss Cuffins tittered romantically. 'Another living in Mid Uist to whom we issued a Milperm in October last year to travel to Glasgow via Mallan. Her Christian name is Measag.'

'What?'

Miss Cuffins had pronounced it 'Meesag,' but even if she had pronounced it properly as 'Mesac' Major Quiblick would probably have said 'what'? He regarded all Gaelic Christian names as a threat to Security Intelligence.

'Do you think Meesag could be a mistake for Minnie?' she asked hopefully.

Major Quiblick shook his head.

'Who's the third?'

'Another Mrs Patrick Macdonald in Mid Uist who had a Milperm to go to East Uist last July. Her Christian names are Mary Angustina. Do you think they could have been run together into . . . oh, but isn't "Minnie" short for "Mary"?' she gulped in the excitement of the chase.

'No,' Major Quiblick said firmly. He was always inclined to be restive under Miss Cuffins' eager helpfulness.

'I'll look through all the Macdonalds in the card index if you like, Major Quiblick, in case we have the husband's name wrong,' she suggested.

'No, no, no. You'll be up till midnight if you're going to look through all the Macdonalds in our card index. Don't bother any more. Will you ask Lieutenant Boggust to come along to my room? Good night, Miss Cuffins, and thank you.'

When Miss Cuffins was gone Major Quiblick picked up the telephone receiver and asked to be put through to the police-station.

'Is that you, Sergeant Macfarlane? Oh, I wonder if you can help me. I want to trace a Mid Uist woman whose Christian name is Minnie and whose surname may be Macdonald . . . the only Minnie you know is what? . . . whisky? . . . Oh, I see, it's what they call this contraband stuff . . . why? . . . oh, short for *Cabinet Minister*? . . . I don't know why they didn't call it "Cabby" — ha-ha! . . . Well, I think we shall have to do something about it, Sergeant . . . I knew they were relaxing the rules about Military Permits for people travelling from one island to another much too soon . . . you think it was about time? . . . well, I suppose it's always the same when we're at war . . . the police think the military authorities are trespassing on their preserves . . . all right, thank you, Sergeant. Good night.'

'My opinion of the police in the Highlands and Islands gets lower and lower, Boggust,' Major Quiblick told his subaltern, who had come into the room while he was talking to Sergeant Macfarlane on the telephone.

'Well, they're bound to be rather primitive out here, sir,' said Lieutenant Boggust who had taken a dislike to the Gael on his native heath since that week-end he spent at the Snorvig Hotel.

'It appears that Minnie is the name given to the whisky in that ship which was wrecked off Little Todday.'

'The one Waggett was worrying us about?'

'That's it. I'm beginning to wonder if Waggett wasn't right after all. You remember he was stressing the likelihood of careless talk if the people's tongues were loosened by whisky? Well, as you know, I didn't really think we could interfere merely on the grounds that it *might* lead to careless talk. And anyway, although in principle these fellows with relations at sea and in the army have no business to be saying where their ships and units are, still, I didn't think it was a serious menace to Security. But now this whisky is reaching Nobost, and if Ruskin succumbs today it may be Beard tomorrow, and who's to say it won't be Briggs or Pershore the next day?' Briggs and Pershore were the two staff-sergeants. 'I can't run the risk of careless talk by our own people. Now, I don't want to interfere in anything which isn't our pigeon. Those Navy fellows at Portrose are as touchy as a lot of schoolgirls. Nor do I want to give those Home Guard dug-outs an inflated idea of their own importance. I think I'll get Ferguson the Excise fellow to come round and see me and suggest that he and I pay a surprise visit to Snorvig in MacWilliam's motor-boat. Then if he reports that the whisky situation is as serious as it sounds I'll establish an S.I.C. control on Snorvig and Kiltod and get Milperm to make permits again necessary for travelling to and from the Toddays.'

'Will that mean my going to Snorvig?' Lieutenant Boggust asked in a depressed voice.

'I expect it will until the situation is restored.'

It was on the next morning that Captain Waggett's letter reached Nobost Lodge.

'I say, things do sound pretty sticky in those two confounded Islands,' Major Quiblick commented gravely. 'Apparently they're selling these cases of whisky at three pounds.'

'Three pounds a dozen for whisky?' his subaltern gulped. 'It must be most frightful hooch.'

'No, according to Waggett it's first-class stuff. They were selling it for two pounds a case up to last week.'

'My God, sir, no wonder Ruskin took the dressing-down you gave him so calmly. Really good whisky at three and six a bottle. It's the kind of thing my old grandfather talks about. And when I was in Snorvig a month ago I could only get one small whisky every other day.'

'If you did go over to Snorvig, you'd have to be very careful, Boggust,' the Major said in a meaning voice.

'I might have a case put in my cabin, sir, like that urn. Or how would it be if I took a black box with me? They'd think it was a regular part of my luggage. Two pounds a dozen,' he murmured to himself.

'It's three pounds a dozen now,' his chief reminded him.

'Well, that's six bottles for you, sir, and six bottles for me at the price of what we're paying now for one.'

'I wonder if you could get hold of two cases.'

'I'll have a jolly good try, sir,' the Subaltern promised with enthusiasm.

When Tom Ferguson the Exciseman came along from Nobost to the Lodge that morning, Major Quiblick told him how much worried he was by the evidence he had just received that illicit whisky was being smuggled into Mid Uist.

'Well, I'll be perfectly frank with you, Major, and admit that I'm beginning to be more than a bitty worried myself,' said Tom Ferguson, a sharp-nosed little man in a suit of Glenurquhart tweed, with the sing-song accent of Aberdeen. 'I thought at first it would be wiser to leave things to the salvage people, but it seems the ship has broken in half and they've all gone away till the fine weather. And now I hear they're selling the stuff. Well, of course, that's something I've just got to inquire into, even if it means a few prosecutions.'

'A few prosecutions won't do any harm,' said Major Quiblick sternly.

'Ay, but I've been treated very well since I was in Nobost, and the last thing I want is to bring the police into it and the sheriff and perhaps get a few old friends of mine heavily fined, ay, or perhaps even sent to prison. If they'd only keep off selling the stuff. Do you know this chap Waggett?'

'I've met him,' said the Major.

'Well, he's an interfering bumptious kind of a chap, and I don't at all like giving him the pleasure of thinking he's cock of the roost. However,

I've had a letter from big Roderick MacRurie at the Snorvig Hotel and I can see I've just got to do something.'

'What about you and I paying a surprise visit in MacWilliam's boat?' Major Quiblick asked.

'That's all right in summer, Major. I'm not so fond of a twenty-mile trip round these waters in the *Pearl* at this time of the year.'

'We'll pick our day, and it'll be convenient to have our own boat. The Todday boats would probably warn the people there.'

'And do you think John MacWilliam won't be warning them? John must have made half a dozen trips to the wreck and come back with the *Pearl* loaded every time.'

'You surprise me. I should have thought he was a thoroughly reliable fellow.'

'So he is,' said the Exciseman. 'Could I catch a single bottle? Not one. Well, well, I suppose we'd better take John. We might make it Monday, weather permitting.'

'That's all right for me,' the Major said. 'By the way, Mr Ferguson, what kind of a woman is Mrs Patrick Macdonald?'

'Which one? The wife of Padruig Ruadh or Padruig Og? They're brothers.'

'The one whose husband is serving in India with the Clanranalds.'

'Oh, that's Measag.'

'Is she all right? One of my men seems to have struck up a friendship with her. I mean to say is she a chatterbox?'

'She'd talk the head off a donkey, but there's no harm in her otherwise. She likes to have lots of laddies sitting around in her kitchen, and they get up to all sorts of larks, but I don't think you need worry at all about your men.'

'You heard, I suppose, that they're selling this stuff at three pounds a case, Mr Ferguson?' the Major asked.

'Ay, and they'll be selling it at twice that presently.'

'You don't think it would be better if you and Major Quiblick went down with MacWilliam tomorrow?' Lieutenant Boggust put in.

'No, no, I can't get away before Monday,' the Exciseman said quickly.

'All right, then, Mr Ferguson, we'll make it Monday,' Major Quiblick decided.

Chapter 16

ALARMS AND EXCURSIONS

The Sergeant-major's visit to Joseph Macroon when the latter was in Inverness for the meetings of the County Council had not been successful in pinning him down to a definite acceptance of the proposed date for his daughter's marriage.

'Ah well, we'll see about it later, Sergeant,' he had procrastinated.

'Yes, but it's already the end of March,' the Sergeant-major had argued. 'Peggy must know as soon as possible when it's to be because of her clothes.'

'Ah, clothes,' Joseph had groaned. 'That's all they think about. Clothes.'

'Women have got to think about clothes. And once Peggy is married you won't have to bother about her clothes any more. That'll be my job.'

However, no arrangements the Sergeant-major could produce had been strong enough to extract from Joseph a clear-cut answer about the date of the wedding, and he wrote to her:

My darling Peggy,

I've just come back from a run over to see your Dad in Inverness, and I can't get him to give the O.K. to us being married on April 28th. He doesn't say no but he doesn't seem able to bring himself to say yes. I believe he can't think of anything just now except Minnie. From what I can make out he and Roderick MacRurie had a bit of a row. Your Dad's going down to Edinburgh now to see the Department of Agriculture about getting their support for his application for a licence to sell spirits in Kiltod. I think he sees a profit of something like 600 per cent. And very nice too if it doesn't land him in gaol and which in my opinion it will. I do hope when he gets back you'll tell him your mind is made up and if he doesn't want you to be married from your own home you can easily be married from your sister's home in Glasgow. Father MacIntyre reckons I'll be ready for you know what in about a fortnight. I wish you could be there. Do I think about you all the time, my darling Peggy? Yes, all the time, and the more I think about you the more I know you're the only girl in the world. If love was whisky I wouldn't half be one over the eight. With love and kisses.

I am for ever your fond and loving

Fred

P.S. Mind you get onto your Dad to hurry up and fix the day. I think Father James would say a word if you asked him. He told me once the raichach had been held the wedding had got to come off pretty soon afterwards. Anyway I've told my old Ma she's got to travel Bank Holiday and cross with me on the Tuesday.

After Joseph Macroon's dilly-dallying it is satisfactory to be able to record that George Campbell had stood no more nonsense from his mother after the night of the *rèiteach*. When Catriona went to tea with her future mother-in-law, Mrs Campbell was as nearly pleasant as she had ever been in her life. There was no more talk of removing her furniture or herself, and she gave Catriona thirty coupons.

At the end of March Norman Macleod had received his summons to report for service.

'So you'll be off into the blue tomorrow,' Dr Maclaren had said, lifting his glass of Over the Border to pledge the schoolmaster.

'That's right, Doctor. Off into the Air Force blue,' Norman had laughed.

'Well, it's satisfactory to know that Catriona will be married next month.'

'Yes, yes. George broke the old lady's spirit that night right enough.'

'She'll probably make a good grandmother,' the Doctor had prophesied. 'It's often the way. Good luck to you, Norman, and I hope you'll not be away too long. By the way, what's happening to all that whisky stored away in the loft of the schoolhouse.'

'Och, it's been most of it distributed,' Norman had replied. 'I've hidden my own particular nest-egg in a safe place.'

'Well, I'll miss you a lot, Norman,' the Doctor had assured him warmly. Then they had shaken hands and Norman had gone down to the pier, where his sister and George Campbell were waiting to see him aboard.

'If I can get leave so soon,' he had promised Catriona, 'I'll come and give you away to George in Glasgow.'

When Major Quiblick and Tom Ferguson the Exciseman reached Snorvig from Nobost on that Monday in the front of April the first person they called on was the landlord of the hotel.

'Och, I'm glad you've come, Mr Ferguson,' said Roderick. 'You won't find any of the stuff, but maybe the sight of you will serve as a pit of a warning, and it would be a good thing if you said a word to Macrae the constaple. He's taking it all chust a bit too easy. I have plenty whisky chust now and it's ferry annoying to hear of the stuff being bought and sold.'

'Who are the chief culprits?' Major Quiblick asked.

'Och, I'll name no names. They're all culprits if it comes to that. Are you from the Excise yourself?'

'No, no, Mr MacRurie,' Ferguson put in. 'This is Major Quiblick, the head of the Security Intelligence Corps at Nobost.'

'Ach, you're the man who wrote me a letter complaining of the atmosphere in my hotel! Do you know the Tuke of Ross, Major Quibalick?'

'Quiblick.'

'I said Quibalick. It's a name I won't be forgetting in a hurry. I wass neffer after having such a letter before. Do you know the Tuke of Ross?'

'I know who you mean,' the Major replied. 'I don't know the Duke personally.'

'Well, there's no finer chentleman in the whole of the country, and the Tuke himself said to me that the air in the Snorvig Hotel was better than the air in his own castle. I took a good deal of offence at what you were writing to me, Major Quibalick.'

'I'm afraid there's a war on, Mr MacRurie, and some of us haven't the time to think about whether we hurt people's feelings. We're fighting for our existence as a nation.'

'Aren't we fighting as hard in Snorvig as you are?' Roderick demanded.

'I should like to think so.'

'And you can think so as much as you like. Are you here about the whisky yourself?'

'Major Quiblick is worried about careless talk,' said Ferguson, with a touch of malice.

'Ay, and so he may be. He was talking pretty careless himself when he was crumpling about the atmosphere in my hotel.'

'I don't think we shall get much help in that quarter, Mr Ferguson,' the Major observed to the Exciseman as they made their way down from the hotel to the police-station.

'Roderick just wants to give them a wee fright,' said Tom Ferguson. 'He wouldn't like to get any of them into trouble.'

'Oh no, of course not,' the Major commented bitterly. 'Like everybody else in these islands he simply doesn't realize there's a war on.'

By Major Quiblick's standards neither did Constable Macrae appear to realize that there was a war on. Instead of welcoming the opportunity to display the majestic authority of the Law and in doing so perhaps earn promotion for himself, he seemed to resent what he called work that didn't properly come under the police at all.

'I have quite enough to do, Major, without making myself responsible for ships. If the Navy aren't interested and the Salvage people aren't interested and . . .'

'The Excise *is* interested now,' Ferguson put in.

'Ay, now, when all the damage is done,' the Constable complained. 'The *Cabinet Minister* was wrecked just a month ago, and this is the first time we've had a sight of you down here, Mr Ferguson.'

'Yes, yes, Constable, I know, I know. We've been very busy. Very busy indeed. Yes, yes, short-handed and all that,' said the Exciseman. 'I'm not criticizing the police at all. No, no, no. But perhaps you'd come across with us to Little Todday and just take a wee walk round. I'll do the same myself. And that's about all we can do. I'm a wee bitty worried about this selling of the stuff.'

'I'm sure you will be, Mr Ferguson,' said the Constable. 'But what can you expect? There must be hundreds of cases hidden away by now all over the two islands. Whisky's so plentiful that some of them are using it to wash their hands.'

'To wash their hands?' Major Quiblick gasped.

'Och, soap's pretty difficult to get just now,' the Constable told him. 'And it takes off grease fine.'

The Major shook his head.

'They'll be using it for cleaning their windows and floors next.'

'Och, the women do that now,' said the Constable.

'It was certainly high time we intervened,' Major Quiblick observed to the Exciseman. 'I wonder if we should ask Waggett to come along with us?'

'Captain Waggett?' the Constable exclaimed. 'What has he to do with it at all?'

'I don't think we want him, Major,' said Ferguson.

'Indeed, and we do not, Mr Ferguson,' the Constable declared. 'I wouldn't want General Montgomery himself on a job like this, and I certainly don't want a man who thinks he's General Montgomery and isn't him at all.'

'I agree with Constable Macrae,' said Ferguson.

'Oh, I don't press for him,' said the Major. 'This is no job for amateurs.'

So when MacWilliam's motor-boat the *Pearl* set out for Little Todday Captain Waggett was left behind.

'Extraordinary,' he commented to his wife, when in battledress he stood watching through a pair of glasses the progress of the *Pearl* across the Coolish. 'Quite extraordinary. It's entirely through my initiative that action is being taken at last, and nobody comes near me. It would be comic if it weren't really rather tragic.' He sighed. 'Well, I suppose if one does a good job one must expect jealousy. It was the same in the last war. The professional soldiers couldn't bear me always being right then. You remember when I . . .'

'Yes, dear,' Mrs Waggett replied automatically.

Captain Waggett turned upon his wife those light-grey eyes of his which had been watching the *Pearl*.

'Look here, Dolly, you mustn't let this war get you down. I hadn't said what I was going to say, so how can you possibly remember?'

'I'm sorry, Paul,' she apologized tactfully. 'So stupid of me.'

Her husband continued relentlessly.

'I was going to say you remember when I told the Brigadier that the Germans would make their main thrust against us at Haut Camembert and not at Petits Fours?'

'Yes, of course, dear.'

'Well, when I was right, as I always was, not one of the fellows at G.H.Q. had the generosity to admit that if it hadn't been for my foresight we might have had a repetition of what happened to the Fifth Army in March 1918. Of course, I'm not comparing this whisky business to France and Flanders in the last war, but *plus ce change*, as the French say, *plus ce le même chose*.'

One of the few facts of her education which had remained in Mrs Waggett's memory was the gender of '*chose*', but in all the years of her married life she had never summoned up the courage to impart that fact to her husband. His glasses were turned again upon the *Pearl*.

'Tch!' he ejaculated.

'Oh dear, what is it now, Paul?'

'They're going round to the wreck first. Of course, if I'd been with them I should have pointed out that by the time they landed on Little Todday every case would be safely hidden.'

And in justice to Captain Waggett it has to be admitted that he was right – perfectly right.

Peat-stacks became a little larger than they usually were at this time of the year. Ricks suggested that the cattle had eaten less hay than usual this winter. Loose floorboards were nailed down. Corks bobbed about in waters where hitherto none had bobbed. Turf recently disturbed was trodden level again as carefully as on a golf-course. In one household only was there anything in the nature of a panic. This was at the post-office where Joseph Macroon would not be back from Edinburgh until the *Island Queen* brought him over from Obaig next day. The news that a strange motor-boat with the Exciseman, the Constable, and an officer in uniform was headed for Kiltod from Snorvig struck Peggy and Kate Anne with dismay.

'A *Mhuire*, *Mhuire*, what will we do if they come here?' Peggy asked tremulously. 'They'll put my father in prison if they find all that whisky in the shed.'

'Don't be saying such a thing, *a Pheigi*,' her sister adjured her. 'They mustn't be finding it. Where's Kenny?'

'Och, Kenny!' Peggy scoffed. 'It would just be a fine excitement for Kenny if his father was taken away to prison.'

'What will we do then?' Kate Anne asked in much agitation.

Peggy took her father's decrepit spy-glass and went outside the shop to watch the hostile boat.

'He's looking terribly fierce,' she said to her sister.

'Who is?'

'The Constable. A *Mhuire mhàthair*, just as black as a crow. And there's a soldier with him right enough. The other will be the Exciseman from Nobost. They're just coming straight for us.'

'There's Kenny down by the quay,' said Kate Anne. 'Kenny!' she cried. 'A *Choinnich!*'

But their young brother paid no attention. He was absorbed in watching the approach of the *Pearl*.

'Will they be taking us away with them if they find all that whisky?' Kate Anne asked.

'Och, I don't know what they'll be doing,' said Peggy almost in despair.

'Will I run up to the Chapel House and ask Father James what we'd better do?' Kate Anne suggested as a last hope.

'Father James will be thinking about his own whisky,' her sister replied. 'He'll just be laughing at us. Och, there's only one thing we can do. We must just empty it all away.'

'What will himself be saying when he comes back from Edinburgh and finds all his whisky gone?' Kate Anne asked.

'Don't be daft, Kate Anne. If he comes back from Edinburgh and finds us gone and his whisky too, what will he be saying then at all?'

'Where would we be gone to?'

'To prison. Where else?'

'To prison? Us?' Kate Anne gasped. '*A Dhia*, Peggy, come on and pour it all away before they get here.'

At this moment the decrepit spy-glass, which only Joseph Macroon himself knew how to nurse, collapsed in Peggy's hands, and without waiting to see which direction the hostile boat was taking, she led the way at a run toward her father's big shed at the back in which the lumber of years was stored.

'We'll never get all these bottles out before they catch us,' Kate Anne declared when they pulled away the tarpaulin from the pile of cases.

'We'll try anyway,' said Peggy resolutely. 'Maybe they won't be coming here first. Get a hammer and a chisel and don't be standing there like a dummy. I'm sure it's me that will be glad when I'm married. Going off to Edinburgh like that and leaving us here with all this whisky! Wait you till my father comes back tomorrow and see what I'll be telling him.'

As fast as the girls could pull them out of the cases they opened the bottles and poured out the liquid gold on the floor of the shed. Highland Hope and Highland Heart, Tartan Milk and Tartan Perfection, Stag's Breath and Stalker's Joy, yes, even Stalker's Joy, which Joseph had finally decided was the brand he liked best of all and of which he had collected a dozen bottles for his own consumption, all were blended ruthlessly upon the earthen floor of the big shed for only the air to taste.

'*A Mhuire, Mhuire*, I feel quite funny, Kate Anne,' said Peggy when nothing remained of the contents of at least a couple of hundred bottles of whisky except the heady fumes.

'I'm just going round inside my head like a top,' her sister declared.

The two girls emerged from the shed to recover themselves, as their brother appeared in front of the post-office.

'Where's the Constable?' Peggy asked.

'Och, the boat went round to the bay,' Kenny told them. 'They'll be taking a look at the wreck.'

'Did they not come here at all?' Peggy asked.

'No, but maybe they will later. The Exciseman from Nobost will be looking for Minnie. *Mac an diabhoil*, he won't be finding much of it ashore.'

'He won't be finding any here,' Peggy announced proudly.

'Och, he won't be looking here,' her brother asserted scornfully. 'He and the old man are too good friends.'

'Even if he did look he wouldn't be finding any,' Peggy said. 'Kate Anne and me have emptied it all away.'

'You're after emptying away all the Minnie in the shed?' Kenny exclaimed. '*A Dhia*, the old man will be wild when he comes back tomorrow. Oh boy, will he be wild? He has plenty Minnie put away safe on Poppay, but that won't make him any less wild to be losing the stuff here.'

Kenny had been perspicacious when he was sure that Tom Ferguson would not put an old friend to the inconvenience of raiding his premises for contraband.

When the Exciseman, the Constable, and the Major reached Kiltod late in the afternoon after calling at some twenty houses in the island, they did not even look in at the post-office but went straight down to the quay and boarded the *Pearl* which had come back from Macroon's Bay to wait for them in the harbour.

'Well, they've been warned now,' said Ferguson.

'Ay, they've been warned right enough,' the Constable agreed, with a hint of cynicism in his tone.

'Yes, I'm sure our visit has done a lot of good,' Major Quiblick decided. 'I don't think it will be necessary for me to put back permits to travel between Great and Little Todday. I was thinking of sending my subaltern down for a week or two to establish an S.I.C. Control, but I *don't* think that should be necessary after our visit.'

Did John MacWilliam blink at the westering sun as he made his way aft to take the helm or did he wink at Major Quiblick?

'I'll have a wee walk round Snorvig tomorrow morning,' said the Exciseman, 'and then I expect you'll be wanting to get back to Loch Stew, John.'

'I'd like to start back by about eleven o'clock if that suits you, Mr Ferguson.'

'Is that all right for you, Major?'

'That'll suit me,' said Major Quiblick in whose attitude there was discernible a serene good-will toward his fellow men of which he had hitherto shown not a sign. 'I suppose we ought to look in on Waggett,' he added, as the *Pearl* cleared the diminutive harbour of Kiltod and set out for Snorvig.

'I don't think I'll be bothered with him, Major,' said the Exciseman. 'We've had an amusing day trying to catch muckle whales with wee sprats, and I'd rather have a crack with Roderick.'

Captain Waggett was inclined to stand on his dignity with Major Quiblick when the latter arrived at Snorvig House, but his visitor made himself so agreeable that finally he was invited into the den.

'I could have told you before you started, Quiblick, that you would find nothing if you gave them time to cover up their traces.'

'The idea was to warn them, Waggett.'

'When you've lived in these islands as long as I have, you'll know that warnings are no use at all. No use at all,' Captain Waggett repeated firmly. 'I've warned them about almost everything under the sun without the slightest effect. They think they know best. They're very pleasant to you on the surface and at first you think they are paying attention to what you say; but underneath they simply go their own way. Bilingual and double-faced, that's what the people are here. Can I offer you a glass of whisky on which duty has been paid?'

'Oh, thanks very much,' said the Major. 'I'd like a peg. It's thirsty work tramping about over Little Todday.'

'Do you know what they're selling it at now?' Captain Waggett asked as he unlocked his tantalus.

'Three pounds a case,' said the Major quickly.

'Five pounds,' Captain Waggett corrected. 'Soda?'

'Thank you, just a spot. Five pounds, eh? Really? I – er – heard it was three pounds.'

'Five or three,' Captain Waggett observed, 'it's equally disgraceful.'

'Oh, quite, quite. Most disgraceful,' the Major agreed, without a vestige in his tone of wounded morality. 'Five pounds,' he repeated pensively. 'Is that the price on Great Todday?'

'A corporal in the Snorvig section of my company offered me a case for five pounds this afternoon. I gave him a rare wigging. No use, of course. I don't delude myself. However, he saw that I was angry.'

'I should be deuced angry if one of my corporals offered me a case for five pounds,' Major Quiblick declared.

The Major spoke sincerely. Thanks to John MacWilliam's skill he had secured two cases at three pounds that afternoon. They travelled back with him and the Exciseman to Nobost the following morning.

'You know, Boggust,' he said to his subaltern, 'I had great difficulty in resisting the temptation to tell that fellow Waggett I'd only paid three pounds a case. He was so damn cocksure he knew more about it than I did.'

'That *would* have been careless talk, sir,' said the Subaltern.

Then they pledged one another in glasses of Trusty Friend.

'This is wizard stuff,' the Subaltern sighed.

'Tophole,' his Commanding Officer agreed.

'It was a jolly sporting effort of yours, sir, to bring the stuff back, with Ferguson aboard.'

Major Quiblick smiled.

'That's an old Intelligence trick,' he said complacently.

The return of Joseph Macroon from Edinburgh, where he had not succeeded in persuading the Department of Agriculture to support his notion of applying for a licence to sell spirituous liquor at Kiltod, was less happy that Tuesday than the return of Major Quiblick to Nobost.

As soon as the *Morning Star* brought him across from the *Island Queen* he went to his shed, having heard on the pier of the activity on Little Todday the previous day. He opened the door. He sniffed the air. He muttered something under his breath. He darted forward and pulled away the tarpaulin. He gazed at the hillock of empty bottles. He groaned. He took from his head the ceremonious bowler he had been wearing to keep his end up in Edinburgh. He flung it down on the whisky-soaked earthen floor, and hurried away to his own room at the back of the shop.

'A Pheigi! A Chatriona! A Choinnich!' he cried. '*Cà bheil sibh? Thigibh an so! Thigibh! Thigibh! A Dhia nan Gràs, cà bheil sibh?*'

'What's the matter, Father?' Peggy asked coming in from the post-office. 'Kenny's away back to Snorvig for the mail. And Kate Anne's away with him.'

'My whisky! Who's after throwing away all my whisky?'

'Kate Anne and I were afraid the Constable was coming here. They were all over the island yesterday and everybody was hiding away their Minnie as hard as they could be.'

'*A Dhia*, then why weren't the two of you hiding it?' the stricken father moaned.

'How could we be hiding all those cases?' Peggy asked indignantly. 'Kate Anne and me nearly killed ourselves opening them and emptying out the bottles. I don't know how many there were.'

'Eighteen cases,' Joseph groaned. 'Two hundred and sixteen bottles, and twelve of them Stalker's Joy, the best of all. Daughters? *Ochòin mo thruaighe!* They're just a misery and a burden to a man.'

King Lear himself was speaking.

'I'm sure Kate Anne and me did it for the best,' said Peggy.

'Your mother would never have done such a fool of a thing for the best,' Joseph reproached her. 'Never. She had more sense in her. Daughters? Clothes and cigarettes and all this sticklips.'

'I'm sure it's not me that wants to be a burden to you,' Peggy avowed. 'I don't want to be a man's daughter at all. I want to be a man's wife. And it's just yourself that's keeping me back. If you'll say the word now Father James can be giving it out in church next Sunday, and Fred and me can be married in Easter Week.'

'Indeed, and I'd sooner see you married than pouring away any more of my Stalker's Joy on me,' her father affirmed. 'There never was such a whisky.'

So on April 11th the banns of marriage between Alfred Ernest Odd and Peigi Ealasaid Nic Ròin were read for the first time without any objection from Iosaiph Mac Ròin. Two days later Peggy left Little Todday on a visit to her sister in Glasgow where she would assemble a hasty trousseau.

When she went on board the *Island Queen* her luggage was larger than it usually was by two wooden boxes wrapped in brown paper and addressed to Lt-Colonel A. Lindsay-Wolseley, D.S.O., Tummie House, Fort Augustus S.O., and Captain G. F. Grant, M.C., H.Q., 8th Bn. Inv. H.G., Fort Augustus, the explanation of which may be found in the following letter:

Ness Cottage
Tummie
Fort Augustus S.O.
7 / 4 / 43

My darling Peggy,

Your telegram this morning made me go all of a doodah with excitement. Please read above address carefully because it is where you and me will be living like two lovebirds in a nest this very month as ever is. It's a treat. There's a quite a lot of flowers blooming now and I'm getting the garden to rights already for the veges and which you'll be cooking with your own dear hands by summer. I'm to be received into the Church next Saturday and on Sunday I'm making my first Communion and which will make me feel like when I first paraded as a drummer boy in the sweet bye and bye. So if you're at early Mass in dear old Kiltod think of your loving Fred going through it in Drumsticket. I would have liked to have got over to do this with you but the Colonel has been so good about this cottage which is furnished a treat that as he's giving me ten days' leave for the honeymoon and which means we could take my old Ma back to Nottingham and you could see what it's like there, I didn't like to ask to come over to the islands just now. There's a night attack on against C Company at Glenbogle Castle with Captain Cameron of Kilwhillie and D Company in support of Major MacDonald of Ben Nevis, and the Colonel's rather anxious to knock sparks out of them with the attacking force. And that brings me to something I want to ask. Can you get hold of two cases of Minnie for the Colonel and the Adjutant? I believe £3 is the price per case, and I enclose notes with addressed labels to stick on. If you leave them at the St Ninian's Hotel, Obaig, the Colonel will send and call for them. I'm sorry to cause you this trouble when you go to Glasgow next Tuesday but I'd like to do something for the Colonel and Captain Grant because they've both been very kind to me. Of course I'm not paying for the Minnie only just getting it for them. Don't find somebody in Glasgow you like better than me. I've scrounged 23 coupons for you and which I enclose. I can't hardly believe that you and me will be aboard the good ship 'Darby and Joan' 21 days from now. Do you remember when you said I was 21 years older than you and I knew you'd worked it out for yourself? *If* you were the only girl in the world? You *are* the only girl in the world for

Your ever most loving and devoted

Fred

Chapter 17

MRS ODD

On the afternoon of Easter Sunday Sergeant-major Odd went down to Glasgow to meet his mother who was arriving at St Enoch's station next day from Nottingham in time to catch the last train to Obaig and go on board the *Island Queen* that night. Mrs Odd was now seventy-one, a hale old woman, small and plump, with white hair, a fresh complexion, and a wonderfully quick step. Nobody who saw her alight from that train would have given her a day more than sixty.

'Ah, here you are, Mar. Have you had a good journey up?' her son asked.

'I've had a lovely journey. Couldn't have been more comfortable if I'd been in my own chair.' She turned back to address a private of the Highland Light Infantry who had been in the compartment with her. 'Good-bye, Harry Lauder the Second,' she said. 'And don't forget if you're ever in Nottingham again to look in and have a cup of tea and plenty of cigarettes. You've got my address. Now, mind you don't forget.' She turned back to her son. 'I didn't introjuice you. He's a bit shy, poor lad, and as Scotch as a good bottle of whisky. "What's your name?" I said after he'd put my bag up on the rack for me, and you could have knocked me down with a feather when he said "my name's Lauder". "Not Harry Lauder for goodness' sake?" I said, and he said, "No, Jimmy Lauder," and I said, "Oh, well, you'll be Harry Lauder the Second to me," and after that we got on a treat, though I couldn't understand more than three words in ten of what he was mumbling. Well, how do you feel, Fred, now you're almost on the brink. Shiverified? And how did you get on with your religious business?'

'It was quite all right, Ma.'

'I always remember your poor old Dad saying to me once, when you was blaring round the house with a tin trumpet and he was trying to get his Sunday afternoon snooze, "That blessed kid'll join the Salvation Army the way he's going," and I said, "Army, if you like, Ernest, but there won't be much salvation about it, if I know the young Turk." That was when we were living in Graves Road, Fulham. Oh, I'd properly sized you up already. And now you're going to be married. Well, I never expected to be a grandmother on the right side of the blanket, as they say, and when you went off to Africa, "Yes," I said to myself, "that's the last we'll hear of poor Peggy." Well, I respeck that girl, Fred. A girl who can hold a man like you for two years and turn him religious at the end of it must have a lot in her.'

'She has, Ma. She's a jewel.'

'I never thought there was much in a jool,' said Mrs Odd. 'Expensive glass that's what I call joolery.'

'Well, you know what I mean.'

'That's all right, Fred. Your Ma knows. She's a girl in a thousand, eh?'

'She's a girl in a million,' Sergeant-major Odd declared fervidly.

'Good job everybody isn't so dainty as you, Fred. There'd be marriage queues on top of all the others. What they won't queue up for nowadays! I won't do it myself. I said to Mr Dumpleton the other day – that's my butcher – I said, "I haven't gone one over the allotted span, Mr Dumpleton, to spend the rest of what I've got left in the tail-end of a kite." '

'You won't find any queuing up in Little Todday, Mar. I hope we get a fine day tomorrow for the crossing.'

When Mrs Odd was shown the berth in her cabin on the *Island Queen* she asked what it was.

'That's where you sleep, Ma,' her son told her.

'Yes, if I was a canary-bird,' she declared, 'it'ud make a comfortable perch. Or if I was Blondin I mightn't fall off it. But being what I am, that's no bed for me.'

'You're in the lower berth,' said the stewardess, 'and you'll have the cabin to yourself.'

'I should hope so,' Mrs Odd commented. 'You don't mean to tell me you ever try and pack two into this what-not? That would be a concentration camp and no mistake.'

However, next morning when the Sergeant-major came along to inquire if his mother was ready for breakfast he found she had slept well.

'Except for some Nosey Parker who put his head round the door to ask for my permit. "I thought this was a free country, Ribbingtrop," I said.'

'But you have got a permit,' her son pointed out.

'That doesn't say anybody's got to be woken up before sunrise to wave it about like a flag, does it?' the old lady demanded. 'I told him to clear out and come back at a Christian hour.'

'What did he say?'

'I don't know what he said or didn't say. I turned over – well, squeezed over – and went to sleep again.'

Later on the Sergeant-major took his mother up to the wheel-house to introduce her to Captain MacKechnie.

'Well, this is a life on the ocean wave and no mistake,' she exclaimed as they came to the top of the companion. 'What a pity your dear old Dad isn't here to enjoy it with us. He was such a one for the sea. Get him aboard the *Margate Belle* and he was in his element. And he was always seasick. Never mind, he'd just go to the side looking as green as a gooseberry on Whit-sunday and then come back humming *Nancy Lee* as cheerful as a cricket until he went green again.'

'This is my mother, Captain MacKechnie,' said the Sergeant-major. 'I thought you wouldn't mind me bringing her up to meet you.'

'Ferry glad you did, Sarchant. Ferry glad to meet you, Mistress Ott,' the Captain squeaked cordially as he shook her hand. 'You'll be pretty excited about the wetting, Mrs Ott? He picked a fine curl for himself. Oh yess, chust a real pewty.'

'And I'll lay you know what a fine girl is, Captain MacKechnie,' Mrs Odd told him.

The skipper of the *Island Queen* laughed high with delight at this.

'Look at that now, Sarchant,' he chuckled, shaking with self-congratulatory mirth. 'Wait you till I tell my missus that. Ah, well, we're all very proud that the Sarchant has chosen an Island curl for himself. He's ferry much liked is the Sarchant. I neffer heard anything but praise for him. Has he introduced you to Minnie yet, Mistress Ott?'

'Minnie?' the old lady repeated. 'You don't mean to say you've got another girl up here, Fred?'

'Ferry good. Ferry good,' the Skipper chuckled, slapping his leg. 'Yess, yess, that's a good one right enough.'

'Minnie is what they call that whisky ship I was telling you about, Ma,' the Sergeant-major explained.

'You'll please come along to my cappin and tap the steward before you go ashore,' Captain MacKechnie invited them. 'I'd like to trink to your happiness, Sarchant, as I can't be at the wetting myself.'

The bens of Great Todday were in sight when Mrs Odd and her son went along to tap the steward.

'Well, here's to you, Sarchant, and here's to you, Mistress Ott, and may all your trupples be little ones!' Captain MacKechnie wished, raising his glass.

'That's a big lot of whisky for an old woman,' Mrs Odd said, eyeing her own.

'Och, you won't notice it, Mistress Ott,' the Skipper assured her. 'It's Caberfèidh. The antlers of the stack. Ay, it's a grand whisky. Mackenzie and Mackenzie of Inverness.

'Well, seeing I've waited twenty years and more for my son to turn sensible,' said Mrs Odd, 'here goes.'

And she drained her dram with a verve that the Biffer himself might have envied.

'By Chinko, that's the right way to put down a tram, Mistress Ott,' her host declared enthusiastically. 'I don't like to see a woman pecking at it like a hen. Not at all.'

'A nice reputation I'll have presently,' said Mrs Odd. 'It's a good thing you're getting married tomorrow, Fred.'

Once the date of the wedding had been definitely fixed Joseph Macroon had stinted nothing to make it a memorable occasion. A hoard of sugar, the existence of which had been unsuspected by his family, was drawn upon for the cake. He had allowed Peggy a generous sum for her trousseau. Now he was on the pier waiting to welcome the Sergeant-major and Mrs Odd.

'That's him,' said the former, from where they were standing on the upper deck.

'That's who?' asked his mother.

'My future par-in-lore in the red knitted cap.'

'Now who does he remind me of?' Mrs Odd exclaimed. 'I know. Will Atkins.'

'Will Atkins? Who's he?'

'The feller who had it in for Robinson Crusoe in the panto. Oh, he's the spitting image of Will Atkins. And who's that big dark feller?'

'That's Roderick MacRurie who has the hotel here in Snorvig.'

'Yes, and he'd need an hotel to live in. What a whopper, eh? And who's Boatrace Bill?'

The Sergeant-major guessed that this name was inspired by Captain Waggett's light-blue tweed suit latticed with dark blue.

'That's Captain Waggett who commands the Todday company of the Home Guard.'

'Thinks quite a lot of himself, doesn't he?' Mrs Odd commented.

A few minutes later she was being greeted by Joseph Macroon on the pier.

'I'm proud to welcome you, Mistress Odd,' he told her. 'You've come a long way, I believe.'

'Nottingham. Was you ever in Nottingham?'

'No, I was never there. It'll be a fine city, I daresay.'

'Not so bad. It's not dear old London of course, but what place is?'

'I was never there either.'

'You was never in London?' Mrs Odd gasped. 'Well, if that hasn't torn it!'

Joseph looked round apprehensively to see what had been torn, and at that moment Duncan Bàn came hurrying up.

'I never heard her blowing,' he explained. 'I was away up the hill having a crack with Alec Mackinnon, and when I looked round there she was.'

'This is Mr Duncan Macroon with who you and me are staying tonight,' said the Sergeant-major.

'*Fàilte do'n dùthaich,*' Duncan bubbled as he warmly wrung the old lady's hand. 'Do you know what that means, Mistress Odd?'

'I can't say I do,' she told him, beaming. 'But I suppose it's a bit of this Garlic you all gabble among yourselves.'

'Welcome to the country. And I never welcomed anybody more heartily,' Duncan declared. 'My goodness, I can see where Fred got that twinkle in his eye. Well now, Joseph, will we go right across, or will we wait for the mails?'

'You'd better be going across right away with Mistress Odd, and the *Morning Star* can come back for me,' Joseph replied.

Kenny was inclined to be a bit shy with Mrs Odd at first, but it was not long before she had him laughing and by the time they reached Kiltod he was suggesting taking her round tomorrow morning early to have a look at the *Cabinet Minister.*

'You let me go in and see Peggy by myself for a moment, Fred,' his mother said when they reached the post-office.

She found Peggy in the little room behind the shop.

'My goodness, you're taller than I expected, my dear. You must be nearly as tall as Fred,' she said as she pulled Peggy down to kiss her after the first formal handshake.

'Well, you've made Fred happy and I see you're going to make his old mother just as happy. He's a lucky man and I'm a lucky old woman.'

'You're being terribly kind, Mrs Odd,' Peggy murmured.

'And what a pleasure to be able to see a girl blush again,' Mrs Odd exclaimed. 'I'd almost forgotten what it looked like.'

'I hope you don't mind Fred becoming a Catholic, Mrs Odd,' Peggy almost whispered.

'I wouldn't mind not if he'd become a Weslean. I'm good old Church of England myself, and I haven't missed a harvest festival in donkey's years, but I don't think Fred has been inside any kind of a church since he was a nipper before he met you. Yes, you've done something I wouldn't have believed anybody could do with Fred, and now what you've got to do is make me a granny as soon as poss. There you go blushing again. Well, really, it's a treat to see it. All these Ats and Whats and Wrens and Whens and Waafs, and those saucy little hussies with their lipstick and powder. Well, I'm not going to make a nuisance of myself now. I'm sure you'll have lots to do, with the wedding tomorrow, and we'll have a good talk when we go away together on Thursday. I'm glad you'll be able to see the place which will be your own one day. It's nothing grand, mind you, but it's cosy. And there's a lovely big room at the back for a nursery.'

Mrs Odd took the two hands of her future daughter-in-law in her own.

'Yes, Fred's waited a long while, but you was worth waiting for.'

One more house Mrs Odd had to visit before she got into the trap in which she was to drive to Tigh nam Bàrd and that was Father Macalister's.

'Well, really, you know, Sergeant, your mother's a wonderful woman,' the parish priest avowed. 'Fancy travelling all the way from that peculiar place where she lives just to see you married. Oh, by Jingo, good shooting! And now you'll take a small refreshment, Mrs Odd.'

'I don't know as I ought, Father Macalister. I had some Caperfay as he called it with Captain MacKechnie, and I thought "Yes, you'll be cutting capers yourself, Elizar Odd, if you do this sort of thing." '

'Ah well, I think you'll manage a small sensation with me. Thanks be to God, we're in a position to offer it these days.'

'Minnie, eh?'

'Ay, Saint Minnie we call her now.'

The parish priest went to his cupboard, and pondered the choice.

'All the Year Round,' he decided. 'Just the smallest sensation, Mrs Odd. Oh, really beautiful stuff. You'll just think you're sipping cream. Really a baby in arms would hardly know it was whisky. *Uisge beatha*. Water of Life!'

'That's Garlic I suppose?'

'Ay, Gaelic it is. What a pity you don't know our glorious language.'

'Say that again, will you, Father Macalister.'

'*Uisge beatha*.'

'I see. Something like a sneeze and then a yawn,' said Mrs Odd.

'Ay, ay, that's just what it is. Something between a sneeze and a yawn. Did you hear that, Duncan? Ah well, really now, I never heard a better description of it. Something between a sneeze and a yawn. I won't forget that, Duncan. And you won't forget it either, my boy.'

'I won't forget it, Father,' the poet assured him.

'You'll enjoy Duncan's company, Mrs Odd,' the priest went on. 'And tomorrow my friend here is to marry a lovely and beautiful girl.' He raised his glass. 'Ah well, Sergeant, you know I wish you everything you can wish for yourself,' he said in his richest bass.

'I know you do, Father. And if I might take advantage of this opportunity I'd like to say on behalf of Peggy and myself how much we owe to you and my friend Duncan here. The course of true love never does run smooth, they say, and certainly the course of true love for Peggy and I ran very wonky for a time – very wonky. However, thanks to Father Macalister here . . .'

'And St Minnie,' the priest interposed.

'All is now going according.'

The Sergeant-major drained his glass.

'Well, I suppose we ought to be going along,' he said. 'You've got quite a bit of a drive yet, Mar, and I expect you're feeling a bit tired. You've had two long days, and you'll have a long journey back Thursday.'

'Oh, I'm feeling quite bobbish,' said his mother. 'Or if I'm not, the whisky is.'

'It'll do you no harm, Mrs Odd,' Father Macalister assured her sonorously. 'In fact it'll do you a power of good.'

Although the clock said half past six, double summer time made it still golden afternoon, and the myriad daisies on the machair were only just beginning to close their petals. Wheatears flashed their white rumps as they dipped in flight ahead of the trap. Stonechats with ebon heads and chestnut breasts clicked beside the track. Oyster-catchers,

Bride's pages, were whistling gleefully to welcome the ebb of the tide on Tràigh Swish.

'Lovely, isn't it, Ma?' the Sergeant-major exclaimed contentedly.

'Oh, it's beautiful,' his mother agreed.

'Are you riding comfortable, Mistress Odd?' asked Duncan.

'Very comfortable, thank you. And what a treat to look at the back of a horse for a change instead of the back of a taxi-driver. Not but what me and taxi-drivers don't get on. You hear a lot of people say they're disobliging. That's not my experience of 'em at all. I went down to see Aunt Lou last August Bank, Fred, and when I got to St Pancras there wasn't a taxi to be seen.

' "Where do you want to go, mum?" the porter asked, and when I said "Peckham," he said, "You'll never get no taxi to take you to Peckham, never. There's a war on." Oh, what a dismal Jimmy! "Yes," I said, "you won't blow up Hitler if they drop you over Berlin, will you?" Well, just as I was thinking I'd have to get that South London Tube, a taxi drove up and deposited an elderly party in trousers. "Hi," I said, "are you engaged?" "Where do you want to go, mum?" he asked. I looked him straight in the eyes and "Peckham," I said. "All right, jump in, Mar," he said, and I reely couldn't help but smile the way that porter stood staring after us when we drove off. He couldn't have stared more if I'd have been the Queen.'

'Duncan doesn't know where Peckham is,' the Sergeant-major reminded his mother.

'Doesn't he? Oh well, you go to the South Pole and take the first turning to the right,' Mrs Odd told him.

'I was never in London at all,' Duncan told her.

'Goodness gracious me, that's the second one who's said that to me inside an hour. What do you do with yourselves up here? Don't you want to go to London, Mr Macroon?'

'No, I don't believe I do at all.'

'Well, I suppose there's no accounting for tastes,' the old lady decided. 'And mind you, I don't say it isn't beautiful here. It is beautiful. Very beautiful. All the same, there's something about dear old London if you're a Cockney born and bred like what I am that makes you think London's the best place in all the world. And London done well in the war, mind you. Yes, London can take it, but Hitler can't take London. What a man, eh? Well, it's really not fair to other men to call him a man at all. A freak, that's what he is. I remember going to Barnum's freaks at Olympia in '99 – not so long after you was born, Fred, and very glad I was you had come into the world or you might have been in the freak business yourself – where was I? Oh yes, well, I sore a freak there called Jo-jo, the Dog-faced man from Siberia, and believe me, he was a human being beside Hitler. Goodness, am I letting my tongue wag? That's this Minnie as you call it. Well, I mean to say, first caperfaying with Captain MacKechnie and then All the Year Round with Father Macalister, and if I'd have had any more of it I'd have been going round with the year, that's one sure thing. What's the matter with that cow?'

An Ayrshire cow was prancing about the machair ahead of the trap.

'She's after having a dram herself,' said Duncan.

'Go on. You don't mean to say you give your cows whisky?' Mrs Odd exclaimed.

'He's pulling your leg, Ma,' said the Sergeant-major.

'I knew he must be. But, seriously, is it all right? It won't come prancing into us, will it, Mr Macroon?'

'No, no, don't you be worrying yourself, Mistress Odd,' her host reassured her.

'That reminds me, what relation exactly are you to my Fred's Peggy?'

'Och, we're pretty far away from one another.'

'But you are cousins?'

'Ay, we're distant sort of cousins.'

'So when Fred and Peggy are married, you'll be a sort of relative of mine. Oh, I'm going to call you "Duncan". I'll tell you what it is. It's always on the tip of my tongue to say Macaroon instead of Macroon. That's Fred's handwriting, that is. When he wrote first and told me he was engaged to a girl called Peggy Macroon, I read it Macaroon, and in fact I told all my friends she was called Macaroon. I remember Mr Hewitson, my greengrocer, who likes a joke, and which is unusual for a greengrocer because most of the greengrocers I've known never make jokes – I think they're always worried whether they'll sell out whatever it is before it goes rotten – well, this Mr Hewitson said to me, "I suppose your son's getting married on his sweet ration, Mrs Odd?"

' "I'm sure I hope not," I said, "I know Fred's style, and he won't want something he can put in his waistcoat pocket and forget she's there." So I'll call you "Duncan" if you don't mind.'

'I'll be very pleased if you'll be calling me Duncan, Mistress Odd. I don't care at all for Mr Macroon, and if anybody calls me Lieutenant Macroon I just feel in a mind to give him a slosh in the jaw. Did you see Captain Waggett on the pier?'

'Wasn't that the feller that looked like the Boatrace, Fred? Yes, I sore him.'

'Then you've seen our aristocracy,' Duncan chuckled.

'I'll tell you somebody who I did like,' Mrs Odd said. 'And that was Father Macalister.'

'There's no better man anywhere,' Duncan declared.

'I'll add "hear, hear" to that,' said the Sergeant-major.

'Oh, I could see that the moment I set eyes on him,' Mrs Odd said. 'And what a voice! I never heard anything like it since I sat close to the double-bass in the orchestra at some play Mr and Mrs Hewitson and me went to. Mrs H. kept nudging me to look at the stage, but I couldn't take my eyes off this double-bass. A very old man he was, with a beard as big as a doormat, but what a rumble he got out of that instrument of his! You know it sort of tickled my tummy the way a toothcomb and tissue-paper used to tickle your lips when you was a kiddie. And Father Macalister's voice had the same kind of a rumble.'

'You can see my house now,' said Duncan pointing to Tigh nam Bàrd. 'The House of the Bard.'

'What's it barred against?'

'No, no, Ma. Bard means poyt,' the Sergeant-major put in.

'Are you a poyt then?' Mrs Odd asked.

'Och, yes, I'm a poet.'

'You mean you write songs and things in rhyme?' she pressed.

'In Garlic, Ma,' her son explained.

'I only knew one feller who wrote rhymes,' said Mrs Odd. 'Jack Bewick his name was. He lived in the same street where I lived when I was a girl. Off the London Road. Islington way. And I remember he frightened the life out of us once, writing a rhyme about Jack the Ripper. There was something about "sliver" and "liver". I know he got all us girls screaming before he was done.'

'Ay, Jack the Ripper,' said Duncan. 'I remember my grandmother used to talk about him. They were always afraid he would come out to the Islands and start his games here. There was a fellow called Stewart, a big joker he was – ach – you heard him give a *port a beul* at your *rèiteach*, Sergeant. Well, Michael was coming back from Kiltod one night, and he thought he'd play a joke on two chaps he saw coming along. So he put his coat up round his face and stopped them and asked where he could have a night's lodging. He could put on any kind of a voice he liked, and they didn't know who he was from Adam himself. Well, they said they didn't know where he could find a lodging at all, and he pointed to Joseph's house – it was his father's then – old John Macroon – and they said he'd never find a lodging there, because you'll understand, Fred, Peggy's grandfather was a bit of a tough nut altogether. Well, Michael drew himself up as tall as he could and he had a voice as big as Father Macalister's when he liked. "I can find a lodging anywhere," he says. "Do you know who I am? I'm Jack the Ripper." *A Dhia nan gràs*, one of them called out and fell down on his back in the ditch saying Hail Marys as fast as he could and crossing himself nineteen to the dozen but the other took to his heels, and by Jingo, he roused the whole island and Michael saw them coming along for him with pitchforks and scythes and guns and he had to take to his heels himself.'

This tale about Jack the Ripper brought them to Tigh nam Bàrd.

'Make yourself at home, Mistress Odd,' said the host. 'Do you like lobster, please?'

'Do I like lobster?' Mrs Odd exclaimed. 'I never finished eating lobster yet but what I could have eaten another clore.'

Duncan Bàn exhibited the lobsters he had secured for his guests.

'What a pair of mammoths!' she gasped in admiration. 'Look at 'em, Fred. Well, I mean, you'd only have to put them two in sentry-boxes outside Buckingham Palace and the Household Brigade could go home to bed.'

Chapter 18

THE WEDDING

The wedding was timed for five o'clock in the afternoon because
everybody in Little Todday, including Father Macalister himself, had a
deep antipathy to what was still known in the Islands as Lloyd George's
time, from the head of the Government which introduced the novelty
during the First World War. The bridegroom-to-be walked in to Kiltod
to make his Communion with his bride-to-be beside him, and then he
parted from her until they would meet, never to part again he hoped, for
the marriage ceremony.

Later on that morning Duncan drove his two guests to the head of
Bàgh Mhic Ròin where Kenny met them with the *Morning Star* and took
them out to see the half of the *Cabinet Minister* that was left lying on the
Gobha, with the other half almost completely submerged.

'And that's where it all comes from, is it?' said Mrs Odd. 'Well, I
never thought I'd live to see a proper shipwreck after seeing so many in
panto.'

'Would you like to come down into the hold, Mrs Odd?' Kenny
asked. 'I'll take you down if you like. You have to go down a rope.'

'I think that's a bit beyond my mother, Kenny,' said the Sergeant-
major. 'No, it's not that you couldn't do it, Ma,' he added quickly. 'But
you'd get covered with a sort of black oil, and don't forget I'm getting
married this afternoon.'

'Och, I wouldn't be spoiling an adventure for anything,' Duncan
urged in support. 'But you'd come out looking like a Hottentot, Mistress
Odd, and your clothes would be in a terrible mess.'

So the old lady allowed herself to be dissuaded from descending into
the hold of the *Cabinet Minister*, once she had made it clear that it was
not her lack of physical capacity which was in question. As the *Morning
Star* chugged slowly round the wrecked ship she was much delighted by
the hundreds of puffins swimming in the water all round them.

'I never saw such comical-looking objecks,' she declared. 'They're a
bit like a bookie I used to know — Sam Orgles. He died of heart failure
coming home from Hurst Park. A nice feller he was too. Never owed

nobody a farthing. What is it you call these birds? Puffins? Yes, that's right. Well, funny thing, but this Sam Orgles used to puff a lot.'

Anything more that might have transpired about Sam Orgles was interrupted by the sudden appearance from the water of the head of an Atlantic seal, just in front of the *Morning Star*.

'Whatever was that?' Mrs Odd exclaimed as the animal dived again and was lost to view. 'A seal? Well, talk about likenesses! I said these puffins reminded me of Sam Orgles, but that *was* Mr Dumpleton.'

'Who's Mr Dumpleton?' Duncan Bàn asked.

'My butcher in Nottingham. Yes, that seal was Mr Dumpleton to the life. Same pop eyes and thick neck and bulging forehead. I won't half pull his leg when I get back. "You've started early this year with your bathing," I'll say to him. I only wish Mr Hewitson looked like a seal — he's my greengrocer — because Mr H. is more one for a good laugh than what Mr D. is. But really that likeness! It was uncanny. If he'd stayed up above water for another minute I'd have been asking him for a nice undercut.'

When Mrs Odd returned from her marine excursion, her son took her for a walk to Tràigh Swish.

'What sands, Fred!' she exclaimed. 'I mean to say sands like that put Margate off the map. Margate's nowhere. Nowhere at all. Or Ramsgate either. A pity they aren't full of people.'

'I don't know so much about that, Mar. I think crowds of people'ud spoil them,' he objected.

'Well, I like to see people enjoying theirselves. This'ud be a proper paradise for kids, and there isn't a soul in sight from one end of it to the other. It's wasted, away up here.'

'It wasn't wasted for me,' said the Sergeant-major. 'Two years ago all but a day I told Peggy I loved her just about where you and me are sitting on the grass now. It was on a Sunday actually, and the date was April 27th. It was a lovely day the same as what it is now, and the macker was covered with daisies the same as what it is now.'

'Macker? What's that?'

'Macker's what they call all this grassy land. Garlic. And I remember Peggy was making herself a bracelet out of daisies while I was telling her the old old story, and I took the bracelet from her and stuck it in this pocket.' He pointed to the pocket over his heart. 'And I've got that withered daisy-bracelet put away in my blotter, and where it'll remain till death do us part.'

'She wouldn't have you at first, would she, Fred?'

'Well, she wouldn't say "yes"; but mark you, she didn't say "no" either. Oh, I firmly believe that if I hadn't have been sent off to Devonshire and then to Africar in the autumn of '41 you'd have been Granny Odd today. Still, there you are, war's war, and human beings get pushed about like luggage in time of war.'

'That's quite right, Fred, pushed about and bumped about a good deal in the pushing. Well, I'm glad I'm not Hitler. Fancy going to bed every night and knowing that millions of people all over the world were wishing you'd never wake up. Oh well, you've had to wait two years, Fred; but as I told Peggy yesterday afternoon when I went in and had those few words with her alone, she was worth waiting for.'

Mother and son sat silent for a minute or two, gazing at the pale-blue ocean breaking placidly upon the lonely expanse of long white beach.

'What's that bird I can hear singing as sweet as a canary?' Mrs Odd asked presently.

'That's a lark, Ma.'

'Yes, he sounds as if he was enjoying himself, the pretty dear,' she said. 'Well, you may grumble at having had to wait so long for Peggy, but you're a lucky feller, Fred. Most men when they reach forty-five have forgotten what it was to be in love, and here are you as soppy as a kid in a Sunday school making goo-goo eyes at the girl who lives round the corner. Well, when you're lying snug with Peggy in your arms tonight, do you know where I shall be?'

'In bed too I should hope.'

'Oh no, I shall be out here.'

'Out here?' the Sergeant-major exclaimed.

'Yes, Duncan's invited me out here to see the fairies by the light of the moon.'

'He's apt to come out here and drink a lot,' the Sergeant-major warned his mother.

'Never mind. If he shows me fairies whether he's twopence on the can or as sober and la-di-da as one of them B.B.C. announcers, I'll go back to Nottingham very pleased with myself. Did he ever tell you about that fairy who came in regular three winters ago and washed all his clothes for him?'

'I have heard him talk about her, yes,' the Sergeant-major admitted cautiously.

'Well, what a godsend for the man! I mean to say, if there's one thing that's gone to pieces more than anything in this blessed war it's laundries. I still do most of my own washing, as you know. But three weeks ago I sent a sheet to the laundry, and really when it came back Peggy could have worn it for a bridal veil it was so full of holes.'

'I think Duncan was imagining this fairy washerwoman, Ma,' her son argued. 'I don't think you ought to take him quite seriously. He's a good chap. I wouldn't want a better for a best man. But he does put away the whisky sometimes.'

'You mean to say his fairies are just the D.T.s?'

'No, I wouldn't go so far as that. I think it's more his fanciful nature. And which *is* very fanciful.'

'Well, you never know. I'm not going to feel sure of anything I mightn't see after that seal who came up and had a squint at us. I mean, look at the story about this seal-woman who was the mother of all these Macroons. Well, I wouldn't have believed that if I hadn't seen with my own orbs that seal who was the living double of my butcher in Nottingham. And after all Macroon, by what Duncan Bang tells me, means "son of the seal" in Garlic. There must have been something in it for them to get their name in the first place. You don't go calling anybody the son of a seal for nothing,' Mrs Odd declared firmly.

'Yes, but it was all a long time ago,' her son pointed out.

'So was Adam and Eve, and if a big snake started off talking to Eve and edging her on to eat fruit strickly forbidden for her to eat, don't tell me a seal couldn't have been half-human once upon a time.'

'Yes, but this fairy of Duncan's was supposed to have done his washing for him in the first winter of this war,' said the Sergeant-major. 'That's not very long ago.'

'Well, perhaps I won't meet her. Or again perhaps I will. Anyway, this beach'll look like a transformation scene by moonlight and I'm going to make the most of my holiday. We may not see fairies in Nottingham any more, or even in dear old London, but that doesn't say we mightn't see them here. And if a fairy had have looked over your shoulder when you was courting Peggy here two years ago, would you have been as surprised as all that?'

The Sergeant-major tossed his head.

'Perhaps I shouldn't,' he agreed with a smile.

Mrs Odd had been invited down to Kiltod to join in a small family dinner before the ceremony in church. The bridegroom and his best man were bidden to present themselves at the bride's house to lead the procession to the wedding sharp at a quarter to five. Neither of Peggy's two married sisters had been able to leave the cares of wartime households to be present, and John, her elder brother, was away at sea; but Peigi Bheag, the schoolteacher at Barra, was at home, and determined to follow her younger sister's example by marrying Neil MacNeil in the summer holidays. The rest of the company was made up of aunts and uncles and cousins living in Little Todday.

'A Dhia, your mother's a very fine woman,' Joseph Macroon said to his all but son-in-law when the Sergeant-major supported by Duncan Macroon arrived at the house of the bride's father. 'Full of stories. She took my mind off that catastrophe.'

'What catastrophe?' the Sergeant-major asked.

'The whisky catastrophe. I was thinking about those two hundred and sixteen bottles when I was putting out the bottles for this evening.'

The procession for church was lined up ready for to start. First went the bridegroom, who had so far broken with the professional etiquette of years of soldiering as to stick a nosegay of daisies in his uniform, with his bride upon his arm, she in a bridal dress of real white silk made up from that of her eldest sister, Peigi Mhòr, who was as tall as herself. Then came Duncan Bàn Macroon with Kate Anne, the bridesmaid, in white artificial silk, obtained it must be confessed through the kindly offices of a case of Minnie. Joseph Macroon, his ceremonial bowler bearing the scars of that whisky catastrophe, went next with Mrs Odd upon his arm, the old lady beaming with delight. Other couples of relations followed, and on either side of the procession Kenny and a young friend of his fired off shot-guns into the air all the way up to the church.

After the ceremony a much longer procession formed up to walk round and be greeted by as many families as possible before it was time to gather at the tables that had been spread in the parish hall. Many friends had come over from Great Todday in the *Flying Fish* and the *Kittiwake*, all of whom took part in the procession. Over the green machair in the golden light of that afternoon at April's end the long line of couples walked laughing and chatting, with not so much firing as Kenny and his friends would have liked owing to the famine of cartridges. Even the few that were fired made Captain Waggett shake his head censoriously.

'They've no business to be wasting ammunition like that,' he told his wife who was on his arm. 'I'm surprised Sergeant-major Odd doesn't stop it. They simply will not remember there's a war on.'

'Oh well, Paul, people only get married once,' she pleaded. 'That is, I mean, nice people.'

'I'm glad we're going to be married in Glasgow,' George Campbell was saying to Catriona Macleod.

'Would you be ashamed, then, to be walking with me in front just now?' she asked.

'No, darling, of course not, but it is very public. And I feel relieved to think that when we go off tomorrow the Sergeant-major and Peggy will get all the attention. They may forget we're going to be married at all,' he added hopefully.

'Don't you be thinking that, George,' she told him, and with justice, considering the number of her girl friends in Great Todday with whom Catriona had discussed that going away.

The houses at which the bride and bridegroom stopped to be greeted were all flying small flags, including at two the Japanese flag the nationality of which was unknown to those who flew it. Anyway, what did it matter? The flags were not flown to celebrate an international event but to express in colour the pleasure of the people of Little Todday that Peigi Ealasaid was married to the Sarchant.

'Och, they're good people, right enough,' the Biffer declared to Bean a'Bhiffer who was moving along upon his arm with her usual placidity. 'I'll never forget the way they welcomed us that night when Drooby and I went over to fetch the first case of Minnie we ever had.'

And to Bean Ailein on his arm Drooby was expressing the same sentiments.

Dr Maclaren had taken for his partner Roderick MacRurie's daughter Annag, who was representing her father at the wedding.

'And when are you going to be walking at the head of a procession like this?' he asked.

'Och, indeed, I don't know, Doctor,' she replied sadly. 'I believe I'll soon be on the shelf.'

'Ay, you'll soon be twenty-one, Annag,' he chuckled. 'Never mind, I believe the war will be over before you're an old *cailleach*, and he'll be home again.'

'I don't know at all what you're talking about, Doctor.'

'Oh no, you don't know, do you?'

'It's a pity George Campbell and Catriona aren't being married in

Snorvig,' she said, changing the subject. 'We could have had some fine fun.'

'George wasn't taking any risks,' the Doctor laughed. 'George didn't see himself being undressed by half a dozen of his friends at the end of the evening and bedded with the bride.'

'Och, really, Doctor, what terrible things you say!'

'Now, don't be a humbug, Annag. You know perfectly well you'd have been in the lead yourself at undressing the bride.'

'What you think about!'

'What I think about at this moment is what a foolish old bachelor I feel.'

He looked round at the merry procession following the bride and bridegroom over the green machair on that golden afternoon — Alec Mackinnon and the teacher from a small school on the other side of Little Todday, Andrew Thomson and Mrs Thomson, Andrew Chisholm and Mrs Chisholm, John Beaton and Mrs Beaton, Angus MacCormac and Bean Aonghais, Sammy MacCodrum and Bean Shomhairle, Hugh Macroon and Bean Uisdein, Jockey Stewart and Bean Yockey, old Michael Macroon the joker with his plump grand-niece Peigi Bheag whose heart was in Barra with her own young man and wasn't bothering about a young partner as Neil himself was not there, couple after couple of them, and twenty couples more. Good wishes from every house they passed and shrill cheers from the children. Flags waving in the gentle breeze. The daisies already crimson with sleep. The whimbrels in the distance crying that May was almost here. Larks and wheatears and stonechats everywhere.

'Peggy, darling Peggy,' the bridegroom turned to murmur to his bride. 'I never thought anybody *could* be as happy as what I am.'

'*Mo ghràidh*,' she murmured back, her deep-blue slanting eyes alive.

'What *does* that mean? I've wanted to ask a lot of people, but I never would.'

'It means "my love",' she told him tenderly. 'It means my love, *a ghràidh mo chridhe*.'

'Mar isn't half enjoying herself with your dad,' exclaimed the bridegroom, too much overcome by emotion to say a word in reply to the exquisitely welcome words from his Peggy.

'I think she's just a beautiful *cailleach*, Fred. She's been so sweet to me.'

'She's going out on Tràigh Swish with Duncan tonight, looking for fairies.'

'I'm sure if anybody would be seeing them, it's herself would be seeing them,' Peggy replied.

When the procession reached the parish hall, the feast had been spread by Kate Anne with the help of her friends Flora, Morag, and Mairead and some of the older women. Muscular fowls and cold mutton were in abundance. Bottles of beer, tactfully ordered in quantity from Big Roderick, were waiting to prepare the way for the whisky, half a dozen bottles of which had also been tactfully ordered from Roderick. Pre-war pickles had been unearthed. Synthetic fruit juices were there to sustain those who did not drink beer or whisky until tea was served. There were heaps of chalk-white Glasgow bread interspersed with healthier home-made scones and bannocks. The wedding-cake owing to a mishap in the baking rose like the leaning tower of Pisa in the middle of the table.

Father Macalister sat on the bride's right, Mrs Odd sat on his other side. Duncan Bàn was next. Old Bean Sheumais Mhìceil, the senior matriarch of the Macroons, sat next the bridegroom, and on the other side was her nephew Joseph.

'A bhòbh bhòbh,' Joseph had muttered to himself when he found that Mrs Waggett was to be on his other side.

Before the speeches Duncan Bàn was called upon to read out the sheaf of telegrams which had arrived during the morning, half of them in Gaelic half in English and at least a dozen of them expressing a hope that all the troubles of the married pair might be little ones.

'Ah well, Mrs Odd,' said the parish priest with a deep sigh, 'original eloquence is pretty rare. Thank God, he's nearly come to the end of them.'

There were many speeches, but the substance of most of them has already been heard at the rèiteach. On this occasion Joseph Macroon, under the influence of the whisky catastrophe and the failure to obtain any support for his proposed licence to sell spirituous liquors in Little Todday, made no allusion either to a new road or a new school. He was content to be the father of the bride. Captain Waggett, too, kept himself strictly to the utterance of the conventional speech made at weddings. He made no allusion to the *Cabinet Minister*.

The only really new contribution to the convivial oratory of Kiltod was the speech made by Mrs Odd in rising to reply to the toast proposed to her both by Duncan Bàn and Joseph Macroon.

'Well, I can't very well say I'm not accustomed to talking because it's a well-known fact that I can talk the hind-legs off a donkey, as the saying goes. All the same, ladies and gentlemen, this is the first time in all my life as I've got up on my tootsies and made a regular speech. Well, first of all I must say what a joy it has been to an old woman to find her only son making such a sensible choice as what Fred has made in marrying my daughter-in-lore Peggy. You'll often hear that mothers-in-lore are a nuisance, and which in fact I think they very often are. Well, my son will tell you I've never tried to interfere with him ever since he was on his own. Mind you, I don't say there weren't times when I wanted to interfere, yes, and when I felt I ought to interfere. But I never did, and I'm certainly not going to start in trying to interfere now. If he doesn't know his own mind at his age, nobody else is going to know it for him, that's one sure thing.

'And I'll tell you this, ladies and gentlemen, apart from falling in love with my daughter-in-lore, he fell in love with Little Todday itself.'

'Good shooting!' ejaculated Father Macalister.

'And I don't blame him,' the old lady went on. 'I've fallen in love with Little Todday myself.' (*Loud applause.*) 'Unfortunately my stay here this time will be all too short, but make no mistake about it, I'm coming back to spend a real holiday here as soon as ever I can. Let 'em try and ask at the railway station if my journey is really necessary and see what answer they get from me. Protected Area? This isn't the only area that needs a bit of protection these days. There's plenty of areas where I live in Nottingham wants a bit of police protection. But then I always was a bit of a Radical. My old man often used to say to me, "Eliza," he used to say, "you're a proper Radical." So you haven't seen the last of me. I don't know whether Duncan Bang here will invite me back to stay with him . . .'

'Don't you be afraid of that, Mistress Odd,' Duncan bubbled.

'And I hope my son's father-in-lore'll ask me.'

'You'll have the freedom of Little Todday, Mrs Odd,' the parish priest proclaimed in his most sonorous bass.

'Well, for once in my life I don't know as I've anything much more to say except to thank you one and all for your kindness to me and my son. I can't hardly believe that I only landed here yesterday afternoon, for I never felt so much at home since I left dear old London. And the only time I ever saw fairyland before was the other side of the footlights.'

'*A Dhia*, what kind of lights are they at all?' Joseph muttered.

'The lighting at a theatre,' Mrs Waggett whispered to him.

'But now here I am right in the middle of fairyland. God bless you all!'

The old lady sat down amid a tumult of applause.

'That was really beautiful, Mrs Odd,' Father Macalister assured her. 'You'll need a small sensation after that. What have you there, Duncan?'

'White Label, Father. Duty paid.'

'Ay, the white label of a blameless life, Mr Waggett. The duty on this has been paid,' said the parish priest, with a profound sigh.

'I'm very glad to hear it, Father Macalister.'

'I'm sure you will be, Mr Waggett. I'm sure you will be.'

'Did you get this from Ruairidh Mór, Joseph?' he asked, turning to his host.

'I did, Father.'

'Ay, you're a great diplomat, Joseph,' the priest assured him gravely.

When the bridal feast was eaten and the speeches all made, the hall was cleared for a dance. The absence of so many of the island's young men made this less of a jollification than usual, and there were more songs than dances. Duncan Bàn, of course, had composed a special one, and his epithalamium was received with rapturous applause. Joseph Macroon delivered one of the *sgeulachdan* or tales for which he was famous. Her inability to follow the Gaelic was a grief to Mrs Odd, for she was sure by the expression on her host's face and the laughter of the audience that the tale he was telling was a really saucy one. Father Macalister, who sang seldom nowadays, gave them two songs which put the audience into an ecstasy.

At last the time came for the bridal reel which was danced only by the bride, the bridegroom, the bridesmaid, and the *fleasgach* or best man. Neither the Sergeant-major nor Duncan Bàn was a first-class performer at a reel, but any awkwardness they displayed was more than made up for by the grace and beauty of the dancing of the two girls, whose white forms in a shower of pre-war confetti unearthed for the occasion like the pickles made Mrs Odd declare that they could knock sparks off anybody she'd seen in the panto for donkey's years.

'But Fred's very clumsy,' she declared. 'Very clumsy indeed. He gets that from his father. I was always very quick on my tootsies.'

More songs followed, and then about ten o'clock came the last reel.

'Now you're going to see something very peculiar, Mrs Odd,' Father Macalister told her. 'After they've been dancing for a while you'll see a couple of the girls come in and steal away the bride and another girl will take her place. That's to cheat the fairies in case they took it into their heads to steal away the bride themselves. They'll think the bride is still dancing.'

'So there *are* fairies about?' Mrs Odd asked, looking at the priest very seriously.

'That's the idea. Then in a minute you'll see the bridegroom look round and find that the bride has vanished, and two or three friends of his will come along and lead him away to where she is, and somebody else will take his place to cheat the fairies again.'

The parish priest did not add that these friends would then proceed to undress the bridegroom and bring him along to the room of the bride who would already have been undressed by her guardians.

As a matter of fact, owing to the Sergeant-major's comparative seniority and his not being a native, he escaped the further attentions of those who led him away from the hall after the mischief of the fairies had been foiled by the stealing away of the bride by Flora, Morag, and Mairead. They were joined, when the last reel had been danced, by Kate Anne and Peigi Bheag, who had taken her sister's place in the reel. If the bridegroom escaped, the bride was spared nothing, and the shrieks of mirth coming from the bridal chamber made the bridegroom wonder what on earth was happening.

Back in the hall the party still went on.

'Unfortunately, you'll be leaving us tomorrow, Mrs Odd,' Father Macalister told her, 'but if you lived here there would have been a gathering in your house tomorrow night. That's what we call the *bainis tighe* or house wedding.'

'You don't mean to let anyone forget they've been married on Little Todday,' Mrs Odd observed. 'But I'm sorry I haven't got a house here. We'd have made a proper night of it again tomorrow.'

At about eleven the guests from over the water gathered to make their way down to the harbour, and the wedding party broke up, although at Joseph's house the uproarious friends of the bride were still making as much noise as ever, and the Sergeant-major in his pyjamas kept coming out of his dressing-room and then dodging back into it again as another peal of mirth came from the bridal chamber.

'Aren't you glad we're being married quietly in Glasgow, Catriona?' George Campbell asked when they heard the laughter coming from the post-office on their way down to the harbour.

'I don't know. It would have been fun here right enough,' Catriona said a little wistfully. 'Still, it wouldn't have been much fun with Norman away,' she added. 'I hope he'll get leave to come to Glasgow for us on Saturday.'

'Well, well,' said Dr Maclaren, overtaking them at that moment, 'if I weren't the only doctor in the two islands I'd come to Glasgow and give you away myself, Catriona. And how's your mother bearing up, George?'

'She's fine, thank you, Doctor.'

'Well, see and ask me up to have a meal with you, Catriona, when you and George get back.'

'We surely will, Doctor.'

'I'll be glad when Norman gets back. You know, I miss that brother of yours a lot. That's quite a nice wee lassie they've put in charge of Watasett school.'

'Effie MacNaughton,' said Catriona. 'Yes, she's very nice. She'd make you a good wife, Doctor.'

'Ach, get away with you. I'm too old a hand to be caught now. Duncan Bàn and I were born to be bachelors.'

'You never know. I'm sure George never thought he'd be anything but a bachelor for the rest of his days,' Catriona laughed.

'And he would have been if it hadn't been for what Father Macalister calls St Minnie,' the Doctor chuckled. 'There wasn't quite so much of it this evening as there was at the rèiteach. Joseph's not going to take any risks. It's fetching five pounds a case now. And I hear the Excise people are likely to make an example of one or two presently. Ah well, all good things come to an end,' he sighed.

While the Great Todday guests were making their way down to the harbour, Duncan Macroon was harnessing up his pony preparatory to driving Mrs Odd back to Tigh nam Bàrd. Soon she was seated beside him and jogging homeward along the metalled track that ran westward over the machair from Kiltod, a humpbacked moon in full silver shining to the south. After a couple of miles they turned off to take the grassy track that led to Duncan's house, driving now in the moon's eye. Now that the rattle of the heels and the clip-clop of the pony's hooves were muffled the long sigh of the Atlantic was audible.

'Just like when you hold a shell to your ears,' Mrs Odd commented.

'Well, I must say I think it's a much nicer way of winding up a wedding than flinging a lot of rice and old shoes at a hired motor-car. But *did* these fairies ever steal away a bride?'

'Och, I believe they will have once upon a time,' Duncan replied. 'Otherwise why should we still be taking such precautions?'

'Um, that's quite right,' the old lady agreed pensively. 'As you say there'd be no sense in carrying on like that, would there? Still, these fairies would have had a tricky job carrying off Peggy. She's no wurzit.'

'Wurzit? What's that at all?' Duncan asked.

'Well, I suppose it's short for "where is it?" It's what we used to call anybody who was a bit smallified. And you wouldn't call my daughter-in-law small, would you?'

'That wouldn't trouble the fairies,' Duncan assured her.

'It wouldn't? But I always thought fairies were such teeny-weenies. Of course at the panto they're usually a lot of whopping fat kids, but the County Council would create if they employed tiny tots.'

'Ay, they're wee right enough, the fairies, but they're terrible strong,' Duncan declared. 'Look at the *sluagh* and what it can do.'

'The slewer. Whatever on earth's that?' she exclaimed.

'It isn't on earth at all, Mistress Odd . . .'

'Here, I don't want to interrupt, but I meant to say this before. I like being called Mistress Odd. But go on about this slewer.'

'The *sluagh* is the fairy host, thousands and thousands and thousands of small glittering craytures. My grandfather saw them once.'

'He did?'

'Ay, just about where we are now.'

'Good gracious! What did they do?'

'They didn't do anything at all. They just swept past him like a wind of gold at sunrise on a summer morning. He was lucky, though. There was a cousin of my grandfather's living in Little Todday then, and the *sluagh* would never be leaving him alone at all. Micheal Macroon was his name. He'd be sitting in his room and he would hear the *sluagh* coming for him. "Hold the door, friends," he used to call out, and they'd be holding the door as hard as they could. But it was no use at all. In the door would come, and there'd be a great rushing like a wind and Michael would be gone.'

'Gone?' Mrs Odd ejaculated.

'And the next thing would be that Michael would turn up again from where the *sluagh* took him. They took him to Islay once, and they took him to the top of the Clisham . . . that's a big hill in Harris. And once they took him over to Ireland . . .'

'To Ireland?' she interjected in amazement. 'Go on, you're kidding, Duncan.'

'No, no, it's as true as I'm standing here. It was nearly three weeks before he got back to Little Todday.'

'And your grandfather saw these slewers just about where we're standing now?'

'Just about here.'

'Well, I wouldn't mind if they took me to Nottingham, even if they do sound a bit bloodthirsty. It'ud save a lot of messing about in trains. It wouldn't half give Mr Dumpleton a shock if he saw me arriving like a golden blitz. It's a pity these slewers can't get hold of Hitler and drop him inside one of these volcanoes. That'ud be well on the way to where he's going one day. Well, I'm glad they didn't cop Fred tonight. He'd have felt a bit chilly on top of a mounting.' She chuckled to herself. 'You know, it's wicked of me to say it, but I reely should have had to laugh. Poor Fred! What a disappointment!'

'Well, maybe we'll see the *sluagh* when we go on the Tràigh presently,' said Duncan.

'I'd sooner see this fairy washerwoman of yours. But wait a moment, Duncan, what size was she? I mean to say, if she wasn't bigger than half a dot how did she manage your washing?'

'She was about the size of a large midget. Och, she'd be all of two foot tall. We used to have great talks together.'

'In Garlic I take it?'

'Och yes, she'd never be talking the English.'

'What sort of clothes did she wear?'

'She had a green dress and a green cloak, and when she was washing for me she would put her cloak over a chair and lay her hat on it. A tall hat it was with a point to it. And when she'd finished the washing she'd climb up and sit in my grandmother's chair. Och, she was the sweetest wee crayture you ever saw, with a voice as soft as the falling dew. I remember fine the last night she came. It was a clear warm night in June, and when she was after finishing my washing she climbed up into the chair and she said, "O Duncan Bàn," she said, "O Duncan Bàn, you'll never be seeing me again, and who's going to be washing your clothes for you next winter I'm sure I don't know." And when I was going to speak back to her the kind wee crayture was gone.'

'And you've never seen her since?' Mrs Odd asked in awe.

'Never a glimpse of her since the month of June 1940.'

They drove on in silence till they reached Tigh nam Bàrd, and after Duncan had fed the pony he came back to ask his guest if she still felt inclined to come on the Tràigh.

'I wouldn't miss that treat for anything,' she declared.

So they walked down to the long stretch of sand gleaming with the silver of the moon. Presently they sat down upon a tussock of grass and listened to the melodious lapping of the tide all the length of the beach, and to the vast whisper of the ocean upon that tranquil midnight.

Duncan produced a bottle of Bard's Bounty and poured out a dram for his guest and himself.

'Here's to when we meet again, Mrs Odd. And don't be forgetting that there's always a room for you at Tigh nam Bàrd.'

'And we will meet again,' she declared. 'I've been making plans, I have. How about if I was to build myself a little house on Little Todday? And then when Fred and Peggy come down to Nottingham after the war and take over the shop I could make myself scarce, and they could come up here for their holidays while I looked after the business in Nottingham.'

'You needn't build yourself a house, Mistress Odd. In fact, the way the rascals are carrying on, you wouldn't be able to build yourself a house just now, I believe. But there's a house just about half a mile away from my own, which I'm sure you could get for a reasonable price. I'll show it to you tomorrow morning before you go away.'

'That would be grand.'

'Ay, it would be grand right enough. I believe you really have fallen in love with Little Todday, Mistress Odd.'

'Except for dear old London I never liked a place so much in all my life,' she affirmed.

'Mind you, it was pretty glum before St Minnie arrived,' he told her. 'And it may be pretty glum again when St Minnie is gone. Och, but it won't be glum when the war is over and the boys are home from the sea.'

'Duncan, why didn't you ever marry?' she asked suddenly.

'Och, that's a sad story. And she didn't leave me with a kind word like my dear fairy. No, no, just rang me up on the telephone when I went back to the University after my grandmother died and said she was going to marry quite another chap altogether.'

'Well, all I've got to say is she was a very silly girl,' Mrs Odd declared vigorously. 'Very silly indeed.'

'Have another dram of Bard's Bounty, Mistress Odd.'

'One more, and one more for yourself, Duncan Bang, and then I'm going to toddle back and get to bed.'

They pledged one another again.

'Well, I've talked a lot and laughed a lot and shed one or two quiet tears in Little Todday,' Mrs Odd said. 'Still, I've done as much in other places. But I've never drunk so much anywhere as what I've drunk in Little Todday. And I don't suppose I ever will again. Well, thank goodness, we haven't got an early start. I'm going to have a jolly good lay in bed tomorrow morning. Do you know what time they got me up on Monday so as to get here for the wedding? Four o'clock. What a game, eh? It was the first time I've felt my age since years ago they let our rooms over our head in Margate and me and my late husband had to sleep on the beach and it come on to pour about four o'clock in the morning. Fred was warm enough. He was in Indiar at the time, and I wished I was. It was a year after he became a drummer-boy. Well, if I stay jabbering much longer I'll be sleeping on the beach here, and, not being a fairy myself, I'd get a nice go of the rheumatics.'

Mrs Odd rose and they walked back to Duncan Bàn's house. In the doorway she paused to look back for a moment at the silver rim of the Atlantic beyond the moon-drenched machair. A curlew fluted somewhere by the tide's edge.

'Tootle-oo to you,' she said. 'But you'll be seeing me again.'

And the curlew fluted once more.

GLOSSARY OF THE GAELIC EXPRESSIONS

The pronunciation indicated in brackets is only approximate

CHAPTER 1

CHAPTER 2

CHAPTER 3

CHAPTER 4

CHAPTER 5

CHAPTER 6

341 *Ruairidh Mór* (rooary mor) Big Roderick

352 *Céilidh* (cayley) literally visit, but used for any entertainment

CHAPTER 7

354 *matà* (matah) then

354 *Feumaidh mi falbh* (faym-ey me falav) I must be going

355 *Seall, Uisdein* (shoul, ooshdjin) Look, Hugh

355 *chaca* (hahca) dirt

356 *Nach ist thu* (nach isht oo) Will you not be quiet

357 *sìthein* (shee-in) fairy hill

358 *bean* (ben) literally woman. Used for wife. I do not know how to write the genitive of Jockey in Gaelic, but the effect is of 'Y' in English

359 *A Mhuire mhàthair* (a voorye vahair) O Mary Mother. *Mhuire* is reserved in Gaelic for the Blessed Virgin. *Màiri* is used as a Christian name

359 *a Chairistiona* (a haristcheeona) O Christina

361 *siorram* (shirra) sheriff

361 *cailleach* (calyach) old woman

363 *dreathan-donn* (dreean down) brown wren

363 *Seadh gu dearbh* (shay gu jerrav) Yes indeed

365 *Am bheil Gàidhlig agaibh?* ('m vail ga-ylic acav) Have you Gaelic?

369 *Co tha'n sud?* (co hah'n shüt) Who is there?

CHAPTER 8

373 *A Chruthadair* (a chrooatir) O Creator. A variant of *Cruithear* which is also spelt *Cruithfhear*

374 *Móran taing* (moran tang) Many thanks

377 *poit dhubh* (poytch goo) black pot

377 *Leodhasach* (lyosach) Lewisman

379 *Mac an diabhoil* (mac an jeeol) son of the devil

CHAPTER 9

388 *Ceart gu leoir* (carst gul-yor) right in plenty

388 *Eisd* (eeshd) listen

388 *Todach* a Toddayman

393 *a chàirdean* (a haarshtjan) O friends

CHAPTER 10

400 *tha* (hah) it is

400 *chan 'eil* (hahn-yale) it is not

402 *Glè mhath* (clay vah) very good

403 *deoch an doruis* (joch an doris) drink at the door

CHAPTER 11

418 *mo chridhe* (mo chree) my heart

CHAPTER 12

421 *Thig a stigh* (hick a sty) Come in
422 *Sgoileir Dubh* (skolir dooh) dark scholar, literally black. *Dubh*, *bàn* (fair) and *ruadh* (red-haired) with more rarely *donn* (brown) are common additions to names and occupations
424 *Peigi Ealasaid Nic Ròin*, i.e. Peggy Elizabeth Macroon. Gaelic 'Mac' is used only for the male 'son'. *Nic*, a contraction of *nighean*, is used for unmarried woman. *Ròn* means 'seal'
425 *pìobaireachd* (peeparack) tune on the bagpipe
427 *Suas am pìobaire* (suas am peepera) up the piper
427 *port a beul* (porst a bale) mouth music
428 *a Dhrooby, a Bhiffer* (a grooby, a viffer) aspirated for the vocative
430 *A ghràidh* (a gry) O love
431 *pitheid* (pee-itch) parrot
433 *Tigh nam Bàrd* (ty nam bahrst) House of the Bard
435 *cailin* (callin) maid

CHAPTER 16

486 *Cà bheil sibh? Thigibh an so* (ca vale shiv? Hickiv an sho) Where are you? Come here
487 *Ochòin, mo thruaighe* (ochone, mo roo-y) alas, my grief

CHAPTER 18

507 *A bhòbh bhòbh* (a vov vov) exclamation of depression
509 *sgeulachdan* (skaylackan) tales
510 *bainis tighe* (banish ty) wedding of the house
512 *sluagh* literally people

THE RIVAL MONSTER

To Harold Raymond, Ian Parsons & Norah Smallwood
from an Affectionate Author

CONTENTS

Chapter 1

THE LETHAL SAUCER

On an afternoon in March when the world was supposed to be at peace again Roderick MacRurie, the landlord of the Snorvig Hotel on the island of Great Todday, and Joseph Macroon, the postmaster and principal merchant of Kiltod, the metropolis of Little Todday, emerged from the meeting of the Inverness-shire County Council and walked along together in the direction of the Porridge Hotel, the renowned hostelry of the Northern capital.

Big Roderick MacRurie's bulk, of which the austerity of a long war had not robbed him of an ounce, seemed to bound as lightly along the pavement as a balloon; his black tufted eyebrows stuck out as aggressively as two Sitka spruces planted by the Forestry Commission on some really good grazing land; he was humming to himself the refrain of the song *Red Rory's Galley*, which celebrates the piratical exploits of his clan in the days when Scotland really did stand where it did. The reason for Big Roderick's lightness of foot and heart was that he had succeeded in persuading his fellow councillors to make a grant for the construction of a pier at Garryboo, a crofting township whose exposure to the full fury of the westerly Atlantic gales had been a grievance for years and had led at the last County Council election to a unanimous vote against the hotel-keeper, who was accused of always favouring Snorvig at the expense of the rest of the island.

'Ah, well, well, Choseph, it's the people of Garryboo will be pleased when Cheorge Campbell puts my telegraph up on the school door to say the pier has been granted to them. Ay, ay, they'll be ferry well pleased right enough.'

'Ah, I believe they will,' Joseph Macroon agreed without warmth. Joseph was a much smaller man, but this afternoon he seemed to weigh twice as much as Roderick, so unwontedly did his trim white moustache droop at the corners.

'It was a pity right enough about the lobster-pool for Little Todday,' Roderick went on. 'Every member from the islands voted for it, but these stink-in-the-muds from the east of the county crudge us every farthing. Ay, ay, chust a parcel of skinnyflints.'

'You had your pier,' Joseph Macroon muttered sombrely.

'Ach, you had your new school at Kiltod two years ago,' Roderick reminded him.

'Not before the old one was a pure disgrace to the county. *A Dhia*, if Hitler had invaded us I would have been ashamed for the man to see it.'

Joseph Macroon walked on in silence; the more he thought about that pier which Roderick MacRurie had extracted from the Council, the more depressed he felt about his own failure to extract a lobster-pool.

'All the priests were after voting for you, Ruairidh,' he said at last.

'Ay, they did that,' the hotel-keeper agreed.

'But some of the ministers were not after voting for me.'

'Och, I wouldn't say it was a religious matter at all, Choseph,' Roderick protested. '*A Chruitheir*, what religion at all has a lobster? No, no, it was chust a piece of what they call economicality.'

'And lobsters fetching six shillings each from the buyers if we can get them fresh to market. What economicality is there in that?' Joseph demanded sternly. '*A Dhia*, it's a wonderful price. There never was such a price for lobsters.'

By this time the two Islandmen had reached the entrance of the Porridge Hotel and as they passed into the lounge they were greeted by John Maclean, the dapper porter.

'A lovely day we've had. I hope today's wind-up of the Council was successful.'

'Ay, it was pretty successful right enough,' Roderick declared.

'It wasn't successful at all, at all,' declared Joseph simultaneously.

'We all enjoyed the film, Mr Macroon,' the porter said. 'I went three times myself.'

'Is it *Whisky Galore* you'll be talking about?' Joseph asked indignantly. 'What kind of fillum is it that was after turning me into a Protestant and never had so much as one view of Little Todday from one end of the fillum to the other? I don't call that a fillum at all. Just a piece of ignorance.'

'Ah, well, Mr Macroon, it gave us all a good laugh in Inverness,' the porter insisted. 'And the monster has been very lively this month. I believe we will have a splendid season. We're booked right up from July on.'

'It was pretty queer nobody in Inverness saw the monster when the war was still going strong,' Joseph observed sardonically. 'I suppose the Military Permit Office wouldn't give her a permit to be showing herself.'

'They reckoned the monster was disturbed by the depth charges they were dropping on these submarines, and laid up for the duration,' the porter pointed out. 'But it's lively enough again now. Two of the monks at Fort Augustus saw its tail last week, which would appear to be forked.'

'Ay, it would be,' Joseph muttered.

'And the very same evening Willie Bayne, who's taken on Charlie Macintosh's job as traveller for Duthie's Dreadnought Sheep Dip, heard what he thought was the water boiling in his radiator just before he came to the road up to Drumsticket and when he pulled up the bonnet it wasn't his radiator at all. No, no. It was something snorting at him from the lochside, but it was too dark by then to make out just what it was. Oh, yes, and Ben Nevis was telling me only this morning he saw it the day before yesterday for the twelfth time. Near Tummie it was. He got quite annoyed with Colonel Lindsay-Wolseley because the Colonel said it was an otter he'd been watching for the last month. "Otter?" Ben Nevis shouted. "Do you think I've lived to be seventy this month to start imagining at my age that otters are eighty feet long? Don't be ridiculous, Lindsay-Wolseley." Yes, that's what he said to the Colonel. "Don't be ridiculous." I don't believe the Colonel was too pleased.'

'Look at that now,' said Joseph Macroon. 'You wouldn't think that a man who's after seeing the monster twelve times would be grudging the people of Little Todday a lobster-pool. But he voted against us this afternoon.'

The two Islandmen, after a much needed couple of drams, entered the car which the kind-hearted ratepayers provided for their long journey to Obaig, where early next morning they would board the *Island Queen* for Snorvig. With them was Father Macintyre, the priest of St Bunian's, Drumsticket, who gently chaffed Joseph Macroon in Gaelic about the ignoring of Little Todday in the film *Whisky Galore*.

'I never would have believed that Roderick here was such a Hitler. No wonder he managed to get that pier for Garryboo this afternoon.'

But Joseph Macroon felt too strongly about Roderick MacRurie's success over the pier and his own failure over the lobster-pool to smile. He withdrew into that vagueness which was always his refuge against the inconvenient demands of the present.

'Ay, ay, Father,' he murmured, and gazed from the window of the car at the steely water of the loch.

It was twilight when the car reached the Chapel House in Drumsticket; immediately Father Macintyre alighted he was surrounded by a small crowd of excited parishioners who had been waiting for his arrival.

'Father, Father, the monster has been killed,' he was told.

'He wasn't shot by the Colonel or Sir Hubert,' the priest assured them, 'for both guns were at the Council meeting.'

'No, no, it was killed by a flying teapot.'

'Sure as death, it's true, Father. It was Coinneach Mór who saw it happen.'

Joseph Macroon turned gloomily to his companion.

'Ach, let you and I be getting on our way, Roderick. It's all stupidity on the mainland. Not enough sense in them to keep lobsters fresh and keening now for a dead water-horse. Good night, Father, we've a long road before we get back to the West.'

'And civilization,' the priest added with a chuckle. *'Beannachd leibh*. And I hope the monster's ghost won't be on your tracks.'

It was not until the *Scottish Daily Tale* of two days later reached the islands of Great and Little Todday that the two Councillors realized how near they had been to the epicentrum of an earth-shaking event on that March evening.

LOCH NESS MONSTER HIT BY A FLYING
SAUCER?
GROAN HEARD BY DRUMSTICKET MAN
MAY HAVE BEEN DEATH AGONY
AMAZING STORY

The people of the remote Inverness-shire village of Drumsticket some ten miles from Fort Augustus were on tenterhooks yesterday when a representative of the *Scottish Daily Tale* arrived to investigate the amazing story told by Mr Kenneth MacLennan, head stalker on the Cloy estate of the well-known sportsman, Sir Hubert Bottley, Bart.

Mr MacLennan, a fine figure of a Highlander of the old school, gave our representative a vivid account of the amazing occurrence:

'I had been over to Tummie House to see Colonel Lindsay-Wolseley on a matter of business, and finding that the Colonel was in Inverness at a Council meeting I was walking back home when just before I came to the turning off the lochside road to Drumsticket I was aware of a bright light travelling at great speed down the loch from the direction of Inverness about twenty feet above the surface of the water. As it drew nearer the front of the missile became a sort of orange-red. I was reminded of the end of a cigar when it is being puffed.'

'It was not a circular disc then?'

'Definitely no,' replied Mr MacLennan. 'But that doesn't say it was the shape of a cigar. I would prefer to compare it to the spout of a teapot. Well, to cut a long story short, just after this flying spout passed close to where I was standing, out of the loch came something I can only describe as a huge horse's head on top of a snaky neck. At the same time I heard a kind of loud hissing noise, but whether this was made by the monster or the flying saucer as you can call this spout I wouldn't care to say. Then suddenly there was a blinding flash and I heard a groan like a cow in agony but much louder of course. I must have shut my eyes for a moment, for I don't mind admitting I was extremely scared, and when I looked again there was nothing there except a quantity of bubbles on the surface of the loch.'

'Do you think the monster tried to attack this flying saucer, Mr MacLennan?'

'I wouldn't care to express an opinion on that. All I'm prepared to say is that it's a possibility.'

'Had you ever seen the monster before?'

'Never,' Mr MacLennan answered emphatically. 'In fact, until today's amazing occurrence I was inclined to disbelieve in the monster, which only goes to show how wrong anybody can be.'

'And had you had any previous experience of flying saucers?'

'Only in the newspapers,' Mr MacLennan replied.

'But this flying object was definitely not like a saucer?'

'As I've said, it more nearly resembled the spout of a teapot.'

Comment in Drumsticket and Cloy on this amazing story told by Mr Kenneth MacLennan testified warmly to his reputation as an accurate observer of nature.

Anxiety about the fate of the monster is of course widespread on Loch Ness side where, ever since the first alarming stories of its ferocity had been demonstrated to be devoid of credibility, it has long been regarded with the genuine affection that is typical of the 'true and tender North'.

Provost Hugh Macpherson, O.B.E., said last night:

'If the monster has indeed been killed Inverness will have suffered the greatest blow since the Battle of Culloden. We are hopeful, however, that the monster succeeded in diving to safety in time. It will indeed be an ironical stroke of fate if a creature in whose existence many presumptuous persons affect to disbelieve should be lost to Loch Ness by the action of a phenomenon which many other people do not accept as an established fact.'

The *Scottish Daily Tale* is privileged to offer its readers a symposium of public opinion collected from various prominent Invernessians and others:

MacDonald of Ben Nevis

'I do not believe in these things called flying saucers and therefore I do not believe that the Loch Ness Monster, which I saw for the twelfth time less than a week ago, is dead. I consider that Kenneth MacLennan, whom I have known for years as one of the finest stalkers in the North, was dazzled by the sudden appearance of the sun just as the monster emerged.'

Sir Hubert Bottley of Cloy, Bart.

'Coinneach Mór (Big Kenneth) as we all call him is not the kind of man to spread a fairy tale. I am satisfied that the eyes of a man whose professional powers of observation have never been at fault since I have had the privilege of enjoying his services as head stalker would not have been deceived. At the same time Coinneach Mór definitely refuses to commit himself to the assertion that this flying saucer or teapot spout, as he insists it resembled, actually hit the monster. The groan he heard may easily have been an expression of rage at the unwarranted attack made upon it.'

Dr Angus Macfadyen, the famous Celtic historian

'I am not qualified to express an opinion about the destructive powers of these mysterious phenomena generally known as "flying saucers", but I hesitate to believe that an animal which has existed since the days of St Columba at least would at this date fall a victim to a "flying saucer". This is to stretch the long arm of coincidence too far for even the most credulous historian. While I have no doubt whatever in the existence of the Loch Ness Monster I am not yet completely satisfied that the "flying saucers" have been identified as such and I deprecate any premature theories about their possible provenance in the present state of our knowledge. It will be a sad day if the existence of the Loch Ness Monster is finally established in the teeth of sceptics by its failure to appear again and I hope that a stricter watch than ever will be maintained all along Loch Ness. The reappearance of the monster shortly after V day was to many of us a sign that peace had indeed come again to our distracted world.'

Professor Andrew Fleming, the great biopsychical expert

'My researches into biopsychics have led me to recognize what are vulgarly called "flying saucers" as an attempt by highly developed insects from the planet Mars to communicate with our planet. Unfortunately for reasons which we are unable to explain at present these devoted emissaries become incandescent as they approach the Earth and finally vanish altogether. I might put forward, very tentatively, a suggestion that Mr Kenneth MacLennan enjoyed the privilege of witnessing the "blinding flash" which accompanies the moment of dissolution. I wish I could be equally convinced by the evidence hitherto adduced in favour of the reality of the Loch Ness Monster. How then, it may be asked, did Mr MacLennan, who has so accurately observed the phenomenon of a flying saucer, imagine the appearance of the monster? I venture to put forward an explanation which may be startling to many at first but in my opinion deserves the fullest consideration. If, as seems certain, the flying saucer is the vehicle of a super-insect it may be that Mr MacLennan enjoyed the unique experience of actually seeing one of these insects desperately attempting to counter the effect of its passage through space by magnifying its own corporeal entity, and thus appearing to resemble the popular conception of the Loch Ness Monster. I make this suggestion with the greatest reserve, for the science of biopsychics is still in the empirical stage. We are, indeed, at present groping in the dark.'

Mr Hector Hamish Mackay, the historian and topographer

'I refuse to despair. I believe that the Loch Ness Monster succeeded in avoiding the flying saucer. It may well be that its mane was singed as the saucer passed over it which would account for the loud groan heard by Mr MacLennan. As readers of the *Scottish Daily Tale* are aware, I have long been convinced that there are two monsters, a male and a female, the latter of which lays her eggs on a shelf in the submarine passage between Loch Ness and the North Sea. If by misfortune one of the monsters *has* been killed by this flying saucer I feel sure that the survivor will seek a mate in the "dark, unfathomed caves of ocean" and that it may not be long before we hear of a "sea-serpent" having been sighted off our coasts. Verb. sap.'

'Och, it would be fine right enough if we could be seeing one of these Verb Saps off Great Todday,' Roderick MacRurie observed to his wife that evening after he had read the article in the *Scottish Daily Tale*.

'What are you saying, Roderick?' Mrs MacRurie exclaimed. 'I never heard tell of a Verb Sap before. Is Joseph Macroon after getting one for Little Todday?'

'What would a Verb Sap be doing in Little Todday? It's no place at all for the crayture. But there would be a beautiful run for it up Loch Sleeport or Loch Bob.'

'I don't know at all what you're talking about, Roderick,' his wife said.

'Ah, woman, you're icknorant right enough. A Verb Sap is a huge great monster, – a kind of *each uisge* but bicker.'

'We're wanting no Verb Saps or water-horses on Great Todday,' Mrs MacRurie declared firmly. 'It's bad enough with the children all turning into Hitlers and Hoolickans.'

'Do you mind how many towrists were coming last summer to hear the seals singing on Poppay and Pillay? Choseph was for effer sending the *Morning Star* to bring them over to Little Todday. Ay, and the Biffer would always be taking parties in the *Kittiwake*. "I would be ashamed, *a Bhiffer*," I was after saying to him once, "I would be townright ashamed to be showing off the seals on Poppay and Pillay to towrists and you a Great Todday man and a MacRurie and your great-grandfather the brother of my own great-grandfather." Ay, and Mr Hector Hamish Mackay himself who's a good friend of my own likes to blow about these tam seals.'*

'*Isd, a Ruairidh*, I wish you wouldn't be using such terrible bad words,' his wife protested.

'Ach, it would make the Minister use bad words the way Choseph Macroon will always be sniffing around for towrists like a dock after pitches . . .'

'Roderick!'

'It's chust the plain truth, wife, I'm after telling you.'

'Too plain indeed.'

'And that's why I'm after saying it would be fine if a Verb Sap would be seen off Great Todday. That would be putting the noses of these tam seals out of their joints.'

---

* 'But hark! What is that melodious moaning we hear in the west? It is the singing of the seals on Poppay and Pillay, the twin small isles that guard the extremities of Little Todday, their fantastic shapes standing out dark against the blood-stained western sky. Would that the present scribe possessed the musical genius of Mrs Kennedy Fraser that he might set down in due notation their melodious moanings.'

Faerie Lands Forlorn, by Hector Hamish Mackay.

Chapter 2

BEN NEVIS INVESTIGATES

Many an anxious eye was turned towards the waters of Loch Ness during the weeks that followed Kenneth MacLennan's remarkable adventure, but not even the ebullient optimism of Ben Nevis was able to imagine that the monster had been seen again. The head stalker himself, a tall lean man with dark hair now grizzled, a big aquiline nose, and a headland of a chin, never wavered in his account of what had happened on that March day.

'I haven't the slightest doubt you saw the monster, MacLennan,' the Chieftain assured him when he and the Laird of Cloy paid the head stalker a visit in his little house, soon after the event which had roused an interest unequalled since the monster appeared about ten years before the outbreak of the Second World War, and seemed likely to make it a better public-relations officer for Inverness than ever.

'Yes, I'm sure you saw the monster,' the Chieftain went on fervidly, 'but this flying saucer . . .'

'It was more like a spout, Ben Nevis,' the stalker put in.

'Well, flying teapot, spout, or whatever it was,' the Chieftain barked, 'I think you were so excited at seeing the monster – and I don't blame you, I've seen it twelve times now, but I'm just as excited as I was when Johnnie Macpherson, my driver, heard me see it the first time – yes, I think you were so excited that when the sun suddenly came out over those beastly deodars planted by these Forestry nincompoops on the other side of the loch you thought it was a flying teacup. I mean, all this flying crockery has been worked up by the papers. That's why these Communist fellows are always dodging behind the Iron Curtain into Russia.'

'I don't quite get that one, Donald,' said Sir Hubert Bottley, looking more than usually plump and florid between the eagle countenances of Ben Nevis and Coinnneach Mór. 'Are they trying to dodge the flying saucers?'

The Chieftain guffawed genially.

'No, what I mean is everybody's paying so much attention to these flying saucers that they get away with those atom bomb secrets. Suppose you and I, Bertie, had gone off on the scent of flying saucers when the war was on? We should have made even bigger fools of ourselves than all those Military Permit Office nincompoops.'

'I didn't believe there was a monster in Loch Ness till I saw him with my own eyes, Ben Nevis,' MacLennan affirmed gravely. 'And I didn't believe in those flying saucers till I saw one with my own eyes.'

'You're a bit of a Doubting Thomas, what?' Mac 'ic Eachainn woofed.

'I can only mind one peculiar thing like that happening to me before,' said MacLennan. 'Did I ever tell you the story of the fox that carried off my deerstalker cap, Sir Hubert?'

'No, you never told me that one, Coinneach.'

'Well, it was when I went as an obligement for a couple of seasons to Sir Simon Mackenzie of Battledore over in Wester Ross.'

'I never knew you were ever with old Battledore, MacLennan,' the Chieftain put in. 'Grand old boy! We don't produce them like that today.'

'Och, I wouldn't be saying that, Ben Nevis,' said Coinneach Mór with the faintest hint of an approving smile upon his lean, stern countenance.

'Ah, I'm afraid you're a bit of a flatterer, MacLennan,' said Ben Nevis, who was nevertheless obviously pleased by the compliment. 'But I interrupted your story.'

'Well, one day in October when the wind was blowing hard from the west I was out on the braes of Meall Oona and I lifted my gun to a fox that was moving quickly through the heather about fifty yards below, but just as I fired the wind got into the deerstalker cap I was wearing and carried it away down the brae.'

'Like a flying saucer, what?' the Chieftain guffawed.

'Well, I missed my bold fox,' MacLennan continued. 'And what's more I missed my cap, for when I went down to look for it it was nowhere to be seen. It had just clean vanished away. I was a bit annoyed because I was pretty fond of that cap. Well, the winter passed away and when it came to spring I was walking again on the braes of Meall Oona and I saw a fox again slinking along the way they will. I thought he was carrying a rabbit in his mouth, and this time I got my bold fellow. But what do you think he was really carrying in his mouth?'

'Your deerstalker, I suppose,' the Chieftain woofed.

'Ay, it was my deerstalker right enough, Ben Nevis.'

'It was? Extraordinary!'

'And what do you think I found in my cap? Ten eggs he must have stolen from the chicken-runs at Battledore House.'

'Good lord!' Ben Nevis ejaculated.

'Ay, he'd been using my cap as a basket to carry eggs to his cubs. Did you ever hear the like of that before?'

'No, I never did. Of course when Hugh Cameron of Kilwhillie and I went out to India — you remember, Bertie, when Hugh and I went out to India after my boy Hector's Colonel got worried about that woman he was getting mixed up with in Tallulaghabad?'

'I do indeed,' said Bottley.

'Well, we saw some pretty extraordinary things then. I mean to say I saw a fellow put a mango-stone — you know what a mango is, MacLennan?'

'I don't believe I do, Ben Nevis.'

'Well, it's a kind of a cross between a large plum and a small pumpkin, if you know what I mean. Well, this mango wallah planted the stone and about ten minutes later it had grown into a great bush. I always remember it, Bertie, because it's about the only time I ever heard Hugh Cameron make a joke. He said "what a pity we can't take this fellow home to teach the Forestry Commission how to grow trees". Oh yes, the older I grow the more I realize the truth of what my chaplain, old Mr Fletcher, said when some duffer was arguing that the monster didn't exist. "There are more things in heaven and on earth, Antonio, than are dreamed by your philosophers." I thought that was very good. It comes in old Shakespeare's play *Macbeth*.'

'Yet you're not believing I saw this flying saucer, Ben Nevis,' Kenneth MacLennan pointed out.

'By Jove, you've rather got me there. I say, he's rather got me there, hasn't he, Bertie? Well, I believe you saw this flying teacup or saucer or whatever it was, MacLennan. But I don't believe it hit the monster. I will not believe that.'

'But the monster hasn't been seen since,' Bottley reminded the Chieftain.

'It's lain up like this before. After all I've only seen it twelve times in the last fifteen years or so. That fellah What's His Name may be right. It's probably mating. The spring's the time for that.'

'Not for stags, Ben Nevis,' the stalker put in.

'By Jove, if the monster started rutting next October that would put the cat among the pigeons, what? But I hope this fellah What's His

Name doesn't go putting ideas into the heads of these islanders that the monster is going to pay them a visit. I didn't like what he said about the possibility of the remaining monster going to search for a mate in the Minch. I took strong exception to that. These islanders would steal anything. They're quite capable of stealing our monster.'

In spite of his firm declaration of confidence in the monster's survival Ben Nevis was worried by his inability to shake Kenneth MacLennan's account of the flying saucer. He could no longer comfort himself with the explanation that Bertie Bottley's head stalker had mistaken the sun for a flying saucer, and therefore he had to face up to the depressing possibility of the monster's death. Hector Hamish Mackay's belief in the existence of two monsters was no consolation when accompanied by the theory that the bereaved survivor, widow or widower, would go gallivanting off to the Atlantic Ocean in search of a mate. The Chieftain decided to look in at Tummie House on his way back to Glenbogle; he felt that an argument with Colonel Lindsay-Wolseley would restore his spirits.

'We'll call at Tummie on our way home, Johnnie,' he told his driver. 'And don't drive too fast up that ghastly road to the house.'

Johnnie Macpherson looked at the Chieftain compassionately.

'You're getting pretty old, right enough, Ben Nevis,' he observed.

'Getting old? What do you mean, Johnnie? If you're as active as I am when you're seventy, you'll do well.'

'You're getting nervous, Ben Nevis,' Johnnie Macpherson explained imperturbably.

'Nervous? I never heard such a preposterous statement in my life. Just because they've kept me off the Roads Committee for over thirty years our roads in Inverness-shire are the worst in the Highlands.'

'They're worse in Ross-shire and in Sutherland, too, what roads there are,' Johnnie Macpherson argued. 'And this is a pretty good road we're on now.'

'That's because it didn't come out of the rates. It was a Government grant. But because it's a good road there's no reason to go scorching along it at forty miles an hour. If the monster saw us he'd think we were another flying saucer. I made the greatest mistake in my life, Johnnie, when I let you persuade me to get rid of the old Daimler and buy this beastly new stream-lined contraption. One of these days I shall bump my head so hard when I'm getting into it that I'll get really angry.'

'You're always so impatient, Ben Nevis.'

'So would you be impatient if you were as big as me and had to squeeze in and out like a cork in a bottle.'

Presently they came to the turning off to Tummie and after a winding climb safely reached the gates of Tummie House, a cosy Victorian residence nestling among trees with a fine view of the country on both sides of the loch.

'Well, this is a pleasure, Ben Nevis,' said Mrs Lindsay-Wolseley, her round jolly face beaming.

'I thought Wolseley would like to hear about a talk I've just had with Bertie Bottley's head stalker.'

The Colonel came in at that moment.

'So you've been talking to MacLennan, Ben Nevis? I must say I am surprised to find a solid chap like MacLennan spreading such a fairy tale.'

'Fairy tale?' Mac 'ic Eachainn gasped, incapable for the moment of further speech.

'I must say I'm often reminded up here of India in the old days. You used to hear the same sort of fantastic story going round on the Frontier.'

'Are you seriously trying to tell me, Wolseley, that you doubt MacLennan's story?'

'I certainly do.'

'In other words that he invented it?'

'I don't think it was deliberate invention. I think he saw something and that a lively imagination did the rest.'

'Look here, Lindsay-Wolseley. You and I have known each other quite a few years now, and we've occasionally had our little differences – I won't go into them now – but for you to sit there and tell me that MacLennan has been pulling my leg is really a bit too much.'

Mrs Lindsay-Wolseley began to laugh; she was one of those happy wives who enjoy masculine absurdity, and she did not feel that her husband needed from her a display of prickly defensive conjugality.

'I didn't say MacLennan was pulling your leg, Ben Nevis,' the Colonel insisted. 'I said that MacLennan was deceived by his own lively imagination. You and I had it out the other day about imagination when you fancied that clutch of otters I've been watching for a month was the monster.'

'And you mean to tell me MacLennan thought that the animal he saw attacked by a flying saucer was an otter? If that's what's happened to his eyesight, the sooner Bertie Bottley gets another stalker the better. He'll find himself being dragged about all over Cloy to stalk an earwig which MacLennan fancied was a royal. And what about this flying saucer? I suppose you'll tell me that was a midge which got in his eye?'

'I understand from that interview with you in the *Daily Tale* that you yourself didn't accept the flying saucer. I thought you believed the sun got into his eye,' the Colonel said.

'That was before I'd had an opportunity of going into the matter with MacLennan. The only thing I don't believe is that this infernal flying thing hit the monster.'

'Oh, I agree with you there, Ben Nevis,' the Colonel chuckled.

'Alec, Alec,' Mrs Lindsay-Wolseley murmured.

'Let him go on, Mrs Wolseley,' the Chieftain said loftily. 'I'm merely sorry for him. Some people can disbelieve anything. Look at poor old Chamberlain, he didn't believe that Hitler was out for our blood. You'd have thought a fellow would hesitate before he told a fellow who'd seen the monster twelve times that it was an optical delusion. Look here, Lindsay-Wolseley, suppose I told you that those otters you've been goggling at were an optical delusion. You'd have a right to feel pretty annoyed, wouldn't you?'

'There's a difference between an otter and a prehistoric monster, Ben Nevis.'

'Yes, there's a difference of anything up to eighty or ninety feet of solid flesh, which makes it much easier to have an optical delusion about an otter than about the monster. In fact, you may have seen the monster yourself without realizing it.'

'Ninety feet of solid flesh?' the Colonel queried.

'You may have seen the monster's humps and thought they were a clutch of otters.'

'It's usually the other way round,' the Colonel commented drily.

'It's hopeless to argue with Lindsay-Wolseley when he's in one of these moods,' Ben Nevis declared, turning to the Colonel's wife. 'For him black's white and there's an end to it.'

'Well, let's leave the monster out of it,' said the Colonel. 'You haven't seen a flying saucer yet, have you?'

'I don't want to see one,' Ben Nevis replied.

'But you believe that people have seen them?'

'I do now since my crack with MacLennan and Bertie Bottley this afternoon.'

'And what do you think is the explanation of them?'

'I think it's probably some Communist plot to stir up trouble. I think these Bolshies of ours are trying to pretend that their friends the Russians have got a secret weapon if you know what I mean. You're Convener of the Police Committee on the Council, Lindsay-Wolseley. I think you ought to put your bloodhounds on the trail, what? Not that I think they'll discover anything. Not one of your observant county police has managed to see the monster yet. And then you expect them to catch salmon-poachers and deer stealers and Communists letting off flying saucers. It would be laughable if we weren't always having to fork out money for the police which ought to be spent on roads.'

'Well, if Hector Hamish Mackay is correct – good writer that chap, it's a pity he never came out to India – well, as I was saying, if his theory is correct we shall be hearing of the monster in the Islands presently. Is that why you voted against a lobster-pool for Little Todday?'

'What's a lobster-pool got to do with the monster?'

'It would make a good nesting-place, wouldn't it?'

'Alec, Alec, don't be so naughty,' Mrs Lindsay-Wolseley put in. 'Don't pay any attention to him, Ben Nevis.'

'My dear Mrs Wolseley, if I'd paid attention to Lindsay-Wolseley all these years I wouldn't have driven those hikers out of Glenbogle; I wouldn't have rescued that boot of ours from that fellow Waggett; and we'd still have that beetroot-headed ninny Constable MacGillivray mooning about in my country.'

'Sergeant MacGillivray,' said the Colonel sharply. 'He was promoted.'

'He's no longer mooning round at Kenspeckle, thank goodness,' said Ben Nevis.

'You lost a good man when Sergeant MacGillivray went to Snorvig.'

'That's your opinion, Wolseley. You only saw MacGillivray in his police-station, filling up forms and all that sort of time-wasting fiddle-faddle. You didn't see him puffing up Glenbogle on that idiotic bicycle of his. So he's gone to Snorvig, has he?'

'Where he is much happier than he was at Kenspeckle.'

'Well, as he never had the gumption to see the monster in Loch Ness he's not likely to see it in the Toddays,' the Chieftain guffawed, as he supposed, sarcastically.

There is no doubt that in spite of the apparent confidence of that last remark Donald MacDonald, Twenty-third of Ben Nevis, was worried about the monster's future. If Hector Hamish Mackay was right in believing that there were two monsters and if Kenneth MacLennan was right in believing that one of them had been destroyed by a flying saucer, the possibility of the survivor's quitting the scene of its bereavement could not be ruled out.

'By Jove, what a duffer I am!' the Chieftain bellowed suddenly as the car turned out of the narrow winding road up to Tummie to reach the main road beside the loch. The loudness of the sudden bellow caused even the cool-headed, calm-handed Johnnie Macpherson to swerve slightly.

'Ach, I wish you wouldn't be giving a great shout like that, Ben Nevis, after sitting so quiet. I might have put the car into the loch and started another big nonsense in the papers.'

'I'm always warning you, Johnnie, not to drive so fast in this wretched new drainpipe of a car I was badgered into buying.'

'It sounds louder when you shout in this car than it used to in the old Daimler right enough, Ben Nevis.'

'Well, I suddenly remembered something.'

'I never heard any man's memory going off with a bang like yours will,' grumbled Johnnie Macpherson, who was still feeling ruffled by the swerve.

'I suddenly remembered about my ancestor Hector MacDonald, the First of Ben Nevis. You know how he was pursued by two water-horses from sunrise to sunset all over Glenbogle and the country round and how he killed them both at sunset with a claymore he found stuck in a granite boulder.'

'Och, ay, Ben Nevis,' Johnnie Macpherson replied with a touch of impatience. 'And about the fairy woman who appeared and handed him over all the land inside the line along which the *eich uisge* chased him. Och, it's a *sgeulachd* you'll be hearing from any of them at a *céilidh*.'

'Well, what does the story prove?'

'I wouldn't be knowing, Ben Nevis.'

'It proves that once upon a time there were water-horses living in Loch Hoch or Loch Hoo — Loch Hoo more probably, and you mark my words, Johnnie, if the monster leaves Loch Ness it's much more likely to go to Loch Hoo than out to the Islands.'

'My goodness, I'd like to see the Minister's face if he met it on the Strathdiddle road,' said Johnnie Macpherson with a chuckle.

The Chieftain guffawed with relish. The Reverend Alexander Munro, the Minister of the United Free Church of Strathdiddle and Strathdun, was not a favourite of his.

'I'm afraid that won't happen, Johnnie; I don't expect the monster to go overland to Loch Hoo. No, my notion is that there may be a subterranean passage between Loch Hoch or Loch Hoo and Loch Ness. I must tell Major MacIsaac to warn all my people up there not to get scared if they see the monster.'

And as soon as the Chieftain reached Glenbogle Castle he told Toker, his butler, to telephone for the Chamberlain to come and see him.

'I'm expecting to hear that the monster has been seen in Loch Hoo, Toker.'

'Indeed, sir? That will certainly be stirring news for the B.B.C.'

'I'm not going to have any of this wireless nonsense up here, Toker.'

'I was referring to Mr Stuart Hibberd's announcement of it in the Six o'clock News, sir.'

'You know I never listen to this wireless nonsense. I can't stand all this mouthing about in a box with everybody sitting gaping like a lot of ninnies.'

The butler withdrew to summon Major Norman MacIsaac, whose air of gentle melancholy and strong resemblance to the White Knight were in marked contrast to the boisterous energy of the Chieftain he served.

'Ah, there you are, MacIsaac. I've been going very carefully into this flying saucer business, and it looks to me as if the monster has almost certainly left Loch Ness.'

The Chamberlain blinked.

'And I feel as certain as one can feel about anything while this Bolshie Government of ours is still in power that we shall soon be hearing of its being seen in Loch Hoo.'

This time Major MacIsaac seemed to jib like an old dapple-grey horse at some strange object in its path.

'But why in Loch Hoo, Ben Nevis?'

'Because there's a subterranean passage between Loch Hoo and Loch Ness.'

'But Loch Hoo is at least a thousand feet higher than Loch Ness.'

'Well, what of it? I suppose a subterranean passage can go uphill, can't it?'

'But how could the water remain in Loch Hoo if there's a sort of great drain-pipe running down from it into Loch Ness?'

'The answer to that is that it does. You get more argumentative every year, MacIsaac. I suppose it comes from people always asking you to do some repairs the Estate can't afford. But I wish you wouldn't always argue with me. Especially when there's nothing to argue about. Anyway, never mind how the water stays in Loch Hoo. This fellow Epstein has upset all our old-fashioned notions about gravity. What I've asked you to come round and see me about is warning the people up in Strathdiddle. And in Strathdun too, because there's an off chance that the monster may go to Loch Hoch. I don't want any humbug from the Minister. If the people see the monster on a Sunday let them see it on a Sunday. I will not have the Reverend Mr Munro laying off about it in the pulpit. But that's by the way. The point is I don't want to hear a lot of old wives' tales about sheep being carried off and chickens and children and all that sort of thing. Make it clear that the monster is not carn . . . well, you know what I mean. It grazes like a cow on weeds under water.'

'I wish cows would graze on weeds above water,' the Chamberlain sighed gently. 'If we could persuade cows to graze on ragwort and bracken the Highlands would be rich.'

'There you go, arguing again. The point is whatever the monster eats it isn't carn . . . well, you know what I mean.'

'Don't you think, Ben Nevis, it would be better to wait until somebody reports that the monster has been seen in Loch Hoo?'

'No, I don't, MacIsaac. You know it has always been my policy to take my people into my confidence. Look at that hiker business. As soon as I told them I wanted nobody to give refreshments to hikers nobody did except a few of these Bolshies you get everywhere today. Thank God, the old clan spirit is not dead in my country. Even Lindsay-Wolseley recognizes that, though he has some dunderheaded idea that the monster is an otter. Even his wife had to pull him up over that this afternoon.'

'Are we to expect flying saucers in Glenbogle?' the Chamberlain inquired gently.

'I suppose you want to argue now that we ought to have a lightning-conductor on the Raven's Tower. I will not spoil it with one of these beastly modern contraptions.'

'I wasn't thinking about lightning-conductors, Ben Nevis. I was merely asking you a question.'

'Just for the pleasure of hearing me say "I don't know", I suppose?'

The Chieftain rang the bell.

'Major MacIsaac will take a dram, Toker.'

And when the decanter of Glenbogle's Pride was brought the Chieftain poured a hefty dram for himself and for his Chamberlain.

'Slahnjervaw, MacIsaac,' he said before he drained the glass. 'And slahnjervaw to the monster.'

'*Slàinte mhór*,' Major MacIsaac echoed.

'It's an extraordinary thing, you know, when you come to think about it, that after eight hundred years a water-horse should come back to Glenbogle. History repeats itself, they say. Well, there you are.'

'I hope it won't chase you round the country from sunrise to sunset,' said the Chamberlain, venturing upon a mild joke after that hefty dram.

The Chieftain guffawed genially.

'No, they're not carn . . . what the devil is that word, MacIsaac?'

'Carnivorous.'

'No, no, they're not carnivorous nowadays. Carnivorous, carnivorous,' Mac 'ic Eachainn murmured as he poured himself out another hefty dram.

Chapter 3

WAGGETT IS SCEPTICAL

About a month after Ben Nevis had established to his own satisfaction the probability of the monster's having quitted the dangerous area of Loch Ness for the comparatively protected water of Loch Hoo, Paul Waggett was sitting in his den at Snorvig House, reading the letters which his wife had just brought back from the post office after the arrival of the *Island Queen*. The war, with all the responsibilities it had brought him as commander of the Home Guard Company of the islands of Great and Little Todday, had aged him slightly. However, he liked to think that every grey hair on his head was a veteran of active service and that none of them was a dull product of the humdrum war of attrition conducted by time against middle-age. If there certainly were a few more grey hairs the pink of his complexion had been preserved by the moist westerly air, and if his name had been, to him unaccountably, forgotten in the awards of the Order of the British Empire, his face and head were now a noble representation of its ribbon. His devotion to exercise and dislike of lolling about reading in a chair had preserved his figure. His light-grey eyes were still able to light up under the influence of curiosity, greed, cocksureness, and sporting concentration. He was in fact at fifty-eight to all intents the same Paul Waggett who had decided thirteen years ago to abandon chartered accountancy in London for the life of a Highland sportsman.

Mrs Waggett, who was ten years younger than her husband, had also worn well. How far the help of peroxide had been called upon to preserve the fair fluffiness of her hair we need not inquire. The roses of her youthful complexion had been pot-pourri for so long now that the only change noticeable since the great days of 1940 was in the appearance on her small nose of one or two little purplish veins like the streaks upon a chaffinch's egg.

Paddy, the outsize Irish setter, had gone on to the canine Valhalla soon after the wreck of the *Cabinet Minister*, and his place had been taken by a Golden Labrador retriever called Monty in honour of the military commander in whom Paul Waggett believed he could discern the closest mental kinship to himself of any general of the Second World War.

'Most extraordinary,' he used to murmur reverently, his sharp slightly upturned nose seeming to sniff out a mystery of transcendental tactics. 'Monty always does exactly what I think to myself I would do if I were in his place. Most extraordinary!'

And when the golden tail of the retriever thumped the floor to acknowledge the mention of his name Paul Waggett would fancy that Field-Marshal Montgomery himself was acknowledging the endorsement of his tactics by an unknown master.

On this fine afternoon at the end of April Paul Waggett was inclined to feel a faint sentimental regret for the great days of war. His post was lacking in interest, and the prospect of not being able to shoot a bird for nearly four months did not please him. He recognized the necessity of a close season during the time of breeding, but he could not help wishing that birds would stagger the business. If he had read *Locksley Hall* he would have wished that the wanton lapwing would get himself another crest in autumn when grouse and snipe and woodcock were available for killing, so that he would be able to kill plovers in the spring.

'Of course, the war was a heavy strain on me, Dolly,' he said to his wife, 'but I can't help feeling it was a mistake to disband the Home Guard. I should have been perfectly willing to carry on here.'

'Yes, dear, I'm sure you would,' Mrs Waggett agreed. 'But I rather doubt if you would have had proper support from the people. Look when you tried to start badminton in the Snorvig hall. Nobody turned up after the first few evenings.'

'And the children were allowed to use the shuttlecocks for toy boats,' Waggett added on a note of disillusioned reminiscence. 'Oh, I know the people here have no idea of the importance of games apart from progressive whist. Still, if the Home Guard hadn't been disbanded I should have been able to set an example.'

'You always do that, Paul.'

'I try in my own humble way,' her husband sighed, the expression of complacency on his countenance not quite in keeping with the modesty of the statement. 'But don't worry, old lady. It's only just over three months to the Twelfth, isn't it, Monty?'

The dog confirmed with an assenting tail his master's calculation.

'And since Norman Macleod left Watasett for a school on the mainland there have definitely been more grouse. Definitely.'

'I hear Catriona Campbell is going to have another baby.'

This was the sister of Norman Macleod and wife of the schoolmaster at Garryboo, the crofting township for which Roderick MacRurie had secured a pier at the last Council meeting.

'It's all that people seem to think about nowadays,' Waggett observed severely. 'The chicks are very late,' he added. 'Hadn't the Biffer got back from Kiltod when the boat came in?'

The chicks were Muriel and Elsie, the twin daughters of the house, who since their demobilization from the Waafs had been at home and from time to time the subject of parental debates about their matrimonial future. Their father, who admired in their blondine fluffiness what he had once admired in their mother, had been surprised that neither of them had won the heart and hand of an officer in the R.A.F. His inability to understand the young men of today became one of his favourite remarks.

'You know what a chatterbox Archie MacRurie is,' Mrs Waggett reminded her husband. 'And the chicks themselves intended to pay quite a round of visits on Little Todday.'

'I hope the chicks will bring back some eggs.'

This was a family joke at which Mrs Waggett tittered dutifully; she had hardly finished when the door of the den opened with such an unwonted burst that Monty leapt to his feet and started to bark wildly.

'Lie down, sir. Lie down at once,' his master snapped, all the old crisp force of military authority crackling again in his voice.

The golden labrador was so much abashed that he turned to lie down with eyes averted from his master's displeasure and in doing so knocked over the small table that held the two or three dull letters of the post.

'Chicks, chicks,' their mother reproached them. 'You know Daddo doesn't like us to rush into his den.'

'Daddo! Mumsy!' the two young women exclaimed. 'A monster came up in the sea off Pillay this afternoon!'

'With a head like a hornless bull,' cried Muriel, who was dressed in smoky-blue tweed.

'And it snarled at him,' added Elsie, who was also dressed in smoky-blue tweed.

The twin sisters were if possible even more alike now in their mid-twenties than they had been as little girls, and when they wore similar clothes they were indistinguishable.

'Rubbish!' their father exclaimed. 'Didn't I tell you when that idiotic story came out in the *Daily Tale* some weeks ago that it was nothing but a press stunt.'

'But this wasn't in the paper, Daddo,' Muriel pointed out. 'It was Kenny Macroon who saw it. He was setting lobster-pots round the Gobha.'

Paul Waggett frowned. That dark rock between the tiny isle of Pillay and Little Todday had wrecked the *Cabinet Minister* and had therefore been responsible for the deplorable behaviour of the islanders over the ship's cargo of whisky. He thoroughly disapproved of the Gobha and was in no mood to tolerate its reappearance in the news as the haunt of a monster.

'The sooner Joseph Macroon gets that idle young rascal of his into a decent job the better,' he observed censoriously. 'Even if lobsters are fetching a fantastic price it's demoralizing for a young man to spend his day messing about for an hour or two every day with lobster-pots and loafing away the rest of his time.'

'But, Daddo,' Muriel insisted, 'I'm sure Kenny thought he saw a monster. We were at the post office in Kiltod when he arrived with the news and his eyes were starting out of his head.'

'You can take it from me, Muriel, that his father put him up to it. Big Roderick was saying to me only the other day he was sure Joseph would be putting it round that the Loch Ness Monster had come out to the Islands just to pay out the Inverness County Council for turning down his lobster-pool. Hornless bull, did you say?'

'Oh, but much bigger than any ordinary bull,' Elsie replied.

'There's a perfectly simple explanation,' her father said. 'As indeed there always is for everything,' he added loftily. 'If Kenny Macroon saw anything, which I doubt, he saw a Polled Angus which had been drowned crossing the ford from Mid Uist to Pendicula. The Department of Agriculture sent a Polled Angus bull to Nobost last year. You may remember when they sent one here and I gave them a lesson by importing a Hereford at my own expense because I consider the Polled Angus is a ridiculous animal for the Islands.'

'But Kenny said the head of this monster was much, much bigger than a bull's,' Muriel insisted.

'Of course,' her father commented, tossing his nose scornfully. 'We all know that a drowned animal swells up.'

'But it snarled at Kenny,' said Elsie.

'Gases,' Paul Waggett declared in the tone of Goethe replying to one of Eckermann's more foolish questions.

'Oh, yes, and I forgot,' Muriel put in, 'it had a mane.'

Paul Waggett regarded his daughter compassionately.

'There is such a thing as sea-weed, chick,' he reminded her with a kindly smile. 'Well, did you bring back Mumsy any eggs?'

The twins looked at one another in consternation. 'We left the basket in the post office at Kiltod,' one of them gasped.

Paul Waggett shook his head sadly.

'It's an extraordinary thing that you were both able to look after a barrage balloon in the war and now you don't seem able to look after a basket of eggs.'

'Well, everybody was frightfully excited, Daddo,' Muriel urged in excuse.

'There was a certain amount of excitement during the war as I remember,' her father observed. 'That wouldn't have been accepted as an excuse for letting your barrage balloon float away from Birmingham.'

'It couldn't have done that unless we'd cut it loose,' Muriel pointed out.

Paul Waggett knitted his brows in what he believed was an expression of disillusioned paternity.

'You never used to argue with me like this once upon a time,' he murmured, and bending over he sought from Monty's golden coat the warmth of responsive uncritical admiration he had once never failed to find in his little daughters. 'Did they, old pal?' he asked with a sigh. The dog sighed a profoundly sympathetic response, rejoicing in his master's pats.

Up in their own room, the three gable windows of which looked out over the roofs of Snorvig across the Coolish to the green island of Little Todday, the twins discussed what they decided was the pre-war attitude of their father to life in general and the monster sighted by Kenny Macroon in particular.

'You know, Elsie, it's a most frightful thing to say, but I think Daddo is getting old.'

'Well, of course he *is* fifty-eight.'

The twins shook their fluffy heads.

'You don't think he is going gaga, do you?' Muriel asked apprehensively.

'No, I don't think he is actually going gaga,' said Muriel in a brave attempt to be optimistic. 'But I think he's got into a rut.'

'And Mumsy too,' her sister added.

'Yes, they're both in it,' Muriel agreed. 'I mean to say, it was stupid of us to leave the eggs over in Kiltod, but Daddo did talk rot about barrage balloons.'

The twins gazed at one another, like two boys who have just cracked a plate-glass window with a catapult: never had either of them in her most intimate self-censoring ventured to whisper such a word about her father's opinions, let alone utter it aloud. Both were sharply aware of the impiety and in a spasm of remorse tried to re-establish their father on that pedestal where they had worshipped him all their lives as an infallible being, and no doubt would have continued to do so if the Second World War had not cast its dark shadow upon domestic life.

'Perhaps it really was a dead bull that Kenny saw,' Elsie suggested.

'Yes, perhaps it was,' her twin concurred.

'And Daddo does know a good deal about bulls,' Elsie went on, even if he doesn't know very much about balloons.'

'But of course he never had a chance to see a barrage balloon in action because he was indispensable here,' Muriel said in reproach of her own impatience over her father's ignorance.

Downstairs in the den Paul Waggett, without touching the tragic heights of King Lear on the subject of undutiful daughters, was impressing his wife with the shock it had been to his paternal affection when Muriel had almost accused him of not understanding the principles underlying the duty of its crew toward a barrage balloon.

'I was quite staggered for a moment, Dolly.'

'I'm sure you were, dear,' she murmured soothingly.

'Of course it's all this growth of Communism. Even the chicks have come under its poisonous influence.'

'Paul, you don't really think that, do you?' his wife exclaimed.

'I'm afraid I do, Dolly,' he sighed. 'It's the same kind of spirit in the chicks as made a lot of silly young people go and vote against Churchill at the election.'

Suddenly his face was rapt with self-esteem, his light-grey eyes were twinkling.

Mrs Waggett knew the signal: her husband was going to make a joke. She waited for it, her whole mind concentrated upon not missing the point when it came. She had managed to do that once or twice even when she had been warned of a joke's approach, and Paul never forgot to remind her of these failures.

'Yes, I'm afraid, Dolly, our chicks are Rhode Island Reds,' he said, the words bubbling in his mouth with amusement at his own wit.

It cost Mrs Waggett something of an effort to laugh as heartily as was expected of her. She could not see anything funny in comparing the twins to hens. And why Rhode Island Reds? If Paul must compare them to hens, why not Light Sussex, the effect of whose plumage was much more like the colour of their hair? However, she laughed away as earnestly as a studio audience at a comic turn on the radio, and Paul was luckily so much amused by his own joke that he did not notice anything at all forced about her laughter.

'Still, it's nothing to joke about,' he said, becoming abruptly serious. 'It's what keeps me from letting them go and stay as paying guests with your sister Gladys at Norwood, which from another point of view might be a good thing.'

'You mean they don't meet enough young men in the Islands?' the mother asked.

For one mad exquisite moment a vision of them all moving from the Outer Isles to one of the Outer Suburbs of London glowed in Mrs Waggett's imagination, but she did not venture to tell this bright dream to her husband.

'Of course, Tom Gorringe himself is quite sound.'

'And so is Gladys,' Mrs Waggett insisted eagerly. 'Don't you remember you thought they wouldn't give her a military permit to come here because she used to attend meetings of the British Union of Fascists before the war? And I can't imagine anybody less Communist than Tom and Gladys.'

Paul Waggett smiled indulgently.

'If we send the chicks to Norwood to give them a chance to meet some young men, they can't spend all their time with Tom and Gladys,' he pointed out. 'No, I'm afraid they'll have to put up with the old folks at home. Yes, I'm afraid so, old lady,' he wound up, and on his countenance was an expression of impregnable self-sufficiency which might have annoyed some people but to his wife was reassuring. 'Well, I think I'll take a stroll along to the hotel and hear what they're saying there about this nonsensical tale from Little Todday.'

It was not Paul Waggett's habit to frequent the bar of the Snorvig

Hotel when it was full of customers. He preferred a cosy chat with Roderick MacRurie in his own snug parlour when the bar was closed. However, he felt it was his duty to lose no time in casting doubt upon the story which his daughters had brought back from Kiltod.

'Good evening, Archie,' he said to a crofter, something under sixty years old, with a nose and chin on him like a lobster's claw and a fierce red complexion. This was the Biffer whose little boat the *Kittiwake* was a feature of the rocky coast of Great Todday. Archie MacRurie was talking to a brawny fisherman, whose nickname, the origin of which had never been discovered, was Drooby. Neither Drooby nor the Biffer looked elated by the entrance of Paul Waggett, but the good manners of the Outer Hebrides made them greet him cordially enough.

'I suppose you've all been laughing at this nonsensical story that's been going round Little Todday?'

'What story would that be, Mr Waggett?' asked Drooby cautiously.

'Surely Archie has told you about young Kenny Macroon's encounter with a sea monster?'

'Ay, it was a pretty queer kind of an encounter too,' said the Biffer quickly.

'And him in the *Morning Star* with one of the plugs choked and not able to move at all. It was after putting a great fear on him.'

'Ach, it would do that right enough,' said Drooby, drawing heavily on his tightly packed pipe. 'The *Morning Star* is no kind of a craft at all in which to meet even a sailfish.'

'Ay, one of them puggers was nearly after upsetting me once in the *Kittiwake*. Ay, they're puggers right enough.'

'Well, perhaps the monster that Kenny Macroon thought he saw was one of these basking sharks, or sailfish as you call them.'

'I never heard tell of a sailfish with a head on her like yon bull the Department sent to Snorvig a year or so before the war.'

'Well, I suppose it is possible that young Macroon did see a drowned cow or even possibly a drowned bull,' Waggett conceded. 'Yes, I suppose it is just possible.'

'Why would a cow be wanting to drown herself at all?' put in Angus MacCormac, a big crofter from Garryboo, with a heavy white moustache.

'I'm not suggesting the cow committed suicide,' Waggett snapped impatiently. 'It may have fallen over a cliff in one of the islands north.'

Angus MacCormac gathered his moustache with a rugged hand and blew through it incredulously.

'I never heard tell of a cow who was after jumping off a cliff into the sea,' he declared. 'Sheep, yes, because sheep are so daring when the hunger is on them and the grass in a crack of the cliff is so green. Ach, not at all. It's no kind of a cow Kenny Iosaiph would be seeing.'

'You don't seriously believe that it *was* a monster?' Waggett asked, almost irritably.

By now the rest of those standing at the bar were listening to the argument, and a murmur of agreement had hailed Angus MacCormac's disbelief in the cow theory.

'Does nobody mind when the *each uisge* was seen in Loch Skinny?' one of the company asked.

'Oh, please, don't let us revive that old story,' protested Waggett. 'The only Yak Ooshker ever seen in Loch Skinny was poaching my salmon.'

'Oh, well, well, Mr Wackett,' said Sammy MacCodrum, another Garryboo crofter, a little man with a high voice and a huge nose, 'if you were effer seeing a salmon in Loch Skinny you were seeing something much more difficult to see there than a *each uisge*.'

Now if there was one thing that really did annoy Paul Waggett it was for anybody to hint that the Skinny, the fishing of which was rented to him by the Department of Agriculture, was not a renowned if diminutive haunt of salmon.

'If everybody from Garryboo or Knockdown didn't poach, there would always be plenty of salmon in the Skinny. And they are not poached by Yak Ooshkers, let me add.'

Big Roderick, the landlord, had been listening attentively to this conversation without saying a word. He was in fact making up his mind whether to segregate the monster as it were on Little Todday and disown it for Great Todday or whether, Joseph Macroon being as fly as he all too well knew him to be, it would be wiser to form an alliance and exploit the monster as an attraction to the visitors of both islands. He had not been too pleased when a film company had turned the two Toddays into one island and on top of that used the Island of Barra to supply their scenery. From what he had heard tourists had been thronging to Barra under the impression that the *Cabinet Minister* was wrecked there, when as everybody knew except these ignorant London folk it was never wrecked there at all. However, he did not think it would be tactful to mention the film in front of Mr Waggett, who had never been able to understand why his efforts to help the revenue had been regarded as a subject for laughter all over the world, by what they had been writing in the newspapers.

'I believe we would be wise to wait a while,' he declared as he measured a dram for Paul Waggett and offered him the bottle of fizzy lemonade with which he liked to dilute his whisky. Waggett seldom took a dram in public and the spectacle of him drinking whisky and fizzy lemonade with apparent enjoyment could still shed an awestruck silence over the bar of the Snorvig Hotel.

'Wait for what?' Waggett asked, putting down his glass.

'Ach, chust wait,' said Big Roderick. 'We would be looking pretty foolish if Kenny Iosaiph was seeing a monster right enough and we were not believing him and then we were after seeing this huge great Verb Sap ourself.'

'Verb Sap?' Waggett exclaimed.

'Ay, that's the name they were giving this crayture in the *Daily Tale*,' Roderick told him.

'But, my dear Roderick,' Waggett protested, 'Verb Sap means – well, it's short for something. I don't exactly remember what, but it's the same as "Amen" or "Enough said".'

'Ay, ay, well, we won't be saying any more at all about this Verb Sap chust now. We'll chust wait,' said Roderick firmly.

And round the bar of Snorvig Hotel the conversation reverted to the prospect of a dry spell for the peat-cutting which might soon be starting.

When he reached his den Paul Waggett looked for a dictionary which he knew he had somewhere; he found it at last supporting an occasional table, one of the legs of which had been broken when he had trodden on Monty's tail and the table had been knocked over by the dog suddenly roused from sleep.

'Yes, of course,' he muttered to himself. Then he lifted the receiver.

'Wackett wants you on the telephone,' Roderick MacRurie's barboy informed him.

'Hullo! Is that you, Roderick? I remembered on my way up to the House that verb sap is short for verbum sapienti.'

The hotel-keeper put his hand over the mouthpiece and turned to his wife.

'Och, the man's trying to say something to me in Gaelic and nobody can ever be understanding what he's trying to say. *Glé mhath, glé mhath*, Mr Wackett. You're getting on fine with the Gaelic,' Roderick said with a faintly insincere enthusiasm when he addressed himself to the mouthpiece.

'Verbum sapienti is Latin not Gaelic,' the instructor snapped. 'It has nothing whatever to do with mythical monsters. In fact it means literally "a word to the wise".'

'A Chruitheir, what a man,' Roderick grumbled to his wife. 'There's nothing wise in him. Pulling me away from the bar like that to blow about the Latin and the Grik that's at him.'

Chapter 4

THE TODDAY MONSTER

Any suspicion in Roderick MacRurie's mind that his fellow councillor had staged the appearance of a monster off Little Todday in order to pay him out for his success in obtaining a pier for Garryboo at the expense of the lobster-pool for Kiltod would have been dispelled if he could have crossed the Coolish that evening and joined the company that thronged Joseph Macroon's shop to hear Kenny tell and re-tell the story of his adventure. It would have been perfectly clear that whatever it was that Kenny had seen, he was convinced that he had seen a strange monster such as nobody on Little Todday had ever seen before. Kenny himself was now a tall and lively young man of twenty-two with merry eyes who as his father's only son was debarred from exploring the world as he would have liked to do. Joseph had the good sense not to insist on his son's being kept too close to the grindstone and he encouraged his activity over lobsters. Indeed, if the County Council had not turned down the scheme for a lobster-pool, he had intended to buy a larger boat, for the old *Morning Star* was by now growing decrepit.

After Peggy Ealasaid became Mrs Alfred Odd and went to live in Nottingham when the war was over, Joseph's youngest daughter Kate Anne looked after the post office. When she married Michael Macdonald, a son of Alan Macdonald who had one of the best crofts on the island, Kate Anne and her husband stayed on in Kiltod with Joseph. Kate Anne was small, with her father's shrewd light-blue eyes and quick movements, and he was inclined to discern in his grandson Iosaiph Òg a miniature of himself which gratified him. Peggy like her mother before her had started off with two daughters – Lucy called after her husband's mother and Catherine called after her own mother.

Mrs Odd herself was away in Nottingham at the moment and not expected back just yet. She had carried out her intention of retiring to Little Todday for half the year and had bought the little house near the croft of Duncan Bàn Macroon on the door of which was painted *Bow Bells*, though it was more generally known as Mistress Odd's House, or in Gaelic, *Tigh Mhistress Ott*.

The only noticeable addition to the buildings of Todaigh Beag since the adventures of the island in wartime was the new school at Kiltod of which Andrew Chisholm, the headmaster, generally known as the *Sgoileir Dubh* or Dark Scholar, and Joseph Macroon were equally proud, though Father James Macalister, the parish priest, always called it the Bad Egg and warned the *Sgoileir Dubh* that one day Waggett would be poaching it in revenge for the barnacle geese and plover shot by the people of Little Todday without regard to his rights as the shooting tenant of the Department of Agriculture. The licence to sell beer for consumption off the premises was not interpreted quite so strictly according to the letter of the law as it would have been if Sergeant MacGillivray had been happening to pay one of his visits to the island; but Sergeant MacGillivray was not the man to proceed suddenly anywhere and when he intended to visit Little Todday he always communicated his intention beforehand to Joseph Macroon, and therefore nobody this evening was worrying about the letter of the law. Indeed, it may be claimed that nobody on Little Todday had worried at all about the letter of the law since the seal-woman bore seven sons to that exiled son of Clan Donald and thus populated the island with Macroons in the dim past. In the dark days of the whisky drought Joseph Macroon, exasperated by his fellow councillors' obstinate opposition to a new school for Kiltod, had contemplated installing and equipping an illicit still, and the Excise may be grateful that the drought was relieved because if Joseph Macroon had decided to get busy with the black pot the source of the spirit in circulation would never have been discovered.

The thronged shop of Joseph Macroon was a cheerful sight on this fine evening at the end of April. Kenny Macroon was sitting on the counter and telling his tale afresh to everybody who came in to hear it. Old Bean Sheumais Mhiceil, the senior matriarch of the Macroons and now not far from ninety, had been sitting on a sack of potatoes in a corner for the last two hours and must have heard Kenny's story three dozen times already — but the slightest hint by her great-grand-daughter Flora about going home to bed was waved away impatiently by a knotted old hand. 'Isd thu! Bith sàmhach! Nach isd thu, a Fhlorag! I want to be hearing about the monaster. Ach, it's me that wishes it was twenty years gone back and himself could be hearing Coinneach telling about the monaster. He would chust have been in his ellimans. There was neffer a man so liking it of a good story whateffer as your big grandfather Seumas, God rest his soul.'

It is a tribute to Kenny Macroon's absolute sincerity that in spite of the temptation over many a repetition of his tale to exaggerate the size of the monster he did not add a foot to its stature. He insisted in spite of several attempts to make him compare the head he had seen emerge from the water to a horse that it was much more like that of a bull, except of course for the mane which he agreed was more equine than bovine. He was equally firm over the noise that the monster had made. It was not a groan or a sigh or a roar or a hoot or a bark or a gurgle or a hiss or even a growl: it was a snarl. It resembled the noise made by an unfriendly dog as it retreats when one stoops to pick up a stone to fling at it, but it was naturally a good deal louder than the snarl of the ordinary collie. He should estimate the size of the head that suddenly appeared out of the water as three times that of an ordinary bull, but he admitted that it gave him a terrible fright and that it may have appeared larger than in fact it was. He had been blowing through the choked plug at the time and was thankful he was not standing up, for if he had been he was sure he should have toppled back overboard.

'And no horns, *a bhalaich?*' the rich bass of Father James Macalister suddenly asked from the door of the shop where he had arrived in time to hear Kenny's account.

'No horns, Father.'

'*Taing do Dhia*,' the priest devoutly bombilated. 'I was afraid it was Satan himself who was taking a look at us on Todaidh Beag.'

Nobody on Little Todday was ever perfectly sure whether Father James was laughing, and one or two in the audience crossed themselves in gratitude to Almighty God for having been spared a visit from the Tempter.

'And it really snarled at you, *a Choinnich?*' the priest asked.

'Yes, Father.'

'Ah, well, well, I believe when the Excisemen blew up the *Cabinet Minister* and put all that good whisky in Davy Jones's locker, Davy Jones himself was warning you to keep off the grass.'

'*A Dhia*, what's Maighstir Seumas after saying?' Jocky Stewart, a little sandy-haired crofter, turned to ask of Hugh Macroon, whose shrewd eyes twinkled in that bald domed head of his.

'Och, he's just talking the way he always will be,' said Hugh in that slow voice of his which lent an air of wisdom to his lightest remark.

But later on that evening, when Kenny Macroon had been examined and cross-examined by Father Macalister in his own cosy room at the

Chapel House, the parish priest had to recognize that Kenny had seen something genuinely unusual in the water round the dark rock called the Gobha.

'And you're sure it wasn't a big seal, *a bhalaich*?'

'I've seen plenty seals, Father, but I never saw a seal like this, big or small.'

'And it didn't look at you?'

'No, Father, thank God. It was down before I saw the face on it.'

The priest exhaled a gusty sigh; he was puzzled.

Next day, taking advantage of the fine weather, the Biffer went off to set some pots on the other side of Ard Snor, the headland which shelters Snorvig from the fierce north-west. That evening he held the attention of the company round the bar in the Snorvig Hotel without having recourse to any of the club-bore tricks of the ancient mariner to make guests listen to him.

'I'd rounded Ard Snor on the way home and I was keeping in close to the land for a shot at a *sgarbh*, the way they'll always be sitting on Sgeir Geal in the afternoon and just as the *Kittiwake* was passing Uamh na Snaoiseanaich* my heart was after nearly dropping out of my mouth I was so scared. Ah, boys, you never saw the like of what I was seeing. A great head was staring at me out of the cave the size of a sack of barley with two eyes as big as pancakes. And the teeth on the mouth of it! *A Thighearna*, I never saw the like of such teeth on a hayrake. I was feeling all chewed up inside of me just to be looking at teeth like that. I tell you, boys, I just put the tiller hard to port and swung the *Kittiwake* away from the shore and prayed to the Lord to let me get away before I was swallowed up like Jonah. Boys, the sweat was pouring down me and when I got home Ealasaid was asking me where was I being because my nose was still red, but the rest of me was as white as chalk.'

'Was the crayture after making a noise when you came upon it in Uamh na Snaoiseanaich, Airchie?' somebody asked.

'Ay, I was forgetting about that. Noise, do you say? It was the queerest noise a man would be hearing at all. If you could be thinking of a cow that would be barking at you like a dog or a dog that would be bellowing at you like a cow and put the two noises in the foghorn of the *Island Queen*, you'd be having a sort of an idea what kind of a noise this crayture was after making when it was seeing me and the *Kittiwake*.'

* The Cave of the Snuff-taker, so called because every few minutes or so the sea would break inside with the effect of a great sneeze.

'Look at that now,' said Big Roderick cheerfully. 'My friend Mr Mackay was right enough when he said we'd be having one of these Verb Saps from Loch Ness out in the Islands. When we were talking yesterday I had it in my mind that Joseph Macroon had put young Kenny up to it, but not at all. Oh, well, well, they'll be feeling pretty annoyed in Inverness when they hear about the Todday Monster.'

'You don't think they'll try and pay us out by doing nothing about the Garryboo pier?' asked Murdo MacCodrum, who as the only lorry owner in Garryboo was looking forward to a profitable monopoly.

'Ach, they would not do a dirty trick on me like that,' the councillor protested. 'You can't be playing quick and loose with a pier.'

At this moment Andrew Thomson, the bank-agent, a swarthy man, so extremely shy as to seem disagreeable to those who did not know him, came into the bar. The ordeal of asking for his dram every evening still made him gulp so much that one might have supposed he was drinking it before the glass was on the counter.

'Good evening, everybody,' he scowled in an effort to be affable.

'You'll have heard about the monster, Mr Thomson?' somebody asked.

'Imphm,' the banker muttered.

And then overcome by the notion of having to express an opinion upon the phenomenon he swallowed his dram, turned on his heels, and walked out of the bar in a dusky blush.

'I wonder what will he be saying about it to the *Obaig Chimes*,' somebody speculated, for it was generally believed in Snorvig that the occasional items of news about Great and Little Todday communicated to the *Obaig Chimes* emanated from Andrew Thomson. In fact it was Mrs Thomson who supplied news of great events in the two islands like sales of work and progressive whist drives.

'Ach, we've something much too high for the *Obaig Chimes*,' Roderick MacRurie declared. 'I believe I'll send a telegraph to that fellow in Glasgow who was here last summer and wrote a big piece about the road to the isles in the *Daily Tale*. He enjoyed himself fine at the hotel. What was his name? Ian . . . Ian . . . Ian Carmichael. Ay, that's it . . . Ian Carmichael.'

Big Roderick did not add that his brother Donald, the postmaster of Snorvig, had let him know of a telegram sent off by Joseph Macroon to the same Ian Carmichael this very morning. It would not do for the people of Todaidh Mór to think that Todaidh Beag was responsible for interesting the press.

'We've had a follow-up to that telegram yesterday from Little Todday, Mr Donaldson,' said Ian Carmichael to the Editor of the *Scottish Daily Tale*, and as he said this he could not resist glancing at the strip of blue sky just visible above the ravine of high grimy Glasgow buildings in which the offices of the newspaper were situated. 'Look at this.'

James Donaldson read the two telegrams on his big desk:

Advise investigation of huge strange creature seen by Kenneth Macroon yesterday in water near Gobha rock on which steamship Cabinet Minister was wrecked during war Little Todday believes forecast of Daily Tale that Loch Ness Monster would take refuge from flying saucepans is all correct and that monster has duly arrived in good order
Joseph Macroon
Merchant
Kiltod
Little Todday
Outer Isles
by Obaig

This afternoon enormous verb sap monster was seen looking out of cave below Ard Snor on Great Todday by Archie MacRurie crofter fisherman highly reliable and respected member of community verb sap in question showed signs of very terrible ferocity but Archie MacRurie was able to escape in his boat and tell the tale of the Lord's great mercy to him we have reports that a verb sap was seen between Pillay and Little Todday previous day which is now believed true in Snorvig suggest immediate investigation of this strange occurrence happy to reserve rooms for you in hotel on notification of your possible time of arrival
Roderick MacRurie
Snorvig Hotel
Great Todday
Outer Isles

'What on earth's he mean by a verb sap?' the Editor asked.

'I couldn't make out at first, Mr Donaldson,' chuckled Carmichael, a fresh-complexioned, rather good-looking young man. 'Then I turned back to our files for March and I think our friend Roderick hasn't quite understood what Hector Hamish Mackay meant by verb sap.'

'It's a silly out-of-date expression anyway,' said the Editor severely. 'I don't know why the sub didn't take it out. I suppose you think you are ear-marked for this investigation?'

'Well, I know the people there, Mr Donaldson. I mean to say I could get busy right away, and this second telegram from Snorvig does look as if something strange had been seen. And I thought as I handled the flying saucer business in March you'd like to keep everything in one key.'

'Losh, I wish sometimes I were a young reporter again,' said the Editor, and this time it was his eye that was turned in the direction of the strip of blue sky above the ravine.

While young Ian Carmichael, with a light heart, was westward bound the monster was seen for the third time.

During the war the Little Todday platoon of the Home Guard had made a surprise landing on Garryboo in gasmasks and acutely frightened Morag and Annag, the two eldest daughters of Bean Shomhairle, the wife of Samuel MacCodrum. Morag and Annag were now away in service on the mainland, and it was the duty of Chrissie and Lizzie, their younger sisters, to carry up any flotsam or jetsam marked down by their father in the course of beachcombing operations, for the building of the pier for Garryboo had not yet started, and the low rocky promontory of Ardvanish, a mile away from the few houses of the township clustered together below the road round the island, was a lonely enough spot, seldom visited except by beachcombers at low tide. After school on the afternoon following the Biffer's adventure by Uamh na Snaoiseanaich, the Cave of the Snuff-taker, Chrissie and Lizzie MacCodrum were sent off to bring back a ship's grating which their father had left on Ardvanish that morning. They dallied for a while to weave the first daisy-chain of the year from the flowers with which the fine weather already starred the green machair land between the township and the sea, the only stretch of such grass in Great Todday, where the soil was almost all rocky moorland, although its sister island was entirely machair land.

'A Thighearna, Lizzie, we'll be late for tea,' said her sister, and the two little girls started to run towards the sea.

Suddenly Chrissie stopped and with something between a gasp and a scream clutched Lizzie's arm.

'What is it at all?' she quavered.

There was no gasp from Lizzie; a wild shriek pierced the quiet afternoon air, and a moment later she was running back to Garryboo as fast as she could, followed by her sister.

Ten minutes later, breathless and half-sobbing, they burst into their mother's kitchen. Bean Shomhairle was spreading jam on slices of bread under the hopeful eyes of her two youngest children, both boys, and the irruption of Chrissie and Lizzie nearly made her cut herself.

In a stream of indignant Gaelic she threatened her daughters with the severest belting they had ever experienced unless they could explain what they meant by their behaviour.

'A huge animal was coming out of the sea on Tràigh Bhuidhe,' said Chrissie.

'Bigger than an elephant,' said Lizzie.

'What do you know about elephants, you silly girl?' her mother demanded. 'You never saw such a thing in your life.'

'Mr Campbell showed us a picture of an elephant in school, with tusks sticking out in front like huge teeth.'

At this moment the father of the household came in to hear of his daughters' adventure.

'Right enough the Biffer saw teeth on the monster in Uamh na Snaoiseanaich,' said Sammy MacCodrum. 'They put him in mind of a hayrake they were so long and so fierce. How pick was this crayture on the *tràigh*?'

'We only saw its head coming out of the sea,' said Chrissie. 'We were running away as fast as we could.'

'We were afraid it would come after us,' Lizzie explained.

'It's mouth was wide open,' said Chrissie, 'and we could see its teeth. Och, they were terrible!' She shuddered at the memory.

'Get on with your tea,' their father told his daughters. 'I'm going down to the *tràigh* to see what I can see and later I'll take you both in to Snorvig in the lorry.'

'Are you daft, *a Shomhairle*,' his wife ejaculated.

'Ach, I want the Biffer to hear the story from themselves, wife. They'll be thinking in Snorvig that we're just seeing the monster in Garryboo to make them feel so small.'

There was no sign of the monster when Sammy MacCodrum reached Tràigh Bhuidhe or Vooey as it was usually printed in maps and guidebooks, but the achievement of his daughters filled him with such elation that he picked up the ship's grating on the promontory and carried it all the way back to the croft himself.

In spite of his wife's protests Sammy persisted with his plan of taking the two little girls into Snorvig, and although they were both sick most of the way home on the lorry after all the lemonade they drank and all the cakes they ate Chrissie and Lizzie considered that evening to be the finest they had yet spent. It may be added that the Biffer, far from resenting the appearance of the monster at Garryboo, was delighted to have the size of its teeth confirmed by independent eye-witnesses.

Next day Ian Carmichael reached the Islands and it was not long before the *Daily Tale* was able to publish the story.

HAS MONSTER DESERTED LOCH NESS?
STRANGE CREATURE ASTOUNDS ISLANDERS
AMAZING STORY

The people of the two remote islands of Great and Little Todday are again making headlines in the news, and by an amazing coincidence the dark rock called the Gobha (pronounced Gowa and meaning blacksmith) on which the S.S. *Cabinet Minister* with a cargo of whisky was wrecked in March 1943 is the scene of the first appearance of the monster whose advent has literally convulsed the Outer Hebrides from the Butt of Lewis to Barra Head.

Last Monday week Kenneth Macroon, the son of Mr Joseph Macroon, the postmaster and principal merchant of Kiltod who represents Little Todday on the Inverness County Council, was setting his lobster-pots round the Gobha. This black rock rises from a submerged reef some two hundred yards from the dark cliffs on the eastern face of the tiny island of Pillay which lies about a mile off the north of Little Todday. It was a calm cloudless morning and while Kenneth Macroon was engaged in adjusting the machinery of his little motor-boat, the *Morning Star*, he heard a curious noise which he describes as like the 'snarling of an unfriendly dog'. Looking up he saw what seemed to be the back of an immense bull with a mane disappearing below the water. When young Macroon came back to Kiltod with his amazing story he was sharply questioned by Father James Macalister, whose Gaelic broadcasts have from time to time given so much pleasure to listeners on Scottish Regional, whether what he had seen might not have been the head of an unusually large seal, but young Macroon claims to have seen enough seals to know that this strange head which snarled at him was three or four times as large as any seal.

Interviewed by a special representative of the *Daily Tale* Mr Kenneth Macroon said:

'In spite of the mane which was clearly visible I would prefer to compare the back of the head I saw to that of a hornless bull about three times as big as the head of an ordinary bull. But I was so frightened that I would not care to be too sure. It may have been more than three times as big.'

'But not less.'

'Definitely not less,' Mr Kenneth Macroon declared.

'And you heard this strange creature snarl before it dived.'

'That is the nearest description I can give of the noise it made.'

The day after the monster appeared to Mr Kenneth Macroon it was seen in even more dramatic circumstances by Mr Archie MacRurie on the coast of Great Todday. Mr MacRurie had also been taking advantage of the clement weather to set his lobster-pots and when he was returning to Snorvig, the harbour and the chief town of the two Toddays, he passed with his boat, the *Kittiwake*, close under the headland of Ard Snor which shelters Snorvig from the north-west, and as he passed what is called the Cave of the Snuff-taker, on account of the effect of a mighty sneeze produced by waves breaking inside at certain stages of the tide, Mr MacRurie was amazed to see an immense head staring at him from the cave.

'Did this alarm you, Mr MacRurie?' our representative asked.

'Wouldn't you be frightened if you saw a head as big as a sack of barley with two eyes like pancakes staring at you from a cave, and wouldn't you be fit to drop down dead with fright if you saw this head had a mouthful of teeth like a hayrake and was making a noise like a fog-horn?'

'Did you notice the mane which Kenneth Macroon saw?'

'I couldn't see the back of the creature's head and I wasn't going to hang around for that.'

'You steered for Snorvig?'

'I did indeed, and glad I was to get safely into the harbour.'

Perhaps the most amazing encounter was on the following afternoon when Christina and Elizabeth MacCodrum, the two daughters of Mr Samuel MacCodrum, a crofter of Garryboo, which is a small village some five miles north of Snorvig, actually saw the monster emerging from the sea on the sandy beach called Traigh Vooey.

Our representative called at Garryboo School where Mr George Campbell, the headmaster, kindly allowed our representative to interrupt the little girls' studies by interviewing them.

'And I believe you both saw these teeth, Christina and Elizabeth?'

'Yes, we did. They were terrible and we were so frightened that we ran all the way home.'

Our representative tried to obtain a more detailed description of the teeth, but the little girls had evidently been too much shaken by their amazing experience to be able to say more than that these teeth were as big as elephants' tusks and that the head of the monster itself was as big as an elephant's.

There is no doubt whatever that the Todday Monster has already been seen by four credible eye-witnesses in circumstances which are at least as convincing and in some respects are even more convincing than those which have attended the many appearances of the Loch Ness Monster at intervals during the last fifteen years.

The question which will certainly be widely debated is whether the Todday

Monster is the Loch Ness Monster itself, a survivor of two Loch Ness monsters, or a new monster altogether which has appeared for the first time.

Mr Hector Hamish Mackay, who has always maintained that there were two monsters in Loch Ness, expressed his satisfaction at the news from the Islands.

'This bears out my theory,' he told the *Daily Tale*. 'What we have to ascertain now is whether the Todday Monster is male or female. There is, however, another possibility. Both the Loch Ness monsters disturbed by the flying saucers may have gone to seek sanctuary among the Outer Isles. We are not yet in a position to say that the monster seen off Little Todday is identical with the one seen in the cave of Great Todday. But whether the dead body of one monster is now lying on the fathomless bottom of Loch Ness or whether both managed to escape, what does seem certain is that there is no longer a monster in Loch Ness.'

Chapter 5

BEN NEVIS AND THE EDITOR

On the day that Ian Carmichael's story of the Todday Monster appeared in the *Daily Tale* the Lady of Ben Nevis was sitting in the chintzy privacy of her own room in Glenbogle Castle which was still known as the Yellow Drawing-Room, though it had not been either yellow or a drawing-room for nearly forty years. The post had just arrived and Mrs MacDonald's tranquil and majestic shape loomed above the annual report of the Kenspeckle Branch of the Women's Rural Institute, of which she was the President, like one of Glenbogle's guardian bens above a lochan. She was just saying to herself how satisfactory the attendance at the winter ceilidhs had been when she heard from some part of the castle a sound like the agonized roar of a love-tormented stag in October. A few moments later Mac 'ic Eachainn burst into the room, his countenance aflame, his beaked nose aglow.

'Trixie! Trixie!' he shouted. 'Look at this abominable rag! Read what these scoundrels say! I've never been so absolutely furious in my life! I've told Johnnie to bring the car round at once! I'm going to Glasgow to horsewhip the editor of this beastly rag! I'll . . . I'll . . . I'll . . .' speech failed him.

He spread the morning's issue of the *Daily Tale* on his wife's table, obliterating with its noisome pages the annual report of the Kenspeckle Branch of the W.R.I.

'Read it, Trixie, read it,' he gasped, flinging himself down into one of Mrs MacDonald's chintz-covered armchairs. 'No longer a monster in Loch Ness! Good lord, we'll be told next that Lochiel has gone to spend a week-end with Molotov and MacCailein Mór's flying the red flag over Inveraray. As a matter of fact, I wouldn't be so surprised if a Campbell did fly the red flag.' He guffawed bitterly.

'Don't work yourself up, Donald,' his wife boomed as gently as the soft diapason of an organ in some glimmering cathedral at evensong. 'Let me read what the paper says.'

'You'll never read such foul and filthy dunderheaded damnable nonsense . . . you'll . . .'

'I certainly shan't if you keep interrupting me,' the Lady of Ben Nevis put in severely.

The Chieftain, breathing heavily, refrained from saying anything more while his wife perused the account of the monster seen in the Islands.

'Well, you know I never attach undue importance to what the papers say,' Mrs MacDonald commented when she had read the offending article. 'And I thought you yourself believed the monster might go to Loch Hoo.'

'What I said was that if the monster had been driven out of Loch Ness by this flying brute it was more likely to take refuge in Loch Hoo or Loch Hoch than go gallivanting off to the Islands. I don't accept the fact that the monster *has* been driven out of Loch Ness. This fellow Hector Hamish Mackay is nothing but a miserable mushy writing nincompoop.'

'Nobody *has* seen the monster since that curious story told by Hubert Bottley's head stalker.'

'Well, practically nobody saw it all through the war. I think it lay up. It's probably lying up again. And I don't blame the creature. I should jolly well lie up if one of these flying saucers came skating across the top of my head. What I object to is this peprosterous idea that the monster has gone to the Islands. I tell you what, Trixie, if any more of this drivelling fat-headedness goes on I shall get Tom Rawstorne to take me out to the Islands in the *Banshee* and investigate for myself, and if I find that these Islanders have somehow lured our monster out there I'll jolly well get it back to Loch Ness somehow. Mind you, I don't believe it is our monster. I don't believe our monster could have curled itself up inside one of these finicking little caves you find beside the sea. If it was in Prince Charlie's cave on Ben Booey there might be something in this pettifogging story.'

Toker came in at this moment to say that Macpherson had brought the car round, and that Mrs Parsall wanted to know if Ben Nevis would take a picnic lunch with him.

'Donald, you aren't seriously thinking of going to Glasgow?' his wife protested.

'I jolly well am, Trixie. I'm determined to get to the bottom of this outrageous yarn, and if the editor or whatever he's called of this vile rag tries any of his Clydeside Bolshie impudence with me I shall give him the soundest thrashing he's ever had in his life. Tell Mrs Parsall to put up a picnic lunch, Toker, and don't forget a bottle of Glenbogle's Pride.'

'Certainly not, Ben Nevis.'

The butler withdrew.

'Donald, there are times when I think you're just seven instead of being just seventy,' his wife sighed profoundly. 'All I can hope is that the long drive will cool you down sufficiently not to cause a scandal in Glasgow.'

'It never cools me down when I drive through Glencoe,' the MacDonald Chieftain declared. 'You know my blood always boils when I drive through Glencoe.'

An hour or so later Ben Nevis halted the car outside the King's House where the Campbells gathered on that February night.

'We'll eat our lunch outside, Johnnie,' he proclaimed. 'I won't soil my brogues by crossing the threshold of such an accursed house.'

When lunch was eaten, Mac 'ic Eachainn gave Johnnie Macpherson a dram and poured out one for himself.

'This is where those infernal Campbells gathered on that appalling night, Johnnie.'

'I believe they did, Ben Nevis.'

'Gathered like a lot of beastly vultures. Down with Campbell of Glenlyon, down with that brute Dalrymple, down with Breadalbane . . . wait a moment, there's one more to down.'

He poured out another dram.

'Down with Dutch William!' He emptied his glass. 'I feel better now, Johnnie. You know the way that contraption in front of a car sometimes boils.'

'Not the radiator of this car, Ben Nevis,' Johnnie Macpherson said indignantly.

'Well, practically all the way up the glen I was boiling like one of these contraptions, but I feel cooler now. Hector, the Thirteenth of Ben Nevis, had married a daughter of MacDonald of Glencoe about fifty years before this abominable massacre and so you can understand my boiling over, Johnnie.'

'Ay, it was a bad business right enough, Ben Nevis.'

'Well, we must be getting on to Glasgow,' said the Chieftain. 'I don't think you'd better have another dram, Johnnie, or you'll be tearing through Tyndrum at forty miles an hour.'

In fact Johnnie Macpherson left Tyndrum behind him at fifty-five miles an hour, but the cockles of Mac 'ic Eachainn's heart had been warmed by Glenbogle's Pride, and his triumph over the ghosts of dead

Campbells made him feel so benign that he fancied Johnnie was driving rather more slowly than usual and told him he could add five miles to the speed; it was not until they reached Loch Lomondside that he said, 'Steady now, Johnnie.'

The janitor of the *Daily Tale* offices was used to kilted visitors and, being a strong Conservative, was inclined to regard them all with disapproval as Scottish Nationalists anxious to disturb the even tenor of Caledonia's life. When this kilted visitor demanded an immediate interview with the Editor he asked if he had an appointment.

'Certainly not, I want to see the Editor.'

'Who shall I say?'

'Ben Nevis,' the Chieftain roared.

'Ben Nevis?' the janitor repeated in bewilderment.

'MacDonald of Ben Nevis, you ninny,' the Chieftain roared again.

For a moment the janitor was under the impression that one of the trams in Buchanan Street had crashed through the doors of the *Daily Tale's* offices.

'I'll ask if Mr Donaldson will see you, sir,' the janitor said, almost obsequiously.

'Donaldson? Is this fellow's name Donaldson?'

'The Editor is Mr James Donaldson.'

'Good lord, a clansman! Extraordinary behaviour for one of my fellow clansmen!' Ben Nevis ejaculated.

A minute later the Chieftain was in the lift under the escort of a small page-boy who as an embryo Nationalist looked up at him with stern approval.

'Are you a Scottish Nationalist, mister?' he asked in a high Glasgow voice.

'Am I what?' the Chieftain gasped.

'A Scottish Nationalist? Ma father is.'

'Who the devil is your father?'

'Och, he's the Secretary of the Gorbals Branch of the League for Scottish Independence. He wears the kilt to meetings the same as you do. His name's MacDonald. Hector MacDonald. I'm Donald MacDonald masel'.'

It took a good deal to deprive Ben Nevis of the power of speech, but that page-boy of his own clan, three feet ten inches tall, achieved what Lochiel had never managed to achieve, nor Simon Lovat before him, at many a session of the Inverness County Council. In fact it was a temporarily subdued Ben Nevis that was shown into James Donaldson's editorial office.

'This is a great honour, Ben Nevis,' said the Editor, offering his hand. 'I hope you weren't kept waiting too long.'

'How do you do, Mr Donaldson? I've come about this article, as I think you call them, in this morning's *Daily Tale*.'

'Do sit down, Ben Nevis. I wonder if I might have the privilege of offering you a little refreshment? I'm afraid it's not the famous Glenbogle's Pride, but it's a decent malt whisky.'

'Oh, thanks very much . . . perhaps, a small dram.'

Ben Nevis found that it was indeed an excellent malt whisky and he began to wonder if this editor chap, who after all was a MacDonald even if he used this vile English variant of it for his name, might not be a more reasonable kind of fellow than he had been supposing.

'You were interested by the news from the Islands in our morning's issue? Young Ian Carmichael whom I sent out to look into the strange business is a bright lad and you can rely on his report.'

'What I took exception to was that disgusting statement at the end by this writing fellow.'

'Old Hector Hamish Mackay? Ah, well, you know, he's a great enthusiast.'

'That doesn't entitle him to say in this cock-a-whoop way that the Monster has left Loch Ness for the Islands.'

'Don't worry, Ben Nevis, our man will test that hypothesis.'

'I hope he'll make it clear that it was just a hytop . . . just a piece of dunder-headed theorizing and nothing more. As soon as I read that preposterous speculation I got into my car and drove straight to Glasgow.'

'You've had a long drive. May I give you the other half of that dram?'

The Chieftain surrendered to the invitation and this time he drank the Editor's health.

'Slahnjervaw, Mr Donaldson. I wonder why you call yourself Donaldson. I mean to say it's a queer sort of place, Glasgow, but after all it isn't England.'

'I used to be on at my old dad about that,' said the Editor. 'But I'll be frank and admit that I've stuck to it because there are more MacDonalds than Donaldsons in Glasgow.'

Ben Nevis remembered his diminutive namesake in the lift.

'Yes, I see what you mean.'

'Don't you think it would be helpful if I sent Hector Hamish Mackay out to the Toddays to try and clear up the mystery?'

'As long as he doesn't insist on pretending that this jumped up jackanapes in the Toddays is the Loch Ness Monster. I warn you, Mr Donaldson, that if he does I shall go to Snorvig myself and deport him. I don't suppose you ever heard of my expedition to Great Todday to rescue a left-footed boot which these islanders had stolen from my Home Guard Company.'

'I never did,' said the Editor. 'I wish we could have covered such a remarkable expedition.'

'Well, as a matter of fact it happened just when Hitler invaded Russia and you were probably jolly busy emptying whitewash over the Russians, what?'

'I hope that if you do decide to lead another expedition to the Islands you'll give us the tip beforehand. There ought to be a splendid story in it. Will you go over in the *Island Queen*?'

'Good Lord, no, my friend Tom Rawstorne will lend me his yacht the *Banshee*. If these rascally islanders go on arguing that this monster of theirs is the Loch Ness Monster I must do something about it. I must prove that they're wrong. And if this writing fellow Mackay tries to argue with me I shall deport him. I suppose he's entered into some kind of beastly alliance with that fellow Wig . . . Wog . . . Waggett. Yes that's his name.'

'This telegram we had this morning may interest you, Ben Nevis,' said the Editor, pushing a piece of paper across the table.

Paul Waggett owner Snorvig House interviewed last night quote consider monster delusion of mass suggestion and attempt emulate Inverness exploitation of equally imaginary monster for gullible tourists unquote urge important secure investigation Hector Hamish Mackay soonest possible personally convinced Todday people have seen something outside ordinary experience
Carmichael

The countenance of Ben Nevis was darkened by an angry flush.

'Loch Ness Monster imaginary,' he exclaimed in stupefaction. 'Imaginary? I don't know what the world's coming to. I really don't. This fellow Waggett was the prime mover in that boot business. He's completely unscrupulous. Oh, I see this expedition of mine is going to be absolutely necessary.'

'And when do you propose to set out?'

'I shall wait till June, and if the Monster has not been seen before then I shall choose a fine spell and go into the whole matter personally.'

'I believe you don't accept the flying saucer as a fact?'

'I didn't when that reporter fellow of yours came and saw me in Glenbogle. However, after going into it with Kenneth MacLennan I decided that some kind of a something did go whizzing down the loch, but I refuse to believe that the Monster was hit.'

'You think that the Todday monster has no connection with the Loch Ness Monster?'

'I hope not, because if it should turn out to be our monster I shall have to discover some way of getting it back to Loch Ness. You must remember I've seen our monster twelve times. I shall know at a glance whether this Todday monster is ours or not. Meanwhile, I do hope that you'll not encourage people to think that the Loch Ness Monster was killed by this flying brute or that it has been frightened away from Loch Ness.'

'Are you returning to Glenbogle at once?' the Editor asked.

'I intended to drive back after dinner,' the Chieftain told him.

'I wonder if you'd give me the very great pleasure of dining with me at a rather good new restaurant we have in Glasgow?' the Editor asked.

'That's very kind of you, Mr Donaldson.'

'I thought with your permission I would like to publish the substance of our talk and I'd like you to vet it before we go to press. Perhaps you'll be kind enough to call in for me about half past six and we could go on to dinner. I do think it's important that the *Daily Tale* should be able to present an authoritative point of view like yours.'

'You mustn't breathe a word about this expedition of mine.'

'Of course not.'

'This'll be the third expedition of a MacDonald of Ben Nevis to Todday. Yes, an ancestor of mine went over once and hanged the MacRurie of the time in his own chimney. Yes, by Jove, he did. Smoked him like a ham and delivered the result to King James IV in Holyrood, poor chap.'

'Well, well, I daresay he deserved it.'

'I didn't mean this scoundrelly MacRurie. I was thinking of King James IV. Flodden and all that, if you know what I mean.'

'The Flowers of the Forest?'

The Chieftain sighed deeply.

'The Flowers of the Forest. Exactly.'

The Editor replenished his glass.

'Slahnjer,' the Chieftain woofed.

'Slahnje,' the Editor echoed.

At half past six Ben Nevis returned to the offices of the *Daily Tale* where the Editor invited him to approve the following:

FAMOUS HIGHLAND CHIEFTAIN
VISITS GLASGOW

To-day everybody on the staff of the *Scottish Daily Tale* was walking more jauntily after a visit from no less a Highland personality than Donald MacDonald, Twenty-third of Ben Nevis, who drove specially from Glenbogle Castle to discuss with the Editor of the *Scottish Daily Tale* the right approach to the amazing problem set by the monster whose appearance in the sea around Great and Little Todday was exclusively announced in the *Scottish Daily Tale* yesterday, and caused a profound sensation throughout the country.

Ben Nevis believes that Mr Hector Hamish Mackay is premature in suggesting that the monster already seen by four witnesses may be the Loch Ness Monster or its mate. He does not reject Mr Mackay's theory that there may be two Loch Ness Monsters, but he does not consider that theory to be an established fact, and he is unwilling to admit on the evidence available at present that the Loch Ness Monster or its supposed mate was killed by a flying saucer. At first he was inclined to disbelieve in the phenomenon of a flying saucer, but after discussing the matter with Mr Kenneth MacLennan, the original witness of the amazing incident, he is now firmly convinced that it happened exactly as Mr MacLennan described it. He maintains, however, that the monster was not actually hit but succeeded in diving to safety, and that its failure to appear since is due to the natural resentment it felt at the intrusion upon its peaceful domain of this flying saucer. He confidently expects at any time to hear of the re-emergence of the Loch Ness Monster from its temporary retirement and refuses to consider for a moment the theory that one monster was killed and that the survivor is now searching for a mate on the western seaboard. He shrewdly points out that we know nothing of the breeding season or habits of these monsters, nor even whether they are viviparous or oviparous . . .

'What's that?' the Chieftain interposed to ask. 'Vipiferous or opiferous?'

The Editor explained.

'Well, I think you'd better use shorter words. I'm sure some of your readers won't know what on earth you're talking about.'

'I believe you're right,' James Donaldson agreed and amended the sentence.

. . . whether the young are born alive or hatched from eggs. He does not pour cold water on Mr Mackay's speculation that the monsters may, like eels, go far out to sea to reproduce themselves, but he doubts if in the state of our present knowledge we have the right to put forward theories in which what he scathingly calls 'these scientific know-alls' would be delighted to pick holes.

When asked whether he considered the Todday Monster was of the same species of monster as the hoary denizen of Loch Ness, Ben Nevis replied that he was prepared to wait until he had seen the Todday Monster before committing himself to an opinion. When he was informed that Mr Paul Waggett of Snorvig House had expressed his disbelief in the Todday Monster the MacDonald Chieftain replied tersely that some people could disbelieve anything. When further informed that Mr Waggett did not believe in the Loch Ness Monster Ben Nevis retorted that such an attitude made any opinion expressed by Mr Waggett about the Todday Monster utterly valueless.

The *Scottish Daily Tale* desires to take this opportunity of congratulating a famous Highland Chieftain upon the robust health with which he carries his seventy years and of wishing him many more years of such health. Figures like Ben Nevis grow more rare all the time, and after the inspiring visit we received from this Chieftain of high degree and ancient lineage the *Scottish Daily Tale* echoes with enthusiasm the motto of this branch of mighty Clan Donald, 'Ben Nevis Gu Brath – Ben Nevis for Ever.'

In *Happy Days Among the Heather* by Hector Hamish Mackay we read:

'In the year 1546 a party of marauding Macintoshes were surprised by the MacDonalds of Ben Nevis led by Mac 'ic Eachainn in person and every single one of them killed. Some years later Clan Chattan took its revenge for this defeat by descending on Strath Diddle, when the young men were raiding the Cameron country to the south, and baking thirty-two old and infirm MacDonalds in an oven. For this Hector the ninth of Ben Nevis exacted a terrible penalty from Clan Chattan when, marching through a stormy December night in the year 1549, he caught the Macintoshes unawares on a Sunday morning and burned forty-five of them in church. While the unfortunate victims of Hector's vengeance were burning, Hector's piper Angus MacQuat improvised a tune and played it to drown their shrieks. This tune, called *Mac 'ic Eachainn's Return to Glenbogle*, is still played by a MacQuat whenever MacDonald of Ben Nevis returns after spending even a single night away from his Castle.'

'Will your piper be waiting your return from Glasgow?' the Chieftain was asked.

'Certainly,' he replied. 'Angus will be there.'

The prophecy made by Ben Nevis was fulfilled. When at 4 a.m. Johnnie Macpherson drove up to the front door of Glenbogle Castle Angus MacQuat, who had been dozing in the Great Hall among the antlers and Lochaber axes, woke as if at the touch of an unseen hand warning him that the Chieftain was come home. He hastily inflated the bag of his pipe and by the time Ben Nevis had extracted himself from the car and come surging through the front door Angus was marching up and down the Great Hall in full blast.

Ben Nevis beamed at him patriarchally, and when the wind had been emptied from the bag he poured out three hefty drams of Glenbogle's Pride, one for Johnnie Macpherson, one for his piper and one for himself.

'Well, I enjoyed myself in Glasgow,' said Mac 'ic Eachainn, now safely returned. 'Extraordinary thing, the boy who took me up in the lift was called Donald MacDonald.'

'Och, there's hundreds of Donald MacDonalds in Glasgow, Ben Nevis,' Johnnie Macpherson assured him a little impatiently.

'Are there, Johnnie? Well, Glasgow isn't really such a queer place as I thought it was.' The Chieftain yawned widely. 'Good night to you both.'

On his way to his own room Ben Nevis put his head round the door of his wife's room.

'Yes, I'm awake, Donald. I heard the pipes. Well?'

'Very decent fellow, this editor of the *Daily Tale*. Donaldson, his name is. A fellow clansman. I've told him to come and stay with us any time he feels like it. Extraordinary things newspapers. I've just been reading what they call an interview with me which you'll all be reading tomorrow. I don't know how they do it. And the boy in the lift, about the size of a shrimp, told me his name was Donald MacDonald. Oh, yes, and we damned all Campbells on our way through Glencoe and then damned them again on our way back. It was quite eerie in the moonlight. I shouldn't have been a bit surprised to see a lot of ghosts covered with blood.'

'Really, Donald!'

'This clansman James Donaldson is keen as mustard on the Monster. I was very pleased with his attitude and he understands absolutely why I object to the notion that the Monster has left Loch Ness. So I shall drive in to Inverness tomorrow and try to get rid of what we used to call alarm and despondency in the war.'

Chapter 6

MRS ODD ARRIVES

The account of the Todday Monster in the English editions of the *Daily Tale* was merely a brief paragraph, for the paper shortage meant rationing of news and naturally the women of England were more interested in the love-affair of a divorced film-star than in a Hebridean monster. Nevertheless, brief though that paragraph was, it acted on Mrs Odd like a galvanic shock.

The old lady had just finished washing up after breakfast and was sitting in the little parlour at the back of the shop in Nottingham. Her son, the ex-sergeant-major, was serving customers across the counter with the packets of gaspers for which they craved. Her daughter-in-law Peggy was upstairs with both hands for housework and one eye for Lucy, aged three, and Catherine, aged two, who were capable jointly or indeed separately of extraordinary destructiveness.

'Well, if anybody had of told me I was going to be grandma to a couple of walking buzz-bombs,' the old lady had exclaimed when the crash was louder than usual, 'well, you was always one for blowing round the house with a tin trumpet, Fred, but you was a dome of silence beside these two terrors you've landed on Nottingham. Goose Fair? Goose Fair's the crip in dear old St Paul's beside what it's like in our house. Not that I mind. I like to hear children enjoying themselves, I do.'

Mrs Odd was now seventy-five, but with her fresh complexion, snow white hair and lively step she did not look a day older than when she attended her son's wedding on Little Todday, and her bright eyes were reading the newspaper without glasses.

'Good land alive,' she ejaculated, and jumping up from the leather-covered armchair, which became Ma's chair after Pa had relinquished it over fifteen years earlier, she was behind the counter just as Fred was handing a packet of gaspers to a customer.

'Fred, the Loch Ness Monster has arrived on Little Todday and I'm off back tonight so as I can catch the *Island Queen* tomorrow morning. You read your *Daily Tale* this morning, Mr Quidling?' she asked the customer.

'Not yet, no Mrs Odd,' the customer replied gloomily. 'I don't get a chance to see it till after my tea, and I only see it then if the Missus doesn't want it.'

'I couldn't be bothered to tell that old spoilsport about the monster,' Mrs Odd said to her son when Mr Quidling had left the shop. 'Still, I suppose it preyed on his mind when people started in calling him Quisling during the war, though, goodness me, you'd think anybody 'ud only be too glad to give people a chance of a bit of fun at such a time. Still, what's the good in talking? Some people is only happy when they're miserable. Yes, I reckon I'll get the connexion from St Pancras and give Captain MacKechnie a surprise tomorrow morning. I'll send a telegram to young Kenny so as he can meet me when I get to Snorvig. He can come back for his father later. You know the way your par-in-lore always hangs around while they're sorting the post. And I'll send a telegram to Duncan Bang to meet me at Kiltod with his pony and trap and drive me to Bow Bells. I wonder if Duncan has seen the monster yet.'

'I reckon you'd better get off as soon as you can, Ma,' her son advised. 'Otherwise you'll be seeing a monster in the Trent. You was going anyway in another fortnight.'

It was a calm sparkling morning when Captain Donald MacKechnie, the skipper of the *Island Queen*, who from the bridge was eyeing the arrival of passengers from the train, heard a loud 'ship ahoy!' and looked down to see Mrs Odd beaming up at him.

A minute later they were shaking hands cordially.

'Ah, well, well, Mistress Ott, it's glad I am to be seeing yourself on such a fine morning,' the Skipper declared in his high voice. '*Fàilte d'on duthaich*. Welcome to the country. Will you be taking a wee dram chust to settle the smell of the train?'

'At half past six in the morning?' Mrs Odd exclaimed. 'What a nerve! But I'll have one with you after my lunch. Well, they say all the nice girls love a sailor, and I'm not surprised, I'm not. Now, I'm not going to interrupt you with your tiddley-bits. I know you won't be fit for a good old chin-wag till you're well out on the briny and nothing to bump into before Great Todday.'

'It's yourself that's a ferry wise woman, Mistress Ott,' Captain MacKechnie assured her. 'And how's the Sarchant and Peigi Ealasaid?'

'Both in the pink and hoping for a little corporal next autumn.'

'Is that so? Ah, ferry coot, ferry coot. And the two wee curlies?'

'Oh, a proper pair of terrors. What a set out we had only the day before yesterday when young Luce edged young Kitty on to try and drink some of that black-currant vitamings out of a tin and Kitty got the juice all over her face. Peggy thought she'd cut herself and started in to holler for Fred to fetch a doctor, and of course it wasn't blood at all, it was just black-currant juice. But look here, don't start me off chattering when you've got to get them all aboard the *Margate Belle*.'

'The market pell?' Captain MacKechnie echoed in a puzzled voice.

'Yes, the good old *Margate Belle*. Oh dear, what times I've had in her in the sweet long ago. Packed like sardines and all enjoying ourselves. Well, tootle-oo till after lunch.'

When the *Island Queen* had nothing between her and America except Great and Little Todday, and the Atlantic, a silvery-blue expanse, was breathing as gently as a sleeping nymph, Mrs Odd joined Captain MacKechnie in his cabin.

'I'm afraid I haven't a drop of Minnie left,' he told her.

Minnie was the endearing diminutive by which the whisky saved from the wreck of the *Cabinet Minister* had been known.

'Drunk it all, eh? I should say so!'

'Ay, and there were still gallons of that peautiful stuff when the excisemen sent it all to the pottom of the sea. Ay, Covernments are queer craytures, right enough. What would a fish be making of such peautiful whisky? There's no fish alive that isn't a teetotaller, Mistress Ott.'

'What a shocking waste, eh?'

'You've said the ferry words. Chust a shocking waste. Still, you won't find this too bad at all.'

He took the cork out of a bottle and poured the golden liquid into a glass.

'Here, I don't want to roll ashore at Snorvig like a barrel,' Mrs Odd protested.

'You won't be rolling at all on any whisky they give us today. *Slàinte mhath!* And I'm ferry proud to be offering you a welcome to the land of pens and clens and heroes. Ay, *tìr nam beann, nan gleann, nan gaisgeach*.'

'And now what about this monster?' Mrs Odd asked. 'Have you seen it?'

'No, no,' said Captain MacKechnie cautiously. 'But I believe it will have been seen right enough. Kenny Macroon, Airchie MacRurie – that's the Biffer – and Sammy MacCodrum's two little curls. Ach, it would be a pold man who would be saying like Mr Wackett that the monster is chust a nothing at all.'

'Waggett doesn't believe anybody sore a monster? Oh dear, oh dear, what a dismal Jimmy that feller is. Good land alive, anybody would think with all this austerity, and which I say means eating horse instead of good old roast beef, well, really anybody would think it was time we had somethink to cheer us up. Well, as soon as I read that bit in the *Daily Tale* about the Loch Ness Monster being seen in Little Todday and Great Todday I was off like a bullet out of a gun. I mean to say, I don't want to miss seeing this monster. Certainly not. Oh dear, what a pity they can't get it down to dear old London. What a drore it would be in the Zoo. Well, look at that Giant Pandar all the kids went so potty over.'

Captain MacKechnie looked puzzled.

'You know,' Mrs Odd said. 'That animal as looked like a teddy-bear dressed up for a pierrot.'

'Pierrot?' echoed the Skipper. He felt he should be familiar with anything that had to do with piers, but he was baffled.

'You know what a pierrot is. Those fellers with white faces and black pongpongs you'll hear singing on the pier, and on the beach too.'

'Is it oyster-catchers you're meaning, Mistress Ott?'

It was her turn to look puzzled.

'Well, I daresay they do catch oysters when there's an R in the month. And whelks and winkles when there isn't if it comes to that.'

'Ach, you'll have another dram, Mistress Ott,' the Skipper pressed.

'No, thanks, one's enough, or I'll be seeing monsters with pink spots. And I think I'll go and have a bit of a lay down now. I was arguing the point all night with the train.'

Mrs Odd retired to a corner of the saloon and drowsed gently until the *Island Queen* warned Snorvig with a series of long hoots that she was arriving.

The first person she met as she stepped ashore from the gang-board was Paul Waggett dressed in the suit of light blue tweed latticed with dark blue which with the passage of years had lost that bright Putney to Mortlake look.

'Hullo, Mr Waggett, how are you? What lovely weather the monster has brought with him, hasn't he? Well, I haven't wasted much time in getting here. It's a real excitement, isn't it?'

Paul Waggett stiffened.

'More excitement than real, I'm afraid, Mrs Odd,' he said, his nose expressing a superior scepticism, his lips trying to soften that superiority with a compassionate smile for weaker minds than his own.

'Oh, go on with you,' she laughed, digging him in the ribs. 'Don't be such an unbelieving Chinee.'

Any protest Waggett may have been on the point of making was quashed by the arrival of Joseph Macroon.

'Welcome back, Mistress Odd. How are they all in Nottingham?'

'Oh, everything in the garden's lovely in Nottingham. So the monster's come to Todday.'

'Ay, ay, the crayture reported here all correct. Kenny will tell you about it when you're crossing to Kiltod. The daisies are looking beautiful on Little Todday.'

While the *Morning Star* was chugging across the Coolish, as the stretch of water separating the two islands was called, Kenny Macroon gave Mrs Odd a full account of the monster's various appearances. Since Chrissie and Lizzie MacCodrum had seen it coming out of the sea by Tràigh Vooey, claims to have seen it had been put in from the banks of Loch Skinny and Loch Bob, but the general feeling was that both appearances were due to the jealousy of the people of Knockdown and Bobanish and indeed of the whole east side of Great Todday at the attention which the appearance of the monster had secured for the west side of Great Todday and for Little Todday. In fact jealousy was growing. A Nobost man had brought news of the monster's having been sighted off Mid Uist and Mr Carmichael, the *Daily Tale* representative, had chartered Drooby's *Flying Fish* to investigate that story, which everybody in both Toddays was sure was devoid of the least foundation.

'We'll be hearing from Peigi Bheag in a minute that the monster has been seen by the Coddy in Barra.'

Peigi Bheag was Joseph Macroon's third daughter and was now married to Neil MacNeil, one of the Barra schoolmasters. The Coddy exercised in Barra the same kind of influence as Roderick MacRurie in Great Todday or Kenny's father in Little Todday, and it may be added that both Roderick and Joseph recognized in the Coddy a foeman worthy of their steel. If the Coddy made up his mind to evacuate the monster to Barra it would be by no means an easy job to prevent him. He had already, according to general belief, persuaded the 'fillums' to deprive the Toddays of the *Cabinet Minister* and substitute for them the coast of Barra. Indeed, he had somehow managed to appear in the film of *Whisky*

Galore himself in the act of pouring out whisky from a pig at the *réiteach*, and though Big Roderick and Joseph Macroon had both appeared by name neither had been invited to appear in person.

'Well, we must keep a sharp look-out on Little Todday,' Mrs Odd declared. 'I know I shall and that's one sure thing. Ah, there's Duncan Bang. I wonder he hasn't seen the monster yet.'

Duncan Bàn Macroon was a Gaelic poet who when he inherited a croft from his grandmother had abandoned the University and the career intended for him as a schoolmaster. It was he who had found for Mrs Odd the cottage. Here he was on the pier at Kiltod, a man already in his forties but seeming always young with his glowing countenance and tumbled fair hair and eyes of kingfisher-blue.

'Ah, well, well, Mistress Odd, it's glad we are to have you back with us in the Isles of the Blest,' he said warmly, and soon he with Mrs Odd and her luggage were jogging in the trap on the only metalled road in the island, which ran from Kiltod to Tràigh Swish, a long beach of white sand facing the Atlantic. After a couple of miles they turned off to take the track that led across the rolling green machair to Duncan's own house called the House of the Bard, and a couple of hundred yards beyond Tigh nam Bàrd to a thatched cottage with thick white walls and small deep-set windows. This was Bow Bells.

The cottage was sheltered from the fury of the west by mounds of close-cropped grass starred with daisies and primroses, and above the sweet silence in which Bow Bells was set could be heard the long sigh of the ocean on this tranquil afternoon, a sigh that could sink to a whisper or rise to a moan and from a moan to a roar when the wind blew.

'Come in, Duncan, I've got something for you,' Mrs Odd told him.

It was a bottle of whisky.

'I oughtn't to encourage you,' she told him. 'But I like encouraging people.'

'*A Dhia*, you oughtn't to be spending your money on me, the terrible price that whisky is in these degenerate days. But you're quite right, Mistress Odd. There's nothing I like better than encouraging people whether it's whisky or piping or poetry. You'll just take a wee dram with me right off the reel.'

'But I had a whopper with Captain MacKechnie in his cabin. I can't have another so soon.'

'Yes, and you can now,' the poet insisted. 'Old friends don't meet again every day.'

So Mrs Odd and Duncan Bàn pledged one another.

'And here's jolly good luck to the monster,' she added. 'Funny you not having seen it yet. I mean to say when you think of all those fairies you've seen, most of them no bigger than wurzits, you'd have thought you was bound to see the monster.'

'Ah, well, he may not be so far away at all just now. Meanwhile, Florag Yocky will be coming along and I'll be away back home.'

Presently Florag, a fifteen-year-old daughter of Jocky Stewart, arrived to give Mrs Odd a hand with her unpacking. She was a plump apple-cheeked girl who devoted a couple of hours every morning to Mrs Odd when she was at Bow Bells and the rest of the day to work on her father's croft.

'Well, isn't it grand to be back on the island, Flo!' the old lady exclaimed. 'My goodness, you've widened out since last October, haven't you? You'll be as big a woman as your mother yet.'

Florag's mother, Bean Yocky, was the largest of several large women on the island, and her daughter pulled a face at the prospect.

'Don't you be looking down your nose at a bit of ombompong, Flo. Ombompong is much better for a girl than being all skin and grief. Well, it stands to reason. No man wants to cuddle a living skelington or a rasher of wind.'

'I wouldn't like to be so big as my mother,' Florag protested.

'Well, I daresay she is a bit too much Jumbo's only rival,' Mrs Odd admitted. 'But that's because she's tall with it. You take more after your dad. How is he?'

'He's quite all right.'

'How many cows has he got now?'

'Four cows, two heifers, and six stirks.'

'Good land alive. Buffalo Bill the Second! Look, I've brought you this.'

Mrs Odd presented Florag with a printed cotton frock.

'If it's too small for you give it to your sister Annie and I'll get you another one.'

However, fortunately for Florag's anxiety about her figure, the frock was not too small.

'It's lovely,' Florag breathed reverently. 'It's really lovely, Mistress Odd.'

'Yes, if the monster catches sight of you in that frock you'll get the best view of him anybody's had yet.'

'*A Mhuire, Mhuire*, don't be saying such a thing, Mistress Odd,' Florag gasped.

'Wouldn't you like to get a good view of this mysterious creature?'

'Indeed, no, I'd be falling down dead with fright, I'm sure.'

'Oh, well, if we all thought alike it would be a dull world,' said Mrs Odd. 'Now, there's nothing would give me more pleasure than to look out of the window at this very moment and see the monster rolling in through the garden gate.'

As she spoke there was a loud rap on the door and Florag screamed.

'*A Mhuire Mhathair*, it's coming to attack us.'

But it was Father James Macalister come to greet Mrs Odd.

'Duncan was telling me you'd just arrived. Well, well, *ceud mìle fàilte*,' he said sonorously.

'Well, whatever it is, the same to you, Father James. Florag thought you was the monster.'

'Ay, and she'll be sure I am next Sunday if she and the rest of the choir don't sing more in tune.' He shook his head reproachfully. 'Oh, great sticks, it was really terrible. Do you know what cacophony is, *a Fhlorag?*'

'No, Father,' she mumbled.

'Well, you'll know what it is next Sunday if you do it again. And how's Peigi Ealasaid and my old friend the Sergeant-major?'

'Both in the best of pink,' Mrs Odd told him. 'And the two kids too. We're expecting another in September. And which means I'll have to get back earlier this year.'

'All the same, it's great news. Is Peggy giving them plenty of Gaelic?'

'Oh, she lays into them in Garlic all right when they're naughty, and that means most of the time.'

'Good shooting! The naughtier they are the better I'll be pleased.'

'All I hope is I'll get a peep at the monster before I go back to Nottingham.'

'Ah, well, I hope you will. But you know it's a strange business right enough. The Biffer was over yesterday morning telling me what he saw in that cave, and if he saw it, and he's a good man is Airchie, it's something none of us have ever seen before.'

That evening in spite of anything Florag could say to dissuade her Mrs Odd went for a walk by herself along Tràigh Swish.

To her immense disappointment she saw nothing that the moonlight could charm into the shape of a monster. There was only the shimmering expanse of the Atlantic and the run of the sea lacing the white sand and the call of the whimbrel to welcome the merry month of May.

A month passed without anybody on either of the Toddays even imagining that he or she had seen the monster. Ian Carmichael went back to Glasgow after investigating one or two claims from other islands that it had been seen. The Editor of the *Scottish Daily Tale* decided that the story from which he had hoped so much had petered out like all too many another, and cancelled the arrangement for Hector Hamish Mackay to visit the two Toddays. Even the weather proved that it had flattered only to deceive and during the second week of that disillusioning month turned to a cold drench of rain followed by a chill wind from the east that blew for ten days and threatened to ruin the grazing.

It was, in the words of Mrs Odd, really chronic, and the only cheerful person on the two islands was Paul Waggett, who stopped all he met to let them hear him congratulate himself on his own acumen in having refused from the first to accept the appearance of the monster as a fact.

At home he lost no opportunity of reminding his twin daughters how lucky they were to have such a judicious father and thus had been prevented from indulging in the credulity of the many.

'Boys,' said the Biffer one evening in the Snorvig bar, 'I never came so near to hitting a man as I came to hitting Wackett this afternoon. Do you know what the clown was after asking me?' A sympathetic murmur of interrogation was heard. 'He was asking me as chicky as you like if I wass after seeing any more otters in Uamh na Snaoiseanaich. Me who has taken more otters than any man in Todaidh Mór!'

'*Seadh, seadh!*' the company agreed.

' "The Lord forgive you, Mr Wackett," I wass saying. "The Lord forgive you," just like that, "if you're after thinking it was an otter I was seeing," and I was minded to say "And if you think yon crayture was an otter you'll be thinking Sahtan is the minister," ay, and I would have said it if I wasn't thinking with the evil that's in him he would be running to the Reverend Angus and telling him I wass after saying he was no better than Sahtan. And I wouldn't like to be hurting the feelings of the wee man, I wouldn't that. *A Chruitheir*, the clown will be asking next if it was a cock-lobster or a hen-lobster I was seeing in Uamh na Snaoiseanaich. Well, well, well, well!'

The Biffer called for a dram, and stood for ten minutes in moody and silent reflection upon the enormity of Paul Waggett's insinuation.

'*Mac an diabhuil*,' he muttered at last, and then he walked out of the bar without even bidding the company good-night.

'Ah, poor Airchie,' said somebody. 'He took it very bad that Wackett would be saying it was an otter he was seeing.'

'He'd petter not be saying to me that it wass an otter Chrissie and Lizzie were seeing of Tràigh Vooey,' said Sammy MacCodrum fiercely. 'He'd have plenty enough to say if the Home Cart was telling him that Hitler wass chust an otter.'

'*Bhitheadh gu dearbh*,' the company murmured in approval.

Over on the mainland the spirits of Ben Nevis rose steadily under the absence of any more news of a monster in the Islands. Indeed, they became boisterous when a rumour reached Glenbogle that one of the monks at Fort Augustus had sighted the monster in Loch Ness apparently as lively as ever. However, the rumour proved baseless. No monk at Fort Augustus had caught a glimpse of the monster since those two novices who had reported the appearance of its forked tail. Nor was the story believed of a tinker who declared that as he was trudging behind his cart between Drumnadrochit and Inverness just after dark a huge head had come out of the loch and drenched him with water. It was generally believed that he had fallen into the loch and invented the story to quieten his wife who was known everywhere as a relentless scold with a tongue as long as the monster itself.

However, as the weeks went by without any news of the monster even the high spirits of Ben Nevis began to flag. He enjoyed a brief exhilaration when word came from the clachan of Ballyhoo that old Ailean Ruadh, now close on ninety, had seen a strange dark object in Loch Hoo. Alas, when he reached the old man's little black house in which he lived alone he found that he had merely expressed a wish that he could be seeing something in the waters of Loch Hoo because he was sure that if he did, himself, and that was Ben Nevis, would be bringing him a bottle of whisky, the taste of which he had not savoured for 'munss *agus* munss *agus* munss,' so hard was it for him with the 'roomatiss' that was on him to get Lloyd George's pension for himself and a dram in Kenspeckle at the same time.

Ben Nevis was shocked by the old man's invalid state and gave orders that a bottle of Glenbogle's Pride was to be sent to him once a month to fortify the brief time that was obviously all that was left to him in this world.

In Inverness itself pessimism deepened steadily. There was now a growing body of defeatist opinion to argue that the monster really had been killed by a flying saucer, and the fact that catastrophe had occurred in the month of March meant that the problem of the monster's fate could be written off as an attraction for the summer season. It was small consolation to be able to feel more certain than ever that the monster must have been real because it had not been seen since its collision with the flying saucer. As for the Todday Monster, people in Inverness just smiled contemptuously and recalled that for the last fifteen years monsters had been appearing at intervals all over the world but had all vanished as soon as their appearance had been reported. The only permanent feature in the world of monsters had been the Loch Ness Monster and except during the war nobody could remember nearly three months passing without seeing at least one of its humps. Not even a hump had been signalled since that flying saucer had gone whizzing down the loch on its destructive mission.

'Och, it's like driving a funeral to be driving Ben Nevis beside the loch these days,' grumbled Johnnie Macpherson. 'And there's no arguing with the man. It's always "you're driving too fast, Johnnie," and me crawling along at ten miles an hour for him to think every dirty little bit of an old log he sees may be the monster and squeezing himself out of the car just to squeeze himself in again and tell me it's only a bit of wood and then grunting and grumbling to himself because he hasn't got the old Daimler any more. It's just getting on my nerves altogether, and the wind as cold as if it was winter.'

And then, when the only monsters left in the world all seemed to have retired behind the Iron Curtain, the east wind died away, leaving a blue sky behind it, to welcome June, and the Todday Monster appeared again on the unimpeachable testimony of Mrs Odd.

Chapter 7

MRS ODD AND THE MONSTER

'Many and fair are the long white beaches that stretch beside the western shores of the islands at the edge of the mighty Atlantic, but none is fairer than lovely Tràigh Swish of Little Todday. Philologists differ about the origin of the name. So let us fly backwards out of the prosaic present upon "the viewless wings of poesy" and accept the derivation from Suis, a Norse princess of long ago who, legend relates, flung herself into the ocean from that grey rock which marks the southern boundary of the strand. Alas, her love for a young bard of Todaidh Beag, as Little Todday is called in the old sweet speech of the Gael, was foredoomed.'

Little did Hector Hamish Mackay think when he wrote those words in *Faerie Lands Forlorn*, which none need hesitate to call the romantic vade cum mecum of everybody privileged to explore the Outer Isles, little did he think that one day that grey rock, or rather to be more precise, that small grey headland, after a placid existence for hundreds of years ever since a Norse princess chose it as a medium for suicide, would again inspire his eloquence.

The topographer himself, whose pages in the words of an enthusiastic reviewer are 'literally scented with the breath of the moorland and hold in their magical descriptions the sound of the sea as in a shell', was a small man in a kilt with slightly shrivelled but well-weathered knees, a prim Edinburgh accent, and spectacles.

Disappointed by the cancellation of his assignment to the Todday Monster by the editor of the *Scottish Daily Tale*, he had found the east wind that May more than usually trying, and when at the beginning of June the weather forecast of the B.B.C. announced a spell of fine weather along the western seaboard of Scotland the topographer was seized with an impulse to take the road to the isles without bothering about getting his expenses guaranteed by the *Daily Tale*. It was probably nothing more remarkable than a mild attack of wanderlust, but in a new and revised edition of *Faerie Lands Forlorn* Mr Mackay has speculated whether that sudden impulse to go west may not have had a supernatural prompting; it must be admitted that the coincidence of his arrival at Snorvig when he did was most remarkable, even if we can find a prosaic explanation for the voice that seemed to whisper in his ear 'Go at once to Kiltod' in the fact that every room in the Snorvig Hotel was taken by the members of the Land Court, who were in session to decide disputes about the removal of neighbours' landmarks and the trespasses of cows and hens.

Certainly Hector Hamish Mackay did go to Kiltod as soon as Joseph Macroon had put the mailbags and the stores in the *Morning Star* and without doubt he did decide, after a delicious high tea in which a lobster with a larger and juicier claw than Edinburgh ever dreamed of played a noble part, to walk across the island to Tràigh Swish. We may attribute that walk to the prompting of a voice that whispered in his ear the place we should visit or, if we insist on the humdrum, to the prompting of the topographer's own digestion.

Mr Mackay avoided the metalled road and followed the winding grassy tracks across the undulating machair dotted with grazing cows and stirks, gilded with buttercups and powdered with eyebright and daisies. From time to time Mr Mackay would plant in the turf his stout cromag cut from a hazel and indulge in a kind of pole-jump, his glasses flashing in the eye of the westering sun as he leapt triumphantly from one knoll to another. Mr Mackay reached the edge of rolling dunes that backed the length of the long white beach between Carraig an Ròin and Ard Swish. He debated whether he should walk north, where the sand was firm by the edge of the tide which had began to flow about half an hour ago, toward the grey rock shaped like an immense seal which legend related was the petrified shape of the seal-woman from whom the Macroons sprang, or whether he should turn southward to Ard Swish. He chose the latter direction and was within forty yards of the narrow natural arch which led through Ard Swish to a small cave beyond Tràigh Veck (Bheag) when suddenly from the arch appeared a plump rosy-faced old woman with snow-white hair.

'The monster, the monster,' she was crying. 'Come on, Rob Roy, or whatever you call yourself. It's the monster.'

Mr Mackay ran up the beach in a diagonal as fast as he could on sand that grew softer as he neared the headland, the end of which was never unwashed by the sea even at the lowest ebb of a spring tide.

Mrs Odd, for of course it was she, had turned back under the natural arch and a moment or two later Mr Mackay found her standing in the further entrance of the arch gazing out to sea.

'You weren't nippy enough,' she said. 'It was here when I came hollering through to tell you to hurry.'

'I did run as fast as I could,' Mr Mackay panted. 'But what was it you saw?'

'What was it I sore? I saw the monster as near as you're standing to me now,' she declared.

'You did? Please tell me all about it. My name is Mackay – Hector Hamish Mackay.'

'Hi! Hi! Hi! Mr Mackay, take me with you when you fly, back to the Isle of Skye,' she hummed. 'Here, are you the feller as wrote that book Duncan Bang gave me the loan of to read? I remember your name because I remember it looked like a sneeze in the middle, and Duncan said it was the same as James. "Well," I said, "poor old James must have had a shocking bad cold in the head when he wrote his name like that." Yes, and you spelt "fairy" wrong, and which did surprise me because I thought people as wrote books had to know how to spell.'

'Spenser spelt it the way I do.'

'Then Spencer ought to have known better. I lay Marks wouldn't have spelt it that way or his name wouldn't have been Marks. Yes, but never mind about the alphabet, it's the monster I want to talk about.'

'So do I,' said Mr Mackay fervidly.

'Well, sit down and I'll tell you about it. I'm Mrs Odd. Mistress Odd they call me here, and which I'm bound to say I like.'

'We still use the prefix in Edinburgh.'

'In Eddingborough, do you? I'll have to pop in and have a look at Eddingborough one of these days. Yes, my boy Fred married the fourth of Joseph Macroon's Peggies. We all live in Nottingham. But every summer I come to Little Todday and where I have a cottage near Duncan Bang. My goodness, won't Duncan be hopping mad when he hears I've seen the monster and he hasn't.'

'I know Duncan Bàn Macroon well. It's high time a volume of his poetry was published. He's a real bard.'

'Well, to get on with my story. As soon as I read about the monster in the *Daily Tale* wild horses couldn't have kept me in Nottingham, and up I came to Little Todday. There's hardly a day passed since I came up but what I've gone for a peep at the sea, and the weather has been chronic until now, but the monster wasn't having any, and that feller

Waggett was sniffing about there being no such a thing as the monster. An invention, he called it. "Well," I said, "Mr Waggett, so was arioplanes an invention, but that doesn't say there's no such a thing as an arioplane as you'd soon have found out if you'd been in dear old London when there was a war on." Oh, I've no patience with that nosey-parkering Know All. And fancy calling that great yellow dog of his "Monty". What a liberty! Just for the pleasure of ordering him about and swanking he's a Commandering-Chief himself. I only wish the monster could have got his teeth into him the same as he nearly did into me.'

'His teeth?'

'I never saw such teeth on any animal. Well, I said to myself, "shall I walk up the beach or down the beach this afternoon?" And I picked a dandelion and blew its fluff off the same as we used to blow them when we was kids for he loves me and he loves me not when anybody was potty on some soppy boy. And the last bit of fluff said "down the beach". So I took my umbreller, and which I always do, wet or fine, because you never know what you want to poke at when you're out for a toddle. And a good job it was I did take my umbreller, for if I hadn't of I reckon the monster would have been worrying me instead of worrying the beach like a dog worries a rat.'

'But where was this creature and what was it like?' Mr Mackay asked.

'I'm telling you, I was walking down the beach to what they call Ard Swish and when I come to the arch, and which is more of a tunnel really, I thought I'd have a look see on the other side as the tide was out. So I walked through thinking to myself how strong it smelt of bloaters, and when I come out on the other side I saw a brute as big as an elephant cloring up the sand with its teeth and I said "Oo-er!" and whipped open my umbreller, and which I always do if one of Buffalo Bill's cows come prancing about too close for comfort. And the monster let out a noise something between a bark and a moo and a groan and went plunging down the beach into the water, and I came running back through the arch and saw you and hollered out but you was too slow and when you got here the monster had dived and where it is now, well, that's anybody's guess.'

'Do you think it could have been an exceptionally large seal?' Mr Mackay asked.

'Don't be silly, my dear man. I know what seals look like. Good land alive, when I've been out lobstering with Kenny I've seen any number of seals bobbing up out of the water all round us and all of 'em looking the spitting image of my butcher in Nottingham. Name of Dumpleton. Well, poor old Dumpleton wouldn't win a prize for his face at a beauty competition, but he doesn't wear his teeth outside. And what teeth! Like a row of pickaxes. Well, I'm not easily scared, but when I sore it cloring up the sand . . . well, you can see for yourself what a mess it's made of the beach.'

And sure enough when Mr Mackay looked at the sand it was scored and striated in every direction, and not a footmark anywhere to suggest that a human being had been elaborating a hoax.

'Could you give me some idea of the shape of this strange creature, Mistress Odd?' Mr Mackay asked.

'It was no shape at all, only just a whopper, but mark you when I came out of the arch and saw this large animal cloring up the beach I was properly scared, and I daresay if I hadn't of opened my umbreller it would have clawed me up the same as the beach. One thing I noticed, the brute's head was covered with hair.'

'Like a horse's mane?' Mr Mackay asked quickly.

'No, more like Jo-Jo.'

'I beg your pardon?'

'Jo-Jo, the dog-faced man from Siberia.'

'I'm afraid I still don't quite follow. Not a Communist?'

'Communist, no. They wasn't invented then. One of Barnum's Freaks.'

'Ah, I never saw them, I'm afraid. You may remember, Mistress Odd, that young Kenny Macroon compared the back of the head of the creature he saw to a hornless bull.'

'That's right, it was all hunched up like a bull and a kind of yellowish-brown colour on top. But Kenny only saw the brute's back. He never saw those shocking teeth.'

'Yes, of course, the teeth. And it was the teeth which impressed Archie MacRurie and MacCodrum's two little girls.'

'Well, small wonder. Look at the beach. That was done by these teeth. I tell you they was like pickaxes.'

'Most interesting, most interesting,' Mr Mackay murmured to himself. 'Oh dear, oh dear, if only that sand hadn't been so soft.'

He gazed across the empty ocean.

'It looks as if I will have to abandon my theory,' he said at last. 'No, I don't think this mysterious creature can be the Loch Ness Monster.'

Five days later the readers of the *Scottish Daily Tale* were invited by the Editor to study carefully the article contributed by Mr Hector Hamish Mackay and try to win £250 offered by the *Daily Tale* for the first properly authenticated photograph of the monster whose existence had been reported from various islands in the Outer Hebrides, and more particularly from Great and Little Todday. The article in question will still be fresh in the public memory, but no apology is offered for taking advantage of Mr Hector Hamish Mackay's generous permission to reproduce it here:

Edinburgh had been ravaged for nearly a fortnight by a ruthless and persistent east wind and even I than whom our noble capital knows no more devoted citizen was beginning to weary of such an unkind May. I mention this because I do not want to exclude a natural explanation for the sudden impulse to leave Edinburgh and revisit the Western Isles. Nevertheless, as will presently transpire, I cannot but regard it as something more fatefully* pregnant than a mere coincidence, for if I had not made up my mind to board the good ship *Island Queen* just when I did I should have missed almost the greatest thrill of a life that has been granted more than a modicum of thrills. Do we not all too often dismiss the 'divinity that shapes our ends' as coincidence? I trow we do.

Nor did what I must with all reverence call the guiding hand of Providence relax its grasp upon my shoulder when I reached the picturesque little port of Snorvig in Great Todday, for I was unable to enjoy the lavish cheer of mine host and old friend Roderick MacRurie owing to the demands made upon the spatial accommodation of the Snorvig Hotel by the 'most potent, grave, and reverend signiors' of the Land Court. As a result I begged shelter of another old friend Joseph Macroon at his hospitable house in Kiltod, the diminutive port of Little Todday, two miles away across the strait that divides the two islands. From here after a sumptuous tea I set out across the rolling machair, which for the benefit of those unfamiliar with the tongue our first parents spoke in Eden, means the grassy land found all along the west of the Outer Isles. I was all agog to see again the three-mile long beach of Tràigh Swish on whose glittering white sands the breakers of the mighty Atlantic murmur or roar according to Neptune's mood.

I might have turned in either direction. The guiding hand of Providence turned my steps in a southerly direction toward the granite headland known as Ard Swish which is pierced by a natural arch some ten yards long which leads to a small sandy cove beyond known as Tràigh Veck, or more correctly Bheag.

As I drew near I was hailed by a female form and bidden to make all haste. Alas, in spite of my efforts I arrived just too late to see the Todday Monster which only a minute or two before had been savagely tearing up the beach with its huge teeth.

* An overzealous sub-editor changed 'fatefully' to 'fatally' in the original article.

But I was able to see the scars this creature of the primeval deep had made and I was able to note that there was not a single footprint upon that beach, proving conclusively that Mrs Lucy Odd had not ventured beyond the opening of the arch from which she had seen the monster. Mrs Odd is the mother of ex-Sergeant-major Alfred Odd, who when occupied with the business of Mars during the war in training the stalwart men of the two Toddays to resist invasion was smiled upon by Venus, or in other words wooed and won Peggy Macroon, one of Mr Joseph Macroon's lovely daughters.

A word about Mrs Lucy Odd. She is a Londoner born and bred, and for a woman some years past the allotted span of a truly remarkable vigour and alertness. Her courage may be realized when instead of fainting or fleeing when she surprised the monster upon the beach of Tràigh Veck she opened her umbrella and drove it back into the sea. Mrs Odd's encounter with the monster confirms the existence of its unusual teeth which had already been noted by Mr Archie MacRurie of Snorvig and by little Cairistiona and Ealasaid MacCodrum of Garryboo. Mr Kenneth Macroon, it may be recalled, only saw the monster's yellowish-brown back.

I have never had the slightest doubt about the accuracy of the previous stories, but I confess that until I saw with my own eyes the condition of the sand in Tràigh Veck I had been inclined to suppose that the teeth of the monster may not have been quite so large as it now appears certain they are. In venturing that opinion I allowed my judgement to be influenced by prejudice and freely admit it. I had put forward a suggestion, based on my belief in the existence of a male and female Loch Ness Monster, that if one of them had been killed by the flying saucer the survivor would probably seek another mate for itself on our western seaboard. Therefore, let me be frank, I was anxious to identify the Todday Monster with what we know about the Loch Ness Monster. That theory is no longer tenable. The Todday Monster is as large as an elephant according to Mrs Odd, but it definitely lacks the length of body we have learned to associate with the Loch Ness Monster. I discard as fanciful and even absurd the theory that the Loch Ness Monster in the manner of certain lizards disencumbered itself of its tail when it met the flying saucer.

I shall remind such theorists that not a single one of the authenticated descriptions of the Loch Ness Monster makes any mention of these enormous teeth which are the outstanding feature of the Todday Monster. The story that it had been seen crossing the road by Drumnadrochit with a sheep in its mouth was almost immediately discredited. Everything we know about the Loch Ness Monster indicates that it is – I still hope I do not have to say 'was' – a placid and even amiable vegetarian. The grief felt in Inverness when the news was published of its possible slaughter by a flying saucer expressed the genuine affection which the Loch Ness Monster had roused all over the North.

Furthermore, another characteristic of the Loch Ness Monster is – or was – its mane. Those who have seen the Todday Monster are unanimous in declaring that it does not possess a mane, and though Mr Kenneth Macroon who saw the back of the Todday Monster was at first under the impression that he saw a mane he is convinced that this mane was in fact a long streamer of sea-weed the yellowish-brown tint of which led him to suppose that it formed part of a capillary growth on the monster's neck.

There were a few theorists who maintained the possibility of the Loch Ness Monster's mane having been burnt off by the flying saucer. I find it easier to believe that the monster which had been observed at close quarters by five people in Great and Little Todday has revealed the existence of a great mammal or saurian hitherto unknown to science. We are only at the beginning of what should be a period of intensive observation throughout the length of our western seaboard. The new monster has probably been sighted in several other islands besides Great and Little Todday, and there is no reason why we should not presently hear from Lewis or Harris or Barra, not to mention the Inner Isles, of as close an encounter with it as was enjoyed by Mrs Odd on Little Todday.

I am myself determined to devote the whole of this summer to searching for the monster, for I cannot believe that the guiding hand of Providence directed me to Tràigh Swish at that moment merely to leave my curiosity baulked.

In conclusion, I should like to express to the people of Inverness-shire my sincere hope that the Loch Ness Monster or its mate will soon be seen rushing across the silvery water in sportive zest. At any rate, wherever the Loch Ness Monster may be at the present moment the people of Inverness-shire can feel completely confident that it has not emigrated to the West.

And yet one more word. While admittedly the Todday Monster's teeth must make the most ardent naturalist pause and reflect before he decides that it is as harmless as the Loch Ness Monster, I think the fact of its retreat before Mrs Odd's expanded umbrella may well be an indication that it is a shy, even a timorous creature in spite of its teeth, and that, given the requisite prudence, there is no reason why what in the world of the silver screen is called a 'close up' should not be obtained of it.

'Of course, that's the kind of thing that gives the Press a bad name,' Paul Waggett commented after he had read Hector Mackay's article. 'I'm glad *my* paper hasn't lost its head.'

'But all the people here are sure that Mrs Odd did see the monster,' one of the chicks cheeped.

'The people here will believe anything,' said Waggett severely. 'Only the other day Calum MacKillop was assuring me that if you stuck hairs from a horse's tail in a burn they would turn into eels. And when I told him that was nonsense he was ready to argue with me that he had seen it happen, starting with the eyes.'

'But, Daddo, Mrs Odd can't have just imagined she saw a monster as big as an elephant,' said Muriel.

'And Mr Mackay saw the marks on the beach made by the monster's teeth just after Mrs Odd saw it,' Elsie added.

'I don't know where you two girls get your credulity from,' said their father, looking sternly at his wife, who was longing to keep out of the domestic argument by concentrating hard on her knitting.

'Oh, I'm sure you're right, Paul,' she said hastily.

'Of course, I'm right. This is just a disgraceful stunt. £250 reward! That means we shall have all the ragtag and bobtail of the country swarming up here this summer and running wild over both islands, disturbing the birds and upsetting the fish on the excuse that they're looking for a monster which every sensible man knows doesn't exist.'

Over in Glenbogle the reaction of Ben Nevis to the article of Hector Hamish Mackay was almost entirely favourable at first.

'I'm glad this writing chap has discovered that he was wrong,' he observed, 'and what is more that he's had the decency to admit his mistake. Of course it was a peprosterous theory, but the more peprosterous any theory is nowadays with this Bolshie Government of ours the more nincompoops there are ready to gobble it up like a lot of quacking ducks. The only thing I don't quite like is the way this writing fellow talks as if there was a possibility that our monster had been killed by this flying brute. I don't accept that, Trixie.'

'Donald dear, I know you don't,' the Lady of Ben Nevis boomed gently.

And in the tone of her reply there was a hint of her having had ample opportunity already to appreciate her husband's point of view in this matter.

'However, he's not gloating as I'm told they have been in Argyll. Just let me hear that one of these Campbells claims to have seen our monster in Loch Fyne or Loch Awe. That's what I said to Hugh Cameron the other day. "Hugh," I said, "if these Campbells try and pretend they've got our monster in Loch Fyne or Loch Awe I shall send round the fiery cross. If Lochiel and Sleat like to stand for that sort of thing I'm jolly well not going to. I'll march through the Pass of Brander with my pipers playing *Macdonald is here*. By Jove, I'll march through Inveraray itself if they aren't careful." '

'I hope Hugh didn't encourage you in such wild nonsense.'

'Wild nonsense? Ha – Ha! Dear old Trixie, you're still stuffed with all these cautious English ideas, aren't you? As a matter of fact, Hugh himself wasn't as much excited by the idea as I thought he would be. Apparently, he got what Dr MacGregor calls a chill on the liver during that infernal east wind, so I suppose the old boy was feeling low. However, young Walter Dutton, whom he's going to formally adopt as the heir to Kilwhillie this autumn, had a gleam in his eye. A good lad that. Pity he has to go back to his regiment in a day or two.'

'He's an extremely nice young man with very good manners,' Mrs MacDonald said. 'And I hope you won't fill his head with wild notions, Donald.'

'You never could understand what I feel about Campbells, Trixie. And of course Macintoshes too.'

'I've had plenty of opportunity to learn,' she observed.

It was with thoughts of Campbell's unscrupulousness playing leapfrog with anxious glances at Loch Ness that Ben Nevis drove to Inverness next day.

'Good morning, Ben Nevis. I hope you're keeping well in this lovely June weather,' said Maclean, the dapper porter, after the Chieftain had extricated himself from the swing-door of the Porridge Hotel, which he swung with such vigour that he had to go round with it twice before he emerged in the hall.

'I always keep well, Maclean, but Kilwhillie has had what they call a chill on the liver.'

'Tut-tut. I'm sorry to be hearing that. Nasty things livers.'

'Beastly!' the Chieftain woofed. 'Well, you've seen in the *Daily Tale* that this writing fellow Mackay has given up his idiotic notion about our monster having gone to the Islands?'

'I did indeed, Ben Nevis. But they're not at all pleased about it in Inverness.'

'Do you mean to say they wanted our monster to go gallivanting off to the Islands? That's that Bolshie Councillor Macaulay from Lewis, I suppose. I always say I have a great respect for Lewismen, but once a Lewisman gets an idea into his head nothing will knock it out, nothing. I'm glad he's the only Lewisman we have on the Inverness-shire Council. I'm told nobody dares say a word in Dingwall at the Ross-shire meetings for fear of upsetting them all in Stornoway.'

'No, no, Ben Nevis, it wasn't that anybody here wanted the Loch Ness Monster to go to the Islands. The trouble is Obaig.'

'You don't mean to say Dunstaffnage is saying he's seen our monster in Loch Etive?'

'No, no, no, Ben Nevis, the Captain of Dunstaffnage hasn't said a word about the monster. No, it's the hotels.'

'Hotels?'

'Yes, the hotels here think that the *Daily Tale* was put up to offer this £250 reward by the Obaig people. They reckon this monster in the Islands will be a big attraction to the Americans.'

'What do Americans want with £250? They're rolling in dollars.'

'Ach, it's not the money, Ben Nevis. It's the advertisement. They're reckoning in Obaig that, whatever the weather, they'll have the best season ever.'

'Well, of course I had a feeling that the Argyll people would cash in on this. I was saying so to Kilwhillie. You're a Maclean.'

'I'm a Maclean right enough.'

'Well, I don't have to tell you that you simply cannot trust a Campbell. I never thought about this hotel business. My idea was they might try and say our monster had gone to Loch Fyne or Loch Awe, and in that case I was prepared to take strong measures. But this sneaking hotel business is just the way the Campbells would go to work. However, I'll stop their little game.'

'And how will you be doing that?' Maclean asked.

And for answer Ben Nevis indulged in a gesture in which few had seen him indulge. He put a finger to his great eagle's beak and winked slowly at the dapper porter of the Porridge Hotel.

Chapter 8

LOVE AT FIRST SIGHT

Mr Sydney Prew, the Secretary of the National Union of Hikers, sat in his office at 702 Gower Street and, his lips tightly pursed, looked at what he called the mountain of correspondence on his desk.

'I've never known so many inquiries about camping sites for so early in June, Miss Wriggleston.'

Mr Prew's amanuensis, a thin woman in her mid-forties, sighed sympathetically. She had not yet abandoned hope of luring Mr Prew into matrimony, though she had been luring away now for over ten years and all her friends assured her that he was a confirmed old maid.

'It's this monster they've been seeing in the Hebrides, Mr Prew.'

'Yes, yes, I'm sure it is,' he agreed. 'Dear me, it's about twelve years since I was in the Highlands, and I've never been to the Islands at all. I'd like to go before I retire from active service.'

'Retire, Mr Prew?' Miss Wriggleston echoed apprehensively.

'Well, in another three years when I shall be sixty I think it will be my duty to resign and give way to a younger pair of knees.'

Mr Prew tittered to himself at this affectionate little allusion to the hiker's costume.

'Not that I shall give up hiking of course,' he added quickly. 'No indeed. To paraphrase that grand song of Harry Lauder's, I intend to hike right on to the end of the road.'

The shrivelled little man with the eyes of a kindly old maid gazed out of the grimy window of the Gower Street office at the June sky above Bloomsbury. Could Miss Wriggleston but have known it, he had divested himself of his trousers in fancy and was pulling on the old shorts to feel once more the light summer breeze playing round his spidery legs.

'I think I shall suggest to the Acting President that I will take my vacation in a week or two's time, instead of waiting until August as usual.'

'I wish I could take mine then,' Miss Wriggleston said.

'Yes, well, I'm afraid the office cannot spare both of us simultaneously.'

He did not think that his amanuensis had seriously intended to sigh for the unattainable in the shape of a hiking duet with himself, but it was just as well to make its utter unattainableness perfectly clear. He turned back to the mountain of letters.

'Nobody loves young people more than I do, but I do think they are getting rather lazy,' he commented after reading through another half dozen. 'One can understand inquiries about how to get to Great Todday, but I do not think it necessary to ask whether it is better to go from Euston or King's Cross to Glasgow and certainly not to ask us to send them a selection of trains.'

Just then there was a knock on the door, and a young man in his mid-twenties came into the office, a large but lanky young man with dark wavy hair, a good-looking, indeed a handsome young man in a slightly farouche way.

'Oh, good morning,' he said, scowling with shyness. 'I'm sorry to bother you but I was told you might be able to help me.'

'Quite, quite. We're always glad to do that. You're a member of the N.U.H. of course?'

'I beg your pardon?'

'The National Union of Hikers.'

'Well, I'm not actually, but I'd like to be. It was Lord Buntingdon who advised me to come and see you.'

'Ah, Lord Buntingdon, our revered President.'

'Yes, he very kindly asked me down to Ouse Hall to study his tortoises. It's the most wonderful collection of tortoises in the world.'

'I know, I know,' said Mr Prew crisply. 'Though, alas, I'm not' – he played for a moment with the word 'testudinologist' but rejected it – 'I'm not a tortoise man myself. May I have your name?'

'Brownsworth. W. W. Brownsworth.'

'Might we have the prefix in full? Miss Wriggleston, will you be good enough?'

'William Waterlow Brownsworth, 22 Wilberforce Gardens, sw7.'

'The annual subscription is five shillings,' said Miss Wriggleston brightly when she had entered those details. 'You'd like a badge, of course?'

'Oh, thank you very much.'

She took from a drawer the green badge with the device of two crossed staffs in white above the motto – *Hike On, Hike Ever.*

'That will be another half a crown.'

Brownsworth forked out.

'Let me shake hands to welcome the latest member of our great Union, and a friend of Lord Buntingdon,' said Mr Prew.

Brownsworth gulped.

'I don't think I can exactly call him a friend. I mean to say when I wrote to ask him if I could visit his tortoises he very kindly asked me to come down to Ouse Hall and when I told him that I was a keen member of the Society of Palaeontological Research and wanted to go into the question of this mysterious creature reported from the Hebrides he advised me to consult you about accommodation and all that sort of thing. He said you knew every corner of Britain.'

'Oh, that's too generous of Lord Buntingdon. Wonderful man, isn't he? Almost the last great Liberal we have left. Dear me, I fear that such peers as Lord Buntingdon will ere long themselves pass into the domain of palaeontology.'

'I spent a fortnight last year investigating the Loch Ness Monster in the hope of being able to link it up with a plesiosaurus, an ichthyosaurus, or indeed with any of the megalosaurs.'

'Quite, quite. Most interesting, I imagine.'

'I wasn't satisfied by the evidence,' said Brownsworth. 'To be frank, I'm not convinced that the Loch Ness Monster exists. The evidence for the existence of this strange creature on the western seaboard of Scotland looks on paper much more solid.'

'I wouldn't know,' said Mr Prew, who found in the catchphrase of the moment an elixir of youth.

'So I thought I would go and investigate for myself on this island, Great Todday, and what I was wondering about is accommodation.'

Mr Prew shook his head.

'I'm afraid a good many people are wondering about that. There is an hotel at Snorvig, the port of Great Todday, and one Joseph Macroon can board and lodge three or four visitors on Little Todday. Some of the crofters on both islands offer accommodation in the season to visitors who do not ask for the amenities of a fashionable seaside resort. However, I have been satisfied that for the rest of the summer there is no possibility of accommodating any more visitors.'

'I see,' said the young palaeontologist in a depressed voice. Then he brightened. 'But couldn't I camp out?'

'My dear sir, of course you can camp out,' Mr Prew replied with enthusiasm. 'And I fancy I may venture to presume that Lord Buntingdon sent you to me because with that extraordinary sagacity of his he expected that if you wanted to spend any time in Great or Little Todday you would only be able to carry out such a project if you were prepared to camp out.'

'And Mr Prew has forgotten more about camping out than most people ever knew,' Miss Wriggleston interposed.

'I'm afraid Miss Wriggleston's enthusiasm makes for exaggeration,' said Mr Prew modestly. 'But I suppose I have studied the art of camping out more intensively than most people. Where haven't I camped out? The Gobi Desert, the Kalahari Desert, the island of Tiburon in the Californian Gulf, on the slopes of Cotopaxi, in Patagonia, among the hairy Ainus in northern Japan, and perhaps most often of all in that wild no man's land where Burma marches with China.'

'I say I do envy you, Mr Prew,' the young palaeontologist gulped in admiration.

'Oh, I mustn't give you the idea that I have actually visited those places in the flesh. No, no. I'm afraid I must wait until my ship comes home before I manage to do that.' And then, feeling that his phraseology was becoming a little old-fashioned, he suddenly leant across his desk, and pointing at his visitor and allowing his kindly old maid's eyes to glitter with a demoniac knowledgeableness he ejaculated:

'Sez you!'

Brownsworth was sure that he was meant to laugh at this point, but he was not perfectly sure and so instead he twisted his mouth into a clumsy smile.

'But don't be downhearted,' said Mr Prew, who did not realize that his visitor was smiling. 'I do know a great deal from practical experience about camping out in the Highlands, and I don't think the technique for camping out in the Islands will vary greatly. In any case, I shall soon know, for I am planning to visit Great and Little Todday myself before June is over. I beg your pardon, Miss Wriggleston?'

'I didn't say anything, Mr Prew.'

This was true. Miss Wriggleston had only released an involuntary sigh.

'By the way, I ought to warn you my information is that Great Todday is a Protestant island, whereas Little Todday is Roman Catholic.'

'That doesn't worry me one way or the other,' said Brownsworth, whose study of primeval life had discouraged the spirit of sectarianism.

'Quite, quite. But I thought you should know, though of course the

N.U.H. is all embracing. Indeed, we have quite a few Communists. Oh yes, rather. We will not have nudists, though. The Nudist Ramblers' Association has been trying to muscle in for years now, but we have always firmly rejected their repeated applications to be affiliated. Mind you, I've nothing against nudists myself. Not at all. But you see, a lot of hotels all over the country use our green signboards with N.U.H. on them, and you just can't run the risk of Nudist Ramblers trying to obtain accommodation and of course inevitably being refused. The next thing would be that some of our jolly young people would arrive rather lightly clad as they often are, and the proprietor thinking they were more nudists would refuse them accommodation. Well, now, if you're going to camp out on either of the Toddays this is what you'll want.'

Ten minutes later Brownsworth was on his way to the store recommended by Mr Prew for the provision of a camping outfit.

'And I do hope you'll win the £250 prize offered by the *Daily Tale*,' Mr Prew had assured him before they parted.

'I'm only interested in the palaeontological side of this business,' the young scientist had replied.

'And you will let Lord Buntingdon know that we looked after you in Gower Street. I won't say good-bye. Just *au revoir*, because I think we shall be meeting again.'

'A very good type,' the Secretary of the N.U.H. observed to his amanuensis. 'I do like to see hiking pinned on to a definite object. That's true democracy.'

Muriel Waggett and her mother were on the pier at Snorvig on the day that Brownsworth came down the gangway from the *Island Queen* with that look which hikers under the weight of their camping equipment share with John Bunyan's Christian under the weight of his sins.

'Another of these trippers hoping to win that money,' said Mrs Waggett.

A minute later Brownsworth had unbuckled himself from his load and, head erect, was standing beside it on the pier to look round him. In that moment Muriel Waggett, who as a Waaf had regarded with frigid indifference over months some of the bushiest moustaches in the Royal Air Force, fell in love.

'Poor young men,' said Mrs Waggett, 'I'm afraid they're all going to be very disappointed.'

Muriel would have liked to stand up for this handsome stranger's chance, but the cunning which Cupid injects in female hearts with the virus of love warned her to be cautious.

'I couldn't care less,' she said severely.

That night when Paul Waggett tuned in to the Brains Trust, which always gave him a much relished opportunity to expose human fallibility at a post-mortem in which he was the intellectual coroner, a listener from Peckham Rye asked the Brains Trust if it believed in love at first sight. A laddered bluestocking from the London School of Economics having knocked out a hopefully romantic Tory M.P. in the last round, the Question Master summed up in the style of the Delphic Oracle and left Peckham Rye as uncertain of what the Brains Trust believed about love at first sight as once upon a time Athens was about the strategy to be adopted against Sparta.

'I couldn't understand what the Brains Trust believed about love at first sight,' Muriel Waggett said when her father had switched off and the intellectual inquest began.

'Well, I think it's all hooey,' Elsie commented.

'I don't know what *you* know about it,' Muriel snapped.

'I know as much as you do anyway,' her twin snapped back.

The effort to preserve her self-control which this challenge cost Muriel may be imagined.

'What does Daddo think?' she muttered.

'Daddo thinks it's nothing but imagination,' he declared loftily. 'And we've all had a lesson about the effect of that over this imaginary monster. I suppose there was the usual mob of trippers from the *Island Queen*. Well, nobody was more anxious than I was to stop Hitler, nobody, but I sometimes wonder if we haven't fallen out of the frying-pan into the fire, as the saying goes. You remember what a fuss the Toddayites kicked up when I tried to make arrangements about the scorched earth policy? And who would have had to bear the brunt of such a policy? I should. Scorched earth would have ruined my shooting on the Toddays for years. Well, the Germans did *not* manage to occupy Todday and so as luck would have it the local opposition to the scorched earth policy didn't matter so much as it might have. You know, Mumsy, if I had my way now I would apply the scorched earth policy to all those trippers who are swarming over the island to look for this imaginary monster.'

'Oh, Paul, you wouldn't really burn down all the houses?' his wife exclaimed.

'No, no, no, of course not,' he said impatiently. 'What I mean is that the Toddayites ought to refuse to supply them with anything. Anything,' he repeated in a dream of thwarted ferocity. 'But, of course, they think first of their pockets. They have an opportunity of overcharging these trippers for eggs and milk and butter and everything else, and they can't resist it. Do you know I drove right round the island this morning and couldn't get an egg anywhere?'

'But our hens are still laying quite well, Daddo,' one of the chicks put in.

'We can never have too many eggs in waterglass,' said their father. 'And this is the time to get them. The same with butter.'

'Butter in waterglass?' Mrs Waggett exclaimed.

'Of course not, Dolly. I mean the same scarcity of butter,' he said in a voice that tried to express an infinite sufferance of human stupidity. 'I couldn't get so much as half a pound of butter. I actually found three of these hikers fishing in Loch Skinny and when I told them that the fishing was strictly preserved, do you know what one of them said? "I always heard the Scotch were mean." I made what I thought was rather a neat retort. "Well," I said, "I happen to be an Englishman and I've always heard that an Englishman's home was his castle." '

'You must have made him feel rather small,' said Mrs Waggett with conjugal flattery. 'What did he say to that?'

'Most insolent. He turned round to his fellow poachers and said "Look what lives in an aquarium." '

'How disgusting, Paul.'

'Oh, I paid no attention. All I said was, "Well, you've been warned." And then I found three more of these trippers fishing in Loch Sleeport and when I told them fishing was strictly forbidden one of them said he hadn't fought with the Eighth Army in Africa to be stopped fishing at home. If only Monty wasn't so friendly with everybody I should have been tempted to set him at these poachers, and let them know they were back in the Eighth Army. And then Sergeant MacGillivray wasn't very helpful. He said he was afraid he hadn't time to go round the island stopping poachers because he was kept so busy stopping the kids in Snorvig from pulling the pegs out of these tents. "Well, Sergeant," I said, "I think my trout more important than these trippers' tents." It obviously made no impression on him at all. I think the world's going mad.'

'There's some music on the cinema organ for half an hour in the Light

Programme,' Mrs Waggett reminded him soothingly after consulting the *Radio Times*.

'Oh, that's good,' her husband said, and soon he was sitting back listening, all problems insular and mundane banished by the music drawn by St Cecilia up aloft from the silver organ-pipes of Paradise.

That night Muriel was lying awake, wondering whether the member of the Brains Trust who had said that love at first sight implied an immediate mutual attraction between two people was right. The good-looking hiker had not seemed to notice her, but after all, if he had fallen in love with her at first sight he would not have wanted people on the pier to know he had. Had not she herself pretended not to have noticed him when Mumsy had said she was afraid so many people were going to be disappointed?

'I saw rather an attractive hiker talking to Archie MacRurie while I was waiting for the post,' Elsie murmured through the darkness.

Muriel's heart began to thump. She and her twin could not each have seen an attractive hiker; they must have seen the same one.

'Oh, what was he like?' she asked, making the bed creak to conceal any quavers in her voice.

'Tall with dark wavy hair and a sort of intense look,' her twin replied.

'He sounds rather like Bungo Jones,' said Muriel.

'Not a bit like Bungo Jones,' Elsie snapped back. Squadron-Leader Bungo Jones had been for several months the main topic of Elsie's letters from Lancashire during the war to her twin in the Midlands.

'He had dark wavy hair, hadn't he?' Muriel reminded her twin.

'So what?' Elsie snapped again.

'Oh, all right,' Muriel grumbled. 'But if you've no objection I want to get to sleep.'

'I'm not stopping you,' said Elsie.

With a simultaneous movement the twins turned over and lay back to back in their two beds.

Elsie was soon asleep, but Muriel stayed awake for a long time, wondering how she could manage to meet the handsome stranger before Elsie managed to meet him, and how after she had succeeded in meeting him she could conceal from Elsie the fact that she had met him. How her heart would have leapt could she have known that, while she lay sleepless in the big bedroom she shared with Elsie at Snorvig House, out on Ard Snor the handsome stranger himself, equally sleepless, was wondering to himself who was the fair fluffy-haired girl he had seen on the pier. It would have given another kind of a leap if she had known that he was under the impression that he had seen her for the second time when she was coming out of the post-office.

It might put an undue strain upon romantic licence to suggest that it was the thought of a fair fluffy-haired girl he fancied he had encountered twice that was depriving Bill Brownsworth of sleep. It was not. This insomnia was induced by trying to sleep on a waterproof sheet spread upon the hard ground of Ard Snor beneath a tent so low that if he sat up his head touched the canvas. Obedient to Mr Prew's instructions to excavate a small depression for his shoulder-blade he had unfortunately disturbed a metropolis of ants and after holding out against the agitated population for twenty minutes he had had to pitch his tent at a safe distance from the little brutes. This time he decided to dispense with any earthly receptacle for his shoulder-blades and they were not long in letting him know that they resented such neglect of their comfort. Unable to sleep he put out his hand for his matches in order to light the lantern which Mr Prew had impressed on him as a vital accessory to camping out; but where he thought his matches were there was a large slug; he grasped that instead, and yelled with horror. If there were any other campers in the vicinity they might have been forgiven for supposing that the Todday Monster had found a victim.

Brownsworth was annoyed with himself when he found what had caused him to yell like that. He felt, and rightly, that it was humiliating for a palaeontologist bent upon solving the riddle of a primeval monster to be frightened by a slug. He could not quite bring himself to overcome his guilt complex by picking the disgusting gasteropod up in his fingers and ejecting it from his tent. So he emptied a two-ounce tin of tobacco into his pouch, coaxed the slug into the tin with a twig from a dwarf sallow, and flung it forth. Then he snuggled down into his sleeping bag and started to read Commander Gould on sea serpents. Suddenly over the top of the volume appeared a yellow, green, and purple monstrosity diabolically arched with a face like a drunken navvy and a threadlike pink forked tail waving above it. Bill Brownsworth, hurling the book away, leapt up so violently that he brought the tent down on top of himself, and after a free for all in which he burnt his cheek on the lantern, got some toothpaste in his eye and upset the pail of water he had fetched from a lochan a quarter of a mile away for his morning toilet he found himself further from sleep than ever.

Bill Brownsworth was a palaeontologist, not an entomologist, and he may be excused for not immediately recognizing the caterpillar of the puss-moth for what it was, but that does not excuse a palaeontologist who has deliberately pitched his tent as near as the lie of the land allowed to the sea-cave in which Archie MacRurie had seen the monster for surrendering to the terror which the caterpillar hoped it was inspiring in the enemy who had interrupted its meal on sallow leaves.

The dawn was dove-grey in the sky above Ben Stickla and Ben Bustival before Bill Brownsworth at last fell asleep in his tent, and the sun was high before he woke to a cloudless morning. The discomforts and discomfitures of the night were forgotten in the placid beauty of the scene. The green carpet of Little Todday was spread out on the other side of the pale blue water of the Coolish. The smoke of Snorvig was sapphirine above the dark-tiled roofs. The sands of Garryboo, the only yellow sands in miles of white beaches up the western seaboard of the Outer Isles, may never have seemed so yellow as now they seemed against the azure of the Atlantic. Ben Bustival and Ben Stickla rose dark against the morning sunlight and though neither reached 1500 feet they seemed as majestic as the mighty bens of the mainland.

Bill Brownsworth strolled down the headland to stand above Uamh na Snaoiseanaich – the Snuff-taker's Cave – from which even on so tranquil a morning he could still hear from time to time the sound of a gentle sneeze. His palaeontological self-respect was restored, and the man who had yelled at the touch of a slug and leapt at the sight of a puss-moth caterpillar peered down now into the water at the base of Ard Snor ready to defy the teeth of any monstrous survival, palaeozoic, mesozoic, or cainozoic.

Presently Brownsworth set out with his pail to secure water for his toilet from the lochan further up the headland. He was glad to see no other tent was in sight and made up his mind to take advantage of the good weather by chartering Archie MacRurie's boat and examining the Snuff-taker's Cave from the sea.

Bill Brownsworth's toilet did not worry him, but the cooking of his breakfast did. In spite of the apparently windless air the flame of the spirit lamp seemed to want to burn everywhere except under the little kettle where it ought to be burning, and then long before there was a sign of boiling the flame expired. He lighted another methylated cube and when that was exhausted the water in the kettle was still only lukewarm. He had been so intent on his preparations for a cup of tea that he had not noticed the approach of a young woman with fair fluffy hair in smoky-blue tweed.

'Won't it boil?' he heard a pleasant sympathetic voice ask.

'Oh, hello,' he said and to his great surprise he did not feel in the least shy. 'No, the methylated spirit doesn't seem to last long enough.'

'Let me try,' she offered.

And with that curious command over the inanimate which women possess, the kettle was boiling away merrily in a minute or two.

'Extraordinary,' Bill Brownsworth ejaculated.

'Not so much tea,' Muriel Waggett said quickly. 'Let me make it.'

'Thanks awfully. I say, didn't I see you on the pier yesterday when the boat arrived?' he asked.

She nodded.

'I was with my mother.'

'And then I saw you again in the post-office.'

Muriel made a lightning-like decision.

'Yes, you did.'

Of course, he would have to know sooner or later that she had a twin sister, but if she were clever it might be too late for Elsie to do anything about it.

'I say, I've only got one cup,' said Bill Brownsworth.

'I don't mind,' Muriel assured him tenderly.

'I say, what's your name?'

'Muriel. Muriel Waggett. What's yours?'

'Bill. Bill Brownsworth.'

And as they sipped tea in turns from Bill's only cup both of them thought that it was the most delicious cup of tea either of them had ever drunk, and since both of them hated condensed milk such enjoyment should have convinced even a laddered bluestocking in the Brains Trust that there *was* such a thing as love at first sight.

Chapter 9

CABLE, TELEPHONE, AND POST

On the morning of the day when Bill Brownsworth and Muriel Waggett established the existence of the phenomenon known as love at first sight, Ben Nevis received a telegram from America, waving which like a flag he rushed off in a state of high excitement to find his wife.

'Trixie! Trixie!' he bellowed. 'Trixie, where on earth are you? Trixie!'

In the Great Hall Toker informed him, with a hint of reproachfulness in his tone, that Mrs MacDonald had driven into Fort William.

'What the deuce has she gone to Fort William for?' the Chieftain asked.

'Mrs MacDonald is meeting Miss Mary and Miss Catriona, sir.'

'Oh, I forgot. Of course. They were coming back from London last night, weren't they?'

'They were, sir.'

Cheated of his pleasure in announcing the news in the cablegram to his wife the Chieftain announced it to his butler; he had to tell somebody.

'Mr and Mrs Royde are sailing almost at once from New York and hope to be at Knocknacolly in about a fortnight, Toker.'

'We must hope that the spell of clement weather which we are enjoying will still be with us when they arrive, sir.'

Chester Royde was the young American financier who had bought the forest and lodge of Knocknacolly some years previously from Hugh Cameron of Kilwhillie, and he and his wife Carrie, a Canadian Macdonald before she married Chester, had managed to spend a few weeks almost every year in the house they had built on the site of the old lodge. They never arrived usually until the beginning of August.

'Yes, poor souls, they have had it rather wet once or twice. The interesting thing is that Mr and Mrs Royde have been hearing about this monster in the islands over in America and Mr Royde wants to charter a yacht to go and dig this brute out of its lair. Get me Mr Rawstorne on the telephone. And don't go away while I'm talking through it in case I want you for the machinery.'

Nothing could have revealed to Toker more clearly the tremendous excitement of Mac 'ic Eachainn than his intention to make use of an instrument he abominated.

'Hullo . . . hullo . . . hullo! Is that you, Tom? This is Donald Ben Nevis speaking. You knew that, did you? How on earth . . . well, if I don't shout into the beastly thing I can't hear what anybody says. Yes, I can hear you all right . . . I never suggested you were deaf . . . well, don't let's start an argument on this beastly contraption . . . look here, Tom, you know you said you thought you might be able to take the *Banshee* over to the islands later in June . . . I know it wasn't certain . . . well, look here, Chester and Carrie Royde have just heard about this monster and they're sailing right away. Royde wants to charter a yacht to hunt this monster and I thought it was a deal right up your street . . . of course he'll pay for it . . . well, you don't want to soak him if you know what I mean, because although he's as rich as Croesus he hates being soaked . . . well, charge him the top price you'd charge anybody else . . . you'd better cable him direct . . . and do it right away, Tom . . . he'll probably be cabling some confounded agent or other . . . you know what Americans are . . . they call it hustling. I don't know why they can't call it bustling, the same as we do . . . How are you keeping, Tom? . . . good . . . well, we don't want a long conversation on this beastly contraption. You'll cable Royde at once, won't you?'

'Do I ring this idiotic bell now or just put it back on the stand?' Ben Nevis asked his butler.

Toker stepped forward to relieve his master of the receiver.

'I can't think why the telephone was ever invented,' Ben Nevis declared.

'It can be an extremely convenient method of rapid communication, sir.'

'Yes, I suppose it is,' the Chieftain admitted grudgingly. 'Now tell Johnnie to bring the car round at once. I want to go to Kilwhillie.'

'The car will hardly be back from Fort William just yet, sir.'

'Oh lord, I wish trains wouldn't arrive from London just when I want the car. Well, I'd better go in the lorry.'

But the lorry turned out to be away on some estate job in Strathdun.

'I suppose I shall have to telephone again. Kilwhillie won't like it, of course. He hates the beastly thing as much as I do. And don't go away Toker, in case the machinery goes wrong.'

'Kilwhillie is quite an adept with the telephone these days, sir. He has rung me up himself on more than one occasion.'

'Go ahead then.'

'Ben Nevis would like the Laird to speak to him . . . Oh, this is Toker speaking, sir . . . Ben Nevis wishes to speak with you.'

The butler handed over the receiver.

'Hullo! Hullo! . . . is that you, Hugh? . . . how are you? . . . and the liver is all right again? . . . I was coming over to see you but Trixie has taken the car to Fort William to meet the two girls on their way back from that horrible place London . . . look here, I've had a cable from Chester and Carrie Royde to say they're coming over almost at once because Chester wants to charter Tom Rawstorne's *Banshee* and have a go at this monster out in the islands . . . we've simply got to kill this blundering tale that's going round about our monster having gone off to the islands . . . and I'll do it if I have to tow this island brute back behind the *Banshee* . . . what's that? . . . you've had a cable from America too? . . . from Yu-Yu? . . . she'll love a good hunt for this island monster . . . oh, she's not coming herself? . . . Deirdre and her husband . . . I never remember his name . . . oh, yes, Wilbur Carboy . . . well, that'll be splendid . . . of course they can come with us . . . I'm sure little Deirdre's as keen as mustard . . . she saw our monster once, you remember . . . we'll put them up at Glenbogle if you're fussing about these preparations for Walter Dutton's birthday . . . but you've got nearly four months to get ready for that . . . nonsense, Hugh, of course you must come on this expedition . . . I never can understand your objection to the sea . . . I'm never seasick . . . yes, well, we can't argue about our insides on this beastly telephone . . . it always pings at me when I start arguing on it . . . I'll come over and see you to-morrow, Hugh.'

Ben Nevis hung up the receiver and shook his head at his butler.

'Can you understand why some people are always seasick, Toker?'

'I believe, sir, it's a matter of the constitution. Some gentlemen and many ladies are allergic to the motion of the sea, and Mr Rawstorne's yacht has the reputation of being what in nautical parlance is called a lively craft.'

'Did you say allergic just now?'

'I did, sir.'

'Allergic?'

'Allergic, sir.'

'Where do you get hold of these extraordinary words, Toker?'

'I pick them up, sir, in the course of my reading.'

'I don't pick up words in that way. They seem to stick to you like burrs.'

'I often delve in the dictionary, sir, in my spare time.'

'Allergic,' the Chieftain repeated to himself. 'Do you think they'd know that word in Inverness?'

'I think it extremely possible, sir.'

'Do you think if I asked those nincompoops on the Roads Committee why they're so allergic to a road up Glenbogle they'd know what I was talking about?'

'I feel sure some of them would, sir.'

'A-L-U-R-G-I-C?'

'A-double-L-E-R-G-I-C, sir.'

'I suppose you're certain it is allérgic and not állergic?'

'I have never heard the latter pronunciation, sir.'

At that moment Toker caught sight of the car returning from Fort William.

'The car, sir,' he said and hurried to the front door followed by the Chieftain.

'Ah, here you are at last. I was getting rather allergic to waiting for you. Ha-ha-ha!' He guffawed with boisterous glee over his new word. 'Enjoy yourselves in that horrible place London?'

The two hefty daughters of Mac 'ic Eachainn extracted themselves from the car to greet their father.

'Chester and Carrie Royde are coming over almost at once. So are Deirdre and her husband — I never can remember his name. We've got Tom Rawstorne's *Banshee* and we're going to rout out this Todday monster.'

'Oh, good-oh,' said Mary MacDonald gruffly; Catriona grunted endorsement.

The Chieftain's plan to pursue the Todday monster to its lair was threatened by the apparent ubiquity of the quarry. Where was its lair? Or indeed had it a lair at all?

Hector Hamish Mackay used to say afterwards that without the help of Bill Brownsworth he believed his reason would have given way under the strain of trying to keep in touch with what was generally known as the Todday monster, though as is made clear by the selection below of letters from the correspondence of the *Scottish Daily Tale*, not all of which were published in its columns and some of which were addressed personally to Mr Mackay himself, many of these correspondents much resented the monster's affiliation to Todday and blamed Mr Mackay for it.

Sir,

I do not know why you persist in writing of the 'Todday' Monster. Are you aware that it has been seen on no less than seven occasions on both the west and east coasts of Lewis – in Loch Seaforth and Loch Erisort on the east and in Loch Roag and Uig Bay on the west. A Bernera woman, who was gathering crotal close to where the bridge linking Bernera with Lewis should have been built years ago, looked up from her creel to see the monster glaring at her, round the corner of a high rock. Hearing its teeth champing the woman fainted and but for the fact that the tide was ebbing at the time she might easily have been drowned.

Yours, etc.,

Leodshasach

Sir,

I sometimes ask myself if there is anything that the people of Lewis will not claim for themselves as we in Harris know too well to our cost. If the monster is to bear the prefix of any island we in Harris would much prefer it to be called the Todday Monster than the Lewis Monster. But why not the Long Island Monster?

Incidentally, you will be interested to know that the Long Island Monster has been seen twice by the schoolchildren of Scarp in the water of the strait which separates Scarp from Hushinish. I will remind you that the *each uisge* or water-horse has been a recurring phenomenon through the centuries in the natural fauna of the beautiful Island of Harris, whereas no *authentic* example of one having been seen on the Island of Lewis is recorded.

Yours, etc.,

Indignant Harrisman

Sir,

Why the Long Island Monster? It has been seen at eleven different points on both the east and west coasts of Skye from Sleat to Trotternish.

Yours, etc.,

Sgiathanach

Dear Mr Mackay,

I am at present staying in the beautiful island of Harris in connection with my researches into the problem whether the late Sir James Barrie was in fact a changeling himself and therefore whether the story of Mary Rose may not have been partly autobiographical. Naturally in the course of my researches I have had to spend many hours in solitary meditation upon the small island in one of the Harris lochs which all are agreed inspired Barrie to write his masterpiece.

You spoke in your article of the guiding hand of Providence. On June 11th – numerologists will recognize the significance of the date – June=6, $1+1=2$, $6+2=8$, the number of Fate – I had myself put ashore on the island by the gillie who makes himself responsible for my transport. I looked at the time on my watch when I stepped ashore and noted that it was exactly six minutes past eleven. $1+1=2$, $2+6=8$, the number of Fate again. I had arranged to remain on the island until 4 p.m., having brought with me some sandwiches, at which hour my gillie, Angus Macleod, was to call for me. You, Mr Mackay, who are a man of imagination, will understand the mysterious drowsiness which is apt to overtake anybody in tune with the infinite who finds himself under the spell of the magical west of which nobody has written with more appropriate eloquence than yourself. To such a drowsiness I succumbed on June 11th and fell fast asleep. Suddenly I awoke with a feeling that something was watching me, and to my amazement I saw beyond a knoll covered with bell-heather an arched neck about ten feet long surmounted by the head of a large horse with eyes that reminded me of a crocodile. I lay without moving a muscle and almost holding my breath, for I must admit that I have never felt more frightened in my life. Presently the neck of the monster began to develop a kind of upward corkscrew motion and opened its mouth wide. Supposing that it was about to attack me I uttered a cry of terror which apparently alarmed the monster, for with a rapid downward corkscrew motion the neck and head vanished.

I am ashamed to say that my fears got the better of my scientific curiosity and instead of trying to see what happened to the monster, I lay where I was without moving.

It has occurred to me since that the monster may have been yawning when it opened its mouth, for I perceived no sign of those long teeth which have figured in other accounts and the monster I saw approximated much more nearly to the descriptions of those who have seen the Loch Ness Monster. Consequently I have asked myself whether your original hypothesis that one of the Loch Ness Monsters had left Loch Ness to seek another mate after the death of the original mate may not be the true explanation of the phenomenon. I ask myself further whether the condition of the beach on Little Todday may not have been caused by this corkscrew motion of the monster's neck rather than by its teeth. Perhaps you will consider this tentative suggestion of mine and let me know what you think of it?

Finally, may I say that when after the monster's departure I looked at my watch the time was seven minutes past two which, allowing for a minute for the withdrawal of the monster after I shouted, would make the time when I saw it first six minutes past two. $6+2=8$, the number of Fate yet again. From then until four minutes past four when Angus Macleod came for me in the boat (4 + 4 = 8!) nothing unusual happened. I cannot help being glad that no monster visited the island while the late Sir James Barrie was, as I believe, recapturing from its atmosphere his own memories of fairyland before he was brought to Thrums as a changeling.

It would have been almost impossible for the great dramatist to avoid mentioning the monster in *Mary Rose*, in which case some of the more materially minded members of the audience might have come away from the Haymarket Theatre with the impression that Mary Rose herself had been swallowed up by a monster instead of being carried off by the fairies.

I have written to you at some length about my extraordinary experience on 'the island that likes to be visited' because I revere you as a writer whose life has been dedicated to damming the dark and turbid flood of materialism which threatens to sweep away all that is most sacred in the life of our country.

If you have time to give me the benefit of your observations upon my experience will you be good enough to write to me c/o Mr Tom Cameron, Tarbert Hotel, Isle of Harris.

Yours faithfully with

my sincerest homage,

Wilfred Cartwright

author of *Why I am a Psychometrist*, *The Secret of Numbers*, *On the Threshold of the Beyond*, *The Illusion of Time*, etc., etc.

P.S. It occurs to me that my experience as a psychometrist might be of use in determining the whereabouts of the Todday Monster, could I be brought in contact with some spot which shows physical evidence of the monster's attentions. I regret to say that when I walked round the island after my alarming experience on June 11th I could find no visible sign by the disturbance of the vegetation of the passage of a great body, and so I was unable to employ my psychometrical gifts to any advantage. The absence of any visible sign of the monster's having landed on the island suggests to me that the long neck and horse's head I saw may have been extruded directly from the water. The place I fell asleep was within a dozen yards of the loch and if one allows a length of twenty feet for the whole neck it could easily have been seen by me. If those who estimate the total length of the Loch Ness Monster at round about eighty feet are right it could surely rear itself twenty feet from the water with consummate ease.

Nobost Hotel,
Mid Uist,
June 9

Sir,

Last Sunday morning while I was walking along the path on the north side of Loch Stew to note what prospect there was of an early run of sea-trout I saw the back of what looked like a large yellowish-brown hornless bull emerge from the water and almost instantly submerge, having presumably scented my proximity. I saw nothing of any mane, but I did see what appeared to be large tufts of hair sticking out on either side of its head.

Yours, etc.,

Henry Hotblack

Lt.-Col. (retd)

Free Presbyterian Manse,
Gibberdale,
East Uist

Sir,

We were disagreeably surprised in East Uist to read Colonel Hotblack's letter in your issue of yesterday. Nobody in East Uist would venture to profane the Lord's Day by thirsting after fish on the Sabbath.

During the war we had occasion to protest more than once against aeroplanes using the East Uist aerodrome on the Sabbath, and now that the war is over we resent strongly the notion that monsters can rouse worldly thoughts on the day which the Lord our God has set aside for His service.

We know that our neighbours on Mid Uist do not see eye to eye to us in this matter of Sabbath observance, but we hope that they will pay regard to our feelings in East Uist and do all that they can to prevent visitors like Colonel Hotblack from encouraging idle sightseers to offend the Lord by staring at fish or at monsters on the Sabbath.

Yours etc.,

(Revd) John MacCodrum

To Hector Hamish Mackay.

How much have you been paid by those well-known robbers, Joseph Macroon and Roderick MacRurie, to pretend that this monster is their personal property? You cannot be ignorant that this monster has visited every island in turn and though you pretend to be such an authority on the islands and have written a lot of inaccurate nonsense about them in books that I wouldn't dirty my fingers to open you are nothing better than a tout for interested parties.

Fair Play

Sir,

We in Inverness are surprised that you should lend your columns to the wild speculations of Mr Hector Hamish Mackay, and we are astonished that Mr Mackay, who in the past has enjoyed our hospitality in no mean fashion, should turn round and bite the hands that fed him by lending himself to the exploitation of a chimera.

Yours etc.,

Disgusted Invernessian

Sir,

We in Obaig take strong exception to the attack on Mr Hector Hamish Mackay made by your anonymous correspondent who signs himself 'Disgusted Invernessian.' We recognize the devotion with which Mr Mackay is trying to establish the identity of the Islands Monster. 'Disgusted Invernessian' would do more to assist the spread of knowledge if he refrained from abuse of a Scottish writer to whose slogan 'See the Highlands and the Islands First' in his brilliant series of broadcasts last year we Gaels owe an immense debt of gratitude. 'Disgusted Invernessian's' annoyance at the loss of the Loch Ness Monster through 'enemy action' should not lead him into intemperate abuse. We sympathize with the chagrin of the 'Capital of the North', but that will not keep the 'Capital of the West' from doing all it can do to welcome the great influx of visitors who are now thronging to Obaig and after they have enjoyed the famous hospitality of the 'Capital of the West' speeding them on their way to the Isles of Enchantment.

Yours etc.,

Obaig Gu Brath

Sir,

We should be glad to know by what right 'Obaig Gu Brath' claims the title of Capital of the West for Obaig. The Capital of the West is and always will be Fort William.

We are, Sir,

Your obedient Servants,

Donald MacDonald of Ben Nevis

Hugh Cameron of Kilwhillie

'Oh dear, oh dear,' Mr Mackay sighed to Bill Brownsworth as he looked at the letters scattered over the table in the parlour at Joseph Macroon's house. 'And here's a letter from my editor':

Dear Mr Mackay,

I feel that when you have looked through this correspondence you will probably want to follow the track of the 'monster' right up the Long Island. I think too it would be as well if you visited Skye also. It will not do for the *Scottish Daily Tale* to give the least impression of prejudice in favour of any particular island, especially of the islands with so comparatively small a population as Great and Little Todday. I suggest that it might be better if you didn't visit Inverness or the neighbourhood just at present. The feeling is rather strong, especially in Glen Urquhart where, I'm sorry to say, many people have cancelled their orders for the *Daily Tale* because they think we have taken up a hostile attitude to the Loch Ness Monster. I am sure that if you can get some really good stories from Lewis any suspicion of bias will vanish, and it will go a long way to offset the effect of that letter from the Wee Free Minister in East Uist.

I expect you'll be able to leave the Toddays in the hands of a reliable man who could telephone to us in case of emergency.

Please get up round all the Long Island as soon as possible. Carmichael has gone to Inverness.

Yours sincerely,

James Donaldson

P.S. We had a great laugh yesterday, when our wee Marjorie announced that she had seen a Teddy Monster in Vincent Square. The creature in question was the Lord Provost in his robes!

'I don't understand why the Inverness-shire people should be annoyed with me,' said the topographer. 'Surely I made it quite plain that I had abandoned my theory that the Loch Ness Monster has gone to the islands? People cannot read their papers intelligently. However, *magna est veritas et prevalebit*,' he concluded solemnly. 'Will you hold the fort while I'm away, Brownsworth?'

The young palaeontologist had no hesitation in agreeing, not the least cogent of his reasons for doing so being the chance it gave him of occupying Mr Mackay's room in Kiltod. He and the topographer had met when the Biffer asked Brownsworth if he would mind Mr Mackay's company in the *Kittiwake* while they took advantage of the fine weather to explore the Snuff-taker's Cave. Bill Brownsworth would have much preferred to enjoy Muriel Waggett's company in the *Kittiwake*, but she had exclaimed in alarm at the prospect of the gossip it would cause in Snorvig if she were to be seen out alone with a stranger to the island.

'You see, Father's position here must be remembered. In a way he's really the equivalent of the Laird and I mustn't give the people a chance to gossip.'

Muriel did not add that if she went out in the *Kittiwake* with Bill her twin sister would undoubtedly hear about it and would resent having been omitted from the invitation. She had not yet told Bill Brownsworth that she had a sister and had warned him not to greet her even if he saw her alone in Snorvig. She had taken this precaution in case he should meet Elsie and, imagining Elsie to be herself, give the game away.

In fact Bill Brownsworth did meet Elsie once or twice and with the audacity that love at first sight inspires he had tried to convey to her without other people's noticing it how glad he was to see her, and he had much admired the way his love was able to receive the quick signals of affection without turning a single fair hair.

'I saw that rather good-looking hiker in Snorvig,' Elsie would say, for Elsie was pleasurably aware of attracting his dark fervid glances. 'Couldn't we get Daddo to ask him up to the house?'

'You know what he feels about trippers,' Muriel had always replied. She was determined not to run any risk of changing the focus of love at first sight.

In the end after three stolen meetings on Ard Snor Muriel had told Bill she thought it would be better if he went over to Little Todday and camped out there.

'But I shan't see you then, Muriel,' he exclaimed in dismay.

'I'll find an excuse to come over and we'll be able to go for a long walk together,' she promised.

'But why can't I go to your father and say we want to be engaged?'

'Oh, no, Bill, no. He's awfully conventional and if you went to him dressed in shorts and said you wanted to marry me he'd never understand that you wouldn't be dressed like that all the time.'

'Surely I could make it clear, that I'm only dressed like this because I'm investigating this monster?'

'Yes, but he doesn't believe in the monster. You couldn't say anything that would annoy him more. You couldn't, really.'

'Well, we can't go on for ever being afraid to tell your father. It's like the Brownings in Wimpole Street.'

'But you never suggested an elopement, Bill. That would be rather marvellous, wouldn't it?'

'I don't see any point at all in an elopement,' Bill Brownsworth demurred. 'That would upset my people. And if I get this Readership in Palaeontology at Norwich University next autumn, which I've every hope of doing, we can be married.'

'Darling, how marvellous!'

'And if I can only identify this monster I'm bound to get that Readership. I mean to say, if it turns out to be a survival my name will be . . . well, it'll be world-famous.'

'But even if you did find the monster it would be better to meet Daddo for the first time in some other connection. He hates being wrong. I thought I'd get my friend Rosemary Smith to ask me down to stay with her in London and then I could write and say I'd met you in her house, and Mr Smith is a company director whom Daddo used to know.'

'Well, of course we don't want to upset your father, I see that,' said Bill. 'And you think I ought to go over and camp out on Little Todday?'

'Oh, I do, darling. I really do.'

'As a matter of fact Hector Hamish Mackay strongly advised me to make a thorough exploration both of Pillay and of Poppay, and of course there's that beach in Little Todday. Try Swish it's called.'

'I know. I'm sure you'll be wise to go over there.'

Bill Brownsworth was not so sure that he had done well to choose the machair for a camping-site when on his first night he was woken, from a nightmare that the candidate he feared most as a competitor for the Readership at Norwich was trying to smother him in a silo, to find that he was being fanned by a blast of hot air smelling of damp grass. As he sat up with a start he heard a loud snort and a moment later he was sitting up under the stars, his tent having been whisked off him. Fortunately the stirk disembarrassed itself of the canvas before it went thudding off, but he did not at all enjoy the job of pitching his tent again to the accompaniment of a thunderous tattoo of hooves all round him in a kind of infernal rodeo.

However, if Bill's night was disturbed he enjoyed sitting at a table again for breakfast with Mr Mackay in Kiltod, and when the topographer left him in charge of any news about the monster with the chance of sleeping once more in a bed Bill Brownsworth was glad that he had surrendered to Muriel's discretion.

Visitors who enjoyed Joseph Macroon's board spoke with less enthusiasm of his beds; Bill Brownsworth thought he had never slept in so comfortable a bed in his life. Those fresh from urban luxury used to wonder sometimes if board did not include with those high teas soaring to the zenith on lobsters and cream the bed to which they retired later.

'I don't know why Mr Mackay told me his bed was so hard,' Bill Brownsworth said to his host, who was wearing that red knitted woollen cap, which, when he was busy among the lumber heaped up in the great shed at the back of the house, made him look so much like a troll.

'Was he after telling you the bed was hard?'

'Yes, I can't think why. I found it extraordinarily comfortable,' said Bill with enthusiasm.

'I'm sure you would. Will you be wanting the *Morning Star* today?'

'I thought I'd like to land on Pillay if it's possible and have a look round.'

'Ay, I believe you'll be able to land quite O.K.'

'Did you see that report about the monster being sighted in Barra?'

'Ay, in Northbay,' said Joseph. 'That's where the Coddy lives. He'll be putting his net out and trying to keep it there. But I believe the monster'll be one too many even for the Coddy.'

Chapter 10

THE PILLAY MANIFESTATION

The small island of Pillay extends to something over three hundred acres. It rises up from the sea along its western face in a series of rocky terraces at first and then by steep grassy braes to the summit, which consists of a level plateau of rough herbage and heather dotted with numerous small lochans. On the east the cliff falls sheer to the sea for about three hundred feet in a magnificent sweep of black basaltic columns whitened by the droppings of innumerable seabirds. The northward side is equally sheer but not so high, and all along the southern end the shore is strewn with huge fragments of basalt from which it is an arduous climb to reach the braes above. The only landing-place is below a small hook-shaped headland running north-west from the coast of the island below which a ledge of rock provides a rough quay. However, the little bay formed by the headland faces due west and only after a spell of calm weather such as the islands were experiencing this June did the heavy groundswell allow a boat to get alongside the rocky ledge. The origin of the name Pillay is in dispute. Some Gaelic topographers say it means 'the island of the winnowing', others argue for a purely Norse derivation from a word cognate with pillow, but the majority agree that it means 'the island of the return' because so many people had tried to land there and failed.

The grazing was good, and one or two of the crofters of Little Todday had sheep on Pillay, but the difficulty of performing the various operations that sheep require through the year, coupled with the heavy losses over the cliffs, did not tempt their neighbours to envy them.

Unsuitable though the island was for sheep, Pillay offered an ideal breeding-place to the grey Atlantic seals, the young of which are born on land early in October and have to be taught to take to water in the lochans before they descend to the wild November seas.

The Macroons, owing to their legendary descent from a seal-woman, had never persecuted the breeding seals either on Pillay or Poppay, its sister isle off the south of Little Todday. It can be imagined how much they resented the theory put forward in some papers that the Todday Monster was nothing more than an outsize grey seal.

There were no seals ashore on Pillay on this lovely June day when Kenny Macroon took Bill Brownsworth across in the *Morning Star* to land him safely in the little bay called Fearvig. Yet even on such a placid day there was enough groundswell to make it impossible for Kenny to leave his boat, and he went off to look at his lobster-pots round the Gobha while Brownsworth poked around on shore.

Brownsworth found when he had scrambled over the rocks to the head of Fearvig that the sand uncovered by the tide was ploughed in every direction similarly to the way Mackay had described the state of the beach beyond Ard Swish where Mrs Odd had seen the monster and that the dry sand above high water showed marks which appeared to be the movement of a huge body across it. He was so excited by this discovery that he lifted up his voice and uttered several resounding 'hurrahs!' From the other side of the headland which was not more than fifty feet high his shouts were answered by a noise between a bark, a bellow, and a whistle.

In a fever of excitement Brownsworth scrambled up to the top of the headland not without difficulty, but to his intense mortification when he was able to look down at the other side he could see nothing except the black boulders and shattered columns of basalt along the base of the dark cliffs, and nowhere in the ocean so much as a speck.

He remained for an hour on the watch, but he heard nothing and saw nothing. Then he scrambled down again into Fearvig to re-examine the condition of the sand. The longer he looked at it the more difficult was it to escape from the conviction that these striations were made by the huge teeth of some great animal unknown to zoology. He decided when Kenny took him back to Kiltod to go and call on Mrs Odd. She might have some clue which she had failed to pass on to Hector Mackay.

'Do you still think the noise you heard was more like a snarl than anything else?' he asked Kenny Macroon when the latter was pointing out the place where he had seen the monster's back submerge.

'Just the very same,' Kenny insisted.

'You didn't hear anything like a whistle?'

Kenny shook his head.

Brownsworth had made up his mind not to say anything about the state of the beach in Fearvig or about the noise he had heard on the other side of the headland, for he did not want inquisitive people to land on Pillay.

'I think I'll go and camp out on Pillay,' he announced.

'You could never be doing that,' Kenny told him.

'Why not?'

'Every why. You might be there for months before anybody could take you off, and there are *bòcain*. No so many *bòcain* as there are on Poppay, but plenty *bòcain* right enough.'

'Bokun?' Brownsworth echoed.

'Ghosts.'

'I don't believe in ghosts,' said Brownsworth severely.

Kenny shrugged his shoulders. He was not going to argue with this poor ignorant Sasunnach about the existence of ghosts because his pride would not allow him to run the risk of being laughed at.

'But of course I couldn't afford to be cut off on Pillay,' Brownsworth admitted.

'If landing there wasn't so difficult we would have put the whisky there.'

'Whisky? Oh, the whisky from the *Cabinet Minister*?'

'Ay,' said Kenny. 'We did try and make the Excise Officers think we'd hidden a lot of the stuff there, but they were too cunning.' He spat overboard. 'Ach, it would have done the Excise a lot of good to be cut off on Pillay for a few months. They'd have been pretty tired of eating sheep and nothing else. It would have been a good lesson for them right enough.' He spat overboard again.

That afternoon Bill Brownsworth walked across the island to call on Mrs Odd. Normally he would have been much too shy to introduce himself to a stranger, but his palaeontological enthusiasm had been so pumped up by the evidence of the monster's propinquity he had found on Pillay that he would have introduced himself to a Duchess at a Charity Bazaar if she had been in recent contact with the monster.

'Good afternoon,' said Mrs Odd cordially. 'I suppose you've come about the monster?'

'Well, yes, I have as a matter of fact.'

'Don't look so frightened. I'm no monster myself. And I'm getting used to questions by now. "Here," I said to one of these walking catechisms, "What do you think I am, a Sunday School?" But come on in. What paper are you from?'

'I'm not from any paper, Mrs Odd. I'm a palaeontologist.'

'A what? You'll sprain your jore, if you start in trying to swallow the dictionary all at one go. Would you like a cup of tea?'

'That's very kind of you.'

'Oh, I'm always glad for the excuse of a cup of tea. My son Fred always says he never knew any teetotaller so fond of an occasional drink of something else so long as it wasn't coffee. Oh, I can't abide coffee. Nutshells and water is what I call coffee. Would you like a dram before you have your tea? Did you hear that? I am getting Scotchified, aren't I? But I'm a true Cockney myself. Yes, born within sound of Bow bells. Where do you come from?'

'South Kensington.'

'Where the Natural History Museum is, eh? Oh dear, how I used to love going there when I was a kid. We used to like stroking the whales. Well, they was the only thing anyone could stroke, because I suppose they couldn't afford to put glass over such whoppers, could they? So we got the smell as well. And it was a smell. Like damp linoleum. But us kiddies liked it.'

By now Bill Brownsworth was seated in an armchair and the old lady was watching the kettle.

'I'm a friend of Mr Hector Hamish Mackay,' he told her. 'He was going to bring me round to call on you, but he has had to go up to Lewis and Harris, and probably Skye.'

'Oh, he was bound to go sky-rocketing with a name like that. Hi! Hi! Mr Mackay, take me with you when you fly, back to the Isle of Skye,' Mrs Odd warbled. 'But you take it from me, young man, he won't find the monster anywhere but in the Toddays.'

'As a palaeontologist . . .'

'There you go again. And what's in the pail when it's at home?'

'I am studying extinct animals and so naturally I am tremendously interested in this mysterious creature which has been seen here.'

'Exstinct? It's no more exstinct than you and me are. If you'd seen it prancing about Try Veck as lively as a penny toy on the pavement you'd have soon seen how exstinct it was.'

'Yes, but it appears to be a survival, and if the fact of a survival could be established and identified palaeontological research . . .'

'Look here, young man, don't you try and say that word till you've drunk up your tea, or it'll be returning on you.'

'Mrs Odd . . . by the way my name's Brownsworth . . . I believe the noise you heard this creature emit was something between a bark and a bellow?'

'And a yawn.'

'Not a whistle?'

'No, there wasn't no whistle. What makes you ask that? I've been asked a lot of funny noises, but that's a new one on me.'

'Well, I wonder . . .' Bill Brownsworth hesitated.

'Go on.'

'I wonder if you can keep a secret?'

'Me keep a secret? What, I'm the grave's only rival with a good secret, I am.'

Brownsworth decided to be frank, and told Mrs Odd about his experience on Pillay that morning.

'But you'll understand why I want to keep quiet about it for the moment because I do not want everybody to go exploring on Pillay and frightening the creature away.'

'Besides getting two hundred and fifty golden soverings from the *Daily Tale*.'

'No, this is not a matter of money, Mrs Odd. This is science.'

'Yes, of course. That's what the doctors tell you. But they don't forget to send in the bill, do they? Or they didn't until this National Health come in and people could get ill for nothing. But get back to this here whistle you heard. What kind of a whistle was it? A sort of a guard's whistle or a look round and let's see your face, Gladys, you've got pretty legs whistle or . . . well, I mean to say, whistle? That can mean anything, can't it?'

'It came at the end of this noise between a bark and a bay and a bellow.'

'It's a proper one-man band, this monster, isn't it? No, I never heard no whistle myself, but poor Sneezer was puffing so hard when he came through the arch he'd have drowned any whistle with his wheezing.'

'Sneezer? Did you say sneezer?'

'Hector Tishoo Mackay. Though there's no hectoring about him. Oh, I like the man, I do. But if I had cocoanut knees like what he has I'd keep out of kilts. No, don't look at yours. They haven't got knobs on like Sneezer's. But really, you know, men are funny. First they aren't happy till they're old enough to leave off knickerbockers and get into trousers and then they aren't happy till they've got out of trousers back into knickerbockers again. And women! If a girl's got legs like a couple of bolsters depend upon it she won't be happy till she can show them off in these shorts as they call them.'

'Couldn't you give me some idea of the teeth?' Bill Brownsworth interposed earnestly.

'Teeth? Oh, the monster's teeth. I'd forgotten about the monster for a moment, thinking about these young dreams in shorts. Well, as I've said, they was more like pickaxes than teeth. It takes a lot to scare Lucy Odd, but I don't mind telling you I was properly scared and no mistake when it started in champing at me with these unnatural grinders. If you'll take my advice, and which of course you won't, you'll watch your step before you go mouching around Pillay on your lonesome. You don't want for Sneezer to come back and find nothing of you left excepting a plate of Irish stew and half a mince-pie.'

Bill Brownsworth thanked Mrs Odd for her solicitude and then in another burst of frankness suddenly confided in her that he had become engaged since he arrived in Todday.

'You have?' she exclaimed. 'Not to one of these female Robinson Crusoes in a tent?'

'No, she lives in Great Todday.'

'There must be something in the air in these islands. My Fred came here in the war to teach the Home Guard how to make an Aunt Sally of that blaring Hitler, and he turned me into a granny instead.'

'He married one of Joseph Macroon's daughters, didn't he?'

'That's right. A lovely girl if ever there was. If you pick yourself another Peggy, never mind about this reward for the monster, you'll go back to dear old London a richer man than what you came.'

Bill Brownsworth was on the verge of revealing to Mrs Odd whom he had picked when there was a knock at the door and the rich voice of Father Macalister was heard asking if anybody was at home.

'Hick into the stye, Father James,' Mrs Odd called out. 'That's the Garlic for "come in",' she told the young palaeontologist.

'Hullo, hullo,' the sonorous bass reverberated. 'Have you seen Duncan anywhere, Mistress Odd?'

'I sore him this morning.'

'Was he in good order?'

'He couldn't be better.'

'Good shooting. I've just had a telegram from the B.B.C. to say they're sending over to make some recordings of us all at home and I want to see Duncan about it.'

'This is . . . and now I've forgotten your name,' Mrs Odd said to her visitor.

'Brownsworth.'

'That's right. I could only think of Ha'porth, and I knew it wasn't that.'

'Welcome to Tìr nan Òg, Mr Brownsworth,' Father Macalister said. 'You'll be here to meet the monster, I suppose. *Am bheil Gàidhlig agaibh?'*

Brownsworth looked bewildered.

'He's asking you if you can parlyview Garlic?' Mrs Odd explained.

'No, I'm afraid I can't.'

Father Macalister sighed deeply.

'Ah, well, well. And what will you say if you do meet the monster, for depend upon it, my boy, the monster won't understand a word of this new-fangled language called English.'

'Mr Brownsworth is a pail . . . well, he's a pail of something, but he'll have to tell you what's in the pail himself.'

'A palaeontologist,' Brownsworth elucidated.

The priest nodded gravely.

'And a very respectable beautiful thing to be,' he declared sonorously. 'Ay, ay. But you mustn't laugh at our monster, Mr Brownsworth. You must let Mr Waggett do that.'

'I haven't met Mr Waggett yet,' the young man gulped.

'Have you not? Oh, well, you've missed a treat. You really have. Ay, ay, he'll tell you more about us than we know about ourselves. Well, well, I must be going. Tingaloori, Mrs Odd.'

'Tingaloori, Father.'

'Is that Gaelic for "good-bye"?' Bill Brownsworth asked.

The priest threw his head back in a mighty gust of laughter.

'Oh, that's a beauty. No, no, Mr Brownsworth. It's just a little word of my own.'

'Isn't it Garlic at all?' Mrs Odd exclaimed. 'Well, aren't you the giddy limit, Father James. And me telling everyone in Nottingham it's how you say "so long" in Garlic.'

Brownsworth said that he too must be getting back to Kiltod.

'Roll right along with me, my boy,' the priest urged.

And so sympathetic did Bill Brownsworth find his company that to him he did tell the story of his experience on Pillay as they walked across the machair together.

'There's something pretty strange in these waters,' the priest said with conviction. 'What do you think yourself?'

'I'm completely baffled at present,' Brownsworth replied. 'If only I could catch a glimpse of this creature. According to the descriptions of it I've been given it doesn't conform to any reconstruction we have made so far from the fossilized remains of any creature discovered in the course of excavations. I suppose Kenny Macroon is right in advising me not to camp out on Pillay?'

'He's dead right, Mr Brownsworth. Now Poppay is different.'

'But the creature hasn't been seen on Poppay.'

'Not yet, but while there's life there's hope.'

'Mr Mackay has gone up to Lewis to investigate reports from there.'

'Poor old Hector Hamish,' said the priest. 'Ay, ay, the Leodhasaich will chew him up if he doesn't admit that the monster is their exclusive property. And he daren't go near Inverness for a while.'

'I investigated the stories of the Loch Ness Monster last year,' Brownsworth told his companion. 'And I couldn't find anything like the evidence I've found for the creature here, quite apart from my own extraordinary experience on Pillay.'

'Could you not? Ah, well, if you take my advice you'll leave the Loch Ness Monster alone. Poor old Hector Hamish is in sad disgrace for suggesting it might have left Loch Ness for the Isles of the Blest.'

'He was rather worried about some of the letters he received.'

'Ay, ay, I'm sure he will have been.'

'Don't you think I ought to wire him to come back? I mean to say he might be rather annoyed with me if I didn't let him know what happened this morning.'

'You'd be doing him a kind action, Mr Brownsworth. Besides, he ought to be here when the B.B.C. invade us. I'm sure they're hoping to be able to broadcast the noise of the monster. And listeners to Scottish Regional will be thinking they've tuned in to the Third Programme by mistake.'

So when he got back to Kiltod, Brownsworth telegraphed to Stornoway:

Almost met our friend this morning strongly urge you return Kiltod soonest possible
Brownsworth

Three or four days later Paul Waggett received by mistake the *Daily*

Tale instead of his own paper. This did happen sometimes and when it did he was always in ruffled spirits, for as he used to say, 'How can I keep in touch with the international situation unless I have my own paper?'

On this occasion his annoyance was fed by the following headlines:

EXPERT ON TRACK OF MONSTER
AMAZING ADVENTURE OF YOUNG SCIENTIST

William Waterlow Brownsworth, who is considered one of the most promising of our younger palaeontologists (palaeontology is the study of extinct creatures), has had an amazing experience on the small island of Pillay lying off the north-west corner of Little Todday. Taking advantage of the recent spell of calm settled weather in the west of Scotland Mr Brownsworth undertook what is regarded as the dangerous task of landing upon Pillay. His boatman having put him ashore went off to look at his lobster-pots, and Mr Brownsworth with characteristic enthusiasm set about the task of making a meticulous examination of the beach in the little bay of Fearvig which affords the only possible landing-place in Pillay. To his amazement he discovered that the sand below high-water mark had been gashed and ploughed in the same way as the beach on Little Todday seen by Hector Hamish Mackay and Mrs Odd, of whose experience the *Daily Tale* was able to give that exclusive account which caused a world-wide sensation.

Mr Brownsworth further discovered in the soft sand above high-water mark clear signs of an immense creature having dragged its great bulk across it.

HARROWING BELLOW

In the natural exultation of his discovery the young palaeontologist emitted what he calls a 'whoop of triumph'. No sooner had the echoes died away among the forbidding cliffs of Pillay than from the other side of the low narrow headland which protects the little bay from the north-west Mr Brownsworth heard his whoop answered by what he describes as a 'harrowing bellow' such as might be emitted by a bull the size of a mammoth, but partaking also of the baying of a gigantic hound and ending in a sort of whistle. Pressed to be more precise about the whistling Mr Brownsworth said that it resembled at first the noise of an infuriated or terrified horse but was definitely a whistle and not a shriek.

Without hesitating Mr Brownsworth ran toward the headland and desperately scaled it in order to obtain if possible a sight of the creature which had uttered this nerve-shattering roar. However, when at last the young palaeontologist achieved the summit it was too late for the reward which his courage deserved. There was no living creature in sight.

Asked if he was not frightened by the noise Mr Brownsworth replied modestly:

'I was really too excited by the prospect of seeing the monster to have time to think about being frightened.'

The amazing adventure of Mr Brownsworth on Pillay will undoubtedly stimulate still further the already intense interest which has been aroused all over the world by this mysterious visitant to the Western Isles. The *Daily Tale*'s offer of £250 to the first person successful in obtaining a photograph of this creature is still open, and we take this opportunity of reminding readers that while the fact of the monster's appearance having been recorded first from Great and Little Todday has led to its becoming generally known as the Todday Monster, numerous authentic reports from the rest of the Long Island and Skye indicate that its presence is not confined to the Toddays.

Mr Hector Hamish Mackay, who has been gathering evidence of the monster's visits to other islands besides the Toddays, wished to repeat and stress his conviction that the Todday Monster is an entirely different creature from the Loch Ness Monster, and that he no longer attaches any importance at all to what he calls his 'too hasty speculation' that the Loch Ness Monster or its possible mate, angered by the flying saucer's aggression, had deserted Loch Ness.

The *Scottish Daily Tale* associates itself with this expression of opinion from Mr Hector Hamish Mackay, and pending the re-appearance of the Loch Ness Monster, has empowered its special representative to investigate any report which may suggest that the Loch Ness Monster escaped injury. Meanwhile, the *Scottish Daily Tale* ventures to express its profound sympathy with the people of Inverness-shire in the ordeal of anxiety through which they have been passing since the flying saucer was seen in March and the painful story of its encounter with the Loch Ness Monster was first reported in the columns of the *Scottish Daily Tale*.

'Poppycock!' Paul Waggett snapped. 'Complete and utter poppycock! Where are the chicks?'

'What, dear?' his wife asked, anxiously disentangling her mind from the pull-over she was knitting, and the impression that something had gone wrong with their fowls.

'There's a disgraceful story in this horrible rag which they've sent up from the post-office instead of my own paper.'

'Oh dear, how careless of them.'

At that moment Muriel came into the room to hear with a shiver of apprehension her father say:

'One of these disgusting trippers called Brownsworth has apparently been writing up this stunt for the Press.'

'Brownsworth?' she murmured unhappily.

'William Waterloo – no, Waterlow Brownsworth,' her father repeated. 'What has he done?'

'He's been telling some cock-and-bull story to the *Daily Tale* about seeing the footprints of this imaginary monster on Pillay and hearing it roar. I suppose he's staying on Little Todday. I shall go over tomorrow morning and warn him that the Pillay shooting belongs to me. It's one of the best places for barnacle geese anywhere in winter. Anywhere!'

'I'm sure it is,' said Mrs Waggett soothingly. 'But you never can get there in the winter, can you, dear?'

'That's no reason, Dolly, why I should allow these trippers to go tramping all over Pillay as if it were Hampstead Heath. It's bad enough having to let the Little Todday crofters put sheep on it.'

'I don't suppose he knew he was trespassing, Daddo,' Muriel put in.

'Then the sooner he does know the better,' Paul Waggett replied. 'He'll be under no illusions about shooting rights when I have talked to him. Calls himself a . . .' he turned back to the newspaper.

'A palaeontologist?' Muriel asked.

'How did you get hold of that word?' her father asked sharply.

'Oh, I heard somebody – it must have been the Minister – say something about there being a palaeontologist on Little Todday. I meant to ask you what it meant, Daddo.'

This was a deliberate and skilful diversion by Muriel. Her father smiled with superior knowledge.

'Palaeontology is the study of extinct creatures,' he explained, after another glance at the paper. 'So presumably a palaeontologist is somebody who studies extinct creatures.'

'Thank you, Daddo. I did so wonder what it meant.'

'And thanks to Daddo now you know,' said Daddo benignly.

'All the same,' thought Muriel, 'I'll have to see Bill somehow and warn him not to argue with Daddo if he does meet him. This makes it quite impossible for Bill to ask Daddo about our engagement yet. How lucky Elsie didn't hear me come out with "palaeontologist" like that. She wouldn't have believed I'd heard it from the Reverend Angus.'

Over in Kiltod Hector Hamish Mackay read the account of Bill Brownsworth's adventure with considerable satisfaction. The Editor had handled the whole business with great tact, and the people of Inverness should surely recognize that the last thing he had wanted was to offend them over the Loch Ness Monster. The stories he had heard all the way up the Long Island had none of them possessed anything like the circumstantial detail of the stories in Great and Little Todday, but the *Daily Tale* had not suggested the slightest prejudice on his part and he might surely expect that the abusive letters he had been receiving would now cease.

'You did perfectly right to fetch me back, Brownsworth,' he assured Bill. 'And I think the story has been really well handled.'

'I've never seen my name in print before,' the young man said. 'It's a curious sensation. Rather like leaving the door of a bathroom unlocked and having somebody fling it wide open. I wonder what my people will say.'

'I would imagine they'd be delighted to find how keenly you are pursuing your researches.'

'Oh, I expect it will be all right,' said Bill a little doubtfully. 'But my father's rather a retiring sort of chap. He was awfully annoyed when one of our maids blew up the geyser and there was a paragraph about it in the *Kensington Courant*. He said that kind of thing was an intrusion upon the English idea of family life.'

'An unknown monster is hardly on a par with a geyser,' Mr Mackay suggested.

'No, of course it isn't. If only we could establish what it is I shouldn't mind.'

'*Dum spiro spero*, as our friends the Romans used to say. I am confident that you and I are going to establish what this creature is. My head is buzzing with plans. What a triumph if we could put this B.B.C. unit in touch with it. It would be a landmark in broadcasting. By the way, you're holding to your plan of camping out in Tràigh Veck?'

'Absolutely.'

'Courageous. Very courageous, I think. But where should we be today if scientists had not been prepared to take risks? "Light, give me more light," as Goethe said before he died. Still, you always have an avenue of escape through the arch to Tràigh Swish.'

'Oh, rather,' Bill Brownsworth agreed.

When Paul Waggett sent along to inquire if the Biffer would be crossing to Kiltod next morning word came back that he was taking Dr Maclaren over and that no doubt the Doctor would be glad to give him a lift.

'That means I can only take one chick with me,' Waggett ruled. '*Quis?*'

'*Ego*,' the twins cried in one voice.

Their father ruled that it was a dead heat. 'I shall have to toss for it.' He tossed a penny in the air, caught it on the back of one hand as he simultaneously clapped it down with his other hand, and with the smile of a juggler who had displayed a dexterity beyond the emulation of anybody in the audience he asked who was going to call.

'I will,' said Muriel.

'Muriel will call,' said her father in the tone of a Daniel come to judgement.

'Heads,' Muriel quavered.

But when the paternal hand was lifted it was tails.

'Hard cheese,' said Elsie, accepting her victory like the good sports-girl she was.

Muriel's tradition of accepting defeat in the same spirit was hardly proof against the bitterness of her disappointment.

'Weren't you going to bike over to see Mrs Beaton at Bobanish tomorrow morning?' she reminded her twin.

'Oh, that'll keep,' said Elsie ruthlessly.

'But why can't we both go?' Muriel pressed.

'You know I don't like being under an obligation to Dr Maclaren,' her father replied. 'That's why I'm not taking Monty. He's going to be disappointed too, poor old boy.'

Muriel was afraid to make an appeal to Elsie's better nature and persuade her to surrender her place in the *Kittiwake*, for she would at once become suspicious of such anxiety to go over to Kiltod. She consoled herself with the thought that if her father intended to warn Bill about the shooting on Pillay he would probably want to see him

alone. Oh dear, why hadn't she called 'tails' instead of calling 'heads'?
She felt sure that if she went down to the pier Dr Maclaren would
invite her to come aboard, but that would annoy Daddo who had
such a thing about knowing how to accept defeat with a smile. He
was always trying to teach the people here to be sporting, and when
the Garryboo tug-of-war team had walked off the field last August at
the Todday Games because, they said, Daddo had favoured the
Snorvig team, he had been thoroughly upset. No, she must not go
down to the pier, and anyway, if she did go over to Kiltod she
probably would not have a chance to warn Bill not to argue with
Daddo either about the shooting on Pillay or the monster. Surely Bill
would realize that he must be tactful for the sake of their future
happiness, but oh, why hadn't she called 'tails'?

'Well, Waggett,' said jovial Dr Maclaren next morning, 'going over
to see that nobody on Little Todday poaches the monster?'

Waggett gave a tired smile. He always found Dr Maclaren's boisterous
facetiousness wearisome. 'I don't think that there's any danger of that,'
he said.

'I wouldn't put it past our friend Airchie,' said the Doctor, looking
down at the crofter who was blowing away at a choked plug.

'Nor would I if the monster really existed,' said Waggett.

The Biffer's spit overboard was not intended as a contemptuous
gesture; in the agitation Waggett's scepticism caused him he
had managed to ingurgitate a mouthful of petrol from the choked
plug.

'Really existed?' he exclaimed indignantly, 'was it an otter that young
chap from down in England somewhere was hearing on Pillay?'

'No, it was probably a seal.'

'I'll talk to you about that when we're clear of the pier,' said the
Biffer.

The Doctor rubbed his hands in pleasurable anticipation, and when
the *Kittiwake* was requiring no more attention from her owner than a
light hand on the tiller he returned to Waggett's seal.

'So you think it was a seal, eh?' he asked.

'Of course. It was obviously a seal that Kenny Macroon saw. It was
obviously a seal that Sammy MacCodrum's girls saw. It was probably a
seal that Mrs Odd saw, if she saw anything at all.'

'And was it a seal I was seeing in Uamh na Snaoiseanaich?' the Biffer
demanded.

'I've told you already, Archie. I think you saw a large otter.'

The *Kittiwake* herself seemed shocked by such a suggestion, and the engine began to splutter indignantly.

'Mr Wackett, if I wass to be telling you that yon great yellow dog of yours wass a canary bird would you be thinking I wass wise?'

'No, I certainly shouldn't.'

'Well, then, and I don't think you're so very wise if you think that a great beast with teeth on him like a hayrake is an otter. Man, I'm telling you the cave was full of the crayture.'

'You have your opinion, Archie. I have mine,' said Waggett with gracious obstinacy.

'Och, I think you're being a bit hasty in your opinions, Waggett, I don't believe our friend Airchie could mistake an otter for the kind of beast he saw.'

'Well, what is it, Doctor?'

'That's what we're all anxious to learn.'

'And I'm very, very much afraid you'll have to go on being anxious,' said Paul Waggett, with kindly and condescending sympathy. 'Yes, I'm afraid it's just another case of auto-suggestion.'

'Like your road blocks to stop German tanks on Great Todday,' the Doctor said with a grin.

'I don't accept that comparison. It's not a patriotic duty to imagine this ridiculous monster, and the country's no longer in a state of emergency.'

Elsie feared that tempers were rising and, brave girl, she drew her father's fire upon herself.

'Wouldn't it be fun, Daddo, if the monster suddenly came up beside us in the Coolish?'

'So as to attract a few more of these trippers, I suppose,' he said distastefully. 'That isn't my notion of fun.'

'And it wouldn't be my notion of a fun at all,' said the Biffer. 'She might be clawing the gunwale from the *Kittiwake* herself with those teeth. Och, it would be a pure disaster if the crayture was to come up beside us.'

By tacit consent the conversation was allowed to drift away from the monster to less controversial topics and in due course the *Kittiwake* was brought alongside of the steps in the tiny harbour of Kiltod.

'*A Dhia*,' Joseph Macroon had muttered to Hector Hamish Mackay. 'Here's Waggett, what's he come over to plague us about now?'

'I'll go and speak to him,' said Mr Mackay. Joseph Macroon sighed with relief.

'Ay, if you can steer him away I'll be much obliged to you, Mr Mackay. I've a lot of work this morning, and I must be getting the trap for the Doctor. Kenny's away to his pots.'

The topographer greeted Waggett cordially on the quay while Doctor Maclaren went on to Joseph's house.

'Mr Waggett, I believe. My name is Mackay. I had intended to call upon you, but I was summoned to the other side of the Long Island. Stirring times here, eh, Mr Waggett?'

'I'm afraid I don't appreciate so much stir, Mr Mackay. You may be aware that I have the shooting and fishing rights over both Great and Little Todday.'

'Yes, yes, I know that.'

'And owing to the popular agitation in the Press about this imaginary monster both islands are infested with trippers.'

'Oh, hardly infested,' the topographer objected. 'I agree there may be a few more visitors than usual, but that's all to the good from the point of view of the people here.'

'Not from the point of view of my grouse and salmon,' said Waggett sternly.

'Why, yes. I know there are a couple of brace of old grouse who were brought here from Ireland by Sir Robert Smith-Cockin when he owned the two islands, but salmon? I've never heard of a salmon in any of the streams of Great Todday. Never. Why, a salmon would cause as much excitement as the monster.'

Paul Waggett stiffened.

'I consider that remark quite uncalled for, Mr Mackay. In fact, I take the very strongest exception to it,' he said.

'My dear sir, if I may venture to say so, you are taking my little pleasantry too seriously altogether, but at the risk of causing you still further offence I must remind you of the old Gaelic proverb which says of a stupid man that his brains are like MacRuaridh's salmon. In other words, that his brains are non-existent.'

'I am not in the habit of paying attention to Gaelic proverbs,' said Paul Waggett. 'I regard Gaelic proverbs as old wives' tales. All superstition is to me equally objectionable, and I think a man like you should be ashamed to encourage this nonsense about an imaginary monster for the sake of what is obviously a Press stunt.'

'The sincere pursuit of truth can never be a Press stunt, Mr Waggett,' the topographer insisted.

'That is where I'm afraid you and I must agree to differ,' said Waggett loftily. *Verbum sapienti*. However, the reason why I have come over to Kiltod this morning is to interview this so-called . . . this so-called scientist who was trespassing on Pillay recently. I believe you are in touch with him.'

'I have been in touch with Mr Brownsworth, certainly. An enthusiastic and most courageous searcher after the truth.'

'Where is he to be found?'

'He is now camping on Tràigh Veck, which was the scene of Mrs Odd's encounter with this strange creature.'

At this moment Waggett caught sight of the trap waiting to take Dr Maclaren on his rounds. He did not like to be under an obligation to the Doctor, but the walk to the other side of the island was long enough to make a lift for some of the way attractive on this sunny morning. Besides, Joseph Macroon charged quite enough for the trap at the ratepayers' expense to give one of them a certain satisfaction in letting Joseph know that full value was being obtained from his bill.

Joseph himself was not too well pleased at Waggett's getting a free ride, but at any rate it would take him out of the way and that was something.

'Room for two little ones?' Waggett asked.

Doctor Maclaren beckoned Elsie and him into the trap.

'I'll be turning off some time before Tràigh Swish,' he warned them.

'Beggars can't be choosers,' said Waggett with a gracious smile.

Bill Brownsworth had pitched his tent where the blown sand, bound by marram grass and silverweed, had remained in a cosy hollow of the dunes about twenty yards inland from Tràigh Veck, and therefore he was out of sight of the beach when Paul Waggett and Elsie emerged upon it from the arch under Ard Swish.

'Nobody here,' said Waggett petulantly.

'He may have gone for a walk,' Elsie suggested.

'There's no sign of any encampment. Curious ideas of truth that man Mackay has.'

Bill Brownsworth was reading an absorbing account of the discovery of a large clutch of fossilized dinosaurs' eggs in Central Asia when he heard voices and, jumping up a moment later, was on the point of shouting 'Muriel!' when he saw the stern figure of Muriel's father just behind her.

'Oh, good morning,' the stern figure, to whom Bill Brownsworth had hoped to be introduced as a prospective son-in-law in happy circumstances, said with cold hauteur.

'Good morning, sir,' he replied.

Paul Waggett was gratified at being called 'sir'. Even when he commanded the Todday Home Guard it was only Sergeant-major Odd who ever called him 'sir', the others had had the greatest difficulty even in addressing him as 'Captain Waggett' rather than 'Mr Waggett'. He was indeed so much gratified by this young man's obvious respect for him that he smiled a lofty smile. This was just as well because Bill Brownsworth himself at that moment had not been able to check giving Elsie a lover's quick smile.

'I understand that you recently landed on Pillay, Mr Brownsworth.'

'Yes, I did, sir.'

This second 'sir' acted upon Paul Waggett's heart like borax upon hard water.

'Well, I don't want to be unduly severe,' he said, 'and of course you may not have realized that the shooting on Pillay is leased to me by the Department of Agriculture.'

'I had no intention of shooting anything, sir.'

'Quite. Quite. I appreciate that, but as a matter of principle I like people to ask my permission before they land on Pillay.'

'I'm sorry, sir. I hadn't realized I was trespassing. In fact I understood from young Macroon that it was very rarely possible for anybody to land on Pillay.'

'That may be so, but the principle remains. In autumn Pillay is a wonderful place for barnacle geese, and I do not want them to be disturbed by indiscriminate shooting. I had a very unpleasant experience two or three years ago over my barnacle geese.'

'I'm sorry to hear that, sir.'

'Yes, the people here happened to get hold of a lot of whisky, and having soaked some barley in it they proceeded to scatter this doctored barley all over the feeding-ground of the geese on Little Todday. What was the result? The unfortunate birds were all staggering about in a state of intoxication and the people here were able to knock as many as they wanted on the head. The most unsporting thing I ever heard of in my life. So naturally I'm anxious to do all I can to protect these unfortunate geese and give them a refuge on Pillay.'

'I fully appreciate that, sir. But there are no geese on Pillay at this season of the year, and I should be very glad to have your formal permission to land again on Pillay if the opportunity occurs.'

Suddenly Paul Waggett thought of a really good joke.

'On this wildgoose chase after an imaginary monster, eh?' he asked, gurgling with amusement at his own humour.

Bill Brownsworth remembered Muriel's warning; taking advantage of the preoccupation of what he hoped was his future father-in-law with his own joke he flashed an ardent glance at Elsie and covered its fire with a blink.

'I am far from suggesting, sir, that the creature I heard on Pillay has yet been positively identified as a primeval survival.'

'You suggested that in the *Daily Tale*,' the sceptic reminded him sternly.

'I only told Mr Hector Hamish Mackay about my experience. Apart from him the only other person I told was the parish-priest here – Father Macalister.'

'Father Macalister?' Waggett echoed, with a slow headshake of disapproval. 'I'm afraid Father Macalister can always be relied upon to make the most of anything. Are you a Roman Catholic?'

'Oh, no.'

'Well, you know what Roman Catholics are. They revel in superstition. I think you can take it from me that what you heard was a seal.'

'And the marks in the sand?'

'Razor-fish. Perfectly simple explanation. By the way, don't let Joseph Macroon persuade you that razor-fish are edible. He persuaded me once when I was a newcomer to the islands, and I never had such indigestion in my life. I don't think a bicycle tyre would have given me such indigestion.'

'I shall remember your advice, sir.'

'I'm always anxious to help strangers. The people here take a lot of knowing. But I suppose I understand them as well as any Englishman *can* hope to understand them.'

'I suppose you speak Gaelic, sir?'

'Oh, I don't pretend to be a Gaelic scholar. But I get along in it. The trouble is the people are so awfully stupid about their own language. Or it may be, of course, that they don't want other people to speak it, and so deliberately pretend they can't understand their own language when somebody talks to them in it. Well, I'm glad to have met you, Mr Brownsworth. When you're over in Snorvig Mrs Waggett and I will be glad to see you at Snorvig House.'

'I'm afraid I haven't got any proper clothes for calling, sir.'

'Come just as you are,' said Paul Waggett kindly. 'We lead the simple life here. Some rather good shooting and some rather particularly good fishing,' he added dreamily. 'Yes, yes, call in just as you are. This is my daughter.'

Bill Brownsworth clasped Elsie's hand with such warmth and let it go with such reluctance that Elsie felt sure that the deference which this handsome young man had shown to her father must have been inspired by his interest in herself, and when her father was in the arch she turned to look back. How right she had been! The handsome young man was kissing his hand to her. Elsie looked quickly to see if Daddo was safely ahead. And then she kissed her own hand in response. 'Bungo Jones,' she thought scornfully as she hurried on through the arch. Oh, well, poor Muriel shouldn't have called 'heads'. If she had called 'tails' she might have met this young man. 'I wonder when he'll come and call. If I only knew I'd manage to get Muriel to be out,' she said to herself.

Bill Brownsworth went back to his sandy hollow, but the account of the large clutch of fossilized dinosaurs' eggs seemed less important than it had been before the visit of Muriel and her father to Tràigh Veck. How lovingly Muriel must be thinking of him at this moment! How proud she must be feeling of the good impression he had obviously made on her father! She had worried about introducing him in shorts as a suitor for her hand. That was nothing to worry over now.

Indeed, Bill Brownsworth had reason to feel optimistic. That afternoon the shooting tenant of the Department of Agriculture expressed to his wife his gratified astonishment at finding their trespasser upon Pillay so comparatively unobjectionable.

'I've invited him to call at Snorvig House, Dolly,' he informed her.

'That will be very nice, dear.'

'I found him quite reasonable as soon as I explained that the noise he heard was made by a seal and that the marks on the beach were razor-fish. Obviously this fellow Mackay has used him as a tool in order to keep this Press stunt going for his own advantage. He was rather shy about calling in shorts, but I put him at his ease about that. I told him we were leading the simple life here and that he need not feel embarrassment.'

'How kind of you, Paul!'

'We older folk have to face up to our responsibilities towards the younger generation,' he said weightily. 'I've never forgotten that with the chicks.'

'I know, dear. You've been an elder brother to them as well as a wonderful Daddo.'

Just then Muriel came in with the tea things.

'I've been telling Mumsy about our expedition to Little Todday. This young man Brownsworth seems quite a gentleman. I was pleasantly surprised. In fact, I've invited him to come over and call on us.'

'Careful, Muriel darling,' her mother interposed anxiously. The thrill her father's announcement gave her had caused Muriel to make an unwonted clatter with the cups and saucers.

'He's not at all pig-headed about this imaginary monster, I'm glad to say. But he's been encouraged by this fellow Mackay, and also, of course, by Father Macalister. I hope he isn't trying to proselytize him. He's quite incorrigible. He actually tried to proselytize me once.'

'Paul, you never told me that,' his wife exclaimed in horror.

'Yes, I was only trying to be pleasant and put him at his ease. I said "Ah, well, Father Macalister, we all work in the same vineyard." And then he gave one of those affected sighs of his and said "Very true, Colonel . . ." you remember that maddening habit he had of calling me Colonel when I was commanding the Todday Home Guard. "Very true, Colonel, but we planted it." '

'What an extraordinary thing to say!'

'Proselytizing.'

'And what did you reply?'

'I can't remember exactly what I said, but he saw it was no use trying to proselytize me. I'm told that the B.B.C. have asked him to arrange a ceilidh for them. They're sending a recording unit. And who do you think they've asked to get together people here?'

'Mr Morrison?'

'As a matter of fact they did ask him, and he, without referring to me, suggested Alec Mackinnon, who is going to do it.'

While her mother and father were lamenting the folly of the B.B.C. in entrusting their recording unit to the guidance of the Minister and the Headmaster of Snorvig School, Muriel was wondering how she could bring the conversation back from the B.B.C. to Bill Browns-worth.

'Perhaps the B.B.C. want to give listeners the latest news about the monster,' she said.

'The B.B.C. are very stupid,' her father observed contemptuously, 'and as you know I've written several times to tell them how to improve their programmes, but I don't think even the B.B.C. would be so stupid as to broadcast a lot of nonsense about an imaginary monster, even in this Third Programme of theirs. Well, if that young man comes to call on us to say Father Macalister has asked him to gabble a lot of rubbish into the microphone he won't be asked to call again.'

'I'm sure he won't do that, Daddo.'

And as she expressed this conviction Muriel told herself that somehow she must see Bill and warn him how much the course of true love would be smoothed if he could give her father an assurance that nobody should ever persuade him to come to the microphone and talk about the monster.

'No, that's what Elsie said,' her father informed her. 'Where is Elsie?'

Muriel had no desire at that moment to know where Elsie was.

'I told her I was taking in the tea things,' she replied with a touch of irritation. 'Must I go and shout all over the house for her?'

Fortune which had been so unkind to Muriel over the toss made up for her malice next day. Elsie had set off on her bicycle to Bobanish to pay that visit to Mrs Beaton, the wife of the schoolmaster, when word came over from Kiltod that Mrs Hugh Macroon had a White Leghorn cockerel from her noted strain of layers.

'Oh, Paul, what a pity you didn't call in to see Mrs Macroon,' the henwife exclaimed.

'I could hardly know that she had a cockerel for you without being advised beforehand, could I, Dolly?' he asked with courtly patience.

'No, dear, of course not. But I did so want one of Mrs Macroon's Leghorns. They're the best layers in either of the islands.'

'Well, Muriel didn't come with me yesterday. Why doesn't she go over in the *Morning Star*? It'll be coming back to meet the boat.'

Thus it fell out to Muriel's delight that she was able to cross to Little Todday without arousing any possible suspicion of her willingness to undertake the transport of the Leghorn cockerel.

'Oh, I didn't mean for you to come all the way over from Snorvig,' said Mrs Hugh Macroon, a prim dapper little woman of something over fifty with hair already grey. 'Not at all. I was just anxious to know if Mrs Waggett was still wanting the cockerel. Hugh would have brought it over for her, which is it? Muriel or Elsie? *A Mhuire Mhuire*, you're both so like to the other there's no telling.'

'This is Muriel. Elsie came over yesterday with my father.'

'Now you won't want to be carrying a live cockerel all the way back to Kiltod. Hugh will bring it to Joseph Macroon's. He's going in to meet the *Island Queen*.'

'That's awfully kind of him, Bean Uisdean. *Moran taing*.'

'Look at that now. And isn't it you that's getting on well with the Gaelic?'

'Being away all through the war didn't help my Gaelic much,' Muriel said.

'Och, that terrible war! But God was very good to me to bring back Michael safe from North Africa and Anthony without a torpedo in four years. Wasn't it just wonderful? And he's doing fine too. Yes, yes. Second mate in the *Highland Maid*, and off to South America last week. You'll take a cup o' tay.'

After a pleasant gossip over a cup of tea with Mrs Hugh Macroon Muriel announced her intention of taking a walk along Tràigh Swish.

'Perhaps I'll see the monster, Bean Uisdean.'

'Indeed, and I hope you won't. Mistress Odd was telling me about it, and I was really shivering. Poor soul, she might have been eaten alive, and I believe she would have been right enough except she had her umbrella. God was very good to her. So do you be careful, Muriel *eudail*.'

Muriel did feel rather apprehensive as she walked through the arch under Ard Swish to Tràigh Veck, and her heart gave a jump when she saw Bill on all fours beside the edge of the tide, for she had a sudden fear that he had been wounded by the monster in a savage encounter.

'Bill! Bill! Are you hurt?' she cried.

To her relief he rose unscathed.

'What are you doing, Bill darling?'

'I was examining the effect of razor-fish on the sand. I didn't like to contradict your father yesterday, but I think he's wrong. The marks I saw were quite different from these.'

'Oh Bill,' she said when his arms were round her, 'you were wonderful yesterday. I was so proud of you. I knew how much you must love me when you didn't argue with Daddo about the monster.'

'Well, I remembered your warning. He was awfully kind to me.'

'I know. He liked you awfully. Oh, Bill, I'm so happy. And fancy his inviting you to our house. All the same you won't be in too much of a hurry to tell him we want to be married in shorts?'

'I'm not proposing to be married in shorts,' said Bill, who must have been infected with the facetiousness of his sweetheart's father.

'Don't be silly. You know what I mean. But oh, Bill, darling Bill, I can't tell you how happy I am. And what do you think of Elsie?'

'Who's Elsie?'

'My sister.'

'Your . . . your sister?' Bill gasped. 'You never told me you had a sister.'

'I know. It was naughty of me, but I was afraid she would be jealous. It would be too frightful if she fell in love with you. And you never can tell with twins. But as it is everything has worked out splendidly.'

'Yes, oh yes,' Bill mumbled doubtfully. He was thinking of that kiss which Elsie had blown him in response to the kisses he had blown to her.

'You'll come and call on us very soon? And if you handle Daddo as tactfully as you did yesterday, he'll probably ask you to dinner. Well, perhaps not to dinner. He's rather conventional. He might think coming to dinner in shorts wouldn't do. But anyway he's sure to ask you to come again, and then perhaps again, and then you can go to London and if you get this appointment at Norwich I'll get Rosemary Smith to ask you to dinner, and I'll write to Daddo and say you've proposed to me, and of course you'll write to him and he won't be prejudiced against you as he might have been if he didn't know you. He was terribly prejudiced against you after he read that account of your adventure on Pillay in the *Daily Tale*. But you handled him quite marvellously yesterday. When will you come and call? Tomorrow?'

'I don't think I'll be able to come tomorrow,' Bill said.

'The next day?' she pressed.

'I don't think I'll be able to manage the next day either. But of course I will come.'

'Bill, why do you keep looking at me in such a strange way?' Muriel asked.

'I didn't mean to look at you in a strange way. It's the glare from this white sand probably.'

'But you seem so cold.'

'Do I? I suppose it was going along on my hands and knees to examine these razor-fish marks.'

'I meant cold in manner,' Muriel explained reproachfully.

'You're imagining things,' said Bill, putting his arm round her.

'Kiss me,' she murmured. And after he had kissed her she said, 'Bill, why do you keep looking over my shoulder at the arch?'

'Oh, I suppose I've got in the habit of keeping an eye open all the time. It's the monster. I'm on the look-out all the time.'

'You weren't thinking of Elsie, were you?' Muriel asked with that horrible clarity of perception which jealousy promotes.

'Why on earth should I be thinking of Elsie? I didn't know she existed until you told me just now. I mean to say, of course I realized she existed as soon as I saw her, but I didn't know her name was Elsie until you told me just now. I like the name Muriel much better.'

'Do you, Bill? I'm glad.'

'Much better,' he repeated fervidly.

'I'm awfully glad I didn't tell you I had a twin sister,' said Muriel firmly. 'You might have liked her better than me.'

'How could I possibly do that?'

'And I'm awfully glad I didn't tell Elsie about you. She's much more jealous than I am.'

'Is she?' said Bill, his heart sinking.

'And she might not have been able to resist telling Daddo about you and me on the way back. I think she rather liked you herself.'

'Do you? What makes you think that?' Bill asked apprehensively.

'Oh, just a twin's instinct.'

'I see,' he gulped miserably.

'Well, you don't mind, do you?'

'No, of course not. I'm in love with you, aren't I?'

'You are so strange today, Bill.'

'Well, as a matter of fact I'm rather worried. I may have to go back to London sooner than I expected.'

'Bill!'

'I may have to consult some books. I can't afford to make any mistake about this monster.'

'But you can't go back to London without coming to see us first.'

'Can't I? No, no, of course I can't. Oh, I expect it'll be all right.'

But on her way back to Kiltod with the Leghorn cockerel Muriel was worried. The luck which had given her an opportunity to come over to

Little Todday and see Bill did not seem to have been so bountiful as she had supposed it was.

On reaching the pier at Snorvig Muriel found everybody in a high state of excitement. Murdoch MacCodrum had just arrived in the Garryboo lorry with the news that Jemima Ross, the assistant at George Campbell's School, had been chased for two hundred yards along Tràigh Vooey by the monster, which was as large as two elephants and moved as fast as his own lorry.

Chapter 12

PAUL WAGGETT, K.C.

When George Campbell, the headmaster of Garryboo School, married Catriona Macleod, his mother, as she had threatened she would, left the Schoolhouse and went to live with her sister in Glasgow. Here, still unreconciled, the old lady had died a year ago. It had been Mrs Campbell's plan that George should marry Jemima Ross, his assistant teacher, over whom she felt she had established in advance the influence which she believed a mother should always have over her son's wife. Jemima Ross, in spite of her disappointment, did not apply for a transfer when her headmaster married, and though George Campbell himself would have been glad to lose her he had not the heart to make her position unpleasant.

So Jemima Ross stayed on, still lodging where she had lodged for the last six years with Mrs Angus MacCormac. She was a carroty wisp of a woman now close upon thirty, the daughter of a Black Isle man who had married a Skye woman and settled in Skye. The general opinion of Jemima Ross in Garryboo was that she was inquisitive and, like so many inquisitive people, a gossip; she had a significantly long thin nose. She was a good disciplinarian, though the parents of her pupils considered that she used the strap to excess; she was at the same time a good teacher, so good indeed that George Campbell, who was as conscientious a man as there was in the two islands, would, apart from his natural kindness, not have felt justified in trying to get her transferred.

When school was over that June day Miss Ross had gone down to Ardvanish Point to gather for herself some carrageen or sea-moss, which, when cooked with milk, makes a pudding resembling cornflour with a faint flavour of iodine. While bending over to gather the sea-moss from the rocks she had heard what she described as a noise like somebody beating a carpet accompanied by a snarling bark. She had looked up and to her horror she had seen a huge animal galloping towards her along Tràigh Vooey. She had dropped the carrageen in a panic, hurried as fast as she could along the flat slippery rocks of Ardvanish Point, fearful of falling and being seized by the monster, until she reached the safety of the grass, and had run all the way back to Garryboo to collapse in Mrs Angus MacCormac's kitchen from exhaustion and fright.

These were the hard facts of Miss Jemima Ross's alarming experience. The story that the monster chased her for two hundred yards along Tràigh Vooey, tearing out pieces of her skirt with its teeth, must be regarded as an exaggeration of what occurred, and it is a tribute to Mr Mackay's zeal for the truth, the whole truth, and nothing but the truth, that in the account of Miss Ross's adventure which he sent to the *Daily Tale* he did not try to pander to the public's appetite for sensationalism.

'What we can now consider an established fact,' he said to Bill Brownsworth, 'is that this mysterious creature is capable of moving with speed upon dry land. I confess that I should not care to find it gaining on me rapidly half way along Tràigh Swish. Even you, Brownsworth, with youth and long legs in your favour, might feel a little nervous in such circumstances, eh?'

'I certainly might,' Bill agreed.

'There's one thing. This latest appearance of the Todday Monster makes it imperative for you to remain here,' said Mr Mackay. 'You can't afford to run away from what may be a scientific discovery of supreme importance. You'd never be able to look knowledge in the face again.'

'Yes, I think I ought to stay,' Bill assented.

'You think?' Mr Mackay exclaimed. 'You *know* you ought to stay.'

That evening Bill Brownsworth wrote to his friend Dick Spinnage. They had been at the same prep. school together; they had been at St James's School together; they had been at London University together; they had been together on active service in the latter part of the war. To write to Dick Spinnage was to address his *alter ego*.

June 16

c/o Post Office, Kiltod,
Little Todday,
Outer Hebrides

Dear Dick,

Since I wrote to you about my secret engagement to Muriel Waggett a most awkward thing has happened. Her father came to see me about trespassing on this small island where he rents the shooting, and as a matter of fact we got on very well together, which made me feel quite bucked. With him was what I thought was Muriel and of course every time I could do so without her father seeing me I tried to show her how pleased I was to see her. At the end of the interview he said 'This is my daughter' and of course I thought he was introducing me to Muriel. And when he had disappeared under a natural arch which joins the little beach above which I'm camping to a much larger beach beyond, I kissed my hand to what I thought was Muriel and *she kissed her hand back to me*. And it wasn't Muriel at all!! It was her twin sister Elsie. Muriel herself came to see me next day and I only just managed not to let her know I'd made this ghastly mistake. Her father had asked me to go and call on the family in Snorvig and naturally Muriel was very keen I should call as soon as possible, the idea being that I should rather suck up to the old gentleman and then that we should meet in the autumn in London and she would write and say I'd proposed to her and all would be quite O.K. Well, after this ghastly mistake I didn't see how I could possibly go and call. It really has put me in a frightful position. Even you, Dick, who's had much more to do with girls than I have would find it pretty frightful. So I told Muriel that I might have to go back to London at once to consult some books and that seemed to strike rather a low note. Anyway, this 'monster' has been seen again and what is more it has been seen moving at a rapid pace along a beach on Great Todday. I can't go away when I may be on the verge of identifying this creature. You know how keen I am to get this Readership at Norwich. Do give me your advice. Muriel says that her sister is very jealous and I think Muriel is inclined to be jealous herself. I always thought twins saw eye to eye about everything, but I realize that if one made love to twins simultaneously it could cause very unpleasant complications. If I tell Muriel that in a way it's her fault because she never told me that she had a twin sister I shall be quite justified, but you know how unreasonable girls are and she'll be watching her sister and me all the time like a hawk. And then there's Elsie to consider. It occurs to me now that I may have several times given her looks – you know what I mean – when I've met her in Snorvig – thinking all the time it was Muriel. You know I'm not conceited about girls, but I think she was attracted. She must have been to kiss her hand like that. You've no idea how much alike they are – identical really. I sweat when I think that it might have been Elsie who came to see me and that I might have found myself engaged to her quite easily. Another complication is that Mr Waggett does not believe in the existence of this 'monster' and if I'm to keep in with him I can't make the monster an excuse for not calling. I mean if I say I'm always on the look-out for it and don't like to leave my post of observation, he'll be prejudiced against me over Muriel.

The only way out of this ghastly muddle is for you to help me. Do you think you could possibly get a fortnight's leave from your firm now and come up here? One's always reading about friends who fall in love with the same girl. It's possible, isn't it, that you might fall in love with Elsie Waggett? At any rate even if you didn't fall in love with her you could give her the impression that you had and I could say to Muriel something like 'I'm glad Dick Spinnage didn't meet you before I did or I shouldn't have had much chance'. However, the important thing is that you must, if you possibly can, come up here. We can discuss the plan of action when you get here.

Bring your camera. You might easily have the luck to get a snap of this animal, in which case £250 would be rather pleasant.

Wire me as soon as you get this. What worries me is that Elsie may tell Muriel about my having kissed my hand to her and then of course Muriel will get suspicious and ask me why I didn't tell her I had made this mistake.

You won't have to camp out. I've arranged with a very nice chap called Duncan Macroon to give you a bed in his house. So you won't have to wear shorts, which will apparently make a good impression on Mr Waggett.

I'm sorry to inflict this huge letter on you, Dick, but I really am in a spot and I know you're the only person who can get me out of it.

Yours aye,
Bill

'Will nothing stop this fellow Mackay?' Paul Waggett demanded, flourishing a copy of the *Daily Tale* outside the post office in Snorvig so violently that Monty, under the impression that he was being urged to attack something, rushed at Simon MacRurie's middle-aged collie which was lying peaceably in the sun outside his shop. Monadh retreated yelping within to be pursued by Monty round the customers' legs. There was a stream of excited Gaelic which became more excited when Monty's master pursued Monty in turn and after bumping into half-a-dozen cailleachs at last managed to seize the golden retriever by the collar.

'That dog of yours is too savage altogether, Mr Waggett,' said Simon MacRurie severely.

Simon was the leading merchant in Snorvig and an elder of the church with a great idea of his own importance in the eyes of God and of his fellow-men.

'He wouldn't hurt a child,' Waggett snapped irritably.

'You want to keep him on a lead,' the merchant insisted.

'I have him under perfect control. But I was upset by this disgraceful story about Miss Ross in the *Daily Tale*.'

'Ah, poor soul,' said Mrs Angus MacCormac who was shopping. 'And wasn't she almost dead in our kitchen chair. Oh, dear dear. I was really sorry for the poor soul, she was that scared. "*Och, a Bhean Aognhais*," she says to me, "I'm nearly killed dead by the monaster. Run? You were never seeing anything run so fast in all your life." Indeed, yes, that's just what she was saying, and "*m'eudail*, Miss Ross dear," I was saying to her, "don't be frightened, for the Lord has kept you safe and brought you back to us and I'm sure there's nobody in Garryboo so pleased as me to be seeing you when you are in our choir." Ach, poor soul, she was away down to Ardvanish just to be getting herself some carrageen for a wee pudding, and if she had not been hearing that terrible thump-thump on the Tràigh it's herself would have been just nothing better than a pudding in another minute.'

'Nothing but complete hysteria,' said Waggett loftily. 'I don't believe a word of it.'

And before Mrs Angus MacCormac could reply he had stalked out of the shop, the dignity of his exit being slightly marred by Monty's looking round to growl at Monadh and having to be dragged after his master.

'Oh, well, well, they're queer right enough these Engelish peoples,' Mrs MacCormac observed. 'Just stick the noses of them up into the air and believe nothing at all.'

The paragraph in the *Scottish Daily Tale* which had roused Paul Waggett's indignation was as follows:

MONSTER PURSUES TODDAY SCHOOLTEACHER AMAZING ESCAPE

On Wednesday last Miss Jemima Ross, the much respected assistant teacher at Garryboo School in Great Todday, took advantage of this glorious June weather to gather carrageen from the rocks below Ardvanish Point which juts out into the sea at the north end of Tràigh Vooey and affords a precarious shelter to the fishermen of Garryboo pending the erection of a pier on which it is understood work will begin this summer under the enlightened auspices of the Inverness-shire County Council. Carrageen or sea-moss is a sea-weed which when dried and cooked with milk provides a succulent dish reminiscent of a cornflour pudding.

Miss Ross was engaged upon her task which necessitated stooping and therefore she was unaware of the danger lurking in the vicinity, upon those yellow sands unto which she in her innocence had come. Suddenly the schoolteacher, her mind preoccupied with visions of the pudding she was going to make, heard behind her what she describes as a dull thud repeated at intervals and accompanied by a kind of snarling bark. She looked up, curious to know what could cause such an unwonted sound upon those tranquil sands, when to her horror and amazement she saw advancing along them at a rapid pace a huge monster which she estimates as larger than an elephant according to her recollection of the elephant she saw on a visit she once paid to the Edinburgh Zoo.

'Did you observe any teeth, Miss Ross?' we asked.

'I was too frightened to observe anything except the size of this monster and the way it was galloping towards me as fast as a man running.'

Miss Ross dropped her basket of carrageen and somehow managed to reach the grassy land at the head of Ardvanish Point which itself is covered with flat slippery rocks. Without looking back she ran up the slight incline all the way to Garryboo to reach the house of Mr and Mrs Angus MacCormac with whom she has resided ever since she was first appointed to Garryboo School six years ago.

It will be remembered that Tràigh Vooey was where Christina and Elizabeth MacCodrum encountered the monster, and Miss Ross's experience confirms that of her young pupils on whose story some strangely incredulous people have ventured to cast doubt. We hope that this latest appearance of the Todday Monster has taught such sceptics a lesson.

One wonders, a little anxiously, what was the object of the mysterious visitant from the deep in approaching Miss Ross at such speed. Can it be that, like the sea-monster from which Perseus rescued Andromeda in the days of yore, the Todday Monster is also carnivorous?

Meanwhile, the excitement is intense and those ardent young adventurers who have flocked to Great and Little Todday in the hope of winning the prize of £250 offered by the *Scottish Daily Tale* for the first authenticated photograph of the monster are more ardent than ever. An element of danger has been definitely added to the explorer's task, and who responds more quickly to danger than the youth of Britain? In the classic words of Field-Marshal Montgomery on the eve of Alamein, the *Scottish Daily Tale* wishes those adventurers 'Good Hunting!'

'There's only one thing I can do about this, Dolly,' her husband announced, 'I must see Jemima Ross myself and make her admit that she got into a panic about nothing.'

'Do you think . . . of course, you know best, dear . . . but you know what the people here are like. They don't really want anybody to disprove the existence of the monster.'

'Of course they don't. That's all the more reason for trying to get at the truth of this matter. I'm not going to encourage people to imagine monsters just because they're able to charge these trippers more for their board and lodging.'

So after tea Paul Waggett with Monty set off in his car to Garryboo. He called first at the Schoolhouse to let George Campbell know that he intended to interview Miss Ross.

'Why, it's Mr Waggett,' exclaimed Catriona Campbell, to whose skirts was clinging a small boy of two and a half with eyes as bright and as dark as her own. 'Say "how d'ye do," Iain,' she bade him. Whereupon Iain tried to turn his mother's skirts into a cave in which he could hide from this intruder.

'He's awful shy, Mr Waggett. You'll just have to excuse him. *Och, Iain, na bith gòrach.*'

But Iain, called after his grandfather Iain Macleod up at Knockdown, was determined to be foolish. Indeed, if the visitor had been the monster itself he could hardly have displayed a more apprehensive agitation. Then the visitor smiled, and that finished Iain off; he began to howl.

'Och, Iain, you really make me feel ashamed of you. Please go into the sitting-room, Mr Waggett, and I'll fetch George.'

She showed him into the flimsy sitting-room which, though hardly ten years old, looked as prematurely aged as all the rest of the buildings erected in the Islands since 1920.

George Campbell would always be shy, but he was a much less shy George than in the days when his old Gorgon of a mother ruled the Schoolhouse of Garryboo. He was over forty now, but he looked younger than he did in the days when he was Sergeant in command of the Garryboo section of the Home Guard.

'Will you take a little something to refresh you after your drive, Mr Waggett?'

'No, thank you, Mr Campbell. I never drink anything when I'm driving. I'm the only careful driver in Todday, and I'm bound to have an accident one day because all the lorry-drivers here are so reckless and I wouldn't like anybody to be able to say that I'd had even one dram. I've come up to talk to you about this latest disgraceful stunt in the *Daily Tale*. You must be feeling very annoyed at such rubbish being printed about Garryboo?'

'Och, I think we've all rather enjoyed it, Mr Waggett.'

'Enjoyed it?'

'We were beginning to feel in Todaidh Mór that they were keeping the monster shut up on Todaidh Beag.'

'I should have thought you'd have been only too glad to think that such nonsense was confined to Little Todday. One expects Father Macalister to encourage this kind of credulity. After all, where would Roman Catholics be without their credulity? But I think Great Todday should try to set an example.'

'You wouldn't say surely that this monster was entirely imagination, would you, Mr Waggett?'

'Entirely. Do you remember what difficulty I had when the war was on to convince the people here that Hitler might invade us?'

'Yes, it was pretty difficult.'

'And yet now they're ready to believe in a real impossibility like this monster. Don't you consider that perverse and pig-headed?'

'I wouldn't call it that, Mr Waggett. Here in Garryboo we have had pretty definite evidence that some kind of a strange creature is round about these waters.'

'Evidence? You're an M.A. of Glasgow University, aren't you?'

'I am.'

'Extraordinary! I never expected to hear an M.A. of Glasgow University tell me he believed in the existence of a prehistoric monster.'

'I'm not prepared to say that this creature is prehistoric, Mr Waggett. We just don't know what it is, but I think we can feel quite sure that it is something nobody here has seen before.'

Paul Waggett sighed.

'I'm disappointed by your attitude, Mr Campbell. I came to Garryboo this afternoon in the hope of trying to convince Miss Ross that this creature she is supposed to have seen galloping towards her on Tràigh Vooey was either a seal or an hallucination, but what chance have I got of doing that if her own headmaster encourages her hysterical behaviour?'

George Campbell might have added that he was well aware of his subordinate's weaknesses, but he was far too loyal to do that.

'Have you any objection to my examining her about this alleged monster?' Waggett asked. 'All sorts of outrageous stories about the incident are now circulating in Snorvig. One of my daughters came in to tea to tell us that old Ben Yacken William was going round telling everybody that this imaginary monster had bitten off the top half of Miss Ross's skirt. I think she was making vulgar jokes about the – er – result, but of course I don't encourage my daughters to report that sort of thing.'

'Ah, well, Mr Waggett, Bean Eachainn Uilleim is famous for being a bit of a wag . . .' George Campbell broke off with a blush . . . 'I mean a bit of a comic.'

'Personally I never find vulgarity comic. But to come back to what I was saying. Have you any objection to my interviewing Miss Ross?'

'It has really nothing to do with me, Mr Waggett.'

'Well, you know what my attitude always was in the Home Guard.

Never listen to any complaints over the head of a man's commanding officer. So I wanted to approach Miss Ross through the proper channels.'

Soon after this the stickler for military etiquette called at the MacCormac house, where Angus blew at him through his big moustache while his wife went to fetch down Miss Ross from her room.

'You'll take a cup of tea, Mr Wackett, please,' he was urged when he and the teacher had been shown into the parlour.

'No, thank you.'

'You'll take a dram, maybe?' the big crofter asked, cupping his moustache.

'Thank you, no, Angus. I never touch anything alcoholic when I'm driving my car.'

Angus and his wife withdrew and left their lodger with her visitor.

'Please sit down, Miss Ross,' Paul Waggett urged.

The thin carroty young woman with the pointed nose sat down in an armchair covered with green velvet; so did Waggett. They sat for a moment in silence under the stony gaze of an enlarged photograph of Angus MacCormac's grandfather, whose beard was to his grandson's big moustache as a haystack to a haycock.

'I thought I would like to ask what exactly you did see on Tràigh Vooey, Miss Ross?'

'Quite so, Mr Waggett. Yes, I'm sure I understand. Will you be wanting to write something in the papers about it?' the schoolteacher asked, with a hint of hunger, for she had already developed an appetite for publicity on the strength of her appearance in the columns of the *Daily Tale*.

'I do not write for the papers,' said Waggett coldly. 'I am merely anxious to arrive at the truth of this business.'

'Oh, it's just what they say in the paper. I was terrified. I was picking carrageen . . .'

'Yes, I know what you were doing, Miss Ross. I want to hear from your own lips what exactly you saw.'

'I saw this huge creature galloping at me and I was so frightened . . .'

'Yes, I know what you did, Miss Ross,' Waggett interposed. 'I want to know what exactly you saw.'

'I've told you.'

'Huge creature may mean anything . . . a rhinoceros or a hippopotamus or an elephant . . .'

'It was more like an elephant.'

'Have you ever seen a hippopotamus?'

'No, I never have, Mr Waggett.'

'Then how do you know it was more like an elephant? Had this monster got a trunk?'

'I didn't mean it looked like an elephant. I meant it was as big as an elephant.'

'Did you see its legs?'

'I didn't have time. I was too frightened.'

'But you say it was galloping. How do you know it was galloping if you didn't see its legs?'

'It was going up and down.'

'Like the motion of a seal when it is disturbed and makes for the water.'

'It was much bigger than a seal.'

'I said like the motion of a seal.'

'And much quicker than a seal.'

Waggett smiled with weary patience.

'I am not trying to suggest that you were suffering from an hallucination, Miss Ross,' he said kindly. 'I accept the fact that you did see something, but could you go into the witness box and declare on oath that what you saw was not a seal?'

'I never thought it was a seal.'

'I daresay not, but it was a long way from you, wasn't it?'

'Indeed, thank goodness it was, Mr Waggett.'

'So I suggest that you saw this big seal slithering along down to the water and with your mind full of the monster you thought it was larger than it really was.'

Miss Ross was not going to sacrifice her heroine status as easily as that.

'I'm not accustomed to imagining things, Mr Waggett,' she said, her thin lips closing tightly on this statement.

'We can all be wrong, Miss Ross. I've been wrong myself once or twice,' he added generously.

'I did not imagine anything I didn't see,' Miss Ross repeated obstinately. 'If I'd been given to imagining I would have been imagining these teeth, but I didn't see those big teeth the others have seen.'

'Or thought they saw,' Waggett corrected.

'I don't care to be always criticizing other people,' said Miss Ross.

Waggett would have liked to tell her that this was her reputation all over Great Todday, but he refrained on the principle of *noblesse oblige*.

'Well, I see you're determined to believe that you saw the monster.'

'I'm determined to believe my own eyes, yes, Mr Waggett.'

'And so I'm afraid there's nothing more for me to say, Miss Ross,' he replied with dignity.

The only satisfaction Paul Waggett derived from his visit to Garryboo was his ability to be able to say to his wife that night just before he put out the light:

'I sometimes regret, Dolly, I didn't take up the Law instead of Chartered Accountancy.'

'Do you, dear?'

'I think I should have made an extraordinarily good cross-examiner.'

'I'm sure you would, Paul.'

'Oh, well,' he decided philosophically, 'I suppose if I had been a leading barrister I should still be grinding away down in the Law Courts instead of leading the simple life here, though if this nonsense about an imaginary monster continues much longer we might as well go and live in one of these holiday camps. However, the papers will get tired of this monster soon. They even got tired of the war towards the end.'

On this remark Waggett put out the light and prepared himself to recede from the petty irritations of the moment into a self-satisfied sleep.

'What are you doing, Dolly?' he asked presently with a touch of irritation.

'I was feeling for my biscuit, Paul. I'm sorry I disturbed you,' she said with conjugal humility.

'I hope you haven't been reading this nonsense in the papers about night starvation,' he asked severely.

'What's that, dear?'

'Another of these Press stunts,' he told her.

On the other side of the Minch the account of Miss Ross's adventure, which had so much annoyed Paul Waggett, filled Ben Nevis with renewed zest for the expedition he was planning.

'This is certainly not our monster, MacIsaac,' he told his Chamberlain. 'Not that I ever thought it was. Our monster has never chased women and children anywhere on Loch Ness side. You can't name a single instance of that, MacIsaac. That's what infuriates me. Our monster wouldn't hurt a fly and yet it's being forced to lie up because of these vile flying saucers whizzing about all over the place. No, I never thought for a moment our monster had gone to the islands. All the same, with so many nincompoops and dunderheads cluttering up the countryside since this Bolshie Government . . .' a sudden thought darkened the Chieftain's brow . . . 'let them try to nationalize our monster. Mind you, MacIsaac, they're quite capable of it. But let them try. I think they'll find they've bitten off more than they can chew at the Scottish Office. Where was I? Oh yes, I was going to say now that this island monster is definitely proved not to be the Loch Ness Monster I think you ought to warn my people in Strathdiddle and Strathdun to be on the alert. Ha-ha! Do you remember when those War Office bigwigs, all wig and no brain, told us that the Home Guard always had to be in a state of suspicious alertness?'

'I do indeed, Ben Nevis.'

'Well, that's what I want my people in Strathdiddle and Strathdun to be in case our monster is lying up in that tunnel between Loch Hoo and Loch Ness. And don't let them think it's going to copy the habits of this Todday monster and start chasing women and children and what not. Well, I'm bound to say I am a little relieved that it's not our monster. I was beginning to think I'd bitten off more than I could chew, if you know what I mean, when I said if I found these Islanders had stolen our monster I'd bring it back to Loch Ness myself. It might have been rather a job, and as you know, when I say I'll do a thing I always do it. Mind you, MacIsaac, I don't blame this Todday monster for chasing these Islanders. If they had their way they'd double the rates, building them piers and lobster-pools and bridges and I don't know what not.'

'Yes, they're rather grasping,' his Chamberlain agreed.

'Rather grasping? If you'd heard that fellow Roderick MacRurie screwing a pier out of us at the last Council meeting for some one-eyed township called Garryboo. Garryboo? Why, that's where this Todday monster has been chasing this schoolteacher. I suppose if Chester Royde and I make a big game show out of our expedition we should have all these blood-sport ninnies on our track. The head of this Todday monster would look jolly well in the Great Hall with half a dozen Lochaber axes on each side of it. Still, I suppose it wouldn't do. They'd be saying we were as bad as flying saucers.'

'No, I don't think it would do, Ben Nevis.'

'Well, the Knocknacolly party will be here in less than a week now. Perfect weather which looks like lasting. It's going to be a splendid expedition. I simply cannot understand why people go and commit suicide. It's extraordinary, isn't it? I'll tell you what I will do, MacIsaac. I'll ask Bertie Bottley to let me have Kenneth MacLennan for a week. He'll be able to say definitely that this Todday monster is not the Loch Ness Monster he saw attacked by that beastly flying saucer. That will stop all argument once and for all. People think I'm prejudiced for some reason or other. By Jove, I've got it,' the Chieftain suddenly bellowed. 'What a duffer I am!'

His Chamberlain waited as on so many other previous occasions he had waited for the announcement of some plan which it would require all his tact to dissuade the Chieftain from trying to carry out.

'We'll try and frighten this Todday monster away from the two Toddays. Then it'll probably go north and we shan't hear any more of this Campbell jiggery-pokery about Obaig being the capital of the West. Of course, we don't want it to go too far north or else those Mackenzies and Macraes will be cashing in on it and they're almost as bad as the Campbells.'

'Yes, I see your point of view, Ben Nevis, but may I utter a word of warning?'

'Oh, of course you'll have to do that, MacIsaac. You've been croaking away at me like a raven for over twenty-five years. I ought to be used to it by now. Well, croak away.'

'It occurred to me that you couldn't be sure the monster or whatever it is . . .'

'Monster or whatever it is? What else could it be? Look here, MacIsaac, for goodness sake, don't you start being a Doubting Thomas. All right, go on.'

'I was going to say you couldn't be sure the monster would go north if you succeeded in frightening it away from Todday, Ben Nevis. It might go south. It might go to Tiree or even to Mull, and nothing would suit the people of Obaig better than that.'

'Yes, I see what you mean,' said the Chieftain in a tone which from any other lips than his would be described as pensive. 'Oh, well, whatever we decide to do, it's going to be a jolly expedition. How poor old Murdoch would have loved it!'

The Chieftain's second son, Lieut.-Commander Murdoch MacDonald, had been killed in the last few months of the war.

'Yes, yes, a sad thought,' said the Chamberlain. 'And it's a pity Young Ben Nevis can't be with us.'

'Oh, well, Hector and Pel . . . he and Penelope are enjoying themselves in Kenya. She's a great girl, MacIsaac. I couldn't have wished for a better daughter-in-law, but I only wish he'd picked a different name. I'm always saying Pelenope instead of Penelope. Well, I think we'd better have a dram and drink slahnjervaw to the Todday monster. I was a bit allergic to it at first if you know what I mean – ha-ha! – but I'm getting quite fond of it now that it's been discovered by this fellow Mackay to be carnivorous and therefore definitely not even a distant relation to our dear old Loch Ness Monster. Hullo, here's Toker with the whisky. How did you know I was going to ring for the decanter, Toker? Wonderful chap, Toker,' he said to his Chamberlain when the butler had retired. 'Always seems to know what I want just at the very moment I want it.'

While Ben Nevis was looking forward with the liveliest anticipation to the cruise of the *Banshee* when his friends arrived from America, at the headquarters of the B.B.C. in Queen Margaret's Drive, Glasgow, some of the moving spirits of Scottish Regional were hardly less excited by the prospects of their visit to Great and Little Todday.

'It would be wonderful,' said Francis Urquhart, who was to be in charge of the outside broadcasting equipment, 'if we could get a broadcast of this monster.'

'Ay, it would be great. It really would,' agreed Duncan MacColl, to whom was entrusted the task of co-ordinating all Gaelic activity on the air.

'The only thing that worries me,' said Francis Urquhart, 'is whether we can land the equipment on Little Todday.'

'I rather doubt it, Frank. But of course I don't want to butt in on the technical side. In fact, I've already written to Father Macalister to ask if he can manage the *céilidh* in the Snorvig Hall. He's just as popular in Great Todday as he is in his own parish. The snag is that we want to record a *luadh*.'

'A what?'

'A *luadh* or waulking is a gathering to shrink the tweed, and it's done by about a dozen women who sit on either side of a long table and shrink the tweed to the accompaniment of waulking songs. Of course, it's not actually done any more in the Toddays as it was once upon a time, but the Little Todday women, thanks to Father James himself, have kept up the traditional singing. The question is whether the Little Todday women will agree to come over to Snorvig.'

'Why wouldn't they?'

'It's always tricky to arrange a combined operation between the islands. Local feeling, you know. However, I hope Father James will exercise his influence. I don't really think you'll ever get the equipment across to Kiltod. That's why I was so pleased to read about this Garryboo appearance again. If we could only get a recording of those noises. You'd enjoy doing the O.B. wouldn't you, Frank, if the monster was galloping along the beach.'

'I'd enjoy it fine,' said Francis Urquhart. 'I don't know how much the engineer would enjoy it?'

'They'd be quite safe inside the wagon. It would be a terrific thrill for listeners.'

At this moment the Director came in.

'London has just been through to suggest that Howard Marshall should come up on the chance of our being able to establish contact with the Todday monster.'

'What?' exclaimed Francis Urquhart. 'Why don't they send Wilfred Pickles up as well and Richard Dimbleby and the whole bl . . .'

'Now don't get excited, Urquhart,' the Director interrupted. 'I'm going to ask if we get a good recording whether they won't take it on Home and Light . . . they might take it on Third as well. After all, it has a great scientific interest.'

'But what does London want to interfere for at all? The damned monster didn't bob up in the Thames. Och, I've nothing against Howard Marshall, but I think a monster in the Hebrides is entirely a matter for Scottish Regional.'

'Well, I had put that point of view to them.'

'Point of view!' Francis Urquhart scoffed. 'When did London ever understand our point of view up here?'

'Now, don't worry, Urquhart. I shall suggest how very unlikely it is that we shall have the luck to be on the spot at the same time as this mysterious creature and that the main preoccupation of the unit will be recording the local atmosphere – talks with old men, and the economic position, and of course a *cèilidh*. Well, obviously you and MacColl will have to look after all that, and if – a very large "if" too – if this mysterious creature does materialize, why, then, you'll be perfectly able to handle the emergency. I think it will be all right.'

The Director withdrew on this optimistic note.

'Just because we won't take their cricket broadcasts,' Francis Urquhart commented bitterly. 'I'm sure that's the reason they want to send

Howard Marshall up here. It's nothing whatever to do with the Todday monster. It's just a trick to make us take their cricket broadcasts on Scottish Regional. If I were Director I'd say "we'll take your cricket broadcasts if you'll take Duncan MacColl's Gaelic quarter of an hour". That would bring in a few letters from listeners to the Light Programme.'

Meanwhile, over in Little Todday, Bill Brownsworth was waiting anxiously for a reply from Dick Spinnage. Something much worse had happened to him than he had foreseen when he sent that SOS to his friend.

Chapter 13

A SLIGHT MISUNDERSTANDING

———

Although Bill Brownsworth would have preferred not to go near Great Todday until he had the support of his friend Dick Spinnage, he had allowed himself to be persuaded by Hector Hamish Mackay to accompany him on his second visit to Miss Ross at Garryboo.

'I want you to watch her very carefully, Brownsworth, and tell me quite frankly if you think she is an hysterical subject.'

'But I don't know anything about female hysteria,' he protested.

'In the prehistoric Eden you fancy there would have been no hysteria?'

'I shouldn't care to commit myself to so general a statement as that,' the young palaeontologist said.

'No, but you could observe Miss Ross closely while she is answering my questions and let me have your impressions of her reliability as a witness.'

'But you've talked to her yourself and you were satisfied of her reliability when you gave her story to the *Daily Tale*.'

'Yes, but I've just had this rather peculiar letter from Mr Waggett which I feel I cannot ignore without running the risk of his writing over my head to James Donaldson, and you know what editors are.'

'Well, I don't really,' said Bill Brownsworth, who was disinclined to admit his knowledge of anything that would take him over to Great Todday without Dick Spinnage.

'Editors are extremely sensitive people.'

'Are they?' Bill Brownsworth asked in surprise. Had he been driven into expressing an opinion about editors he would have been likely to venture a comparison between their hides and those of the megalosaurians with which he was more familiar.

The topographer gave him the letter he had received from Paul Waggett:

Snorvig House,
Great Todday,
June 20th

Dear Mr Mackay,

I read with astonishment what I assume was your report to the Scottish Daily Tale on the subject of the alleged 'monster' to Miss Jemima Ross, the assistant teacher at Garryboo School.

As soon as I had read this report I made it my business to interview Miss Ross and obtain from her an admission that what she had seen was nothing more unusual than a large grey Atlantic seal slithering down from Traigh Vooey into the water. I do not wish to suggest either that Miss Ross deliberately exaggerated the occurrence or that you allowed your pen to exaggerate it. At the same time, in the interest of truth, I shall feel it my duty to notify the Editor of the Scottish Daily Tale of the true facts of what happened and if he fails to publish my communication I shall notify the rest of the Scottish Press of what I consider his deliberate intention to work up a sensation with the object of obtaining publicity for his paper.

I do not wish to be unfair to you, and therefore I take this opportunity of warning you that Miss Ross has the reputation of being a gossip of which you may not have been aware when you encouraged her to talk so freely about this imaginary monster. Verbum sapienti.

Yours faithfully,
Paul Waggett

'Of course, I don't know how far our friend Waggett has involved himself in the risk of a slander action by accusing Miss Ross of being a gossip,' the topographer observed, 'but I'm afraid Donaldson won't consider that. He will be entirely concerned with his own position in regard to other editors, and if Miss Ross has admitted that it was a seal, he and I will both be in an extremely awkward position. So, quite apart from the value of your opinion about Miss Ross's emotional condition, it is really essential for me to have a third person present when I interrogate her, for my professional reputation is at stake, Brownsworth.'

So with a prayer to fortune that they would not meet any of the Waggett family Bill Brownsworth had accompanied Hector Hamish Mackay to Garryboo.

From the point of view of the latter the expedition had been a complete success because not only had Miss Ross denied indignantly any admission to Paul Waggett that the creature she saw was a seal but George Campbell had testified warmly in favour of her accuracy as an observer of nature.

'Very satisfactory. Very satisfactory indeed,' the topographer had declared when they landed again at Kiltod, and inasmuch as Bill Brownsworth had not caught sight of any of the Waggett family he had been able to echo Mr Mackay's enthusiasm with sincerity. Indeed, he had been sufficiently impressed by Miss Ross's account of her adventure when not being antagonized by Waggett's forensic ambitions to be anxious to get back as soon as possible to Tràigh Veck in the hope of enjoying a similar adventure himself.

'I'd like you to see the letter I propose to send to Waggett.'

So Bill Brownsworth had waited for the counter-attack.

'I think that will put him in his place,' said Hector Hamish Mackay:

> c/o Mr Joseph Macroon,
> Kiltod,
> Little Todday,
> June 21st

Dear Mr Waggett,

I received your letter and at once charged myself with the duty of re-examining Miss Jemima Ross. I am satisfied that you were mistaken in supposing her to have admitted that the creature she saw was a grey Atlantic seal.

I was discreet enough not to mention to Miss Ross that you had accused her of being a gossip because I would not wish to involve anybody in an action for slander, particularly somebody who is as ardently concerned as I am to ascertain the truth.

I may mention that I was accompanied by Mr William Brownsworth, a rising young palaeontologist, who, like myself, was completely satisfied by the bona fides of Miss Ross and was unable to detect in her the slightest tendency toward hyperbolism.

Yours faithfully,
Hector Hamish Mackay

'I say, would you mind very much leaving out that last bit about me?' Bill Brownsworth asked anxiously.

'But why? I want to impress this fellow Waggett with the fact that I am not playing a lone hand in this matter.'

'Yes, I know, but I've got rather a special reason for not wanting you to mention me to Mr Waggett in connection with this creature.'

'Come, come, Brownsworth, creature is hardly the word for poor little Miss Ross, who surely deserves your chivalrous support.'

'I mean in connection with the monster. I told you he came to warn me about trespassing on Pillay, and well, . . . I can't explain yet exactly why I don't want you to mention me in connection with this creature . . .

with this monster, but it is rather important for me that you don't. And anyway, if he thinks what I heard on Pillay was the noise of a seal he won't pay any attention to my opinion.'

'As you will, Brownsworth,' said the topographer, the east wind of Edinburgh giving a bite to his agreement. 'But I take it you have no objection to my quoting you to my Editor?'

'Oh, none at all.'

Bill Brownsworth reached his camp in the sandy hollow above Tràigh Veck on that warm afternoon, still without any word from Dick Spinnage, and decided to take off his shirt and have a nap. He awoke with that sense of danger in the vicinity which is so usual an alarm clock to men of action in adventure stories.

'The monster' was his first thought, and he hastily pulled on his shoes in case he had to clamber over rocks. Then he sprang up just as Muriel (or was it Elsie?), just as Elsie (or was it Muriel?) emerged from the arch.

'Hullo, darling!' he exclaimed with all the ardour he could infuse into what was so often a nonchalant greeting, and while congratulating himself on the presence of mind which had saved him from saying 'Muriel', cursing himself within the same instant for the lack of it which had not saved him from saying 'darling'.

Then, with what those at a safe distance from such a desperate situation as Bill Brownsworth's may censure as a stupid gesture, he held out his arms. Bill himself argued that if the apparition in a flowered cotton frock he had never seen before melted into his arms he could assume that it was Muriel. The apparition duly melted, but as the apparition's lips met his he was assailed by a horrible doubt whether they were not in fact the lips of Elsie. After all, if Muriel had fallen in love with him at first sight her twin sister might have fallen in love with him with equal celerity, which would account for what otherwise might have seemed too easy a surrender.

'All well at home?' Bill asked in the hope that whichever girl it was would mention the other in reply.

'Father's still on the warpath,' Muriel or Elsie replied.

'On the warpath?' Bill echoed with a frown of apprehension.

'Against the monster.'

'Yes, of course. I was afraid at first you meant me.'

'Oh, no, he's taken quite a fancy to you. But you know that.'

A dead end. Either of the sisters might have told him this; in fact, Muriel already had. He tried a bolder approach.

'How's your sister?'

'She came over to Kiltod with me.'

Bill Brownsworth hoped that whichever girl it was would attribute the beads upon his forehead to the normal sudatory effect of the sun.

'She may be coming along here,' he suggested gloomily.

'Oh, no. Don't worry. She's having tea with old Mrs Odd.'

'But won't she be wondering where you are?'

'Not a bit. I told her I was going to see Mrs Hugh Macroon.'

Another dead end! Muriel had been to see Mrs Hugh Macroon the last time she visited Tràigh Veck. It must be Muriel after all. Oh, yes, of course it was Muriel. He was letting himself get into a stew about nothing.

'I've written to ask my greatest friend, Dick Spinnage, to come and stay with me,' said Bill Brownsworth. 'Wouldn't it be wonderful if he fell in love with your sister and she fell in love with him? We could have a double wedding.'

'A double wedding,' she murmured softly, with a sweet emotion.

'Dick and I have been friends ever since our prep. school. The other chaps nicknamed us Bill and Coo, though Dick was also called Turnip Tops, and at St James's he was called Topsy.'

'And didn't you have a nickname?'

'No, I was always Bill.'

'Bill. I'm glad. I love the name Bill.'

Bill Brownsworth was again a prey to doubt. He had a sudden macabre suspicion that she did not know until this moment that his name was Bill. Oh, he was worrying himself needlessly. He mustn't start fancying horrors. Muriel was often saying how much she liked the name Bill.

Then he felt beads of sweat glistening upon his forehead beyond even the power of a tropical sun to precipitate. If this was not Muriel he had practically proposed to her sister. What mad impulse had lured him into talking about a double wedding? If this was Elsie she must now be supposing that Dick Spinnage had been invited here to fall in love with Muriel. If this was Elsie she must be supposing that she was to be his own bride at this double wedding.

'It's frightfully hot,' he gulped, mopping his forehead.

'Is your friend Dick Spinnage good-looking?' she asked.

'Oh, awfully good-looking. He's rather like Ivor Novello.'

'I say!'

'You think your sister will like him?'

'I'm jolly sure she will. But he might not fall in love with her, might he?'

'I'm positive he will. Our tastes are identical. That's why I'm so keen for him to come up here.'

'When's he coming?'

'I don't know exactly. I was hoping for a telegram this morning.'

'Perhaps he'll be on the *Island Queen* when she arrives this afternoon. I'll tell you what Muriel says about him when we meet again.'

Bill Brownsworth had a momentary impression that somebody had caught him a sharp crack on the head with a hammer.

'Muriel?' he repeated in a hollow voice.

'That's my sister's name.'

'Oh, is it? I thought it was Elsie.'

'Did you think I was Muriel?'

'No, of course not. I just got the names the wrong way round.'

When Elsie had departed to pick up her sister and go back to meet the *Island Queen* Bill Brownsworth could have kicked himself the full length of Tràigh Swish for not having given a bold affirmative to that question. The words he ought to have said flowed now that she was no longer able to hear them.

'Yes, I did think you were Muriel. Otherwise I shouldn't have asked you to kiss me. It is only right to tell you that Muriel and I are engaged. We fell in love with one another at first sight. She wished our engagement to be kept a secret at present because she didn't know how your father would take it. When he came to speak to me about trespassing on Pillay I thought it was Muriel who came with him.'

That was what he ought to have said, and although he might have made a lifelong enemy of his future sister-in-law by saying it that would have been better than the deplorable position in which he had left himself out of sheer cowardice. It had been bad enough when he had mistaken Elsie for Muriel the first time, but it was nothing to the situation he had brought about by talking about a double wedding. It was the sort of thing one might say in a bad dream, but not in reality. What else could Elsie imagine but that he had been making her a proposal of marriage? He recalled with a heavy heart the tone of her voice when she had murmured 'a double wedding' with all too evident a pleasure at the prospect. The tone of her voice tolled in his ears with the solemn melancholy of a passing-bell.

The only crumb of comfort he could extract from this disastrous meeting was Elsie's awe when he had said that Dick Spinnage was rather like Ivor Novello. Obviously if he had not made such a mess of things she would have been quite prepared to fall for Dick. And he had not exaggerated. If Dick were a composer and a dramatist and a singer and an actor and his profile were enhanced by the meretricious glamour of the footlights he would be rather like Ivor Novello.

But what was the good of all these comparisons between Dick and Ivor Novello? Dick had failed him; Dick had not even written; his appeal had been coldly ignored by his best friend. For the rest of that afternoon Bill Brownsworth gave himself up to self-recrimination. It was so easy to explain the misunderstanding to Elsie when Elsie was not there, and then from being worried about what Elsie would say and do he began to be even more worried about what Muriel would say and do. In his anxiety about Elsie he had forgotten the explanation he would owe to Muriel. Muriel would say, and she would have a right to say it, that if he was capable of mixing her up with her twin sister he could hardly be as much in love with her as he pretended to be. Muriel would not believe that her outward resemblance to Elsie could deceive one who truly loved her. She was bound to resent the slight upon her personality.

Then he fell back upon a day dream. Dick had arrived and had made an immediate impression upon Elsie.

'I'm sorry for poor Bill, Elsie, but I love you, and all's fair in love and war. You love me. I will tell Bill what has happened, and when he knows that you love his best friend I feel somehow that Bill will turn to Muriel, and that Muriel will console him. You and she are superficially very much alike, but I love you and I do not love Muriel. I know Bill. He will face up to facts. The one thing he would not be able to stand would be for you to give yourself to him when all the while you were in love with me. That would be a mortal blow to poor old Bill, and he would be bound to find out the truth. He analyses everything. Science is his god. We should never be able to keep the truth from him. So let me tell Bill tonight that fate has brought you and me together and that bitterly sorry as I am to step between him and the girl he loves, I cannot live a lie.'

Bill Brownsworth was in the middle of this vicarious eloquence when he heard his name shouted from the arch, and saw Kenny Macroon.

'I've brought along a friend of yours, Mr Brownsworth, who came by the boat.'

Bill's heart leapt with joy. He jumped up and ran to greet his longed-for friend, but as he reached the arch he heard a prim voice say,

'Eureka.'

And it was not Dick Spinnage. It was Mr Sydney Prew, the Secretary of the National Union of Hikers, bowed down beneath a weight of camping equipment, the dark hairs between the top of his stockings and the bottom of his shorts fluttering in the light June breeze.

'Yes, here I am,' said Mr Prew. 'And full of plans to contact the monster. Yes, some of the jolly young people here and I have already discussed the possibility of forming non-stop monster patrols. Lord Buntingdon is intensely interested and desired to be remembered to you. He of course, loyal as ever to the Testudinaceae, does not conceal his hope that the monster may prove to be a great turtle hitherto unknown to testudinaceous experts. And this is your camp? Delightful. You'll not object to my teaming up with you tonight? I want to hear of your adventures round a roaring camp-fire. And don't think I'm going to upset your commissariat. Oh, no. An old timer like myself doesn't do that. I hope you like "Spam"? I always say there's nothing like "Spam" for giving a spice to life.'

Bill Brownsworth was dimly aware of the grin on Kenny Macroon's face as in a daze he led Mr Prew to the sandy hollow above Tràigh Veck.

Chapter 14

THE POPPAY MANIFESTATION

The small isle of Poppay lies rather nearer to the south coast of Little
Todday than Pillay to the north coast. Moreover, unless a south-westerly
gale is blowing hard Poppay can be reached without difficulty, there
being a well-protected small bay facing north-east with a wide shelf of
rock by which a boat may be moored on a clean bottom and lie snug
enough in any weather and at any state of the tide. Bàgh nam Marbh or
the Bay of the Dead is so called because in the old days Poppay was the
burial-place of the Macroons. The body was put aboard from Tràigh
nam Marbh, the Strand of the Dead, at the south-east end of Little
Todday and ferried across to its last resting-place. The old burial-ground
lay above the sands of Bàgh nam Marbh at the bottom of a long brae
sloping up to the cliffs which fall sheer to the sea in columns of dark
basalt along the northern and western faces of Poppay. The grass grows
rank in the old burial-ground, and in one corner of it are the crumbling
walls of a little ancient church, in another a cock-eyed Celtic cross. If
tombstones ever marked where the dead slept none of them remains
today. Yet this old burial-ground, disused for nearly two centuries,
preserves an almost eerie solemnity, so that the visitor who sits in the
lush grass beside a small burn that winds down the brae, the banks of
which when it reaches the level of the burial-ground are bright in the
month of June with golden flags, is apt to look over his shoulder from
time to time, under the impression that he is being watched by an
invisible presence. He is not surprised to be told that Poppay is the
resort of *bòcain* whose haunting influence extends to Tràigh nam Marbh
on Little Todday, a strand along which no native of the Islands likes to
walk without a companion in the flesh.

Beyond the burn the rocky southerly horn of Bàgh nam Marbh rises
more steeply to a terrace of sparse greenery which gives access to a large
cave called Uamh nan Cnàmh, the Cave of the Bones, in which according
to legend a Macroon chief with a strong sense of conjugal duty had
starved his wife to death for having gazed, as he imagined amorously, at
the eldest son of the MacRurie Chief of the time.

The origin of the name Poppay is in dispute, but most philologists now accept it as a variant of Pabbay — the Priest's Island. There is, however, a small but noisy minority which prefers to seek for the etymology of the name in *pìòb* — Pipe Island — from a fancied resemblance to a piper of an isolated basaltic fragment rising from the sea just off the point of the northerly horn of Bàgh nam Marbh. Certainly this rock is still known as *Am Piobair*, but, as Mr John Lorne Campbell of Canna has observed sternly, 'there is no excuse for flouting every canon of etymology in order to gratify a taste for the facile picturesque. Poppay is clearly a piece of debased eighteenth-century topography for Pabbay, and indeed, on a rare map of Todaidh Mór and Todaidh Beag in my possession dated 1780, I find Pobbay. After the deliberate efforts of the S.P.C.K., financed from London, to extirpate Gaelic and Latin from the Islands and Wester Inverness through the latter half of the eighteenth century, it is a matter for grateful surprise that corrupt nomenclature like Poppay is not more frequent.'

The mind of Joseph Macroon was not disturbed by etymological problems as he sat in the prow of the *Morning Star* on the anniversary of the famous invasion of the Toddays by Major Donald MacDonald of Ben Nevis and C Company of the 8th Battalion of the Inverness-shire Home Guard to recover a left-footed boot which he considered had been stolen from him by Captain Paul Waggett of G Company. It was just such another tranquil and sunny June morning again. The reason for Joseph Macroon's visit to Poppay was to extract from what was left of his share of the whisky saved from the wreck of the *Cabinet Minister* a bottle of Stalker's Joy, in order to present it to Mr Hector Hamish Mackay whose loyal championship of Little and Great Todday against the jealous attempts by other islands to claim their monster he felt merited a gesture of appreciation.

Joseph Macroon was esteemed as hard a man at a bargain as anybody in the Long Island, but when he gave he gave generously, and in giving Mr Mackay a bottle of Stalker's Joy he was giving him a bottle of the brand that was his own special favourite.

In choosing Poppay as the repository for his liquid treasure Joseph was actuated by the desire to protect it as much against the people of Little Todday as against the Excise. Poppay was no place at all for a nocturnal excursion on account of its ghostly population, and if anybody had visited his hiding-place during the day-time Joseph could not have failed to hear of such a raid.

Kenny Macroon knew that his father had concealed the whisky in Uamh nan Cnàmh, but even he had never ventured to linger long enough in that haunted cave to discover exactly where, and on this morning he remained in the *Morning Star* moored to the rocky shelf in Bàgh nam Marbh, while his father went off through the rank grass of the burial-ground a foot or two above the sandy beach toward the steep rocky slope that led up to the Cave of the Bones, the terrace in front of which was some thirty feet above the sea.

As Kenny watched his father's red knitted cap going up the slope he thought to himself that the *bodach* was still pretty lively. If this was the reflection that occurred to him when his father was on the way up it occurred to him much more forcibly when he saw his father coming down.

'*A Dhia*,' Kenny muttered to himself. 'I never saw the old man move so fast since he heard the shooting and thought the Germans had landed on Tràigh nam Marbh. *A Dhia*, he is running like a pony with a cleg biting him.'

Kenny watched his father's red cap bobbing above the rank grass of the burial-ground, and when he hailed him to find out what was the matter as his father reached the corner of the beach near the landing-place, for answer he snatched his red knitted cap from his head, fell on his knees, crossed himself and said three Hail Marys, followed by a Paternoster and three more Hail Marys.

'Och, he will be making an Act of Contrition now. *Dé rud, athair?*'

Joseph waved his hands for his son not to interrupt his devotions. When they were finished he came along the shelf and got back into the boat.

'Are you after seeing a *bòcan?*' Kenny asked.

'I'm after seeing a fearful terrible thing, *a Choinnich*. Ah, well, God forgive me that I would even be wondering if the Biffer wasn't seeing so much as he said he was after seeing. Ay, ay, God forgive me. Teeth? *A Dhia na Gràs*, it was a terrible thing right enough. I was just bending over to get a bottle of Stalker's Joy for Mr Mackay when I was after hearing . . . snarl were you saying? . . . not at all . . . it was more of a roar with a whistle on the end of it from the far back of the cave and then I saw it looking at me.' Joseph crossed himself again. 'And the eyes of it!' He shuddered. 'But the teeth were the worst.'

'Like pickaxes Mistress Odd said they were,' Kenny reminded him.

'Och, pickaxes,' Joseph scoffed. 'A pickaxe wouldn't be seeming much bigger than a toothpick besides such huge great weapons. Och, well, it will cost me a new statue for St Tod for getting me away from those teeth. I've been meaning to get one for him ever since the roof of the Chapel leaked on to his mitre and turned the face of him as green as grass. "Poor old St Tod," Maighstir Seumas was for ever saying with a quick look at me and me knowing what he was wanting would be looking the other way. Ay, ay, I'll tell Father James to order a new statue right away and I'll pay for it, carriage and all. *A Dhia*, it's me that's glad I'm not a Protestant this day, or there would be a few more bones in Uamh nan Cnàmh right enough, for it was St Tod himself who pulled me out of the business, and the holy man will have the best statue my money can buy for him. There won't be a better statue in Morar or Moidart, no, nor in Mid Uist or Barra.'

'Did you get the whisky?'

'How would I be getting the whisky?' Joseph demanded indignantly. 'Is it whisky I would be thinking of when I was staring into two eyes you wouldn't see the like of in Hell itself.' He crossed himself again. 'Ay, ay, poor Airchie, it was just as well he was in the *Kittiwake*, for he'd never have come out of Uamh na Snaoiseanaich alive, and not a saint for the poor soul to call on to help him.'

During the journey back to Kiltod Joseph Macroon sat in the bows of the *Morning Star*, shaking his head from time to time in grave reflection on God's mercy to him as a Catholic.

'Did you hear about wee Jonathan Munro in school, *athair*?' his son asked.

'What was that?'

Jonathan Munro was the only young Protestant in the Kiltod School.

'Why, when Miss MacDonald was taking the infants Michael Anthony Macroon held up his hand and said Jonathan Munro had made a big swear. "Och," says Miss MacDonald, "what was that at all?" "Please, miss, Jonathan Munro was saying that God is a Protestant." '

'Ay, ay, look at that now,' said Joseph sombrely; in his present mood of chastened gratitude for his safety he did not think the story at all funny.

When Kenny stopped the engine of the *Morning Star* to come quietly alongside the stone steps down from the quay of Kiltod's diminutive harbour, his father said in tones that left his son in no doubt that he expected him to pay attention.

'You'll not be saying a word to anybody about Poppay, Kenny. Not a word, mind you, not a word. I'll be seeing Father James myself just now.'

Joseph Macroon walked along to the Chapel House where the parish priest who was saying his office laid down the breviary and motioned his visitor to the armchair on the other side of the fireplace.

'I've been thinking, Father James, that it looks pretty bad for St Tod to have that kind of a green face on him, and Little Todday so full of towrists.'

'Ay, ay, it looks pretty bad right enough, *a Iosaiph*,' replied the priest, pondering his leading parishioner's remark the way a chess-player will consider the gambit offered him by his opponent.

'So, I've been saying to myself, *a Mhaighstir Sheumais*, wouldn't it be a good idea now if there was to be a new statue.'

'Oh, a glorious beautiful idea it would be, right enough,' Father James agreed. 'But if you're suggesting a whip round to subscribe for a new statue, Joseph, you'll be waiting till the contributions have been collected for my coal.'

'It's not a collection I would be making at all,' said Joseph Macroon, with a touch of self-righteousness in the tone of his reply. 'And if it's coal for the year that you're thinking about, Father, you needn't be thinking at all because the puffer will be here early next month and your coal is on order all correct. No, no, Father, I was thinking I would be offering the Chapel a new statue of St Tod and paying for it myself, carriage as well.'

'Good shooting!' the priest approved sonorously.

'That was a nice wee statue of St Anthony the Sgoileir Dubh was after giving when the new school was built, but a patron saint oughtn't to be squeezed into nothing at all like that, and so I'd like St Tod to be able to hold his own with Our Lady, Star of the Sea, on the other side of the Chapel. And that means just twice as big as he is now.' Joseph hummed to himself for a moment or two. 'It'll cost me the price of a new engine second-hand for the *Morning Star*, but if we get that lobster-pool maybe I'll buy a new boat next year.'

'And will I put the order for St Tod in hand, Joseph?'

'You'll do that, Father, please, right away.'

'Would you say it was too early in the day, Joseph, for a sensation?' the priest asked.

'It would be too early on most days, Father, but I believe I'd take a sensation today. I believe it's what I need to restore the balance.'

The priest rose and went to a cupboard in the corner from which he produced a bottle of Stag's Breath and a couple of dram glasses.

'*Slainte mhór*, Father,' said Joseph, draining the glass.

'*Slainte mhath, a Iosaiph*,' the priest responded. 'And I hope St Tod will give you your lobster-pool.'

'Och, it's not to be getting something out of the man I'm giving the statue to the Chapel.'

'Is it not, Joseph?'

'No, no, Father, it's for a favour received.'

And Joseph Macroon went on to tell Father Macalister the story of his alarming experience on Poppay.

'You'll be telling Mr Waggett that story you've just been telling me, Joseph.'

'Indeed, and I'll be doing no such thing, Father. And it's just because I don't want a soul except yourself to know what happened to me in Uamh nan Cnàmh that I'm after telling you.'

'Ay, but you haven't told me the whole story, Joseph,' said the priest. 'You haven't told me about the Minnie you have hidden in Uamh nan Cnàmh.'

Joseph was on the verge of crossing himself, so slight was seeming to him at that moment the difference between Father James Macalister and the Devil himself.

'Ah, well, well, you know too much and that's the truth, *a Mhaigstir Sheumais*. Ay, there may be a little Minnie left right enough,' Joseph admitted, and then added hastily, 'but it's little enough, more's the pity, and there will be none left at all if these towrists and visitors go looking for the monster and find the Minnie.'

'Ay, ay, you'll do well to move it, Joseph. How many bottles have you?'

'Och, there might be half-a-dozen or perhaps a full dozen.'

'Or a couple of dozen and a half-a-dozen more. You'd better be moving it pretty quickly, Joseph.'

'I wouldn't go into Uamh nan Cnàmh and see those eyes looking at me and those terrible teeth for all the whisky in the country. But that's not to say I'm wanting these towrists to clear me out. Och, I don't know what to do about it at all, at all.'

The priest leant back in his chair and looked up to the ceiling for inspiration.

'This is what you'll do, Joseph,' he announced at last in a voice an oracle would have envied. 'You'll tell Mr Mackay just how things are . . .'

'Och, if I tell him I'll be in the papers right away.'

'You'll tell Mr Mackay and young Brownsworth and you'll ask them to get your Minnie away if the coast's clear and what you'll do with it after that is your own business except that you'll be giving me two bottles of King's Own if there's any of it left.'

'There's no King's Own, Father. I never saw another bottle of it after my daughters broke a dozen bottles on me when they thought the Excise was after it. *Obh bh'obh*, what a terrible day that was!'

'Well, well, you'll be giving me a couple of bottles of whatever you have. And you'll be giving Mr Mackay a couple of bottles.'

'Wasn't I going to fetch a bottle of Stalker's Joy for him when the monster nearly had me in his jaws?'

'And if young Brownsworth gets a photograph of the monster and wins £250 you'll be telling him that we want a new stove in the sacristy and that's the way he can show his gratitude for a favour received.'

'I'll do that, Father.'

'Ay, and you won't be putting into his head, Joseph, that you're expecting anything for yourself out of that £250.'

'Would I ever do a thing like that?'

'No, no, I couldn't imagine your doing such a thing. That's just why I was telling you that you wouldn't be doing it, because I know you wouldn't like St Tod to be under an obligation to a Protestant.'

'Certainly not, Father James. That would be taking the gilt off the gingerbread for his goodness to me altogether.'

'It certainly would. And now there's something else you can do. The B.B.C. have let me know that they won't be able to give their broadcast from Little Todday and they want me to arrange a *luadh* in Snorvig. I'll be telling the *cailleachan* in Church on Sunday from the altar that they'll be going over to Snorvig and when you open the shop after Mass you'll not be listening to any nonsense about the people of Snorvig sitting back to criticize them. I've spoken to the Dot and they'll all go in the *St Dot*.'

The Dot was the name under which Donald Macroon, a small swarthy taciturn man, was generally known, and his sizeable fishing-boat, the *St Tod*, was always called the *St Dot* by Father Macalister.

'Alec Mackinnon is arranging for the performers from Great Todday and we'll just have Duncan Bàn from here with Andrew Chisholm and

Michael Gillies for some piping and old Michael Stewart for a *port a beul*.'

'I'll do what you say, Father,' said Joseph Macroon.

'By all the holy crows, and you certainly will, Joseph, or you'll find me much less inclined than St Tod to get you out of a predicament.'

'What a man,' Joseph Macroon reflected as he walked over to his shop from the Chapel House. 'Ay, ay, he got back at me right enough for not letting him have a bottle of the real Mackay that time he had nothing but altar wine for a dram last month and the wind in the east. But how did he know I had any Minnie left in Uamh nan Cnàmh? It would be the Devil who was wanting a long spoon if he was taking brose with Maighstir Seumais. What a man, what a man! Och, if I save the Minnie from those towrists it's three bottles of Stalker's Joy I'll be giving him.'

Hector Hamish Mackay and Bill Brownsworth were impressed by Joseph Macroon's adventure on Poppay. To his relief the topographer was as much against giving the news to the papers as he was himself while a bottle of Minnie remained in the Cave of the Bones.

'What we have to guard against now,' said Mr Mackay, 'is the possibility of idle trippers landing on Poppay and disturbing the monster.'

'They can't be getting there except by boat,' said Joseph. 'I'll be seeing the Biffer and Drooby and I'm sure they'll never be putting a towrist alone on Poppay from Todaidh Mór.'

'What about Mr Waggett?' Bill Brownsworth asked. 'Doesn't he have the shooting on Poppay?'

'Ay, he goes there missing more snipe than he hits in the autumn, but there's nothing for him to shoot at just now, *taing do Dhia*.'

'Yes, but there was nothing for him to shoot at on Pillay,' Brownsworth pointed out. 'But he wasn't at all pleased that I had landed there. And then he's very much against the idea that the monster really exists. He may want to go to Poppay and contradict Mr Macroon's story.'

'There's no contradiction in it,' said Joseph indignantly. 'You can't be contradicting the nose on a man's face. Ach, but what's the sense in bothering about Waggett? If it isn't in the papers he'll know nothing about Poppay. There's just one little thing, though, and if you can both help me here I'll be much obliged. You'll be going to have a look at the cave?'

'We certainly will,' said Mr Mackay.

'If you find when you get there that the monster isn't at home, will you give a call to Kenny and you'll be able to get the whisky safe aboard the *Morning Star* the three of you.'

'Whisky?' Mr Mackay echoed.

'Ay, ay, was I not telling you about the whisky? Yes, I have a few bottles I've been keeping. Yes, in Uamh nan Cnàmh, and I wouldn't like the monster to get at them with those huge teeth of his.'

When Hector Hamish Mackay and Bill Brownsworth landed upon Poppay that afternoon and looked across at the Cave of the Bones their hearts were beating at the prospect of a scientific triumph to which the element of danger in that prospect gave an accelerated tempo. As they made their way through the rank grass of the ancient burial-ground, Mr Mackay related to Bill Brownsworth the legend of the bones, and though this penalty of love was inclined to disturb the thoughts of one whose amorous glances had involved him in getting engaged to two sisters at once, the possibility of meeting the monster face to face banished all worry and Bill Brownsworth strode on, hearing academic voices prophesying fame. He was so preoccupied with that Readership at Norwich University that he strode into a thicket of particularly vicious nettles which attacked his knees with alacrity.

'Look out, nettles!' he warned his companion.

'So I see,' said Mr Mackay, who, though he deplored the myopia which compelled him to wear glasses with the kilt, never allowed vanity to get the better of caution.

When they reached the rocky slope up to the terrace in front of the cave they relieved the anxious strain upon their minds by hushing one another when the steps of either disturbed a loose pebble and sent it clattering down.

'Look,' Bill Brownsworth whispered when they stood upon the sparse vegetation of the terrace. He pointed to a track further along to the right of the cave.

They moved across on tip-toe to find clear evidence of a track beyond the slope leading directly down into the sea below the south-easterly horn of Bàgh nan Marbh.

Mr Sydney Prew, whose company by the way they had had some difficulty in shaking off when they went aboard the *Morning Star*, would have paid his tribute to contemporary youth by ejaculating 'Smashing!' Hector Hamish Mackay chose a word with a larger dignity.

'Stupendous!' he breathed in awe.

Bill Brownsworth, like stout Cortez on a peak in Darien, said nothing, but his brown eyes burned.

'Well,' Mr Mackay whispered, 'it's no longer a case of "excelsior" but of "interior".'

'Every time,' Bill Brownsworth agreed.

'Yes, indeed it is,' Mr Mackay whispered again. 'Do you think one of us ought to stay outside with the camera?'

Brownsworth shook his head.

'I think we both ought to go in,' he insisted. 'It may not come out. In fact, it probably won't.'

'Yes, yes, there's always that probability,' Mr Mackay agreed.

'And in that case,' Brownsworth suggested, 'it would be better if we both saw it. If I count the upper teeth will you count the lower ones? I attach great importance to these teeth from a palaeontological standpoint.'

'Oh, I fully appreciate the importance of these teeth, Brownsworth. Well, interior, eh? Kenny Macroon looks so snug down there in his boat, doesn't he?'

'Hush,' Brownsworth whispered and began to move towards the entrance of the cave.

'Just a moment,' Mr Mackay mumured. 'If the creature charges, mind you I don't believe for a moment it will charge, but if it does I imagine we had better retreat by the same route as we came up.'

'It'll probably go down to the sea by the track it obviously always uses.'

'Yes, exactly,' Mr Mackay whispered.

'But if by luck it does charge straight ahead,' said Brownsworth, 'I shall cut quickly to the left and try to get a snapshot of it as it pursues you down the slope.'

'Yes, I appreciate your strategy,' Mr Mackay said. 'Yes, that ought to make a very effective picture, if the monster doesn't move too quickly and spoil it. Well, in we go, eh? Hush, what was that?' He put a hand on Brownsworth's arm.

'I didn't hear anything.'

'I thought I heard a sort of rumbling noise. Yes, there it is again.'

'Borborhygmus,' Brownsworth whispered.

'What kind of animal is that?' Mr Mackay asked nervously.

'Rumbling in the guts. My guts were rumbling.'

'Of course, of course. My mind was running on something else. Yes, yes, the Greeks had a name for it, eh? Well, in we go.'

And this time they really did go into the cave. It was empty.

'Dash it, what a disappointment!' Mr Mackay exclaimed, in tones more appropriate to enthusiastic relief than to yearning regret.

'However, it's an ill wind that blows nobody any good, Joseph Macroon will get his whisky.'

Following the directions they had been given they penetrated to the further end of the cave where there was a narrow passage terminating in a smaller secondary cave. Here, under a heap of straw, lay seven cases stamped EXPORT ONLY. Besides these there were twelve bottles of whisky buried in a patch of loose soil by the entrance of the cave.

'I say,' Mr Mackay exclaimed, 'Friend Joseph doesn't mind asking favours from his friends. I hope he'll decide that the labourer is worthy of his hire.'

Poor Bill Brownsworth was too much disappointed by their failure to find the monster at home to worry about the transportation of the contraband whisky to the *Morning Star*, and not having been on Little Todday when the *Cabinet Minister* was wrecked he did not realize the risk he ran of appearing as a criminal in the eyes of the man whose son-in-law he hoped to be.

The conveyance of the whisky to the *Morning Star* proved a less arduous task than it threatened to be because Kenny Macroon, who had a less expansive sense than his father of what one could ask others to do for one, insisted on bearing the chief shape of the burden.

'I didn't know the old man had managed to hide all that lot,' he said. 'Isn't it he that's smart? And him girning for ever because Peigi Ealasaid and Kate Anne broke all those bottles on him when they thought the Exciseman was coming to Kiltod. Ah, well, *tha è cho carach ris a mhadaidh ruaidh gu dearbh*. It's only Father James who can take the eyes out of him, and how he's thinking we will be getting all these cases to his store without anybody seeing I don't know at all.'

But Kenny was soon to find out, for as soon as they reached Kiltod with the *Morning Star*'s cargo he was told to take it round to Bàgh Mhic Ròin on the north coast of Little Todday where he was to wait until his father arrived in the grey dusk of the Hebridean summer midnight to take it back in his trap to the big shed at the back of his shop.

'Ay, ay,' said Joseph with a sigh of satisfaction when the whisky was safely housed and hidden behind the junk of years, 'they can put me in the papers now when they've a mind to.'

However, when he informed Mr Mackay accordingly next morning at breakfast, his guest asked him to preserve the strictest secrecy for the present about all the monster's movements on Poppay.

'I understand you, Mr Mackay, you can trust me to keep my mouth shut,' and by a process of reasoning that was peculiar to Joseph Macroon he was able to suppose that any obligation was now entirely on the side of his guest. However, to do him justice he did give Hector Hamish Mackay two bottles, not of Stalker's Joy but of Thistle Cream, which was nearly as good.

'You see, Mr Brownsworth and I do want to be the first in the field.'

'Ay, first in the field,' said Joseph. 'That's always the best place, without a doubt. And the gilt stays on the gingerbread all correct.'

Hector Hamish Mackay had good reason to warn Joseph Macroon against telling everybody about the monster's presence on Poppay. The Secretary of the N.U.H. had lost no time in organizing the hiker's patrols he had mentioned to Bill Brownsworth the previous evening, and while Joseph's whisky was being transported from the Cave of the Bones to the *Morning Star* Mr Prew had taken advantage of the Biffer's arrival at Kiltod to get a passage back with him to Snorvig. In the course of the afternoon he arranged for a non-stop patrol along Tràigh Vooey, which was considered the most likely place for the monster to reappear, and much to Bill Brownsworth's relief he found a note in his tent when he got back to Tràigh Veck that evening after an optimistic meal with Hector Hamish Mackay to say that Mr Prew would be camping himself near Garryboo for the present with a very jolly trio of young men from the Ealing Branch of the N.U.H. He found a second note which, when he read it first, gave him a momentary feeling that he had gone off his head:

> Snorvig House,
> Great Todday,
> June 22nd

Dear Mr Brownsworth,

Mrs Waggett and I will be glad to see you at tea-time tomorrow. I understand that you are a friend of Mr Spinnage, who is staying with us, and who arrived by the boat last night from Obaig.

Yours sincerely,
Paul Waggett

Chapter 15

MOLES

After his stevedore's labour in transporting Joseph Macroon's whisky from the Cave of the Bones Bill Brownsworth should have slept soundly to the soft music of the tranquil ocean upon that night. The shock of the news in Waggett's letter was so severe that sleep did not come to him until the small hours and Mr Mackay had not finished his breakfast when he arrived at Joseph Macroon's.

'The most amazing thing has happened,' he told Mr Mackay.

'You've seen the monster at Tràigh Veck?' the topographer asked eagerly.

'No, no, something much more extraordinary than that. You remember I invited a friend to come and stay with me here?'

'Yes, and you were wondering why you hadn't heard from him.'

'Well, he's here!'

'Is that so very extraordinary?'

'Yes, because he's staying with Mr Waggett. I found a note from Mr Waggett when I got back last night asking me to go over to tea with them this afternoon without a word from Dick Spinnage to explain this extraordinary business. I'm absolutely staggered.'

All sorts of fantastic theories had been chasing one another through Bill Brownsworth's brain during the moth-grey Hebridean night, but in the clear light of morning all seemed equally far-fetched and he would have been ashamed to repeat them to Mr Mackay. He had contemplated taking Mr Mackay into his confidence and asking his advice about his difficult position, but when he saw this prim lifelong bachelor by the clear light of morning he shrank from consulting him about a problem so dependent for its solution on a belief in love at first sight.

'Well, you'll find out the explanation when you go to tea in Snorvig this afternoon. I'm glad Mr Prew has betaken himself and his unpleasant impedimenta to Great Todday, though it will be extremely annoying if he and his officious patrols succeed in establishing contact with the monster. You say Mr Waggett is prejudiced against hikers?'

'Very.'

'A pity,' Mr Mackay commented drily. 'He and Mr Prew seem to have the same kind of boy-scout mind, judging by the stories I heard of him when he commanded the Home Guard here. By the way, the B.B.C. have written to ask if I will say a few words about the monster next week at the *luadh* and *céilidh* which is to be broadcast from the Snorvig Hall. A little plan is simmering at the back of my head, Brownsworth. Of course, it may not materialize, but if it did it would give listeners one of the greatest thrills the microphone has ever given to them. But I see you're not interested,' Mr Mackay concluded with a touch of pettishness. The thought of Mr Prew seemed to bring out the old maid in himself.

'I'm so sorry,' said Bill Brownsworth hastily. 'My mind had gone back for a moment to this extraordinary business about my friend Spinnage. What is your plan?'

'Why, it occurred to me that, if you could be stationed on Poppay and if by a happy turn of fate you could establish the presence of the monster there at the moment when the broadcast begins, it would be a superb dramatic effect if you could reach the Hall when I am actually talking about the monster and announce what you had just seen on Poppay.'

'Wouldn't Mr Waggett be rather annoyed about my trespassing on Poppay?' Brownsworth demurred.

'Really, really, my dear boy,' said Mr Mackay irritably, 'you call yourself a palaeontologist and now with an opportunity to put palaeontology on the map you're prepared to sacrifice that opportunity to the petty self-importance of an English shooting-tenant. After all, if the monster doesn't appear nobody need be any the wiser about your vigil, and if it does appear I hardly think Mr Waggett's shooting rights, for which, by the way, I'm told he pays only £40 a year to the Department, will matter a great deal. It's a thousand pities that we cannot land the broadcasting equipment on Poppay and give listeners a chance to hear the monster for themselves, but that's impossible. As it is, listeners will hear me make the dramatic announcement and you'll be able to say a few words yourself into the microphone.'

'Oh, no, I couldn't possibly do that,' Brownsworth gasped.

'And why not?'

'Well, when I feel embarrassed I get a curious constriction of my throat which makes a kind of gulping noise and that would sound very loud on the microphone – like when somebody pours out a drink in a wireless play. I mean to say, even if an announcer's throat tickles and he gives a little cough, he always begs the pardon of listeners.'

'In that case I'll just have to tell the story myself and when the broadcast is over I'll telephone through to the *Daily Tale* the full account of what you saw on Poppay.'

'Perhaps the monster won't be there,' Brownsworth suggested, with a regrettable note of hopefulness in his voice from a young man whose god was science. 'After all, it wasn't there yesterday afternoon.'

'We'll take a chance, Brownsworth, and meanwhile we'll keep away from Poppay. Perhaps it's just as well that this antipathetic Prew creature is working up these patrols. The more activity there is along Tràigh Vooey and Tràigh Swish the more likely the monster is to appreciate the peace and seclusion of Poppay. That beach down from Uamh nan Cnàmh to the sea, eh? It's like the opening of Beethoven's Fifth Symphony. Fate knocking at the door. I had the same feeling I had in Edinburgh last month when I suddenly made up my mind to take the road to the isles. I haven't the second-sight myself, but I'm always on the edge of it. I have intimations. You know what I'm trying to say?'

'Oh, rather,' Brownsworth assured him. He had not the least idea what Mr Mackay was trying to say, but since reading that note from Paul Waggett the foundations of the scientific approach to life had been so severely shaken that for the nonce he was willing to truckle even to superstition.

After all, it was no more absurd to suppose that the monster might be on Poppay when the broadcast started than to suppose that Dick Spinnage would be staying with the Waggetts at this moment. Indeed, it was much less improbable, and on his way across the Coolish to Snorvig that afternoon Bill Brownsworth began to wonder if conceivably there might not be some more reliable evidence for the phenomena known as flying saucers than he had taken the trouble to examine.

To his relief when the *Morning Star* reached Snorvig, Bill Brownsworth saw Dick Spinnage waiting for him on the pier. At any rate, he would not have had to spend an agonized hour or so hoping for a chance to find out why he was staying with the Waggetts.

'Dick!' he exclaimed, and though he tried to keep reproachfulness out of his voice he could not quite manage it. There came back to him from the past a moment at his prep. school when Dick had had a secret with a boy called Twining whom he hated and when for a week he and Dick had been cutting one another under the emotional strain of threatened friendship.

'Bill!'

There was no trace of apology in Dick's greeting. He stood there in a Donegal tweed suit as apparently sure of his audience's welcome as Ivor Novello himself could always be.

'Why on earth didn't you let me know you were coming to stay with the Waggetts?' Bill asked.

'I did.'

'I never had your letter.'

'I wrote you by return. And then I wrote again.'

'I didn't get that letter either.'

In case the failure of Dick Spinnage's two letters to reach his friend should seem to cast a reflection upon the post office at Snorvig or the postal service of Scotland, here is the text of them as they came back to Dick Spinnage a year later from the New Hebrides by way of Sydney, N.S.W. Nobody at the sorting office for WC2 knew that there were islands off the coast of Scotland called the Outer Hebrides, and as Dick had omitted to add Scotland to the address his letters had been sent to the Pacific.

> Blundell, Blundell, Pickthorn, and Blundell,
> Chartered Accountants,
> 15, Crumple Inn, WC2
> Wednesday

Charles W. Blundell, F.I.C.A.,
Edward R. Pickthorn, F.I.C.A.,
Walter C. Blundell, F.I.C.A.

Dear Bill,

Nothing would suit me better. Old Charles Blundell knows your future father-in-law well. In fact, he was a partner in this firm until he sold out about five years before the war and went up to live in the Hebrides. He's writing to Waggett. I'll be with you in about a week. I think I can handle this business for you all right, though I'm not going to commit myself to falling in love at first sight with the fair Elsie!

Yours aye,
Dick

And the second letter from the same address was:

Dear Bill,

Your future father-in-law has telegraphed inviting me to stay with him. I'm arriving by Thursday's boat from a place called Obaig. I'll look out for you when I get to this island. It's an extraordinary coincidence that things should play into our hands like this.

Yours aye,
Dick

'I thought I'd gone mad when I got Mr Waggett's note to say you were staying with them,' said Bill after his friend had explained what had happened. 'What do you think of my girl?'

'A very nice little girl indeed, Bill. But you certainly said it when you said they were alike. If I'm going to make the running with Elsie I'll have to get them to pin a label on with their names, or I'll be making the running with your girl.'

'I don't think that would matter.'

'Bill!' his friend exclaimed.

'I mean if you could make a mistake like that it would salve Muriel's pride over Elsie. But do you like Elsie?' Bill asked anxiously.

'Oh, she's quite attractive. But her father isn't so hot. Not that I'm suggesting Elsie is hot,' he added quickly.

'Of course you've had more experience with girls than I have,' Bill reminded his friend.

'I suppose I have,' Dick agreed.

'Oh, much more. I mean to say you wouldn't be so likely to fall in love with a girl at first sight as I should.'

'You know,' said Dick a moment or two later, as they were nearing the gateway to Snorvig House, 'I believe it mightn't be a bad idea if I did try to make love to your girl. She'd get annoyed.'

'Yes, I suppose she would,' Bill agreed a little doubtfully. He had a tremendous respect for his friend's sway over the hearts of girls.

'Of course she would,' said Dick. 'And then I'd say "Good lord, I thought it was your sister." I wouldn't do this till just before I was going away because even if I began to have a soft spot for Elsie I really couldn't face our late partner at Blundell's as a father-in-law. And then when I was apologizing to your girl I'd tell her you'd made the same mistake over Elsie and how badly you felt about it.'

'I believe you've hit on it, Dick,' said Bill. 'Of course, if you *could* fall in love with Elsie I'd be tremendously bucked because it would be so grand to have you as my brother-in-law.'

'I wouldn't be your brother-in-law. I'd be Muriel's. And you wouldn't be mine. You'd be Elsie's.'

'Well, it's more or less the same thing,' said Bill. 'I mean to say we could go off on our holidays together. In fact, we might share a house.'

'Too risky, Bill,' said Dick, who was a good deal stronger on neontology than his friend.

'Still, if you could fall in love with Elsie,' Bill said as they reached the gateway of Snorvig House, 'I do think your other plan will put things right.'

Paul Waggett was happy with two young men in front of whom he could show off as a country gentleman and he enjoyed the opportunity it gave him of demonstrating to his wife and daughters the amount of deference he was able to secure from those who really knew what a sportsman was.

'Come along, Brownsworth. I'm glad you were able to get over this afternoon. You haven't met Mrs Waggett. Dolly, this is Mr Brownsworth. You've met this daughter, but you haven't met my other daughter, Muriel.'

Bill Brownsworth was grateful to a state of affairs which allowed him to treat both sisters as strangers and indeed, if the uncomplicated existence of this family leading the simple life was not to be tangled up, demanded that he should. He was so much afraid of letting Muriel or Elsie fancy that he was paying more attention to her twin than to herself that he was unable to give himself an opportunity of searching for any distinctive marks on either twin that would secure him in future against confusing one with the other.

'Of course, it's a great pity you chose June for your visit, Spinnage. We *might* get a salmon in Loch Skinny and we *might* get a good run of sea-trout in Loch Sleeport, but it's a bit early. I suppose Charlie Blundell is becoming just as much of a stickler as his old dad was about holidays. That was really the reason why I sold out. I said to myself "what's the use of slaving on just for the sake of making a little more money?" I had enough to buy Snorvig House and, though I say it, I wouldn't exchange my shooting and fishing here for any in Scotland or England. I wouldn't really. Grouse, cock, plover, snipe, geese, salmon, sea-trout, what more does anybody want? I don't miss the pheasants and partridges. I mean to say, every year I used to be one of a syndicate for a pheasant and partridge shoot somewhere in the Home Counties, but, I'll be quite frank with you, Spinnage, I didn't really enjoy shooting with a syndicate. I found the gamekeepers thought about nothing but squeezing every tip they could out of the members. It was too commercial for me altogether.

I sometimes wish I had a small forest here – but I don't care for stalking so much as all that. I was offered an eight-head forest last year in Wester Inverness, but I said "no." '

Mrs Waggett and his daughters looked up at this revelation; it was the first they had heard of such an offer. They did not know it had been made to all the readers of *The Field*, an odd copy of which Daddo had picked up in the smoking-room of one of the Obaig hotels.

'Have you done much stalking, sir?' Dick Spinnage asked.

'No, no. I don't really care for it. You ought to have come up for the Twelfth; oughtn't he, Monty, old boy.'

The golden retriever thumped the floor with his tail.

'Wonderful mouth,' said Monty's master dreamily. 'Of course, I trained him myself. I never lose a bird. Unless I make a boss shot of course,' he added, smiling broadly at such a magnificent joke against himself. 'But I'm a fairly good shot,' he added modestly. 'I think any gun who can count on eleven brace of snipe out of twelve in the rough going we sometimes get here can call himself a fairly good shot. I had a wonderful Irish setter who died three years ago. He outgrew his strength, poor old Paddy. The people here were frightened of him. I used to say to the children "if you don't run away he won't run after you." But you can't teach these Islanders anything. They've been boxed up here for hundreds of years, and they think they know everything. It would be funny if it wasn't sometimes so pathetic. When I was in command of the Home Guard Company here I tried to explain to them the importance of the blackout. And what do you think they used to argue? They actually used to argue that because the harbour lights were showing all the way up the Long Island there was no point in bothering about chinks in their windows. I used to try and explain the principle of the thing. Quite useless. They just don't believe in principles. You've heard about that whisky ship? I can't tell you what a responsibility it was for me. All they could see was that there was a cargo of whisky and therefore it must be theirs. They regard law and order as their natural enemies. Of course, they used to be pirates in days gone by, but what I say is they've never stopped being pirates. Still, if you want to enjoy the pleasure of living far from the maddening crowd you have to take the rough with the smooth, and of course an Englishman is always at a disadvantage. Clannishness. That's the trouble. Look what's happened here over this imaginary monster. Why do you suppose everybody here is determined to believe it exists? Clannishness. Why do you suppose the people in Inverness get so annoyed if anybody ventures to doubt if the Loch Ness Monster exists? Clannishness. The whole of Scotland is ridden with clannishness. I wonder what would happen to England if all the Smiths suddenly started getting clannish. Fellows like Hector Hamish Mackay flatter this clannishness in order to sell their books. He gives the people here an entirely false sense of their own importance. You've noticed that, of course,' he said turning to Bill Brownsworth, whose desire to propitiate what he hoped was his future father-in-law would not drive him into criticism of a man who had shown him so much kindness and hospitality.

'No, sir, I can't say I have noticed that,' he said, looking quickly to see if Muriel was showing signs of agitation at what bordered upon a contradiction. He did notice an apprehensive look in her eyes, but he noticed something that was to him much more important; he noticed that just behind the lobe of her left ear she had a small beige-coloured mole. It was an exquisite oasis in a desert of similarity.

'Have you read any of Mackay's books?' Paul Waggett asked.

'I've read the one about these islands, sir.'

'Well, you must have noticed the way he flatters the people here. You'd think to read *Faerie Lands Forlorn* that the people here were all poets. There's no poetry in them. I arranged a poetry reading for them soon after I came to live here, and I read them some of Rudyard Kipling's best known poems and some of Adam Lindsay Gordon's – oh, yes, and Macaulay's poem about the Armada, and *The Charge of the Light Brigade*, and they sat there like a lot of dummies. They just sat like a lot of dummies. Mr Morrison the minister who was quite young then and had only just come to Snorvig was in the chair and he had to flatter them when he was proposing a vote of thanks to me. Yes, he actually complimented the audience on the close attention with which they had tried to follow what for most of them was a foreign tongue in poetry, and they applauded the minister's remarks much more loudly than they applauded my reading. It wasn't that which annoyed me. Not at all. What did annoy me was his suggestion that there was something clever in not being able to understand English poetry. However, it was worse in the Kiltod Hall because Father Macalister deliberately sighed all the time I was reading, and then he made a speech in Gaelic and though I couldn't follow absolutely all he said it was evidently intended to be funny.'

Mrs Waggett shook her head sadly.

'I must say Father Macalister does behave very strangely sometimes for a clergyman,' she sighed.

'But he's not a clergyman, Dolly,' her husband contradicted. 'He's a priest. Priests are not allowed to marry. So they have no sense of responsibility. Every man ought to marry.'

'I do agree with you there, Mr Waggett,' said Bill Brownsworth fervidly.

'I consider celibacy *most* unhealthy,' Paul Waggett declared, his nose tilting upward as if the very word had an unpleasant smell. 'Are you engaged, Brownsworth?' he asked.

Brownsworth was saved from replying by swallowing some tea the wrong way, and by the time he had recovered from coughing his host was holding forth on the iniquities of what he called a gang of hikers who were camping out on the machair above Tràigh Vooey.

'I warned the fellow who was apparently in charge – a most objectionable type – that I had the shooting rights and could not allow any camping where he was, and what do you think he had the impudence to reply? "I have sought and obtained permission from the Garryboo crofters to camp here." I was quite staggered for a moment. And then he produced his card. Sydney Prew, National Union of Hikers. One of these Communist agitators, no doubt. I suppose he thinks he'll curry favour here by supporting this idiotic imaginary monster.'

'I don't think he's a Communist, sir,' Bill gulped. 'The National Union of Hikers is the same kind of organization as the Cyclists Touring Club.'

'I distrust any organization which doesn't respect shooting and fishing rights,' Waggett declared. 'I've notified Sergeant MacGillivray that this gang of hikers is swarming all over Garryboo signalling to one another like a lot of boy scouts, but of course it's a waste of time. Sergeant MacGillivray's only idea is to keep the peace.'

'Well, that is what the police are for, isn't it, sir?' said Dick Spinnage.

'But you mustn't misunderstand what I said about boy scouts,' Waggett went on, deciding to ignore his guest's interjection. 'Oh, no, I'm a keen supporter of the scout movement. In fact, I tried to start a troop here, but the only thing they cared about was blowing their whistles all day long for about a week and nearly driving my old Irish setter mad and then it all petered out and I saw their sisters wearing the MacRurie tartan scarves with which I'd presented them. So I gave it up.'

When Bill Brownsworth said it was time for him to be getting back to Kiltod and Dick Spinnage volunteered to walk down to the pier with him their host had been talking for twenty minutes about the Normandy landings in which both of them had taken part. Dick Spinnage had made one effort to check the flow of information by mentioning this fact, but it only made their host more eloquent, for, as he said, they would appreciate all the more the problems by which Montgomery was faced and the curious way in which his solution of them had always coincided with his own.

'Why don't you two girls walk as far as the pier with us?' Dick suggested.

Bill, as always, was dazzled by his friend's assurance, especially when Daddo said graciously:

'Run along, chicks, a breath of air will do you good.'

Then Dick became even more dazzling.

'Why don't we charter this chap – the Biffer or Buffer or whatever he's called – and have a picnic supper over the water? I'll bring them safely back, sir.'

'What does Mumsy say?' Daddo asked.

'I think it would be very nice for them, Paul.'

So that was that.

'Why do you keep looking at my hair, Bill?' Muriel asked as they walked down to the pier. 'Is it untidy?'

'I was looking at that mole behind your ear.'

'Behind my left ear?'

'Yes.'

'Elsie has one too, just in the same place.'

That exquisite oasis in a desert of similarity was nothing but a mirage after all. How fortunate he had not notified Dick of it as a landmark!

'Oh, Bill, isn't it wonderful to be together like this?' she sighed.

'Absolutely marvellous.'

'And do you know, I believe Elsie is rather more than a little interested in Dick.'

'Do you really think so?'

'I do really,' she said seriously.

'That would be marvellous.'

'Wouldn't it?'

'Oh, absolutely.'

'I wonder if Dick's interested in her.'

'I think he is definitely,' Bill affirmed.

'Of course he is very attractive.'

'I'm jolly glad you didn't meet him before you met me.'

'Don't be silly.'

'Well, he might have fallen in love with you.'

'Wouldn't Elsie be jealous if he had?' she murmured.

'You think she would?' Bill asked anxiously.

'Imagine what I should feel if I thought you were attracted by Elsie.'

'Well, I couldn't be, could I?'

'You know, I did have one horrid moment when I thought you had been rather attracted by her. She talked about you an awful lot that night when you met her on Tràigh Veck.'

'I don't know why.'

'I think she was very attracted by you,' Muriel said, her blue eyes open wide.

'But not since Dick came,' Bill urged quickly.

'No, I think she's more interested in Dick now.'

'That's what I mean. You might be attracted by Dick if he made love to you.'

'But, Bill, your best friend would never do such a thing. It would be frightfully dishonourable,' Muriel exclaimed in obvious revolt against such unromantic behaviour.

'Oh, yes, absolutely the end,' he agreed.

'Why, I'd as soon imagine your making love to Elsie.'

'That's what I mean. It's unthinkable.'

'All the same I wouldn't trust Elsie,' said Muriel, frowning to herself.

'I say, you oughtn't to say things like that about your sister,' he protested.

Muriel was silent.

'You don't know Elsie,' she said presently.

In the first exhilaration of seeing how well Dick was making the running with Elsie Bill had been tempted to confide in Muriel the absurd mistake he had made in confusing her with her sister, but Muriel's obvious belief that Elsie considered all fair in love and war deterred him. If he had made the mistake only once he felt that he could have carried it off. *'Do you know, the first time I saw Elsie, I actually blew her a kiss, thinking it was you. Ridiculous, wasn't it?'* Muriel might not have liked it, but, after all, in common fairness she would have had to admit that it was ridiculous. But it was the second time. *'Do you know, the second time*

I saw Elsie I actually called her "darling", and talked about a double wedding? Ridiculous, wasn't it?'

'A penny for your thoughts, Bill,' Muriel said suddenly.

'My thoughts?' Bill ejaculated with a startled expression. 'Oh, my thoughts? I really don't know. Not worth a penny anyway.'

'I wondered if you were thinking about me.'

'Muriel! As if I'd say my thoughts about you weren't worth a penny!'

'You were looking so worried, Bill. Is anything worrying you?'

'No, I was just wondering where we'd have supper.'

'Oh, on Tràigh Veck, of course.'

'You don't think that's too far?' Bill demurred. He would have preferred any background to that of the natural arch for this picnic.

'We could hire Joseph Macroon's trap, couldn't we?' she suggested.

Later he was grateful to Muriel's happy suggestion, for Dick drove with Elsie beside him, and so Bill, sitting with Muriel at the back, was able to discover that Elsie had a very small coffee-coloured mole under her right ear.

'Don't move, darling,' he said to Muriel as he looked round behind her neck.

'What is it, Bill?' she asked nervously.

'Nothing much,' he said, flipping away an imaginary something with his finger. 'Only a ladybird.'

'You did give me a fright.'

'I thought it was another mole.'

'No, I haven't got a mole there. Elsie has, though.'

'Has she?' said Bill, in a tone which he hoped conveyed the utter indifference he would like Muriel to think he felt about her sister's moles.

'Yes, Mumsy used to say that when we were tiny tots Elsie's other mole was the only way she could be sure which was which.'

'Really?' said Bill. 'That was rather ingenious of your mother. Haven't you got moles anywhere else?'

'Bill!' Muriel exclaimed. 'Aren't you dreadful?'

He blushed, for he was naturally an old-fashioned young man and his passion for palaeontology had preserved his old-fashioned notions.

'I say, I'm awfully sorry. One gets in the habit of asking questions like that when one's identifying fossilized remains.'

Muriel laughed.

'What's the joke at the back?' Dick Spinnage turned round to ask.

'Bill's been comparing Elsie and me to fossilized remains,' Muriel told him.

'I like that!' Elsie expostulated without a trace of indignation because she was wondering if Muriel was feeling frightfully jealous of the way she herself had obviously made such a completely contrary impression upon Dick.

The picnic on Tràigh Veck was a complete success, and the scenic effects, combined with superlative lighting, made Dick Spinnage look more like Ivor Novello than ever, so that when after supper he suggested taking Elsie for a stroll along Tràigh Swish, Bill felt buoyantly sure that his friend would be bewitched by the magical atmosphere into making love to Elsie and possibly even into proposing to her.

'Well, you may say what you like, darling,' he murmured to Muriel, 'but I'm jolly glad I had the luck to meet you before Dick arrived. I wouldn't have had a chance.'

'But, Bill, I fell in love with you at first sight.'

'Yes, but you might have fallen in love with Dick at first sight, and if you had Elsie wouldn't have had a chance.'

'Oh, Bill, I do love you,' she sighed rapturously.

Bill may not have had much experience of women, but by falling in love with a twin he had discovered a great deal about them in a very short time.

'If Dick does propose to Elsie,' he said, when kisses required an interval of words, 'I shall tell your father before I leave that I want to marry you. I meant to talk about my prospects in an indirect way this afternoon, but your father didn't give me a good opportunity.'

'Poor old Daddo, he doesn't often get a chance of holding forth except to Mumsy and us and he did enjoy himself. I'm afraid when Elsie and I get married he's going to feel rather lost up here. Of course, Mumsy is longing to go and live near Aunt Gladys in Norwood. Still, *que voulez-vous?* Daughters must get married some day.'

'Oh, rather,' Bill agreed, 'every time. But I wish your father wasn't so prejudiced against this mysterious creature or monster. I mean to say if I do succeed in identifying it he'll be so annoyed to find he's wrong. However, don't let's look on the gloomy side. Things have gone so much better for us than we could have dreamed of only a day or two ago.'

'What's the time, Bill?' Muriel asked. 'We mustn't be too late.'

'Half past kissing time. Time to kiss again,' said Bill. 'I had a nurse who always used to say that when I asked her the time. I used to get furious with her. Now it seems a pretty sound remark.'

While the girls were getting themselves adjusted for the crossing to Snorvig, Bill had an opportunity to talk to Dick for a minute or two.

'You didn't propose to Elsie this evening?' he asked hopefully.

'No, I certainly didn't. Mind you, she's not a bad little girl, and I was strongly tempted to put an arm round her, but I thought of you, Bill, and resisted the temptation.'

'Thought of me?' Bill exclaimed.

'Well, if you're serious about marrying Muriel it would hardly do for your best friend to start making love to her sister without serious intentions.'

'I wish you would marry Elsie,' Bill sighed.

'I couldn't take old Waggett as an in-law. I simply couldn't, Bill. I never heard a man talk so much. Thank god, he left Blundell *ad lib.* before I joined the outfit. Mind you, I daresay he could be quite useful as a father-in-law in the way of hurrying on that partnership. Charlie Blundell spoke of him with real affection and said he was a great loss to the firm. I suppose he talked out even the Income Tax people.'

'Well, if you're not going to propose to Elsie, Dick, you *must* carry out this plan about Muriel. It's more important than ever now because if Elsie has fallen badly for you she'll be so disappointed and jealous that she may enjoy upsetting Muriel.'

'I won't let you down, Bill.'

'Listen, Dick. This is very important. In case you aren't perfectly sure that it is Muriel look at the back of her right ear.'

'What?'

'If it's Muriel there won't be a very small coffee-coloured mole.'

'So what?'

'But if it's Elsie there will be. They both have much paler moles under their left ears.'

'Bill, for heaven's sake have a heart. It may be your technique to go sniffing around the moles at the back of a girl's ears, but, boy, believe me it isn't mine.'

'I don't want to go sniffing around their moles. The point is that if you're in the least doubt which girl it is you can always make sure.'

'I see, Muriel's got a coffee-coloured mole and Elsie hasn't.'

'No, the other way round, Dick,' Bill protested. 'They both have paler moles, but only Elsie has this coffee-coloured mole.'

'*Café noir* or *café au lait?*'

'Compared with the others more like *café noir*,' said Bill very seriously.

'Don't worry. I'll be safer with my own instinct than your moles,' Dick assured him. 'I was never in a moment's doubt this evening which was which.'

'It was quite easy. One of them had a light green tweed wrap and the other a pale blue one. And anyway, Muriel was with me all the time. I don't want to fuss, but, after all, I did make the same mistake myself twice.'

Dick smiled.

'I shan't, Bill. But wait a minute. Suppose when I tell Muriel I thought it was Elsie's she tells Elsie? I'd be hooked myself.'

'No, you wouldn't. Elsie might be annoyed, of course, but that won't matter to you.'

'Oh, I expect it'll be all right. I hear the girls coming.'

'Well, if you're at all doubtful, don't forget that Elsie has a coffee-coloured mole under her right ear,' Bill muttered.

'What are you two whispering about?' Elsie asked.

'Bill was giving me some tips about natural history,' Dick told her with a grin. 'Well, it's been a grand evening, Bill. When are you coming over to Snorvig?'

'I'll probably come over the day after tomorrow,' he said. 'The day after tomorrow,' he repeated, giving his friend a dark grimly earnest look such as the villain in an old-fashioned melodrama used to give the hero to disturb an audience of happy unsophisticated playgoers with a promise of trouble brewing for the heroine in the near future.

'All the same,' he thought when he had waved the *Kittiwake* out on to the oxidized silver of the Coolish in the breathless gloaming, 'all the same, it would be much simpler if Dick proposed to Elsie.'

Bill turned in to Joseph Macroon's again to have a talk with Mr Mackay before he went back to his tent.

'Ah, good, I'm glad you looked in, Brownsworth. I've just had a telegram from the B.B.C. Would you care to read it?'

Delighted you will give five minutes talk at ceilidh about monster stop we propose arrive with our unit on Tuesday boat stop ceilidh will start 7.45 Thursday and run till 9 stop full programme will be arranged in consultation with Father Macalister and Mr Mackinnon of Snorvig School stop we shall make recordings round Great Todday of characteristic Hebridean scenes and shall appreciate any cooperation you care to give stop understand Ben Nevis will be at Snorvig with yacht suggest possibility of recording interview with him and suggesting to Father Macalister possibility of inviting Ben Nevis to say a few words at ceilidh and should again appreciate your cooperation as experienced broadcaster

Duncan MacColl

'It's a very nice telegram, I think,' said Mr Mackay. 'It's always pleasant to know that one's efforts are appreciated. And here's another nice telegram from the *Daily Tale*.'

Carmichael accompanying Ben Nevis to Snorvig stop you should do utmost to effect his contact with subject of your interesting letter just received stop your work has been usefullest

Donaldson

'I don't quite understand how Ben Nevis comes into this,' said Bill Brownsworth in bewilderment.

'Oh, he's a great enthusiast for the Loch Ness Monster.'

'Ben Nevis? Ben Nevis, did you say?'

'Yes, yes, Donald MacDonald of Ben Nevis. One of the last of the rare old Chieftains. A great figure.' Suddenly Mr Mackay realized Bill Brownsworth's perplexity. 'Oh, laddie, laddie, you didn't think Ben Nevis was the mountain? Oh, dear, that's rich. Oh, I must tell Father Macalister that one. That would be a case of the mountain coming to Mahomet with a vengeance. We must have a dram of Thistle Cream on that one.'

When he had set the glasses on the table and poured out the drams Mr Mackay returned to the exciting future.

'I decided to write at once to Mr Donaldson, the Editor, giving him in the strictest confidence our news about Poppay and proposing to him our plan of action. He's evidently delighted. Young Carmichael is a capital lad. You'll like him and of course he'll be able to be with you on Poppay in case the monster appears at the right moment. Oh, it's great, it's splendid. If only the monster will appear. It'll be one of the supreme moments in broadcasting. And, look here, if you're thinking about the photograph, don't worry. I'm sure if Carmichael gets one you'll be given the credit, ay, and the cash too. Really, I don't think I've ever felt quite so excited in the whole of my life. No, not even when I thought I saw Oscar Slater sitting opposite me in one of the Leith trams. But we must be as close as oysters over Poppay. We don't want that fellow Prew starting non-stop patrols there. The monster must be persuaded that it has found a quiet spot in Uamh nan Cnàmh. By Jingo, I'd like fine to go over and have a look at Poppay with you tomorrow. But we won't. We'll leave it all to Providence, and I feel certain, do you know, that Providence is not going to let us down. You're not drinking your whisky, man. Drink up, drink up. We've a great week ahead of us.'

Chapter 16

THE OCEAN WAVE

To the disappointment of Ben Nevis, Deirdre and Wilbur Carboy could not reach Scotland in time to sail with the *Banshee*, for it was felt that it would be tempting fortune too hard to postpone the expedition and risk a change in this lovely June weather.

'But I do wish you'd have one more shot to persuade Hugh to come with us,' the Chieftain said to Chester Royde. The laird of Knocknacolly, in spite of having put on weight during the last decade, did not look much older than when he and Carrie came to stay at Glenbogle Castle a year or two before the second war. The double chin he had had when he was twenty-five was a rather larger double to-day, his complexion was pastier, and his pugnose was now approximating to a bulldog's nose. Nevertheless, with the heavy work of a great financial house increasingly upon his shoulders Chester Royde gave an impression of the liveliest vigour. As for Carrie Royde, with her red hair and beautiful complexion, she seemed not a day older.

The laird of Kilwhillie was adamant.

'No, I will not take part in this expedition,' he declared firmly. 'I dislike the sea and I am much too busy getting ready for Walter's birthday at the beginning of October when we are to have the formal ceremony of adopting him as my heir.'

'Now look, Hugh,' said Chester, 'if you'll join in this monster chase, Carrie and I will stay over here till after your celebrations. And what's more, we'll somehow get Myrtle and Alan over. They've got this tropical bug pretty badly and are bumming around in the West Indies just now, but I'm going to make a big point of their coming over.'

Myrtle was Chester Royde's sister who had married the Scottish poet, Alan MacMillan.

'Nothing will give me greater pleasure than to welcome Myrtle and Alan,' said Kilwhillie. 'But I will not cross the Minch.'

'But, Hugh, I've got a crackerjack new gun. It's an elephant gun and you'd be pretty sore if I bagged this island monster and you weren't there.'

'I shall be pretty sore, as you put it, if you do bag it,' said Kilwhillie severely. 'I never heard of such an outrageous proposal. Do you mean to tell me that Donald Ben Nevis is prepared to take part in such a piece of vandalism? It's the kind of thing I should expect from General MacArthur.'

When his visitors had gone Kilwhillie took the receiver from the telephone, the expression on his face that of a man who is removing a noxious reptile from his slipper.

'I wish to speak to Ben Nevis, Toker,' he said when the Glenbogle butler acknowledged his ring.

'Certainly, Kilwhillie. Will you hold on, sir, please, till I can find Ben Nevis?'

A minute later Kilwhillie blinked for a moment as the receiver suddenly vibrated.

'I can hear you perfectly well, Donald,' he said coldly. 'Chester Royde has just been here trying to persuade me to cross the Minch with you. I will not cross the Minch . . . yes, I daresay the Minch and the Atlantic are both as smooth as a mill pond at present. I have no intention of finding out for myself what they're like. That's not what I've rung up about . . . Chester Royde has just announced to me that he has bought a new elephant gun with which he's proposing to make an attempt to bag this monster, as he puts it. Were you aware of this disgraceful project? . . . the likelihood of his hitting it does not enter into the question . . . you did, in fact, know that this project was afoot . . . well, all I can say is that I am appalled by such a piece of vulgarity . . . yes, I did say vulgarity . . . I'm sorry if you think my language is too strong, Donald, but I don't think any language could be too strong for this disgraceful vandalism, and I must stand by what I have said . . . What would you say if you heard that I was abetting an American millionaire in an attempt to take the life of the Loch Ness Monster? . . . *you'd* be appalled, precisely . . . if Chester Royde wants to go shooting with this elephant gun of his, let him shoot a few film-stars or members of the present Government or crooners as they're called or any other kind of public nuisance . . . I don't agree that doing your best to dissuade Royde is enough. You can make it clear to him that either you go or the elephant gun goes to the Islands, and that Chester must choose which . . . I'm sorry, Donald, I'm not interested in the rest of your party. All I am concerned with is this disgraceful gun.'

Kilwhillie put the receiver back.

'Is anything the matter, Donald?' the Chieftain's wife asked when she found him sitting by the telephone in a state as near to dejection as it was possible for Mac 'ic Eachainn to achieve.

'That was Hugh on the telephone. He rang me up.'

'How is he?'

'I think this liver of his is still causing trouble. He suggested that Chester Royde should shoot all the members of this Bolshie Government of ours.'

'Shoot them?' Mrs MacDonald boomed in amazement.

'Yes, he has a new elephant gun.'

'Did you say shoot them?' Mrs MacDonald asked.

'Yes, the poor old boy's obviously rather under the weather.'

'The weather could hardly be better,' Mrs MacDonald commented, 'The weather is no excuse for Hugh Cameron's extraordinary proposal.'

'Yes, well, Chester Royde isn't likely to fall in with it,' said the Chieftain.

'Indeed, I shouldn't think so. I hope Dr Macgregor knows about these extraordinary ideas of Hugh's. I'm sure he'd rule out visits from you as much too exciting for him.'

'Look here, you're making a molehill out of a mountain, Trixie, you really are. I'm sorry Hugh won't come with us in the *Banshee* because I think the sea breezes would have blown away his liver and all that sort of thing. However, he won't come with us and that's the end of it.'

The Roydes were dining at Glenbogle that night and when the financier and the Chieftain were sitting over their port the latter said:

'I've been thinking about this plan of yours to shoot this island monster, Chester, and I'm getting a little worried about it.'

'You are?'

'Yes, I really am. You see, it might put it into somebody's head to have a shot at our monster and if they did I think you'd be blamed. There's some word when a tinker breaks into an alms box in a church and takes the cash — I can't remember for a moment what the word is, but that's what people in the North would think shooting at our monster was. Now, you wouldn't like to be accused of encouraging what this word is that I can't remember. That's why I hate those vile crossword puzzles they print all over the place nowadays.'

'Is it "sacrilege" you're trying to say, Ben Nevis?'

'That's the brute, yes. Bravo, Chester. Sacrilege. Sacrilege. Well, they're very allergic to sacrilege up here if you know what I mean.'

'But I thought the Loch Ness Monster had been taken for a ride by this flying saucer, Ben Nevis. I don't see why we need worry any about the Loch Ness Monster.'

'But nobody up here believes that our dear old monster was killed by this flying saucer. We think it's lying low. And though I regard these islanders as a set of robbers I don't feel easy in my mind about shooting their monster. Hugh Cameron feels the same.'

'You're telling me,' Chester exclaimed. 'When I told him about this new gun of mine and how I was hoping to bag this island monster he looked at me as if . . . well, you know the way Kilwhillie can look at anybody as he'd been dead a fortnight and it was time to ring and have him taken away. Still, I don't want to upset anybody up here. I certainly don't. So if you think this new gun of mine had better be left behind, that's O.K. with me.'

'Very good of you, Chester. Fill up your glass. I don't much care for port myself. Always think it tastes a bit like stewed plums, if you know what I mean. Yes, I'm very grateful to you for being so — er — co-operative. Wonderful thing co-operativeness except, of course, when these Bolshies down in Whitehall try to nationalize it. You don't mind Kenneth MacLennan coming with us? He's the chap that saw the outrage in Loch Ness in March and I want him as an eyewitness to stop all this nonsensical bubble-babble about the island monster being our monster.'

'Sure, bring him along.'

'And there's one more thing. The Editor of the *Scottish Daily Tale*, who's a fellow clansman of mine, wants to have a representative on board in case of any excitement. I promised him he should come if you've no objection. A very decent young chap called Carmichael. He's been round Loch Ness trying to find evidence that our monster is still there.'

'Sure, bring him along too.'

'Well, then we shall be you and Carrie and me, Catriona and Mary, Bertie Bottley, this lad Carmichael, and Kenneth MacLennan, and of course Toker as Chief Steward, what? Oh, yes, and I'm bringing my piper, Angus MacQuat. I asked Tom Rawstorne, but I'm glad to say he can't come, because owners can be an awful nuisance on board their own yachts. So fussy about scratches on the deck and all that sort of old-maidish stuff. We sail on Tuesday morning from Axedge, and I'm looking forward to a wonderful cruise. If we don't have any luck in the Toddays we can carry on up to Nobost, and for that matter right up the Long Island as far as Stornoway.'

It was a drive of over twenty-five miles to the little port of Axedge which lay about three miles up the wooded banks of lovely Loch Dooin on the Lochaber side. Ben Nevis, with Catriona and Mary, drove with Chester and Carrie Royde in the Knocknacolly Rolls-Royce. Johnnie Macpherson took Angus MacQuat, Toker, and two cases of Glenbogle's Pride in the Glenbogle car.

'I'm sorry old Hugh isn't with us, Carrie,' the Chieftain said. 'I knew it was going to be a glorious morning.'

'It's just too bad he hates the sea so terribly,' Carrie said.

'All imagination of course,' the Chieftain commented scornfully.

'No, no, I'm not going to stand for that, Ben Nevis,' she protested. 'I've been terribly sea-sick once or twice even when crossing in the *Ruritania* and that certainly wasn't imagination.'

'Extraordinary!' the Chieftain woofed. 'Nobody looking at you would ever suppose you could be sea-sick. But Hugh isn't happy on board ship until he *is* sea-sick. I remember when he and I sailed to Bombay how miserable he was. I got quite worried once when a pretty girl asked him if he would judge the costumes in the fancy-dress dance. I thought for a moment he was going to throw her overboard. I did really.'

The *Banshee* was a trim craft and as she lay beside the little pier at Axedge on that flawless morning in June those who would presently entrust themselves to her for the eighty-mile voyage felt as confident of her graceful seaworthiness as if she were the mighty *Ruritania* or *Ecstatic*.

'I'd like to sail at eleven o'clock to catch the tide,' Captain Gillies told his passengers with a dark glance at the Chieftain's brogues.

'We ought to be able to do that, Captain,' said Chester Royde.

'Sir Hubert Bottley isn't here yet,' Captain Gillies observed sternly. He had had to wait for the laird of Cloy on one or two previous occasions.

'Oh, he'll be here in good time,' Ben Nevis barked genially. 'In fact, there he is now.'

The Bottley Bentley had just emerged from the woods at the head of the loch, and presently its plump amiable owner was greeting everybody.

'Ah, there you are, MacLennan,' said Ben Nevis. 'I'm glad you were able to come. I want you to tell Mr Royde that story about the fox which pinched your deerstalker.'

'Say, that sounds a pretty good story,' Chester Royde commented.

'One of the finest stalkers in the north,' Ben Nevis observed, without embarrassing the eagle-beaked Coinneach Mór who was perfectly aware of his own skill. 'I wish you had him at Knocknacolly.'

'Look here, Donald,' said Bottley with a grin, 'we have all our work cut out to deal with black-market deer-poachers without your trying to poach my head stalker.'

'I know,' Ben Nevis barked. 'We've got to do something about it, too. There won't be a deer or salmon left unless we're allowed a free hand with these ruffians. Lindsay-Wolseley, of course, was as sticky as a blob of glue when I put up to him the idea of setting mantraps. He said mantraps were illegal. "So's poaching" I reminded him. And then he started some dunderheaded argument about two blacks not making a white or two whites not making a black. Hopeless. The North-West Frontier must have been like a Sunday School when Wolseley was soldiering up there.'

At this moment young Ian Carmichael of the *Daily Tale* came up to salute Ben Nevis and was introduced to Chester and Carrie Royde.

'Glad to have you with us on this trip, Mr Carmichael.'

'I assure you your kindness is much appreciated, sir. Have you seen this morning's *Daily Tale*? I brought one with me from Fort William. There are two or three paragraphs you might care to see.'

The young reporter handed Chester Royde a copy of the current issue, and he read out the following:

'Lively interest has been roused by the news that Mr Chester Royde, Jr, of the great financial house of New York, has joined hands with MacDonald of Ben Nevis to lead an expedition in search of the Island Monster with the object of disproving once and for all its connection with the Loch Ness Monster. The famous Lochaber Chieftain attaches the greatest importance to this in view of what he scathingly calls "the attempts of interested parties" to encourage the idea that the Loch Ness Monster has deserted the mainland for the islands. Sir Hubert Bottley of Cloy, who is accompanying the expedition himself, has lent the services of his head-stalker, Mr Kenneth MacLennan. Inasmuch as it was Mr MacLennan who last March, as first reported in the *Daily Tale*, was an eyewitness of the amazing collision between the Loch Ness Monster and a flying saucer, general gratification will be felt at the news that Coinneach Mor (Big Kenneth) as he is affectionately called on Loch Ness side, will be at hand if and when the Island monster shows itself.

'A special representative of the *Scottish Daily Tale* will accompany the expedition which will sail this morning from Loch Dooin in Mr T. Rawstorne's S.Y. *Banshee*, and our readers will be kept in close touch with the latest developments of this amazing story which, without at present being able for obvious reasons to say more, are likely to prove nothing less than sensational.

'It is a matter of particular satisfaction to the *Scottish Daily Tale*, which believes that the future happiness and prosperity of the world depends upon a continuous strengthening of the bonds which link the British Commonwealth with the United States, that the expedition of the *Banshee* is a joint operation.'

'Why, I think that's very, very sweet,' said Carrie, smiling at Ian Carmichael whom she suspected rightly of having written this puff preliminary. Ian Carmichael blushed. Carrie Royde's eyes were as fatal to good-looking young men as depth-charges to submarines.

Soon after the *Banshee* cast off to the strains of *Clan Donald is Here* and *Over the Sea to Skye* piped by Angus MacQuat. Ben Nevis, his countenance glowing, announced that it was time to tap the steward and Toker was bidden to bring in a bottle of Glenbogle's Pride to toast the expedition. Long gone were the days when Chester Royde drowned the noble liquid with soda and chilled it with ice, at any rate on this side of the Atlantic. What he did with highballs on the other side was, so far as Ben Nevis was concerned, wrapped in a merciful oblivion.

'Gee, this is certainly a great whisky, Ben Nevis,' he declared reverently after putting down a couple of drams.

'Well, of course I'm rather prejudiced, but I don't think there's anything to touch it,' said the Chieftain with a touch of complacency. 'Slahnjervaw, everybody.'

'I wonder what the old bean would say if we sank a dram instead of this horrible sherry,' Catriona muttered to her sister.

Mary tried the experiment.

'Slahnjervaw, father,' she boomed in that deep voice which both daughters had inherited from their mother.

'Slahnjer . . .' and then the Chieftain stopped. He was privately not at all displeased that one of his hefty daughters should be a chip of the old block, but in fancy he was on the mat in the yellow drawing-room at Glenbogle trying to explain to his wife why he had not immediately asserted himself as a father when Mary took a dram at eleven o'clock in the morning. Before he could decide what to say Catriona had followed her sister's example. The attention of Ben Nevis was distracted from his daughters by a signal from Toker.

'What is it?'

'Might I have a word with you, sir, for a moment in your cabin?'

'What on earth's the matter?' he asked when the butler had closed the door of the cabin.

'It's a little question of footwear, sir,' Toker replied.

'Footwear?'

'Yes, sir, Captain Gillies observed that there were tacks on your brogues and, if I may be permitted a rather vulgar expression, went off the deep end about them to me. Being well aware of the peppery nature of many sea-captains, I let him — er — do the talking until he cooled down and returned to the navigation of the yacht.'

'What's the matter with the tacks in my brogues?' the Chieftain barked.

'Apparently, sir, the effect of them upon the deck of a yacht is deleterious. Definitely deleterious.'

'In other words, Captain Gillies is allergic to my brogues, what?'

'That would express the present condition of the Captain's mind with absolute accuracy, sir.'

'I see, well, what am I to do about it?'

'I have ventured to inquire whether the yacht's stores were capable of coping with the emergency, sir, and I have succeeded in procuring a pair of what in the days of my youth we used to call sandshoes.'

Toker went to a locker and produced a pair of heelless rubber-soled shoes the uppers of which were of speckled black and grey canvas.

'Good lord, Toker, I can't wear those,' the Chieftain protested. 'I shall look as if I were wearing a couple of flounders with that beastly dark skin on top.'

'Nevertheless, sir, I venture to hope that you will humour Captain Gillies in this little matter.'

'Little matter? It isn't a little matter to expect me to go bouncing about the deck like a tennis ball.'

'I think, sir, if you would kindly try them on you will find them less objectionable when worn than they appear upon their own. You may have observed, sir, that Sir Hubert and Mr Royde are both in nautical attire and wearing rubber-soled buckskin shoes, and it would unquestionably relieve the Captain's solicitude for the condition of the deck if you could see your way to indulge in this matter. There is, of course, an alternative. You could wear your buckled patent-leather evening brogues, but I thought the notion of wearing these with a tweed doublet might be distasteful.'

'It certainly would be, Toker. It would be disgusting. I don't want to look like a piper at a wedding.'

'Precisely, sir. And if you will sit down I will ascertain if the pair of sandshoes I have chosen are comfortable.'

'You are without exception the most persistent fellah I ever knew, Toker,' said the Chieftain.

'Thank you, sir,' the butler replied as he offered Ben Nevis a shoe-horn. '*Nil desperandum* has always been my favourite motto. And of course *sic itur ad astra.*'

'Now don't you start talking about sea-sickness.'

'Excuse me, sir. I was quoting Latin. *Sic itur ad astra*. Thus do we reach the stars.'

'I was always very allergic to Latin when I was at Harrow. Never could see any point in it. *Mensa*, a table. *Mensa*. O table. Whoever wants to talk to a table in any language? If I'm reduced to talking to tables I'll talk to them in English. *Mensa*, O table! I think Latin is a wooden-headed language.'

'How do you find the shoes, sir?'

The Chieftain got up and stamped about the cabin.

'Well, they don't feel as beastly as they look. So I suppose I can stand them while we're actually at sea.'

'I feel sure Captain Gillies will much appreciate your conciliatory attitude, sir.'

'I suppose, my boy Murdoch would have supported the Captain, wouldn't he?'

'I think the Commander undoubtedly would have, sir.'

The Chieftain sighed gustily, and blew his nose. 'I wish he were with us, Toker.'

'Indeed, sir, we all wish the Commander were with us.'

'Well, I'd better be getting back on deck,' Ben Nevis said. 'Lunch is at one, isn't it?'

'Yes, sir, I thought with the appetite for which the sea is famous you would prefer lunch half-an-hour before your usual hour.'

'Quite right. In fact, I'm beginning to feel quite peckish already.'

'You are, sir? I wonder if you would like a cup of cold consommé now? It won't spoil your appetite for lunch, but it will remove that feeling of the watched pot which never boils.'

'I think we'd all like a cup of consommé. And by the way, Toker, when you're handing round the whisky I think it would be better to pass by Miss Catriona and Miss Mary.'

'I always do, sir. The young ladies were drinking sherry just now.'

'They weren't. That's just it. They were drinking whisky. I was wondering what to do about it when you called me away about these shoes. Mind you, I think whisky is much better for them than these ghastly cocktails tasting of hair oil and methylated spirits, but I don't think their mother would quite understand.'

'It might perplex Mrs MacDonald, sir.'

Conscious of having carried out his paternal duty, Ben Nevis rejoined the others.

'I see you've put on a pair of winged sandals, Donald,' the laird of Cloy said in that high voice so often heard from the lips of plump men.

'They're not sandals; they're sandshoes, Bertie. Toker managed to get hold of a pair for me. Did you say "winged"? What on earth are you talking about?'

'Perseus and Andromeda and all that,' said Bottley.

'Who on earth are Persus and Romeda?' Ben Nevis asked.

The laird of Cloy giggled.

'Perseus put on a pair of winged sandals to rescue Andromeda from the sea-monster.'

Ben Nevis shook his head.

'I expect it's very funny, Bertie, but it's beyond me. Do you know what he's talking about, Chester?'

The financier shook his head.

'Of course you do, Chester,' Carrie Royde put in, and before he could reveal the full extent of his ignorance she related the ancient story.

'This fellow Perseus seems to have been a bit of a flying saucer, what?' said Ben Nevis when Carrie had finished. 'Do you believe that yarn, Bertie? It sounds to me a pretty tall story. It's a pity, though, we can't get hold of a Gorgon's head. By Jove, this Bolshie Government of ours would be an absolute quarry before I'd finished with them. But all we've got is Gorgonzola, what? And not much of that.'

Mac 'ic Eachainn was so pleased with this joke that he forgave the laird of Cloy for what he had been inclined to condemn as showing off.

After lunch Toker found an opportunity to talk to Ian Carmichael on a subject near to his heart.

'Will you excuse me, sir, but during lunch I happened to overhear you comment on the fact that Mr Hector Hamish Mackay is at present on the island of Little Todday.'

'Yes, he's working there for our set up.'

'I had divined as much from his recent articles in the *Daily Tale*. Will you think it presumptuous on my part to ask you to give me a chance of telling Mr Hector Hamish Mackay what his books have meant to me for many years?'

'Och, I'm sure he'll be delighted.'

'You think he will? On one occasion I did write to tell him what a world of romance his book *Faerie Lands Forlorn* had revealed to me, and I received from Mr Hector Hamish Mackay a gracious acknowledgement. That note is among my most treasured possessions. I have heard him broadcast, but it has never been my good fortune to come into personal contact with him and I am, if I may use an expression which Mr Mackay himself would never use, all agog, Mr Carmichael, to tell a great writer in my own inadequate words how much I venerate his poetic eloquence. It was most painful when I heard Ben Nevis stigmatize him as a mushy nincompoop because in the first flush of excitement caused by the news of the flying saucer's attack on the Loch Ness Monster Mr Mackay ventured to speculate whether the monster's bereaved mate might not seek a refuge in the Islands. However, Mr Mackay has since then expressed his conviction that the Island Monster is, as the old Romans used to say, *suo genere*, and I have no doubt whatever that as they also used to say, Mr Mackay is now *persona grata* with Ben Nevis. Please forgive me for expressing myself at such length, but I was anxious to let you know how earnestly I was hoping to have an opportunity of offering my homage to a master of the English language.'

'I'll make it my business to see that you do get this opportunity, Mr Toker,' the young reporter promised with that pleasant smile which extracted so much useful information for his paper.

'Toker, sir, if you don't mind,' the butler murmured gently. 'I do not wish to sail under false colours. If the occasion presents itself will you just say "this is Toker, the butler at Glenbogle Castle, who is one of your most ardent admirers." '

'I'll do that. You can rely on me, Toker.'

'I am extremely obliged, sir. In the hope of having this opportunity to let Mr Hector Hamish Mackay know of my admiration for him I have ventured to bring with me a selection of his books in which I shall be so bold as to ask him to inscribe his name. *Happy Days Among the Heather, Faerie Lands Forlorn, The Glamour of the Glens, In the Footsteps of Prince Charlie, Came Ye by Athol?, By Loch and Ben, Wandering in Wester Ross*, and last but by no means least one of his earliest books, *Land of Heart's Desire* — a gem, Mr Carmichael, a gem of purest ray serene as our great English poet Gray has it. Do you think I shall be trespassing too far on Mr Mackay's indulgence if I ask him to inscribe these eight books?'

'I'm sure he'll be pleased to sign them.'

'Thank you, sir. You have taken a great weight from my mind. May I get you any refreshment?'

'No, thanks, Toker. I'm not going to touch a drop of anything till we've had a definite "yes" or "no" to this monster. I've a feeling that we're going to surprise the world in the next three or four days, and I want to have a clear head.'

'Bravo, sir. Bravo, indeed. Self-abnegation is the corner-stone of scientific research, as Professor Honeywood says in his *Compendium of Science for Everyman*. I check my pleasure in romantic dreams by keeping in touch as far as I am able with the latest developments of science.'

'Well, I hope we're going to give science a nasty poke in the eye by producing a prehistoric monster for them. Losh, it'll be the biggest scoop ever.'

It was about six o'clock of a golden afternoon when the *Banshee* entered the Coolish and dropped anchor about three hundred yards from Snorvig harbour. The *Island Queen* had already arrived and was moored along the pier. Ian Carmichael went ashore at once, and presently came back to ask if Mr Mackay could pay his respects to Ben Nevis. The Chieftain looked at his sandshoes. The notion of receiving Hector Hamish Mackay in sandshoes displeased him, but he did not want to rouse the hostility of Captain Gillies by putting on his heavy brogues. The skipper of the *Banshee* had already been sniffing the air suspiciously and saying that if there was the least sign of a change in the weather he would have to weigh anchor and make for Nobost in Mid Uist. Ben Nevis believed him capable of going to Nobost merely to pay him out for the tacks in his brogues.

'I think he'd better dine with us, Carmichael, and you too of course.'

'That's awfully good of you, sir. I'll go ashore right away, but I'm afraid I've only this old tweed doublet and I don't expect Mr Mackay will have glad rags.'

'Glad rags?'

'Evening dress.'

'Extraordinary,' the Chieftain woofed.

Ian Carmichael was not sure whether his host meant the expression or the lack of evening clothes was extraordinary.

'Well, I shall expect you both at eight. Don't bother about dressing.'

Ben Nevis himself put on his tartan doublet buttoned up to the neck with eagles' heads of silver and set off by a lace jabot; this allowed him to wear his buckled brogues with propriety. It was a majestic figure that received Mr Mackay and Ian Carmichael on deck that evening.

'I am really incapable of expressing in suitable words what this privilege means to me, Ben Nevis,' said the topographer.

'Will you take a dram?'

'Many thanks.'

'Or would you prefer one of these cocktails?'

'Indeed, I never drink cocktails.'

'Quite right,' the Chieftain barked approvingly. 'When I was in India I used to have to drink something they called a gimlet. I made rather a good joke once. I said, "I suppose you call this beastly mixture of gin and lime a gimlet because it's such a boring drink?" Ha-ha-ha!'

If Hector Hamish Mackay was overwhelmed by meeting Ben Nevis, Toker was not less overwhelmed by meeting Hector Hamish Mackay. Ganymede could not have served Zeus with a cup of nectar more reverently than Toker poured out a hefty dram of Glenbogle's Pride for his most esteemed author. Indeed, in his emotion he very nearly offered the whisky to Catriona and Mary instead of the sherry.

Presently the strains of *Beinn Nibheis Gu Brath*, the tune which had heralded Mac 'ic Eachainn's dinner from time immemorial, were heard and the party moved below to the saloon.

'I wonder if your piper will give me the pleasure of hearing *Iomradh Mhic 'ic Eachainn*. I remember once as a lad passing by Glenbogle Castle when your revered father was still alive and hearing his piper playing it under his window early on a fine morning in May. I have never forgotten what was for me a most thrilling experience.'

Ben Nevis was gratified by this and when presently the topographer asked for *M'Eudail, M'Eudail, Mac 'ic Eachainn*, Ben Nevis began to warm towards him, and soon he was in a glow when Mr Mackay said:

'Although I think that the Clanranald Macdonalds claim this melody under the name *M'Eudail, M'Eudail, Mac 'ic Ailein* I have always maintained that the Ben Nevis Macdonalds have the prior claim.'

'Well, we don't press the point too hard,' said Ben Nevis tolerantly. 'After all, it's a domestic matter if you know what I mean. Of course, if the Campbells or the Macintoshes tried to poach one of our tunes that would be different. We wouldn't stand for that. I was after your blood when you started that peprosterous idea about the Loch Ness Monster having gone to the Islands.'

'That was based on my theory that there were probably a male and female monster in Loch Ness, and when the news about the flying saucer was first published I was anxious to look at the bright side because the death of the Loch Ness Monster seemed to me to strike a blow at the very roots of Highland life.'

'Well, of course, I maintain that the monster took what these flying fellahs call evasive action,' said the Chieftain. 'I will never believe that our monster was killed.'

'I think you're right, Ben Nevis. At any rate, this island monster clearly has no connection at all with the Loch Ness Monster and I have said as much in the columns of the *Daily Tale* in no uncertain fashion. I believe Mr Donaldson, our Editor, had the privilege of meeting you recently.'

'And I found him a very pleasant sensible fellah,' said the Chieftain.

'And an admirable editor. Now, as you know, Mr Donaldson is particularly interested in your visit to Great Todday, and he has sent our young friend Carmichael to cover what he believes may be one of the greatest stories in the history of journalism.'

'It won't be much of a story if we don't see this monster,' said Ben Nevis.

Mr Mackay lowered his voice.

'If I might have a word with you in private after dinner, Ben Nevis, I have a most important communication for your ears alone.'

So after dinner the conversation was resumed in the smoking-saloon while the rest of the party sat on deck, watching a glorious sunset.

'Well, perhaps now you'll put me in the picture,' said Mac 'ic Eachainn after he and Mr Mackay had drunk a couple of potent drams.

'I have discovered a cave which the monster is in the habit of frequenting and though I have not actually seen the monster a young palaeontologist and myself are quite satisfied . . .'

'A young what?' Ben Nevis interjected.

'A young expert on the remains of prehistoric creatures.'

'But you didn't say that at first.'

'Palaeontologist.'

'What an extraordinary word! Pal . . . say it again slowly syllable by syllable.'

'Pal-ae-ont-ologist.'

The Chieftain muttered to himself for a moment or two. Then he rang the bell.

'Oh, Toker,' he said when his butler came in. 'I forgot to say that if a young . . .' Ben Nevis drew his breath like a defiant stag . . . 'if a young pal-ae-ont-ologist comes aboard you can show him down into the smoking-saloon.'

'Very good, Ben Nevis,' said the butler.

'You know what a pal, a pal-ae-ont-ologist is, Toker?'

'I believe, sir, it is the word for one who studies the fossilized remains of the prehistoric monsters that used in days of yore to roam the earth.'

'Yes. Quite,' said Ben Nevis in a subdued voice. 'By the way what's his name, Mr Mackay?'

'Brownsworth.'

'All right, Toker, that's all I wanted to say.' This was not perfectly true. What Ben Nevis had wanted to say was that at last he had found a word to make Toker blink.

'Extraordinary chap, my butler,' he said to Mr Mackay. 'He's a walking dictionary. And by the way he's a great reader of your books. He's apparently brought a whole packet of them with him and wants you to write your name in them.'

'Certainly. I shall be delighted.'

'That's very kind of you. He didn't tell me, but he told young Carmichael, who asked me if I would mind if Toker asked you. But to get back to this . . . Good lord, the name's gone already.'

'Palaeontologist.'

'It's no use. I shall never remember it. What's he called — Brown something.'

'Brownsworth.'

'You were saying?'

'Young Brownsworth and I discovered unmistakable signs that the monster resorts to a cave on the little island of Poppay known as the Cave of the Bones. Uamh nan Cnàmh.'

'We've got a cave with the same name on Ben Gorm,' the Chieftain exclaimed. 'Macintosh bones they were, the remains of some Macintoshes who were smoked to death in it in the days of Hector the Sixth.'

'I've told the story in my book *The Glamour of the Glens*. Well, as soon as I'd established the fact of the monster's frequenting this cave I decided that not a word should be said about it in the Press because I did not want all those hikers . . .'

'Hikers? Did you say hikers?'

'There are quite a few camped out on both islands, all hoping to win this £250 offered by the *Daily Tale*.'

'Well, let's hope this monster is carnivorous,' said Ben Nevis.

'So far not a word has leaked out about the monster using this cave on Poppay and I thought that when we had this *céilidh* broadcast from Snorvig on Thursday it would be a wonderful dramatic stroke if young Brownsworth could arrive at the *céilidh* and bring news that the monster was at that very moment in its cave. Then I thought I would announce this to listeners and tell them that Ben Nevis in person was going over at once to Poppay to establish once and for all that it was not the Loch Ness Monster and that if all went well the programme later in the evening would be interrupted for a minute or two to give listeners the latest news. And now you understand why I was so secretive at dinner. I shall tell young Carmichael, of course, because he will have to stay behind on Poppay when Brownsworth brings word to the *céilidh*. Mr Donaldson knows; you know; and I know; but nobody else knows except Joseph Macroon . . .'

'Well, if Joseph Macroon knows he'll try and put the monster on the rates. He'll probably want us to build a pool for him and a new pier.'

'It was, in fact, Joseph Macroon who discovered the monster's refuge, and pretty scared he was by what he saw. And now there's one more favour I have to ask. The B.B.C. are most anxious that you should say a few words into the microphone at the *céilidh* in order to give listeners the pleasure of hearing your voice.'

'What, talk on the wireless? I wouldn't know what to do.'

'It's as simple as talking into a telephone,' Mr Mackay urged.

'I don't call that very simple. In fact, I never knew anything more complicated.'

'Well, I won't press you now, but it would give a very great deal of pleasure to thousands. And now if you'll excuse me I think I must be wending. I have to cross to Kiltod.'

'You'll have a jockendorrus?'

'Well, I can't say "no" to that old Highland custom. And you will not breathe a word to anybody about the monster's probable where-abouts?'

'I shan't say a word,' The Chieftain raised his glass. 'Well, slahnjervaw to the monster.'

'*Slàinte mhòr*.'

'And don't forget to write your name in Toker's books,' Ben Nevis said. 'He deserves it after knowing what a . . . well, you remember the word.'

That night in the cabin he was sharing with Kenneth MacLennan Toker sat up in his bunk and played with his eight signed copies of Hector Hamish Mackay's works as a little girl plays with her dolls.

Chapter 17

THE CAVE OF THE BONES

Possibly stimulated by that whacking *deoch an doruis* which Ben Nevis gave him, possibly moved by Toker's recognition of him as a figure in Scottish literature to be mentioned in the same breath as Ossian, Hector Hamish Mackay suggested taking Ian Carmichael to Poppay in order to effect a reconnaissance of the monster's movements.

'I'll consult Joseph Macroon and if he's willing for Kenny to take us there tonight in the *Morning Star* I think it would be a good thing for you to see the lie of the land, Carmichael.'

The young reporter did not require either a *deoch an doruis* or Toker's homage to support Mr Mackay's suggestion with enthusiasm, and at midnight they boarded the *Morning Star* with the avowed intention of fishing for pollack, though Joseph Macroon was taken into their confidence and impressed once more with the need of strict secrecy, a need which he in turn passed on to his son.

Those who have never experienced the magic of a fine Hebridean midnight at the end of June may have difficulty in imagining the romantic exaltation of Hector Hamish Mackay and Ian Carmichael as the *Morning Star* chugged past Tràigh nam Marbh to reach Bàgh nam Marbh in Poppay. The sea was tarnished silver; a luminous glow in the western sky had hardly faded when the eastern sky came to life in lavender and rose; the landscape seemed to quiver like the wings of grey moths. It was, however, the quality of the air itself, combining the twilight of evening with the twilight of dawn, which gave the time and the scene a peculiar magic, and which it is beyond the power of any painter to portray or the skill of any writer to evoke.

When the *Morning Star* came alongside the landing-place in the Bay of the Dead, Mr Mackay and young Carmichael stepped ashore on tiptoe not so much because they were thinking about moving quietly to avoid disturbing the monster but because the visible world seemed to be a whisper which they must be chary of interrupting.

Ghost moths came dancing up from the rank herbage as they walked silently across the ancient burial-ground; a corncrake rasped.

'Losh, what was that?' Carmichael asked apprehensively.

The topographer told him.

'A queer noise for a bird to make,' the young man commented.

'I'm awful fond of that noise,' said Mr Mackay with a sigh. 'It takes me back to the summers when I was young. The bird grows rarer every year on the mainland. But not another word. We're getting near the slope up to the cave. Try not to kick down any loose stones. When we reach the terrace in front of the cave I will approach and listen from the right of the entrance and you will approach and listen from the left. Both of us must keep out of the monster's sight if we possibly can. The way down to the sea about which I told you is on the left as we stand and if the monster does show itself I think you'd be wise to get over to the right and give it a clear road. Now then, on we go. And as quietly as possible.'

In years to come Hector Hamish Mackay would declare that one of the supreme moments of his life was the moment when he cautiously put his ear round the corner of Uamh nan Cnàmh and heard from its innermost depths a brobdingnagian snore, and he would always add that the greatest temptation he had ever resisted was the temptation to lure the monster from its den that night and satisfy his curiosity once and for all.

'Indeed, I don't know how I was able to come away and leave the mystery unprobed, Carmichael,' he said, when they were making their way back to the *Morning Star* across the burial-ground.

'It's all just luck, Mr Mackay. We're playing for big stakes and I'm sure Mr Donaldson would agree that they are worth it. If the monster isn't at home on Thursday evening when the *céilidh* is being broadcast we can feel fairly sure of finding it later on that night and we'll get a flashlight picture. If we'd disturbed it tonight we couldn't have had a photograph and people might have said we were just inventing the whole thing as a stunt for our paper. But what a snore! Losh, I haven't heard such a snore since I shared a wee room in a cottage with a Paisley commercial when the bus ran into a snowdrift in Sutherland last winter.'

'Yes, yes, I'm sure we've done the right thing,' Mr Mackay agreed. 'And we've certainly done the honourable thing. Young Brownsworth might have thought that I'd double-crossed him. He's kept his word and never been near Poppay since we rescued Joseph Macroon's whisky, and the temptation to a rising young palaeontologist must have been great.

Well, well, if that snore is the nearest I ever get to the monster I shall always maintain that we did the right thing.'

Presently they reached the landing-place.

'Och, it's myself that's glad to see you, Mr Mackay,' said Kenny in a tone of relief. 'I didn't like being down here alone at all, at all. I was all the time thinking I could see *bòcain* walking about.'

'Ay, it's a haunted spot, Kenny. I'd have felt a bit nervous myself if I'd been alone. I certainly would. Well, the monster's in Uamh nan Cnàmh at this very moment.'

'Are you after seeing it?'

'No, but we're after hearing it. It's asleep in the cave and snoring like an earthquake. But not a word of this to a living soul, Kenny. We must be patient till Thursday comes.'

'It wasn't a stirk you heard snoring?' Kenny suggested. 'A stirk can snore pretty loud.'

'A stirk would have to be the size of three bulls to sound as loud as the noise we heard in the Cave of the Bones,' Mr Mackay declared.

'Or a commercial traveller,' added Carmichael. 'And it couldn't have been a commercial traveller.'

'It may be a bit early for the crayture to go to its bed by the time the *céilidh* will be starting,' Kenny suggested.

'I'd thought of that,' the topographer said. 'But the B.B.C. wanted the *céilidh* to finish in time for the nine o'clock news. We must just take our chance, and I've a feeling that the monster is not going to let us down.'

It was two o'clock before Hector Hamish Mackay and Ian Carmichael went to bed, and the eastern sky above the bens of Great Todday was already lavender.

Next morning they went over to see Bill Brownsworth at Tràigh Veck to let him know about the snoring in the cave.

'I felt a wee bit guilty by going over to Poppay without you, Brownsworth, but I wanted to take the opportunity of showing Carmichael the lie of the land and I knew you'd understand.'

'Oh, rather,' said Brownsworth.

'I've arranged for Kenny Macroon to land you and Carmichael to-morrow at half past seven. Then you'll both reconnoitre the cave and if the monster is at home Carmichael is to hold the pass while Kenny takes you over to Snorvig as quickly as he can. If the monster comes out before the *Banshee* . . .'

'The *Banshee?*' Brownsworth echoed.

'The *Banshee* is the yacht with Ben Nevis and his party. As soon as you arrive like a messenger in a Greek play with the news, the *Banshee*, which will have steam up, will take Ben Nevis and his party, myself, Father Macalister and possibly one or two others over to Poppay and the secret of the monster will be revealed. Should the monster emerge before you get back Carmichael will secure a photograph, and I think I'm right in saying that the credit of this photograph will be given to you accompanied by the no doubt welcome cash in recognition of your co-operation.'

'That's what Mr Donaldson would wish,' said the young reporter.

'But that's hardly fair on Carmichael,' Brownsworth objected.

'Forget it,' Carmichael said. 'It's all in the day's work for me.'

'I wish I could persuade you to come to the microphone yourself, Brownsworth,' said Mr Mackay. 'Would you not try the effect?'

'But I know I should gulp,' Brownsworth protested.

'I really don't think a gulp would matter. What do you say, Carmichael?'

'Och, I think a good gulp would add to the effect. It would suggest Brownsworth's excitement,' Carmichael replied.

'Why don't you try the effect?' Mr Mackay urged. 'Let's suppose that this beach is the hall and the natural arch the entrance. You and Carmichael have established the monster's whereabouts and Kenny Macroon has brought you over to Snorvig — by the way, I hope he won't have trouble with his engine on Thursday; that would be a disaster. Shall I show you my idea of the entrance? Mind you, Urquhart and MacColl, the two B.B.C. chaps, may not agree to this handling of the situation, but my notion would be to interrupt whoever is singing or talking at the *céilidh*. That can be settled later.'

Hector Hamish Mackay disappeared into the natural arch to prepare his entrance, and it happened a moment later that one of Jocky Stewart's cows which had been wandering came down on to Tràig Veck pursued by Jocky's daughter Florag, who, when not herding her father's cattle, helped Mrs Odd in the house.

Florag thumped the cow's stern with a stick and adjured it in angry Gaelic to get back on to the machair.

'*Suas thu, a Bhuttercup, suas, suas, a nighinn an diabhuil.*'

Through the natural arch came Hector Hamish Mackay.

'Great news, great news,' he cried. 'The monster is . . .'

The remainder of the messenger's announcement was drowned by a piercing shriek from Florag as she ran up the sandy slope.

'A *Mhuire Mhathair*, the monster, the monster,' Florag screamed. 'Oh, God help me, what will I do?' And as she made this appeal she tripped over a tussock of marram and fell prone.

The effect of Hector Hamish Mackay waving his cromag and flashing his glasses in the entrance of the arch, combined with Florag's screams, excited Buttercup the cow and she began to prance round the beach, lowering her head and kicking her heels in the air, and obviously perfectly ready to jump over the moon if the moon had been there to be jumped over. Every time that Mr Mackay attempted to cross the beach and join the others the cow, which was an Ayrshire, lowered her horns and drove him hurriedly back into the shelter of the natural arch; it was not until Brownsworth and Carmichael between them had managed to convince Florag that the monster was not in the neighbourhood that she was persuaded to get up and exercise her authority over Buttercup.

'Well, there's not likely to be a cow in the Snorvig Hall, Brownsworth,' said Mr Mackay. 'So I'll try again.'

He emerged from the natural arch for the second time.

'Great news, great news, the monster is in its den on the island of Poppay. That's what I should like you to say, Brownsworth. Then I'll go to the microphone and tell listeners that under the leadership of Ben Nevis some of us are going to beard the monster in its den, after which Francis Urquhart will inform listeners that the programme will be interrupted later on in the evening in the event of there being any news. Surely, Brownsworth, you could manage that one simple sentence? Great news, great news, the monster is in its den on the island of Poppay. Try.'

Brownsworth felt that he could not disappoint Mr Mackay, who had been so kind to him. He retired into the natural arch, from which he emerged awkwardly, his cheeks duskily blushing with embarrassment.

'Great news, great news,' he mumbled. And then he gulped over and over again with a sound of corks being pulled out of his gullet one after another. He was quite unable to release the news.

'Yes, I see your point, Brownsworth,' said Mr Mackay. 'One or two gulps would really be quite effective, but a series of them without any words to follow might puzzle listeners. It's a pity, but it can't be helped. You'll just have to beckon me and quietly tell me the situation on Poppay so that I can make the announcement.'

'If the cave is empty when Brownsworth and I go to Poppay tomorrow, would you like one of us to come over and let you know?' Carmichael asked.

'Oh, certainly, certainly, but I refuse to consider such a possibility. You're making me wonder now whether you and I shouldn't have routed out the monster last night when we heard it snoring in Uamh nan Cnàmh. Well, I must be getting back to Kiltod. The B.B.C. boys are coming over to make final arrangements with Father Macalister. What will you do, Carmichael?'

'I thought I'd take a run around Great Todday. I don't want to spend the day here in case there are any news hounds around on the look out for a tip. And I also want to tell Ben Nevis about the snoring last night. Why don't you come over with me, Brownsworth?'

'Well, I will. I want to see my friend Spinnage if I can.'

Bill Brownsworth did not have to cross the Coolish to see Dick Spinnage. When they all three reached Kiltod Dick Spinnage was with Francis Urquhart and Duncan MacColl in the *Kittiwake*, which was just coming alongside the harbour steps.

The two B.B.C. men went off with Hector Hamish Mackay to visit Father James, and Carmichael asked the Biffer if he would take him over to have a look at Uamh na Snaoiseanaich in a loud voice for the benefit of various visitors who were hanging around, staring at what they felt were people in the know.

'They'll be two hours at least with Father Macalister,' Carmichael said.

'Yes, yes, come aboard, Mr Carmichael,' said the Biffer. 'I'll take you over. Plenty time. Plenty time.'

'Are you coming, Brownsworth?' Carmichael asked.

'I must talk to you, Bill,' Dick Spinnage muttered to his friend. 'Something frightful has happened.'

So the *Kittiwake* went off without them.

'Bill,' said Dick Spinnage when the two friends, remote from human company, were seated on a green knoll on the buttercup-gilded and daisy-silvered machair, 'Bill, why on earth did you tell me Muriel had a coffee-coloured mole under her right ear?'

'The last thing I said to you, Dick, on the night of our picnic was to remember that, if you were in any doubt which girl was which, Elsie had a coffee-coloured mole at the back of her right ear.'

'You said Muriel.'

'No, you said Muriel and I said "no, not Muriel, Elsie." But what has happened?' Bill asked anxiously.

'What's happened? Wait till you hear what's happened. Last night, having taken particular note of this coffee-coloured mole, I asked Muriel to come for a stroll to look at the sunset.'

'But if she had a coffee-coloured mole it wasn't Muriel you asked.'

'You're telling me, Bill. But I thought it was Muriel, and to keep the promise I made you . . .'

'That was awfully decent of you, Dick,' Bill put in affectionately.

'Oh, well, a promise is a promise. Anyway, feeling perfectly sure that it was Muriel, I suggested sitting down by the edge of the cliff and after I'd been talking in rather a gooey way for a bit I put my arm round her waist, expecting she'd freeze the way any girl just engaged to somebody would freeze if his best friend started to make the running – any decent girl that is. Well, you can imagine that I was a bit shocked when the girl I thought was madly in love with my best friend, instead of saying right out of the refrigerator "please, don't do that" cuddled up close and put her head on my shoulder with a kind of steamy sigh. I can tell you, Bill, that shook me. It shook me from every point of view. I thought how you and I had planned this business and then I thought Bill's never going to believe that his girl cuddled up to me like this without a lot of come hither stuff on my part beforehand. You see, Bill, you've always had rather an exaggerated idea of my attraction for girls and, dash it, I didn't see how I was going to tell you that Muriel was n.b.g. as a girl to marry. Well, there was I with my arm still round her waist and her head on my shoulder, and I had a sudden feeling that perhaps it wasn't Muriel at all but Elsie. And then I caught sight of that coffee-coloured mole and knew it was Muriel right enough.'

'But, Dick, I did try to impress on you that it was Elsie who had the coffee-coloured mole.'

'All right, Bill, don't ride it. Riding that damn mole won't get me out of the mess I'm in. Well, to go on, there was I as I thought in the position of having tried to seduce my best friend's girl.'

'I think you're putting it rather too strongly,' Bill suggested modestly.

'Don't interrupt, Bill. So I said to myself, hell knows no fury like a woman scorned and it's no use my telling Muriel at this moment that I thought she was Elsie. That'll only make her vicious. I decided to take the line of having been irresistibly tempted by her and asking her to forgive me. So I said, "you and I oughtn't to be doing this, you know," and she cuddled up closer and said, "why not?" "Well," I said, "after all I'm Bill's best friend and I feel rather a worm." "What's Bill got to do with you and me?" she asked. That punch fairly made my teeth rattle and I looked again to see if I could have been mistaken about that mole. But no . . .'

'But I did keep telling you it was Elsie who had that coffee-coloured . . .'

'Don't ride it, Bill, don't ride it,' Dick snapped irritably. 'Do you think if I hadn't been absolutely sure it was Muriel I wouldn't have known how to handle it? Where was I? Oh, yes, "What's Bill got to do with you and me?" And then, like an absolute ass, I lost my head and decided to pretend I thought it was Elsie. I know, I know. I make no excuses. Don't harp on that mole, Bill. "Well," I said, "I had an idea, Elsie, that you and Bill had an understanding. Bill talked to me of meeting you that day in Tràigh Veck and I got the impression that you and he had this understanding." "Oh, no," she said, "there was never anything between Bill and me. Indeed, I think he's keen on Muriel and I'm pretty sure Muriel has fallen for him. Otherwise, she'd have been jealous of me over you." You can imagine what I felt when I realized that it wasn't Muriel at all. Of course at that moment I ought to have removed her head from my shoulder and taken my arm from her waist and said, "I've no business to be flirting with you, Elsie, because I'm already engaged to a girl in London." '

'But you aren't, Dick.'

'I know I'm not, I wish you wouldn't interrupt. Where was I? "I've behaved rottenly and all I can hope is that you'll forgive me." But instead of that I kissed her!'

'But why didn't you say you thought she was Muriel and tell her that I'd made just the same mistake at Tràigh Veck?' Bill asked. 'That would have put everything right both for you and for me.'

'Oh, Bill, don't make me laugh. I never felt less like laughing. Tell a girl that two men one after another have only made themselves agreeable because they thought she was her twin sister? But never mind what I ought to have done. Listen to what I have done. When I kissed her she went into a sort of doodah, and said, "Oh, Dick darling, you don't mind if I tell Muriel tonight that we're engaged? I've never had a secret from my twin sister." So apparently I'm engaged to Elsie, and I don't see how I can get out of it. I mean to say if old Waggett writes to Charlie Blundell and tells him I've played pitch and toss with his daughter's heart it might lead to my losing that partnership.'

'But if he writes to tell Blundell that he's very pleased about his daughter's engagement you'll probably be a partner before you know where you are,' said Bill eagerly. 'And you do like Elsie, don't you?'

'I'm really quite keen on Elsie, as a matter of fact. But think of old Waggett as a father-in-law,' Dick groaned.

'Well, I hope he's going to be my father-in-law too. Really, Dick, I don't know why you're so upset. I'm tremendously pleased about this.'

'Bill,' said Dick sharply, 'are you sure you didn't deliberately tell me that Muriel had a coffee-coloured mole at the back of her right ear?'

'Dick, I warned you that Muriel *didn't* have a coffee-coloured mole. You got it wrong once and I corrected you. I really am not to blame over this. Of course I can't help being pleased about it. I think I'll go over to Snorvig this afternoon and tell Mr Waggett that I want to marry Muriel.'

'No,' said Dick firmly. 'Neither you nor I will say a word to old Waggett. If you think I'm going to spend the next two or three days listening to the old man talking about marriage from the time of Adam and Eve, think again. No, no, Bill, not a word until we're well out of reach of his tongue. I shall sound Charlie Blundell first. I shall tell him I want to marry Waggett's daughter and ask him what about it. Then if he makes a firm date for the partnership I shall write to Waggett.'

'Yes, that's all very well for you, Dick, but I'd like to fix up things about Muriel before we discover the monster because Mr Waggett . . .'

'Don't keep on calling him Mr Waggett, Bill, as if you were a small boy talking about a master to another master.'

'Well, Waggett,' Bill gulped, 'doesn't believe this monster exists and I don't want him to be prejudiced against me.'

'It won't do, Bill. We must both wait until we are out of range of the old man's tongue. I've made it quite clear to Elsie that she must say nothing to her father until I'm off the island. I'd rather he went on talking about the Normandy landings than matrimony through the ages. And if and when you and I do get married, we've somehow got to keep old Waggett safely parked in the Outer Hebrides. Well, now I've got it off my chest, Bill, I don't feel quite so gloomy, and if Charlie Blundell comes up to scratch I believe I'll feel quite cheerful.'

'You can imagine how happy I feel, Dick, and if I discover the monster and get that Readership at Norwich I shall be the happiest chap in the country. Fancy you and me being brothers-in-law.'

'We won't be brothers-in-law. I've explained that to you already. You're as much muddled about our relationship as I was about our sister-in-laws' moles. And one more stipulation, Bill.'

'What's that?'

'You are not to call old Waggett "Daddo",' said Dick Spinnage sternly.

Chapter 18

NO LONGER RIVALS

At half past seven sharp as Bill Brownsworth and Ian Carmichael stepped ashore on Poppay from the *Morning Star* the doors of the Snorvig hall were closed. On the platform were Ben Nevis in his tartan doublet buttoned with silver eagles' heads; Chester Royde and Hubert Bottley in white mess jackets; Catriona and Mary MacDonald, each with a sash of Ben Nevis MacDonald tartan; Paul Waggett in a dinner-jacket and black tie, which for some reason caused a certain amount of giggling among the Snorvig school choir until Alec Mackinnon, the tall thin swarthy schoolmaster, threatened to eject them and strike their action song out of the programme; Mrs Waggett with Muriel, Elsie, and Dick Spinnage, the last named also in a dinner-jacket, much to his host's gratification; Dr Maclaren, deplorably in a stained old Lovat tweed suit; the Reverend Angus Morrison and his wife; John Beaton, the burly schoolmaster of Bobanish, and his wife, demonstrating by their presence that Bobanish was not in the least jealous because the Snorvig school choir and the Garryboo school choir had been chosen to represent the juvenile talent of Great Todday; big Roderick MacRurie, Simon MacRurie, Andrew Thomson, the bank agent, and Mrs Thomson, with several more local notabilities. Donald MacRurie, from whose post office the broadcast was being sent over the sea to the mainland listeners, remained at home, under the impression that his supervision was required for the success of the transmission. George and Catriona Campbell were down in the body of the hall giving final words of advice to the Garryboo choir. Alec Mackinnon was ubiquitous. Father Macalister was shaking his fist at the team of old, young, and middle-aged women who were to uphold the fame of Little Todday at the *luadh*.

A narrow trestle-table about fourteen feet long was set out in the middle of the hall with benches on either side and on the table lay a piece of blanketing folded back on itself in the shape of a U. If the waulking had been a genuine process of shrinking and fulling, the blanket would have been soaking in a tub of diluted ammonia; but the weaving of tweed and blankets had almost died out in the Toddays and a waulking today was only an illustration of what it was once upon a time, and indeed unless Father Macalister had insisted on a *luadh* from time to time in the Kiltod hall it would have become extinct even as an illustration of the past. The parish priest had had some difficulty in overcoming Todaidh Beag's fear of being derided by Todaidh Mór, but in the end he had prevailed and at half past six the women were all aboard Dot MacDonald's large fishing-boat, the *St Tod*. Bean Yockey, the wife of Jockey Stewart; Bean Uisdein, the wife of Hugh Macroon; Joseph Macroon's daughter, Kate Anne Macdonald; Kate Anne's friends Morag and Mairead – these were some of the party. The older women wore long voluminous skirts of drugget with red or green or blue lines, but the younger women were no longer willing to wear such old-fashioned garb and looked somewhat frivolous in printed cotton frocks. The principal singer was Florag's grandmother, Bean Iosaiph Sheumais, now close on seventy, but treated by her mother, Bean Sheumais Mhicèil, aged ninety, as if she were the same age as Florag.

The singer's duty was to sing a narrative song of innumerable verses the chorus of which, consisting of 'hiro-hivo, huva-haro' and other sounds without meaning, was taken up by the women who, each grasping in both hands a section of the blanketing or cloth to be waulked, banged it down upon the table in front of them in time with the singer. Toward the end of the waulking what was called a clapping song was sung, the tempo of which was much faster and the rhythm much more exhilarating. Then like Maenads the women sang the chorus more loudly, banged the cloth down more and more rapidly, and induced in themselves and in the audience a kind of dithyrambic frenzy.

Besides the Little Todday women for the *luadh* old Michael Stewart went over to sing a rousing *port a beul*.

'But where's Duncan Bàn?' Father Macalister asked.

Mrs Odd shook her head.

'Duncan Bang's better at home, Father James.'

'Is that so? Ah, well, poor Duncan. I expect he got too excited.'

'He was very excited.'

'But you're coming over with us, Mistress Odd,' the parish priest had said when all the women were aboard the *St Tod*. 'Isn't that beautiful now?'

'And what's more, Father James, I'm going to be one of the looers myself.'

'Good shooting! You'll just be knocking sparks out of them.'

'Yes, Florag and me have been horoheaving away for a week and more. Talk of the Oxford and Cambridge boat-race, it's a funeral beside Florag's mother and the rest of them. "Good land alive," I said, "if you bang that pore blanket about much harder it'll be a sheet not a blanket at all." Horo-hiro! Hara-hiva! Horo-hivo! Huva-hara!'

The rest of the women were so much enchanted by Mrs Odd's rendering of a chorus that they all forgot they ought to feel sea-sick on the glassy Coolish and they were still laughing when they trooped up the steps to the pier and walked along through Snorvig to the hall. When the doors were closed a quarter of an hour before the broadcast began the Little Todday women were sitting on the bench that ran right round the hall. It had been decided to restrict admission to those who could find seats on this bench and, except for the trestle-table with the blanket, the middle of the hall was empty to give the B.B.C. equipment fair play.

'So that's Ben Nevis, is it?' Mrs Odd said to Bean Uisdein. 'What's he wearing that bib under his chin for? He doesn't look a dribbler.'

'Och, he's a very fine man, Mistress Odd.'

'He *is* a fine man. My boy Fred thought he was the finest man he ever knew.'

Father Macalister overheard this and presently went along to ask the Chieftain if he would have a word with the mother of Sergeant-major Odd, who had seen the monster.

Ben Nevis plunged down from the platform and Father Macalister brought along Mrs Odd.

'Jolly glad to meet the mother of my old friend Sergeant-major Odd,' he barked, shaking her by the hand. 'How is he?'

'Oh, he's in the best of pink, thanks. Has two little girls now and hoping for a little boy this September.'

'Jolly good,' the Chieftain woofed. 'And so you saw this Todday monster, eh?'

Mrs Odd gave him an account of her adventure on Tràigh Veck.

'Well, I've seen the Loch Ness Monster twelve times.'

'Have you reelly?'

'But it didn't have these long teeth, Mrs Odd.'

'Well, it wouldn't do if every monster looked like the next, would it?' Mrs Odd said.

'Absolute silence, now,' Francis Urquhart was calling.

'I'll get back to my seat. Jolly glad to have met you, Mrs Odd. Remember me to the Sergeant-major.'

'I will. He'll be listening to us on the wireless tonight. That is if he can get Scotland in Nottingham and which he can't always.'

'Please,' said Francis Urquhart in a reproachful voice.

'Wireless Willie's giving us the bird,' said Mrs Odd with a twinkle.

'Look out, Donald. You'll wreck the programme if you aren't careful,' Hubert Bottley chuckled.

When Ben Nevis was back on the platform Francis Urquhart addressed the gathering.

'Now, listen, ladies and gentlemen. In exactly another five minutes we shall be on the air and that means that every sound in this hall will be broadcast as soon as the green light turns red. So will you please try not to cough more than you can help and under no circumstances talk to one another. Absolute silence, please. And when you are applauding the items will you please not clap until I raise my hand and will you please stop clapping the moment I drop it.'

Duncan MacColl went across to the platform and asked Ben Nevis to join them round the microphone.

'It will start everything so splendidly, Ben Nevis, if you would say a few words when I give you the cue.'

'What do I want a cue for?' the mystified Chieftain asked.

'To know when to speak into the microphone. And remember, please, not too close. As I suggested this afternoon, just fancy that the microphone is an old friend you've been talking to in your natural voice.'

'I lay you fifty dollars, Carrie, that Donald Ben Nevis blows up the microphone,' Chester Royde murmured to his wife.

Bertie Bottley began to giggle.

'Silence, please, absolute silence,' Urquhart entreated. The red light glowed.

'A Thighearna,' whispered Bean Shomhairle to Sammy MacCodrum, 'it's terrible like Sahtan's eye looking at you.'

'Ist, woman,' her husband adjured with a nudge.

'This is the parish hall of Snorvig, the picturesque little port of Great Todday,' Duncan MacColl announced, 'where you are invited to join us at a céilidh which is being held on this lovely June evening in the land of perpetual youth – Tir nan Òg. You will hear songs and piping. You will hear the dance-compelling port a beul or mouth-music when the singer takes the place of the fiddle or the pipe. You will hear an old tale or two and you will hear Hector Hamish Mackay give you the latest news of the Island Monster. And last but by no means least you will hear the women of Little Todday waulking the cloth. We are privileged this evening to have with us MacDonald of Ben Nevis, who has come all the way from Lochaber to take part in this *céilidh*. I am now going to ask him to say a few words.'

'Where's this cue?' Ben Nevis asked as he stepped forward to the microphone.

'You've had it,' Duncan MacColl whispered as he pointed to the microphone.

'I haven't,' Ben Nevis whispered back hoarsely.

Duncan MacColl pointed to the microphone again.

'Now, now, now,' he whispered.

'This is the first time I've tried talking into this wireless contraption,' Ben Nevis told Scotland. 'But I'm jolly glad to be here at one of our grand old Highland gatherings. I've come over to Great Todday in order to get a glimpse of this monster which some duffers believe is the Loch Ness Monster.'

Francis Urquhart was signalling to Duncan MacColl to get Ben Nevis away from the microphone; he was afraid that elderly ladies all over Scotland were by now ringing up the B.B.C. to ask if the Communists were blowing up Glasgow. Urquhart tried to indicate to Ben Nevis that he was speaking too close to the microphone, but the Chieftain mistook his intention and, putting his mouth about an inch away, he bellowed into it more loudly than ever.

'They'll think the monster has gotten a hold of him,' Chester Royde laughed. 'He'll fuse every radio in the country.'

It was Toker who saved the situation. He advanced with a light-footed dignity and offered his master a glass of water.

Ben Nevis looked round. Toker put his finger to his lips and pointed to the microphone. The Chieftain recognized that in Toker's opinion he had said enough and followed his butler across the hall to the platform.

'What's this for?' he muttered hoarsely, looking at the glass of water.

'Your voice was failing, sir.'

'I was afraid I was talking too loudly.'

'You were talking much too loudly, sir.'

'How, was my voice failing then?'

'It was failing to adapt itself to the microphone, sir.'

'I see,' Ben Nevis murmured to himself, and then he took his seat again on the platform, wondering what difference it would have made if they had given him a cue to hold.

The *céilidh* progressed like many another *céilidh*. It was half past eight when the *luadh* started, and a hope may be expressed here that television will reach Scotland before the *luadh* is extinct, because those who have only heard a *luadh* over the air cannot have the slightest idea of the spectacle.

'Gee,' exclaimed Chester Royde, 'the Carroway Indians have nothing on this. Gee, it's great. Attagirl!'

'Don't talk so loud, Chester,' Carrie warned him, 'they'll hear you.'

'I don't give a darn if they hear me or not. Gee, this is the best thing I ever saw. Look at that big woman over there. She's shaking like a jelly.'

'I say, Mary, I've a jolly good mind to go down and join in,' said Catriona MacDonald to her sister.

'Good-oh,' Mary ejaculated. 'I'm all for it.'

And to loud applause from the company the two hefty daughters of Ben Nevis took their places in the team, one on either side of the table.

Thud – thud – thud – thud – thud – thud.

The bodies of the women swung to right and swung to left as they banged the blanket on the table. Father Macalister's voice was like a bourdon behind the chorus. Hiro-horo! Hiro-hivo! Huva-hiva! Hive-huva!

Thud – thud – thud – thud – thud – thud.

Duncan MacColl kept up a running commentary.

'The increase in speed marks the beginning of the end of the waulking. The blanket is nearly shrunk as it should be. Oh, I wish you could see these women from Little Todday. What drive! What rhythm! They've finished. They're all breathless. One or two of them are leaning over the trestle-table as oarsmen lean over their oars at the end of a race. The audience are wildly enthusiastic. Mr Chester Royde, Jr, the American financier who is here and who was adopted by the Carroway Indians into their tribe under the name of Butting Moose, says that a Carroway war dance is a tame affair compared with this Hebridean waulking. And now I am going to call upon Hector Hamish Mackay to tell us the latest news about the mysterious visitant to these shores which is generally known as the Island Monster. Mr Mackay.'

Duncan MacColl yielded the microphone to Mr Mackay.

'Good evening, everybody. We've had a wonderful evening here in Snorvig and we hope that you have all enjoyed yourselves as much as we have here with all the fine singing and piping and fiddling and that wonderful waulking you've just heard. The time is going on, but I'm told that listeners would be glad to hear from me the latest news of the monster. It remains a mystery at present, but my personal investigations lead me to suppose that the monster, which has been reported from various places right up the Long Island, has returned to Great and Little Todday, unable, perhaps like some of us, to resist the charm of these exquisite little islands which sum up in themselves all the magic of the legend-haunted West. As many of you have read, the Island Monster was first seen by Mr Kenneth Macroon between Little Todday and the much smaller and wilder island of Pillay, a mile or so north of it. It was seen again in the Snuff-taker's Cave on Great Todday by Mr Archie MacRurie; it was seen on Tràigh Vooey, the beautiful beach of yellow sand which is almost unique in the Long Island where all the beaches on the western seaboard are a dazzling white. Yes, there it was seen by the two little daughters of Mr and Mrs Samuel MacCodrum of Garryboo, a crofting township of Great Todday.'

At the mention of her name Bean Shomhairle was seized with irrepressible giggles, and the more loudly she was hushed the more she giggled. Paul Waggett, who had been feeling throughout the evening that he had not been playing the prominent part in the proceedings to which as the owner of Snorvig House he felt he was entitled, and who was furious with what he considered this unwarrantable advertisement of an imaginary monster, came down from the platform with his nose in the air and told Sammy MacCodrum that if he could not quieten his wife he must take her out of the hall. Meanwhile, Mr Mackay, who was much too experienced a broadcaster to be upset by such a trifling incident, went on:

'The monster was seen again by Miss Jemima Ross, a teacher at Garryboo School, the performance of whose choir of boys and girls has given us so much pleasure this evening. Perhaps the most dramatic encounter was that with Mrs Odd on Little Todday, an encounter in which I myself was within an ace of partaking. Mrs Odd, who is a native of London, has taken these outermost isles to her heart and was one of that sturdy team whose waulking of the cloth has been perhaps the most notable item in a splendid programme.

'Since then I, in co-operation with three determined investigators, have established with all reasonable certainty the monster's lair or den or refuge . . .'

At this moment Bill Brownsworth entered the hall.

'One moment, please. I believe I am on the verge of being able to make a most important announcement. Could we have a tune from one of our pipers while I interrupt my talk to obtain the latest news?'

Michael Gillies, the Little Todday piper, was bidden to play and with a nice courtesy thrilled the company with the stirring strains of *Clan Donald is Here*.

'I'm getting rather fond of these Islanders, Bertie. I believe I've been wrong about them,' said Ben Nevis to the laird of Cloy. 'That fellah's a good piper. He must come on board the *Banshee* and have a dram with me. Angus!'

Angus MacQuat drew near.

'Who's that piper?'

'Michael Gillies, Ben Nevis.'

'He's a good piper.'

'He's a very good piper, Ben Nevis.'

'Bring him on board the *Banshee*. I want to give him a dram.'

'I'll do that, Ben Nevis.'

The strains of *Clan Donald is Here* died away and Mr Mackay approached the microphone again.

'I'm sure all listeners will share in the excitement of us all here when I say that a messenger has arrived hotfoot from the little isle of Poppay off the south coast of Todaidh Beag to say that the monster is at this very moment beyond all shadow of doubt lying up in what is called the Cave of the Bones. Steam is up on the good ship *Banshee* and under the inspiring leadership of MacDonald of Ben Nevis, famed in Gaelic lore and legend as Mac 'ic Eachainn, the Son of the Son of Hector, the first Chieftain of that great line of which the present Ben Nevis is the twenty-third representative, we will immediately cross the Coolish, the strait that divides Great Todday from Little Todday. I am sure that listeners will accept our excuses for leaving the *céilidh* before it is finished. Do you hear the pipers? Led by Angus MacQuat, the hereditary piper of the MacDonalds of Ben Nevis, they are playing that grand martial tune, *Mac 'ic Eachainn's March to Sheriffmuir*. Oh, I wish you could see the scene. Ben Nevis is marching out of the hall, his head high, a noble representative of our country's most cherished traditions. He is followed by Mr Chester Royde, Jr, in this combined operation by Scotland and

America. Sir Hubert Bottley of Cloy goes next; Miss Catriona and Miss Mary MacDonald of Ben Nevis follow. And now as the pipers precede the expeditionary force down to the pier I hand over to Duncan MacColl and prepare to hurry after them, conscious that listeners all over Scotland are wishing us God-speed at this tremendous moment.'

Hector Hamish Mackay hurried away without seeing that Paul Waggett, with Dick Spinnage and his twin daughters, were also leaving the hall.

Duncan MacColl now came to the microphone.

'I must regret that we cannot give listeners an opportunity to share in the dramatic series of events that the announcement of Hector Hamish Mackay seems to promise, but as soon as we receive news from Poppay we shall interrupt the programme in the course of the evening to give Scottish listeners the latest information. And now the last item at our *céilidh* is an action song by the boys and girls of Snorvig School. Snorvig School are the present holders of the Shiant Shield which is competed for by schools every year at the National Mòd and they hope to defend their title at the Mòd held in Obaig at the end of September. After the action song we shall conclude the *céilidh* in time-honoured fashion by singing *Oidche Mhath Leibh's Beannachd Leibh*, good-night to you and good-bye, in which I hope our Gaelic-speaking listeners in the isles and on the mainland will all join us.'

But we, too, must leave the *céilidh* and follow the pipes with Mr Mackay and Bill Brownsworth.

'Now, I'm anxious to have a few more details, Brownsworth,' said the topographer. 'Let me have your story from the beginning.'

'Carmichael and I landed at exactly half past seven and started at once to reconnoitre. We reached the cave and listened without showing ourselves, but we could learn nothing. Then I decided to go in and I reached as far as the smaller second cave beyond, but there was nothing there. Carmichael and I decided that it would be best to return to the landing-place and give the creature a chance to retire. This summertime rather upsets things. The sun doesn't set here till well after half past nine at this time of year. We went back to the cave at eight o'clock. There was still nothing. Then we went back a third time at a quarter past eight. Carmichael was slightly in front of me and as he reached the top of the slope up to the terrace he saw the back of a large body disappearing into the cave. He whispered to me and I slithered back down the slope and ran as fast as I could across the burial-ground. My knees are still burning with nettle-stings. Kenny saw me hurrying and, thank goodness, he was able to start the engine at once. You know the rest. Carmichael is going to try to cover the creature's path down to the sea so that if it leaves the cave he'll be able to get a snap of it.'

'A large body is vague. Wasn't he able to give a better idea of the size?'

'He said it was definitely not as large as an elephant, but I think he was too excited to get an accurate idea of the creature. He did say that what he saw rather reminded him of a huge seal.'

'That's what our friend Mr Waggett believes it is. But I never heard of a seal climbing up a steep rough path like that from the sea.'

At this moment Waggett himself overtook them.

'Good evening, Mr Mackay. Good evening, Brownsworth, I couldn't help overhearing what you said, and I think it's pretty obvious that I am right. If this monster isn't entirely imaginary, it is nothing more extraordinary than a common or garden seal.'

'But, Mr Waggett, you've not seen this path up from the sea. No seal could climb that.'

Bill Brownsworth had dropped behind to walk with Muriel; he had no desire to argue about the alpine ability of seals with his future father-in-law.

'Oh, darling,' she murmured, 'I think we must tell Daddo about us. Dick wants to wait till he gets to London and then write about him and Elsie.'

'I want to tell him. But I'm a bit worried about this monster. You see, it really is there and I think your father will blame me if he's wrong.'

'But perhaps he won't be wrong,' said Muriel. 'He's going over to Poppay in the Biffer's boat. Dick and Elsie and I are going with him. Do come too, Bill.'

'I'm afraid I really must stay with Mr Mackay, and he's going across in the yacht. I'll see you over on Poppay presently.'

Bill Brownsworth overtook Hector Hamish Mackay, and they hurried along to where the *Banshee*'s motor-boat was waiting at the pier.

'I never met such an obstinate fellow as Waggett in all my life,' Mr Mackay sniffed. 'His cocksureness really is nothing less than exasperating.'

'He's going over to Poppay to prove that he's right,' said Bill Brownsworth. 'I hope he won't get there before us and disturb the creature and perhaps make it take to the water.'

'Young Carmichael will soon put a stop to that,' the topographer said.

'But if Mr Waggett is the shooting tenant of Poppay he may claim that the creature is his property.'

'I think not,' Mr Mackay said firmly.

Ben Nevis was already in the motor-boat when they reached the pier, and Mr Mackay asked if they might come over with him to Poppay.

'This is Brownsworth, the rising young palaeontologist about whom I was speaking.'

'Come aboard, come aboard. Very glad to meet you,' the Chieftain shouted up.

'Be careful not to say anything derogatory about the Loch Ness Monster, Brownsworth,' Mr Mackay warned him in a low voice as they went down the steps to board the motor-boat.

'So you're one of these thats, are you?' Ben Nevis woofed genially. 'Did you come into contact with the Loch Ness Monster at all?'

'I was up in Inverness for a fortnight last year, sir,' Brownsworth replied, 'but I wasn't lucky enough to see it.'

'Ah, pity. I believe I've seen it oftener than anybody. Twelve times, to be exact. It's a great sight. But I suppose Kenneth MacLennan here had the finest view of the lot. He saw it attacked by this flying saucer.' Ben Nevis introduced Bill Brownsworth to the rest of the party. 'Now tell us all about this Poppay business. I think we'll drop Toker and my piper. Oh, dash it, Angus, we were going to give that Todday piper a dram. Look here, I know what we'll do. We'll go straight across to Poppay and then you go back in the motor-boat, Toker, and ask Captain Gillies, with my compliments, if he'll bring the *Banshee* over and stand off Poppay, sending the motor-boat to the landing-place. And, Angus, you stay here and get hold of that piper. Good lord, what a duffer I am! We've forgotten Father Macalister. Look here, Angus, you tell Father Macalister we're expecting him to have a cold snack with us in the *Banshee* when we've solved this problem of the monster, and I'd like Sergeant-major Odd's mother to come along too, and we'd better have Joseph Macroon and Big Roderick. You see to it, Angus. I suppose I ought to ask this chap Waggett, too, oughtn't I?'

'I think Mr Waggett is going across to Poppay, of which he has the shooting rights,' said Mr Mackay.

'He's jolly well not going to shoot the monster. I would never include a monster in any shooting I let. Off we go, coxswain.'

'Wait a minute, Donald,' said the laird of Cloy. 'You haven't made proper arrangements to fetch Father Macalister and any others from Snorvig. Wouldn't it be better if we ran alongside the *Banshee* first, and told Captain Gillies the programme?'

Thus it was settled, much to the gratification of Toker, who was able to give orders to the yacht's stewards and with a clear conscience go over to Poppay in the motor-boat with the rest of the party. The motor-boat was then to return at once to Snorvig, pick up there the invited guests, put them aboard the *Banshee* and then fetch what it was hoped would be a band of triumphant discoverers from Poppay.

The slight delay involved in these directions and preparations gave Paul Waggett time to reach Poppay at the same moment as the motor-boat. He had never known the Biffer to get the *Kittiwake* so quickly on her way with such good will.

'You know, perhaps, that I am the shooting-tenant of Poppay,' Waggett reminded the Chieftain. 'Well, of course I'm delighted for you to land here, Ben Nevis, but I think you ought to prepare for a disappointment. I must confess I was rather shocked when I heard Mr Mackay make that announcement over the microphone.'

'We will agree to differ over that, Mr Waggett,' said Mr Mackay acidly. 'I am perfectly satisfied that we shall not be disappointed.'

'Personally, I don't believe that there is anything in the cave,' Waggett maintained. 'But I make one reservation. It may be a large seal.'

'*A Chruitheir*, what a man,' the Biffer muttered to Kenneth MacLennan.

'Well, it's no use standing here arguing about it,' Ben Nevis woofed. 'The sooner we get to the cave the sooner we shall find out who is right.'

'Your brogues, sir,' Toker said gently. 'I think you will need tacks up that slope.'

The ancient burial-ground had seen many a procession in the past when a Macroon Chief was borne to his last resting-place by mournful clansmen, but it had never witnessed quite such a variegated procession as moved through the rank herbage on this June evening just before sunset, such a mixture of kilts and shorts and frocks and plus-fours and dinner-jackets and whites.

'I wonder if we oughtn't to get down on our hands and knees. What do you say, MacLennan?' the Chieftain asked. 'Don't you think we ought to do a little stalking?'

'I'm not going to crawl on my hands and knees through these darned nettles for any monster,' Chester Royde declared.

'We're in white, Donald,' Bottley protested.

'I know, that's what's worrying me,' Ben Nevis replied. 'I'm so afraid the monster will bolt when he sees you and Chester walking about like Dr Livingstone and all that. I don't know why you didn't both get into something quieter when we went back to the yacht.'

'Young Carmichael will be close to the cave, Ben Nevis,' Mr Mackay reminded him. 'And if the monster had already come out he would surely have warned us.'

'Yes, I suppose you're right,' the Chieftain agreed, with a regretful note in his voice, for he would have enjoyed directing everybody in a stalk.

They found Ian Carmichael with his camera by the edge of the terrace on the landward side.

'I began to think you were never coming,' he said. 'We've only a few minutes left for a possible photograph.'

Paul Waggett stepped forward.

'I propose to go into the cave by myself,' he said grandly. 'And when I have satisfied myself that there is nothing there, except possibly a seal, I shall come out and you will then be able to satisfy yourselves that there is nothing there except possibly a seal.'

'Daddo!' Muriel exclaimed apprehensively; under the influence of Bill Brownsworth she did not feel so confident as her father in there being nothing there. He paid no heed and with uptilted nose he and his dinner-jacket disappeared into the mouth of the cave.

'You'd better all keep to the landward side of the terrace,' Mr Mackay urged. 'The monster will probably make for the water by its usual path.'

Suddenly they heard within the cave a noise between a bellow and a bark and a whistle.

'That's the very noise I heard on Pillay,' Bill Brownsworth exclaimed.

He had hardly spoken when Paul Waggett came running out of the cave, followed by a huge form.

'Got him,' Ian Carmichael shouted in triumph as his camera clicked.

'It's a walrus,' cried Chester Royde. 'Look out everybody. Oh, gee, why didn't you let me bring that new gun of mine, Ben Nevis? A walrus at bay is an ugly creature.'

By this time Waggett was over the terrace and slithering down the slope, the walrus in noisy pursuit and slithering down, it seemed to the alarmed onlookers, rather more quickly than the shooting-tenant.

Bill Brownsworth, feeling that now was his chance to win a bride, rushed forward and slithered down the slope behind the walrus.

Waggett reached the bottom of the slope and started to run across the burial-ground.

The walrus galumphed after him. Bill Brownsworth, shouting and waving his arms, managed to overtake the walrus and distract its attention from Waggett. For a moment as the walrus uttered again that noise between a bark, a bellow, and a whistle, it looked as if those fearsome eighteen-inch tusks would be buried in the body of the devoted young palaeontologist. Then to the relief of everybody the huge beast turned away and went galumphing down into the sea. Its head and tusks and bristling moustache were presently lost to sight in the golden waters of the Coolish.

'I ought to have guessed it was a walrus,' said Bill Brownsworth, 'when I saw those marks on the beach on Pillay. It must have been digging up shellfish, and of course it would have used its tusks as an ice-axe to get up to the cave here.'

'Well, I must admit I hadn't thought of a walrus,' said Waggett to Bill Brownsworth. 'But a walrus is only a large kind of a seal. So I was really right all the time. However,' he added graciously, 'I might have had rather a job with those tusks if you hadn't succeeded in diverting the brute's attention. Thank you, Brownsworth.'

'Before the others come, may I ask you something, sir?'

'I'm afraid I never had any first-hand experience of walruses before this evening, but . . .'

'No, I didn't want to ask you anything about walruses, sir. I wanted to ask you if I may marry Muriel.'

'This is rather sudden, Brownsworth.'

'I love her very much and she loves me. We fell in love . . .' then the young man remembered that the father-in-law to whom he aspired did not believe in love at first sight, and he substituted 'with one another.'

'Well, we can't discuss this sort of thing with all these people about. You'd better come over and see me tomorrow,' said Paul Waggett.

The others were now gathering round, congratulating Paul Waggett on his escape and Bill Brownsworth on his courageous diversion.

'That wasn't the monster you saw in Loch Ness, MacLennan, eh?' said the Chieftain triumphantly.

MacLennan shook his head.

'The monster I saw was a lot bigger than that. And I'm afraid he's a dead monster now, Ben Nevis. Ay, I think yon devil of a flaming machine was one too many for the poor crayture.'

'I don't believe it, MacLennan, and I never will believe it,' the Chieftain roared, almost as loudly as a walrus. 'What do you say, Mr Mackay?'

'Oh, I'm hoping more than ever now that the Loch Ness Monster will show itself again very soon. Still, we've had a really unique experience to-night.'

'Extraordinary thing, Mr Mackay,' said the Chieftain, 'when that brute came charging out of the cave after Mr Waggett, do you know what I was reminded of?'

'I don't know at all, Ben Nevis.'

'I was reminded of my ancestor, Hector, the Fourth of Ben Nevis.'

'Hector of the Tusk!' Mr Mackay exclaimed.

'That's the very chap. We've got a painting of him at Glenbogle. He used to nick felons he'd condemned to death in the back of the head with this tusk to avoid any muddle over who was and who wasn't to be put to death. This nick he used to make was called Mackickyacken's kiss. Pockvickickyacken in Gaelic. Of course, this walrus had two tusks and my ancestor only had one, but he had very much the same kind of moustache as this walrus.'

At this moment there sounded from the steep brae above the burial-ground a noise that made Ben Nevis and Chester Royde stare at one another.

'Cooee! Cooee! Wolla-wolla-wolla-wolla! Oo-hoo! oo-hoo!'

'Good lord, Chester, that's the sound of hikers,' Ben Nevis exclaimed.

'It certainly is. I haven't heard that noise for some years,' said Chester Royde, 'but I'll never forget it. Gee, it brings back that wonderful time we had at Glenbogle before the war.'

'There they are,' said Ben Nevis pointing to four figures in shorts bounding with the agility of goats down the brae.

A minute or two later Ben Nevis was saluted by Mr Sydney Prew and three members of the Ealing Branch of the N.U.H.

'Good lord,' he gasped.

'I hope you will let bygones be bygones, Mr MacDonald,' said the secretary, 'and allow me to offer you the congratulations of the National Union of Hikers on your successful solution of the mystery of the Todday

Monster. My young friends here and I were hot on the scent, but you just beat us.'

The Secretary and the three members of the Ealing Branch saluted again with their staffs, and went off to find their boat.

'Extraordinary!' Ben Nevis muttered to himself as he started off to join the others. 'Well, I hope everybody will come back and have a cold snack in the *Banshee*. You'll come, Mr Waggett, and your daughters and your friend there. Where's Mrs Waggett?'

'I'll go across to Snorvig and fetch her in the *Kittiwake* if I may,' said Paul Waggett, who was much gratified by this invitation.

'Yes, of course, the more the merrier, what?'

Bill Brownsworth took Dick Spinnage aside and told him that he'd broken the news to Mr Waggett about wanting to marry Muriel.

'Why don't you tell him about Elsie now? I'm sure this is the right moment, Dick. I'll come over with you in the *Kittiwake*, if you like, when we go to fetch Mrs Waggett.'

And Dick Spinnage took his friend's advice.

'Your dress and trousers are in rather a mess, Paul,' said his wife as she finished a rapid toilet before going out to the *Banshee*. 'And, oh dear, there's a piece torn out of the seat. Was that the walrus's tusks?'

'It may have been, Dolly,' he said.

'Oh, Paul, I didn't realize how near I was to losing you.' Her eyes filled with tears.

'Well, we're losing the chicks instead, old lady. Still, we couldn't expect to keep them with us for ever, could we?'

He put his hand to the seat of his dress trousers. 'Good gracious, Dolly,' he exclaimed. 'I've lost about six square inches. I'll have to put on my blue serge suit.'

'Will you announce the chicks' engagement this evening, Paul?'

'I think so, old lady. They seem quite eligible young men. I shall write to Charlie Blundell at once. I'm sure he'll arrange a partnership as soon as possible. Of course, Bill's prospects rather depend on his getting this appointment at Norwich, but we must be optimistic. And we mustn't forget that he may have saved me from losing more than just a bit out of my dress trousers. Another thing I like about him is his willingness to admit that I was right about this monster all the time and that a walrus is just another kind of seal.'

And Paul Waggett went on being right. Bill Brownsworth did get a

Readership at Norwich University that autumn and Dick Spinnage did get his partnership in Blundell, Blundell, Pickthorn, and Blundell. What is more, Bill Brownsworth was given £250 by the *Scottish Daily Tale* for the snap Ian Carmichael obtained of the walrus close on his future father-in-law's heels.

The picture had as caption:

NARROW ESCAPE OF ISLAND LAIRD
THE POPPAY WALRUS ALMOST CLAIMS
A VICTIM

When Paul Waggett read about himself as an island laird he was too happy to mind about the somewhat undignified attitude in which he had been photographed.

It was a merry evening on board the *Banshee*, and thanks to American hospitality those who liked champagne were able to hold their own with those who preferred whisky. Everybody was happy. The engaged couples were toasted. Paul Waggett did not feel that he was playing second fiddle over the walrus. Mrs Waggett dreamed of going to live at Norwood near her sister Gladys. Francis Urquhart and Duncan MacColl were sure that Scottish Regional had provided listeners with one of the most memorable outside broadcasts since the fleet was lit up on that genial evening once upon a time. Hector Hamish Mackay was looking forward to the talk which he would no doubt be invited to give and which he might not unreasonably hope would find a place in the Home Service, possibly even in the Third Programme as a repeat. Mrs Odd had visions of disorganizing the meat ration in Nottingham when she related the story of the walrus to her butcher, Mr Dumpleton.

'Though, mind you, I shan't tell him he's the walking double of the walrus except he doesn't wear his teeth outside. I don't know why I didn't reckernize him when I saw the walrus on Try Veck. I suppose I was a bit flustered by those tusks. And which I certainly thought was a lot more than two. I suppose it was the way it was chewing up the beach. Pore thing, I daresay if we'd have fed it with winkles it would have got as tame as young Catherine's guinea-pig.'

Yes, everybody was happy; even Captain Gillies gave up casting dark glances at marks on his deck.

But the peak of the evening was reached when Ian Carmichael, flushed with the praise he had received for the story he had telephoned to the

Scottish Daily Tale, came back to the *Banshee* with a telegram for Ben Nevis which Donald MacRurie had given him.

Few who saw the Chieftain's countenance as he read that telegram will ever forget its expression of an ultimate, indeed a seraphic happiness, the attainment of which is granted to very few human beings.

'Listen to this,' he bellowed. 'It's a telegram from Kilwhillie. Listen. Listen. Sent off from Kenspeckle just about the time the walrus came out of the cave on Poppay. Listen, everybody. Listen!

'Monster seen by me between Foyers and Kenspeckle this evening at eight seventeen stop eight humps definite and probable ninth stop monster was moving rapidly towards the middle of the loch where it submerged stop am satisfied it has completely recovered from encounter with flying saucer

Hugh Cameron'

The Chieftain beamed at the company; a grateful emotion had deprived him for a moment of speech.

'There's nobody in Inverness-shire better pleased to hear that news than myself, Ben Nevis,' Kenneth MacLennan declared.

Then the stalker raised his glass.

'*Slàinte mhath* to the Loch Ness Monster,' he said gravely. '*A h'uile latha a chi's nach fhaic.*'

'Slahnjervaw,' Ben Nevis woofed from the bottom of his great heart.

And as the eagle-beaked Chieftain and the eagle-beaked head-stalker gazed at one another and swallowed each a powerful dram of Glenbogle's Pride, Angus MacQuat and Michael Gillies piped the moving strains of *M'Eudail, M'Eudail, Mac 'ic Eachainn*.

'Och, I believe we will be having our lobster-pool for Todaidh Beag right enough, *a Ruairidh*,' Joseph Macroon murmured to Big Roderick.

'Ay, I believe you will, Choseph. And we might get a grant for the road between Knockdown and Bobanish.'

Then Father Macalister rose.

'*A Chàirdean*, before this glorious and beautiful evening comes to a close I want to thank our visitors for their glorious and beautiful hospitality. We wish Kilwhillie were with us at this moment, but we are glad that he has been able to give us such great news about the Loch Ness Monster. And will you now please give a thought to our Todday Monster, to Old Bill who has gone off to find himself a Better Hole. Let us wish him a safe return to his icy home.'

*

Postscript

About a month later Mr Hector Hamish Mackay, back in Edinburgh, received the following letter:

Glenbogle Castle,
Inverness-shire,
July 28th

Sir,

The memory of your recent kindness in appending your esteemed autograph to some of your wonderful books has emboldened me to inflict upon you the enclosed. It is the first time I have ventured to communicate to anybody my audacious attempts to express my deeper feelings in rhyme, and I hope you will excuse the liberty. I listened to your broadcast about the strayed walrus with moist eyes.

Yours respectfully,
William Toker

> Arctic amphibian of the frozen north,
> Who ventured far from boreal strands to roam,
> You have a friend beside the Firth of Forth
> Who wishes you a safe return to home.
>
> Arctic amphibian, an unerring eye
> Has guided Caledonia's master pen,
> And eke the voice of Hector H. Mackay
> To tell your story to the ears of men.
>
> Your visit to the Islands of the West
> Has been immortalized in jewelled words;
> And now, O wandering walrus, be at rest,
> Browsing on sea-weed with familiar herds.

W.T.

GLOSSARY OF THE GAELIC EXPRESSIONS

The pronunciation indicated in brackets is only approximate

FOR THE BEST IN PAPERBACKS, LOOK FOR THE

In every corner of the world, on every subject under the sun, Penguin represents quality and variety – the very best in publishing today.

For complete information about books available from Penguin – including Puffins, Penguin Classics and Arkana – and how to order them, write to us at the appropriate address below. Please note that for copyright reasons the selection of books varies from country to country.

In the United Kingdom: Please write to *Dept E.P., Penguin Books Ltd, Harmondsworth, Middlesex, UB7 0DA.*

If you have any difficulty in obtaining a title, please send your order with the correct money, plus ten per cent for postage and packaging, to *PO Box No 11, West Drayton, Middlesex*

In the United States: Please write to *Dept BA, Penguin, 299 Murray Hill Parkway, East Rutherford, New Jersey 07073*

In Canada: Please write to *Penguin Books Canada Ltd, 2801 John Street, Markham, Ontario L3R 1B4*

In Australia: Please write to the *Marketing Department, Penguin Books Australia Ltd, P.O. Box 257, Ringwood, Victoria 3134*

In New Zealand: Please write to the *Marketing Department, Penguin Books (NZ) Ltd, Private Bag, Takapuna, Auckland 9*

In India: Please write to *Penguin Overseas Ltd, 706 Eros Apartments, 56 Nehru Place, New Delhi, 110019*

In the Netherlands: Please write to *Penguin Books Netherlands B.V., Postbus 3507, 1001 AH, Amsterdam*

In West Germany: Please write to *Penguin Books Ltd, Friedrichstrasse 10–12, D–6000 Frankfurt/Main 1*

In Spain: Please write to *Alhambra Longman S.A., Fernandez de la Hoz 9, E–28010 Madrid*

In Italy: Please write to *Penguin Italia s.r.l., Via Como 4, I-20096 Pioltello (Milano)*

In France: Please write to *Penguin Books Ltd, 39 Rue de Montmorency, F-75003 Paris*

In Japan: Please write to *Longman Penguin Japan Co Ltd, Yamaguchi Building, 2–12–9 Kanda Jimbocho, Chiyoda-Ku, Tokyo 101*

The Fly in the Ointment   Alice Thomas Ellis

Poor mousey Margaret doesn't look a bit like a girl who is about to be married. Perhaps, Lili speculates idly, she is marrying Syl on the rebound? This deliciously malicious comedy completes the trilogy begun with *The Clothes in the Wardrobe* and *The Skeleton in the Cupboard*.

Raney   Clyde Edgerton

Raney would have thought a man could get married without getting drunk. As for the honeymoon at the Holiday Inn – no amount of advice from her aunts could have prepared her for *that*. 'Splendid … what James Thurber might have written had he lived in North Carolina' – *Washington Post*

Orders for New York   Leslie Thomas

One foggy June evening back in 1942, a party of Nazi saboteurs landed in the USA. As retired war correspondent Michael Findlater turned up more about the Nazi double betrayer who led them to the electric chair, he realized that someone else still remembered 1942 – and that someone wanted him dead.

Traveller   Richard Adams

General Robert E. Lee and Traveller have become the stuff of legend: a brave man and his brave steed suffering together in complete accord through the bloody campaigns of the American Civil War. Traveller's simple, vivid reminiscences draw us irresistibly back... 'His best novel since *Watership Down*' – Ruth Rendell

Adam Hardrow   David Fraser

The first volume in an enthralling saga of men and war. Mobilized for France in September 1939, Second Lieutenant Adam Hardrow is ardent to prove himself in battle. But he is soon to learn about the realities of war and the men he fights it with – and their wives and daughters too..

A CHOICE OF PENGUIN FICTION

The House of Stairs Barbara Vine

'A masterly and hypnotic synthesis of past, present and terrifying future … both compelling and disturbing' – *Sunday Times*. 'Not only … a quietly smouldering suspense novel but also … an accurately atmospheric portrayal of London in the heady '60s. Literally unputdownable' – *Time Out*

Summer People Marge Piercy

Every summer the noisy city people migrate to Cape Cod, disrupting the peace of its permanent community. Dinah grits her teeth until the woods are hers again. Willie shrugs and takes on their carpentry jobs. Only Susan envies their glamour and excitement – and her envy swells to obsession… 'A brilliant and demanding novel' – *Cosmopolitan*

The Trick of It Michael Frayn

'This short and delightful book is pure pleasure … This is a book about who owns the livingness of the living writer; it is funny, moving, intricately constructed and done with an observant wisdom' – Malcolm Bradbury. 'Brilliantly funny, perceptive and, at the death, chilling' – *Sunday Telegraph*

Your Lover Just Called John Updike

Stories of Joan and Richard Maple – a couple multiplied by love and divided by lovers. Here is a portrait of a modern American marriage in all its mundane moments as only John Updike could draw it.

The Best of Roald Dahl

Twenty perfect bedtime stories for those who relish sleepless nights, chosen from his bestsellers – *Over to You, Someone Like You, Kiss Kiss* and *Switch Bitch*.

PENGUIN OMNIBUSES

Perfick! Perfick! H. E. Bates

The adventures of the irrepressible Larkin family, in four novels: *The Darling Buds of May*, *A Breath of French Air*, *When the Green Woods Laugh* and *Oh! To Be in England*.

The Complete Novels of George Orwell

Burmese Days, *A Clergyman's Daughter*, *Keep the Aspidistra Flying*, *Coming Up for Air* – and, of course, the world-famous *Animal Farm* and *Nineteen Eighty-Four* – together in one volume. These six novels display all the powerful imagination that placed Orwell firmly beside Blake and Lawrence in the great tradition of prophetic moralists.

Enderby Anthony Burgess

'These three novels are the richest and most verbally dazzling comedies Burgess has written' – *Listener*. Containing the three volumes *Inside Mr Enderby*, *Enderby Outside* and *The Clockwork Testament*.

The Complete Saki

Macabre, acid and very funny, Saki's work drives a knife into the upper crust of English Edwardian life. Here are the effete and dashing heroes, the tea on the lawn, the smell of gunshot, the half-felt menace of disturbing undercurrents … all in this magnificent omnibus.

Italian Folktales Italo Calvino

Greeted with overwhelming enthusiasm and praise, Calvino's anthology is already a classic. These tales have been gathered from every region of Italy and retold in Calvino's own inspired and sensuous language. 'A magic book and a classic' – *Time*

FOR THE BEST IN PAPERBACKS, LOOK FOR THE

PENGUIN OMNIBUSES

Life at Thrush Green   Miss Read

Gossip, squabbles, domestic drama and the quiet rhythms of country living – this is the world of Miss Read. And here, in one volume, is some of the best of that world: *Thrush Green*, *Winter in Thrush Green* and *News from Thrush Green*.

The Alexander Trilogy   Mary Renault

'One of this century's most original works of art' – Gore Vidal. Mary Renault's masterly evocation of ancient Greece and of Alexander the Great, published in one volume: *Fire From Heaven*, *The Persian Boy* and *Funeral Games*.

The Stories of William Trevor

'Trevor's short stories are a joy' – *Spectator*. 'Trevor packs into each separate five or six thousand words more richness, more laughter, more ache, more multifarious human-ness than many good writers manage to get into a whole novel' – *Punch*

The First Rumpole Omnibus   John Mortimer

'A fruity, foxy masterpiece, defender of our wilting faith in mankind' – *Sunday Times*. Here is Horace Rumpole, triumphantly celebrated in this first omnibus edition: *Rumpole of the Bailey*, *The Trials of Rumpole* and *Rumpole's Return*.

The Best of Roald Dahl

Twenty tales to curdle your blood and scorch your soul, chosen from his bestsellers *Over to You*, *Someone Like You*, *Kiss, Kiss* and *Switch Bitch*.